RIFTBORN

RIFTBORN

THE RIFT BRIDE BOOK II

ADA DART

PAINTED BLIND PUBLISHING
LITERARY ALCHEMY

PAINTED BLIND
PUBLISHING
LITERARY ALCHEMY

Riftborn: Book II of The Rift Bride
© 2022 Ada Dart
ISBN: 978-1-957469-11-9

Text: Ada Dart
Book & Cover Design: M. F. Sullivan

Ada Dart Online: adadartromance.com
Painted Blind Publishing: paintedblindpublishing.com

*Reader discretion is encouraged.
For spoiler reasons, triggers
and tags are available
on the author's website,
adadartromance.com*

My name is Thecla Farrow.

*After discovering my unique nature
as both altered and riftborn,
Malin Farrow, Master of Gudrune,
took me as his consort.*

*His closest footman, Eleison,
is my mate alongside him,
equal in love if not in status.*

*And, in the shadows,
a wretched demon pursues me
while calling itself my slave.*

*But that is not even
half of the story.*

*It is just the beginning
of our secrets.*

THOUGH IT'S TRUE Duke Montagne arrived during an inauspicious week, my husband would have been enraged by his message no matter the circumstances. We had been married four months, including the honeymoon—long enough one might have anticipated the glow of love to tarnish, even if only by some unpredicted doubt.

But everything in my private world still glowed with gold's perfection. Malin Farrow, Master of the territory into which I had been born—and now my doting husband—was obsessed with me. To feel so desired was thrilling, I confess. Passion flooded his grim features, the spark of lust lending hunger to his dark eyes, if I happened past an open meeting room and called his attention away from whatever poor soul was having his career, family or very life calmly threatened in exchange for some task left undone. I could persuade my dear Malin to cancel a weekend business trip with the right torrent of semi-private tears and the slow revelation of their source while I lay in his lap so he might kiss me, pet me, bargain me back to happiness. He took me everywhere he could in that fabulous city of Saalast, and promised he still had more to show—both within our territory of Gudrune and without.

Yet, even as every evening found Malin more eager to see me, the compassion he showed my mate's need for me was never in short supply. Toward Eleison, as toward me, Malin was patient and infinitely kind. Toward the rest of the world, he was another man altogether.

What I did not understand, in those early days, was that the purposes served by these two vastly different dispositions were ultimately the same.

The morning began with blood, which disappointed us both when he noticed it on himself after he finished waking me up. My smile faded a few degrees, but Malin tutted once and moved along.

"Never mind," he adjured me, brushing back my disarrayed hair to admire my face in the filtered morning light. "Never mind… when the time is right, it'll happen. I feel it, darling. Don't you?"

Though I nodded, a little pain still tugged at me. I had never particularly idealized being a mother for my own sake. However, upon marrying a man thirty years my senior and perceiving his hope that I might rectify his childless condition, the idea of motherhood struck me with new tenderness. He had done so much for me: sparing me and elevating me; loving me and teaching me.

I could weave my tapestries and save his life, but Malin loved me so intensely, had given me so much—risking my life to produce his heir was the grandest gesture I could conceive.

Of course, Malin was not the only man who intensely loved me. While I trailed my hand over his brow, then across the scar that extended up into a white streak through his otherwise steeling crown of gold, his dark eyes shut with bliss.

They shot open again when an unexpected knock rattled our bedroom door.

"What in the blazes—"

While glancing toward the clock, Malin pulled the covers over me before I even thought to do it myself. I would have laughed were I not concerned that this interruption signaled an emergency—a knock at our bedroom door was unheard of, let alone at such an hour. If Charlotte needed to communicate something before Malin was out and about in the apartment or the rest of the Saalast house, she would leave a note with the breakfast set at our table.

But, once Malin had thrown on his dressing gown and jerked open the door, his shoulders relaxed. His tone changed to something pleasant; almost airy.

"Oh! You had me concerned—"

"Don't be too glad to see me." Eleison's gruff response brightened my mood, too, and I straightened up with a happy gasp for the nearness of my mate.

Then, remembering my present condition, I fought my cringe into a blushing smile while Malin stepped aside.

Oh! The sight of either man alone has always caused me a sweet pain, but together they resemble the dearest manifestation of love I have ever known. Two divergent aspects of one sensual god! After so many years, the vision warms my face and heart in a warm aurora of emotion.

Then, when my love for them both was still so very new, it left me nearly faint with thrill. I couldn't have cared less about whatever bad news Eleison brought. It was hardly six-thirty, and there he was in his dark blue suit with those radiant crimson eyes clear and crisp and wide-awake as they swept hungrily over the scraps of flesh left bare by the sheet.

"I know someone who's always glad to see you," Malin rejoined fondly, jerking his head toward me. "Why don't you two say good-morning while you tell me the bad news, Eleison...it'll go down easier if at least one of us is having fun."

With only the barest second of hesitation—still the lingering glance of an intensely loyal servant toward his master's offered liberty—Eleison prowled into the bedroom and didn't look back as Malin shut the door behind him. Flush with delight, more acutely aware than ever of my nakedness under the sheets, I reached for my mate. Eleison bent his head toward me, his arms sliding around my waist, his nose brushing mine without further contact.

"Hey," he murmured.

I searched his face, drinking in that addictive combination of profound, barely contained desire and slight jealousy that had a way of making him seem so stern with me. "Good morning, Eleison," I whispered back, my face's warmth increasing by the second.

"You two are going to have to get used to kissing in front of me sometime..."

With a sort of guilty chuckle and a brief shutting of his eyes, Eleison gave in.

Oh…I had thought Malin's love had satisfied me for the morning, but the devouring pressure of Eleison's kiss reawakened me to lust. While my mate's tongue brushed mine, then slid in to take control of my mouth, my husband's dark gaze drank us in with unfettered admiration.

"There…that's much better, isn't it. No reason to hide anything anymore, is there? Let's all be grateful we understand each other. Celebrate your love for Thecla openly, Eleison…I want you to."

Drawing back from my gasping lips, one knee perched on the edge of the bed upon which he sank into a sitting position beside me, Eleison chuckled to Malin. "I don't know if you'll say that in a minute…remember not to shoot the messenger, now…"

"Let me hear it," Malin said amid a sigh, crossing to his dressing room with an expression arranged to exhibit neutrality.

"Duke Montagne is here."

"Aleister's in Saalast? That's not like him—"

"No, he's not just in Saalast. He's *here*."

Malin stopped on the threshold of the dressing room to turn an arched brow upon Eleison. "He's *here*?"

"We are settling him into a room as we speak."

"It's six-thirty in the morning!"

Spreading his hands as an excuse to slide one arm around my waist and draw me, sighing softly, against his side, Eleison said, "Took the train."

""Took the train,"" repeated Malin with a shake of his head. "Well, that's annoying, but I don't see why it's cause for alarm. Not that we don't love your visits…you should greet us every morning."

While Malin disappeared into the dressing room with the flick of a light switch, I whispered to Eleison, "You should."

My mate smiled softly, his big, warm hand running up and down my bare flank. I wished he would touch me everywhere with those hands. Wished he and Malin *both* would, at once, as they had not yet.

Alas, such bliss was not in the cards for that morning.

"The reason I came to prepare you about Duke Montagne being here is, uh—it seems like the Overseer sent him."

The rooms grew so quiet I heard a maid laugh from the floor below us. Eleison watched the dressing room's empty doorway in anticipation of a response.

It didn't come.

"I'm not sure why she sent him," he filled the air by saying, "but—I thought I should let you know."

"No, no," Malin said briskly, striding out of the room with his trousers unbuttoned around his waist and a shirt in his hands. "You did the right thing."

But his face had changed. All that lurid mischief, that devilish pleasure, had disappeared. His angular features now formed a hard mask: serious, with his black eyes as dead and distant as those painted upon a sarcophagus.

Clearing my throat, I asked with some reluctance, "Does the Overseer normally send emissaries to you?"

"Not for a long time," Malin said in a tone that was, to say the least, preoccupied. With his shirt still in his hands, he crossed to the bathroom and stepped inside. "Excuse me a moment."

The door shut; Eleison and I looked at one another with a shared cringe. While their relationship extended back some time before my birth, I was vaguely aware of Malin's fraught history with the Overseer of the continent. They had gone to war against one another, which was an extraordinary occurrence in the relatively stable political landscape of our era; even more extraordinarily, his skill as a military tactician made him the victor. He not only kept Gudrune and his head, but expanded his territory and made his reputation clear. Malin Farrow was not a man to be trifled with, even by the Overseer.

It was therefore no surprise that he was so displeased to hear from her…but it was a little alarming. Only rarely did I observe Malin in such a dark turn; and when he took them, he avoided me. As though to keep from exposing me to something unfit, or contagious.

Sensing my disturbance, Eleison brushed his nose over my hair and bent to kiss my neck.

"Hey," he murmured again, that same bedroom tone he'd used on greeting me.

"Hello," I managed to whisper beneath the gasp his lips inspired.

"You smell like sex…" His lip curled against my throat just enough for me to feel the edges of his teeth. "And like Malin… which makes me want to fuck you right now to fix that…"

Moaning, especially as he drew the sheets down from my bosom to allow his kisses to descend, I warned him, "I'm bleeding this morning."

"Does it bother you?"

"Well—not as such, but—"

"Doesn't bother me, either." While Eleison's lips brushed over the bead of my left nipple, I choked to find myself outrageously sensitive. My fingers carded back through his perfectly styled black hair, my caress messing it to no complaint. His hands, traversing over my body, itched to slide beneath the sheets to tantalize my thighs, and what lay between—but, inhaling in frustration, he confessed, "There's no time this morning, though…and I can already tell that Malin's going to need you to distract him tonight."

I whimpered as his head raised to deliver another kiss to my lips. When we parted, I stroked his chest beneath his black tie and begged, "Come spend the evening with us."

I knew what would happen next; the sigh, the glance away, the sort of quiet half-smile he exhibited in lieu of baring his teeth.

"Thecla…"

"Please, Eleison…don't be so shy. You love me. Malin knows that, just like you know he loves me, and I love both of you. He's right…what is there to hide?"

Snorting slightly, my jealous mate flicked a glance toward the shut door where water ran for Malin's morning shave. "Your husband's body, if I get too jealous."

I didn't hide my frown. "That's not funny, Eleison."

"Sorry."

"You love Malin, don't you? Why does anybody need to be jealous of anyone else?"

His sigh was deep, a little guilty. While his hand raised to my cheek, I leaned into his caress and soon found myself pressed totally against his chest while he answered me.

"It's hard to explain what I feel. I accept it—everything about our relationships, I mean. And I'm humbled; eternally grateful that Malin is so generous about us. I know it's shitty to be jealous when he's gone to such lengths to embrace my relationship with you. But…I can't help it."

His nose once again brushed my flesh, his lips parting as he fully absorbed the scent of the sweat drying upon my neck.

"When I smell your body…when I smell another man on your body…the animal in me wakes up. The thoughts I have— they're not always mine." As if to emphasize his point, the gritting of his jaw gave his words the low timbre of a growl. I stroked his face, trailed my nails through his hair, and tried not to swoon before his beastly temperament.

After being altered for so long—after spending so many Rift Events transforming into a borro to protect the country properties where Malin frequently worked—Eleison had been in dire straits before Fate delivered us to one another. The biochemical benefits of our mating bond had effectively saved his life, stabilizing him against the Rift and allowing him to keep his humanity for as long as we loved one another.

But, much as Malin's tenebrous soul seemed lighter when he took shelter in my company, Eleison had a way of affecting the opposite change. My mate was a quiet but ultimately affable man to others, soft-spoken yet pleasant, charming, wry; but when we were alone, I felt the animal in him. The beast stared through his eyes, filling his mind with demands beneath which he sometimes collapsed. It felt as if the stabilization process was really a compartmentalization—a redirection of his inner animal's appetites away from the world and into me.

And oh, I loved it.

"Maybe," I whispered as his lips brushed over the curve of my shoulder, "if your borro is so jealous, that should tell you something."

"Yeah?"

"You wouldn't have to feel jealous if you would let go and enjoy yourself with us." My fingers curling against his scalp, I tilted his head back to gaze into his eyes. "You're jealous," I observed, "because Malin spends time with me when he wants to, and does it without concern—but you're still always thinking about him. About giving him time with me, or respecting him, or not displaying our relationship. But…"

I bit my lip and stroked along the starched collar of Eleison's shirt, allowing it to guide me to the tie I used to draw his mouth toward mine.

"I want to display our relationship, Eleison." My nose brushed his; our lips grazed. I murmured on, "I want you to feel as relaxed, as free with me, as Malin does. If you want me, come and take me. If you want me tonight…have me tonight. I'm sure it won't interrupt Malin's intentions. Only enhance them."

Eleison's brooding features remained firm in uncertainty. Pouting, I stroked down the length of the tie I still held.

"Please, think about it…I bounce between you two like a shuttlecock. As much as I adore spending time with each of you individually, oh…it would be so especially sweet if I could enjoy both your companionship at the same time."

Nostrils flaring while the water in the washroom stopped, Eleison held my chin between his thumb and forefinger.

"I'll think about it," he told me, his lips damply brushing mine.

While I moaned into his kiss, pressed against the hand-carved headboard by his passion, the door opened and Malin stepped back out.

"Ah"—a sigh of relief curled from him—"you really are a vision together…if only it were any other morning."

Smirking faintly, Eleison tore himself from me and stood. "Maybe another time," he agreed with a quick glance my way.

As grim as Malin still looked, his lips quirked in a dry smile.

"That's promising…I'll hold you to that, Eleison, be careful. Now, darling—"

With another sigh, this of displeasure, Malin filled the spot Eleison had just vacated and took up my hands.

"As much as I hate to ask this of you, knowing you and your schedule…would you, could you, do me the favor of keeping Duke Montagne amused this morning?"

Genuine excitement leapt across my face. In my time as Malin's consort, I felt I had contributed precious little. The household ran itself—or Charlotte made it seem that way—and, as I had no associations with the spouses of the various figures Malin needed to deal with on a semi-daily basis, I was not particularly useful from a political standpoint. All I could do was weave for him, which I had done diligently, and he had by then received three tapestries (two large, plus one small one that, private, remained upon the wall of our honeymoon villa) without ever giving indication he desired I do more than express my creativity for his pleasure.

To be asked this favor, therefore, was thrilling—and intimidating.

"I'd be happy to! I'm not sure how amusing I'll be, exactly—"

"Now, my dear, you're a pleasure to be around. He may not even be up to socializing until he's had some rest. Anyway, you know him—he was one of the courtiers staying overwinter in the country house."

That fact did reduce the pleasure of the task. It was perhaps too strong to say I actively disliked the courtiers…but they had made it clear at the time of my coming to Malin's home that I was not one of their number, and they demonstrated no interest in bridging the gap.

"At least we'll have something to talk about," I said, earning a kiss upon the back of my hand.

"I know, it's a tedious favor to ask when you could be spending the day working on what you'd prefer—but my day was already overbooked. Leave it to Parvati to pick such a bad time for her emissary to arrive…which brings me to my next point."

Head lifting, Malin fixed me with that intense stare of his.

"Don't pry if he's secretive about it…but, if you could uncover even a whiff of why he's here, that information could go a very long way in helping me decide how to treat him."

"Oh!" I laughed as I realized how fun the idea sounded. "Why, I feel like a spy!"

"You are, of course, darling…you're always my little spy, wherever you are. My second set of eyes and ears—my dearest partner of greatness."

Cheeks colored with delight, I smiled into him, and he into me. In a sandalwood haze, my husband bent to steal a kiss. Its unexpected fierceness promised rewards for my obedience.

Then he was gone, and meeting Eleison by the door. I was thrilled to note my mate had watched us and only now turned away to hold the door for his employer. Malin didn't dwell on it and kept thinking aloud to me, "I'll leave it to you to do as you believe is best…perhaps take him to lunch."

Eleison barely repressed a smirk. "Yeah, great idea, sir. Remember that time we went out to—what was that place, Bethlehem, with him?"

"I wish I could forget. Made an absolute ass of himself, oh, Hell…"

I cringed a little. "Is he a drunk?"

"He does like a big, stiff cocktail," said facetious Eleison.

"Who doesn't," quipped Malin, winking at me in a way that made me blush and laugh (and, I confess, find myself excited by new speculation about my husband) before he blew me a kiss. "Anyway, you'll figure it out, I have faith in you…ta-ta, ma chérie, I'll see you in the evening, let's touchpoint sometime afternoon if you can…"

"I love you, Thecla," Eleison told me while he shut the door behind them.

Then, I was alone.

The low chatter and receding footsteps of my beloveds faded off, vanishing in the direction of the foyer and elevator beyond.

Stomach tightening, I hurried up from the bed with a brisk, unhappy glance at the telltale spots upon the sheet beneath me. I recoiled back from it and fetched my robe without taking my eye from the stain; then, rapidly stripping the bed, (which Charlotte would have words with me for later, as usual when I lifted a finger), I bundled the spoiled sheets and hurried to bury them in the hamper of my suite, just down from Malin's.

The little boudoir was where I felt the infernal presence most strongly, but it was also the room where I had paradoxically noticed the smallest amount of interference. The suite was mine, all mine within Malin's apartment, and he had sworn he would not enter it without my explicit permission; Eleison, too, was invited in from time to time, but didn't frequent the Saalast house's master apartment and hadn't yet had occasion to stay overnight in it, let alone let himself into my suite.

The only man who violated the boundary of that room, I was sure, was not a man in so many words.

An empty thing, masquerading as a man.

That old fortune-teller…where was he now?

My skin crawled while the beautiful features of the dharmine emerged from the miasma of my thoughts, its sensual mercury eyes inescapable within their permanently smiling porcelain mask. I peered around the room, finding no trace of it in the flesh.

Typical. In fact, I hadn't seen it in the flesh since the honeymoon—if a very vivid dream (yes, just a dream—only a dream, Thecla, remember!) might be counted as flesh for an entity without true static form.

Yet, though I hadn't set eye on it while sleeping or waking, I knew the dharmine was near me all the time. When my thoughts were not occupied, it seemed to impress itself upon me: gently, but insistently. Like it pressed slow kisses against my very brain. Occasionally, when it was well-fed from feasting upon my sexual pleasure without my consent, thoughts entered my head—thoughts that were external to me.

The dharmine's thoughts. Its words, directed at me as if in conversation.

You needn't fear me, Madame…

"Shut up," I said in the silence, "shut up, you beast, and listen to me."

The thoughts quieted, the pressure lessening. I pointed at the hamper, speaking to my reflection in the vanity mirror for want of another point of focus.

"I know I can't seem to stop you from—hovering around me somehow. From feeding on my pain and pleasure. Not since I opened myself to you. But do not touch my blood, you revolting thing. Do you understand me?"

But your blood is so sweet…and I've sworn, Madame, your blood poisoning will not be my doing, so this is the only means I have to taste of you for now.

I bared my teeth against the chill of fright. "And no more of your blasted prophecies—no more slips from the future!"

I only mean to say, Madame, that I can help you. Didn't the last stains disappear perfectly? No harm done.

Lip curled, I let my hands hang in fists at my side.

"You're swine. It's enough that you intrude into my mind and siphon off the pleasure of my private lovemaking, or gorge yourself on the pains of my womb and my Rift allergy—you don't deserve my blood."

Oh, Madame! You're right, of course.

The pleasure in its tone was undeserved and repulsive. "Don't agree with me, swine."

But I am sorry, Madame...very sorry.

As disgusted as I was by the parasitic demon, there was something about it that was—thrilling. I couldn't admit it to myself then, but that was certainly how I felt in my boudoir when the dharmine fell silent and its presence, so evident since my beloveds' departure that morning, at last abated.

They subsisted on pleasure and pain—to such an extent that even their own pleasure and pain could sustain them. Though at first I had been fearful of the dharmine pursuing me, as the weeks passed and I lived my life unabducted and unharmed, I began to regard its presence as less of a danger and more of a nuisance.

I had taken to speaking sharply to it. When I was alone and the dharmine was there, I found myself unleashing upon it a tongue I never knew I had. Malin had certainly managed to coax out an imperious, rather sadistic side of me during our honeymoon, and he continued whenever he could to coach me in the fine arts of corporal ecstasy, both delivering and receiving.

But the dharmine, inviting my abuse, only received it. And, even though I could feel it taking insidious enjoyment and sustenance in my cruelty…I couldn't care.

Because I enjoyed being cruel *to* it, this beautiful, evil, subservient thing that I could feel very much wished to use me for some purpose I could not divine.

I just wasn't sure what that said about me.

Relieved by its absence, I heaved a sigh to stride from my drawing room.

And ran almost directly into Brea, my eavesdropping lady's maid.

To SAY I had no love for Brea would be an understatement, but when I had taken my bath she got the job of dressing me and seeing to my hair done well enough. I asked her for something elegant that day, mentioning Montagne, and her ears perked with the potential of gossip.

"I was *wondering* what the fuss was about. What's he doing here in Saalast?"

"I'm not sure," I told her cordially, my eyes following the reflections of her deft fingers through my hair. "I suppose we'll all find out once he's had some rest. Do you often listen to me think out loud, Brea?"

Her body stiffened behind mine just a little. "I'm sorry about that, Madame," she told me. "I was just—I thought you might be talking to Master, and I was afraid to interrupt."

"Don't linger next time…you startled me."

"Sorry, Madame."

I had accepted her apology and was ready to proceed, but the air remained thick with the buzzing of her thoughts. After a handful of long seconds during which she finished sweeping a fishtail braid down the side of my head and into a chignon in the back of my neck, she asked, "May I ask, Madame, um—"

Looking at her reflection, I waited.

"Just who *were* you talking to?"

"As I said, Brea…I was thinking out loud. Are we finished?"

"Erm—yes, Madame, you look—"

"Very good, thank you. I'll call for you if I need you later."

With an awkward curtsy, she left.

How immensely I had changed in the course of nine months! Just over half a year, and there I was in the gold-green room of my master: my husband. There I was, in a fine gown whose red silk fell in a stern profile to my ankles but hugged tightly to my waist and bust.

There I was, taking up the necklace of ruby and diamond given to me by my husband on our wedding day.

It was strange to think that, not so long ago, I had lived in one little room over a bookbinder in Lescaut. My clothes had been old: largely handmade, or at least hand-repaired before being passed into my life. I had felt so alien in this glamorous world.

I had thought I was merely human.

When would the mysterious powers of the riftborn make themselves known in me? When would I learn what Eleison felt when the violet light of an Event cracked the sky and he ran with four paws, hunted with fangs and teeth? I had already changed so much, yet I was impatient for so much more.

If only I had mindfully enjoyed the days of my simple, mortal existence! But they were long gone. I had changed, and I wished to change more. As Malin once advised me, I wished to feel worthy of what he had bestowed upon me.

For, though I was the consort of one of the most powerful men in the world, I was still nervous to be expected to entertain a duke on such short notice. It seemed in all the romance paperbacks the maids traded back and forth that there was a duke waiting around every corner, but I had learned while plunging into Malin's libraries since our marriage that in fact the number of duchies on the continent was small. Montagne was a formidable holding in the territory of Elita, which happened to abut the Overseer's capital; and it seemed the Duke Montagne had power in sufficient amounts to travel widely, make friends in Malin's circles, and show up where he pleased, when he pleased…even if that was to a territory master's private residence.

So, it was natural for me to feel anxious before meeting this Aleister fellow…but, I confess, he evaporated my trepidation so quickly that I soon understood why so many unfriendly territories welcomed him with equally open arms.

"Aha!"

Much to my surprise, I discovered him taking breakfast in the rooftop garden with the help of a tip from Charlotte. Having already finished and been in the process of sweeping a lavender napkin across his mouth, the duke saw me first and rose to greet me with hand extended.

"Thecla, it's so good to see you again! Congratulations on the marriage, wish I could have made it to the wedding."

"Oh, we eloped—"

"Really! How romantic…here I had thought my invitation got lost in the mail."

I was so astonished by his changed demeanor that I didn't know what to say in response. Now seeing him again, I could put a face to the name. The Duke Montagne was a dapper gentleman, with a perfectly coiffed princely hairdo of gold curls tamed until the ideal moment, at which point they fell wildly across the edge of his forehead to sharpen his sea green eyes. He was smiling, clean-shaven, somehow feminine in charm and manner—and I distinctly remembered him looking through me like I wasn't there when I was but the titleless pet of the territory master.

All the same, I made myself smile. I was practiced at it, for it was what I did on all those pastoral Lescaut days when I wanted to stay in my little studio reading instead of weaving for somebody else. It was a pleasant smile: professional, but not overly fond.

The duke returned it in spades.

"I'm sure we'll have some fete—some sort of banquet or something eventually." I fluttered my hand in a clumsy wave while producing an informal little laugh. "Perhaps on our anniversary. If you really want to know the truth, I think Malin enjoys formal affairs far more than I do. I'm rather nervous in the public eye."

"Really? But you're so natural at it. Where are you from, again?"

"Oh, uh—"

For the first time, I was embarrassed of Lescaut. The heat in my cheeks spread to my ears while I stammered out a discreet response.

"I'm sure you wouldn't have heard of it…it's very out of the way, but—Montagne! I've heard it's lovely. And you've lived there all your life?"

After a mean snort he pruned before it grew to laughter, the duke slid his hands into the pockets of his trousers and regarded me with private mockery glinting from his eye.

"Yes, dear, of course. Montagne's a hereditary title, just like territory master and everything else…unless a surviving spouse or trustee of some sort is appointed special successor and ratified by the Overseer, but what a pain. Much easier when it's a relative, and easiest of all when, whatever they decide, the person with the title thinks ahead enough to make arrangements while they're living…don't get me started on the nightmare of inter-territory disputes that will spark off when Overseer Parvati dies without a natural or appointed heir. It's all very tedious."

"Of course," I said, inwardly wishing to throw myself over the edge of the roof to escape the embarrassment of a moment I'd be doomed to remember forever. "Yes, of course, how silly of me. You'll have to forgive me, Duke—"

"Please, 'Aleister,' Aleister Hartford, forget the formality."

The tension of my shoulders easing, I nodded and smiled in relief. He smiled back, more organically now, and said, "There, that's what I mean when I say you're a natural in public—you've got such a gentle, genuine look to you. I'm sure Malin is over the moon to have you…a statesman's dream wife!"

After wiggling his finger at me teasingly, Aleister dropped a hand upon my shoulder to walk along toward the stairs with me as though we were a pair of politicians.

And then I realized in a stark bolt of cold reality that we *were* a pair of politicians, and I felt a little nauseous.

"So, *tell* me! How's it *been*? You must be absolutely *dying* to gossip with somebody who knows Malin."

"Oh, no, I—"

"Don't be so shy! You're the territory master's consort—*Malin Farrow*'s consort. I think most people would *enjoy* bragging at least a little…especially after we all gave you such a stony reception back in Karrisregion." He flashed a childish flick of his eyes and a sort of pout, adding, "You must forgive me, Thecla. I was a louse."

"Not at all," I lied, thereby sacrificing any pleasure I might have taken in telling him he was, in fact, some fellow to have treated me so poorly and now speak as if we'd been chums for ages. The reward was the outward appearance, if not the inward experience, of grace and maturity, and Aleister seemed to note that as I went on. "Let's forget it all. Goodness knows, you can see I'm still learning my role here! I knew even less last time I saw you…I can't really blame you for failing to take an interest in me."

Somehow, by some infuriating enchantment of his walking and talking, Aleister had led me down the stairs from the roof without ever announcing his intention to do so. I simply realized that we were walking down the stairs, and that his chatterbox tongue had lulled me into a kind of trance.

"I am curious, though, Aleister—how is it that you know Malin so well you seem able to drop in at a moment's notice?"

With another flashing smile, Aleister slid his hand from my shoulder and back into the pocket of his trousers. "Oh, we go back ten years or so! Shocking to say it out loud, *ten*. Anyway… He's been a mentor to me—as I would suspect he is to you. Though it's not Malin's fault that I'm here, if you want to know the truth…in fact, it's yours!"

Balking a little, particularly as he was there on behalf of the Overseer, I narrowly managed to produce something like a laugh instead of succumbing to the fright threatening to show on my face.

"*My* fault! Really, is that so?"

"It certainly is…but, I'd better wait for that until we can meet with Malin. Just where is the old dog prowling? I'm surprised he hasn't greeted me yet!"

"Yes, well—he expressed his apologies and sent me along in his stead. He is *very* busy today."

"Oh, no! My timing is usually better than this."

"It's a pity! He'll be occupied all day, so far as he told me. I think he might be trying to free up dinner, but I wouldn't count on it…he called the day 'overbooked.'"

Tutting, Aleister said, "Well, there's always tomorrow if he can't speak to me today…but the sooner he sees me, the sooner I'll be out of his hair. Now, my dear Thecla, if you'll excuse me—"

Yawning with theatrical aplomb, hand emerging from his pocket to cover his mouth a little too late, Aleister nodded toward the guest room that had once been my Saalast quarters. "I am bushed. Luxury beds, my eye…no train is meant for sleeping in. Let's go out this afternoon, though! I have to say, Saalast looks cleaner since I was last around…maybe even safer."

It had certainly felt safer to me since the death of Dr. Gall… especially since I embraced our security detail. Where once I was resistant, now I was liberated by them, and I smiled at the thought of hitting the town with Aleister as he left.

"Yes, it's a lovely city. Perhaps we can find a show to take in…rest well, it's a pleasure to have you here…"

When his door shut, I went to the library on the first floor. At the writing desk, I jotted a note.

Dear—
Spoke to Aleister briefly; he's resting now, we may
go out later. Says he's here because of me, won't
explain why until we're with you. Dinner?
Love,
Thecla

A few minutes later, I found just the woman for the delivery. Charlotte, looking about as displeased by the visit as anyone, was in the middle of making coffee for Malin's ongoing meeting. Her eyes had hardened to jade daggers that thrust across me as I entered the kitchen, at which point her cheeks tensed as she braced for further chaos.

"Good morning, Madame. I trust you have already met the duke?"

Just as she had been in my family's little cottage in Lescaut, Charlotte was inscrutable, discreet—yet, having grown close to her over the past months of daily interaction, I could tell by her tone just how thrilled she was.

"He certainly is a character," I said, smiling pleasantly in case any of his staff happened to be within earshot. "Would you leave this with Malin when you bring him that coffee, Charlotte?"

As I slid the note upon her silver tray, she nodded. "Certainly. Anything else?"

Glancing over my shoulder toward the door, I bit back my grin until I could no longer wholly stifle it. "I know you hate talking about men," I whispered to her, "but there's a chance, the smallest chance, that Eleison might come see me with Malin tonight."

One coppery brow arched perhaps a millimeter in what, for her, qualified as a massive show of interest. "Oh?"

"Oh, yes."

"Hm...well, you're right to say that I generally don't care for discussing troubles with men...but, if you make any interesting discoveries in the field of their research, I'd be curious to hear."

Giggling like a schoolgirl at her tacit approval, I whispered, "I'll let you know how it goes…oh, cross your fingers, Charlotte. I just want Eleison to—you know. Relax into our life."

"He will, eventually, when he fully believes it's real."

A little surprised, I pondered, "You think he's worried it might—evaporate?"

"Aren't you?"

"Sometimes," I admitted, "but—less so every day."

Shrugging mildly, Charlotte suggested, "Then he probably feels the same way…it's just taking him longer to believe in it."

Yes, it was true. As usual, Charlotte was right. I was impatient to have everything. Much as, on our honeymoon, I had been impatient to know Malin, I was now similarly impatient for Eleison to grow confident in the arrangement. Perhaps that was what made me so testy those days, the dharmine aside…neither of those very reasonable cravings had been satisfied.

Malin, for instance. By the end of our honeymoon, I had reluctantly come to see I hounded my husband for the details of his past not out of my own desire to be trusted but out of a lack of trust for him; and I had since committed myself to trusting him from the bottom of my heart, and waiting patiently for him to open himself. Yet…that meant I remained unable to fulfill the natural craving to intimately, thoroughly know my husband. To know the contents of his mind and his past and his plans.

I always seemed to be on the other side of some door to his soul, still yearning for entry.

Not long later, I was hard at work weaving when the response came via Charlotte. Yes, dinner, 7 PM, first floor dining room. I was to select the menu.

"I don't suppose," I said with a pitiful look, "that you might assist in that?"

"Only if you can stand to get up from that loom for more than five minutes…"

Stretching, I shot a reluctant look back at it and confessed, "I suppose I should consider myself lucky I stole the time I did today."

"Very mature of you. Oh, and by the by—"

Charlotte paused before we exited the room, her voice lowering.

"The sheets, Madame—they were the ones left in your suite's hamper?"

My cheeks were already tight with cold anger. "Yes, the very same."

"Hm…this is why I wish you would leave the linens for my girls. No one can find a stain anywhere on it."

Though my upper lip attempted to curl into a sneer of disgust, I couldn't let it contort that way before Charlotte. I dared not explain to her—to anyone who did not need, truly need, to know—about the dharmine.

Frankly, the only ones who needed to know were Malin and Eleison, and even then, only one of them was the least bit privy to the secret of its existence.

Though…he was not aware of the way it had steadily developed as a presence in my life.

"Very good. I'm sure it will be discovered eventually…or perhaps it was my imagination."

Charlotte looked at me, her expression probing as always.

"You do," she agreed, opening the door at last, "have a very active imagination."

Y THE AFTERNOON, I discovered that the duke had not only roused, but gone out without me. Content to accept the snub, I wrote a letter to my stepmother and half-sister with only the vaguest shock to reflect I had written them perhaps twice since returning from the honeymoon. I was so desperate to distract myself from the dharmine that some days I wove from the hour Malin left me until the moment Eleison was free from work to join me for supper.

And even then, the dharmine was still there. It was there with me that very day. I had worked my way back to the start of the play and presently depicted the wicked heroine's meeting with the ill-fated king, rendered as a queen in my version. Already reflected as it had been in a freak arrangement of the first tapestry's threads, the dharmine became a witch to be hidden somewhere within each composition, and its silver eyes glinted out at me from the latest textile.

So, really, I was never safe…and there was no excuse for neglecting my family. Out of guilt, I enclosed money—Malin was always filling my purse faster than I could empty it—and dropped the letter into the postbox not five minutes before the postman came down the street.

The timing felt fortuitous until, as my foot set upon the first landing on my way back to my work in progress, the RMS alarmed through the house.

"Extreme Rift Event Advisory," the voice advised. "Seek shelter immediately and follow your local instructions to acquire food in cases of extended isolation. Estimated time until Event: fifteen minutes."

An extreme Rift Event! I grew dizzy and extended a hand to the nearby rail to brace myself. There was no reason for me to be especially afraid, as the average Rift Event tended closer in length to an abbreviated extreme one all the time. I had even lived through an extreme Event of particular note, an awful one that lasted a week, but I was five at the time and hardly understood what was going on. That was, as usual, thanks to my father, who sheltered me from the Events and all the monsters they brought from that baleful other place. I remember having no power, and throwing out some food that had gone bad without the ice box, but Papa had managed to make it seem fun. He had kept us distracted from the Event like always, had continued my lessons by lantern, and never showed the least sign of fear or distress.

It was amazing to me that he was able to do it. Ever since I had kicked my way out of that overturned carriage, I had been afraid of Rift Events as never before. The headaches they brought had gotten subtly worse with each exposure, the latest and longest being Malin's kidnapping. Everything about the Events seemed malicious to me as they never had before.

Well…maybe not everything was malicious.

While the house exploded with the frantic energy of a team of servants shuttering windows and checking the various levels of household staples, I ducked from the way in time to avoid some security officers hurrying down the stairs.

"Now don't you go wandering out in this, Ma'am," teased the security man Ignatius as he strode past with memories of losing me through the window of my weaving room.

"I won't—but someone must look out for Duke Montagne, he's—"

"—awful weather," the duke was just that very moment complaining bitterly to his footman, who entered with him and, at the duke's command, took his coat and left. Smoothing his waistcoat with an unpleasant expression as he conferred with his thoughts, Aleister plucked his watch from his pocket and bent his head to check it.

A big hand, warm and firm, grabbed me by the elbow and pulled me back toward the library.

Gasping, knowing Eleison by instinct, I turned and threw my arms around his neck. That truly animal growl rumbled up from his chest as his lips brushed mine, inhabiting his words like a possessing spirit as he murmured, "I take it you heard the alarm?"

"Of course. Eleison, I'm afraid—"

"Don't be…wow—"

Despite himself and his sense of propriety, Eleison ran his hands over my arms and down into the curve of my waist with a gruff chuckle. "You're shaking like a leaf, baby. You okay?"

Though Eleison had been my mate longer than Malin had been my husband, Eleison had endured a limited number of Rift Events with me. In the country house, he had always been out on the grounds: exposed to the danger, unsafe and destabilized by the Rift. But though he was perfectly safe here in Saalast, and would be able to stay inside with the rest of us while the city was protected by its police and mercenary forces, I trembled before him as I never had.

And I knew why. It was because, without my consenting to properly feed it, Rift Events seemed the only time the dharmine had strength enough to manifest in the flesh.

Now here we were, staring down a prolonged one.

"I'm sorry to be so—so ridiculous." I tried to laugh at my own trembling, but Eleison shook his head.

"You're not ridiculous…Malin sent me. He said you'd need me to settle you down for sure….he was right." One hand supporting the back of my neck, Eleison told me, "You're safe, Thecla."

How I wished I could tell him my true fears! How I longed to share the information on the dharmine with my mate, who had dispatched one of those heinous demons even before he was genetically altered with the DNA of a rift monster.

Yet—I couldn't speak on the matter. I couldn't risk making the dharmine stronger. Not without finding some way to contain it, if it were possible. Perhaps that was the contract I would make with it…the contract that it claimed bound it to me for eternity, even before that contract had been made.

My lips dry, my tongue darting across them, I began to say to Eleison, "I'm safe as long as I'm with you, anyway," but the words were halfway from my mouth when the duke's footfall and shocked scoff interrupted us. We glanced over, still in one another's arms, visible from where we stood just within the doorway of the library.

"Awfully bold, aren't you? Most politician's wives take lovers, but not so early on…and not with the door hanging open. Unless they're into a certain type of risk, of course."

Snorting, Eleison flicked a glance from the duke's foot to his head. "Afternoon, Your Grace. Hope your stay's been pleasant."

"I don't know about pleasant, but it's certainly taking a turn for the intriguing."

Brow arched upon me, Aleister regarded me with new, far keener interest.

"If you don't mind me indulging my favorite hobby—that is, sticking my nose where it doesn't belong—*are* you stepping out on Malin, or do my eyes deceive me?"

"Not at all," I said coolly. "I'm loyal to Malin, just as I'm loyal to my mate here. They're not in competition."

Now both his eyebrows were crawling up to his hairline. Eyes widening with them, Aleister set his hands upon his hips. "*Mate*? What on earth—you mean, that business with altered individuals and pheromones and whatnot? You're *altered!*"

"It would seem I am," I said, nodding. "And as I was falling in love with Malin, it became apparent that Eleison and I were mates; so, we have an understanding."

"Some understanding!" With very real intrigue, Aleister stroked his clean-shaven jaw as though in search of a beard. "Sounds to me like I'd ought to make an appointment over at Sigma while I'm here…oh, what a fun loophole."

"It's not a *loophole*," I told Aleister in unbridled annoyance.

His hand still upon my waist, Eleison spoke up for me.

"It benefits Malin."

"That a fact?" One arm crossed along his diaphragm

to support the hand that covered his smiling mouth, his tone struggling to remain neutral in its level of interest.

My mate didn't flinch from the truth, though his roughly edged tone made it clear he did not relish the interrogation. "Without Thecla, I would be so destabilized by the Rift that I'd be more animal than man. Malin would lose his footman…then where would he be after all these years of getting me used to his ways?"

"Mercy. I suppose that's true, Eleison…and Thecla. Thecla, Thecla! Aren't you just more interesting all the time."

Chuckling to himself, Aleister continued up the stairs while calling after, "And what time should one expect supper here?"

"Seven," I told him, earning a glance back and a respectful nod when I added, "and Malin will be there."

"Very good! I'm looking forward to it."

Upstairs, Aleister's footfalls continued until a door shut.

I sighed, leaning against Eleison's chest with my own knotted by annoyance.

"See," said Eleison with a flick of his eyes. "This is why I'm still reticent to take you out on the town…even to flirt with you the way I'd like." As he spoke, his arms tightened around me, the warmth of his hands running up and down my back a blessed relief. "The more relaxed I am with you, the more normal and casual, the more other people will talk."

"Then let them, as Malin says. I don't care, Eleison—I'd rather explain myself ten thousand times than miss out on a single kiss from you."

"It's not safe. The general public knows you're the rags-to-riches riftborn girl Malin plucked from the streets of Lescaut. The more people know you're altered, the more dangerous it'll be to whatever third generation child you bring into the world someday."

That was true, and had crossed my mind along with Malin's. As my family had been commanded to avoid registering me so that Malin could collect me—a precious commodity, as both a second-generation altered and a riftborn—Malin had been forced to apply for my immediate registration when we were to be married. The Overseer could not say "No" out of public respect to him, but I could not help recalling now that the digital registry file I had recently perused contained an error. Rather than listing my mother as Giselle, Malin had submitted my registry paperwork with my stepmother's name. At least, my stepmother was listed as my birth mother, with the woman who died a few hours into my life nowhere to be found. I hadn't said anything about it at the time of noting the issue.

Now, in Eleison's arms with my cheeks still warm with the frustrated passion of a love I could not seem to share with the world, I wondered if it had been an error, or if it had been a strategic decision made to prevent the Overseer from challenging our marriage. If second-generation altered individuals were rare, third were still practically unheard of; and, if the Overseer felt the territory of Gudrune and its master could not be fully trusted, the last thing she would want would be an altered successor to Malin's position.

So I understood it was in all our best interest to keep things quiet to a certain extent—but I simply could not stand denying Eleison's importance to me, and could not disgrace my love for him by downplaying its validity.

"There must be some way we can spin the relationship to those who would ask—and who merit a response out of station or circumstance, of course. I *want* you to be able to flirt with me, Eleison! I *want* to go out with you, oh!" At the cry of love that escaped me, his eyes lit up, and he bowed his head to ignite my mouth with the fire of his kiss. When he drew away, I remained pressed closely to his chest, his heart keeping the tempo of mine. "It's your privilege as my mate. After all...to me, at least, you're as important as Malin. It's a social promotion, even if it isn't a professional one. Please, Eleison—"

I surveyed the depths of those beautiful eyes, always overflowing with emotion since he had been made more himself by his stabilization.

"You're so dear to me. I want to give you everything I can—so much. Oh, I'm frustrated sometimes when I think of it... if you were a woman and I were a man, I could furnish you with treasures, or—"

"Thecla—you already saved my life."

I faltered, stopped by his observation as much as by the caress of his hand over my cheek. He stared deeply into me, his lowered lids tender but serious.

"I don't want you to ever feel like you need to do anything for me. You already saved me once—and being near you continues to save me. I can live my life again. Be myself again, even with a Rift Event like the one we're about to have. Although, I admit..."

He chuckled, and his lip quirked up from his top row of teeth to reveal the sharp edge of a cuspid.

"I've been feeling a little cagey since finding you like this."

My breathing shallow, I pawed at Eleison's chest and strained against the irresistible energy already whirling within me. "I don't know how he can expect me to help him host dinner in this condition, Eleison—oh, darling, I feel overwhelmed today."

"Come with me," he said simply, sliding me against his shoulder before, against expectation, he stooped and slipped me up off the floor. I cried out, laughing, then sighed in delight for the ease with which Eleison held me.

And, oh…just a bit of delicious fright—awe, perhaps—for his abilities. For the monster within him that seemed to want me, too.

And not in the same way Eleison did.

The man who once kidnapped me from the Saalast streets (for had it not been a real kidnapping, even if by someone I knew, and back to my own home?) was the same man who held me now, but he wasn't. The man who had held me at gunpoint and knifepoint on two separate occasions was also this man, but he wasn't. There was something that came roaring out of him sometimes—just sometimes. And when it did, I ached with desire.

When Eleison had whisked me up several flights of stairs despite whatever reticence he must have felt at the occasional ogling from a passing maid or two, he set me on my feet and whirled to shut the door. Beneath his hand, it slammed so hard it echoed, and I cried out at the noise mere seconds before he was upon me.

His quarters in Saalast were smaller than his apartment in the country house, but I enjoyed them more. In that place, all we had done was fight; in this one, all we did was make love…if one could call it that while Eleison's passion climbed past his senses and into the naked desire to have me. His mouth fiercely plunged against mine, his hands capturing my face and keeping me against his kiss while he forced me back to the bed. I gasped against the scrape of his teeth, the ardent strokes of his tongue, oh, those lips—

"You don't smell like blood to me," he said, that ominous growl prowling beneath the breath of each word as he pushed me down into the dark navy bedclothes of his plush mattress. "You sure you're on your cycle?"

"Maybe not," I stammered, my heart giving a happy little flutter of hope that the spotting was an indication of something else. "Oh, no, maybe not—"

I shivered as his lips and nose moved over my neck and down the declivity of my breasts, a hound seeking traces of his prey's scent. His practiced hands untied the ribbon at the waist of my dress and swiftly saw to its buttons as well as the lace beneath, and I found myself almost screaming in ecstasy to be exposed to him when the bustier was similarly dismissed by his expertise.

The Event left me so sensitive that his very eye upon me was its own bliss. When most of my clothes were away and I managed to get him out of his jacket, I reached the limit of what he permitted me. After catching my hands and pushing them away from his tie, he kissed his way along the path of my stomach.

"I've never felt you shake like this, baby…"

My teeth rattled in my head, the thought of my shaking increasing my awareness of the growing Rift Event; and that, in turn, increasing its power over me. Not unlike the dharmine—

No!

As Eleison slid my panties down my thighs, glancing briefly into their absorbent bandage and confirming, "No blood," before tossing them aside, the room grew a few degrees colder. Gravity, a few ounces of pressure more powerful.

While my mate lowered toward my center, I raised my head to look at him and instead cried out in fear.

The dharmine stood in the room, his lovely smile a strange crossbreed of bliss and malice.

Eleison, thinking my exclamation had been for the contact of his lips, (and it had been, in part), carried on without awareness of the demon that had appeared within his shut door. As my mate's tongue slid to work and his ruby eyes lowered, the dharmine's silver eyes dominated my attention. I could not look away from his marble visage, or that brilliant mane of white hair and the braid into which it was tamed over his shoulder, or the powerful muscles of a dangerously cut torso visible through the fuligin cloak falling to his boots. Even his legs in the dark leather of his trousers were obviously well-hewn. I exhaled shakily, rectifying my gaze to the demon's face and trying desperately to summon the courage to dismiss the thing in Eleison's presence.

"Eleison can't see me," whispered the dharmine. "Not yet... you haven't been keeping up your end of the bargain, Madame."

I wanted to tell him—no, "it," a blasted beast like all creatures from the Rift—I wanted to tell it that I had made no bargain yet, and that I detested its ways as much as I detested its insistence on holding me to a contract I had not yet made, or even envisioned; yet it seemed to understand all that in my face, or mind, and as its smile widened, fangs flashed along with its teeth.

Eleison carried on pleasuring me, his tongue and lips expertly stimulating the pulsating little nerve that was so unbearably sensitive some of his caresses made me scream.

"I suppose I understand your reticence to give up your blood to me, even if it's tissue otherwise wasted...but, if you will not give me your discarded blood, Madame, you must feed me something else. Particularly if I am to fulfill my duties to you...to protect you when not even the beast within you can keep you safe."

I didn't want its damned help. All I knew was that I was afraid it would hurt me—or, worse, hurt Malin or Eleison. Gritting my teeth, I fought to ignore it: I would deny it every scrap of attention I could.

"Oh, please!" I tugged at Eleison's hair, trembling, unable to bear the rapid battery of his tongue while he led me to an edge that fast approached. "Eleison, oh, mate with me—fuck me, please, I'll never stop shaking otherwise, I feel so empty and afraid—"

Without responding by more than a flick of those red eyes up at me, Eleison removed his tie and stripped away dress shirt and undershirt at once. When he lunged upon the bed, both our hands scrambled toward his belt and trousers. As I yanked the strap from his waist, he pushed the fabric down and made me groan with the mere sight of his readiness.

When I raised my eyes from him, I had a second of relief in which I realized the dharmine was gone. Then, Eleison was upon me, over me, pouring kisses into my mouth and setting himself against me without the need of a look or even a hand. Both my men knew my body so well, better all the time—but Eleison, especially, had an approach to it that was natural, confident, pure. As his tongue, still bearing the ghost of my arousal, slid into my mouth, he plunged himself to the hilt in me in one long, steady stroke.

"Oh!" I screamed against his mouth, yielding to his kisses for a few more seconds before screaming again, "Oh, Eleison, yes—yes, please—"

"Holy shit." Almost astonished with desire, Eleison stared into my face while setting his hips to stunning work. "Oh, baby, you really do need it today, don't you..."

"Yes! Yes, please, oh—"

"This is what the Rift does to you while I'm busy running all over the mansion property? Poor girl…must be miserable…I wish all Rift Events were extreme ones now, though…"

He had such a superb way of using his anatomy to exert the most addictive pressure against the roof of my pelvis. While he fucked me senseless, I nodded through a brow furrowed by the intensity of his strokes.

"Yes, yes! Oh, Eleison—when the Events come and Malin has sent you out, extreme or no, I go mad! I need you both, I can't just have him—oh, I can't stand to be left empty for a second, I want a prick in me the whole Event, oh, ah—!"

My words incited him, tweaking his jealousy and his arousal to leave him hard as iron. Eleison rammed into me, the slapping of flesh beneath my lurid words a sensual backbeat along with the rattle of the bed frame around us. Hand fitting to my jaw, his thumb running over my lip, Eleison assessed my face.

"You need it even more than normal, you mean…" While I gave a naughty, guilty sort of laugh, he growled. That bestial noise excited my senses so that, near screaming, I thrust back up against him and tugged at my own hair. He enjoyed my every gesture through heavily lidded eyes, his intent observation of the effect his prick had upon me taking me to a point of no return.

"I never thought I'd be comfortable sharing my mate with another man, let alone Malin…but, you want to know a secret, Thecla?"

"What, oh, what? Tell me, Eleison, please—"

"When you say something that makes me picture you with Malin's prick working nice and deep inside you, I still get jealous… but it turns me on just a little, too."

"Eleison, oh, yes!"

"Like I was telling you this morning…I think of him fucking you, and I think about how hot and eager you are, and I want to reclaim my territory right away."

He bared his teeth while thrusting hard into me, provoking my hips to buck his while my feet dug into the bed against a high rising pressure.

"But," Eleison went on in that sensual growl, his eye streaking across my face, down my body, down to where we were conjoined, then to my face again, "you know, Thecla, baby…the more I think about you and Malin…the more I think I could stand to watch sometime."

As he spoke, my body at last reached its explosion. While my throbbing flesh begged for proof of his passion, his mouth swept down over mine.

And the dharmine, extended along the ceiling above us just as I lay upon the bed below, smiled softly to drink in my ecstasy, then disappeared.

ALTHOUGH THERE WAS no doubt that my husband had sent Eleison to tend to my needs as a gesture of love, said gesture served a calculated purpose. Malin understood even better than I did that I was not going to be able to play hostess unless my fever had been reduced, and although he would have loved to do it himself, Eleison really was his right-hand man.

And my mate had, of course, not hesitated to jump to the task.

We must have been at it on and off for three hours before collapsing into a love-sedated doze that was, thankfully, interrupted by Charlotte's wise knock. "I had a feeling you needed a wake-up call, and I can't seem to locate our dear Brea." She cast a brisk glance past Eleison's shoulder at me, then down to her pocket watch. "Please advise Madame she must be ready to join Master for dinner in forty minutes."

"Thank you, Charlotte," I said with relief, waiting for the door's closure to slide up and into Eleison's bathroom. He followed me, fetching a pair of towels from the cabinet and pursuing me into the glass-enclosed shower.

It was so difficult to resist him…and he was particularly excited by me that afternoon, I'd noticed, even given his usual zeal. The dharmine's words rolled through me again, reminding me that I had as much a beast within me as Eleison had within him. That I was just as subject to the Rift.

The only difference was that the animal within me remained dormant.

Would I be like my mother? Charlotte, midwife that fateful night, once said Giselle possessed ventil DNA. If that were so, whenever that altered part of myself awoke, (if it ever did!), would I not become a ventil, too? A creature not at all unlike a deer?

Would I not be prey to the borro within Eleison, rather than breeding mate?

I had so many questions about myself, and my body's response to the raging Rift Event left me ruminating on the matter more than usual that day. After the shower, when at last we separated long enough to don civilized disguises and look like two dressed human beings, Eleison watched me button my dress to the collar before coming over to help me retie the ribbon at the back of its waist.

"How are you feeling, Thecla? You seem quiet."

"I'm fine, of course…just…oh, well— I'm eager to get this over with, I'll say that!"

I laughed a little, checking the band of Malin's gold ring upon my left ring finger, then the copper bangles upon my wrists, then the tendrils of my loose hair in the mirror. There was no hope of getting it back into Brea's chignon.

I could help you, Madame.

The probe of a tongue from within my ear, rather than without it. Inhaling sharply against the intrusion of the evil spirit, I brushed a few chestnut locks back over my shoulder and smiled up at my mate.

"Shall we?"

I was firm with Eleison about learning to be comfortable with our relationship, but there were still aspects of the power dynamic that grew tricky when he was required to fulfill more traditional assignments. He was my mate, which did elevate him; but he was Malin's footman. Just as Eleison was jealous of my marriage from time to time, so I was occasionally a bit green-eyed over the way he still seemed to put his relationship with Malin at the forefront. As he was, as he put it to me, "on assignment" from the moment we stepped out of his bedroom, Eleison became infuriatingly formal. He walked behind me, respectful and professional, and though the burn of his crimson eyes into the back of my body nearly reduced me to cinders, he made no move to touch me as we progressed downstairs.

And I ached with desire more than ever at his formality, boiling inside of myself to touch him again; to be touched again.

But then we were at the dining room whence emanated jovial male conversation, and as I filled the door Eleison opened for me, Malin and I perked to see one another. He smiled, his knowing eyes sliding over my loose hair, then Eleison at my back. While the duke at his right made similar assessment from behind a full wine glass, Malin stood to take me in his arms and kiss my cheek.

"There you are, darling…gorgeous, as always."

Flush with pleasure at his praise while he drew my seat for me, I glanced between the drinking men and asked, "I'm not late, am I?"

"Oh, dear, no. I gave in and canceled a few things, so Aleister and I were catching up a bit. It's been a busy few months since we last spoke." With a respectful nod to Eleison, who took a customary place about five feet behind Malin's chair and slightly to the right, the territory master reclaimed his seat and went on, "We started with wine in the parlor, and by two or three in it just made more sense to migrate along here."

""Two or three" glasses," I teased, "or bottles?"

Malin laughed in surprise, tapping me on the back of the hand while our guest missed the joke. "Uncle here's got a superb nose for wine," extolled Aleister, nearly sloshing his out of the glass with the swirl of his hand at the wrist. "I can never help but interrogate him for new suggestions whenever I visit... Before you know it, we're plastered."

Malin produced the chuckle of a man who had let his friend outpace him by at least a glass or two, probably more. Ears having perked, however, I said with excitement, "I didn't realize you two were related."

While Aleister laughed into his glass, Malin's smile changed into a sly one that begged curious interpretation. "Not literally, of course. Just a fond nickname from a long time ago...aha, here we are."

The door swung open to permit the smell of food, and about three minutes of arranging and explanation later, we were left to our devices with it. While the men went at it with great gusto and I helped myself to a little duck, Malin glanced over his shoulder.

"Have you eaten? Sit down, Eleison, please, I'll send for another plate..."

"Goodness, yes," agreed Aleister, perhaps a hair too eagerly. "Come sit with us, Eleison, eat! Would you like a drink?"

"No, thanks," he said of the alcohol, sliding down into the empty seat at my left while I glowed in pleasure. "But thank you, sir. I think I'll eat a little."

"Bet you two worked up an appetite," quipped the duke, wiggling his eyebrows while Malin cleared his throat. Scoffing, the younger aristocrat said, "What? Goodness, Malin, you get married and get into this little ménage, but you're suddenly a prude with *me?*"

"I just can't imagine Madame Farrow is eager to have her love life interrogated by a fellow she barely knows…especially not one who so notably snubbed her back in Karrisregion."

Pouting at Malin's admonishment, which was paired with a certain expectant look, Aleister snatched up the other duck leg and said, "Now, Uncle, we've already made up for that…haven't we, Thecla?"

"To the duke's credit," I agreed with a thin smile, "he did apologize."

Beaming at me, Aleister went on, "There, you see? I'm a *real* boy now…two years of having a respectable title changes a man, wouldn't you say."

"Just wait until twenty."

An unaffected shudder wracked Aleister's lithe frame. "Please, Uncle, let's not go that far. I'm still trying to cope with thirty-one…God! I'm just not ready to die, but I don't relish the thought of looking in the mirror to see an old man! No offense."

While Eleison took up a knife and fork that had, thanks to some hidden button of Malin's, been brought to him along with a perfect duplicate of our plates, my mate suggested, "You could always make an appointment over at Sigma…they might even give us a discount on my brother's Stabilify for a month or two if you put me down as your referral."

The duke sighed heftily at that, studying his wine. "You jest, but it really *is* about time to start considering that, if I'm going to consider it at all...nobody wants to be altered at forty, God forbid fifty...end up looking like Malin forever, sorry again, Uncle—crows' feet look good on you, but I can't pull them off."

"In a world with even the possibility of immortality," Malin agreed not unsympathetically, "the decision to age is a statement...so is the decision to die."

"How dramatic. And morbid! I've no interest in dying; nor in talking about death. I'd much rather talk about anything else...like how all this"—he used his fingertip to draw a little triangle between Malin, Eleison and me—"got hashed out!"

Beginning to look annoyed on my behalf, Malin said, "Really, Aleister—"

But I spoke over him, shrugging and plucking up my wine.

"It just worked out this way, as Eleison explained to you upstairs. Eleison knew we were mates before I did, and he kept it to himself because Malin was already courting me." Beneath the table, I slid my red suede pump against Malin's shoe. He watched me all the more intently, his wine glass raising to his lips as I freed my foot and let its stockinged surface tease us both with contact against his ankle.

"I was very, very attracted to Malin," I said, sliding my hand into Eleison's lap to rest upon his thigh, "and to Eleison, who avoided me studiously during my first months in the manor. For a few months I was overwrought! But, gradually, things happened, and...we found ourselves thus."

While Eleison, his hand wrapping around mine, ate by fork alone and listened to my perspective on things with a thoughtful sort of expression, Aleister leaned forward in scandalous interest.

"How did it *develop*, though? I mean, you didn't very well go to Malin and tell him you'd let Eleison have his way with you—or, did you?"

"I longed for the courage," I admitted, my toes sliding up Malin's trouser leg and back down to the top of his shoe. As it trailed up again, he raised his leg and, I thought, meant to shake me off; but then his left hand slipped discreetly beneath the table, and I let my foot slide up over his knee to enjoy his surreptitious caress. My face colored by this and by the story, I continued. "Instead, shamefully craven, I went along with both men, unsure what to do, until that bad business with Dr. Gall."

"Oh, *yes*—I heard all about that. Uncle, we didn't even *talk* about that yet! You were *kidnapped*, the absolute impudence of that—"

"It was harrowing," Malin agreed, his thumb working firmly along the arch of my foot while I tried not to sigh. "Gall had obviously lost his mind, and the question was whether he'd lost it enough to do something like kill me…thankfully, Thecla was heroic."

I smiled mildly. "I just wound up being stalked by some beast on the way to find you, Husband…I didn't do anything special. The Rift animal in question," I explained to Aleister, "dispatched the men paid to hold us there, but in the meantime, Eleison had been injured. So…it was let him die, or tell Malin the truth."

"And we've all lived happily ever after," Eleison said wryly, earning a smile of approval from Malin. My husband released my foot and settled back in his seat while I returned it to its shoe, nodding in agreement.

"I'd say we have…wouldn't you, Thecla?"

"Oh, yes—I'm very happy. Happier than most women on Earth, I'd venture."

"That really is some story," agreed the rather awed duke. "Frankly, Uncle, knowing what I know about you, I'm surprised this hasn't driven you out of your head with jealousy."

"Jealousy is a young man's insecurity that some other man is superior to him...superiority doesn't enter the equation here. Eleison and I adore Thecla, both have our reasons for it, and neither one wants to take her from the other. It's a matter of trust...and, of course, of enjoying Thecla's enjoyment."

"Well, you old dog, I'm glad to hear that marriage hasn't sucked all the fun out of you. I was worried you'd left the last remnants of your libertine days behind you! It's a relief to hear you've pursued a more open model of—"

"Oh," said Malin quickly, "it's not open."

Brows arching in surprise, Aleister asked, "How's that?"

"We're as faithful to one another as any couple...it just happens that my darling consort has an accessory, a mate whom I know to love her as much as I do. Others don't factor into it... do you feel the need for additional attention, darling? Not that I would begrudge it of you if you did..."

I shook my head, laughing as his eyes' reptilian spark of intrigue made visible some passing erotic thought that may or may not have struck him before. "No," I said, shooing away my own images of the dharmine's fixating silver eyes, smiling mouth, powerful hands. "No, I think I'm well seen-to."

"And I'm very satisfied with Thecla, I must say—satisfied as I have never been by the attentions of a single person. And, Eleison? I assume you're content with what Thecla offers you, physically and spiritually?"

Rather than trying to speak around a full mouth, Eleison released my hand to flash a thumb's up.

"You see," said Malin, smiling at Aleister, "we really are a happy little family."

"So I'm beginning to see. Well, well! How unusual…shame you're off-limits, Malin, but I am glad to hear you're satisfied."

"We'll always have our memories," said my husband with an affectionate, roguish smile for the duke. I blushed furiously at confirmation of my growing suspicion, and though I took pleasure to think Malin had just tactfully rebuffed the duke's advances, I couldn't help but find myself flustered by their history.

Suddenly I knew what Eleison meant about the exciting edge of jealousy.

While I wished Malin existed only within some enchanted boundary demarked by our acquaintance, without any history of lovers but with the same magical expertise that made him so addictive in bed, (and let's put Eleison in that same bubble, while we're at it!), my husband at last returned to his dinner. Knife and fork back at work, he said, "But, enough of your prurient talk at the table, Aleister, please…you've kept me waiting for an answer all day. I think we're all dying to know why you've come here."

"Oh! Yes, yes of course—"

Aleister wagged his finger while setting down his glass. "No wonder you've been loading me up tonight. Trying to turn me into a gossip! I assure you, no amount of even this very fine libation could keep me from my professional duties…let's get the business out of the way without crowing much…" At the impatient "hurry it up" wave of Malin's hand, Aleister caught himself mid-drunken ramble and course-corrected. "Oh, uh, all that is to say—it's not very exciting."

The duke gestured toward me, then plucked up his knife and fork while saying, "It's just that Parvati has taken an interest in Madame Farrow here, and has invited her to come stay in Valquist Palace for a week or two to get to know her."

Everything changed.

At my right, Malin's body went rigid. Noting the adjustment as readily as I, Eleison casually set down his cutlery to wipe hands and mouth upon his napkin.

"No," said Malin, not looking up from his plate as the duke went on, now only to me.

"I wasn't too excited by the prospect of chaperoning you at first, but now knowing you a little, Thecla, I must say I think it will be a jolly good—"

"Didn't you hear me?"

For the first time I had seen, Aleister fell silent. With a slow caution that telegraphed deliberate intent to avoid antagonism, he set his knife and fork down against the edges of his plate in favor of his wine again.

"I said "no,"" Malin condescended to repeat, his eyes lowering back to the duck breast he sawed into pieces but did not eat. "Tell Parvati she should have sent a message and spared you the trouble of coming."

As Aleister took his next sip, his Adam's apple bobbing sharply in his throat, his eyes fluttered across the knife working in Malin's right hand. Then, in a silent plea I couldn't seem to answer, they met mine.

I was just as helpless as Aleister was. Never having seen Malin this way, my heart raced. My entire body mirrored the tension of the room and, like the others, I could no longer eat. Only Malin continued, at last remembering to take a bite like an actor resolutely carrying about his stage business while the rest of his company bombed their opening night.

"That's just it, of course." Aleister's tone was unnaturally delicate. He affected a strained smile while the tip of his tongue nervously darted along his wine-stained lower lip. "I *am* the message…and I'm not to return empty-handed."

"You'll have to."

"But, Uncle"—the duke reached for my husband's arm, a familiar and friendly gesture as designed to placate as his boyish smile—"surely it would be—"

Malin slammed his knife into the table two inches from Aleister's hand, which recoiled against a heart that surely hammered like mine. We both, in fact, leapt back from the table, provoking a feral jerk of Malin's head toward me.

"Sit, Thecla," he told me hoarsely, glancing at my plate and then at my ashen face. "You're not hungry?"

"N—no, it's not—"

Lips pursing, stomach tight, I lowered back into my seat beneath the pressure of his stare and somehow managed a smile. The black stars of his eyes wandered down with me, and the hollows of his cheeks lost their strain…or altered it to a familiar expression of lustful promise.

Oh, I longed for him to whip me senseless in that moment! Instead, reaching across the corner of the table, Malin held my hand—squeezed it, really, so hard that the metal of his ring pressed into my skin to remind me I was most deliciously owned by him. I trusted him and his opinion. There had to be a reason he reacted so badly to the idea of my meeting the Overseer.

But the violence of his response was frightening. So frightening that I could only accept it by transfiguring my fear into desire…and as soon as we touched, I realized I enjoyed observing Malin's temper from a close seat when I could do so safe in the knowledge that it was not anger for me.

Seeing that Malin had been temporarily quieted by contact with me—or at least that his features had gone from raging to brooding, his eyes fixed dully into space somewhere around the hand he roughly massaged—Aleister also returned to his seat… but didn't bother scooting it back into the table. From this new, safer distance, his glass artfully balanced upon his crossed knee, he regarded us.

"I know you have a substantial history with Her Governance…but surely you understand, Malin, that's why you don't have a choice."

His jaw clenched and unclenched, a muscle in his neck visibly shifting. Focusing on me, maintaining a strained if breakable calm, my husband ran his broad fingers along mine as he did when marveling over the softness of my skin in our private moments.

Observing these caresses, his mouth tilting in sympathy, Aleister insisted, "I know what your concern is, of course, Uncle."

"My concern is that, from the moment she sets foot in Valquist, Thecla's ear will be filled with—"

He stopped himself, his chest swelling in his suit. Malin released me, leaning back in his chair and folding his hands before him as he regarded the duke.

"I suppose the invitation is not extended to me," he said acidly.

Despite himself, the duke smirked. "No, Uncle, I'm afraid your lifelong exile from the Capital is still in effect."

"So transparent…at least she was intelligent enough to send you." Snatching up his glass and the nearby bottle, Malin topped himself off, gave me a little more, then set the bottle down while ignoring frowning Aleister. "Anybody else would have been returned to her in a box...several boxes. Not that I'm not still thinking about it."

Without batting an eye, Aleister agreed, "She does know a thing or two about politics...and you. But! She knows next to nothing about your lovely bride...can you blame her for her curiosity?"

"Of course I can. I don't give a damn what she does, so long as she leaves me to my private business. It needn't concern her who I've married...or what I'm doing in my territory, for that matter."

"It would be a lovely world if people would mind their business," agreed the duke with a self-incriminating smile, "but, as we are not living in that world...."

His head turned; soon all the men fixed their eyes on me.

"...why don't we ask Thecla?"

I had been so shocked by Malin's temper that what was being offered had barely occurred to me. The conversation seemed so abstract that only now did I become aware of it in a meaningful sense.

Only now did I fully realize I was being invited—commanded, in truth—to meet the overseer of the continent. The very woman who was responsible for managing the territory masters and matrices—and, arguably, the only person on the continent, if not the world, who was more powerful than my husband.

And my husband seemed set on keeping me from such a meeting.

One could not help being curious...and concerned.

Lowering my wine, I smiled politely. "Perhaps you could tell me, Malin, what your reservations are?"

"My reservations," he said, each word carefully measured for tone as well as volume and coming out strained, somehow foreign, as he struggled to shield me from the fallout of his short fuse, "are rooted in several decades of bad blood between myself and Parvati...I do not like the thought of her having unfettered access to you. She might persuade you of anything. She might—"

"But I *love* you, Malin," I insisted, a little saddened that he thought me so easily swayed. He hesitated, in fact, upon being reminded, as though that were a factor he had forgotten to consider. Reaching across to take his hand again, I gripped his great paw in my small one and gazed earnestly into his face. "I would never betray you," I went on to him, my tone lowering to a murmur that made him list toward me with longing in his eyes and parted lips. "Wherever we go in the world, together or apart, no one can say or do anything to dissuade me from the way I feel for you."

"Perhaps not, no...but they might make you regret that devotion."

"That's not possible," I told him firmly.

Eleison, shifting in his seat, drew our attention as he said, "If I might—"

We all looked at him, waiting, and I held my breath in incredulity as he broached the following anecdote: "The first time—well, there was a time Thecla went out by herself, and...I wasn't in my right mind, so I thought I'd stage her kidnapping to teach her a lesson about going out in Saalast alone at night."

While the duke barked out a shocked laugh, Malin's arched brow reflected the intrigue that at last succeeded in cutting through his dark mood. "I'm not sure I've ever heard of this."

Bless Eleison and his understanding of the territory master he had served so long! Though I was embarrassed to have the story dredged up in mixed company, it was the perfect way to handle Malin. Distract him with knowledge he could not resist. Tantalize him. It was not unlike how, when our frighteningly fun games reached a peak I could no longer stand, I sought security in his love. His moods needed pivoting: redirecting, like the momentum of a top.

"I never thought I'd tell you about this," confessed Eleison. "Thecla can give you the details, if you want…hopefully you won't feel the need to discipline me if she does, though that is a matter of your discretion as always, sir…but what I think you should know is, when her life was endangered and she could have screamed and bargained and told her kidnapper about you, your money, anything—she didn't."

While Malin listened to this with grave but sincere interest, the duke laughed and waved his hand.

"Dear me, I wouldn't have hesitated! I'd promise jewels, coins, anything!"

But my husband didn't laugh at all. His calculating eyes turned upon me.

Though his lips were firmly set, he ruminated upon the thumb he ran back and forth along my knuckles.

"Do you remember," Malin said in an unusually chastened tone, "when we first met, Thecla…and we talked about loyalty?"

"Yes," I swore to him, unhesitating. "Yes, I remember— and I take it seriously, what you said to me then."

His nostrils flared; his jaw tensed again.

"I still don't want you to go," he snapped. "I just—can't *believe*"—he threw down my hand so roughly I withdrew it with a cry, but the action had been to keep himself from hurting me, as he slammed the same now empty hand so hard against the edge of the table that I cried out a second, more concerned time—"that odious bitch has the temerity to send *my* friend into *my* territory and *demand* I send *my* wife to meet her without the least—supervision!"

His voice had raised to a shout. Seeing me cringe, Malin shoved himself up from the table with such force that the chair nearly toppled. He caught it at the last second, roughly shoving it back into place and pacing away to face the shuttered window.

"If you distrust Her Governance so much—and I don't blame you, of course, Uncle—why not send Eleison along with her? *He's* not banned from the Capital."

Malin made no reply, his back to us amid his stony silence.

"Look," said the duke with a long, resigned sigh, "you're drunk, I'm drunker, *and* I'm still absolutely bushed. Besides…it's not as though I'm going anywhere while the weather's the way it is. Why don't you take a few days before deciding this is a battle worth fighting, Malin? Think it over—decide at the end of the Rift Event. I mean—"

Laughing a little, Aleister set aside his finally emptied glass. "It isn't as though you'll never see her again."

Malin turned on his heel and strode from the room.

Alarmed, I called uselessly after him. The door slammed in his wake, and the three of us sat in the uncomfortable fog of the silence.

"You must forgive my husband," I said, managing a thin smile after the shock had dulled with several seconds of his absence. "I think we can all agree that Malin is a very passionate man. Eleison—"

He glanced at me, and I inwardly cringed to find myself using him like a common servant.

"Please see to it the kitchen receives my regards and knows how excellent everything was. Would you like help to your room, Aleister?"

"I'm drunk, dear"—the duke responded while Eleison, clearly not as reluctant to take my order as I was to give it, rose to obey—"not stupid, I can remember the way. But…you and I should have a fun chat sometime. When we're on the way to Valquist, *we* can get drunk…I'll pry all the lurid details out of you, oh, yes, I can *hardly* wait…"

Laughing to himself, the duke staggered off while Eleison disappeared into the kitchen.

Alone in the dining room, I let out a long, slow breath and stood to find my husband.

THERE ARE THOSE moments in life wherein we really get to know the people we love. When we see them faced with adversity—when we learn their definition of adversity, to begin with.

More than I was shocked to have Malin's temper displayed so clearly before me, I was taken aback to know it had been triggered by the Overseer's summons. Eleison's support in the matter had placated him only a little; I could tell there was something at work here that I didn't understand, or understood only in part.

And I would continue to understand only in part, unless my husband related me the full volume of his thoughts.

Our apartment was ominously quiet when the elevator let me out on the topmost floor. No boiling tea kettle; no vinyl disc weaving music; no rustling book pages.

Only Malin, seated in the parlor, silent and still as a corpse. He filled his preferred lounge chair, his elbow upon the brown leather arm and his splayed fingers braced across his mouth. Having removed his waistcoat, he now sat in a meditation so intense it seemed to nullify even the sound of my breath.

As he registered that I had stepped around the corner, his black eyes focused out of some other dimension and upon me. Raising from its listless posture on his thigh, his free hand extended.

Unspeaking, I slid into my husband's opened arm and perched upon his knee.

He exhaled, his hand sliding down my back and around my rump to pull me closer to him. His dark eyes searched my face, scrutinizing me as though for any sign of flightiness.

"I want to trust you," Malin told me.

"Then do."

"You don't know what she'll say." His glanced off to some far region of the room while I slid my hand over his shirt and undid a button of his already loosened collar. Even as he inhaled with pleasure when my hand slipped inside his shirt, he emphasized, "I do."

"Then tell me what she'll say so that I won't be shocked by it."

His eyes shut. One great hand rested upon mine, holding it still against his heart through the barrier of his shirt. "I want to, Thecla…darling, I want to, but…"

I slid my hand from the fabric and instead trailed my fingertips over his jaw, lightly sandpapered with the bristle of the day.

"Then don't tell me," I said, "because I've already sworn to you that I won't pry. However reluctantly, I accept your decision not to tell me what you think it best to hide. I told you that on our honeymoon, and I stand by that, Malin. I'll deafen my ears to the sound of your name while I'm there; I'll ask no questions, I'll accept no advice. Master—"

His eye swung back to me while I flowed out of his lap and knelt before him. As he exhaled in low pleasure at the sight, I clasped his hand in both of mine and gazed earnestly into his face.

"I mean what I said. I love you, Master…you're my husband, and so much more. I would never give you up…never trade you, or be seduced away from you. Even if what I do or don't learn over the years affects *me*, it can never affect the way I feel. I swear it."

"You can't know that, Thecla."

"But I can. And so help me, Malin, I have sworn to always love you, and never abandon you. I will *never* abandon you, ever. What your old wife did to you is a nightmare. A betrayal that was ultimately for the best, because it let us be together. But, Master…"

I leaned up toward him as, listening, he bent to meet me.

"…if I ever abandoned you for good, Malin…ever truly betrayed you…you would have my permission to cut off my head."

His nostrils flared into black holes as great as his pupils. Malin's hand slid from mine and caught my chin. His thumb worked along my lower lip, then crept down the edge of my jaw.

My husband bent to kiss me, his lips brushing mine and his tongue exploring my mouth for a long, tender moment that heated my body and cajoled me into leaning up against him.

Just as I did, he pulled away.

"I don't need your permission to cut off your head, Thecla," he told me in that low, cold tone I loved so much. His fingers loosened their hold on my chin that the tip of his index might slide down the column of my throat, following the path of my artery before coming back up by the same route. "I just need an axe, and somebody to clean up after. Strip."

Flush with delirious thrill, as always at his abrupt commands, I rose.

"I didn't tell you to stand," he reminded me haughtily. "I told you to strip."

I trembled all the way back down, my hasty fingers flying across buttons and tugging open the ribbon Eleison had retied. Malin watched, his eyes plunging down my torso until the dress, the shift, the bustier fell away altogether, and there I was before him.

"You're not bleeding yet, after all," he observed when I slid my panties and garters away, his tone lightened by the observation.

"No, sir; I don't seem to be."

"That's excellent. I feel like using you extensively tonight, my hot little harlot…and I would hate if you were in poor condition, because I want you to enjoy what I permit you to enjoy."

I shivered amid my own panted breaths, my desire echoing in my ears with my voice. "Thank you, Master."

"You're such an obedient pet…come here, darling…recline in my arms."

Malin had such a way with me. But a word, a glance, a gesture, and I was breathless with excitement—heated with lust. Thrilled to be invited, I slid into his lap with my nude body curled against him, direct access barred by all his clothes save for the sleeves rolled to his elbows and the arrow of flesh visible at the chest of his open shirt.

"Sometimes, Thecla," he murmured softly, his great hands running down my back, over my rear, along my thigh, down my ankle, "I just want to hold you…to stroke you like a cat while I think through my problems. You send me to a different place… were you frightened at dinner?"

"Yes," I answered honestly, earning a tilt of his head and the passage of his lips over my brow.

"I'm sorry." His breath was rich with wine and warm with love. "That's not how I want to frighten you. I'm better than that, usually…but this is a touchy subject."

Shifting me in his arms so my rump was more favorably positioned for the occasional pat of his hand—and the pressure of his groin—Malin's gaze trailed over my face, down my throat, along my breasts, and into the soft crook of my contorted stomach.

"Thecla," he began, looking up into my face again after a full minute of silence, "would you be tempted to leave me forever if I sent you and Eleison off on this journey together?"

"Not for a second! Oh, Malin—I wish you would believe—"

"I do believe," he told me, catching the hand I had raised toward his face and drawing it to his mouth for a kiss. "I do believe, but that's why this is so frightening…I believe your love. I believe it is beautiful and pure and powerful, Thecla. And…I want to keep it pure."

"We can keep it pure," I whispered while his fingers trailed over my knuckles. "My love for you can always be pure, Malin, but what might tarnish it is discovering from someone else truths you should have told me."

Exhaling heavily, he toyed with my fingers, then clasped my hand to his heart. "But what if the truth itself is enough to tarnish? What will I do? Thecla…if your love ever recedes from me, I'll be crushed."

His lips contorted in a grimace of pain that flexed his scar while our hands squeezed together. When Malin's lips swept down for mine, it was with a crushing, almost agonizingly passionate kiss. I moaned his name, writhing in his lap, my thighs parting to encourage his teasing caresses of my legs and rear to make more progress. He continued holding back, observing me through those wicked bedroom eyes when he drew away from our kiss.

"I should take Eleison's advice...I should lock you up in a tower, someplace far away, with your loom and some books... never let anyone else set eyes on you. Overseer be damned...the Capital, the continent, all of it—"

"Why does she detest you so, Master? I know a little about the war, but—"

"I don't want to speak of it now," he told me firmly, drawn from absent reflections and into the reality of my presence in his arms. "No—I'd rather discuss more pleasant things. Like...ah..."

His hand fell into patting my rear, and I whimpered a little in anticipation of what was to come. "Let's talk about this kidnapping incident between you and Eleison, Thecla...I'm dying of curiosity to know all about it."

My breathing shaky with desire and concern, I whispered, "Do you promise you won't be angry with Eleison?"

"If I am, I promise to take it out on you."

Blushing at a slightly harder slap of my rear on the next pat, I swallowed against my tight throat and began, "Well, let's see...it was that time I went to the theatre."

"I thought you said Eleison came along with you but waited outside."

"He did...only, I didn't know it at the time. I was still being very stubborn, and I didn't want him to come with me...he infuriated me."

"Did you know you were mates by then?"

"Yes, we must have known for some months. I must have known, anyway...he seems to have known from the moment we met."

"How?"

Realizing with a guilty start that I had never told him this either, I raised my right forearm and demonstrated the slight discoloration of the scar Eleison delivered when startled in his borro form. "He tasted me," I confessed to my husband, earning a strange kind of lustful look as he studied the marks. "My blood stabilized him out of the very fit that had provoked him to assume I was a threat, and he knew right away what we were to one another.

"At any rate...the night of the theatre, I had known for a few months, and I was very fed up with him. When he insisted I take him along to protect me, I was outraged. I couldn't believe he thought I was so helpless."

Malin's hand slid back and forth along my thigh again, higher each stroke. "I'm sure, so used to Lescaut, you thought you had it perfectly under control."

"And I'm sure I would have," I said with a small scowl I couldn't help. "I wasn't so completely naive five months ago... oh, but Eleison thought I was...he followed me, Master...he knew I'd forget to check the time the trains shut down, and he knew I'd have to walk home...ah—"

I gasped as Malin's petting trailed over my thigh and down into the track to its apex.

"What did he do to you, Thecla?"

"All I knew was somebody leapt from an alley and put a bag over my head. He had me—handcuffed and locked in a carriage in a moment. Oh, sir—"

I hesitated, but as Malin's fingers teased between the petals of a flower that could not resist his attention, I gazed into those lust-softened eyes and whispered, "He pointed a gun at me."

"Poor Thecla... the men who love you have such wickedness in their hearts...ah...but you love that, don't you..."

Whimpering as his caresses illuminated for the both of us exactly how affected I was, I pressed a kiss to Malin's barely parted lips. "Yes, yes—oh, I wish he would be so rough and frightening with me again…but he doesn't care for the kinds of games you do, Master."

His smile crooked as one thick digit slid inside me, Malin drank in my rapture. "I'm sure most men look at a girl like you, Thecla, and wish to protect her. To love her with a gentle passion. Oh, and I confess I enjoy being gentle with you. But I do not find myself thinking gentle thoughts when I look on you, my wife."

Shuddering as the smooth, confident swirling of his finger and thumb left me not only awash in bliss, but somehow all the more exposed to his gaze, I stroked his cheek and panted to the beat of my pleasure.

"I don't want you to think gently of me," I begged. "Eleison can have his gentle thoughts—I want your wicked ones, Malin! Please, be cruel to me—"

"I think you deserve a spanking after wasting half your dinner and hiding this sexy little anecdote from me, don't you?"

Whining, wishing to protest that I hadn't hidden it so much as not thought about how much he might enjoy it, I instead bit my tongue and forced myself to agree, "Yes, sir—I feel so guilty."

"Then let me absolve you."

His hand slid out from between my thighs and set upon my rear. With a pat, he commanded me to turn over in his lap without a word, and I moaned lightly to feel his unfettered gaze re-memorize every inch of me. Blushing, I braced myself against the edge of the chair, then the floor, as he shifted me more comfortably in his lap and left my backside more easily accessible.

"What does your master want you to say if you need to stop," he asked me, that kindly offered out always extended despite my insistence I would never use it.

"Lescaut," I whispered.

He began.

The surface of his hand was hard as a paddle, and as it cracked with practiced ease against my flesh, I cried out with a shock whose echoes competed with the next blow. Momentarily, my legs twitched; my stomach flinched tight and, as I gripped my husband's ankle, his sadistic chuckling sent excitement rushing all through me.

"What a spankable little ass," Malin said while I moaned and thrashed, his free arm draping over my waist to keep me in place despite my flailing. The beat of his hand remained steady, hard, and almost intolerably fast from the start. "It's lucky you enjoy it, Thecla…lucky you beg for this kind of treatment from me. If not, I would go mad. I would die."

Gasping with an especially hot swat that had a way of echoing through to the front of me, I lifted upon my toes to press my backside higher for him. He sighed, stroking a hot, surely reddened cheek that he then immediately struck again.

"Then let me keep you alive forever, Master…" I lost balance on one foot and bent my knee at the next volley of stinging swats. "Ah! Oh, sir—I can't live without you either, can't you see? Who—oh, oh, who could give me this but you?"

Exhaling sharply, Malin drew my hair away from my face. Then, still laying down a blitz of spanks so heavy they numbed me, he bent to nuzzle my ear.

"When I let you up, you're going to take off my belt. Then you're going to crawl to the bedroom and wait for me."

My body flooded with euphoria at the command. "Yes, yes sir, I understand! Oh—"

Moaning with anticipation as his arm lifted, I slid from his lap and down between his legs. His eyes stayed fixed on mine as I hurried to unbuckle his belt, eager to pull the leather from the loops of his trousers—

And then, in the foyer, the elevator made its grinding approach to our floor.

For half a second, I was frustrated with the interruption, and saw the same thing in his face—then, in the next second, we both arrived at the same conclusion.

"Now who could *that* be," pondered Malin playfully, his dark eyes newly twinkling with mischief. At last, the absolute foulness of his mood had been forgotten with the possibilities he now saw in the night. "Surely it can't be Eleison accepting our invitation...what a fine time he's picked. You're very lucky, you know, dear."

Stopping my hands before I could remove his belt entirely, Malin drew me up into his lap and pressed a fierce kiss to my mouth.

"I was really going to give you a proper hiding tonight... oh, I want to make you *scream*—"

While his teeth bared, his hand slipped up into my hair and clenched there. I cried out in the sting and the thrill.

"Yes, Master," I begged, "I want that, too—"

"But let's not go about things too strongly with Eleison... don't want to scare him off."

Flushed, nodding, I brushed my nose against his and had just stolen a kiss from his warm, wonderful mouth when the elevator doors slid open.

"Hey," called Eleison, "Thecla? You around?"

"In here," I told him while Malin tutted lightly.

"Don't be shy, old boy…if it were up to me, you'd take a room up in the apartment here and feel completely at ease with us…"

His finely polished oxfords echoing down the foyer, Eleison stepped into our parlor just before he looked.

Finding me naked in Malin's lap, he hesitated for a heartbeat, then lowered his eyes with a dry chuckle whose feral rumbling spoke his true mind.

"You really mean 'at ease,' huh…hey, baby."

"I'm so happy you came up, Eleison!" While suppressing, for the sake of conversation, the moans inspired by Malin's kisses along my neck, my voice became almost breathless and laughing. "You picked such a fun time, too…"

"Here I thought I was interrupting."

"Never," Malin and I said at once, exchanging a laugh that was ended when his hands slid down my breasts to make me gasp. My husband went on, a soft smile still highlighting his voice as my mate stalked toward us. "In fact, we were just discussing you."

"I should probably be worried."

"Only pleasant things, Eleison…oh, now—isn't that nice."

Malin was a cad no matter the day or the hour, and he could have found something worth lusting after in the most benign flutter of my eyelid—but I was not sure I felt the weight of his voyeuristic cravings for me until Eleison was with us. Eleison always pulsed with that undercurrent of jealousy when seeing Malin kiss me; but, as my mate bent his head with his fingers catching my chin and his lips ready to devour mine from the first contact, Malin watched with such appreciation I felt as though I were some kind of performance artist. Moaning into

Eleison's mouth, I slid my arms around his neck and let one hand trail into the careful styling of his short black hair. All the time, my husband's heavily lidded eyes never averted; in fact, while one hand teased a tightly beaded nipple that ached with his touch, his other slid down into my lap, trailing between my thighs to further agitate my desire.

"He does have a wonderful way of kissing you, doesn't he, Thecla...forceful. No wonder you want him to take you against your will."

Moaning at Malin's ugly yet true (and inappropriately exciting) words, I was flooded with that rare awareness of my own true helplessness. In the territory master's lap, with his most valuable and violent footman before me, it didn't matter who I was, or what my position was with respect to either. They could do with me whatever they wanted, body and mind, in practical reality and in the dark corners of the law.

And I wanted them to.

Eleison, his growl low against my mouth, turned his lips just from mine to let our noses bump.

"I think I'm going to need a drink," he said, rising while I produced a kind of sad little mewl to unwind my arms from his shoulders. Hearing me, he brushed his knuckle over my cheek. "Don't worry, I'm not going anywhere."

"Why don't we *all* go somewhere, actually," advised Malin, patting my thigh for me to stand. "The bedroom is much more comfortable, don't you think...fix a nightcap for me while you're at it, Eleison..."

"Be there in a minute," called my mate, glancing briefly at us while Malin, his great hand around my forearm, swept me from the parlor and down the hall to our room.

"Do you know," Malin said to me unexpectedly on the way, bending to brush his lips along my hair, "the joy you bring me? The absolute pleasure? You do, don't you, Thecla? I hope you do…I love you."

"I love you," I pledged, my tone adoring and my mind high with excitement. "Oh, yes, Malin—thank you for teaching me so much."

At the boundary of the bedroom, my husband stopped to savagely kiss me. By the force of his mouth and the hand braced upon my cheek, he backed me into the room in such a way that I didn't realize his other hand removed his belt. I only heard the ominous jingle and, glancing down, gasped as he caught me by the hair to hold me in place.

With the strap doubled, Malin stared blackly into my face and whipped my exposed rear in a handful of rapid, sharp strikes up against my flesh.

Moaning, trembling, I cried his name and clutched his shirt in my fists to stay upright. His hand in my hair helped with that, supporting my head to keep my eyes fixed on his as he beat me in a manner so matter-of-fact yet erotic that I felt drunk by the time he shoved me to the bed.

"Malin, oh—fuck me, please! Oh, Husband—"

Exhaling in response to that sensual title that was the only thing more exciting to us both than "Master," Malin studied me sprawled upon the golden sheets of our bed and unbuttoned his shirt. "Sure you wouldn't rather let your mate fuck you, first?"

"Why don't you two go ahead," Eleison said as he stepped into the room, shutting the door with his elbow. Malin glanced back but briefly while stripping off his shirt, an act with which I leaned up to assist.

After setting Malin's drink down on the nightstand, Eleison took his own to the armchair of the small sitting area between the bed and the balcony.

"I hate to cut in," he said as he settled down—as my hands dropped to Malin's trousers. "And, anyway…what's good for the gander is…good for the other gander."

I laughed, and Malin did a little, too. I was overjoyed that my husband had once again become so at-ease…though just having that thought evoked memories of his fit at dinner. The most pleasing shiver of fright rattled through me and, seeing it—perhaps even feeling it—Malin slid a finger along my jaw and pushed me back into the bedspread before finishing the task of stripping his trousers.

"Very decent of you, Eleison…I'm sure you'd like nothing better than to put a bullet in my head and have your way with her this instant, so I appreciate your restraint."

Malin has always been a handsome, almost artfully built man. In his youth, he must have kept as toned as Eleison: in the middle of his fifties, Malin maintained definition most men his age just couldn't. It was all power, that body…and he made me moan as he bent over me, his most devious instrument of sweet torture poised between my legs.

"Besides…I'm sure Thecla is just happy you're here with us."

"Yes!" My body smoldered beneath Malin's kisses, caresses, teases along my torso and between my legs, but I looked instead at my mate. Eleison sat a little straighter in the chair as my eyes fell upon him, his drink poised before his lips. "Yes, oh, Eleison—I love seeing you both apart, I want to be with each of you alone… oh, but I want to be together sometimes, too—ah!"

Malin's first thrust inside me drew my attention back, and I cried out again at the sight of him plunging that brutal dagger between my legs. Trembling, I wrapped one arm around his neck and raised the other hand to quaveringly stroke his face, his beautiful face—especially that scar, a pale stripe sweeping up past his left eye, up the temple of his forehead, up through the hair disarrayed with my caresses.

"That's what I want, too, Eleison," Malin agreed, his voice distant as his attention was otherwise absorbed in me and all the things he could make my body do. "I want to know that you feel fully comfortable…fully a part of Thecla's love."

"You know, Malin…" Eleison's voice sweetened my pleasure until I dug my nails into Malin, inspiring a profound sharpening of his thrusts. "I was concerned about that at first…but I have to give it to you. You've really gone out of your way to make me feel respected. Welcomed. It's not you two, trust me. It's me…"

"I'm sure it is…but look at her."

His hand trailing over my face, Malin pushed my cheek down into the mattress until I faced Eleison. I cried out with pleasure to be pinned there, my face blanched with lust as my eyes found my mate's.

"Look at her pleasure…how sweet it is, how hot it is."

His middle finger trailed against the edges of my lip and I turned, catching the digit in my mouth to suck it. With a low groan, Malin braced his knee against the edge of the bed and pulled me closer to it.

"Who could wish to deny her this? Who could turn away from watching it? I want to keep her so yielding, pliant, forever… and when I lack the stamina, I need someone to help me do that. You certainly seem close, darling."

I whimpered, nodding, my brow furrowed as he addressed me in his tone of casual aside. Every hard hammer up into me increased the power of the coming explosion, which seemed liable to destroy me. "I'm close, oh, Malin! I'm so close—"

"Good."

While I cried out in shock and agony, he pulled from me altogether and chuckled at my rapid protests.

"Please! No, please, but sir—"

"Go let your mate feel how wet you are," Malin commanded in a hot murmur against my ear, his hands fondling every last inch of my body while he kissed and nipped my jaw, my neck. "You're the only one who can break him from his shell, angel...go on..."

Moaning in agreement, I put aside my craving for Malin for now and scrambled up to reach Eleison. While his breath hitched and he barely managed to put aside his glass, I threw myself into my mate's lap and caught his face for a long, slow kiss. My tongue reasoned with his, slowly stoking its power, and soon his strong hands fit to my back.

Then they were sliding down my rear.

"There. That's just lovely, isn't it." Straightening up, Malin took his dressing gown down from its peg by the head of the bed and tugged it on. "We're all adults here, Eleison...we all know each other. Let's be honest about what we want to do."

My hands hastened between our bodies to free Eleison from his trousers, and I smiled in delight to feel his evident pleasure. "Honesty is important," I agreed, my brow furrowing as Eleison's fingers wrapped around the underside of my still stinging nate and slid along the crevice of my pleasure. "Oh, Eleison..."

"You really are soaking wet, aren't you…" Sighing, his teeth grinding with the force of his desire, Eleison flicked a glance between us, then back into my face. "Did Malin whip you just now?"

I moaned faintly and confessed, "He did."

"You sure do love that, huh…good thing he knows how to do it—ah!"

"Oh, Eleison—" I had wasted no more time in mounting him and now, sliding down his glorious prick with Malin's eye upon us, I moaned even before I went to work pleasuring myself upon him. "Eleison, Eleison, you really are so hard—"

"I promise," Malin said, gliding over with his drink to lean against the arm of Eleison's seat and enjoy things from a privileged perspective, "I'll keep most of our little games for our private enjoyment, Eleison—but I hope it won't bother you if you overhear the occasional whipcrack, the odd bedroom command. I'm sure Thecla will be humiliated, but you, my friend…think nothing of it."

Barely able to speak while I worked myself up and down his length, Eleison managed to grunt out the words, "I won't," as his hands fit to my hips.

"You could play, too, Eleison," I assured him, my fingers sliding into my hair to have something to grip as I impaled myself upon that gorgeous, thick cock of his. "Oh, Eleison, I'd love a whipping from you—I want you to tie me up and treat me roughly, just as Master does—"

"Sounded from what Malin said that you want more than that."

Moaning, I bit my lip and nodded. "I want you to ravish me, Eleison—oh, Eleison, I want you to rape me, I want to lose all control to you, I want to fear you—"

The animal in him growling, Eleison kissed me heavily. When his head lifted, Malin slid a paternal arm around Eleison and bent for his turn at my kiss. I lapped the scotch from my husband's lips, already trembling on the edge of ecstasy to be on my mate's cock while I did it.

But what happened next was my true undoing.

"She is a scrumptious little slut," Malin said, nursing his drink for another sip before patting Eleison's arm. "And you have her, you know…as much as I have her, Eleison, you also have Thecla. You have her, and your brother, and fine places to stay, and food like few will ever taste in their lives."

"You're generous, Malin," Eleison managed to observe, the words distant through the tunnel of my ecstasy.

"Don't say that," Malin pleaded. "Dear, Eleison, don't say that…I give you some of these things not because I'm generous, but because it's my duty, or part of our agreement. But there are other things, Eleison, that I give you out of—a deep, personal affection I feel for you."

Eleison glanced over at Malin. My mate's breath quickened as I bent my head to nibble and kiss his ear.

"If you two go off to the capital, and, away from me, decide the spell is broken and you'd prefer running off together—"

"I would never," I moaned, while Eleison protested, "Sir—"

"Just know," Malin continued steadily, his head low over Eleison's, "that I would be broken-hearted by your betrayal just like I would be by Thecla's."

"Sir…"

Eleison steadied his panting breath and raised his head to fix Malin with an intense, earnest stare.

"I swear," Eleison told him, meaning it as deeply as I, "we'll never do that to you. I feel—a lot of affection for you, too, Malin."

Their stares held a crackle of lightning, just as they had on the first night we came to an open agreement about the relationship the three of us needed.

This time, it was Malin who broke the stare; but it was not me whom he kissed.

The sight of Malin and Eleison kissing was so extraordinary, so erotically novel to me, that I at once succumbed to my rising orgasm. While my body gave in to the shocking stimulus and I drowned in pleasure, Eleison growled low against Malin's lips and barely permitted the exploration of his tongue.

Then, as quickly as it had begun, the kiss ended. Eleison turned his face away, his expression more driven than ever, and his next kiss was for me. I drowned in it, groaning his name, then crying out in pleasure as he effortlessly rose from his seat with me still affixed to his pelvis. In one smooth motion, he turned to lay me down against the arm of the chair, his hand under my thigh to open me to him while he pounded deeper.

"Maybe I'll come up more often," he agreed, his forehead against mine, his ruby eyes burning with passion. "I haven't wanted to interrupt, but…you're both so forthcoming…ah, fuck, Thecla—"

"Eleison, Eleison! Yes, please, cum in me, oh—leave me dripping for my husband, please, yes, yes!"

Groaning, Eleison caught my chin in his hand and stared into my eyes. "Have to get you all hot and bothered regularly if you're going to have a baby with him, don't I?"

I cried out, the stroke of his cock in synch with his comment driving me to another climax. Eleison pounded me through it, working himself within my fluttering confines until, snarling my name, he thrust a few harsher times while expelling the cataclysmic heights of his tension."

Moaning, I caught his face in my hands and held him still for my kiss.

It was true that altered individuals like Eleison agreed to medical birth control of various kinds when they signed their consent forms, but it still excited me to no end to feel his emission inside of me—and I certainly knew Malin felt the same. His eyes glittering with mirth, Malin savored the sight of another man's orgasm within his wife the way he savored his drink.

When it was over, Eleison raised his panting head from mine, his eyes searching my face.

I smiled a little, telling him, "You don't have to stay the night if you don't want to."

"It just seems like a little much, still, somehow." He sighed against me while I raised my head to kiss him, another animal growl rising from his heart as he admitted, "And...I still have to get used to...watching."

"There's no rush at all," Malin said, his eyes bouncing quickly across Eleison's cock as it was slid free of my body and tucked away again. "Thecla and I are happy to take things at your pace, Eleison...do what you want, don't do what you don't want. It's as simple as that."

"I love you," I told Eleison by way of agreement, stroking his chest.

"*We* love you," Malin said warmly, the words genuine if less intensely meant than when they were uttered to me. "And the last thing we want to do is scare you off. It's already enough that you visited us tonight."

"You won't scare me off. I'm just…taking it slow. Sort of," he added with a chuckle and a glance down at my body. Pausing, Eleison kissed me one last time before asking, "Is it really okay?"

"Go, darling," I told him, smiling and stroking his cheek. "I'll see you tomorrow."

Looking somehow relieved and reluctant at once, Eleison kissed my brow, told me, "I love you, baby…good night," and rose with a nod to Malin.

After looking for half a second like he wanted to say something else to my husband, my mate turned his head and sauntered from the room to process what had just happened.

Before I had turned from watching Eleison go, Malin was already upon me to press long, thoughtful kisses over the column of my neck. His fingers teased along the drenched cleft of my sex.

"You shouldn't have let him go if you wanted the least prayer of sitting at breakfast tomorrow…go bend over the bed, angel…there's a good girl…ah, Thecla…I adore you so!"

ONDERFUL AS THE night had been, by morning Malin withdrew again into his troubled thoughts. It was disappointing. Then too flippant with youth and too ignorant of Malin's secrets, I had hoped somehow that the momentary distractions of the flesh could ease the serious concerns of his soul—but, of course, my ruling husband's mind was not so easily soothed long-term. I understood a little of his wariness about the Overseer, and I could see already how this trip of mine would represent the first great challenge of our trust, but his silence made me nervous. When asked about his plans he muttered something about a few call-in meetings, as the Rift Event continued without ending. Once his meal was finished, he sat back in his seat with a mug of coffee going cold in his hand, his eyes fixed not on me but somewhere in space to the right of my head.

Finally, buzzing with my customary Rift anxiety along with the tense memories of his tantrum the night before, I set my napkin aside and stood from the table. Malin flicked me a glance, about to stand without comment, but made a small noise of pleasure and relented when I stopped him by sliding into his lap.

"I'm sure your mood is about—that business at dinner, but if I did or said something last night—"

"Thecla, please."

His tone was a little gruff, but measured. His arms sliding around me, Malin pressed his forehead to my decolletage within the folds of my robe while his big hands stroked my body.

"I'm hungover, and yes, still thinking about dinner, and Montagne, and the whole thing…but when you and Eleison cross my mind, it's the one set of thoughts in my whole contemptible head that *don't* bring me misery."

After planting a few slow kisses between my breasts while I sighed, my husband raised his head again and picked up his coffee with me still in his lap. "If anything, I should be the one debriefing *you* about our good time…I don't want to have shocked you, after all."

Laughing, defiant, I assured him, "You can't shock me, Master."

"Oh, dear…"

The glint of his eye, evil as an onyx blade, made me shiver with delight.

"You and I both know that's not at all true…don't tempt me."

Biting my lip, I held the steady stare of those serpent eyes while lowering my mouth upon his. "But I love to tempt you," I said between kisses of his sullen lips, my heart racing as

I gradually enjoyed the growing insistence of his tongue. "I want you to foreswear all your obligations and come make love to me again this instant, Malin…I want you to come tell me all about your histories with other men, the thought excites me."

"Does it? That's good…I wasn't sure how you'd take it."

The heat between us stoked the adrenaline that raced my heart. As his lips moved over my cheek and my jaw, I whimpered with delight, "Though it makes me terribly jealous to think you ever lived without me, and I would never wish for you to love another woman, I'm glad to think that perhaps you and Eleison might cultivate a romantic connection between yourselves. We really *are* a happy family, after all. Oh, yes, I forgot to tell you, darling—there was still no more blood this morning. Perhaps it's just the stress of the Rift making me late, but I'm sure we could try again—"

Groaning, Malin raised his head to kiss and nip my throat in a way that wildly fired my blood.

"You vixen, ah, Thecla—"

His head raised. His mouth caught mine and I grew excited, hopeful—

And then, with a sudden snapping off of lights and devices that was so universal it sounded somehow like an explosion, the power died. With it died the air conditioning, the greatest source of noise in the outage.

Malin, his mouth on mine, growled in fury. He caught my face in his hands and drew back from me. Even in the sudden darkness of the shuttered apartment, his expression was so tense I had no trouble discerning it in his face or tone. The sudden inundation of fury and shadow accented his age, and his teeth bared so frighteningly I nearly cried out.

"Alas…God is testing me this week. Damn this weather—"

Patting me to get me up from his lap, Malin ran a hand over his face and sighed to rise.

"I have some letters to write, since the power isn't cooperating for now."

Though I tried not to exhibit my alarm, Malin stopped the worrying of my hands by holding both in his and looking in my eye.

"I'll have a technician look into the power as soon as possible, darling, but it's probably just the Event affecting the city…so blasted frustrating, if only—ah, never mind."

Bending to kiss my cheek, his hand squeezing mine tight, he said, "Sad to say the generators will have to focus on powering the kitchen and the security system, and if the neighborhood is hit with its own bad patch not even they'll be able to keep those circuits of the house afloat, so it might get a bit stuffy today. A little tightly wound. Just try to stay cool so I don't have to worry about you. Oh, and— Check in on our guest, if you wouldn't mind, and make sure he hasn't taken offense. Not likely, knowing Aleister, but you never do know…"

"Try to have a good day," I called to him as he strode off.

He laughed, one short note as he disappeared toward the exit to the rooftop garden…which—unfortunately for me— provided our only access to the house's main staircase when a power outage rendered the elevator inoperable.

Frustrated that I couldn't help him—and embarrassed, really, that I had even thought it within my capacity in this case—I looked around the dark apartment for a minute or two before remembering a utility closet that Charlotte was always in and out of. I hurried to it, pleased to find a little box of matches, then set about lighting a few of the otherwise decorative candles that ornamented the parlor, the bathroom, my dressing room.

By the time I was finished, Brea was still nowhere to be seen, but I suppressed my annoyance by supposing she was in some way helping the rest of the staff deal with the power loss. I bathed and picked out a simple pink frock and, since it was hot and I dressed alone, a brassiere rather than the more stifling underthings that produced the fashionable darting waists. Likewise, I simply pulled my hair back from my neck and went without jewelry since the day was to be spent working inside.

Frankly, I was among the best-off in the house. Between my loom and the library, all I needed to entertain myself was a book of matches.

Or a friend.

I was just on my way to my workroom when the hollow, rhythmic clatter of ping-pong echoed from the neglected game room. Just as I paused upon the landing to investigate the sound, Brea, of all people, stepped out.

"Madame," she said in surprise, her face falling a little when she realized I was dressed. "Oh—you don't need your hair done today?"

"Not anymore, thank you, Brea..."

While she awkwardly watched from the middle of the floor, I swept past her and into the game room to smile at the guest I'd had a feeling I'd find.

"Good morning, Aleister! You're up early for someone who had so much wine yesterday."

"Oh, no, I'm never hungover from wine. Liquor is all I need to worry about...hello, Thecla."

I stood amazed by Aleister's dexterity as he steadily bounced the ball upon his round paddle, his wrist only jerking from side to side when necessary to keep it centered. Smiling, I asked, "You like playing table tennis, Aleister?"

He smiled and caught the ball with his free hand, snatching it out of the air and flourishing with an elegant shrug.

"I dabble...would you like to play for money?"

Laughing dryly, I took up the paddle from the basket at the table's edge and told him, "I have the feeling I'd regret it, mysteriously...but I'll lose for free anytime."

Eleison had taught me the basic rules of the game one afternoon, while thoroughly trouncing me in what could hardly be considered a "match". It seemed I was doomed to a more humiliating repeat of the same, with Aleister effortlessly sending me after the ball while he struggled against increasingly obvious laughter.

"You really aren't very good at this, Thecla, but I admire your perseverance..."

"Yes, well, I'm better at this than I am at most sports...at least I can get the blasted thing over to you, and hit yours back... sometimes..." Laughing, I lunged after the ball in demonstration and just barely managed to return it. "Eleison has taught me to shoot and throw darts and play a few other games, but some things are only learned by practice."

"That's true...like dealing with Malin."

Cringing as I missed the ball, I confessed while hurrying after it, "I hope you'll excuse him for last night—"

"Dear, dear, I'm not the one lacking experience with his fits. I was wondering how *you'd* be doing! Knowing Malin, he's done his best to keep you in a pretty, polished bell jar."

I neither cared for the duke's tone nor the route of the conversation and served the little ball with a chilly smile.

"My husband has certainly taken care to treat me with kindness, but no man is perfectly calm all the time…heaven knows, I'm not."

With a wry look as he tapped the ball back and I managed to knock it lamely into the net, Aleister remarked, "You don't have to tell me *that,* Thecla…"

"What's that supposed to mean, exactly?"

"It means"—he strode to the midway point to show off by sliding his paddle under the ball and balancing it back to his side—"but a single conversation with you is very revealing to somebody like me. You're a powder keg! What on earth do you have to be so angry about?"

Scoffing, completely missing the ball and, annoyed, setting the paddle down on the edge of the table, I asked in an unexpectedly sharp tone, "*Angry?* Why would I be angry?"

"That's what I just asked you, isn't it…but do you know what I've noticed about women generally, Thecla? You never feel like you have the *right* to be angry. Why is that?"

If I was angry, it was surely because of Aleister and the unnecessary trouble his news had brought into our lives. All the same, I found myself entertaining his question.

"Perhaps men spend so much time getting themselves wound up over trivialities that we women simply don't want to embarrass ourselves in the same fashion."

"Perhaps…though, I confess"—he raised his eyebrows toward me while dropping his paddle back in the basket—"if I were Malin, I also wouldn't want my new spouse going to meet the Overseer alone."

"Why is that, exactly?"

"They're enemies, of course, Thecla, going way back. It's no small thing to be told to stay with the enemy of your husband… but, Malin doesn't really have a choice, and he knows that. Men with power don't generally like to be reminded when there's someone who has more of it than they do."

There was more to Malin's resistance than that, I was sure, but before I could interrogate him, Aleister released a hefty sigh. "Blast this contemptible weather! Can't believe it's knocked out the power…and the air. I'm thirsty. Join me for a drink before all the ice melts?"

With a startled laugh and a glance down at my pocket watch, I shook my head and confessed, "It's a little early for me, but thank you for the invitation…besides, I've work to do."

"Oh, yes, that weaving business Malin told me about…I suppose you don't need electrical power for that, do you. Well, no matter…I'm sure I'll get you nice and drunk for a *real* conversation soon. Ta-ta, Thecla, enjoy your boring day…"

With a sinuous rotation of one delicate wrist, the duke blew me a facetious kiss and strode from the room in search of his drink. I laughed a little and stooped to fetch the lost ball, replacing it and my paddle beside the duke's.

And fingers brushed against the back of my neck.

I cried out, leaping forward, laughing in expectation of Eleison—but the noise was left half-finished when I whirled to discover nothing.

It was there. The dharmine. It was certainly there: had *been* there, perhaps, waiting for me to be alone. My eyes revealed nothing, but I buzzed with its proximity as I might for one of my lovers.

I staggered back and turned only when I reached the end of the ping-pong table. Too afraid to wonder how an extreme Event might empower the demon, rather than demeaning it like usual, I sped for the blessed safety of the loom.

But there was no safety that day.

In fact, it had wanted me to go there.

For half an hour at least, the dharmine let me work. I lit one candle on the table by my side, and, too afraid for more, I let my eyes adjust to the dulled colors of the room before flying into work. The threads wove smoothly that morning! Perhaps it was just my desperation to escape—the dharmine, the lies, myself— but I was thrilled by the flight of the shuttle, the confidence of my fingers, the easy rhythm of my moving feet.

And when I was submerged in the river of creative flow, hands drew my hair back from my shoulders.

Gasping, wincing, I turned toward the door I had not heard open—to the man who stood behind me, his caress continuing down my neck and sliding around my shoulder to rest over my pounding heart.

I saw nothing. The door was not open.

Yet something in the darkness touched me as solidly as might have Malin or Eleison.

"Sh..." The dharmine's sensual whisper came so close against my ear that I jolted again, doubly frightened by the sensation of its breath. "It's all right, Madame...I swear, I won't hurt you...keep working..."

I did. I tried to, anyway, though now my fingers trembled with awful mortal expectations. As the loom once again groaned into motion, the invisible hands of the demon slid from my heart to my breasts. My pulse pounded at the caress, at the circuit of pleasure that had built in me from its first brush in the game room.

Lips touched my neck. I whimpered, struggling to weave while the dharmine seduced me.

"The duke is right...you're always angry, Madame...I feel it burning in the center of your body."

Its mouth opened into a low sigh that dimpled my flesh. While I wove the hidden witch of the tapestry, my own demonic prophet quickly sped my respiration to a pant by nothing more than caresses down my waist, over my abdomen, back up again along my breasts and as high as my face. Between kisses—and the occasional fear-inducing scrape of teeth or tongue against my ear, my pulse—the demon spoke on.

"You should let me help you abate your anger, Madame, please...I'm so eager to help you..."

"You seem to be."

Voice lifting in a faint breath of pleasure to be addressed by me, the dharmine whispered into my ear, "I swear, I am. Tell me what has upset you."

"Don't you know already, demon?"

"Speaking the wishes in your heart gives them form...at least, when they're said to me."

Shivering as its tongue slithered along my jaw, I steadied myself against the pleasure and worked on. "You're like a dog, you know."

"Oh, Madame...I know..."

"Here I thought Eleison was supposed to be the one with an animal inside him...though, I suppose you *are* an animal."

Teeth grinding in my skull, I somehow swept through the work all the faster with these demonic hands fondling my body. Not even our conversation distracted me. I felt no hesitation to let the work unfold beneath my hands while I whispered to the demon flooding my body with greater heights of lust every second.

"I want to love Malin forever—want nothing to come between us. I want to stay in Gudrune with him, and be satisfied."

"I can help you stay in Gudrune, Madame. I swear…if you let me help you, you will not leave this place."

"Very well." My stomach tightened, body braced against the seat while the demon caressed and kissed me in a way that was surely enchanted. At least, it sent streaking through my body bolts of pleasure disproportionate with the mere act of fondling over clothes. "Very well—I'll give you this opportunity, demon—"

"Ah! Madame, yes, please—"

"—but—but what am I to call you when I require you? If you're to serve me—ah—"

An urgent streak of excitement flashed between my thighs, which parted as if in invitation for a lover not there. I cried out, leaning back into the support of those unseen hands. Its lips passed over mine, my head tilting back to receive its kiss despite my better judgment, and I found myself thinking how strangely this might have appeared to someone watching. There I was, my body in tremors, my mouth open for incorporeal kisses, my limbs struggling to maintain their working positions while they fought against the fit of an uncanny orgasm.

"My name, Madame," the demon whispered against my lips as it drew back from the teasing kiss it had lightly delivered, "is Ba'al-Dinon…please, Dinon is fine."

"Very well…very well—oh, blast—"

I gasped, flooded by the demon's caresses, tight as a bow whose arrow was loosed when Dinon's tongue snaked into my mouth. Very, very far into my mouth. The profane penetration promised what it could do but, moreover, seemed to act as a kind of substitute for that penetration my body craved—and which I would certainly never give to such a creature as this.

I did not want to even imagine what could happen if I let that thing take me.

"You'll have to wait and see, Madame," it whispered in that awful, sensually smiling voice that made me crave to behold its gorgeous form again. "For now...I'll help you as you asked."

The hands lifted away from me.

As its presence vanished, the candle flame died at my arm.

GAINST EXPECTATION, I flew on through my work when the dharmine—Dinon—left. I would have thought myself to be distracted, or to have been weakened by whatever vigor he stole from me after feeding on that very pleasure he cultivated.

Far from it. When he disappeared, I felt limber not just in my body but in my mind. I only realized after an hour of weaving that I had forgotten to relight the candle; only half an hour later could I bear to pause long enough to light it. Once, I got up and walked around my room, wondering if I needed a break; but, if I met up with Eleison again, that would be it for the rest of my day. So, remaining secluded, I plowed on through the threads and marveled at my loom's ability to keep up with me.

"I'll bet you didn't know you'd be worked so hard when you arrived here," I told it fondly. "Neither did I."

What a slippery slope it was! One started with speaking to invisible demons, and before one knew it, one was talking to one's loom. Soon I'd be an old lady in an asylum somewhere, talking to her window, her fruit flies…I had to be mad, anyway, to agree to let the dharmine help me.

But that was how desperate I was—how conflicted I was.

All I wanted, of course, was my husband's truth. He had so many secrets that I could not begin to concretely envision the actual shape of whatever he kept from me; and, although that quality was partially a matter of his position and the high-level issues with which he daily wrestled, I was sure that some of what he kept from me also concerned me. And that just wasn't fair. If not for our honeymoon, I would not have tolerated it…but it was clear to me now that Malin wanted to tell me the truth. The problem as he saw it was that he couldn't. I had to accept that for now.

And if Malin was alarmed about somebody trying to exploit that truth to drive a wedge between us, then I was also alarmed without needing to know details. I would rather sit in the dark than know the truth if it would affect the joyful relationship we had barely begun to develop.

I did not want to leave Gudrune without him—so, if Dinon could really keep me where I was, what was the harm in letting him try?

Sometime mid-afternoon, one external stimulus managed to pierce my creative fugue. The heat had risen to become unbearable. Saalast was in the height of a sweltering summer. Without the air conditioning, I gradually found myself lifting my forearm to mop my brow. I had the sense I was swimming through air thickened by the heat, and it occurred to me that if I didn't open my door I might suffocate.

Sighing with reluctance to stop even briefly, I stretched up from my seat, pulled open the door, and paused.

The house thrummed with activity. Soft conversation, hasty footsteps, a general air of intensity that sent me spiraling back to the kidnapping. Frightened, I hurried down the stairs to the first floor.

Before I even noticed Ignatius at his post on the landing, I was staggered by the number of guests in the foyer.

Guests? Well—not really. I looked again, and recognized in hard jaws and bored but serious facades the hallmarks of security officers of various ranks and uniforms. Some police officers were there, and some private men in suits like Eleison or a black shirt like our lesser security staff.

As I stopped before Ignatius, he turned to acknowledge me with a nod and the security officers' informal, "Ma'am."

"What on earth is going on," I whispered with another rapid glance into the milling throng. "Is something the matter?"

"Oh—no, Ma'am. Master Farrow's called some meeting. These are just the security of the people involved."

Relieved as I was to hear nothing was urgently amiss, I was now also curious. What could be so important that Malin had invited people to the house during an extreme Rift Event?

"Did he say what room it's in?" I smiled sweetly, my irony undisguised as I specified, "So I can avoid it."

"It's your house, Ma'am…" Chuckling, giving in to the rapport we had built, Ignatius jerked his chin down the length of the foyer and to the parlor beyond. "They're holding it in the formal dining room. Been at it over an hour…I had the feeling it was gonna be a long one."

"Not as though anyone has much else to do today…thank you, Ignatius, have a good afternoon."

Though I hesitated before stepping into the foyer, and one of the men met my eye in a frank, discouraging sort of way, I reminded myself what Ignatius had just said. It *was* my house, and my husband.

And my territory.

I didn't like to think about it, but it was true. If Malin died before his heir was of age, or if his will otherwise specified such a thing, his death would leave me Matrix of Gudrune. Such circumstances were routinely challenged by the extended relatives of deceased masters, but on the whole, marriage to a territory master was considered a promotion in political responsibility as well as in social rank. Malin had encouraged me from the start to consider him my mentor; so far as I was concerned, understanding his business was part of that mentorship.

So, head high, I willed my face into the same blank, hard mask Malin seemed to effortlessly evoke. To my amazement, those officers in my path moved out from it, sometimes crushing their fellows against walls to make way for me.

I didn't let myself smile until I was through the other side… but oh, it was an effusive smile.

The expression and confidence both faded as I passed through the parlor and into a juncture that led toward the main kitchens, the ballroom, or the dining room, depending on the way one turned. At the end of the little hall to my right, the shut doors of the dining room seemed an ominous dead end barring approach, let alone passage.

Yet Malin's angry tone lured me soundlessly on, reverberating through the wood and echoing down the corridor along with the thump of something against his hand.

"I'm tired of that excuse. Look me in the eyes—look, *look* at me, Platt."

In the pause, I pressed my cheek to the wood of the door.

"Does it look like I care?"

"Maybe you should," said whoever Platt was. "These are your citizens we're talking about."

"That's not what I mean. I care about my citizens. And we all want to care about the people who *might* die. But my citizens, exposed to Rift Events, are *going* to die, Platt. They're going to die whatever we do, however elaborate our contingency plans are, however excellent the infrastructure. And we can't maintain our *fucking infrastructure*"—my ears smarted to hear a word favored in our bedroom repurposed as profanity, which exploded in a kind of snarl as his anger increased—"if we keep losing power due to Rift Events. Each one like this sets us back weeks. Look, where is the—you, give me that report—"

"Here, sir."

Somebody else audibly scrambled through papers before a folder flopped down. Malin's fast stride reminded me of a caged luptich the circus brought through before they settled into favoring slightly more domesticable borros. After snatching the folder from the table and rifling through its contents, Malin threw it down again.

"There," he said as it landed, "see, right there, in black and white—do you understand this trend?"

Platt's chair creaked along with the chairs of a few people near him. "Extreme Rift Events *are* increasing, of course," this poor idiot agreed after a few seconds, tone delicate to avoid antagonizing Malin, "but—"

""But," nothing. *There's* your deaths you're worried about. Do you know how many people here in Saalast are going to die over the next two days? And I don't mean from monsters, or from new altered who have never experienced the hybridization phenomenon." My ears twitched at that, but I couldn't long dwell on it as Malin went harshly on. "I mean from losing power at hospitals, I mean from interference with police communications, I mean this *fucking miserable heat!* We *need* a better solution. Even garden variety Rift Events can limit the use of electricity to a dangerous extent. Did you really look at that report? I don't think you're understanding the numbers—read that bit out loud, Platt, I want to hear you say the words."

Barely repressing a sigh of bitter frustration, this Platt person cleared his throat and shifted in his seat. "Uh—'Horizon's Rift activity data therefore indicates an exponential increase in extreme Rift Events over the coming century, with extreme Events predicted annually in the Gudrune region over the next ten years.'"

Scoffing, Platt finished, "That's not that many. Surely, if we can just—"

"Apparently you don't understand what "exponential" means, so let me spell it out for you. Do you have children?"

"Yeah."

"By the time they die, their children—your grandchildren—will be living in the dark ages. In fifty years"—Malin strode away from the door and up to the head of the table, where I presume he had been sitting long before my arrival—"nine percent of all Rift Events will be extreme events lasting an average of three days. Nearly one in ten Events. Think about that. That's multiple weeks per yer spent like this. I will also remind you that the length of a so-called "typical" Rift Event has been creeping up—they're an average of thirty-six hours now, aren't they, Arthur?"

"Yes, sir," answered the third voice in the conversation.

"We can't keep doing this." Malin thumped into his seat

with a groan of displeasure, his voice muffled as though by hands he pressed over his face. "I'm sick of this—I'm sick of kowtowing to the blasted Overseer when there's an obvious solution."

"All due respect"—Platt again—"I wouldn't say it's 'obvious' at all. It's deliberately unresearched. Theoretical, at best. Unless, of course, you mean to say Gudrune has been engaging in these studies without the Overseer's approval."

"I know that would really upset a bootlicker like you, wouldn't it, Platt…so, go on. Piss off. While you're busy trying to score points by telling her nothing new, let her know what goes on in Gudrune is none of her concern. She knows I don't have the least respect for her; she knows she can't stop me from doing what's right."

"Malin"—still in the hot seat, Platt took a slow, steadying breath, but his voice remained shaky—"I think I can speak for everybody in this room when I say I know you're passionate about this, but—"

"Then stop there. That's all you need to know to recognize that I won't be dissuaded. The Horizon data is too disturbing—and, after my experience with Sigma Labs, I've grown in my distaste for the continent's current policies. It's fine to exploit the Rift Events to keep us treading this feudalist water until our grandchildren are left to die in a hot, angry world full of dharmines and giganturns, but I petition to use the Rift to actively better society, and I'm a criminal for it. And why does she stop me, I ask you? Because it would threaten her power structure. She wants to keep all human society handicapped so she can stay comfortable in Valquist Palace where you, Platt, dream of being installed. Well, dream on."

The chair creaked, and I was surprised to divine by a thump that Malin had kicked his feet upon the table. He was truly a different man in his work than when, alone with me, he was a gentleman until we both craved something more. You may accordingly imagine how excited I was to hear that cruel, derisive tone he turned on me in play drawn naturally out by genuine hatred for his present company.

"I'll say this of the Overseer...she's a good judge of character. As good a judge as I am. And, given what I see when I look at you"—Malin uttered a scornful laugh—"I can't imagine you'll see Valquist Palace outside of a postage stamp."

The tension of the room mounted to a brutal height. I almost pitied the men who had incited my husbands' wrath. Certainly, I was glad I wasn't in the room.

At last Malin spoke again, breaking the silence they had all known better than to fill.

"I've decided to sign off on government funding for Horizon Clean Energy Institute," he announced. "I thought when I invited you all here this morning that I would talk it over with you sensibly and listen to your arguments, but having seen you, I feel less sensible than ever. I feel—stark-raving mad that this room of politicians and climate activists and other synonyms for idiot can't seem to see that there is only one side for us in this war. There is humanity's side, damn you, and I am on it."

"Maybe we're not sure about that," said Platt, the words springing from his mouth as if compelled.

Somebody in the room inhaled sharply.

Malin only laughed.

"You're very lucky this meeting wasn't held ten years ago, Platt, or I would gladly show you just how inhumane I can be. That's enough, all of you—Arthur, when service is restored, call me and we'll talk about how to use the money. Oh, and, wait, you—"

The groaning chairs paused as the rising parties were frozen mid-motion.

"How is the dig going down in Azstoria?"

I hadn't heard this voice yet. A woman's, and nervous. "Excavation is proceeding at a standard pace, sir. I can encourage everyone to move faster, but the normal recycling processes—"

"No, no, I understand. Lithium is always the priority, of course…the more you can find, the better-off we all are."

Feeling cocky because he hadn't been executed on the spot, Platt said, "You're making a mistake, Malin."

""Master Farrow,"" corrected Malin definitively. "Make the mistake one more time and I'll send investigators to scour your office for impropriety in every sector, then let the masses stone you to death in the Saalast streets. I've changed in the past decade. Did you?"

Nobody said anything. Malin slammed the table.

"*Go on*," he snarled. "Get the hell out of here, all of you."

I had intended to dash away and hide in the kitchen while the meeting adjourned—but a new firmness of purpose entered my heart to hear Malin at his duties. Though I'd overheard him working before, this had been new on many levels, and I didn't want to hide my interest. So, I pressed to the wall to wait for the meeting to file out.

The doors blew open, and, their faces made more gaunt in the shrouding of candlelight flickering through the halls, the guests emerged. Fastest and first were a trio of excited, surprisingly young-looking people who spared me a quick glance through two pairs of spectacles but carried on with their conversation without missing a beat. The man in the front—bearded with short blond hair—held a folder depicting an orange sun, broken into rays by an abstract swoop of negative space, rising over the word *HORIZON*. Next came a pair of gray-haired men in suits, one of whom looked at me in surprise, maybe almost fright; I recognized him as someone I had met at that party Malin had hosted to announce our engagement, and went on to divine by the fear in his eyes that this was the Platt my husband had just been berating. The politicians rushed on past me, and more spilled out in their wake.

It seemed I waited forever before, at last, I stepped into the room as the empty door swung shut.

"—and tell Charlotte to bring me some ice water, my God, Eleison, I'm dying of thirst."

"Right away, sir—Thecla!"

I smiled, having not even realized Eleison was in the room for as silent as he was. Malin, his hand having been braced against his forehead, looked sharply up. "Thecla? Oh—dear, what are you doing here?"

"I was eavesdropping on you," I told him flatly, eliciting a smile and a laugh from both men. Eleison's humor was wry, but Malin seemed almost glad.

"What a cheeky girl you are…you know, Eleison, I changed my mind."

Gesturing to the paperwork scattered around the head of the table, Malin got up from his seat with a stretch and said, "Be so kind as to send this upstairs with Charlotte, and the ice water, too…unless you'd care to come up with us?"

"Sir, with all due appreciation: it's ten thousand degrees."

"Yes, well, that's fair…"

"See you later, baby." Eleison smiled to kiss the corner of my mouth and touch the small of my back before going on out through to the corridor. "Let's make sure everybody found their way back to the front door…"

At the disappearance of Eleison's back, the door shut with a gentle click. Malin looked me over on his way to my side, his bared forearms weaving around my waist to draw me close.

"*You* don't mind that it's hot, do you, pet?"

I shivered, assuring him, "Three bodies might be too many when it's so sweltering, he's right…but I won't mind getting sweaty with you, sir."

His smile widened into my favorite of his, the rarest and most gorgeous. A little crooked, a hint of his upper row of teeth, a slight merry crinkling around his eyes and lips. I was surprised it remained, in fact, when I asked, "But that meeting, Master—may I ask what I heard? I'm very curious."

"You can't possibly be interested in such boring matters as the ones I grapple daily."

"I can only name one or two things that interest me more," I confessed. "It didn't sound boring, anyway. You certainly seemed very adamant about—whatever it is."

His lips closed his smile into a smirk, those black eyes assessing me not with any condescension or mistrust but with respect.

"What is it, Malin?"

"Nothing." His knuckle softly brushed along my jaw before he stepped away. "Here," he said with a coaxing finger, "I'll show you."

My heart pattered with excitement as I hurried to the head of the table and eyed the mountain of paperwork, folders, and ratty old files that all looked the same to me. Out of it, Malin selected a stapled packet of documents that formed a copy of a Continental Decree nearly two decades old.

"When my father died and I inherited his position, I was young and ambitious—but I was also very optimistic. Do you know what's on the other side of the Rift, Thecla? Where these monsters are coming from?"

I shook my head. "Some other dimension, but—I'm afraid I don't really understand."

"That's all right, don't be embarrassed. It's complicated. If you want to know the truth, I personally understand it in concept, but when you bog me down in the math and the terms Horizon liked to use throughout their reports before Arthur came onboard, I find myself desperate to cut to the chase.

"In effect, Thecla, Rift Events are places in spacetime where our entropic reality intersects with another universe: one of negative entropy. You know about entropy, don't you, dear?"

"It's like—a measurement of possibility."

"That's an interesting way to put it. In a sense, yes; or, to describe it another way, a measurement of disorder. It describes the potential number of arrangements within a system. The higher the entropy"—he gestured to the wildly disordered pile of paperwork only he could seem to parse—"the more potential arrangements there are, making *desirable* arrangements harder to come by. When we burn coal and the energy is released, entropy is heightened. The solid state is less chaotic, and therefore less entropic, than the gaseous state. As time goes on, reality tends toward heightened entropy. Increasingly efficient, renewable means of energy production must be sought to combat it."

I nodded, and he said, "For the past two thousand years, Thecla, humanity should have been mastering those forms of energy production. Instead, we're barely able to store what we have. Small generators, as you know, work intermittently during an extreme Rift Event, and only when providing power directly to a circuit—to our kitchen, for instance. Something like a residential solar panel won't be able to function under a Rift sky anyway, so no harm done there.

"However, when large generators, say a windmill, are run during Rift Events, they drain stored power rather than providing more, and no one can dream to combat it by any means other than attempting to improve existing methods of energy storage and collection during clear weather. Massive numbers of resources go into lithium recycling every year, and that's just here in Gudrune. Every civilization all over the world is beginning to understand that humankind has hit a ceiling. Unless we can not just create and store energy efficiently and consistently but find a way to continue doing it during Rift Events, mankind will never be able to progress. We'll die here, Thecla—the species will die here."

Quieted, I frowned at the document before me while Malin continued. "What the Overseer doesn't want to hear about is this: that the Rift Events may be harnessed as a resource of clean energy that is renewable for as long as there are Rift Events. One that is dependent on Events, not damaged by them. We must learn to work *with* the Rift, if only in a certain manner of speaking, instead of wanting to have our cake of a world with altered and riftborn while ignoring the greater implication."

"Which is that the Rift Events are getting worse," I whispered, looking into his face, "not better."

"I'm afraid, my darling, that you haven't been born into an easy life…you've chosen to marry an evil man in the middle of trying to repent. One willing to sacrifice everything, anything, even peace in his territory, for the betterment of humanity. No one listens to the only sane man, and sometimes, he doubts his sanity…but I am sure about this, Thecla. The research bears it out.”

He tapped the document before me: the decree which, in as many phrasings as possible, banned experimentation with the Rift, “Rift radiation,” “tachyon particles,” and all other efforts to interact with Rift Events in pursuit of more than general statistical data for the Overseer’s government.

“But I’ve been hamstrung. I fought a war over this, and because backing down on the issue was the only way to maintain my hold on the territory earned during the Expansion while permitting the Overseer to save face, I agreed to play ball and abide by her ban of Rift energy research.”

“Why is she so opposed?”

“She’s worried people will die…but, as I said in the meeting, people are going to die during Rift Events no matter what we do. We had damn well better make good use of those deaths, hadn’t we?”

Before I could ask more, (*How* could people die in the energy research?), the door clicked open and Charlotte’s polite “Oh” drew our attention.

“Ah, Charlotte—come along, Thecla, let’s take this chatter upstairs…perhaps a cool bath is in order for both of us. You know, we’d really ought to get a pool installed in the gym… I’ll get someone on it next week.”

I WAS GLAD I asked Malin my question while we were downstairs, because the heat certainly didn't stop him from falling upon me in a fit of love the moment we rushed in from the violet light of the garden door and sealed it laughingly behind us. His mouth, his hands, his whole body was so stimulating, I confess I myself was hardly deterred. If my head throbbed once or twice with the quick trip from the staircase to our apartment, I hardly noticed it beneath my husband's kisses.

After, though, when we were left shimmering and sticky with sweat, we laughed to mutually admit we needed to air off and lay half a fingertip apart upon the bed. As it always did in the heat, my mind whirred away from my usual inclination toward post-coital doze. Even Malin, who I would have expected to want a few minutes of blissful unconsciousness after such a fraught morning, lay staring into the ceiling with a pensive look.

"Thecla," he broke the silence, his hand sliding over mine, "do you know much about your mother?"

I shook my head, embarrassed. "Not really. Papa was never very comfortable talking about her…I thought it was just because of my stepmother, but now I realize it was because he didn't want me to know she was altered. He must not have wanted to lie about her."

Malin raised my hand toward his face and peered at it through the dark before pressing my knuckles to his lips. "Do you know what she looked like?"

"Oh, sort of. He had a little portrait of her, a photograph, which always amazed me because they're so expensive, or they were when I was a little girl…but I haven't seen it in years. I had it buried with him."

"Why did you do that?"

I smiled sadly, shrugging as he lowered the back of my hand to hold against his hot heart. "I don't know. Because I was very sad, and upset, and at the time Papa died I never wanted to see anything that reminded me of either one of them. Not ever again."

Hesitating, the duke's words from earlier still heavy in my soul, I confessed on to Malin, "I was very angry at my father for dying."

With a noise that was half a laugh, half a sympathetic click of his tongue, my husband asked, "Why?"

"Because…he knew better. He spent my whole life obsessing over the weather, over the security of the house. He was the expert on Rift Events and how to handle them. He was my hero! And then—he let some dharmine get close enough to bite him while he was out helping our neighbors manage an Event."

"Was the dharmine killed?"

I shook my head, staring at the ceiling, unable to look at Malin while I struggled to stay numb to the old pain. "Nobody ever saw it. They just knew my father disappeared from the hunting party. A few hours later he stumbled through our front door, bleeding, panicking. He collapsed. And—"

I raised my free hand to scratch an itch at the edge of my eye, amazed that I managed to go without shedding tears. "He just never woke up. I kept waiting for him, praying for him to wake up. I sat by his bedside for days, watching his hair grow in white. And then, one morning, my mother—my stepmother, I mean—woke me up by sitting on the edge of my bed, and I knew just what she was going to say to me. And she did. She held my hand and said, "He's dead." And that was it."

"I'm sorry."

Lips trembling at last, I shut my eyes and told Malin, "It's fine. It doesn't matter anymore. But—I was so shocked, then. So afraid. I just…I couldn't stand the thought of him anymore, and thinking of my mother made me think of him. I didn't want to keep her picture, so I put it in his suit pocket before they buried him, and I've never regretted it."

Malin exhaled in another expression of sympathy, his hand sliding beneath my head to draw me to his chest. I rolled against him, my ear pressing to that wonderful heart.

"I know she was beautiful, though," I said. "She had auburn hair, and Papa told me that her eyes were striking blue in person…now I realize they must have glowed. Bright, bright blue." I smiled a little, then touched my own somewhat darker hair. "But I take after my father."

"How do you think our children will look?"

Excited by his question, I tilted my face up toward Malin's and enthused, "Oh, I don't know! I suppose, if we have a boy, I'd be happiest if he took after you...but, I don't know, I don't know!" With a girlish laugh, I told him unabashedly, "They'll be *smart* children, whatever the case."

"Oh, little geniuses...between the two of us, they're guaranteed to always be right. Or think that they are."

We laughed, and I raised my head to kiss him; but, when our lips separated, his mood had sobered. One great hand raised to ghost along my cheek.

"You know, for the sake of our children—I don't want you to keep your relationship with Eleison private, of course, but if you might avoid describing him as your mate while abroad...that sounds so insulting to ask of you..."

I shook my head. "I understand. I was worried about Aleister finding out after we let it slip. Please don't worry, though. It won't be hard for me to conceal from the Overseer what I only learned so recently!"

"Well, Aleister's not a problem...and neither is the Overseer. One look at you, two, three, and she'll figure you out. I can't hide your altered heritage from her." While I frowned with concern, he rested his thumb at the corner of my mouth. "Don't worry, please. Much as I detest Parvati, I don't think she would be a danger to our children. It's the rest of Valquist learning that Malin Farrow's heir will be a third generation altered—that's what worries me."

Earnestly, I told him, "I'll protect the secret for as long as I can, Malin."

"I know you will."

Like a drowning man bobbing above the surface, Malin produced the ghost of a smile before letting it fall back into a frown to match mine. "I don't have the power to keep you from the Overseer," he said sadly, "and I trust that you love me more than I have ever trusted anyone in any matter, which I mean without exaggeration…but, darling, I confess…I will be in dire condition until you return to me."

While I frowned, Malin sighed to sit up and snatched a glass of water from the nightstand. "Would that I could go with you… maybe I should ignore the exile and tag along anyway. What's she going to do, arrest me? She'd look like an ass…"

While Malin pulled from the water, I studied the beads across the glass's surface—and perked.

"Charlotte," I said brightly. "That's it!"

"What's that?"

"Why not, instead of sending Brea with me, send Charlotte?" Malin looked back at me with a flex of his lips, then gave a glance of assent toward the ceiling's corner while I went on. "As valuable as Charlotte is to you here, I'm sure she'd be even more valuable to your peace of mind if she came with me. She certainly wouldn't let me run away or anything like that, if that's what you're still worried about."

"Oh, maybe I am a little…but, if I were, volunteering to bring Charlotte along really is a trustworthy gesture. I'll think about it." Delivered in a tone indicating he'd already decided to do it. "Speaking of Charlotte, shall we dress for dinner?"

And undress again quickly afterwards. The stuffy house was so miserable we blew out all the candles after Charlotte cleared the table and disappeared, neither one of us being able to tolerate the sight of fire. Then, back in bed, we lounged around chatting softly in the dark, made love once more, and by some miracle managed to find our ways to sleep.

Malin did, anyway…my sleep was interrupted by the slither of a familiar whisper into my ear.

"Madame…"

As they had during that strange honeymoon dream, in which the dharmine led me to discover the chilling secret of a second Malin in the villa's basement, (which was, I always had to assure myself when the thought crossed my mind, *indisputably* a dream), my eyes flew open to hear Ba'al-Dinon's honeyed voice.

And, as had been the case that time, the bedroom door stood open for me.

"Come see my devotion, Madame…see everything I do to please you…"

My throat tensed with fear and regret. I had been a fool to allow Dinon to help me—I knew that at once, even while I was still yanking on my robe and briskly hurrying from the bedroom. As I caught the shadow of the dharmine's ultra-dark cloak receding through the pitch of the apartment, I had the sudden sense that if I did not learn to deal with this creature properly, my life would be destroyed.

But when I stepped out to the rooftop garden, where Aleister shuffled slowly through rows of marigolds and up to the building's edge, I saw through the pulsing flood of Rift-violeted night that it was not just my life at stake.

"Aleister!" I screamed, rushing toward the sleepwalking duke who pursued some unseen dream figure toward his death. "No! Wake up!"

Heedless of the exposure to the Rift and the effect it would have on my head, I rushed through the maze of flowers and past a bench overlooking the city, and somehow got beyond the little fountain on the other side of that same breakfast table where I'd greeted Aleister forty-eight hours before. My heart pumping with adrenaline so intense I didn't perceive a whit of the obstacle course I had just overcome, I barely caught the back of his nightshirt before he could step off the edge.

The dharmine's ultra-dark cloak flapped in the breeze before us, revealed to me as plainly as he must have been to Aleister.

Quicksilver eyes as bright as comets; vanishing with that same haste.

Behind us, the stairwell door slammed open.

Five minutes, three security guards and one rude awakening later, Aleister sat in the parlor with Malin and I in the couch across from him.

"So sorry about all that," he said with an embarrassed shake of his head and glance into his nightcap. "Don't know if I should be drinking more, or less."

"Knowing you," observed Malin wryly, "I think we both know the answer…has this happened to you before, Aleister?"

"Goodness, no, I don't *sleepwalk*." He laughed, as though somnambulism was something for the rabble, then went on with a slow pull of his scotch on the rocks, "Then again, I don't normally recall dreams, either…but that was a strange one."

"A dream, eh? What—one so depressing it made you want to kill yourself?"

While Aleister laughed at Malin's joke, I intended to smile politely and excuse myself back to bed; but Aleister said, "No, oh, a splendid dream, actually, of a curious man," and the intention fled me.

Clearing my throat, I asked, "What kind of man?"

"Breathtaking," he said, sighing into the glass and slumping back in his seat. "Oh, so lovely…long white hair"—I paled, and

Malin flicked me a brisk glance I didn't fail to note—"and strange silver eyes...a sort of feline smile. You don't happen to have a servant like that in this house, do you?"

Aleister sounded hopeful, and I managed to eek out a laugh while saying apologetically, "No, I'm afraid—not in this one."

"Pity! In the dream, I'm sure he was a servant of yours, Malin...and he was going to lead me to some kind of...secret pleasure room, some harem hidden in the halls of your house. Well, what could I possibly do but follow?" Laughing, shrugging, Aleister drained his glass. "I'm a simple man, with simple needs... and apparently what I need is somebody to handcuff me to the bed at night. Care to volunteer, Uncle?"

"So sorry, Aleister."

"Ah, well...guess I'll try Eleison." While I scoffed, Aleister winked at me cheekily and stretched up from his chair. "Only teasing, Auntie! Goodness. You're so *possessive*...you two certainly are a match. Three. Whatever...good night, Thecla. Thank you for saving my life."

With a wiggle of his fingers, Aleister meandered off to bed.

Malin waited for the garden door to shut before turning to face me.

"That chap he described sounded familiar, didn't he...were you aware the dharmine has been looming around our halls?"

Though I paled to do so, my tongue darting across my lower lip, I confessed in a raw tone, "I thought—I thought it wouldn't trouble anyone but *me*. I—I'm sorry, Malin, I should have—"

"Now—" He caught my hand and held it, looking at me softly despite my expectation. "Nothing to *apologize* about, dear. You *are* its foremost victim. How does it appear? Do you see it with your waking eye?"

Relieved to have the bubble of my own last secret snap beneath the probe of Malin's neutral interest, I explained, "No. Well—sometimes, but briefly. When I do see him, it, I look away. I'm afraid to look at it longer than a few seconds."

"You likely shouldn't. Has it bitten you?"

"No. It tells me that it won't, but I don't know why. It might be lying, but…if it intended to take my blood, I'm sure it would have done so by now."

"Not necessarily…and it certainly is lying, if it's talking to you at all. How often *does* it talk to you, darling?"

Were it not for the affection in Malin's voice, the conversation would have had the tone of a witchfinder's inquest… or a psychiatrist's.

"Perhaps—once a day. Twice, if I'm often alone or unoccupied."

One dark eye widening with the arch of his brow, Malin asked, "That often?"

At my nod, his surprise dissolved into a sterner arrangement of his features. "Thecla"—now he *was* a bit unhappy with me, and I cringed as his hand raised to catch the tip of my chin and keep my gaze fixed to his—"I know it must be hard to tell me the truth when I do so much omitting of my own, but—"

"It's not that." My voice quivered, the words clipped short. As though what I had just said was a lie. "It's just—I don't know. I've wanted to tell you about it, but it's…trying to *please* me. I think—"

My eyes darted toward the foyer, each word a whisper.

"I think that what it tried to do to Aleister tonight was a gesture for me. It came to me while I was weaving today." I pressed closely against Malin and earned the slow exhalation of his desire. As the hand upon my chin slid up to cradle the back of my head, his other arm tightened into the small of my back.

"It took no form," I whispered on, "yet it touched me—sweetly, longingly, as you or Eleison might."

My husband's dark eyes drank in my face, the hint of excitement that edged my frightened words sparking intrigue amid his lightly remonstrative air. "You didn't let it take you," he observed, or hoped.

"Of course not! It's a disgraceful, obsequious animal—and, anyway, I'm frightened to think what could happen. No, Malin. Nor did I permit its hands to reach my lap. It knew I wouldn't, so it refrained. Yet, all the same…oh, I should confess it brought me to an ecstasy."

"So that's how it's feeding from you. I see." With a new light of understanding, (and perhaps even sympathy for my plight), Malin's softening eyes stole a glance into my robe. "I suppose, with a hot, willing young woman such as yourself, it might be wiser to find other methods to feed than short-term ones…however sweet blood must be to their senses."

Shivering as he pushed my robe open to kiss a long route down my breast, I asked "Do you suppose dharmines really find blood sweet? Or is it only that they take pleasure in the hideousness of the—of the act…Malin…"

"Keep talking." His hands trailed over my waist while the vibrations of his lips teased the nerves of one tightening areola. "I interrupted you, darling, I'm so sorry…you were saying something about today, and unlucky Montagne's close call."

"Oh, what *was* I saying? Yes, yes, well…it begged me for some way it could help me. So, I told it"—my stomach tensed with pleasure as my husband's teeth, then tongue, grazed my beaded nipple—"that I didn't want to go away to Valquist."

"Thecla…"

My throat strained as I admitted, "I told it that I wanted to stay here with you, Malin. That I didn't want anything to come between us."

The sound of heartbreak escaping his lips, Malin raised his head to kiss me on the mouth. While his tongue slid in against mine, his hand trailed along my stomach. His fingers disappeared into the shadows of the thicket south.

"You just made me realize how I've failed you these past few days, Thecla."

"Don't say that," I begged, my words breaking off in a soft, "Oh—"

"I have…I've put my own fears into you. You're a lovely woman still blessed with a fresh and open mind, but you've spent your life living in one small place and you're uncomfortable at the thought of more…even now, you've seen perhaps a sliver of what Gudrune can offer you. You've been invited to stay in Valquist Palace…to meet the Overseer of the blasted continent, an honor no matter what I feel about her…you should be excited, and instead I've made you fret over it so much that—"

"You haven't." I moaned through my poorly cobbled words while his fingers exacerbated the excitement provoked by my account of Dinon's caress. "I told the dharmine that because I want to be near you, Malin! Because…I don't want these happy times to be abbreviated."

"Oh, Thecla…"

He looked pained to hear me say such a thing. Through the waves of pleasure he sent rippling through my sensitive, sometimes thrashing frame, Malin told me firmly, "They won't be."

"I know they won't."

"We're going to be together forever," he told me, not with the fanciful dream of a clumsy little boy but with the certainty, the absolute and calculated certainty, of a man who knew something I didn't. "What we have will change. It's the nature of time. Yet, so long as you don't let that change drive us apart, it will represent but a deepening of our love. Don't be afraid, angel—don't ever be afraid. *Do you love me?*"

"Yes! Oh! Malin, yes, I worship you—"

My choice of word inspired that vain smile, that devilish hint of tooth, that I loved so much. I cried out, thrust up to the edge of bliss simply by the way he looked at me amid his petting. But, oh! The glide of his fingers teasing up and down, spreading my flood along the flesh that screamed with me—the teasing trailing down to my begging entrance, brushed but never penetrated before he caressed back up to the crown jewel to which he began paying singular, almost unbearably pleasurable attention! I had found Malin an expert in the art of love. It should have been no surprise that his mere gaze might prove transcendent.

"Then we'll always be together, Thecla...and we'll always find each other when the world tries to separate us."

Whimpering, I caressed his face, his scar, his disarrayed hair. "Please, Malin, please—I need you to take me—"

"Oh, I will...just let Master reward you for your honesty... just relax...ah..."

With a brief glance at some telltale tightening of my thighs, a signal of apogee he had been fast to note, Malin smiled into my eyes.

"That's right, Thecla...give in to me."

"Malin! Please, oh—oh!"

I nearly screamed, the feeling of his third and middle

fingers sliding just barely inside of me such an erotic jolt after the ceaseless, superficial petting that I submitted on the spot. While the orgasm crashed over me and I clutched my husband's robe with a torrid cry, Malin furrowed his brow and moved his lips in that artistic appreciation for my pleasure's contortions.

"That's right, Thecla. Who does it better…Master, or the dharmine wretch?"

"You, Master! Sir—oh, yes, my body is yours, you know it so well! Oh, Master! I love the way you touch me—"

With a low rumble of appreciation in his chest, Malin slowly withdrew his fingers and untied his robe.

"Perhaps it's not such a bad thing you're going off for a little while, darling…yes, ah—so long as you love me, perhaps it's not really so bad…you'll come back to me, won't you…"

Before I could extol his virtues to assure him no force could shake my love, a wonderful omen couched our future in security.

With another explosion of light and noise, the power returned, and we kissed amid our happily shared laughter.

THE NEXT MORNING, a new life inhabited the house. It and all the people in it could breathe again, even if the Rift Event remained steadily aglow on the other side of every shuttered window. Literally overnight, everyone's outlook changed. I had never seen a household of people so glad to be disturbed from sleep by an inundation of light and electronics!

Not all omens were necessarily as pleasant as the return of the power. For instance, I awoke to find my delayed bleeding had not just begun, but made up for lost time. I was so sick with menses my thrashing awoke poor Malin, who called for a hot water bottle and spent our usual pre-dawn lovemaking session holding me gently in his arms while I whimpered and groused.

Yet even the blood seemed a kind of heartening sign. By the time I returned to Saalast after more than half a month away, Malin and I would be ready to try anew, our love revived by the distance.

After one more day, the Rift Event finished; after three more days, my journey to Valquist loomed hatefully on the horizon of my mind. The morning just before the trip, at Malin's request, I hosted my first press conference, which was a kind of event wherein one had to speak on a topic before politely and placidly answering questions. I was sick with anxiety, but the speech Malin and his writer had crafted made my job as straightforward as any actor's.

If I had realized then how hard actors truly worked at their craft, perhaps I would have been more impressed with myself!

The questions from the newspaper and radio people were exceedingly gentle, and I got the impression that this was by Malin's design, for he appeared silently along with me. In addition to cowing the media, his presence tamped down my stage fright simply because I had attended several such events with him before. First, in my debut as his wife; then, a few times when he thought my smiling presence would soften his image, or in some way reinforce the point he was making. Normally, I stood somewhere behind him—generally beside Eleison, which always gave me a little thrill—and smiled and nodded or scowled with displeasure depending on the contents of Malin's speech.

That morning, our roles were reversed. As I read, he watched over the crowd, and I sensed his eyes raking over their number as though daring anyone to ask an unapproved question.

They didn't.

With the conference announcing my visit uneventful, I would have hoped I would feel some relief. Instead, I felt more afraid than ever. There was now nothing between me and the trip to Valquist...although not everyone was as morose as I was.

While I suffered Brea to put up my hair for one last pre-trip dinner and show with Malin, a familiar knock at my door piqued my interest. "Come in!" I beamed as Eleison stepped in and glanced twice at Brea.

"Oh," he said, earning a sidelong glance from the maid.

"Won't be a moment, sir," she said with a bobby pin still stuck in the corner of her mouth, returning her attention to my reflection. "Don't mind me."

But he clearly did—having twigged long before Malin, or perhaps even me, as to my distaste for Brea—and kept our conversation superficial while we were in company.

"Nice job with the press today, Madame."

"Thank you." I allowed a sly half-smile at his formal address. "It was nothing…silly, really. I'm not sure why Gudrune's citizens would even care about my trip!"

"It's symbolic," he said, barely getting the words out before Brea interrupted with a kind of laugh.

"Are you kidding, Madame?"

She no longer flinched beneath my imitation of Malin's stare. A bad sign. "What do you mean," I asked calmly, my eyes lowering to the jewelry box from which I picked a few bracelets.

"Well, it's—you're like a princess from a nursery tale, don't you see?" When I looked back up at her, the earnest glow to her blue eyes was almost endearing. Brea wasn't a bad person, you must understand…just not a good maid. She went on in a dreamy tone, reminding me, "You're a girl from nowhere, and now you're the consort of the territory master! It's a dream. All over Gudrune, women scour the papers you're in for a little taste of your life."

Uncomfortable, I stammered out a laugh while she stepped away to inspect her work. "I don't know about *that*—"

"She's right," said Eleison knowingly. "Your marriage to Malin means something to them. It gives them hope…something to dream about, no matter how impossible. Because you show them it isn't so impossible, right?"

While Brea put away the remainder of the pins and clips, I pondered my reflection and found myself admitting, "I suppose so. Yes...I suppose I hadn't thought of myself that way."

Smiling in encouragement, Brea curtsied. "Enjoy your show, Madame," she said while swishing past Eleison and out of the room.

Maybe she wasn't so bad all the time...she could be charming, at least. Catching myself—boggling at the ease with which I passed judgment over someone who, nine months prior, would have seemed infinitely superior to me in rank, manner, and fortune—I told her "Good-bye" before leaning forward to fix my brows.

At last, my sensual shadow stepped behind me.

"You're sexy in red," Eleison noted while bending to kiss my ear, my jaw, my neck. "Are you excited?"

"Oh, yes, but I'm a little intimidated for my first opera. What if—"

"No!" Laughing, his toothsome smile wide as it flashed across his face, Eleison straightened up behind me and set his hand on the nape of my neck. "I meant about going to the capital," he clarified, his thumb digging into taut muscle and working it loose. I sighed and lowered my hands from my work altogether. "Just you and me...and Charlotte, of course, but I don't think she'll want to watch if she's not getting any."

Laughing to imagine Charlotte's face upon hearing such a joke, I shook my head and confessed, "She's certainly the best chaperone to keep me on-task. You should have seen her eyes glaze over when I was asking for her advice about you and Malin earlier in the year."

"I get the feeling that Charlotte's done her time with men… so, what do you want to do in Valquist? If there's a chance."

Taken aback by the question, I laughed. As melodramatic and moody as Malin had been over the whole thing, the idea of excitement hadn't occurred to me. Now that Eleison was here, I realized this would be my first stretch of time truly alone with my mate. Even during the weeks before the wedding, when Malin forswore his claim to my bed as a courtesy to his friend and footman, I was still seeing my then-husband-to-be a few evenings a week.

Viewed in that light, I could better understand Malin's anxiety about sending me somewhere he felt had the potential to sour me on our marriage…but I hoped I would prove something of my maturity to him.

That drive to prove oneself was the trouble with loving an older man. At least, it was in my case. Yet, that was what kept our love so spectacular, I think.

Eleison and I, our love was solid, somehow immutable. He knew it, I knew it. It was a fact of nature and chemical attraction, and we felt it every time we touched. But Malin and I would never have an intense biochemical link that guaranteed we would overcome all odds. There was nothing external that assured each of the other's love; indeed, we both had incentive to engage in the union lovelessly, and for any number of reasons that varied between us.

And with that knowledge, Malin and I were driven to love one another all the more. It was a war, with each skirmish rooted in the challenge to authentically express our feelings. With every look, every caress, every gesture or gift or promise, we begged each other to believe in our love.

And, each time we did, that love grew hotter—stronger—between us.

Though Eleison shadowed us at dinner and stood looking bored stupid at the opera, he discreetly kissed my cheek in the foyer and thereafter left us alone. Malin turned on me with a look that overflowed my heart with the humbling passion of his love, and as he slid a hand into the small of my back to guide me to the elevator, I already knew how tenderly he would take me that night.

For once, there were none of his games. No rituals or pretenses. He was not rough or stern; not the master of Gudrune. Not the terrifying Malin Farrow, desperate to hide his blackened past from me.

He was my husband, and I was completely his wife.

In the soft light of morning, Malin kissed me awake for one last round of love. Birds sang quietly above the distant sounds of the city's rising traffic. I melted in his arms, linked to him in body, mind, and soul.

Then, it was over. His sweat-dotted brow rested against mine.

As his panting mouth contorted with his frown, a hint of sorrow reddened the edges of his eyes. Mine filled with tears at once, unable to stand the sight. While he tutted and staved off his own emotion to care for mine, I cried like a silly child.

"I don't want to go!"

"Oh, Thecla…you'll have a good time, dear…sh…"

As I wound my arms around his neck and buried my face in his chest, Malin delicately rolled upon his back to hold me in his arms.

"Don't be sad, Thecla…you'll have so much fun that you'll forget all about me, I promise."

"I would never," I choked, but he laughed while gathering my hair from my neck.

"Not in that way…I mean to say, you'll have so much to do and see and experience…you'll probably have to talk to a few more reporters while you're there, you know." He brooded on that for a few seconds before going on. "But, perhaps, if you wouldn't think me too suffocating…you might send me a message on the watch each evening, or call to tell me about your day."

"I will! Oh, but it's so much later out there. Will I interrupt you—"

"No, never. Call me anytime, I don't care. I'll interrupt a man pleading for his life to answer you. The world can wait…it would be good for it to try, from time to time."

Maybe learning to wait would have been good for the world, but it made me suffer. Malin and I left bed only when the inevitable could be delayed no longer. Then, with heavy hearts, we cleaned and dressed ourselves, and I met Brea to have my hair pulled away and tucked under a fascinator whose short silver veil cut down across my brow. The effect made Malin sigh to see me sitting at my vanity.

"My bride…Thecla…"

His hand rubbed over his chest until, wincing as though in pain, Malin knelt at my side and took my hands in his.

"I don't know if I can stand to see you off, darling."

Swallowing back the sorrow constricting my throat, I begged, "But we'll talk tonight, won't we?"

"We'll talk tonight, and tomorrow, and every night so long as you wish it…but seeing you step on that train, unable to come with you while knowing—"

His expression tightened. After bowing over my hands to

kiss them both, he studied my fingers. The gold band upon the third finger of my left hand.

"Thecla," he said softly, raising his eyes to mine with an expression that was earnest, if sad, "whatever you glean—whatever she tells you, or lets slip—promise me that you'll try to forgive me. Even if it takes time…please, swear to me that you'll try."

"You could still tell me yourself," I urged him, "now," but he shook his head before I finished the thought.

"No. There's too much, and no more time."

And why would he choose to reveal what he had not shared, when I was not guaranteed to learn anything?

"I just want to know you fully," I begged him. "I swear… whatever it is, even *if* I can't process it right away, I'll forgive you someday. Please, Malin—I love you so."

I saw it all in his face, revolving again. The wife he never discussed. The history of bloodshed and war. The red door in our honeymoon villa, and the redder room within.

"By the time you know me the way you want to, Thecla," he said with a curious kind of dreaminess to gaze into me, "you'll be far more powerful than me, and I'll have no more secrets left to intrigue you…let your poor old husband hold on to what's his a bit longer."

He spoke in such odd ways! I frowned, but he didn't let me probe. He kissed me, and as he kissed me stood up to take my face in his hands.

"Please, darling," he said, his voice ragged with the unslaked thirst of love, "call me when you think to."

I cried out, reaching up to grab him as he slipped away— but, in a few long, swift strides, the door of my dressing room shut, and I sagged back into my seat with a sorry pang.

Perhaps he was right. Perhaps it was good I was going to Valquist—that we were risking this. I wanted the truth, didn't I? At least to learn the vague shape of what was concealed from me.

But, as sensitive as Malin was to my moods—and as sensitive as I was in turn!—I wasn't sure either one of us would ever have been able to withstand the pressure of in-person revelation. He did not want to look into my face and see *real* pain, or heartbreak… and I was not sure I would want to look into his eyes while he made these confessions, whatever they were.

So it *was* better, perhaps, to hear it from someone else. For the first brick between us to be removed by outside disaster, rather than his hands or mine.

At least, that was what I told myself as Eleison helped me into the coach.

"Oh," sighed Aleister as the door shut. "Thank goodness! Saalast, good-bye…can't say I'll miss you."

Desperate to distract myself, I stooped to small talk. "You come a long way to visit Malin, don't you, Aleister?"

"Oh, yes"—he smiled as we rocked into motion, Charlotte and the duke and I all swaying while Eleison rode up front to smoke beside Aleister's footman—"yes, it's a bit of a slog…though usually I stay a season or two, and usually in his Karrisregion estate, of course."

"You don't find Saalast has anything to commend it? I like it."

"Mm, well, you haven't seen many other cities, have you? Trust me when I say there are finer examples. Saalast *is* better than it used to be, I'll give your husband that…but, well, it's just not safe."

Reflecting grimly on my own brush with the seedier parts of the city, I suggested, "Not all of it, perhaps, but surely every city has its quarrelsome areas."

"Not Valquist, dear. It's pristine, historic, so safe I can walk around without security...wouldn't recommend it for *you*, of course, oh no." He laughed a little while Charlotte and I exchanged a sidelong glance.

"Should I be concerned for my safety, Aleister? If Malin is so detested that he's banned from the city—"

"Let's leave that for the Overseer to determine...I don't want to frighten you, especially since I can tell from your face that you're just bound and determined not to have a good time."

"That's not—"

"Lighten up, Thecla! Good Lord." Swinging the tip of his boot against my gown, then recrossing his legs at the knee, Aleister said, "Maybe now that Malin's not liable to pop around the corner you'll *relax* a little. Start acting like a human...no offense to you and your altered beau, of course."

"Altered *are* human," I reminded him, glancing at Charlotte for assistance. "Or, am I wrong?"

"Altered are capable of reproduction with healthy adult humans, may receive blood transfusions, skin grafts and other organs from unaltered humans, and may maintain their civil liberties in Gudrune so long as they operate within the boundaries of the law and their contractual obligations. In other words," Charlotte agreed, carefully addressing all of this to me and not to the duke, "you are human, Madame, yes."

"For a *certain* definition of human," agreed Aleister, facing the window. "I suppose that's true."

Charlotte's expression communicated everything her mouth could not.

When we arrived at the station, the train was already there; and, I was surprised to find with a flutter of fear, already boarding. Upon finding that nobody else was near as panicked as I, however, I disguised the feeling with neutral interest for our surroundings. We stopped outside the station building, and Eleison found an attendant with whom he engaged himself in soft conversation. The attendant hurried inside, and not two minutes later a suited man with bushy eyebrows and a neat black cap strode out to introduce himself to me.

"Your car is all ready for you, Madame, if you'd follow me to your entrance. Oh, uh—and some journalists are here as well…although, (and I really hate to put any kind of pressure on you, of course), we *were* hoping to depart as close to schedule as possible—"

Unable to disguise my displeasure to hear of more reporters, I turned it toward Eleison in the form of a tight little smile.

"Goodness, well, we don't want to keep them waiting, do we? We'd better hurry through."

"With pleasure," agreed my mate, his warm hand sliding into the small of my back and erasing my anxiety at once.

Boarding the train was an unpleasant experience, fast and frantic after we were led through a short maze of administrative corridors accessible from a side entrance. Then a door opened into the sunlight again, and I caught a glimpse of a great, brilliantly gleaming locomotive rising above us, and somebody cried out, "She's here!"

Then they were on me from all sides, flashbulbs snapping and voices shouting in such disorder that all but one of the questions were lost—and that one I did parse, I could only infer, for most of the first clause was drowned to leave me with only, "—say about your visit with the Overseer?"

Laughing, searching the crowd of reporters through which Eleison and the train crew whisked us, I agreed with my voice raised above the chaos and my smile fixed in no specific direction, "Yes, I—I'm very excited to represent Gudrune!"

While the conductor slid open a gilded door I barely saw, Eleison took me by the hand and said, "Careful," while half-pushing me up the short set of stairs into the train. Charlotte and Aleister hurried after me, both sighing to have made it through the gauntlet.

As Eleison propelled himself aboard, the conductor followed, and the abrupt silence of the shut door seemed apocalyptic.

"Well," the conductor said brightly, his hands clapping together as he looked between the lot of us, "that was exciting! Thank you very much for coming aboard today, Madame Farrow—and all of you. This is your compartment"—he opened the door nearest us just as I was taking in the corridor's long stretch of dark, highly polished wood that gleamed in the light of the windows and reminded me of Malin's apartment—"and your lady's maid will be just next door."

He passed a key over to me while advising, "Please, make yourself comfortable—I'll be with you in just a moment. If you would come with me, Your Grace—"

While the conductor dealt with Aleister, it occurred to me that he had known not to bother with Eleison. With a faint smile and a flush of pleasure I couldn't help, I stepped into the compartment and was dizzied by shock.

As dearly as I loved Lescaut while growing up a peasant in it, my upbringing left me with a lack of imagination for the heights of luxury. Malin casually lived in a way that shocked me, and the compartment his title had secured was but the latest example. My eye first fell upon the full-sized, plushily made bed tucked into an alcove at the far end of the apartment. (Apartment! My pen slipped—but, in truth, it *was* a mobile apartment, no matter how cramped.) As in the corridor, a series of windows ran along a wall of intricately patterned, beautifully gleaming wood with a floral design contrasting the external corridor's stern uniformity. Directly left of the entrance was another door, behind which I was stunned to find a bathroom, and beside which was mounted a bar. Eleison availed himself amid a noise of delight.

Between us and the bed, a sitting area welcomed us, and a small table beside the curtained and presently shuttered windows had been arrayed with beautifully cut fruit in every color, flowers to match, a personal letter of welcome from the president of the railway, and a pair of champagne flutes overturned beside a bucket of ice.

"Never noticed this bar before. It's no wonder Malin doesn't mind going down to the desert." Chuckling, Eleison sniffed the contents of a bottle of scotch he'd just cracked open brand new. "I'm usually stuck in Char's compartment…not that it's bad, but, hell—it doesn't have a private bathroom, for starters."

"I don't feel like I'm on a train." Boggling, I stumbled forward and slid down into a chair at the table. I didn't even recognize some of the fruits piled there; then my eye was caught by an astonishing sight just over Eleison's head.

"They even got our *bags* on the train already somehow! My goodness, Eleison, are they riftborn?"

He laughed in agreement, his low chuckle filling my heart with a shy, almost girlish delight. "They know how to serve the territory master's consort, anyway…one sideways glance from you, and suddenly the company's shut out of Gudrune, or getting hit with some kind of penalty. At the very least, no longer getting the Gudrune hoi polloi to pay for a compartment like this so eagerly."

A knock reverberated upon the door. Eleison stepped out of the way and the mustached conductor from before stepped in, a bottle of champagne tucked in his arm.

"Oh, goodness," I began with a laugh and a glance to Eleison's already poured drink.

"Compliments of the company, Madame, the whole way to Valquist. Please let us know at any point if you'd like more"— he strode in and flipped over one of the two glasses, discreetly removing the other—"or, of course, if you need anything at all. That button will summon your butler, and, if for some reason he isn't available, I'll be by to get you whatever you need. Will you be requiring turndown service?"

Never having so much as stayed in a hotel before, I looked helplessly at Eleison, who shrugged and said, "Sure, she'll be impressed."

With an elegant, polite sort of laugh that carried genuine relief for Eleison's casual demeanor, the conductor said, "Very good. That will be at six, which is coincidentally when the piano player starts his evening in the lounge car. Highly recommended, very pleasant…"

He went on, smothering me in more information than I could absorb or remember. There were three restaurant cars he recommended, as well as a fourth he advised I might prefer to avoid—being as it was, in his words, "For a slightly different class of traveler." The floor below ours in the same car was a private observation area; the other observation area was recommended against for similar reasons as that other restaurant. There was an on-board postal service, they offered recreational amenities including board games and books, I could expect a breakfast spread free of charge delivered to my compartment each morning, and, in the instance of a Rift Event, he assured me particular care would be paid to my car of the train.

"Oh no," I said quickly, "don't tell me that—I'll worry about everyone else aboard."

"We'll take care of them, too, of course," he added with a small laugh. "And, lastly, if you need anything that requires some level of discretion and you would prefer for whatever reason not to bother with the butler, please feel free to ask for me by name. I'm Josko."

If I had been worried I would never be able to remember his name amid all the other details, the uniqueness of it made me smile and relax somehow. "All right," I agreed, very pleased and frankly now far more excited for the trip, "thank you very much."

"Our pleasure! Please, enjoy your journey. Sir." With a nod and a half-bow toward Eleison, Josko flashed one more quick smile and then was gone.

"What's even *happened*?" The breath was caught in my lungs. I looked at Eleison with wide eyes while he locked the door behind the conductor.

"It's really fucking cute how amazed you still are by everything. Haha, hey—"

I had snapped the cloth napkin at the seat of his trousers as he sauntered past to investigate the bed. "You swear so casually, you naughty boy."

"You know, I'm six years older than you."

"Five and a half…though you wouldn't know it sometimes."

He grinned a little, nursing his drink as he lowered upon the foot of the bed. "Pretty cushy," he observed, pushing high the lever that raise the window shutter and laughing as a flash bulb went off in his face. He shut it again. "Maybe we'll save that for when we leave the station…"

I laughed at him, wagging my finger. "Careful, Eleison… if you're nervous about being too public with our relationship, you don't want to get caught in photos drinking whiskey on my bed."

"Oh, I'm not *nervous*. I just don't want to cause problems for Malin—or for you. Come here."

My heart sparked at his command, given while he stretched toward the head of the bed and set his glass upon the nightstand. Eleison was so professionally differential toward me that when the lover came out, his tongue bold and sharp, I was always all aflutter. Leaving the champagne behind, I hurried down the compartment and upon the bed with him. There, I fell into his arms and against his eager kiss.

"Think they'll let me smoke in here," he asked as I settled down with my cheek upon his chest. Laughing, stroking his tie, I tilted my face toward his.

"Will *I* let you, is the better question."

"Fascist. What's that supposed to mean!" While I laughed at his mock incredulity, at his wildly working brows, Eleison raised his head, then his entire upper half to push me over upon my back.

Slowly, heated just to find myself beneath him, I stopped laughing but smiled on as I trailed my fingers over his face.

"It means you're a slave to those damned things…the only one to whom you should really be a slave is me."

With a sly quirk to his own lips, Eleison lowered his head to consume me in another kiss.

Before the hand I slid over his chest was able to make any progress in undoing his tie, a great deal of uncouth banging upon our door interrupted us.

"Thecla, you slut"—the ribald duke shocked me into laughing despite my better judgment, while Eleison rolled his eyes in annoyance and collapsed off me with a groan—"get your hands out of his trousers and come drink with me!"

"Please drink with him," Eleison agreed, veiling his mirth with his own glass. "He's going to be a fu— a nuisance until he's had a few drinks…then he'll still be a nuisance, but at least he'll be more likely to pass out."

"Thecla," called Aleister again, "you can't fool me—"

With a quick kiss of Eleison's cheek, I hurried up to answer the door. Having disposed of his hat and his coat, the duke looked up from a bored examination of the buff of his nails and quit jibbing me at once. "*There* you are," he said, stepping aside, "come on, let's go."

"Where are we going?"

"I don't know about you, but I'm dying of thirst…and I mean that in more ways than one. Let's go slumming!"

As the door shut behind me, I asked, "You mean, on the other side of the train? But—"

"Lost your taste for the common crowd already, eh? I don't blame you…but they have more men to pick from than do the entertainment cars for our station, so there you have it! Off we go—"

"Madame."

Before Aleister could pull me down the corridor by the elbow he had just snatched, Charlotte stepped from her open door to block our way. As the duke stared at the ceiling in disgust, and a flash bulb from one of the few journalists with the foresight to steal into the central platform between two of the station's waiting trains went off to dot my eyes, Charlotte withdrew a sealed letter bearing a familiar hand.

"Master Farrow asked that I convey this to you. Please, read it when convenient."

"Thank you, Charlotte! You know—there's champagne and a whole lot of fruit in the suite, if you'd like some."

Intrigued, Charlotte considered this for about two seconds—or politely pretended to. "Thank you, Madame. I may take you up on that."

"Please, yes, you'll be a help! See you later." I laughed as Aleister whisked me past her, my teeth flashing in an apologetic grimace as she ducked into her compartment to give us extra space. With a fond smile for the yet unread letter, I slid it into a pocket hidden among the folds of my dress.

At the end of our car, Aleister threw open the door.

I FEAR MY depiction of Duke Montagne may seem, at times, uncharitable. The truth is simply that, after enduring such a frosty reception on my arrival into Malin's world, I was unsure how to behave around courtiers.

In Aleister's case, however, I quickly found him to be an easy person to get along with. Near as I could tell, he liked three things: gambling, men, and drinking, and not necessarily in that order. Frankly, I would venture a guess that drinking really *was* his favorite pastime. He certainly sought libations with a shamelessness that made his substance abuse seem fun for those around him, as opposed to a source of concern.

"I *can't* believe you've never been on a train," he enthused with a shake of his head, already two beverages in for my one. "Unbelievable!"

"My town doesn't have any kind of rail. One not far from us was on an industrial route or two, and I suppose it would be easy enough for us to be incorporated into the routes of some of these companies…but why would they?"

"Mm, of course. And what was it called again?"

"Lescaut," I answered, inhibitions unfettered by the concoction of champagne and orange juice I fully intended to emulate—or, goodness, why not just order—every morning for the rest of the trip. While Aleister nodded to himself, I smiled on into the glass. "Oh, it's a nice place, very charming…but it's small. I suppose you would consider it 'quaint.'"

"I'm sure I would. Doesn't mean it's bad, of course"—he threw this in quickly, eager to counter any objections before I could voice them—"just…cute. Say, you there, what was it—Nilsen? Very good."

Sloshing to his feet and sweeping his trouser leg free of droplets, Aleister announced a bit loudly, "Nilsen, the lovely Madame and I are moving to the main observation car—the public one, that is, the fun one—and shall need more drinks—"

Aleister glanced quickly at me, realized my mimosa was still a quarter full, and pressed his fingers against the bottom of the flute until my hand was forced to raise it toward my mouth.

"—more drinks," he continued, gesturing toward my forced sip, "at your earliest convenience." A few solid gold coins passed from his hand into the waiter's, at which point Aleister led me to the far end of the lounge car.

"Just couldn't stand the repressive atmosphere anymore," complained Aleister, dropping his voice only as an actor does to simulate a whisper. "It's too quiet! Reminds me of Malin's country house this winter. Oh, I know you were treated rottenly but my dear, you *must* understand not a one of us wanted to be stuck in that house during snow season. It's made for *outdoor* activities, you know, that lovely garden and all…ladies first—"

Sliding wide the door and gesturing me on to the next car, Aleister finished the drink in his hand and set it on the sideboard. Around, between, beneath the cars, Gudrune cruised steadily by. I hesitated, a little afraid, but the duke plucked the flute from my hand and gestured with it before setting it beside his own glass. "Don't worry, it's safe. Just move quickly."

With but a brief glance down to the wavering platform created by the conjoined cars, I darted to the other side and threw open the next door for us. "There you go," he said with an approving clap of his hands. "You're not the little mouse you think you are, that's for sure…couldn't be! You're Malin's wife."

Was there a little twinge of jealousy there? Maybe… although it came off less like romantic longing and rather more like a stepchild's envy over the reallocated attention of their parent toward a new spouse. As Aleister led me on through the car, I hurried along just behind him and barely took in the restaurant we disgraced by our drunken presence. "I really don't think I'm what you seem to perceive…whatever that is."

"I know you really don't think that, but you're wrong. You never really gave me a good answer about women, you know. Why don't you get properly angry? You get, oh, sad or annoyed, or hurt, or you just shrivel up and die like my dear old mother while Daddy was off on his 'business trips'"—he gestured ironically with his fingers to signal quotation marks before throwing the next door open and this time crossing ahead—"but it's only every once in a while that a woman lets herself express *anger*. Why *is* that?"

The question was a little insulting somehow. Why didn't we let ourselves express anger? Because when we got angry, men got angry. Because, so often, our entire existence was dependent upon abiding by a man's rules, ways—secrecy.

But, in unconscious furtherance of his point, I swallowed back my true opinion and smiled thinly.

"The only answer I have is the one I gave. It must be because we see men get angry, and we feel embarrassed for them."

Scoffing, flicking a scowl, he turned his eyes from me again. "It's embarrassing, perhaps, but a good fit gets things accomplished...just look at Malin."

"Did that really accomplish anything, though?"

"It certainly persuaded me to make sure you have a jolly good time if I ever want to enter Gudrune safely again," said the duke, half to himself.

The train was incredibly long, although Aleister explained as I commented on it that a number of cars would be decoupled at our first layover. "But, with that in mind, it'll still be impressive... it has a number of people to serve going back and forth across the continent, after all. Here we are!"

At last, Aleister threw open a door that inundated us with noise. The public observation car was entirely windowed, with two floors arranged beneath the glass walls that arced into a ceiling. Booths were arranged down each side, and a sharp set of stairs directly to our right turned ninety degrees at a landing and permitted access to a few seats on a higher level.

"Bugger," he muttered with a look around the full tables, "I was hoping for a seat on the first floor...wonder if that old couple will give us their table if we pay—no, never mind, come on, Thecla, let's just go up. Too bad! It's harder to scout from up there..."

As we emerged upon the second floor, though, he looked pleased—very pleased. "Oh, but...it's such a nice view, I suppose—"

Chuckling, Aleister slung himself down into one of the seats that, on the second floor, were arranged in pairs or trios to face the windows. He patted the one beside him, urging me into the seat nearest the stairs.

Before I took him up on it, I noticed the view he had been talking about.

What a handsome man! Stoic, solidly built, the kissably full lips of his bearded mouth relaxed as his blue eyes scanned through the book in his tattooed hands. He gave the impression of rugged, wild masculinity, untamed, without Eleison's sense of constraint or Malin's elegant manner. The stern brow beneath a few errant brown waves of messy hair was clearly not one concerned with society matters.

Yet—there was something so magnetic about him that, when he sensed my gaze had sustained a second too long and his attention flicked up from the page, I was almost shocked to feel the gravity of our eye contact.

He looked a little shocked, too...or seemed to be before I forcefully tore my eyes away and slid into the seat beside Aleister's.

Had I seen this man before?

"What did I tell you," whispered the duke, his eyebrow knowingly arched to see both my look and the new dedication I had to not looking any farther left than his profile. "This is the *fun* observation car."

"Observation" was right. Leaning just past him to see in my periphery that the man had resumed reading his book, I whispered, "I feel like I know him from somewhere."

"You probably do—that's Glenn Stone."

My eyes widened in surprise at my own understanding. This beautiful man had been the hunter at the Torea Festival where Eleison leapt to the rescue of our small party—when I first gained some inkling of what seemed to be my power as riftborn, the latent ability to control animals.

Oblivious to my reflection, Aleister went on, "I heard he was in some sort of accident at one of those—oh, *gross* Torea Festivals, they are just vile. Probably deserved whatever happened to him...although now that I see him up close, I rather wish I'd been one of the doctors at his rehab clinic."

While the duke laughed at his own joke, and I laughed guiltily along because I could relate, the waiter appeared with a tray of drinks—two of Aleister's, I noted with humor and appreciation for the man's foresight. We settled back in and Aleister shamelessly eyeballed the hunter for another few seconds before turning a wry expression on me.

"I don't suppose you can still sympathize with the plight of somebody in an empty bed...not long now before you'll be begging for one for a night or two, frankly. Do you ever sleep?"

I laughed, confessing, "I sleep well, as it happens...Malin likes to retire early."

"I'm sure he does. Does he still tip the maids, as it were?"

Ugh. The mere memory boiled my blood, though I had witnessed nothing but the sound of a whipcrack and had not even been in a formal courtship with him at the time. "Certainly not," I told Aleister, smoothing my skirt over my knees while I turned away to sip from my drink. "You heard him...the relationship's not open."

The duke scoffed in astonishment. "Not even *now*? You left him home in a building—no, a *city* full of nubile beauties who'd suck his dick for his pocket change—"

"*Aleister*," I remonstrated, plainly shocked by his language and gesturing for him to keep his volume down. He ignored me, going right on.

"—and he's to abstain entirely while you're off in Valquist, getting it from Tall, Dark and Sexy every night? You really *are* cruel, Auntie...I like it."

While Aleister laughed crassly to himself, taking a pull of his drink as he did, Stone shut his book. Embarrassment washed through me. We were being loud and inappropriate, and now we'd gone and disturbed a man into leaving the car.

"*Do* lower your voice, Aleister," I begged softly, trying not to cringe as the hunter slipped casually behind us on his way down the stairs. Scents like leather, eucalyptus, the rich bourbon air of masculinity, caught my nose and lingered in the buzzing tissue of my frontal lobe. "There are children downstairs."

But Aleister didn't care. He went on, waving and laughing. "You know, I have to say I'm touched. It's almost inspiring how Malin's grown up in the time that I've known him...and a little sad, of course. He used to throw the *wildest* parties..."

Downstairs, the door opened and shut. I sighed, sagging back into my seat, now free to speak to Aleister more or less privately. "I never realized someone of your rank could have such a coarse tongue," I told him.

"There it is, Thecla, let me have it. Doesn't it feel better to let it out?"

While he, also, rose with a stretch of his legs, I smiled tightly up at him.

"Oh—I haven't even begun to let it out."

The duke laughed in short surprise and nudged my shoulder. "*Now* you're sounding like Malin...better be careful. Or maybe *I* should be...well, it's slim pickings here, so I'm going to wander down through coach and see what else there is to enjoy. You won't get lost if I let you go back to our car on your own, will you, Madame? It's straight"—he pointed up toward the engine—"that way. Just keep walking, you're bound to find it."

I laughed and shook my head. "Thank you, Aleister."

Bowing, flourishing, he said, "You are *welcome*, my dear... have that extra drink of mine, too. Think I'll be switching to wine with my lunch."

"I don't know how you can do it."

"The doctors always told my parents I had an exceptional metabolism as a lad...I suppose that has something to do with it. Bump into you some other time..."

With a wave and a swig, he strolled down the stairs and, despite the movement of the train and his own inebriated state, managed to demonstrate only the slightest hint of a wobble. I shook my head, amazed he could behave such a way without thinking twice about it, and laid my hand in my lap with a contented sigh as Gudrune's green landscape unfurled along the window before me.

That train! Rail remains my favorite method of travel, but that first trip was such a symbol of my new life that it seemed enchanted at the time. From Saalast, we plowed south toward Karrisregion, then would carry on yet farther, until we reached the coast; then, after a layover that would allow us to dine in the city if we wished, we would continue east through the Azstorian desert that marked the better portion of the Expansion.

In other words...in about thirty-six hours, I would be outside Gudrune for the first time in my life.

Even after Malin's hard work registering my name and information with the state, I was nervous. I'd heard that at the border of territories, especially some contested or conservative territories with legislation more prejudicial toward altered, identities were also carefully checked in pursuit of unregistered riftborn. Though I couldn't imagine the train would be indisposed while border guards checked every single passenger's information, (and even if that were the case, I consoled myself, I would still be absolved of potential wrongdoing by mere virtue of my station), leaving Gudrune felt like a kind of exposure. Exposure to threats I had faced all my life without realizing, because Lescaut and the people in it had kept me safe...and exposure of myself to the scrutiny of others in a manner I couldn't control.

Though that, too, had always been present in my life without my knowledge. How many of our neighbors knew the truth about me back in those old Lescaut days? As the mountains pulled away, farther and farther from the verdant countryside through which we plunged, I thought to myself how funny it was that my family had worked to keep me from the man who became my husband. In fact, perhaps they kept me from him exactly long enough to ensure he would *be* my husband—my love.

My heart surged with sparks of longing at the thought of poor Malin Remembering the letter, I slid it from my pocket to break the seal and read the contents.

Dearest,

How sorry I am to not be with you! I've dreamed for months of how fine it will be to take you on your first trip abroad—but, no matter. Perhaps it's best that you enjoy your first trip without my firm-set ways. There's still time for me to show you the things I love about Gudrune and territories beyond.

Will you miss me at all? It's cruel to say I hope you do, but I do. I hope you'll think of me with all the longing I feel for you, and I hope you'll remember that feeling no matter what happens at Valquist. I'm sure it will be very sweet to be alone with Eleison...just don't let it be so sweet that you forget what other delights await you at home.

I more than love you! I worship you. I miss you already. Write me when you can.

Come back to me someday,
Your Sad Hound, Malin

Oh, Malin! I had never known him to be so worried about anything. My teeth sank into my lip while I reread the letter, admired the precision of his script, then carefully refolded and replaced the stationary in its red-lined envelope.

From that same pocket, I withdrew my watch and opened its silver door. The device was still vaguely new to me, as I'd never gotten my head enough above water to afford one while on my own, but I was more used to it all the time and deftly called open its communication features, which were available in text, audio and video. When I selected video, a colorful keyboard of light projected just above the device's small face, substantially larger than the screen for ease of use.

Though my fingers hovered before the keyboard, they hesitated to move.

What could I say that would reassure him? What would make him understand the way he made me feel? How could I get him to see that, in a few hours of our separation, my longing for him was already so acute I could feel it in my bones?

You're right, I wrote to Malin at last, emboldened by the drink and by Aleister's audacious manners of speech. *Eleison is sweet to me. He's never cruel the way you are, Malin.*

I sent the first message and waited, not sure he would see it then—but, a few seconds later, a black dot appeared beside the message to indicate it had been opened. He had seen it, and was stewing in it. Perhaps frightened by it.

I typed on after he had been given a few long, painful seconds alone with it.

> *Only you get to be cruel to me, Master. I wish you were here with me right now—I wish I could feel you.*

The black dot appeared instantaneously this time, and I bit back my smile while the intelligent device advised me, *Malin is typing...*

Thank you for your note, I summarized, shutting the door to torture him with his visibly unread response.

No matter how I wanted to read it.

Smiling against the watch I pressed to my lower lip, I marveled at the grand cerulean expanse of the cloudless country sky, and I drank. A few people gradually made their way to the second floor, and, not recognizing me, smiled to exchange a polite greeting before picking out seats for themselves. They left me alone. Even the dharmine seemed to be leaving me alone, I was surprised to find. It felt like a wonderful vacation from a life where every minute was accounted for, and I was always needed or wanted by someone.

I stayed there nearly an hour, Gudrune easing by me, until we made a stop that was announced over a speaker somewhere below the second-floor platform. Soothed and perhaps more than a little tipsy, I took the cocktail Aleister had willed to me and made my way down the stairs to step out from the train.

It was good to be outside for a moment—to be still for a moment! Ten moments, to be precise. Amazed that the train's passengers could shuffle on and off so quickly, I felt a bit of a rush to get to my intended destination: any restaurant car, as it had occurred to me that lunch was practically over and I stood a chance of getting a seat without waiting.

And, though it was fun to be spoiled in my private compartment, or tempting to go find Eleison to bring him on an impromptu date, there would be time for that later. I wanted to wander by myself, and to be fully present in my experience without another's influence.

The conductor at the door through which I re-entered smiled at me and stepped aside, saying, "Welcome back aboard," as if it had been an hour. I smiled back, realized I had gotten on about a car too soon, and made my way along the corridor, across the coupling, and into the restaurant.

The fourth restaurant—the one I had been advised to avoid.

One could see at a glance it wasn't as carefully tended as the other dining cars which Aleister and I had navigated. No concierge greeted me at the door, but a table did sit empty. I thought of sliding into it to wait, but, as others were finishing their meals and one group was actively settling the bill to leave, I decided to wait by the host's stand and be patient.

About fifteen seconds into my half-focused rumination over the leaves of a potted fern across from me, I heard it—a baritone voice, low and a little amused beneath its raw edge.

"Are you lost?"

I looked to my left.

After the delay of a few seconds, I recognized with a sort of shock the man from the observation car.

Glenn Stone—that wild hunter, that senseless brute.

Eating alone…and talking to me.

FLUSTERED FOR TOO many reasons, (Aleister had just chased him from the car by being crass; Glenn Stone was a baseless tormentor of Rift monsters; said baseless tormentor of monsters was devastatingly, ruggedly handsome, and his blue eyes were impossible to escape), I forced out a laugh for Mr. Stone.

"Lost? No, of course not—I'm waiting for the host. Do I look lost?"

"Maybe a little." His eyes released me from their thrall and lowered to his plate again, which became his focus as he sawed through the final few bites of a lunch that resembled a late breakfast. "Overwhelmed, at least. I just wouldn't have expected to find you in *this* dining car."

"Goodness, well—if you really want to know, I'm overwhelmed by the atmosphere in the *other* restaurants. This lifestyle is still very new to me." Unable to help my curiosity, I bit my lip before daring to ask, "I take it you know who I am?"

With an ironic, quick sort of laugh and a flash of all his teeth, Glenn raised his eyebrows quickly but kept his eyes still on his meal. "Impossible not to, if you live in a city and read the newspapers...I'm almost finished. You can have my table, if you're looking for someplace to sit."

Excited in a guilty way by the invitation, I nevertheless found myself smiling to say, "That's very kind of you, thank you," while sliding into the seat across from his.

Glenn's chin bobbed in a quick nod. Then, perhaps realizing how painful it would be if he persisted in what I sensed was customary silence, he met my gaze in a way that made me realize I had been staring at him.

"Kind of amazing to think you're not used to the, uh... pomp and glamor. You pull it off well enough. Where are you from?"

Taken aback by what almost seemed like a compliment, I confessed for the second time that day, "Lescaut," and earned a suddenly more interested glance from over his coffee mug. I barely registered it, already going on with a self-effacing laugh, "It's just some little place, just south of Karrisregion. Near to the coast, but not near enough to benefit from it or even travel to it without money."

"But nice, though," he said, lowering his mug. "Lescaut is—very nice."

Astonished, I perked. "You know it?"

"I have a cousin who went into business there. I visited him one time for a week or two...it was a nice summer. Good weather. How's the river running these days? The fishing was great."

"Oh, the water was beautiful when I left last winter, it was all the snow—I can't *believe* you know about Lescaut."

Glenn's teeth, straight and white, flashed bright against his beard. "I grant you, it's small…but it's not like they're keeping it out of the atlas."

"Well—maybe I should say that I can't believe you would speak fondly of Lescaut."

His great brows folded over his eyes in undoctored surprise. "You don't like it?"

"No, I love Lescaut! It isn't that. I just mean…well!" I waved a hand at him. "You're a rather *cosmopolitan* man, aren't you— What?" He had laughed at my word choice, his honest mirth crinkling his eyes to accent, along with his beard, the apples of his cheeks. "I mean to say, you *travel*, obviously. You're here, on this train, going—where, out of curiosity?"

"Valquist," he admitted, the very word an ember that drifted into me and lit a slow-growing panic in the background of my heart.

"So you see," I told him without adding that was also my destination, "you *are* a worldly man. Going all the way from Gudrune to the capital!"

"I live in Valquist, actually…I was just visiting Gudrune for—work."

Was he embarrassed by what had happened at the Torea Festival, or could he just divine my distaste for such things?

No…

Was it possible he recognized me from it?

"If you live in Valquist," I told him with a sip of my drink, "that makes your appreciation for Lescaut all the more remarkable, in my estimate. That's all I'll say."

"I don't know…I don't really like the city. Just live there for work…so the Guild can easily find and dispatch me." Investigating the final bite of roast lupella poised upon his fork, Glenn said, "Lescaut is—peaceful. Friendly. It's the kind of place I used to dream of living."

Now it was my turn to laugh. "Who could possibly dream of living in a little place like Lescaut?"

He swallowed that last bite and took up his coffee again, his animated eyebrows emphasizing his points. "Isn't that what everybody wants? A fairy tale town, where you can have your quiet, fairy tale life…let everything else go and fade out into quiet and comfort. A little cottage…friendly neighbors…"

His eyes crossed boldly over my face as he said, "A beautiful wife," then continued dreaming toward the people greeting one another on the station platform outside the window. "Kids, a market to go to on Sundays, a bar where you can meet your friends in the evenings. I don't know…just thinking about it lowers my blood pressure."

Though I laughed, I couldn't help but feel a sudden longing. At the time I had those opportunities, I had taken them all so rarely. "You really do make it sound like a pleasure. Growing up there, I never felt there was anything to do."

"That's the beauty of it. There *isn't* anything to do. Nothing except live, and be with the people who love you."

Smiling into the middle distance, I found myself saying of this abstracted, crisply haloed vision, "That sounds divine."

"It does," he agreed.

When I refocused away from the simple little fantasy, his eyes were set on me.

At the crossing of our stares, Glenn seemed to snap awake. He hid behind his coffee mug, then realized it was empty and set it down.

"But you don't have to worry about anything like that," he said. "You're Thecla Farrow...consort to Malin Farrow. You've got twenty places more beautiful to live...servants to do everything you need. We live on different planets."

My smile fell into insult and my brow furrowed. Half-aware at best of the door to my back sliding open, I began, "You can't say that to me when you don't even—"

"There you are!"

My insult collapsing into embarrassment and just a hint of fright, I turned in my seat to find Eleison loping up with that crooked canine smile. With a brisk glance over my lunch partner and no comment, Eleison set a hand on my shoulder and did what he seldom did: he bent to kiss me in public. As I gasped, my mate's lips and tongue urged the hollow of my mouth to remain open for a few long, intense seconds that sent a clear message to all involved.

By the time Eleison broke the kiss to sit beside me, urging me deeper into the booth, Glenn had removed his billfold to give himself something to look at.

"Uh, Mr. Stone"—I gestured with a flustered, helpless, but ultimately pleased smile—"this is my—companion, Eleison."

"I remember him," was all Glenn said, plucking a complimentary meal voucher from his wallet.

On an impulse, I extended a hand to stop him. "Let me take care of your bill," I told him, "in exchange for the table. And for giving me a chance to think fondly of Lescaut for the first time in too long."

His blue eyes were so gentle they seemed almost hurt. Perhaps they were. "All right," he said with a nod, sliding his wallet way. "Thank you. And..."

Meeting Eleison's brilliant garnet stare, he nodded. "Thank you. You saved my life."

While my heart sank to view the incident at the festival in a different light—my uncontrolled powers had caused this decent-seeming man such suffering!—Eleison nodded back.

"I'm sure you'd do the same for me," said my mate, his tone bearing only a hint of wry challenge.

Nostrils flaring, Glenn slid up from the table, told us, "Enjoy the trip," and made the long walk down the restaurant toward the open seats of coach.

When the door shut behind him, I realized the car had emptied during our conversation. Only Eleison and I sat there now; he looked around in a kind of amazement.

"Slow service," he said, lighting a cigarette since nobody was around to tell him not to. "No wonder Josko suggested we try the others."

Too embarrassed to develop a reasonable response, (Why? Hadn't I only been politely talking with a stranger?), I finished Aleister's drink and agreed, "Yes, well, now that you're here, I'm thinking of taking lunch in our room…"

His free arm sliding around the small of my back to draw me into him, Eleison said, "Sounds nice…but, Thecla—"

I tensed, worried he was going to have something to say about my decision to talk to Glenn (again—why would he?) until Eleison went on in a low tone with respect to the waiters who made their belated appearances.

"I know you and Malin want me to feel respected, and I appreciate that…and I'll lay you down on this table and fuck you in front of anyone who thinks he has a shot with you." Flush with an intermingling of pleasure and fear at his jealousy, I pressed my body more fully to his. "But—once we're in Valquist and you're getting cameras flashed in your face all day, we need to keep our relationship quiet for your sake. I don't just mean hiding that we're mated and you're altered. I mean hiding everything."

"But—"

"It's not social," he said quickly, then amending, "well—it is, but not in the way you're thinking." At a pointed glance from an otherwise helpless waiter who was too busy bussing the table on the other side of the car to say anything out loud, Eleison stubbed his cigarette in the open mouth of Glenn's mug and turned to face me properly.

"Just look at how quickly he hit the road. Altered people aren't regarded the same way outside of Gudrune as we are within it…and you know that even within it, we're not always thought of with warmth."

I frowned. Even though Lescaut had been, to the best of my knowledge, free of any altered people but myself, it still somehow had not occurred to me that other territories might take a less charitable view. I supposed, with Sigma being the heart of the operation and other alteration clinics mere derivatives still dependent upon Sigma's supply of Stabilify, I ought to have expected the citizenry of the distant capital to regard altered with some level of mistrust—but, all the same, I was surprised and annoyed.

"Is that why he left so abruptly?"

"Glenn Stone's pretty anti-alteration on the public record, it's true…but, I'm sure he had plenty of reasons to leave."

I scoffed. "You don't mean to say he's embarrassed about the Torea Festival?"

"I wasn't even thinking about that, but maybe. After all…

you can be anti-alter*ation*, but it's hard to be anti-alter*ed* when one's saved your life. No. What I really mean is—"

My mate's breath was hot on my exposed ear as he lowered his head.

"—when you're attracted to a woman, nothing kills your mood faster than somebody like me showing up."

"Oh..." My leg rubbing along his through the summer-light fabric of my dress, I asked, "You think Glenn was attracted to me, do you?"

"Who isn't?" The growl in his words left me sparkling with desire and I tilted toward him to enjoy his kiss along my earlobe. "You're very sexy, Thecla...whenever you walk into any room, every man has his eye on you."

"I don't know if I care for the thought of that..."

"That's why you need me...so they'll know better."

"That's not the only reason I need you, Eleison."

"Would you two like to order?"

Drawn from our canoodling by the arrival of a waiter at last, I straightened with a guilty smile and confessed, "I think we've changed our mind—but please, let me settle our friend's bill..."

O N THE WHOLE, the train ride was uneventful—
something we all appreciated, having just endured a
grueling period of Rift activity. I had yet to see Eleison
so relaxed, even accounting for that abbreviated period during
which Malin stayed in the country house as we opened the city
one. For the first time I had ever seen, my mate slept in; then,
after ravenously availing himself of some pan au chocolat, (which
I confess I myself savored), a cup of coffee, and a bowl of fruit
gleaming in colors and shapes like gemstones, he pulled me back
into the bed and made long, lazy love to me while the mystical
wastes of the shrub-covered Azstorian desert whipped past our
windows like the endless background of a dream.

Oh, Eleison! Malin focused on sensation, either pleasure or pain, giving or receiving; but Eleison was about being there in the moment. About celebrating his love of and desire for me, with me. Sometimes Eleison smiled when he kissed me, as if he reflected on a luck he simply couldn't believe; and, when things had reached their peak and we lay around recovering in one another's arms, he would lapse into silence and admire my face with such tenderness I felt nearly shy.

It was a wonderful time. Except to go to dinner, or so he might take advantage of a chance to smoke, we hardly left our love-nest. Aleister managed to avoid us the whole rest of the trip, save for a few incidental meetings in the corridor; and Charlotte similarly seemed content to use the transit to unwind. When I did bother leaving our room, it was to chat with her while she embroidered in the private observation floor below us, a comfortable parlor with windows on all sides and fine leather furniture arranged to promote conversation.

Best of all...I did not feel the dharmine. When that thought crossed my mind, I hastily turned my attention to something else, as difficult as that sometimes was; but those fleeting flashes of acknowledgement did not seem to summon him. Eleison and I made love upwards of twice a day every day for the rest of the trip, and not once did I feel that blackening presence edging into my mind.

Pleasing as it was to think Dinon had lost track of me, I was worried. Did that mean he was still lurking around the halls of the Saalast house? Without me around, would he exhibit the tendencies of a poltergeist and act out in destructive protest? How would he feed?

Might he hurt Malin?

Thankfully, my husband was well, though not necessarily in good spirits. "Darling," he said in a ragged tone when I called him during our layover the first evening. "Where are you? How has your trip been so far?"

"Oh, it's been wonderful! We're in Farina—"

"Ah! Isn't it grand?"

"We haven't seen any of it yet, but Eleison and I are going to dinner soon."

"Well...that will be nice, won't it, precious. I have a few places to take you there...a few in Quart, too. Thecla—I'm glad you called."

"Of course...you never wrote me back." I pouted, my plan to tease him by text message having been turned around on me when, later that day, I discovered he had left my message on "read" without reply. "You make me nervous, sir."

"Good—you should be nervous. When you're home again, I promise I'll be just as strict and cruel as you could regret you wished for...and you *will* be my good girl and come home again, won't you?"

"Master—of course, I—"

"I know you will," he said, reassuring himself as much as mollifying me. "I know you will, Thecla...I love you. I trust you. I know I'll have you back in my arms soon enough...I just need to be patient."

My heart ached for Malin's restless insecurity, but there was nothing that could be done—not more than I had done already, as Eleison assured me.

"He knows he's being irrational, Thecla...just keep doing what you're doing. Be patient with him. His wife running off with that boyfriend of hers really got to him."

"I can tell." Sighing, I nestled against the dark hairs of his hard chest while his hands found handles on my hip and waist. "It's a marvel he takes such pleasure in the thought of you and me together—that he lets us do anything at all, given that."

"Sometimes, the only way the brain can cope with a trauma is by eroticizing it."

Shaking my head, I confessed, "Then I don't think I've *ever* been traumatized...not in that way, anyway."

"You're lucky. Not everybody is as blessed."

Refraining from a laugh of surprise, I instead arched a brow up at Eleison and observed, "You sound like you can *relate* to Malin on this."

"I don't know about that...but, well—some traumas are always there. They're inescapable." His crimson eyes unfocused into the distance as he said, "Just there in the background, on the wall of your life, coloring even sex...like one of your tapestries, Thecla."

I somehow felt deprived by my lack of knowledge about Malin, but the truth was that my knowledge of Eleison had its fair share of gaps. There were some things he didn't enjoy talking about, like his parents...especially his mother. The difference, I suppose, was that I didn't sense these things were being *kept* from me. I knew that if it was so important—if I cared to upset him—I could pry open Eleison's heart and extract the pearls of truth from the shell that defended them. His silence was purely a matter of his own distaste for reliving certain events.

With Malin...it was just different. Try as I might not to ponder that difference, time alone with Eleison brought the issue into relief until at last, after three and a half long days aboard the rail, Josko tapped on our door and stepped in only when Eleison opened it for him.

"I just wanted to let you two know that we will be arriving at Valquist in one hour, and have already been instructed in the care of your luggage; but, if you'd like to enjoy one last drink, or—"

"No, thank you—hello, Charlotte!"

Having heard the interruption, Charlotte appeared behind him like a shadow. The conductor jumped in slight surprise, then laughed a little. "Well, then I'll let you enjoy your last hour aboard the Shooting Star without interruption. Thank you again for choosing to ride with us, Madame Farrow. We look forward to bringing you home again."

While the door shut behind him, Charlotte folded her hands at her waist and looked me steadily in the eye.

"*Don't* have one more drink," she advised. "In fact, I would recommend that from now on you avoid imbibing alcohol of any kind and keep your wits about you until you're on the train home again. It's important for Gudrune's security that Parvati find you friendly, but immovable and discreet."

"Security? I doubt I could be of any consequence to the territory's *security*, Charlotte."

"Even if that were true, Parvati is notoriously skilled at reading people, and at mining a casual conversation for information that could be deadly. When you speak with her—and I suspect she will seize as many opportunities as she can to speak with *you*—I recommend you think carefully about what topics to engage, and which topics to avoid."

Lips pursing, I nodded. "All right," I agreed, "thank you for the advice."

"I'll be staying in a room either adjacent to or near yours, so don't hesitate to come to me if you feel uncomfortable. We can decide what needs doing, if anything. For now, Thecla, assume the best. But—"

She touched my hand, a gesture that spoke as many volumes as her use of my given name.

"—I think you should try to understand before we've even arrived—public perception of you in Valquist will be very, very different from what you've experienced in Gudrune. There, children are excited to see you, and adults who keep up with their news are honored when you patronize their shops and restaurants. Here—"

Her sharp jade eyes seared into mine to emphasize her seriousness.

"You're Malin Farrow's wife. That's dangerous for all of us, but especially for you."

My throat tightening as I considered that my husband was a former enemy of the state, I posited, "But Aleister said Valquist is very safe."

"For him, I'm sure it is. For you, Thecla...I would suggest you treat this visit with extreme caution, and that you bring Eleison with you everywhere you can."

I nodded. "I will."

Satisfied, Charlotte patted my hand one last time and said, "All that aside...don't worry too much. I'm sure we'll all start having a little fun once we've been here for a day or two."

One could hope, anyway!

The train's arrival into the city seemed abrupt, as we had traversed a sizable wilderness to get to it, and had in fact chugged through a great number of trees. By the time Valquist appeared as an elaborate vision of curving roads, abrupt industry, and grand buildings of gleaming white sandstone, I was unprepared for the density of the structures rising around us. Even Eleison, far more traveled than I, whistled at the sudden appearance of the city whose aesthetic was less antiquated—and far less brooding—than Saalast's. Beautiful and strange constructions, somehow sensual buildings domed like the ancient cathedrals my father had relished showing me in photographs, gave Valquist's skyline a softness. Almost a femininity, especially against the gradually easing light of early evening.

"Excited," asked Eleison, jostling me, "or just nervous?"

I laughed, plucking at the black lace of the gloves Charlotte had paired with my fascinator. "Can't I be both?"

"I guess so. Try not to be *too* nervous, though…you know I've got you."

I nodded, leaning against his shoulder. "I know. Of course, I know…I'm just having all kinds of absurd thoughts, that's all. What if they, oh, I don't know…"

"Look, Thecla. If there's one thing the Overseer values"— he gestured through the window while the train began to slow— "it's image. If she invited you here to *do* something to you— something malicious, like arrest you, or—" His face darkened and he simply redirected his thoughts to more speakable avenues. "It wouldn't look good for her to make a move like that. Certainly not unprovoked. This whole thing is probably being orchestrated *to* make her look good—like she's open to communicating with Gudrune at a more egalitarian level at long last."

That was what I had been telling myself, but I'd maintained all number of disaster scenarios in the back of my head. Now that the train was slowing to cruise into the station, I was almost sick with them all.

And when I saw a bevy of reporters, nearly identical to the ones I'd left behind, eagerly crowded on the platform, I felt all the sicker. This group was contained: neatly corralled behind a series of velvet ropes that perhaps would have been employed if Malin had deigned to make an appearance at the station with me. Here, in Valquist, things had been arranged with respect for another leader altogether.

"There she is," remarked Eleison. "Madame Overseer, Parvati of Valquist."

Yes, there she was: flanked by security, waiting with a broad, patient smile for the train to fully stop, the Overseer of the Western Continent stood in the center of a carpet that had been literally rolled out for our arrival. While we rolled to a stop, my window revealed her as a flash of caramel face, steel hair, and the dark blue coat that whipped around her in the exhaust of the train to allow the vibrant flash of an orange gown beneath.

Then we slipped just past, and the locomotive groaned to our final stop.

"Here we go," said Eleison, guiding me through the door of our compartment with a firm arm hooked around my waist.

"Don't you look trim, Thecla," Aleister said as we met in the corridor, breaking off a conversation with the footman who went back into the duke's compartment for one last check of something or other. With an impressed, pleased look, he nodded to Charlotte. "You do good work."

"She makes it easy."

Josko, who had been smiling politely by the door, unfolded his hands to say, "One last time: on behalf of the company, thank you for traveling with us. We hope to see you back!"

"Oh no," answered the duke with surprising haste, "thank *you*."

When Josko smiled a little crookedly and turned away to open the door, I got the private joke; and, because I had twigged to it, I was laughing up at Aleister even as Eleison and Charlotte hurried ahead of us. Grinning a bit himself, the duke put a hand on my arm and said, "This is it, dear—hold onto that smile, and all the papers tomorrow morning will belong in picture frames."

With a wink toward Josko, Aleister stepped down and extended a hand to help me. I had no trouble sustaining my smile, rest assured, and even had a hard time restraining my laugh at the amorous duke's unexpected conquest.

As such, when the Overseer first set eyes on me, her smile changed from a photo-ready artifice to genuine relief.

Had she been nervous, too?

"Madame Farrow," she called, her hand extended as Aleister walked me up the carpet to meet her. "Welcome to Valquist—I trust your trip went well."

"It was wonderful." Amid the snaps of cameras and the warm scent of patchouli, I recall being surprised by the strength of her slender hand. "Thank you so much for having me! It's exciting to be here."

The white flood of flash bulbs had tiled my vision in chunks of color, and when these scales fell away, I finally saw Parvati—her brilliant eyes, hazel like mine, were more honey colored than green, and though she had worn the blue mantle for the evening I could tell she was of exceptional fitness. Most remarkably, though she was at least twenty years my husband's senior, she had aged with such grace I almost envied her despite my own still vivid youth. In fact, it shocked me to observe she looked no older than forty aside from the silver lending depth to her dark crown. Even the skin of her face was still firm with the vigor of a far younger woman. In the middle of what had to be her seventies, she nonetheless possessed a natural beauty that seemed as immortal as that of a sculpture in one of Saalast's museums.

I may have continued admiring her forever if she hadn't released my hand and asked, "Should we give them one more picture today?"

With a shy laugh and a little nod, I turned along with her toward the stall of reporters penned in by the rope—and, I now realized, a great number of security agents. While she waved, Parvati slung her other arm around my shoulders, and I was so flustered that I only belatedly remembered to wave along with her. Cameras snapped wildly. I smiled between them all, unsure where to look as the Overseer announced, "This visit marks an important moment in the history of our continent, and I'm sure everyone would love to ask questions, but Madame Farrow has had a long trip! I think I'll let her get some rest. Thank you all for coming!"

With another wave of her hand, Parvati released me and met my eye in an understanding sort of smile. "Unless you wanted to talk to them?"

"Oh, dear God, no!"

I was embarrassed as soon as the words escaped me, but Parvati tipped back her head in a great laugh. "I like your honesty…come on—"

Aleister had already disappeared, remarkably enough. It seemed as if he had dissolved into smoke just as soon as I was the Overseer's problem. After looking around helplessly to find Eleison on the other side of three capital security officers who seemed to be debriefing him, going by his look of intense concentration and the steady nods of his head, I reflected on Charlotte's advice with a cringe.

"Ah, yes, but, my man—"

"Oh, your staff will follow along, don't worry. It's your first time traveling out of territory, isn't it? Somebody checked the records when Malin wrote to me about you—they said it was like you didn't exist."

As she spoke, her voice low, Parvati guided me down the arranged carpet. Her pair of security officials hurried along, and together we rushed through the glass doors of the emptied station that was a work of extraordinary architectural design. As I boggled at the complicated details of the vast glass ceiling, the mosaics of the floor, the polish of the ornate ticket stands, I struggled to remember what Parvati had been saying and could only unconsciously mumble, "Yes, I—I grew up in a very small town."

"Lescaut, wasn't it? Stop me if I'm being too familiar."

Although I was a little frightened by her knowledge of me, I didn't want her to know that and cleared my throat to regain my focus. "Oh, no! If I were you, I'd like a thorough study of anyone coming to visit me…or anyone marrying my enemy."

The words escaped me before I could curtail them. She looked at me in a sidelong way that was not exactly wincing, but was rather the careful maintenance of a practiced expression that had briefly failed at her smiling mouth and crinkled eyes.

"Let's wait until we've had a moment to decompress…this is us—"

She gestured toward the cream-colored carriage which, through the glass wall to which we strode, waited with more security. A little amazed by the reception, I allowed myself to be silently whisked up into an opulent seat. In Malin's carriages, the seats were lined with velvet, and tolerable; in this brilliantly gleaming car of the Overseer, I discovered silk-lined seats with fine rouching that leant exquisite visual interest along with the intricate decorations of the interior itself. To my amazement, there was even a bar, and I laughed at the sight.

"Now Eleison will be *very* sorry," I said of the small array of liquors and glasses tucked into a railed shelf between the two seats.

The Overseer took the seat across from me with an interested smile. "What was that?"

"Oh, nothing—just thinking out loud. Where are we going, exactly?"

"My home, of course. Valquist Palace. I meant what I said. You must be exhausted!"

I had been so prepared to dislike or even be frightened by this woman—so sure I would meet someone even more terrible than Malin—that I was far more unnerved by the ease with which I found myself talking to her.

"It was a wonderful trip and relaxing in its way, but you're right…I'll be glad to sit in a building that doesn't move."

"I'm sure! Did you get the private car? Oh, isn't it wonderful—can I pour you something?"

She extended a hand toward a bottle of clear liquor, or perhaps a seltzer—and though my instinct was to say 'no,' in part due to Charlotte's coaching but in larger part to avoid being a bother, refusal somehow didn't seem the right choice. Why was I worried about troubling the most powerful person in the world? A woman who entertained political guests perhaps even more frequently than Malin, and who had the means to be in fact *endlessly* troubled when she invited it?

"Yes, please," I said, smiling as she smiled. "Whatever you're having."

"I can tell you've spent the last three days on a train…"

"There really *was* a lot of drinking," I confessed, laughing a bit. "It made the travel easier…not that it was bad at all otherwise. Why—"

I wasn't sure why I said it—perhaps because it was the only detail appropriate to share with a stranger.

"I even met Glenn Stone, which was a strange synchronicity because, oh—it's a long story."

"Really!" Her eyebrows raised once she had doled out a few fingers of liquor apiece, then traded the vodka bottle for a seltzer one. "I know Glenn."

"Do you, really? I was surprised to find him such a nice man… Thank you."

Having handed me a glass kept cold by some means hidden within the bar, the Overseer settled back for a sip of her own drink. "Between you and me, the past year of Events haven't gone as smoothly as I'd like them to, so I called him back to town to consult with the city's Rift Event task force. Why were you surprised by him, exactly?"

"Oh, well—I don't know. One doesn't usually think of hunters as charming fellows. Master Farrow brought me to a Torea Festival earlier this year; Glenn was the star hunter."

"No kidding. The one that went bad on him? He just got out of rehab for his injuries from that, you know…"

She all but exploded with these thoughts, unable to contain her own mind and even lowering her drink from her swallowing mouth to express it. While the carriage rocked into motion, I nodded.

"Eleison, my—man back there"—it felt like a betrayal to not call him my mate or at the very least my companion, though he had been the one to most strongly counsel against it—"was the one who saved Glenn from the oris."

"Is that so! No wonder you wanted him to ride with us." With a chuckle that I didn't return, Parvati leaned back in her seat and lowered her glass upon her knee.

Her eyes fixed upon me, and it seemed as though something

as intangible yet oppressive as the dharmine had settled into the carriage with us.

"Thecla, let me be honest with you. When I was a young woman, the whole first ten years I spent as Overseer, I was naive. I thought I could work with anyone—but your husband taught me that, even between heads of state, sometimes people just hate each other."

""Hate" is a strong word," I said, my smile winnowing down. "Especially when it applies to my husband."

"Trust me when I say there's no love lost...he hates me right back. But I'm sure you know that."

Her gaze was unflinching. I couldn't stand it and, thinking of Glenn in the dining car, raised my glass to shield myself as I said, "I can't be sure of his opinion on you because I've never asked the specific details, but I do know he was unhappy to have his bride called away but a few months into our marriage. We understand, though...it's a nice opportunity, isn't it?"

"That's right," she agreed. "It's an excellent chance for me to get to know you, Thecla. I get the sense that you're much easier to work with than your husband."

Though I wished to rejoin her that Malin was easy to work with when the people working with him were reasonable, I simply smiled.

"If nothing else," I agreed, "I look more approachable."

Parvati laughed, a genuine one of agreement. "That's true! Much more. You certainly come off more personably in the papers, though it's always hard to tell when you're looking at something from Gudrune."

"How do you mean?"

"Only that the news is always tailored to the tastes of the state, for better or for worse, even if the bias is only unconscious. Most news tends to be biased *for* its territory, anyway…not even I can influence the tabloids."

She meant the smutty rags that circulated in cities once per week and generally contained outrageous stories about high society figures doing decadent things. The mere thought of such content sent me down other avenues, and the drink had eased my nerves enough to allow me to speak somewhat close to plainly.

"Although I assume my maid, Charlotte, will be located as close to me as possible, would you be so kind as to ensure the same is done with my security man? I prefer him within arm's length for emergencies. Perhaps give him a copy of my key. He's always coming in and out for one reason or another."

Her eyebrow barely twitching in betrayal of her repressed intrigue, the Overseer said, "Of course. I'll ensure he's accessible to you."

"Thank you so much." Feeling in need of some explanation that could avoid controversial subjects, I added quickly, "Without Master Farrow around, I'm feeling rather—exposed, for lack of a better word."

"You know—"

Her eyes so sharply narrowed that her expression of curiosity was almost aggressive. I froze while she set her empty glass aside.

"You're very old-fashioned. That's the second time you've called your husband "Master Farrow.""

I hadn't even realized it and wasn't sure what she was getting at. "How else am I to speak of him to a stranger I know to dislike him?"

Her smile seemed a little smaller.

"I suppose that's fair...it just surprised me. Young people your age aren't so formal nowadays."

"Young people my age aren't often thrust into being political dignitaries," I advised her upon draining my own glass and swallowing back the final mouthful of fiery liquor. "If you're thinking of me as Malin's wife first and a young person second, perhaps you should know I define myself by many other qualities before those two even cross my mind."

"I can certainly tell that." Her voice was melodious with the annoying tone of an older person who hadn't expected to be impressed by a "young person." I tried not to take offense and let her go on, "You know, Thecla...I didn't know what to expect from you! I still don't."

As the carriage rolled to a stop within the black fence of the sprawling, pearlescent palace, Parvati said with sincerity, "But I'm certainly excited to find out."

I N THE ORANGE embrace of a twilight that signaled a lovely night, the palace looked to be made of brass. The next morning, I would find it shiny and white like so many of the other buildings of Valquist. I much preferred my initial impression, although the white interiors into which we stepped were stunning with their pink quartz accents. After the hustle and bustle, my sense of the palace was one of peace, and I sighed with pleasure to be in a proper building with the intent to stay a few days.

Hopefully not *very* long, though. After merely thirty minutes of guarded small talk with the Overseer, I was exhausted. Being on the defense for the next several days was going to wear on me.

"Let me show you to your room for now," she said, hastening to add, "and you've eaten? Good. If you *do* need anything, don't hesitate to call the kitchens with the RMS panel in your room. Up this way…"

Smiling as she did, Parvati led me up a set of stairs along which flowed a red carpet not unlike the one from the train station. "I don't know if Aleister told you, but I've organized a small ball in your honor."

A little shocked, I willed my tone to edge into surprise and away from immense displeasure. "Oh! How nice."

Unconvinced, she glanced at me with a small laugh. "So, he didn't warn you…well, I'm sorry about that, but it *will* be fun. You should learn to expect this sort of thing, for what it's worth. The spouse of a master or matrix is an extension of them…their partner in politics and business. You may find yourself traveling on your husband's behalf a great deal, at least depending on how this visit works out."

"It's thoughtful of you to honor me in such a way. I certainly can't object to getting to know some people from your circle, Madame."

"Please! "Parvati." I appreciate your respect, but we're practically equals, Thecla. Now…"

After taking the first juncture to the left, Parvati led me down a long corridor, past the stern portraits of former Overseers, (most of whom, I noticed, were men), and to the third widely-spaced door. "This is your room, and your lady's maid will be just there." She indicated to the other side of a leafy green palm that grew from a pot for more visual interest in the hall. "I'll see to it your security man has a key, as you requested; but, if you require him, we'll be putting him just around the corner here."

"Good, thank you so very much. And, my luggage—"

"Should already be here, I believe," she said while turning the knob to let me into the recently unlocked suite.

Much as the architecture surrounding Malin seemed sullen

and dark in comparison to that of Valquist, my husband's tendency toward busy maximalist patterns and rooms that functioned as great collages of endless visual interest was starkly contrasted by the spare but artful decorations of Parvati's palace. The simple gold wallpaper above the white wainscotting of my guest suite had no pattern, but instead was the neat backdrop of red velvet drapes hung on either side of the floor-to-ceiling windows. The bed, too, a four-poster on a frame of shining cherry wood with a hand-carved headboard, was crisply made with simple sheets that echoed the walls.

It was a lovely room…and it seemed somehow so sterile that I was even more homesick than I'd been on leaving.

"The washroom is there," she indicated, "the closet there, and the RMS panel"—tapping its metal surface—"has all the call buttons you could need. And, oh—yes, there's your luggage."

As she gestured to one of the smaller bags that Charlotte must have had set aside for me, knowing I would want my books and a few other things that didn't concern her as much as my morning service, I laughed in incredulity.

"I don't know how they did it so fast. It was the same thing when boarding the train."

"Oh, they went on ahead of us…I had our driver take a more scenic route because I wanted to show you around, but instead I got to talking. Maybe tomorrow you'll let me show you Valquist and take you out to brunch?"

"That does sound lovely—I'd be glad to."

"Very good!" Tapping me in the bicep, Parvati smiled and said, "Rest well! The ball is the night after tomorrow, so I hope you'll be recovered by then."

"Hopefully, I will be…thank you, Parvati. Good night…"

The door shut behind her, I locked it and fell into bed with an enormous sigh. Oh, I was exhausted! Maybe it was just the steady stream of libations, as excessive and frequent as if it had been a holiday. I felt like I could collapse into sleep on the spot, my gown still on, the lights still bright, the bedclothes not even pulled back.

But, owing to the cramped spaces aboard the train, I'd been forced to make do with showers for days. Therefore, fingers crossed, I pushed myself up from the bed and opened the door to the bathroom.

A tub of gleaming porcelain smiled at me, and I smiled back from across the black and white tessellation of the long floor.

While the bath filled, I found the towels, fetched a nightgown from the bag, and eagerly stripped…starting with Charlotte's blasted fascinator. But, as I stood in my skivvies, my stockings, and a pale cream bustier, my watch thumped down upon the chaise where I laid my dress. My heart fluttered to recognize my first true moment alone—if I was ever alone in the palace—and I snatched the watch from the folds of my dress with no small amount of glee.

After turning down the water, I hovered around the bathroom while still in my underthings and placed a call to Malin.

"Thecla," he hastened to gasp as he picked up, "finally—"

"Malin! Oh, darling, I miss you."

"You have no idea how much I've missed you." The rumble of craving inhabiting his words sent a shiver down my spine. "Where are you, angel? What are you doing?"

"We've just arrived at the palace. Parvati dropped me off at my suite. It's very nice! But, oh…I wish you were here."

"Trust me…I wish it, too. Thecla…the sound of your voice

is almost too intense for me to bear if I can't see you, can't touch you."

"I don't mean to upset you, Master."

"No, no! Not at all. Far from it. I'm so happy you've called."

I smiled to myself, aglow with the joy of which I'd been deprived since our parting. "I love you, Husband."

"Not as much as I love you, my little bride…oh, delicious Thecla."

He hesitated, then went on in an amorous tone that strained to seem casual, "Have you and Eleison had a nice trip so far?"

"Oh, yes…" My hand, laying as it had upon my heart, slid down to rest upon my breast as I sighed in reminiscence. "It was wonderful. He's usually rough when he's fucking me—he just can't help himself"—I grinned at Malin's staggered little gasp of pleasure—"but, oh, he was sweet and gentle on the train. I think the countryside flying by must have made him romantic."

"Let him take you with the windows open, did you? You exhibitionist…I'll whip you for being a slut when you're home. What are you wearing?"

Embarrassed, excited, I said, "My underwear, sir, and stockings…I was just undressing to take a bath, but I wanted to call you before I unwound. I miss you…I wish you were here to be strict—oh, *very* strict with me!"

"Darling…it's a good thing I'm not. With you begging me like that I might wind up strict enough to finally make you use the safeword. Are you going to let him fuck you tonight?"

"I haven't seen him since we were on the train… If he wants to, then I'm sure I will."

Chuckling, Malin said, "Of course he'll want to, angel…

neither one of us can resist you. Ah! I can't wait for you to come home to me."

"I can't wait, either, Malin…I want to kiss you…I miss your kisses."

"I'll kiss you all night long when you're home, darling. Oh, Thecla—I'd ought to let you go, you must be tired."

I was, but I didn't want to get off the line. I wanted to beg him to stay on it all night, our watches beside us so we could hear each other sleep. That one short conversation made me pine for him in a visceral way…but there was nothing to be done.

"I love you very much, Malin," I repeated to him.

"And I love you. I miss you, gorgeous…tell your mate to give you a good, hard fucking for me."

Shuddering, I whispered, "Yes, sir," and hung up, unable to bring myself to tell him good-bye.

My heart raced as I pressed the shut watch to my lips, longing to kiss him.

I nearly dropped it when Eleison snatched a fistful of my hair and dragged me back to *his* kiss, instead.

"Oh!" I moaned, helpless as he pushed me up against the sink, my hand releasing the watch as he braced me against the cold granite of the counter. Eleison's tongue showed the urgency of a man who had waited too long for this moment, and it occurred to me, as he roughly shoved aside the crotch of my panties and stroked the wet flesh beneath, that he had only been gentle because he'd had no other choice within the close quarters of the train.

Now, in the spacious and somewhat more private rooms of the grand palace, he could take me the way I wanted to be taken by him. Though I cried out and struggled against his grip of my hair, my thighs splayed apart and my body welcomed him unconditionally.

"Very thoughtful of you to see to it I got a key." While his middle finger plunged into me, my body lubricated from simply talking to Malin, Eleison rested his forehead against mine and added, "Not the most discreet, though."

Moaning, I gripped the lapels of his jacket and insisted, "I just don't care, Eleison. If it were up to me, I'd want everyone to know—I want every woman in this blasted city to look at me with envy. Every woman in the *world!* Ah!"

I loved his fingers. Somehow, the excitement that came with a man's penetration never got old—never seemed to become any less intense, or slightly taboo. Even when it was my husband, the man who was by all means entitled to lie with me, the act had a kind of thrilling, invasive quality. I was being *taken.*

But, with Eleison, there was something more to it all. It were as though my body simultaneously craved and feared his. Malin was right to observe the way I responded to my mate as a kind of submission. When Eleison came upon me, a strange urge to protect myself rose up in me—along with the knowledge that I never could defend myself from him if he really wanted to hurt me. My way of relenting to him so easily was perhaps the collaboration of the two battling certainties. The solution to them.

But it certainly was a *happy* solution.

While Eleison yanked down my bustier to lower his mouth to my freed breasts, his finger left me but a moment. Just long enough for him to shrug off his jacket and release himself from his trousers.

I couldn't help but stroke his cock, so achingly hard already, just as soon as it was free. He growled on the contact, the noise vibrating through the walls of the bathroom and echoing sweetly in my body.

"Eleison!" I cried out to feel how hard he was, soon encircling that great shaft as much as my hand could manage it. "Oh, darling—let me kiss it, Eleison, please, let me taste you—"

"Maybe when I've made you cum." His mouth caught mine in a kiss while he snatched my wrist and effortlessly removed it from his prick. "Spread your legs, Madame."

Groaning to be so commanded, I let my thighs part wider. Even then, he set a hand upon my knee to keep me in place; to keep me absolutely exposed to the hard stone pillar that so naturally, effortlessly found the center of my passion.

"I heard you talking to Malin just now…you want it rough, do you?"

"Oh, yes, Eleison, Eleison—yes!"

He didn't delay. As his wonderful cock hammered deeply into me, nearly splitting me in two, I made no effort to hold back my scream.

"Yes! Yes, oh, darling—yes, Eleison, take me! Claim me. Let them all know that I'm your territory."

"You really *don't* care, do you…"

My mouth fell open as though in astonishment while, gripping my hip with one hand and my knee with the other, Eleison roughly plowed me amid intense study of my face. Full of him, exposed to him, I trembled without clear sense of place or purpose other than to savor each rush of his power up into my body.

"No," I half-whispered, my volume constrained only due to the sharply rising pleasure that increased in urgency with his every fast stab. "No, no, oh, Eleison, I want your hand on me in public; I want to kiss you whenever I want; I want to feel your cum sliding between my thighs while I pretend to be some dignified civil servant—oh, Eleison, Eleison—oh!"

His hand shifted from my hip to caress over my abdomen, pressing over the muscles that contracted and fluttered in delight for his penetrations before sliding down to run his thumb over my aching clitoris. I screamed again, arching my hips into his fucking, my back contorting and my panting mouth seeking his.

"I don't care what they think of me," I told him while he withheld his kiss to tease me, his just-parted lips always at least an inch from mine. "I don't care, oh—fuck, let them think I'm a slut. I want them to, Eleison. Just as long as they know you're the one who's made me this way! Fuck, fuck, oh—"

"You're about to cum this quickly, Thecla? Damn…maybe Malin's right."

Looking in my eye, a dark lock falling across his red gaze with his exertions, Eleison told me, "Maybe you really do want me to rape you."

His echo of my previously uttered fantasy was so exciting, so frightening and shocking, that I collapsed into climax on the spot.

"Eleison"—I nearly sobbed, thrashing upon the edge of the sink with an orgasm so powerful that he had to tense his arms around my thighs to keep me from slipping off—"Eleison, oh, *yes*! Please—I'm yours, yours and Malin's. You two can do whatever you'd like to me! Use me, oh, use me for your own pleasure even when it isn't mine—*make* it mine, oh, Eleison, yes, yes, yes—"

Teeth grit, Eleison caught my face in one big hand and held me there for a savage kiss. As his tongue penetrated, his cock withdrew, and I moaned sadly while he twitched against the rumpled silk of my sex. When at last his head snapped sharply back, his great pupils swallowed up mine.

"For you, Thecla…I'll try anything once."

He kissed me one more quick time before forcing himself to step away. Overcome with glee to feel Eleison gradually yielding to any number of games—games with Malin, games with me, games with both of us—I hurried down from the sink and sank to my knees without even thinking of the hard tile floor.

Still gleaming with my pleasure and reddened by its own lust, Eleison's cock bobbed before my face.

"It's frightening," I gasped, raising my hand to caress it, "but so beautiful…you're such a beautiful man, Eleison…"

"You deserve the best," he muttered, his hand stroking hair back from my face as I kissed his cock. While my lips trailed over the shaft, he seemed to hold his breath. "But you don't have to be afraid of it, baby. It likes you."

Giggling, I kissed the tip of his glans and lapped my tongue over the white dot of anticipation that had crowned it. He groaned, laughing as I asked against his hot flesh, "I wonder what it sees in me."

"It's a good judge of character…ah…Thecla…"

Unable to resist any longer, I swallowed him.

Pleasuring Eleison with my mouth was no easy task. I was still getting used to his size in some ways, and taking him too far into my throat was yet a recipe for a lot of choking, sputtering, and drooling embarrassment that he never seemed to mind. I certainly minded, and I looked forward to the day I could pleasure him as confidently as he did me.

Going by his low growl of desire as his hard length was gradually drawn deeper toward my throat, he seemed to think I was already there.

"Fuck…ah, Thecla—Madame—that feels so fucking good, you're so good at this…"

Because he was so large, my hand attended to those regions my mouth couldn't. My fingertips tickled down his shaft, then wrapped around him as tight as they could. My open jaw, meanwhile, worked him up and down, lips striving to stay in contact with my fist.

Between my legs, my free hand worked the lingering heat of my last climax into a brand new one.

"Thecla...oh, fuck...you have such a soft mouth...so warm...I love your tongue, baby—ah, shit—"

I had responded to his praise by running my hampered tongue back and forth over his head, having just barely made it back to the tip at the time. My lips paused there, pursed in a kiss while my hand stroked him at a similar pace to the one I used between my legs.

"I love your cock, Eleison...I love the way it smells, oh, and tastes...so hot, almost sweet, like your sweat, like your skin...I love how wonderfully hard I can make it..."

"You really *do* make it hard, Thecla. Ah, fuck...I don't know if I'd rather cum in your mouth or on your face. The idea of you being covered in my semen is really fucking hot...but I like the thought of you drinking every drop, too."

"Let me swallow it," I begged, "please! If I won't have you between my legs, I want you in my mouth."

"All right," he said, his words panted between the growls that arose as my mouth bobbed down his shaft again. "Fuck—all right, baby. I'll cum in your mouth anytime you want...you ask so sweetly...sweetly for a bad girl, anyway..."

Moaning, I stroked myself a little faster, my head bobbing more eagerly. He exhaled, his hand still combing away my hair but now occasionally pausing at the back of my head as though to urge me on. I pushed myself, eager to learn, and let him fill my mouth until the tip of his thick member brushed the back of my throat.

Barely restraining a cough, I slid back and started again.

Driving Eleison's pleasure was just so spectacular. My own desire flowed from it, and my fingers were soaked as I kept myself suspended near my next orgasm. Everything about it aroused me: the act of service to him; the warm male musk of his flesh; the *feeling* of him, of his occasional twitches and pulses of pleasure.

Of the way, through the ecstasy I delivered, Eleison's cock grew tighter, thicker, harder, until he could not help himself but thrust into my mouth as he would between my legs. Teeth bared, he admired me at work and now almost aggressively shoved my hair away.

"If you really want me to play…gray area games with you," he settled on calling them, his voice almost trembling with the height of his pleasure, "you need a way to tell me to stop—to really stop, if you really want me to. I don't want to hurt you, Thecla, or upset you…but—"

Fire blazed in his eye and he held my head still, fucking himself to orgasm in the depths of my moaning mouth.

"—I like the thought of wrestling you down and giving you a good fucking, whether you want it or not."

My eyelids fluttering, my voice raising in a cry, I slipped over the brink of orgasm and quickly took Eleison with me. Seeing my state, his panting increased, and so did the vigor of his strokes. The tension of his anatomy in my mouth reached a point of no return, his cock now not just hard but tight enough to burst.

Until, to my greater ecstasy, it did.

"Thecla! Fuck—ah, baby—"

With a sigh of bliss, I eagerly swallowed every pulse his cock jetted into the back of my mouth, then drew back a little to collect it upon the tip of my tongue. The white substance was so erotic despite its peculiar taste—somehow reminiscent of his smell, truly his essence compacted within a protein delivery mechanism—that as I licked the final few drops from him, a third, albeit less powerful orgasm bolted through me with the final ministrations of my fingers.

My name still murmuring from his lips, Eleison released his grip on my hair.

Instead, he caught my arm to help me to my feet, whereupon he kissed me.

"Sorry if I interrupted your bath," he said, his words ragged as he pulled away.

As high as high could be, I smiled. "I'm sure it's still warm enough, darling…care to join me?"

14

IN THE MORNING, primed by Malin's schedule and wired from several days of travel, we found ourselves awake at 4 a.m. regardless of the time change. At the very least, Eleison slept restlessly that morning, and it was his restlessness that drew me from slumber.

"I'm dying to work out," he said, sliding against me. "You want to come work out with me?"

Blearily, I managed, "Do you even know where the workout room is?"

"Sure. One of their guys gave me a map." While I laughed, he pressed a kiss to the curve of my throat. I sighed, tempted to protest that we could exercise just as well in the bed; but before I could, he tore himself away. "You sure do make it easy to stay in bed, Thecla."

"I much *prefer* to stay in bed, whenever possible…it's not often, but it does happen."

"Come on." He flipped his pillow over my face. As I shoved it away and forced myself to sit up, he wandered into the bathroom to dress for the walk to his room. "We stayed in bed three mornings in a row…and, anyway, we've got to adjust to the time change. Only one thing for it."

"Malin has brainwashed us all into living like we're in some kind of boot camp," I muttered while my mate emerged, the gorgeous muscles of his stomach tempting an eye that sloped down a path of black hair for what was hidden by low-slung trousers. He caught my stare while slinging on his shirt and left it open with a crooked, knowing smile.

"A little routine never hurt anybody…you'll be glad you did it once it's over."

Jacket, tie and undershirt still slung over his arm, Eleison fixed his vibrant ruby eyes upon my lips before swooping down for a quick but staggering kiss I seemed to feel all over. I gasped him in, my hand sliding up over his chest—

Then he escaped from me, disappearing around the corner of the bed with a merry wink.

"Pick you up in ten minutes," he told me as, despite his size, he moved soundlessly across the floor with respect to the early hour.

Even the door barely made a sound behind him.

If I was very lucky, Charlotte would have neglected to pack any clothes suitable for exercise…but, after turning on the lamp and wincingly digging through the bag, I discovered this was of course not the case. She had thought ahead, and to ease her own burden had made sure I had accessible not just the proper clothes for riding and training, but also a few simple day dresses that didn't call for her help. One, a lovely series of somehow pulsing colors that had no discernable pattern save for the occasional interruption of black, was so pretty that I set it aside for the day, then reluctantly snatched up a pair of leggings, a sports bra, and the boxing shoes I wore when Eleison trained me at home. With a vigorous brush of my teeth and the quick tying back of my hair with a ribbon, I stepped from the room to find Eleison waiting for me…and so effortlessly sexy. The black undershirt he wore clung tightly to his hard torso, while the muscles of his folded arms made me ache to be held.

Then, there were his blasted trousers—a pair of gray sweatpants that, though of a more relaxed fit, nonetheless had the magical quality of somehow emphasizing the position, size, and even general shape of his endowment.

"Are you really going into a public place looking like that," I chided him.

His eyebrows raised and, having just been admiring my figure as I did his, he looked down at himself in befuddlement. "Is something wrong?"

"*Yes*, it's wrong, Eleison…it's awful for you to be so sexy." While his features relaxed into a soft laugh of understanding, I slid up against him in the empty hall and murmured with a pout, "I'll have to flee Valquist a murderess. If other women see you, they'll be crawling all over themselves for your attention."

"And I won't pay them any…anyway, that's the benefit of getting in early. We'll be in and out before anybody else is awake."

The plan was sound. Dying to touch him as we emerged in the main halls of the palace, but trying to respect his concerns about making our affection too public, I instead settled for shamelessly drinking in his beauty as we made our way to the workout room. When we arrived, the equipment visible through a glass pane installed in the door, Eleison whistled softly.

"What a big facility! This is great—there's even room to spar." He grinned. "You want to box a little?"

My lower lip vanished anxiously between my teeth. "Is there time this morning?"

Eleison's chuckle, so husky with understanding, rattled through me like a shudder. He knew just what I meant. Since we had become honest about our relationship, the former sexual tension of the physical training in Karrisregion had transformed into our sensual reality. Any physical contact Eleison and I had was a kind of foreplay. It didn't matter if it was holding hands. Merely touching each other provoked an erotic charge.

And to fight him, to be overpowered by him…such things generally ended one way these days.

"I think the better question," he said, looking back at me with one hand on the handle of the door he pushed wide, "is if we'll make it back to the room—ah—"

His head whipped toward the corner, previously invisible from our angle, and his grip tightened around the handle.

As I peered past him, I fought back a sigh of disappointment.

Of all blasted people, we'd been beaten the Overseer. In a tight tank and a pair of leggings that emphasized the power of her slender legs, Parvati ran upon a whirring treadmill with a confidence and apparent ease that made her seem half her age.

Suddenly, something clicked. There was something objectively different about Parvati—but, what? Was she riftborn, perhaps?

"Oh"—she glanced quickly back over her shoulder at the

sound of the opening door—"good morning!" Her voice was brisk and smiling, raised above the noise of the treadmill and her own exertion. "I'm amazed you're both up so early! I figured I wouldn't see you until brunch, Thecla."

While Eleison and I exchanged a disappointed glance and he separated to warm up before his usual solitary routine, I summoned a smile for my host. "Well, one doesn't want to deviate from one's routine too sharply, and I am an early riser at home."

"Do you run?"

"Ah"—my smile widened into a toothy, good-humored grimace—"I actually do just a bit, since we have a few devices like these at home and Saalast is so *stuffy*, but I'm not sure I could keep pace with you."

"That's the beauty of treadmills," she said, patting the one beside hers, "you don't need to!"

With a guilty laugh and one last glance at Eleison, I mounted the machine and stood stretching my limbs for the first few seconds. As I did, the Overseer spoke to me.

Now—I personally know that when I read a book, my friend, I am not a great one for small talk. When characters discuss the weather, I weep with annoyance.

But, when it was with the Overseer, even small talk seemed directed; scrutinized. When she asked me, "How did you sleep? I hope you found the room comfortable," it was perfectly casual, yet somehow pointed. There was another question running like a current beneath the surface, and it set me on edge even as I courteously responded.

"It's lovely, thank you so much. And spacious! What a relief after that trip."

"Was the bed on the train very cramped?"

"Oh, well, it was nice enough, but—" She was trapping me, and I repressed a furtive glance at Eleison's push-ups. "The compartment just *felt* rather narrow. I've been constrained to two dimensions for half a week now!"

"I'm sure. It's hard to share such a small space, too."

Laughing weakly, not interested in taking her bait, I activated the treadmill and stepped along its surface until its speed enabled a fast jog. "Yes! It's a good thing my husband wasn't with me."

"Does he know?"

My mouth contorted in insult. Unable to respect Eleison's wishes beneath her pointed questions, I was now forced to defend my character. Good thing Malin had never thought it possible for me to conceal my altered nature from Parvati. Perhaps I could shock her out of her curiosity, if our kind really were so reviled in Valquist. Though Eleison minded his business and was busy with his workout, I swore I could feel him listening as I said, "Of course, he knows. Eleison and I are mates. My husband understands that it can't be helped, and he's glad to know I have another good man looking after me with sincere interest."

Interested to hear this, the topaz jewels of her eyes curving into crescents with her slight laugh, the Overseer tossed me a sidelong glance. "No kidding? I hadn't heard about this, somehow."

"Eleison prefers to keep it quiet out of courtesy to my husband—though Master Farrow and I both agree it's best if the two relationships are given the same open respect."

"Interesting. Very interesting, actually. Maybe Malin has changed more than I've given him credit for." I expected her to segue into some sort of gossip about Malin's ex-wife and was instead relieved when she didn't persist. "What kind of mates are you," she asked instead, leaving me a little befuddled.

"I'm sorry, I don't understand the question."

"Oh, that's all right. I forgot. Malin said nobody told you that you were riftborn, right? That was in that first letter—'unregistered through no fault of her own,' I think he put it. Then you probably don't know much about being altered, either, since you look like second-generation... There are actually three different types of mate bonds discernable between altered. The research is all recent, within the past ten years, so I don't even know if Eleison over there will have heard of it."

Curious, I asked, "What are they?"

"There's the mated," she said, her breathing a little staggered between her words after what looked to be thirty minutes of running, now with talking atop it, "the fated, and the bonded."

"What's the difference?"

"Well, under the Three-Tier Model of Altered Relationships"—I somehow didn't roll my eyes at the sanitized researchese—"the weakest link is between the bonded. Two altered, or an altered and a human, who have a child together. The production of offspring changes the altered's brain regardless of sex, and minimal stabilizing influence is achieved. Not much, often has to be supplemented by Stabilify...but they'll still have an easier time than an unmated altered.

"The second pair bond is the mated, which occurs between two altered of the same type. So, two luptich altered might seek one another out during a Rift Event and become a couple as humans afterwards. It's the type of connection most people are thinking about when they say 'mates' in this context."

I nodded. "And, the third?"

"The third type, the fated connection, occurs between two altered of different types. It's not actually a mating bond between their animals in this case, though. It's a predator-prey relationship…and it's rare, but it's said to be the most powerful of the three. It's not just the most stabilizing—it's also, for reasons we don't yet understand, the most rejuvenating. Fated partners tend to stay younger and healthier for longer. They may even be biologically immortal, but we're not sure of that yet since the alteration programs haven't been around long enough to really tell."

If I hadn't already been panting with my own steady running during our conversation, I likely would have gone a bit flush with strange excitement. "I didn't know about that."

Parvati nodded. "The normal drive to stalk and hunt the prey tends to be activated in the predator if their partner is present in a Rift Event, but, because of the partner's stabilizing influence on that predator, such interactions rarely if ever end in violence. It's more like—an abstracted interspecies courtship. So, which are you?"

"I don't really know," was my lackluster response. "My animal—it hasn't expressed itself yet."

Her eyebrows raised, then lowered again in a far more measured, artificial containment of her curiosity. "That's very interesting. No idea at all?"

"I think my mother was a ventil or somesuch— You certainly do know a lot about altered." I panted through my redirection as, to my relief, she dialed her treadmill's speed gradually down.

"It's in my best interest to learn everything I can about all the different types of people on the continent…but certain matters hold a more personal interest, I'll admit. Since Malin knows"—

her treadmill rolled to a full stop and she stood beside me, smiling again as she plucked up her towel to mop her neck and face—"why doesn't Eleison eat brunch with us?"

"Oh, we don't want to cause a fuss—"

"People might be nosey, but I doubt you'll cause a *fuss*. Just think about it. Maybe even take him to the ball. If you want to, of course…I only mean to say, I wouldn't disapprove of it."

Glad to hear her say that, I smiled genuinely. "Thank you."

She nodded, waved to Eleison as he sat up for a break in his current set, then said to us both, "How about we meet up in the front hall around nine-thirty? Oh, and—I hope you don't mind, but there'll be a few reporters there. They'll be sick for a word from you by now… you might want to think about giving them a soundbite or two."

With another wave, this for me, Parvati slipped out the door and let it swing slowly shut behind her.

Eleison wasted no time raking his gaze over me. I endeavored to look as helpless and desirable as one could while still jogging on a machine, my underlip protruded. "I'm having second thoughts about our workout again. Don't you want to join me for a shower?"

His chest heaved with his theatrical sigh. Dismounting his weight bench, Eleison prowled across the floor, launched himself up into the treadmill at my other side, and reached across to my machine to reduce the speed until I rolled to a stop.

"I can swing brunch, because you should have security with you, and it'd might as well be me—and you know I really want to take you out to a few places, which, again, is one thing. But I'm sorry, baby. No matter what she says, I can't accompany you to the ball. There are other people to worry about than the Overseer."

"I don't care about them. Darling, *please!* They've got to find out sometime. Why not let it be now?"

Sighing, sagging against the arm support of the treadmill where he was corralled, Eleison dismounted the device and stepped up into mine. A fine sheen of sweat already covered his neck and arms, but I certainly didn't mind it when he pulled me to his chest.

"I mean it when I say I want everyone to know," I whispered, my mouth tipping up to beg for his kiss. "Oh, Eleison, please. Everyone knows I'm Malin's wife. Why can't they also know you're my beloved, my mate? Why can't we make it normal?"

His head lowered not to my mouth, but to my shoulder. As his kisses trailed toward my neck, he confessed in a murmur, "I *want* it to be normal. I'd love to have the chance to take you to a ball. But the problem isn't so much that we're mates, baby. It's—well, if you have *a* baby."

"So I'm to stand idly by and let society demean myself and that baby—before it's even been conceived, mind!—simply because we're altered?"

"It's not about that. Well—I mean, it is inherently about that with the people of Valquist. But what keeping things as quiet as we can really is, Thecla, is a political strategy meant to protect you. Don't pout...you know that. Even accepting that Parvati will figure it out is part of Malin's politics. We all know a third-generation altered is going to be a huge target for all kinds of bad actors if the information is widely known, especially as Malin's child. But if Parvati likes you well enough to see past Malin, which he seems to be gambling will be the case, then she might be able to offer you some level of protection or public support."

Unable to argue, knowing all this and more, I could only sigh and run my fingertip along the plane of his hard pectoral. "So...you're really not coming to the ball? Even if I invite you?"

He shook his head. "And that's all the more reason to train like normal," he said to my further disappointment. Grinning a bit, landing a full-handed swat upon my rear in what was an acceptable but still insufficient consolation prize for his immediate love, Eleison backed down from the treadmill. His head jerked toward a wall-mounted cabinet he had earlier inspected. "They have training guns in there. Come on…I want you to practice until you could disarm me in your sleep."

Here's to hoping I would have to sometime.

Oh, dear. It was the queerest sensation, but—perhaps owing to the way things happened on the night Eleison's passion at last overwhelmed his reason—I couldn't help a flush of excitement when my mate took the pistol-shaped practice dummy from the cabinet of various other training supplies. We had several of the things at home in the Saalast gym, and the reaction in the hearth of my body was forever the same. Eleison has always had some of the most finely sculpted male hands I've ever seen, corded with the same power that rippled up through his forearm and into his bicep, and the sight of that hand wrapped around a deadly weapon gave me all kinds of frightening, delicious thoughts.

And that was before the training.

Eleison had meant what he said. He was fully dedicated to forcing me to train with him regularly and thoroughly, until my muscle memory would protect me from whatever emergency scenarios seemed to run forever through his mind. While I was embarrassed, he was deadly serious, and he took on every sample scenario between us as though they were real. The prop gun wasn't capable of hurting me, but he was so stern while wielding it that my instincts never seemed to accept it was only a prop.

In general, there were several different approaches he took. Eleison would start on one side of the space and I would start on the other. He would walk toward me, or I would walk toward him. At some point, he would draw, and I would have to evade a pantomime gunshot and disarm him in what always seemed too long, frightfully long, the sight of the prop raising along with his arm enough to cause the jerk-and-twist of my body away, the fly of my hand to his wrist, my other hand raising to twist the weapon—

"Bang," he'd say, having gotten the pistol level with my heart. "You're dead."

"You *cheated*, Eleison, you brat—you knew where I'd be ducking, you swung to the left."

"No complaining. Start again."

Grousing under my breath, I would return to my spot and get ready for the next exercise. We worked in sets that seemed to go on forever, repeating one exercise until I was exhausted. Then and only then did we move on to the next, repeating it forever once again. The second scenario was blocked with us standing closer together, and there was never any telling what he would do in that case. Sometimes he would lull me into a false sense of security by very casually praising some aspect of my prior performance, or asking what I felt like for breakfast later, or—

"Bang," he said, having snatched me by the arm and twisted me back so the base of my skull met the muzzle of the raised prop. "You're dead. Wake up, Thecla."

"It's not the same when it's *you*." I gasped a little as he jutted the fake gun into the back of my neck. "Oh, Eleison, don't—"

"You have to be prepared to accept that it *could* be me. It *was* me, Thecla. I'll never stop thinking about when that bitch converted me to do her and Gall's dirty work. I'll never stop thinking about pointing that gun at you."

As Eleison permitted himself the liberty of lowering his head to brush his lips along my hair, I shuddered to assure him, "I won't, either."

It was really amazing he hadn't twigged to it prior to that moment. There are times when I look back on those early days in our relationship and think Eleison perceived me very differently— perhaps perceived me as Aleister claimed I wrongly depicted myself. But, for whatever reason, the raw whisper of my tone at last perked his ear...and piqued his interest.

"Now, Thecla..." The gun—the *prop* gun, I again had to remind myself—trailed down the back of my neck and along my spine while I shivered in the fearful, shameful pleasure of it. "All this time I thought you hated training. Were you getting shy? Don't tell me you *enjoy* this..."

Jerking me back by that same well-controlled arm, Eleison pulled me against the damp black shirt that fit to his hot chest. While he raised the prop's muzzle into the base of my throat and let it glide up to my jaw, I flinched back with a cry and a gasp that, even to my ears, sounded a bit lewder than mere surprise ought to have made it.

"I don't *hate* training," I told him, the words a whisper, my attention gripped by our reflections in the mirrored wall across from us. He was so fine—and the way he looked at me when he forgot I could see him was oh so sensual in its contentment. The look of a borro in no hurry to feast upon the prey he knew he could enjoy any time it suited him.

Stomach tight against my desire to yield, I let my frustration with my weakness for him serve as a source of strength.

Quicker than I ever had, I jerked my head aside while my left hand twisted the gun down and out of his fingers. At the same time, my right hand snatched his bicep to wrench him down and away from the weapon from which I parted him. "Bang," he said by reflexive surprise half a second after my head had flown clear, a quarter second before the prop was twisted fully from his grip.

Two seconds later, I had stumbled back and wheeled around, the prop gun steady in my hands while I pointed it at Eleison.

"You lived," he commended, his tone as impressed as his crooked smile. Lowering the hands he had raised in a reflexive response of his own, he set one upon the prop and pushed it down to step toward me.

The door opened to permit a couple of softly chatting security men for their workouts. They glanced at us, and I glanced at them. Eleison didn't acknowledge their arrival and continued removing the prop from my hand.

"Now that we're through with training," he said with a roguish cock of his brow, "can I take you up on your suggestion from earlier?"

"Interesting timing," I told him, speaking not of our sudden company but of his discovery that I had cultivated, shall we say, an unfortunate predilection. Taking my meaning just as I intended it, he made no move to hide his widening grin while he replaced the prop.

"Hey, Madame, what can I say...working for Master Farrow has made me open-minded."

THOUGH I HADN'T been pleased to see her at the time, I certainly was satisfied by the results of my conversation with the Overseer. When Eleison and I at last separated long enough for me to go to breakfast and Eleison to have the combination of coffee and cigarette he preferred savoring in monk-like silence, I was newly aglow with anticipation for the rest of the trip.

Perhaps it wouldn't be so bad after all! Why, I was even happy to see Aleister already picking at a bowl of granola and yogurt at one of the small luncheon hall tables—widely berthed in their white-lit, window-lined rotunda, to facilitate intimate chats before a rear view of the palace's sprawling green lawns. I sat before him without invitation and a staff member hurried over with a printed menu of the chef's morning suggestions. While I accepted the paper from his hands, I said to Aleister, "You disappeared so quickly yesterday. I thought you went on home already!"

"God, no, not another day on the blasted train…anyway"—he sighed and sagged back in his seat, scooting away from the table—"you'd ought not to get too close to me. I'm afraid I'm a bit under the weather."

"Oh, no! Have you caught a cold?"

"I'm not sure…I've just been feeling poor since yesterday evening. Can barely finish *this*," he said with annoyance, briskly drumming the bowl's ceramic edge with the back of his spoon. "The Overseer wants me to stay long enough to go to her damned party…I don't think I'll make it there, but she may end up sorry she wished me to stay. I *refuse* to travel sick."

As his hand's definitive slice through the air punctuated his point, the duke crossed his legs and nodded to me. "What about you? You didn't pick up anything from that train, did you?"

"No, not at all. I even worked out today…and I've been by the gym, too."

Taking my meaning with a husky laugh, Aleister plucked up the only glass of water I've ever seen him drink. "Oh, *yes*. Well, that's very nice, thank you…now I'm just sick with jealousy instead of with some virus. *Tell* me about Eleison, would you? I'm desperate to know."

I blushed, lowering my voice as I stuttered, "I don't *know*, Aleister, really—"

"*Please*? What if I'm dying?" Though he started to lean across the table to smack me in the hand, he stopped himself and instead gestured futilely. "Why, what if I have some sort of blood poisoning? What if that Josko fellow was really a dharmine, and—"

I must have paled, for he quickly added, "I'm *kidding*, of course. Don't be silly. Everyone knows dharmines don't come out in good weather."

But it was not his joke that had frightened me. Only the memory his joke had triggered: Dinon, his black cloak fluttering around him, as Aleister mounted the edge of the roof.

Angry thoughts flooded me. While my pallid face colored with fury and I said through a small, tight smile, "Of course, of course not—not to mention, they don't take trains," my surging mind whirled about itself for the dharmine's presence.

Did you do this, I demanded, the message sent off into space and time like a drowning swimmer's shout above waves of terrible memories. Oh, my poor father! His hair so white and his body so gaunt in his deathbed. Eleison's brother was blessed to have avoided that terrible death; Eleison was so good, so generous to have bargained his life and liberty for Kyrie's survival.

As the shadow of the dharmine slowly rose along my spine, calling back to me from some great distance, I spurned him altogether and thought instead of Eleison.

"Since you *must* be dramatic," I told Aleister, my hands laying in my lap to twist my cloth napkin, "Eleison is very—bold. And he's rough, though he doesn't mean to be. He just can't help it."

Sighing, fanning himself a little, Aleister said, "That is the best, isn't it…"

I confess I sighed myself, feeling like a girl gossiping in the market again. "He fusses over me so much when he's through sometimes. Oh, he's so afraid of hurting me…but, between you and me, I wish he would hurt me more."

"I'll bet." Eyes narrowing conspiratorially, Aleister glanced at the distant waiter who patiently awaited my gesture, or perhaps a break in the conversation. "How *big* is it?"

"*Aleister,* really—"

The duke turned his head, exhibiting the second-rate cough of an actor who had once been made aware of the concept of pathetic orphans but had never been near a real one in his life.

Biting back a laugh, I rolled my eyes and held my hands apart at approximate length.

Aleister's eyebrows craned toward his hairline.

"*Really?*"

I scrutinized my estimate and shrugged slightly. "I'd say so."

"And around?"

Unable to resist what now was a matter of strange pride, I estimated that with one hand.

Now his eyes seemed liable to bug out of his head.

"Don't suppose he has any interest in men, does he?"

Ignoring the vivid reproduction my memory painted of that one brutal kiss between my loves, I laughed and shook my head.

Aleister sighed. "And if he's mated to you, I suppose poisoning you and kidnapping him"—my laugh boomed with my shock—"wouldn't do me much good...then he'd just be a miserable wretch all the time, pining after you."

"And trust me," I said, waving the waiter over, "he's already such a sulky boy sometimes...it's so precious, though... Yes, I'll have—"

Once I'd at last ordered—and the waiter, having left me with a small silver tea pot and cup, had scurried off—Aleister remained locked in his morbid fascination.

"Not that I would really *know*, but doesn't it *hurt* you when it's that big?"

"Oh, well, it's a little—it's about practice, I suppose, and adaptation...and excitement. Although there are bound to be occasional accidents no matter what one does…he bruised my cervix once, oh! It felt awful. I had cramps for hours and he felt so sorry. But, I don't know." I laughed wickedly, pouring out a cup of tea while I admitted, "I thought it was very impressive…something to be admired."

"There are worse problems to have in life, at least. You certainly do have Uncle's spirit of adventure. How is it the other way, though? It must be far more comfortable, given your…ceiling on the front side not being a problem from the back."

And I—no longer innocent but still, in so many ways, naive—stared at him blankly.

Aleister's mouth slowly opened. Despite himself, he leaned toward me, then forced himself back into his seat as he spoke.

"You mean to say you have *never* tried—you know, the rear entrance? You have *two men* and you haven't even been *practicing* to take them both at once? Oh, dear girl—"

Laughing, sitting up a little in his seat with a brisk rubbing together of his hands, Aleister said, "You are *very* lucky I'm here to advise you."

"Am I?"

"*Trust* me, you are. There are whole arts of love you're missing out on, but one must be very *careful* about their practice for any number of reasons. Hygiene, obviously, but also one's own well-being. It's very easy to damage one's body…especially with a big man who likes to be rough."

Though I blushed behind my teacup, I forced myself to listen without embarrassment while the duke doled out invaluable knowledge on anal sex. "I'd advise you," he said in that conspiratorial half-murmur, "to pick one of them to practice with a little bit, for starters. One of these days, after all, nature will take its course. You three will be together, one thing will lead to another, and before you know it, you'll be wishing you'd prepared."

"It sounds very—I don't know, uncomfortable."

"No, no, it's wonderful! Even for women, I understand it can be one of the great heights of pleasure. Sensual, intimate, just the right amount of embarrassing to really sweeten the deal. If you're trying it and don't enjoy it, he isn't doing it right, or you may be injured. Most likely, it's the lube. You can *never* have too much lubricant, ever."

The gravity with which he emphasized this suddenly made me realize just *how* invaluable his advice was. I nodded, saying, "All right."

"Since you said Eleison is rough, maybe you'd better ask Malin about it…you'll want him to be gentle, especially at first. He has plenty of experience with it, too." While I cleared my throat at that, Aleister grinned and went on. "Anyway, dear, just *relax* into it. Get yourself used to it before the inevitable…and then, for the love of all that's holy, please *tell* me about the inevitable." While I laughed, he fanned himself again and rose from the table uneasily. "I *am* envious of you, dear, I must admit."

"I'm sure you could maintain a whole household of attractive men in Montagne, Aleister."

"What a load of work…I think I'd rather hear about *your* men, Thecla. Ta-ta, I'm off to sleep the day away. Would you apologize to the Overseer for me? Don't think I'm going to see her today."

"I'll let her know when I meet her. Feel better soon, Aleister."

While he waved and limped uneasily off, I stared grimly into my tea.

In the far distance, the dharmine's ebbing presence still responded to my angry call.

I did not want it with me. I had been soothed by the trip in large part because it was the first time in months I had not, when alone, felt the pressure of the beast straining against the edges of my mind. For once, I was myself, able to think my normal thoughts without rushing to my weaving as I sought to escape it.

But if it had taken the blood of my friend, I would no longer be able to tolerate it.

After breakfast, I frittered away a bit of time by visiting with Charlotte, who fixed up my hair less elaborately than might have Brea, but served as better company…if a stricter satellite of my husband's will.

"I couldn't help but notice," she said wryly, "that at her first chance, the Overseer separated you from us."

While she coiled my hair into a bun that, high at the back of my head, required a deal of sharp tugging, I winced. "Yes, well, I'm not entirely convinced she meant it in a nefarious way—"

Taking the arch of her reflection's brow in stride as the pain cleared, I observed, "But you seem to be convinced enough for both of us, Charlotte."

"There's an old saying, Thecla: "Never attribute to guile what could be attributed to idiocy," or something like that. Well… when it comes to the Overseer, I would encourage you to take the opposite tact."

Turning back to her work, she went on. "Assume every errant word is calculated—every question, designed to mine you for information that might be used against our territory. There is no subject that's safe. The ones that seem to be are likely designed to gauge *you*, and your prospective use to her."

My mouth thinned with anxiety. "I suppose it's no different from how I used to interact with Malin."

"That is an excellent comparison. I would urge you the same caution. Not just with the Overseer, but with the press. Remember—when they ask you a question, no matter what it is, tell them, 'No,' and rephrase the answer in your own way. If a reporter asks you, "Is your name Thecla," you tell them, "Not quite, it's actually Madame Thecla Farrow of Gudrune.""

"They'll find me very annoying if I'm doing that all day!"

"Good. If they're annoyed, it means you're not giving them a chance to control the narrative about you, or to take your words out of context. Just don't let them trick you into saying 'Yes,' whatever you do. If you say 'Yes,' they get to print the question they asked you as though it's a quote from your mouth."

After sliding a final pin into place and lifting her hands to see how it held, Charlotte remained without moving or speaking for several seconds.

When I finally glanced into her looking glass face, she wasn't focused on my hair, but on my reflected eyes.

"What is it?"

"I hope you understand, Thecla, that I don't approve of any of this. I never have."

Thinking she meant the trip, I smiled wanly. "Neither do I...but I have faith it will all work out."

At Eleison's knock, we both straightened our postures. He appeared in the doorway dressed in his usual uniform, with a pin featuring my husband's seal—that twisting serpent beneath an open bud—now adorning his lapel.

"Ready to go?"

In truth, not really. Even after Charlotte's ominous advisory,

I might still have found it tolerable to meet with the Overseer. Especially with Eleison in arm's reach, private discussions with her seemed tense but feasible.

But, as Parvati herself had said, certain forces could not be controlled. I had spoken to a bare handful of journalists in Gudrune, and those with whom I'd interviewed had tossed me only the lightest questions. I had endured one extensive photography session for a women's periodical roughly three weeks after our honeymoon, and even that afternoon's line of questioning had been almost embarrassingly kind. They gave me a puppy to hold while the cameras flashed, and asked me questions about my dreams for the future, my current set of hobbies, my quiet little town in the country.

Even before we met Parvati at the palace's grand front doors that morning, I was sure this press conference would not be like that.

No puppies, for starters.

"You'll do great," the Overseer said once her bevy of busy staff members had given us space, one matronly hand upon my shoulder while her other waved to the journalists. I remained hidden behind a broad, square column supporting the roof of the veranda. My stomach twisted in knots, her assurance somehow agitating my condition.

"It's a good thing we're doing this *before* brunch, Parvati… oh, I feel sick."

My own half-joke brought Aleister to mind. I ground my teeth. If he *did* have blood sickness—if there was even a chance—

"You'll do great! Trust me. What are you worried about? That they'll ask you about being riftborn?"

The idea hadn't concretely occurred to me, but now that

she had put it in my head, it was good a reason as any to weakly nod.

"Don't worry. Malin said in his letter about you that you don't even show any powers, right?"

"Well...there was an incident with rift beasts once—no, twice—but I can't say I understand it in any great detail."

Her eyes narrowing but briefly to hear this, Parvati smiled on. "Then don't worry about it! What you don't know, you can't tell them. Let's get it over with." As she spoke, she linked her arm in mine to walk me into the line of fire. "Trust me...you'll feel much better when it's over."

Though I wasn't so sure of that, I nodded, took a deep breath—and only belatedly remembered to summon up my smile. There were the cameras, cracking and blazing, blinding me as Parvati waved on behalf of us both. "Good morning," she addressed them in a half-shout, her voice projecting across a crowd that seemed larger than the one that met us at the station. "How are we doing today? Well? Good, I'm glad to see you all..."

Somehow, I had expected a safe table to hide behind; instead, there was only a podium, tall and imposing, that would force me to take the questions on my feet. I gladly let Parvati stand behind it first, opting to hover to her left.

"Well, as you all know, this is Madame Farrow's first morning here in Valquist, and I don't know about her, but I'm personally having a very enjoyable visit so far. We've had some pleasant conversations—and I already feel a new optimism about our relations with Gudrune. Yes."

A reporter had raised a hand somewhere in the crowd and stood up, briskly identifying himself and his paper to ask, "Who initiated this visit, Madame Overseer?"

"Good question. I did. When I heard Malin Farrow had taken a wife after all these years, I thought it might be a chance for a fresh start for everyone. And"—she smiled over at me, prompting me to smile automatically back—"I have the feeling I was right. Yes, you, Cora."

"So, to be clear, this visit isn't a response to any behavior of Gudrune's?"

"I think any change in Malin Farrow is worth my interest. But—why don't I let Madame Farrow take the podium for a little while? She's the one you're interested in. I'll help you field questions," she half-whispered to me, turning her face away from the microphone she adjusted down with respect to my height. "Don't worry about picking from them."

After nodding to her, I mustered up another, far more nervous smile and waved to the crowd as we traded places. "Good morning," I said, suddenly aware of how dry my throat and mouth had become. "I'm sure you all have a lot ask me! Oh—"

When what seemed like thirty hands shot into the air all at once, I laughed in anxiety I hadn't a prayer of disguising.

"Let's start in the front. Reynolds—"

"Reynolds Taft, *The Imperial*. Madame Farrow, we have very little information about you and your career history before your marriage to Gudrune's territory master. Do you have any formal diplomatic or political experience?"

"No, goodness. No, I—I look at this, really, as a *personal* visit as much as any effort to rekindle warm feelings between our states."

"Follow-up question—"

"I'll allow you one," Parvati told him.

"So you don't have any specific political goals for this visit?"

Now I was starting to feel embarrassed, like a child who hadn't done her schoolwork. "Erm, well, ah, that is—I wouldn't say so, no. I mean…even if I wanted to, how could I? Perhaps"—I laughed wryly and glanced sidelong at Parvati, happy to throw her under the carriage on this particular subject—"if I could persuade the Overseer to lift my husband's permanent ban from Valquist, that would be a start."

With a dry chuckle of her own and a thin but still good-natured sort of smirk, Parvati pointed out the next reporter while the first sat down. After the usual brisk introduction, the reporter launched into it.

"Madame Farrow, is it true that you're riftborn?"

I faltered a little, smiling weakly to admit, "It would seem I am, though who knows what that really means, if anything."

"Follow-up: Is it true you were unregistered before your marriage to Malin?"

Charlotte's advice flooded my head belatedly, and I cringed to wonder if my last response had been a troublesome one. "No," I rebuffed the journalist. "No, I believe Malin saw to it that I was registered prior to our wedding. Yes?"

A reporter on the aisle had been looking ready to fall out of their seat for my attention. They barely remembered to introduce themself before hastening to ask, "But you admit to spending most of your life to this point unregistered, correct?"

"I admit that my family could have done a bit more paperwork when I was born, but they didn't ask my opinion on the subject…I was an infant at the time."

A few of the more liberal reporters chuckled, being as they were likely to be sympathetic toward the plights of riftborn, and I had a second of gratification before the follow-up was thrown.

"But don't you think it's a little unfair how easily you were able to enter Gudrune's registry as an adult? Most riftborn who consent to join the registry independent of their parents' wishes face a long and arduous process."

"No," I began again, beginning to feel the power of the word. "I don't think it's fair that the process is arduous or lengthy for anyone."

"You object to the treatment of riftborn," the same reporter asked, his observation turned to question by tone as the Overseer warned, "One follow-up, people, let's remember."

"I certainly do object to the treatment of riftborn individuals," I was at last was willing to agree, sending a few heads bowing over hands that scribbled fiercely in notebooks. "And altered individuals, for that matter. You there."

A woman in a suit that was audacious for its Rift-purple tone rose at my gesturing.

"How can it be that you didn't realize you were riftborn? The distinguishing factor between a riftborn and normal human seems to be the development of certain powers, doesn't it?"

"I don't have a power," I half-lied. "There have been recent, small incidents of note, but I'm not ready to speak with confidence about what those instances might mean."

The reporter sat without follow-up. I picked another.

"But it's true," this portly man said, rising to his feet without removing his sunglasses, "that you saved the Gudrune territory master's life during an incident last spring?"

I hesitated, my mouth opening in silence before it closed again in as polite a smile as I could evoke. "No comment," I told him.

"Is that because you're hiding something about the kidnapping, Madame Farrow?"

"What could I possibly be hiding about the time my husband was kidnapped? It was traumatic. I don't want to talk about it."

"You could be hiding," suggested the reporter, audaciously ignoring the Overseer's command that he sit, "the development of a dangerous power."

"I assure you, I'm not."

"Then how did all those mercenaries end up dead?"

Parvati's waving hands froze, then dropped. Looking aggrieved, she said, "I thought I made myself clear—"

"I didn't kill them, if that's what you're asking. Do you think I could?"

"I think," the reporter said, his mirrored lenses staring into me with a malice that almost shocked me, "that you're Malin Farrow's wife. Surely, that must be for a reason."

"My husband is a kind and noble man these days, whatever his history. I pity anyone who can't see him as he is now because they're too consumed with their own bad memories. Someone else, please—"

But the journalist went on, insistent. Parvati waved to one of her security men, who strode over to listen to her whisper as I was asked, "So since you don't care about the Azstorian famine and all the people displaced during the Expansion, I assume you're also saying you don't believe there's any credence to rumors that your husband is a dharmine?"

Even as that baleful dream from my honeymoon appeared to me again—those wicked silver eyes!—I scoffed in disgust.

"What a childish thing to ask. You're allowed to report for the paper when you believe in such fantasies? You'd might as well ask if *I'm* a dharmine."

"Well," he asked, his bald head reflecting the sun along with his ugly little grin, "are you?"

"If I were, you wouldn't have dared ask the question."

"Come on," the security guard could be heard saying while wading into the reporters to catch hold of the putrid reptile.

"Then what about your relationship with your husband's footman, Eleison of Karris?"

My face must have changed more than I wanted it to, for a few people shifted in their seats.

How on *earth* did he know a thing like that already? Was it just the natural drift of rumor between territories? But, no. Then Aleister would have known all about it already. And—the confidence with which this fellow named Eleison—

"You know what," said Parvati, leaning past me, "I think we're going to wrap this up early, before any other tabloid writers give Madame Farrow another reason to change her mind about us." As the press burst into a clamor of protests, the Overseer said, "If you think you have a good question for our guest, maybe we can organize something later in the week…something much, much smaller. Thanks for coming out."

"Thank you," I muttered dryly into the microphone, embarrassed and more enraged than I would have expected myself to be. But it would have been a different situation if the information had come from me.

Somewhere, there was a leak. Was it in *my* traveling party? Surely not. Eleison's feelings about our relationship in the context of Valquist's society were clear. Then there was Charlotte—and she would never have breathed a word. Never would have been in a position to breathe a word. Especially not in so short a time.

The duke? He was sick—he hurried from the train station back to the palace and, so far as I could tell, disappeared directly into his guest suite.

The Overseer, then? I peered carefully at her as, amid an escort of her security and mine, we made our brisk way across the lawn and into the carriage that awaited us. Her expression was tight with a displeasure I believed; when she spoke, I could hear she was truly chagrined.

"That went well, huh?"

"I hope I didn't cause a problem."

My comment earned a glance from both her and Eleison, who walked silently in stride with us.

"You," she asked. "No, of course not! You did excellently. I'm sorry, that was Tony Franklin…he runs my least favorite paper in the tri-territory area, but if I don't let him in, whatever he writes is infinitely worse than it would be if he gets to ask his questions."

"Then I suppose I should thank you for sparing me."

With a slight, bleak sort of smirk, the Overseer ducked into the carriage and settled into her seat from the day before. As I predicted, Eleison's red eyes lit up to land upon the bar when he slid in beside me.

The door shut, and the carriage rocked off.

"I need some kind of aide to help me prepare for speaking when I travel," I told Eleison, expressing my thoughts without regard for the very powerful woman in the car with us. "I don't ever want to be put in a situation like that again."

Trained from years of dealing with Malin's foul turns of mood, Eleison took my temper in stride and removed his watch from his breast pocket. "I'll send a suggestion to Master Farrow."

"Damn this whole situation. It would be so easy to simply tell the truth about myself and Eleison, but instead I keep having to tiptoe around it—I should have stayed up there when you pulled me down," I added in an unnecessary jab at the Overseer, my irritation bubbling up to a scalding fever that looked for blame.

"I suppose you could go fully public," said Parvati, unruffled by my poor turn of mood, "But—think about what that would mean, Thecla."

Sympathetic, his watch snapping shut and tucked away again, Eleison slid his hand over the one that sat in an angry fist upon the seat beside me. I forced my fingers to relax against his, and the contact inspired a cool wave of love to unbind the muscles in my chest.

"Ridiculous," I settled for saying. "What ridiculous questions. They probably think I'm hiding all sorts of things, when the reality is I just don't *know*."

"So you've really never experienced your animal or your power?"

I shook my head at Parvati's question. "No. I've really thought all this time that I was normal. I mean—" I flicked an embarrassed glance at Eleison, who laughed slightly. "That I was an unaltered, typical human. I'm sure they want something very exciting from me, but the reality is that I'm just a weaver from Lescaut who is very blessed. Oh—so blessed—"

Tears streaked over my vision. I clenched my teeth in frustration and slapped my hand over my eyes.

"Is he a *dharmine*," I repeated with derision. "What a *question*."

"It was out of line," Parvati agreed in a cautious tone, "but, well—you have to understand how little we really know about what's going on in Gudrune. Some rumors are hard to shake, even if they're ridiculous."

While accepting Eleison's offered handkerchief to dab at the corners of my eyes, I said, "Yes, I suppose I've got to get used to it. "Grow a thick skin." My mother—my stepmother, I mean—always told me I was too sensitive."

"It's a good quality to be sensitive, but you're probably right, Thecla…the press won't always be kind to you. You'd better adapt to it now."

"Yes, I suppose—oh, I suppose so. Ah—ahem, by the by, Parvati, would—is there a doctor on-staff at the palace?"

Parvati straightened her shoulders. "Why? Are you all right?"

"Me, yes, I'm fine. But—it's the duke. Aleister was feeling ill this morning, though he *looked* fine. And he didn't sound very ill, but…"

My throat clearing with a furtive glance of guilt toward Eleison, I confessed before them both, "I have reason to believe he may have had unwitting contact with an *actual* dharmine, and I'm afraid he might be in the earliest stages of blood poisoning."

While Parvati's eyes widened, Eleison scoffed. "When was this?"

No time like the present, I supposed. Begging Parvati to understand and hoping that Eleison would, too, I said, "That time, with Malin's kidnapping—those men died because a dharmine followed me through the Rift Event and killed them."

Parvati leaned forward just slightly.

Eleison, his face hardened by shock into an angry version of his professional facade, said, "You never told me this."

"Malin and I—we didn't want to speak of it again. I didn't want to speak of it again. I was afraid speaking of it would call it, but it's been about me anyway. Poltergeist activity has surrounded me in subtle ways ever since"—I returned my attention to Parvati, whose intense expression was illegible to me—"and, during the Extreme Rift Event just after his arrival to Gudrune, I personally witnessed the entity trying to lure the duke to his death. There didn't seem to be any outward sign of injury, but—I'm not so sure that matters."

Exhaling, Eleison withdrew his hand from mine to snatch his pocket watch out of his suitcoat. "I have to write to Malin again. Excuse me a moment."

"Do you think," asked the Overseer, searching my face, "that it followed you here?"

"If it is following me," I hedged, "it hasn't reached me yet. I can tell when it's around, and it hasn't been around since the train."

Her thumb running along her jaw in an affectation that resembled a scholarly man stroking his beard, Parvati glanced out the window before saying to me, "You did the right thing by telling me. I'll have the doctor look at him as soon as possible. Don't worry—when it's caught very early, the worst symptoms are often evaded altogether...but, if you sense the dharmine has come here, please let my security know immediately, Thecla."

"Please do," Eleison agreed, snapping shut his watch. "And consider telling your own, too."

NEEDLESS to say, the tour of Valquist did not go to plan. The Overseer was distracted; Eleison was in a sulk the whole time, and must have checked his pocket watch to respond to some message of Malin's on at least six occasions.

For my own part, I absorbed little of the city. There was just too much to behold. We would stop somewhere, Parvati would give us a tour of a neighborhood with a few interesting sights or stores or historical buildings, somebody would be there to take our pictures, and we would be off to the next stop.

The only thing that really caught my eye, for one reason or another, was the tall, broad building at the edge of the river rolling through the trades district. A great crest featuring a rifle crossing a rapier was emblazoned in massive relief above the double doors of the front entrance.

"That's the Hunter's Guild," she explained, gesturing. "Their historic headquarters—the organization has operated out of it for over one thousand years." I made a noise of amazement, regarding the structure beneath the shield of my hand while Parvati observed, "For obvious reasons, they're among the oldest organized trades to establish operations after the Second Dark Age."

"I believe I've heard that…along with smithing. And, of course, weaving."

"Yes, I forget—and you still do it, even now?"

"She's very skilled," Eleison inserted without looking away from the building. The first thing he'd said since leaving the carriage…at least it was kind.

"Is that so? Maybe I'll commission something sometime."

"Oh no," I said with a hasty laugh, "no, I don't think my work belongs in a palace like yours, Parvati…I'd be embarrassed."

The truth was there in my words; it just depended on how you chose to listen to it. I couldn't stand the thought of ever again putting hours of work in for someone else's pleasure. Malin's pleasure was my pleasure, making it very different.

How I pined for him! For my loom, and my little window, and the sights and smells of home. I even caught myself pining for the dharmine just a bit, and I bit back a grimace as it surged toward me across the continent.

Over all, Valquist was a beautiful city, but I was glad when Parvati announced with a sigh and slight smile, "And that's going to have to be our last stop for the day, I think—I have a few calls to make, and the sooner the doctor sees Aleister, the better."

I nodded, settling in my carriage seat. "Thank you very much for arranging that. It's probably nothing, but, with the timing, it would set my mind at ease to know he's been cared for."

"You're really not what I expected you to be, Thecla," she observed with amusement. "I don't think you're what the press expected, either."

Eleison darkly snorted and drew Parvati's attention.

"I can tell you have an opinion about that."

"Gee," my mate said with an insolence that thrilled but embarrassed me, "I can see why you're such a long-lived Overseer…you're perceptive. Yeah, Madame Overseer, I have an opinion about a few things."

As his red eyes darted across me, they slid back to our hostess.

"You sell yourself short," he summarized to Parvati, attempting to turn toward the window and away from the conversation.

"What do you mean by that?"

Parvati's tone was light, unoffended—but there was something mocking in it, as when an adult addresses a child.

"I mean," said Eleison, his tone hard as the gaze he turned back upon her, "you want to sit here and act like a helpless cog in a machine. Like we don't both live with and interact with Malin Farrow on a daily basis. I'm sure your intelligence made you aware of me long before we met today."

"Yes," she agreed.

"Then you know I've worked with him almost a decade. So, while Thecla might be willing to accept that you have no control over the press, you can't fool me."

Curious, I studied the Overseer closely enough to measure the degrees by which her smile tarnished.

"The press here in Valquist is free," she insisted coolly. "It's hardly as if I can tell them what to print, or bar certain journalistic outfits from my conferences just because of a questionable political stance."

"You and I both know that's a lie, Madame Overseer, but I don't want to embarrass you in front of your guest. It's none of my business...you asked."

"I guess I did," she said, that tight smile still cold upon Eleison before it thawed for me.

"Unfortunately, Thecla, I don't think I'll get much of a chance to see you before the ball tomorrow! We might be able to sneak in a lunch together if I rearrange some things—if you're willing, of course."

"Yes, of course."

I said it to be agreeable, but Eleison's hand visibly tightened upon his knee. Ignoring him, sure diplomacy was the best tactic, I smiled on.

"I really am having a very nice time," I told her, endeavoring to sound sincere. "Thank you for inviting me, Parvati...it's been an interesting experience so far."

And it was to continue to be. When we arrived at the palace and parted ways in the foyer, Eleison let her get out of earshot before dropping his voice. "Can we go talk?"

Embarrassingly, I had to remind myself that I was an adult. Not a small child in trouble.

"Yes," I agreed, "I think we'd better."

Behind the shut door of my suite, Eleison wasted no time folding his arms and leaning back against the wall.

"When were you planning to tell me about this dharmine, exactly?"

"I—I don't know, Eleison. I didn't know how to."

"That's not good enough for me."

I studied his shoes and agreed, "No, it's not."

For a few long, truly agonizing heartbeats, he didn't speak. When he did, his voice was oddly hushed.

"I shouldn't have to tell you how I feel about dharmines, Thecla."

With grim reflection on white-haired Kyrie, forever marked by the dharmine that had taken the form of their mother, I nodded. "You don't have to, Eleison. I can already tell."

"Has it ever hurt you?"

"No." I shook my head, swearing to him, "If it had, I certainly *would* have told you. No, it—the only harmful thing it's done has been its attempt on the duke."

"And, you know…killing all those men in that facility."

"Only because—"

My protest froze in my mouth, but it was too late. He had heard that much and now waited, alert, for the rest.

"—only because I commanded it to," I admitted in a whisper that paled him. "Because I invited it to manifest through my attention, in exchange for its service."

Tilting forward at the waist, his eyes wide with shock, Eleison demanded after a stunned second, "Are you *insane*?"

"What choice did I have?" My voice raised and I waved a hand, glancing toward the motion as if off into the past. "I was— *you* were entrapped. Enslaved by that *witch!* Add to that, Malin was as liable to die as you were once that ypron stabbed you. I had to do something to save you both."

His eyes narrowing, Eleison pushed off from the wall and unfolded his arms to pace around the length of the suite. "So you made a deal with a devil."

"I—yes. Yes, I suppose I did."

One hand raising to run along his face, Eleison growled as he stopped before one of the tall windows. "I'm glad you're not dead…but I'm pretty fucking pissed you didn't tell me about this immediately."

"Please, Eleison—I didn't tell Malin, either. Not that it had followed me home, anyway."

"Yeah, he said that in a text message…it does make me feel a little bit better, in a worse way. Thecla—"

With a noise that was such a sharp sigh of agitation it was almost a scoff, Eleison turned away from the light pouring through the window.

"You're not *alone* anymore, you know?" While I bit my lip, guiltily taking his meaning at once, he went on, "You and Malin and I—we all have to learn how to tell each other the truth if we're going to make this work."

"I'm sorry, Eleison."

Chest expanding with another, slower sigh, Eleison made his way back to the bedside where I sadly perched. He sat beside me, his hands sliding around mine.

"I know it's scary, Thecla, and that you feel responsible for bringing the dharmine into the house; but since we're together, your problems are *my* problems, and vice versa. It's not about who's responsible for them, okay? Problems show up, we figure out what we need to do to fix them, and then we do it. It's that simple—it should be that simple."

I nodded steadily, agreeing, "Yes, of course."

"At least I know now. We can figure out a way to trap it— though they're much easier to put down before they've—"

A strange fright bolted through me. I straightened, my hands tightening around his.

"Oh, no—please, Eleison, don't *kill* it."

Looking almost wild with shock—no, horror! oh, it ached my soul—Eleison asked, "Do you *like* this thing?"

"It—no, but it—"

"It's a *parasite*, Thecla! A demon!" Sliding his hands out of mine to pace again, Eleison ran his fingers through his hair. "I feel like I'm going crazy here. Malin is acting like it's no big deal, too. I asked him if he had experienced it at all, you know what he said? "That thing wouldn't dare come near me without a good reason." Like a dharmine gives a shit who Malin is!"

"Eleison—"

I reached for him, but he stepped back. "No, Thecla—don't treat me like I'm the one being irrational here."

"But it hasn't *hurt* me. It's trying to please me."

"It's not a puppy that followed you home through the rain one day! It's a demon. And if I see it, I'm going to do my job no matter what you think you want—no matter what it's convinced you that you think you want."

"Oh—" I cried out, springing up as Eleison strode from the room, "Eleison, please, wait—"

"I need to calm down. Call me if you have an emergency you deign to tell me about."

While the door slammed in his wake, I collapsed upon the floor to weep in a self-pitying heap.

For the first night in over four months, I slept alone.

T HE NEXT DAY, the atmosphere had lost its gloss. The weather was still fine—rain, no Rift Events likely—but Valquist was less lovely to me. It seemed posturing, somehow. Hostile toward me, in a way that made me project a hostility of my own.

But it was not always all projection. After breakfast, I returned to my suite to find a note from the Overseer; she'd made room for a luncheon after all, and advised me to meet her on the back patio around twelve.

One may imagine I was simply overjoyed.

"Thecla"—she smiled and rose from her seat when I emerged from the glass doors, her hand extending for another firm shake—"how are you today? Did you get a chance to go out on your own yet?"

"Oh, no. I'm still catching up on my rest."

"Well, be sure to take some time to explore soon! Valquist is a wonderful city. Oh, but I wanted to let you know—Aleister is fine."

Exhaling, I asked, "Really?"

Parvati smiled kindly at the undisguised relief of my tone. "Yes, really...just some food poisoning, the doctor said. You'll be able to check up on him without risk to yourself in a couple of days."

"I certainly will." While I settled in the chair across from hers, smoothing my gown over my knees, I said with embarrassment, "I am sorry for Eleison's poor mood yesterday—"

"Please, don't apologize. If I hadn't been ready for a harsh opinion, I wouldn't have asked for one. A little critique is good for everybody now and then. Besides...given your relationship, I'm sure it's difficult for him to stand by while journalists pick at everything you say."

I had barely considered the impact the press conference might have had on Eleison before the truth of the dharmine came out. Suddenly, they appeared the same: two separate incidents, neither of which he could protect me from.

Both of which were brought about by Malin.

"I appreciate your charitable position," I said, smiling slightly as a cocktail was set before me. "Eleison is normally very reserved. I was surprised to hear him speaking to you yesterday, but I suppose you're right."

With a slight smile of understanding and a swig of her own drink, the Overseer raised her eyebrows as if in sudden memory and cast a darting glance away. She shifted in her seat, smoothing her napkin over her lap while saying, "Speaking of yesterday—I couldn't help but notice something you mentioned before we spoke to the press. Something about your developing power as a riftborn? What was it, again?"

"Oh, well—"

There again was Charlotte's warning. I cringed to have been asked a question too direct to escape, but I still found myself reluctant to reveal any information Parvati did not already know.

I understood Malin better all the time.

"We're not *really* sure," I qualified, my fingers running up and down the stem of the cool glass. "I mean, it could be a coincidence, but—"

"Go on."

Tongue darting across my lower lip, I lowered my voice and explained to her about the Torea Festival, as well as the giganturn and solitary ypron who had changed or simply dropped the targets of their harassment on the night of the kidnapping. Parvati listened with careful interest.

"And no other times?"

"Well," I said, "no—but I don't go into the Rift very often. It gives me terrible headaches."

"That's interesting. So the dharmine was your first encounter with a Rift monster up-close?"

"There was a lupella when I was young, and on the way to Malin's for the first time our carriage was overturned by a pack of borros. If Eleison hadn't arrived just in time, we would have been done for."

"So your power had no effect that time?"

I shook my head. "I guess not."

"Strange." Though she said this as though in thought, it was somehow affected. "I wonder what the difference was?"

"I don't know."

"Say, Thecla—I'm really interested in this." Sitting forward, she asked, "Would you mind humoring me for an experiment?"

Given the last "experiment" I had endured, I couldn't help my cringe. "What kind, exactly?"

But she was already getting to her feet. "Just to satisfy my curiosity," she said, gesturing toward an outbuilding tucked neatly along the far edge of the distant lawn. A small autocart, open to allow the breeze while it ferried riders from one end of the property to the other, stood waiting for us.

Feeling grim, I followed her to it and let her drive me over.

The closer we grew, the more the scent on the wind was unmistakable—and the more I realized the outbuilding was only a building in the loosest sense of the term. It certainly was a roof; but beneath that roof was a series of open-faced kennels.

"What are those?"

"We release a few guard monsters on the property every night. The luptichs, anyway. Not the ertiz. We tried them first, but they proved less adept at the task...I keep them around anyway, I've got a soft spot for them."

Smiling thinly, I agreed, "Ertiz do seem among the loveliest creatures from the Rift."

As she parked, an animal handler appeared from the one secure portion of the building: a small, enclosed office space at the kennels' end. With a smile and a wave, the handler pulled on a pair of thick gloves while making her way down the rows of kennels. Most of the animals were sleeping, though a few eyed her with a suspicion I could sense even before getting out of the cart.

"I'm not going to be in danger, am I?"

"Oh," said Parvati quickly, "no, no, of course not. In fact, the ertiz I have in mind for this experiment is more likely to kiss you to death than to try and eat you—see?"

She laughed, indicating the likewise laughing handler who had the kennel door open for all of one second before, bushy tail wagging, the sleek ertiz wiggled out to thrash with great excitement at the feet of a human it clearly adored. After weaving a few speedy figure-8s between her feet, it paused before her to roll about, then twisted to nibble harmlessly at her hand while she affixed the lead to its collar. Despite my mood, I giggled at the sight and found myself rather envious. What a cute pet it might make, given the proper conditions and training.

"I didn't realize ertiz were *so* friendly!"

"This one was bred in captivity." At my look of surprise, she spread her hands. "Breeding Rift monsters here on earth in a controlled manner is an excellent way to research them without depending on external factors, like the number of Rift Events in a given year or the question of the animal's condition. This one was the product of an experiment in domestication, and, well…"

Straining at its lead, yelping and yipping as if in conversation, the ertiz wove wildly across the aisle of kennels down which the handler struggled to lead it. The rumble of a luptich's growl reverberated through the air and inspired the unearthly snarls of a few others, which caused the jumpy little ertiz to bounce about in search for a closer exit than the one to which it simultaneously led its handler.

"…as you can see, you still can't really call them *domesticated*…but this one is very friendly."

There was something puppyish about it, with two of its four ears tweaking down in an adorable flop while the higher-frequency pair still rose like horns upon its head. Its eyes were as bright and sweet as could be, and its tail never seemed to stop thrashing—though it grew fluffed to about three times its original, already voluminous size at the outraged snarl emitted by the growling luptich at the end of the row. The leonine beast threw itself at the rattling cage door, its paw, a six-clawed instrument of death, hooking against the grate while the ertiz yelped to get clear of the other animals.

"So what am I supposed to do, exactly?"

"Just try to see if you can get it to do something. Make it calm down...this one never sits still once he's out—aha!"

Scenting us, the ertiz jerked so hard on its lead that it slipped even its expert handler's grip. While the Overseer laughed, the goofy creature pranced up to us, its wet, red nose wiggling with wild interest while it hopped and danced about.

Though I laughed, I was annoyed by all this, really. Did she think I was lying? What reason would I have for such a thing?

Meanwhile, agitated by the movements and noises of the slender ertiz, a few of the leonine luptich growled with displeasure. One of them in particular, imprisoned not far from the end of the row, slapped at the door of its cage. The rattling noise inspired in me a wince that provoked the friendly ertiz to rise up and lay its front paws against my dress. Oh, Charlotte would be so cross— look at the mud on those paws, who knew what else—

Parvati's voice, smug with her question:

"Do you think it's working?"

"What do *you* think," I asked her, unable to modulate my harsh tone while I struggled to push the demanding little Rift vulpine off me. Eventually, sensing the nearness of its keeper in spite of the presence of someone new—and the continuous growling of that now very angry luptich—the ertiz twisted down upon the ground with an almost childlike giddiness. Its long body coiled over itself in the fashion of a snake while it leapt off in a playful evasion of its human friend. It dashed around in circles, ran several yards away, then paused to let the keeper catch up a bit before, its body flowing curiously, the ertiz scrambled back to us.

As the keeper gave chase, calling the ertiz's name between occasional whistles and clicks, I sorted myself out well enough to focus on the point of the experiment. No wonder things weren't working as anticipated! With the merry beast hopping around me, I had barely remembered what it was the Overseer wanted me to do. Now, I could focus.

Now, I imagined being calm. Calm as a lake on a windless day. Calm, so calm, as one is in those precious seconds when one becomes aware of falling asleep, and then it just—happens.

I dreamed of being so calm that I even began to feel calm.

Yet—the ertiz, with boundless energy to have been let free outside its normal schedule, did not.

Nor did the luptich that, enraged and hungry or sleepless or all, slammed itself against the flimsy door of its kennel one more violent time.

When the beast succeeded in propelling itself out of the cage, it seemed almost shocked to find itself free. Its legs went stiff to fight its own momentum, its eyes comically wide above its equally yellow fangs. For the lengths of three or perhaps four inches, its black claws extended from golden paws to gouge furrows in the earth.

Then, wheeling with a snarl, it sprang at the ertiz.

I cried out, falling back against Parvati. Though she flinched, she made no move, as I did, to recoil to the cart. Instead she stood perfectly still, her expression hard with concentration while she watched the unfolding chaos. Like she was still waiting for something to happen. Desperately now, I tried to evoke that calmness—and you may imagine how counter-productive that was!

It didn't matter. While the ertiz went yelping off, having been meanly slapped across the nose but not penetrated deeper than the fur, the keeper managed to slip the lead around the raging luptich's neck by getting behind the beast as it wheeled toward us. While the predator snarled and spat, its great paws thrashing with the promise of death, the increasingly distant ertiz raced up one of a row of cherry trees some three hundred yards from us.

The Overseer watched not it, but me.

"Apparently," I told her thinly, "I can't do it today."

"Apparently not," she agreed, tapping her chin. In one smooth slide of her eyes she looked me up and down, and, before she turned away, produced a noise so singularly annoying it spiked my blood pressure. "Hm."

"What's *hm*?"

"Oh, well, it's just that— When I listened to your stories, I noticed a common thread. Though I don't mean to insult you, it's one I'm not sure you've considered."

My hands resting upon the backs of my hips, I shrugged. "Any sense of direction would be useful here, I'd say."

"The same two people, aside from you, were conscious at the events you mentioned to me...and only one of them is still alive."

Eyes narrowing, I parsed out what she had just told me. A hot breeze seemed only to push the humid air of Valquist unpleasantly around us.

The Overseer resumed her path to the cart.

"Are you coming? Lunch should be served by now."

With a long look at the empty seat beside her, then up at the haze of the humid sky, I told Parvati, "I think I've decided I'm not very hungry after all. Besides! I'm sure tonight there will be so many opportunities for snacking…I don't want to make myself sick."

Her smile was false, and she did not make an effort to sell it to me. "Then let me drive you back, at least."

"Thank you, Madame Overseer"—was my smile was any more believable than hers?—"but I would rather walk."

"Very well…see you tonight, Thecla."

As the cart cruised away, and the keeper, having contained the luptich, hurried off to coax the ertiz down from its tree, I stood numbly for a while before setting off.

I had given Parvati the benefit of the doubt, but clearly Malin was right to mistrust her. This was just the first, smallest thing she could tell me. She had not even told it to me directly. I didn't like her sly manner of leaking information.

I didn't like that she had just revealed my husband was possibly riftborn, just like me.

She was testing the waters of my loyalty. Weighing that loyalty against my curiosity to see which had more control over my heart.

And she was making a fatal miscalculation if she thought I couldn't see that.

In the cool halls of the palace, I made my way up to Eleison's room. When I knocked on the door, there was no answer. Still pouting, I assumed. My eyes rolling, I headed down my corridor and let myself into my room.

And there he was, seated solemnly upon the edge of the bed.

"Hey." He stood, nodding to me. "I was just about to leave, actually. Charlotte said you met the Overseer for lunch."

"She said something I found very distasteful, so I let her know my opinion by leaving our appointment before the meal... Just like I wish I could leave this blasted city, oh—"

Tears welled in my eyes so immediately they couldn't be fought, and my lips trembled in misery. "I'm sorry, Eleison," I said while, looking pained by me, he hurried to take me in his arms. "I'm sorry, you're right—I should tell you the truth of everything, oh, but nobody ever tells *me* anything, and—"

"Hey, Thecla—I forgive you for that, okay?" While he drew my head to his heart, I took a few quivering breaths and let his shirt soak up my tears. "That's not what I'm upset about."

"But you are still upset."

Sighing, Eleison pressed his mouth to the top of my head. He rested it there a long moment before saying, "I'm not upset at *you*, Thecla. But...I'm not happy to think that this thing has put some kind of glamor on you."

I scoffed, a little offended, and raised my hand between us to wipe my eyes until his handkerchief appeared for me. "I'm not so—so weak-*willed*. It doesn't need to glamor me for me to see its use. I'm still thinking straight about this, Eleison. I know it's dangerous; but so is Malin. And so are you."

"Not to *you*, though," he began, though he hesitated to say more. Quieted, no doubt, by his own recently evoked memories of being under Vivian's mind control.

"The dharmine isn't dangerous to me, either," I told him with steadily developing confidence. "It's obsessed with serving me. It says it has a contract with me in the future—one that binds it to me forever, in the present and the past."

"So it's indebting you now to work its will later."

"Perhaps. But even when it was trying to harm the duke, it was doing so in the name of helping me." Biting my lip, I told him, "I know you have good reason to hate dharmines, and I suppose I ultimately can't stop you from trying to kill it if you meet it…but—"

But I trusted the creature not to harm me, and it appeared to have had ample untaken opportunities to harm Eleison.

Besides…if, as the Overseer just demonstrated to me, Malin really was blessed with the gift I had thought to be mine, he was safer than we were.

Not certain what Eleison knew and what I dared tell him about the creature that had manifested itself through me, I could make no defense against his arguments. Further debate would only result in another angry fight. My arms folded across my breasts as I returned my mate's scowl.

"Did you come here for more arguing?"

"No." His tone was sharp before he had it under control enough to say, still with a bit of a gruff edge, "I *meant* to apologize to you. I wanted to see if you'd come somewhere with me."

Lips pursing, having passed up lunch, I kept my arms folded even as I asked, "Where did you have in mind?"

"Have you ever been to a cinema?" As I perked, shaking my head, Eleison asked, "But you've seen moving pictures before, right?"

"Not very often, but there were a few different fellows, drifters who owned projectors and—I suppose by trading among themselves and others—maintained a collection of old pictures."

"How old?"

"Goodness, pre-Rift, I suppose. Who would want to watch anything from after?"

"That's sort of true," Eleison speculated with a dry sort of laugh. "Anyway…Valquist's movie house is about as famous as Saalast's opera house. I know it's not as high-brow as you probably deserve, but—"

"No!" My arms unfolding at last, I pressed myself to him and felt both our hearts swell with love. While Eleison embraced me, his hand in the small of my back so electric that I shivered, his surprised expression relaxed. "Don't say that, Eleison, darling…I love you so. I want to go out with you—to enjoy special things between just us. Besides"—leaning back, I smoothed my dress and fixed my hair and patted his handkerchief along my eyes—"a lot of these pictures are as intelligent as any opera…and a great number of operas are silly drivel when one reads their librettos. Just let me wash my face. Would you like to get a bite together first?"

As ridiculous as it might sound, that afternoon with Eleison was so very fine it was almost worth the price of admission: that petty fight, the sorry mockery from the Overseer, the entire trip to Valquist. Oh! It was so good just to be out with my mate, and only my mate. Much as it had been on the train, our time together seemed to represent the intersection of a different universe. Not the Rift: only a place where Eleison felt at full liberty to express his love for me.

At the restaurant, we were brought to a quiet table that permitted us to sit close together without observation from the public. Eleison's big body was warm against mine, the brushing of our knees or alignment of our feet beneath the table a sweet relief… and, I confess, still something of an illicit thrill. Especially when, giving in, he slid his arm around my back and fit his hand against my shoulder, and worried his thumb against my flesh through the fabric, and turned to kiss my cheek without thinking about it.

But it didn't take him long to warm up in the dark movie house. In fact, just as soon as we sat down, that big arm once again hooked around me. This time, he drew me so close I was practically in his lap. I laughed in surprise, looking around, but even as he said, "What? It's dark," I drew that conclusion and felt at greater ease. Owing in no small part to the end-of-summer temperatures, the theatre was crowded, and among such a throng we were but two more there for the film.

"Back in Karris"—among the theater's anticipatory murmur, Eleison's low voice filled my ear so abruptly that it took me several seconds to realize he was about to discuss his rarely elaborated upon pre-Malin existence—"when my mother was alive, we'd go to the pictures all the time. She loved them. When we saw a good one, it would be all we could talk about. Kyrie'd come along, too, but he was pretty young at the time."

"Does he remember her well, do you think?"

"No. I think—when that dharmine took her form, it somehow tainted the rest of his memories of her." Eleison went quiet for a heartbeat. I feared I'd said the wrong thing and made him clam up again, but he went on after only brief meditation. "I think she'd be really excited if she knew how many films they're starting to make these days."

It was true. The gradually expanding return to industrial society had, just so, begun to increase the availability of leisure time. That increased the interest in leisure activities, and so, over the prior decade or so, there had been a gradual but notable increase in the number of new films being produced here and there around the continent. The sorts of rare old films the wandering projectionists showed were, I had been told, from the Second Renaissance, which included, among many achievements in the arts and sciences, a golden age of picture-making that lasted just over two hundred years. There were long pictures and short pictures, and serialized ones that were hundreds of hours in length if one managed by good connections and good fortune to acquire the entire collection—which was, in most cases, unlikely. They came in color and black-and-white, and the ones from before the Rift represented an extreme, almost magical blend of illusion and life. Many of their greatest artistic achievements were accomplished by technologies which were known but for which the resources simply did not exist anymore.

The Rift had very simply disordered everything. At the time that it arrived, the average serf was wealthier, or at least had a higher standard of living, than all but perhaps the very richest in Lescaut. Perhaps for their time this was not much; but, if such a person were transported to my dear hometown, in my time, with all their worldly belongings and finances, they could have lived like Malin if they would be content to live as luxuriously as one could in a somewhat quaint village. Trade was smoother. I've read that anyone could buy any spice with hardly any effort. There had been ready access to technologies like vaccines in large parts of the world, and humanity had nursed dreams of going into space. We had even, my father told me with pride, achieved that last feat to a limited extent. This had been a golden age for humanity, and the films that were being made now seemed to be mere shadows of that.

The film was two hours, an entertaining space opera—a genre that had fallen out of popularity with mankind's scorned dreams of pioneering vast regions of the galaxy. Now that we had the leisure to dream anew, however, it was an increasingly popular motif in books and films. This one, following the adventures of a space pirate and his intelligent ship, was a fun spectacle. The first in a promised series, it featured the main character's accidental discovery of the ship—some ancient schooner left floating in the void due to a fungus that rendered it too deadly to be recovered. While being pursued by an evil federation that controlled the known planets of the universe, the hero was forced to tame the intelligent feminine mind of the ship while also seeking a cure for the potentially deadly fungal infection wreaking havoc in his lungs.

So I gleaned, anyway, between Eleison's heavy kisses. It was difficult to turn him down! I did try to pay attention, but it always seemed that just as something vital was to happen, his head would bend and his lips would brush my brow. Seconds later we would be upon one another again. It got to be such that, halfway through the movie, I twisted from another spellbinding smooch to slap my hand over his mouth and arch my brows highly in the semi-illuminated dark.

Getting the message with a soft laugh, Eleison tightened his grip on me, drew me against his chest, and contented himself with resting his head atop mine while we watched the picture. The story unfolded with classic beats I recognized from countless adventure tales and ancient plays. It was so fascinating that for all the ways mankind had changed over the aeons, our stories remained universal! Sacred formulae for the invocation of change.

Eleison's heartbeat thudded beneath the soundtrack and the dialogue. The dark, cool room contrasted so deliciously against his warm body that I felt I were the one floating in space.

For just a few seconds, I closed my eyes.

When I opened them again, I was alone.

Fear should have taken me. Yet, in the way of dreams, I could not detect the irregularity. Eleison's absence was, though not desirable, somehow not worth noting with more than a passing glance. The movie played on.

In the center of the screen, a black rectangle slowly expanded up from the floor to take on the proportions of an open doorway.

Another dream was interspersed, visible with heavy, hazy three-dimensionality: my honeymoon. The dharmine had led me through my husband's vineyard home to a darkened doorway just like this one. To a maze beyond.

To that other Malin, silver-eyed and terrifying.

When the doorway at last stood inert in the center of the playing movie, I looked one more time at the place where Eleison ought to have stood. His seat remained empty.

As I turned away, I realized I already stood before the doorway, the flashing lights and colors of the screen around too close to be anything but a halo of meaningless data.

Compelled, I walked into the darkness.

I had intuited some sort of passageway waited on its other side, but I saw nothing. When I stretched my hands, I touched neither walls nor ceiling. There was nothing by which I might make sense of direction.

No door stood behind me anymore.

"Madame."

My spine tightened with the dharmine's echoed voice. Lips dry, I waited for it to come again.

"This way," he called, a whisper at his great distance.

It came from before me: too far away to be seen. Whatever force had driven me through that door now drove me on in pursuit of Dinon's sultry murmur. I walked into the unrelenting darkness, my steps growing longer as my confidence in them increased. Faster, too, as I was imbued with greater urgency.

Just as I feared I had been plunged into some trap, a vague outline made itself distinct against the greater darkness around. My eyes strained to assign it some familiar identity.

But, upon stepping closer, I knew it.

"A loom," I whispered, my hand extending toward its obsidian surface.

Before I touched it, the cheers that greeted the end of the movie jerked me from my slumber.

I struggled to remember where I was. Eleison smiled down at me, then laughed as I scowlingly told him, "You let me miss half the blasted thing!"

"You're so cute when you pout...I just couldn't wake you up, baby. I can tell how tired you are. It was a good movie, though." While I scoffed angrily at his teasing comment, he went on, nose brushing against mine, "I'd be willing to see it with you again when it makes it through Gudrune."

Though I was a bit sour still—especially having been awoken so sharply from such a vivid dream—my mood was bolstered by Eleison's quick kiss at the corner of my mouth. "Let's get out of here while the credits are rolling," he told me, taking my hand.

The daylight of the street, just beginning to soften with early evening, stunned me into a blinking laugh as Eleison navigated me through a side alley into pedestrian traffic. "My goodness, it really was dark in there... Well, Eleison, since you let me sleep through it, it's your responsibility to tell me how it ended!"

Laughing, his eyes creasing and his cheeks outlined by handsome dimples, he asked with raised eyebrows, "Are you sure you want spoilers?"

"I'll have forgotten it all by the time it comes through

Gudrune, anyway. Charlotte's been giving me these blasted romance novels—I'm going through so many that I can't seem to remember where one story ends and another starts."

"Well, if you're sure…what's the last scene you remember?"

It was amazing to me that Eleison could carry on a conversation while doing so many other things. With his free hand, he fished his sunglasses from his breast pocket and slid them on to protect his eyes not from the sun but from scrutiny. His red irises, marking him as altered, would only have drawn attention to us in Valquist—and would have made it all the more obvious how endlessly his eyes scanned the crowd, assessing for threats as he navigated us along the relatively long route back to the Overseer's palace. While doing all this, he kept one arm crooked for me to hold. I pressed to it with perhaps more intimacy than was decent, given everything…but, I just couldn't care.

"Around the time the protagonist was rescuing his girlfriend, I think."

"What! That early on?"

"You're so warm and safe, blast it…when I lean against you I either fall asleep, or—well."

The low rhythm of his chuckle reverberated through my body and my soul. My mate! I squeezed his arm tighter while he consented to explain, "Well, right after that, Divany's girlfriend has to rescue *him* because, uh, he's got that fungal infection or whatever, so she has to work with the ship—oh, and I should mention that she's jealous of the female, uh, mind of the ship—"

"It's a love triangle?"

"Yeah! I'm telling you, you checked out right when you really would have started to like it. Maybe we should have stayed for the second showing after all—"

I laughed, about to tease that then it would be *his* turn to fall asleep—but Eleison's body stiffened. He stopped us at the curb, and without stepping off removed his sunglasses as though to better see.

Something was wrong. It was evident in his newly rigid posture: in the way he shook free of my grip, saying brusquely, "Excuse me," as though I were someone he had bumped into on the sidewalk. While I stood uncertainly in place, he wove across the traffic of the crowded street in pursuit of what I assumed to be some kind of threat.

Instead, to my amazement, he stopped at a newsstand. After coldly regarding something there, he began a tense conversation with the man selling the papers. Why, he even interrupted another person's transaction to do it! Whatever Eleison barged up to ask, the newspaper man looked annoyed, then shook his head. The gesture kept me from any hope of lip-reading his response as he turned away to finish the transaction.

Without hesitating, Eleison reached into the little stand and dragged the man halfway out by the shirt collar.

As the previous patron scurried away, I cried out and scrambled through the traffic in the street. An autohorse jolted to a programmed stop and someone cursed me, but all I could hear above the clamor was the gradually apparent voice of the salesclerk, who stammered, "Two hours ago, maybe! Hour and a half? I don't know, I just—"

"Where are you on the route," my aggrieved mate demanded, giving the clerk a vicious shake. "First or last or middle? What kind of carriage do they use?"

"It's, uh, I don't know, it's just a big white one—"

"Eleison! What—"

After dropping the terrified man, my mate whipped toward me. His look of murderous wrath was so feral I winced. "Just let me handle this," Eleison said, the words a snarl.

I had no idea what he was talking about until, in attempting to look over the side of the stand to check that the clerk was fine, my eye was caught by a familiar face.

My own.

Blood slowly draining from my cheeks, I stepped back from the racks of the newsstand. My ears rang while I read the headline that had been paired with a photograph of my unsmiling face. A fatal shot from those seconds at the start of the press conference.

While Eleison removed his watch to dial Charlotte, I fished out my pocketbook and asked the shaken salesman, "How much for the stack?"

18

DEATH!
WITCHCRAFT!
DECADENT SEX PARTIES!
…HUMAN SACRIFICE?

What we know about Madame Farrow, and what remains to be seen: Capital Voice's exclusive look into the life of Gudrune's consort!

In my suite at the Overseer's palace, Charlotte whipped away the profane issue and rolled it as though to hit a dog. Instead, she tapped her open hand.

"Don't look at it."

"I can't help it. How long will it be available?"

"Looks like it will be in circulation for a week."

"In other words," I observed, "the entire time we're here."

"Very nearly…at least there doesn't appear to be anything in it about your being altered." Gesturing with the tabloid, a sweep of her arm that commanded me aside no matter what our official stations were, Charlotte strode across the room with but a glance at angrily pacing Eleison. "I would strongly advise you not to read it, Madame. It's vulgar libel, as you can tell from the headline."

The rest of the stack had gone in the trash, but two copies remained. One was in Charlotte's hand; the other was in Eleison's, who bared his teeth at something so ugly it made him cease pacing for a fraction of a second, then rustle the pages as if in replacement for wringing someone's neck.

"I don't advise *you* read it, either," Charlotte said, reaching toward his strangled copy.

To my amazement, Eleison—or the beast inside him— growled with the menace of a savage about to take off someone's fingers. Also looking a little stunned, Charlotte withdrew her hand with an arched brow.

"We really *are* far from Gudrune," she noted, "aren't we."

"No shit." His mouth opened as though to say something more, then transfigured into a sneer. Those fiery eyes snapped briskly up to me, then back down to the paper.

Unable to tolerate it, he shredded the booklet with his bare hands.

"I can't believe," I said while the remains gathered at his feet, "that they're allowed to print such—*smut.*"

""Free press,"" reflected growling Eleison. He looked sidelong at Charlotte, who nodded.

"As long as they have someone they can cite as a source— someone to blame, in other words—they can print very nearly anything."

Stunned, I looked between my friends in full befuddlement. "Then, that means—"

"Someone fed them information about you."

"But—who would do that, and how? It's just us."

Eleison regarded the shreds of the paper littering the floor before fetching a trash can into which he could sweep his victim. "Us," he said, "and Montagne, and Montagne's footman."

I scoffed. "That's ridiculous. The duke has been laid up since we've been here! He hasn't had time to talk to anybody but me, and then only for about ten minutes during breakfast. I don't think I've seen him since…and as to the footman, I get the idea that the better part of his salary comes from discretion. I barely even noticed the man in Saalast. Unless Aleister gossiped with him, I doubt he's privy to anything."

"Then it might be somebody else sharing information. I doubt the Overseer would have stooped to doing it herself, but she could have paid someone to inform for her." While Eleison threw down the trash can again, he said, "Whoever it is, they'd better pray they're too important to shoot."

I had never seen Eleison like this. It made me shiver. As I moved toward him, it was with the caution I would show a wild animal. He even seemed to eye me like one: cautious, unsure of my intentions, until I was close enough to slide my hands over his chest and let him embrace me.

Slowly, reverberation by reverberation, the sustained growl from the center of his diaphragm faded off altogether.

"Too bad I can't go to that ball. I'm going to be hunting around the whole time instead. Waiting for Aleister to crawl out of his sickbed so I can wring his neck."

"I'm really not convinced it was Aleister," I said, frowning even as my hands wove around the back of Eleison's neck. "Though I admit, I'm not sure who else could have—"

Glenn Stone, looking between us with true despondency while he left the dining car.

"*Oh*, that—that blasted *hunter*! No wonder that lout from the tabloid already knew about Eleison and I. He must have gone running to the press as soon as he disembarked—Eleison—"

Eleison's expression had hardened. The growling began anew. He released me, snatching up his abandoned suitcoat.

"He's not too important to kill," Eleison mused while my body was clutched by fear. "A little too famous…but not, like, a dignitary or something…"

Why did I care about this hunter I'd met only once? I didn't, of course…I just didn't want Eleison to wind up in shackles as a consequence of that abbreviated encounter. Despite my fright, I found myself clutching my mate's arm.

"Please, darling—"

"I'm not going to *do* anything to Stone, okay?" Eleison's tone was harsh. At my wince, his bared teeth vanished behind a tight frown. His voice lowered, even if his tone could not relax. "I need to talk to Malin."

"As do I," Charlotte said. "Furthermore, Thecla—"

Her mouth sloped in a touch of wry displeasure to even broach the topic with me, and she was right to be wary.

"I know, of course, that the last time I decided it was best for you to stay in your room for a while, the decision didn't go over very well."

"That's a funny way of saying you had me imprisoned in my own bedroom, Charlotte," I said as lightly as I could.

"Her smile razor thin—invisible, really, save for the slight lines that graced the edges of her mouth—Charlotte agreed, "Yes, well! Times were more desperate. However…while you, as Madame Farrow, have no obligation to take my advice—"

"No," I agreed, "I don't."

She went on effortlessly, as though having calculated for the interruption.

"—I *strongly* recommend you bow out of the ball tonight."

"And look like a coward?"

"And look like you have the class to protest indecent treatment with absence, rather than controversy."

Now, of course, I see her point. Rumors will fly no matter what one does or how one responds…but, at the time, it was my first brush with the ugly side of celebrity, and I was hurt by it. Through no fault of my own, I had been dragged to a city that hated my husband so much he wasn't even able to accompany me—and my reward for doing the diplomatic thing was disgrace.

"I don't care for the thought of gossip freely flying while I have no say in it," I told Charlotte in undisguised disgust. "Not with all these—*strangers*, fools who know nothing but what they've read in the gossip columns today, circulating around the ballroom—"

"But they *are* strangers, Madame."

"Charlotte's right," Eleison agreed while fixing his tie. "don't worry what they think."

"*You* seem concerned," I observed.

A miscalculation. The look he shot me was nearly hurt: a brooding, almost adolescent scowl.

"You think I care about image this much? No, baby. I care about having to stand here like a good boy while my mate gets raked over the coals. Don't pretend the Overseer doesn't secretly love this? You can't kid yourself. There's nothing she won't do to punish Malin...and she'll punish you for loving him. And here I am. And I—"

Whatever he was going to say, he stopped himself. That dangerous growl softening just a little as he took my face in his hands, Eleison searched my features.

"I love you, Thecla."

"I love you, oh, darling—"

"I think I'm going to take a walk while I call Malin. Please, Thecla—just tell them you have the duke's illness. Stay in. Whatever you say, no matter how logically and eloquently you rebuff them, they'll only use it as fuel for worse slander."

Misery sweeping over me as the one potentially fun political event of the trip was snatched away, I sank upon the edge of the mattress. "I just want to be *home*," I said, feeling and sounding like an overtired child. "It's *miserable* here. Everything is so—so *sterile*, so *careful*, until the second the facade slips away and you discover how ugly it is underneath. It's like a bad dream, where everything should be so sweet. But it's not. It's just hateful. Oh—I hate it."

"Me, too," agreed Eleison.

"If you want to know what I would do"—Charlotte looked and sounded sympathetic, but her words still had the hard edge of displeasure that could not yet be shaken from any of us—"when the Overseer asks you why you didn't make it to the ball, tell her about the paper. Tell her what you just told us, and demand to know what she wants of you. If she can't give you a concrete, truthful answer, demand to be sent home immediately. She detests Malin, but she doesn't want to provoke him. If you let her know how unacceptable all this is, first in gesture and then in word, she'll respond accordingly."

Numbly, I nodded.

"So," asked Charlotte, "will you be going, or not? If so, we need to get you ready."

The pressure of two gazes, two unhappy wills opposed to mine, was too much for me to bear. I didn't want to capitulate. I wanted to go in defiance of rumor, my head held high.

But, not yet twenty-five, I was still a girl in my dealings with others. Too much of me still wanted to please those I loved and respected; too much of me was eager to make Eleison happy, particularly when he'd spent the last day so upset.

My shoulders sagged. "I wish I had my loom. Will you find some paper and pencils for me, Charlotte? If I can't work, I'd like to at least spend my time doing *something* productive tonight."

The tension melting out of her face just slightly, Charlotte said, "Right away. I'll bring you your dinner, as well. Would you care to see the menu from the party? I'm sure the chef—"

"No, Charlotte, I don't care. Frankly, I'm not very hungry."

"Please eat something," said Eleison. "I might be out late—I don't want to worry about you."

Frowning, I asked, "Where exactly are you going?"

"Like I said…I need a walk. A long walk."

He waited for me to challenge him.

I took his hand and kissed it, my stomach in a curious knot of reluctance.

"Please don't get into trouble, Eleison. I love you too much for that."

"I promise, I won't." Eleison bent to kiss my cheek. "You going to be okay?"

"Of course. Are you?"

"Once I've gotten in a mile or six, probably." With a quick

flash of his crooked smile, he kissed me one last time, then made his way from the room. "I'll tell Malin you said hello."

The door shut behind him.

Alone, I flopped back upon the bed and nursed my sullen thoughts.

Was it better to go, or not go? I was indecisive even once the decision had been made. The trouble was that my personal thoughts had not changed. I still wanted to go to the ball, and I wanted to go very much. But Eleison truly had been tortured by the last few days. The moment we stepped from the train, our pleasant trip dissolved into miserable work.

And for what thanks?

When Charlotte had delivered my drawing supplies, taken some dinner I hardly touched, and left a bottle of wine I touched too much, I dug through the waste basket and assembled what pieces I could of the ugly article.

And it *was* ugly. Written with lascivious, clearly prurient detail, the paper described "blood-soaked orgies" commissioned by my husband, who apparently in this fictional universe was a verifiable dharmine, as was "commonly known" by readers of the *Voice*. My obscure but innocent background had transformed into a period of time raised by witches who worshipped the Rift, which I admit sounded like it would have been exciting if true. Most absurdly among the reconstructed article was the suggestion that Malin had married me only to produce accursed infants, either as sacrifices to keep open the Rift, or to be raised as Malin's unholy heirs in some scheme of world dominion. *The Capital Voice* seemed unable to make up its mind.

Already disgusted, especially given that Malin and I were trying to conceive an heir, I gave up very quickly and tossed the pieces away again. As I did, I imagined the horror my father would have felt to read it.

What would my mother, Giselle, have said of the girl who took her life?

Damn, damn. How I hated this! I detested the thought of spending the night alone with my thoughts. Yet there I was: unable to make myself acceptable for the ball and sneak out without alerting Charlotte. Meanwhile, they were all down there convincing each other I couldn't make it because I hadn't eaten enough babies since leaving Gudrune.

Eleison and Charlotte were right…I shouldn't have read a blasted word.

Angry at the paper and the Overseer—and myself, for being so weak I couldn't make my demands the way Malin might have—I kicked the waste basket, then sat at the adjacent writing desk in a terrible huff.

But, as I took up a piece of charcoal and flipped on the lamp to see what I was doing, my heart eased somewhat.

It seemed like it had been ages since I'd been at work, even if it had been barely more than a week. Still—any time away from my weaving was pure torture. Nothing was the same without the loom…but, at the very least, I could get a step ahead and crack out a new design. Which? I was not committed to producing them in order and had in fact already defied chronology, visiting different scenes of the play depicted as my mood allowed.

And my mood was foul. I was in a strange land where no one could see who I really was. Within me there remained a fragile young woman, the same innocent girl who had naively wandered the circus tents and wept real tears when Charlotte took her from Lescaut. That fragile young woman was crushed to hear strangers say such things about her. She was good and pure and did not deserve it. Not at all.

But...was there not another Thecla? After all—that girl was *inside* me.

What was outside of me? What was I becoming as I moved through the world? How was that girl within me transformed by being Malin Farrow's wife?

I just *wasn't* that girl anymore, I realized while my hand moved in a kind of semi-automation over the page. I insisted on perceiving myself as innocent, when really there was nothing innocent left about me.

The duke right. The way I really was and the way I perceived myself were opposed—as opposed as that tabloid had been to the truth, or perhaps more. At that desk, I snapped awake, fully conscious of how I had changed in the years since my father's death. How I had changed in the past year, alone! I had not one but two lovers, and had access to delights that some would find shocking only because they had no opportunity to experience their richness. I had gone from extremely poor to so wealthy I didn't even really know how much money we had. I had learned, in fact, that I had *never* been who I thought I was—never been a simple human maiden without exceptional quality.

And I had consorted with a dharmine. Had even grown attached to it, I had been forced to admit to myself when Eleison threatened it.

It had killed for me.

Even if that had been in defense, was I still to be called innocent? Did these festering rumors swirling about the capital not contain the smallest seed of a truth?

Instead of finding insult in the truth, was I not better taking control of it?

Slowly, I developed the figures in the center of the design. I had already depicted Macbeth's first, meeting with the monarch she was to depose—but the hero's earlier encounter with the witches and their ill-advised prophecy poured out of me without effort. In my design, the feminized Thane peered into a cauldron tipped toward her by the witch, the dharmine, *my* dharmine—Dinon.

And as I drew, that accursed spirit made haste greater than any I had felt him exhibit. When aware of his distant heat along the ridges of my brain, I vividly imagined him. Specifically, I ruminated upon the last time he had come to me, in the darkness of my workroom.

For the first time, I even let myself want him.

The demon howled in my body, his nearness measurable in the stimulation of my every nerve. I drew until the design sat complete, then wiped off my hands.

"Dinon," I whispered, staring into the charcoal simulacrum of his features, "come to me, Dinon."

His rush toward me grew more urgent—more excited. Lip bitten, I opened my robe at the lap and let my thighs part.

"Hurry, dharmine," I commanded the image, my face flushed as I ran my fingertips along my inner thigh and against the cleft between my legs. "You must be famished. Come, dharmine! Come, servant…your mistress commands you, oh…Dinon—"

As my fingers slipped up over that delicate jewel of delights, one of my guest room's windows slammed open.

19

THE DHARMINE FELL upon me with a shuddering gasp, half-corporeal, his nuzzling lips brushing my ear only to sometimes slip into me, just past the bounds of my skull, and elicit a spike of exotic pleasure just as extreme as any other penetration.

"Madame," gasped Dinon. A cry still fresh upon my lips, my body still tensed with surprise, I pulled my robe shut in instinctive response. "Madame, at last—you called me—"

His dreamy voice was so pleased! Could dharmines experience emotion after all? Just another trap, surely.

"If they're going to tell me I'm a witch," I said darkly, my eyes fluttering shut as his tongue extended to slide along my jaw, "I'll consort with demons as if I'm one. Oh—"

Dinon's hands wasted no time sliding over me, caressing down my breasts and waist as he lowered to his knees behind me. "Look at me, Madame," he begged, trying to slide one hand into my robe.

I caught it, gripping his cold flesh without otherwise observing the pale hand I had stopped.

"I'll look at you if you give your advice, dharmine. I imagine you perceive the tabloid that has upset me tonight?"

"I perceive all things, Madame," the creature whispered, his mouth against the center of my back to press kisses of absolute adoration through the fabric of my robe. "I perceive you have been upset by what you read, although I cannot understand why."

I scoffed. "What do you mean, you can't understand?"

"Your kind are obsessed with taboos I cannot conceive. All behavior is neutral to me. Pleasure and pain sustain me in equal measure. Madame—"

With an almost boyish turn of desperation in his voice, Dinon breathed, "I've starved since you left."

Banishing my natural instinct toward pity, I took up my charcoal again and busied my mind with the basic elements of calculation for the threads my piece would require. While Dinon whimpered to feel my thoughts turn to hard, factual, emotionless matters like arithmetic, I told him in a dismissive tone learned from Malin, "Then you'd better help me figure this out. I'm in no mood to entertain you otherwise."

"I can tell how upset you are."

Of that, I had no doubt. The demon spoke to me always in an awestruck, almost breathless voice, as though I were a marble sculpture in a museum and he some historian overwhelmed by antiquity. Malin got a similar tone from time to time, but his never had the hint of desperation shown by Dinon. In his eagerness to please, the dharmine studied the contents of my mind and heart with something like religious scrutiny, and he went on to prove it.

"What eludes me," he went on, "is the "why" of it all. *Why* does it upset you that someone said those things? They are not true…they are meaningless."

"All the same, I'm upset."

"Perhaps it's because you wonder if you're capable of the things they say of you."

"I'm not worried about eating *babies*," I protested, breaking off my calculations to scribble in annoyance.

The demon chuckled, rising behind me to gather my hair from my neck.

"No…not that. No, but—what was printed could be true in a simpler way."

"What way?"

"It could be true that your finest possible existence is not one that abides by the moral standards humans deem "good." And this, I can tell, bothers you greatly…although, as before, I'm not sure why."

My lips pursed.

"No one wants to be thought of as *evil*," I protested.

"Does your husband mind it?"

"—No." I remained hesitant for another few seconds. The demon waited for me, knowing my thought unfinished. "But…I'm not sure Malin considers himself evil, as such."

"And do *you* need to consider yourself evil, as such? Is that which is not aligned with perfect goodness inherently evil? Can balance not be found between these two extremes of thought? Some simultaneity? Malin is evil to some; but, to you, he is very good. Are these conditions not equally true?"

Somehow, that idea had never occurred to me before. I had lived in a simple world, where I was good, and normal people were good, and anything that deviated or destroyed was bad. Now I had deviated—was, in the eyes of the public, *deviant*—and therefore, to my simple child's judgment, I was now 'bad.' I was even startled to reflect that the girl I had been might have disapproved of me if we met on the road as strangers.

But was that because I was now wrong? Or was it because, inexperienced, my child's mind had inherited an unnuanced, unreasonably puritanical expectation of human behavior?

Slowly lowering the charcoal and once again wiping my smudged hands on my handkerchief, I conceded, "Perhaps there is some virtue to that line of thinking."

"Virtue," Ba'al-Dinon agreed, "and peril, too. All conditions are simultaneously true as I see them, Madame. One may justify anything, if rational enough."

I snorted darkly. "Just look at Malin's lies…"

Holding my breath to do it, I turned upon the swiveling stool that had been paired with the in-built desk.

Oh…the dharmine—no, Dinon—was so incredibly attractive that my thighs splayed a few degrees just to look upon him. It was easy to call him a "demon," and to think of him as little more than some phantasm when I could not see him…but there, before me, standing over me with that serpentine smile, he was every irresistible inch of him a man. The hyper-black cloak that tumbled around his shoulders, much like the low-slung trousers of black leather that clung to his hips, only served to emphasize the cool radiance of his pale chest, his abdomen, the cut of the Adonis belt down into regions undisclosed. It seemed his complexion was white as the mane that, swept back into a plait that hung over his shoulder, made me wonder about Dinon as an individual. Who had he been before being a dharmine? How did he live before I met him?

His smile slightly widened. Very slightly: only as much as my eyes narrowed.

"If you can't refrain from perceiving my thoughts, make your perception useful. If I ask you for the truth about my husband, will you give it to me?"

"I am forbidden from speaking Master Farrow's secrets, Madame…as eternally as I am bound to you, so I am also bound to that."

I sighed, leaning back against the desk. "You're useless, then."

"Ah, Madame…anything but. I did help you just now, didn't I? As you asked."

It was true—he had. The dialectical notion of embracing emotional complexity felt like it had opened a new way of thinking for me. One I had barely begun to probe, and would not until I'd had time to fully reflect on it.

"I suppose so." One arm folding across my waist, I sighed to run my opposite hand first along my jaw, then down my neck and along my breast. I had never so intentionally aggravated a man's desire before—not even with Malin or Eleison, who were always inclined toward amorous thoughts no matter what I did.

Yet, much as I found myself able to speak to Dinon as I otherwise spoke only in my private thoughts, I found myself inclined to treat him cruelly. To tempt him and tease him, because he invited it.

And oh, he made me want to do the same to my other men.

"I'm almost glad you're here," I told him, my hand at rest upon my bosom while he eyed it, my throat, my face in turns. "Though, I'm afraid. If Eleison finds you…well…do I need to tell you that we spoke about you yesterday?"

"How sorry I am to cause quarrels between you and your lover, Madame…but you need not be afraid. Eleison is occupied."

I frowned, the stroke of that hand down my own ribs pausing there at my waist. "With what?"

"He is killing a man," said the demon so flatly I couldn't make sense of it.

When I did, my mouth fell open.

"What do you mean?"

Dinon did not seem bound to protect Eleison's confidence in the way he was Malin's. The demon gestured toward the waste basket.

"He was far more upset than you…but he has *been* upset."

"Yes, but—" I dropped my voice with a fearful glance at the RMS panel and did not think it wise to complete the sentence. Because of their built-in speakers and microphones, it was common knowledge that all such devices were capable of recording speech. Most, of course, were not utilized for such purposes, but I was wary there.

Dinon did not require me to continue aloud, however; and he spoke so plainly I suspected (and would someday find) his speech could not be captured. "Please consider, Madame, that he is out killing this man not out of will alone, but also out of duty."

The ringing in my ears settled to a distant hum. Eleison—killing someone over me right this very second.

"Is there a chance it could go badly for him," I asked, paled by the thought.

"There is always a chance," replied Dinon wisely, "but he is an expert."

Mouth dry, I plucked up my neglected glass of red wine and nursed from its chalice for a few long seconds.

The demonic man before me had killed a score of people on my behalf. I had watched him do it—watched the blood spray from Gall's neck before the idiot toppled over the rail and down to his final end.

But that was to be expected from a dharmine.

From Eleison?

From Eleison—who, in addition to my gallant lover, was Malin's closest servant of close to ten years.

"How many times has Eleison done such things for my husband?"

"Many more than either could remember if pressed."

At once, I was unable to sit still. Lips tight, I rose from my seat and paced to the window left open by Dinon's arrival. Nearer to the empty frame, the night air was rich with the clamor of guests mingling before entering the ball.

"I think I knew that somehow," I confessed to Dinon, pushing the window closed, then pulling shut the curtains. "Yes. Somehow, I knew that about him. We hadn't talked about it. I just—somehow, I never thought about it concretely. Never thought about it…continuing to happen."

While I pulled shut the other set of drapes, Dinon followed my every motion with lustful silver eyes always lidded for the bedroom.

"Does thinking of it concretely change how you perceive him?"

"…Maybe not," I confessed.

Dinon's smile widened enough for me to catch a hint of white teeth. Was that the tip of a fang? I shuddered and polished off my wine in one swig.

"That is truly unconditional love," Dinon observed. "And

is love not among the highest virtues? The most pursued of human experiences? It purifies...justifies."

"I don't know I would call such a thing "justified." But..." With a sniff of derision to remember the gross, sweaty tabloid journalist and the tasteless questions he had asked, I confessed, "I'm not particularly sorry, either. Not as long as Eleison won't be affected."

"No, Madame."

I nodded. "When will he be back?"

"Not until midnight, Madame. He has not killed yet; he is stalking now."

Scoffing, I made my way to the edge of the bed. I perched there, facing Dinon.

"Then I *could* have gone to the ball...blast it, I wish Charlotte didn't have my finery locked up with her..."

"Oh, Madame—you can still go to the party."

I laughed dryly. "In my robe?"

With a chuckle of his own, Dinon studied the leg that gravity revealed. "No man there would dare complain, though their wives would find it in poor taste. No, Madame. Let me help you dress. None there will compare when I'm finished with you."

Excitement flooded through me. Yes—that was just what I wanted. I didn't just want to go to the ball. I wanted to attend it as its most irresistible guest. I wanted to be better than everyone there.

Especially the blasted Overseer.

Though no doubt he could taste my delight on the air, I kept myself coolly disposed toward the dharmine. "I suppose you'll wish to be fed beforehand?"

"Please," the demon begged, genuflecting before me with

his eyes fixed upon mine. "Madame—I can only help you if you feed me—ah—"

With a derisive roll of my eyes, I pulled at the tie of my robe and let its sash fall open.

The simple act of exposing myself to the dharmine gave me such immense pleasure! I wasn't sure it needed to touch me for my ecstasy to sate its hunger. Drawing the robe back from one breast, I opened that same naked thigh to invite the creature's hungry gaze. Lips just parted, Dinon examined every inch of me.

"I suppose you're going to beg to touch me now," I said in a tone of bored resignation, my hand teasing over my thigh and remaining poised just beneath the soaking crevice there. "Go on, get it over with…"

"Oh, Madame…of course, I won't touch you if you don't want me to, but…I know what your body wants…"

"I'm sure you don't need all those powers of yours for that…but I hope you also know, Dinon, that you don't have my permission to fuck me."

"Of course not, Madame. I don't deserve to—although…it would be so sweet for us…"

"Stop trying to tempt me, or instead I'll feed you by giving you a whipping."

"That sounds delicious, Madame…but, ah—"

Eyes closed, the demon leaned forward. The temple of his forehead rested upon my knee as he murmured, "Your desire, your pleasure, your satisfaction, that desire's renewal, over and over…there are few meals as sweet in all the world. Please…I do beg you…"

Those silver eyes opened, focused between my thighs.

"Let me show you."

As gorgeous as he was, Dinon was almost impossible to resist. Especially there at my feet, begging to please me.

Malin did seem fine with the idea, I told myself while setting my hand atop Dinon's head.

Smiling, the dharmine wasted no time. His smile faded only briefly: only into a look of concentration that appeared in the second before his kisses trailed up my thighs. Each tender press of his cool, damp lips exacerbated the state between my legs so that, when the first kiss pressed upon my labia, I felt ready to explode.

And that was just the first contact.

His silver eyes flicking toward me, Dinon opened his mouth and extended a tongue that was long and pointed. The slender organ slithered the length of my sex and I fought back the urge to moan, desperate to downplay the satisfaction this vile creature threatened to bring…but my efforts did not last long. The lapping of his tongue, devoted at first to enjoying the arousal that shone from every petal, slid up to my clitoris. My panting devolved into a long, low groan. With one hand tightening around the bedspread, I used the other to stroke and pat his head.

"Good dharmine," I gasped. How strange! Even then, I felt in total control—despite how vulnerable I ought to have felt every time fangs flashed with lips lifted to kiss some other part. "You're not so bad, after all…good boy, oh, yes—yes!"

My brow furrowed while that long tongue plunged into me, lapping at the interior of my channel in a way that was somehow both disturbing and erotic. The demon's arms slid under my rear while the rest of my robe fell away. Naked, I let it tip me back without complaint. I even spread my legs a little wider for it.

Then, its attention shifted. As though it were the most natural thing in the world, Dinon slid his tongue out and let his kisses trail farther down.

"What are you doing?"

"What I know you want, Madame…"

Before I could inquire further, its fingers slipped expertly around my clitoral nerve. I found myself bucking with surprise. I was so occupied by the wet slide of his fingers over me that I never braced myself for the tongue slithering along my rear.

What a vulgar sensation! I cried out in a combination of pleasure and humiliation, the ecstasy itself somehow increasing that shame. Yet, as the demon's tongue kept lapping, and its fingers worked without having to see, the bliss that rose through me was as novel as the one inspired by Malin's whipping games. I was so absolutely overwhelmed with pleasure that, very quickly, I forgot to be ashamed.

It would be different with Malin no matter what—but, with the demon, nothing mattered. I didn't need to fret over decorum, or communication, or any of the etiquette Malin incorporated to sweeten our pleasure. And sweeten, they did, and inevitably would.

Yet, with the dharmine—

It was like being worshipped by my own shadow.

There was nothing it did not know. Nothing about me it did not see or understand—no dark thought, no errant deed. And, knowing, it had followed me across the continent for a week by some occult means until I provided it with enough thought energy to let it find me. It had wandered all this way to, as ever, beg to serve me, and in manners sweeter all the time.

Gradually, the tip of its swirling tongue probed just within me. I tensed, then relaxed, my legs around its head unbinding a bit—enough for me to realize I had tightened them so much in the first place. At my deliberate acceptance of its intrusion, the demon's tongue slithered a little deeper. Just enough that my nervous system was absolutely rocked by the sensation; by the promises of what could be wrought with more extensive means.

With Malin.

As the husband for whom I pined flashed across my mind, the dharmine slid his finger from my clitoris and into me. The sensation, so unexpectedly pleasurable when I had been focused on Dinon's tongue, was what made me collapse into a fit. The convulsions of ecstasy produced a scream I forced myself to mute, one hand clapping over my mouth. While I moaned behind it, rocked fore and aft by waves of a somehow sharpened pleasure, the dharmine released a long sigh and guided me through it as though he had been doing this to me for years.

When at last Dinon retreated, I felt some energy draining from me in a way I could not explain, and I lay there studying the ceiling a long moment. My legs unbound and, unspeaking, Dinon rose.

"Would you like anything else from me tonight, aside from help before your party?"

"No...yes—yes."

In the clarity of the aftermath, with the lessons of the dharmine somehow fomented by the orgasm, my own little public relations problem was secondary. All I cared about was Eleison's safety.

"I'm very sure Eleison is...professional. I trust him...I don't want him to ever doubt that. But the fact remains that there's always—evidence of something, somewhere."

The demon's inscrutable little smile returned while I sat up without regard for my nudity. Seeing the protrusion in his trousers, I blessed the orgasm for easing my urgent longing to be filled by a man. I instead slid my foot up Dinon's leg and along the outline of his cock. Though he sighed, and his eyes closed lightly, he did not move.

"You're obviously deft in matters of removing stains," I went on while teasing him, using force enough to make him gasp as I added, "regardless of whether you have my permission."

"I'm sorry, Madame…I'm a wretch…but what man is not before you?"

"Cut the flattery, please, and tell me you'll be able to go clean up."

"Yes, Madame. Would you prefer I make the kill?"

His eyes opened, one big hand raising to stroke along my foot. For the audacity, I lowered my leg before he could heighten the caress. I even slid my robe on while he shuddered, his great body vibrating with the power of a lion denied playtime with its keeper.

"No," I said after a few seconds of genuine consideration. "No—I think Eleison needs it. And it will be harder for you, since you may only enter houses where you have been invited, or where the owner is dead."

"Or where *you* have been invited, Madame, since you behold me into existence…but, you are correct."

Unnerved, I cleared my throat. "…If you speak the truth when you say Eleison won't be troubled—"

As though someone else said them in another part of the room—another part of the world!—I heard myself ask, "What do I care?"

"Very good, Madame." Nodding, the dharmine smiled and gestured toward the wall behind me. "Shall we?"

When I turned to follow his indication, a new door had appeared in the wall. Red—red like that strange door hiding the torture chamber in my husband's villa. By all logic, this door ought to have opened into the hallway. I knew without having to touch the knob that it would not.

"Where—"

I glanced over my shoulder while speaking to find Dinon had disappeared.

Had this been a mistake? As devoted as the dharmine claimed to be, I was not sure I could really trust him with anything.

Yet, when I opened that red door to find nothing more than a little closet, empty of everything but a single shoe, I began to think it not a matter of trust but of mockery.

"Is this some joke?"

"Of course not, Madame. Would you like help putting it on?"

"I certainly would—and the dress, too, wherever it is."

Dinon appeared to my left, somewhere out of my periphery, and stepped just into view. "You didn't flinch this time," he said, almost disappointed. His hand trailing through my hair, the tips of his fingers grazing my jaw and neck, Dinon bent to brush his lips over my ear. "Do you recognize the shoe, Madame?"

It took a few long seconds, especially at the brush of Dinon's teeth along my flesh, but I soon recognized the glass beads that decorated the black toe of the simple flat slipper.

"Why—I lost that the night Eleison and I—"

"I found it during the next Rift Event," breathed the lustful creature, the depraved and obsessed creature, his body pressing against mine, his hands sliding over my arms and back. "That was how I knew we were soon to meet…I was so happy…I've been so happy…will you let me please you again, Madame?"

"Eleison's not *half* the dog you are, and borros are practically canines…no. I'll miss the entire ball at this rate. Stop dawdling and dress me, Dinon."

"Yes, Madame."

Breathless with excitement to be addressed by his name, Dinon lunged past me to collect the slipper, then dropped to his knee while I slowly untied the robe. Filled with the desire to torture him with his craving for me, I looked him in those predatory eyes and stood, naked, above him.

While he savored me with deliberately insolent appreciation, I extended a leg. As carefully as he had yet handled me, Dinon fit a firm hand around my ankle and guided the slipper over my foot.

VIBRANT RIFT RADIATION burst around us, so bright it blinded me. It felt as though I had stared straight into the brilliant splits the Rift carved in the pulsating sky.

Wincing, I threw my hand over my eyes too late. As with the flash bulbs, the haze had to gradually clear.

My vision was restored not a moment too soon.

As though the Rift itself had appeared to weave my dress—or had been pulled through space and woven together by Dinon's unholy hands—the eerie violet light twisted around us in tendrils that formed the frame of my dress. Soon it had built layers, developing a marvelously flared skirt that arced from my hips and down to the floor. As it gripped my waist, the solidifying fabric darkened into indigo.

Somewhere, somehow, I remembered Malin. *The solid state is less chaotic, and therefore less entropic, than the gaseous state.*

"You are so wonderful to look upon, Madame. Breathtaking. Will you please sit, so I may fix your hair?"

I wished only to marvel over the dress, whose substance was finer and more inviting to the touch than silk. "Can't you just do it with more—I don't know, sorcery?"

"I could...but I love to fix your hair myself."

"You love to put your hands on me whenever you can, you mean, you dog...very well."

Sighing, I sat at the vanity and tried not to grin while the demon stepped into view. He smiled softly now, his fingertips unhesitating as they trailed through my scalp and into my hair.

"I suppose it's a fair reward for this dress," I allotted. "It is very beautiful."

The mirror revealed elaborate patterns embroidered into the indigo bodice, a starburst of fuligin thread and silver beads. "Are you able to take a thing from one place and bring it to another, or can you only shape new things?"

"Only new things, Madame," he said, his fingertips deftly picking bobby pins out of thin air before expertly curling my hair from the temples of my forehead. "But, if you would like, I could reproduce something for you."

"I'd like Malin's necklace, please. I believe Charlotte packed it, but it's obviously in her room. Probably in a safe."

"Ah...that would be no trouble to fetch for you. Please, wait."

The dharmine disappeared, and I did wait.

All of sixty seconds later, he returned with the familiar case in his hand. "Is this the one, Madame?"

"You know that it is...put it on me, please."

While, with a deft hand, Dinon snapped open the case and

obeyed, I examined his work thus far. My hair was really poised to be stunning; and, once the ruby and its diamond cohorts were around my throat, he returned to his task with fingers that flew quicker than any mortal's.

"Remember, Madame. Your mate will return at midnight, so try to be back by then if you want to get ahead of him."

I nodded. "And this dress?"

"It, and your shoes, will be taken care of when you return."

"Very good, Dinon. You know—"

He paused, his silver eyes fixing upon the reflection of my face rather than his work.

Oh, how desperately my body still yearned for him…and I could see in his sly smile that he knew it.

"—I'm impressed by your devotion."

"Thank you, Madame…you are all I think about. Your pleasure, and Master's."

Like that, he was done. As he stepped back, I looked at myself in shock. In the space of five minutes—six, if you included his time to fetch the necklace—Dinon had turned me into a queen.

"May I"—his tone was coy as he extended a hand into some pocket of air I couldn't perceive—"present you with a small token, Madame? Not that you require additional adornment… but…"

As he drew from that interspace a tiara adorned in ruby and amethyst, I held my breath and nodded. He set it carefully upon my swirling hair, and, as with the dress, I became gradually aware of more detail. Of tiny diamonds that twinkled in perfect rows between the greater gems; of the keratoid spikes that, like the antlers they resembled, were artfully asymmetrical in a subtle but appealing way.

At last, unable to hide my pleasure from the dharmine, I smiled.

"Very good," I told him, aware of a noise that rumbled up from his diaphragm and seemed not unlike the purr of a common housecat. "Yes, Dinon, that's very good…I can see how eager you are to satisfy me."

"Yes, Madame."

"I'll call you if I need you again tonight. For now—go watch over Eleison. When he departs, whatever's happened—"

"I will ensure there is no trace of a crime, Madame."

I nodded. "Very good. Then…I'd ought to go."

"Enjoy the ball," Dinon told me, that omnipresent smile lighting his voice as he helped me up from the vanity with one strong hand. "You'll make a splash."

That was putting it mildly.

I rose with a lurch of vertigo. Somewhere, deep in the center of my head, I felt the first prods of a cousin to the splitting migraines that overwhelmed me when I was exposed to Rift Events. "Perhaps it's a good thing I need to be back by midnight—this gown isn't *harmful* to me, is it?"

"No, Madame, certainly not. Your allergy to Rift radiation is but a complication of your latent abilities. It will go away, eventually."

"When?"

In a certain, somehow mocking way, his smile widened. "Please call me if you need me—ah, please, don't hesitate."

The curtains burst wide and the windows flew open before I even saw Dinon move. When he did move, it was not a matter of registering his movement so much as his sudden absence.

While the windows shut themselves far more slowly, I turned away and hurried from my room.

The corridor seemed longer than normal, yet the sound of chamber music reached me as soon as I stepped through the door. My head high, I made my way toward a security officer stationed to keep lost or snooping guests from wandering into the residences. He looked at me once, twice, then exhibited the slightest jerk of a surprised eyebrow before sliding his pocket watch from his tuxedo. "Madame Farrow," he said, nodding politely. "I'll let Madame Overseer know to expect you."

I nodded, gliding past him and down the stairs to the main hall where guests still trickled through, some of them lightly conversing or ogling the vast ceilings and dramatic entryways of the post-brutalist architecture before checking their coats. Now that I saw the attendees and the splendor with which they were dressed, I was relieved Charlotte had forced the dharmine to improvise. The partygoers of Valquist were cut in the finest haute couture, every woman's dress designed to wow with color and shape and every man neat as a pin in designer tuxedos that were seldom the traditional black. A vibrant rainbow of bodies—one from which one hue was missing until I descended the stairs and made eye contact with an unoccupied concierge to ask, "The ballroom?"

He had some sort of earpiece in. I was impressed to find that, thanks to whatever the guard had mumbled into his watch, this fellow had evidently been waiting for me. "Right this way, Madame Farrow. Shall I announce you?"

Noting my lack of an escort, the concierge offered his elbow, and I rested a hand lightly upon it while saying, "Yes, please do."

Not everyone had read that ridiculous paper, I reminded myself while the clean-cut fellow guided me along the carpet, past the milling guests, and beyond the long row of proudly displayed Overseer portraits. Every step we took, our footfalls grew more muted by the clamor of conversation, the resonance of the cello, the clinking of glasses, the laughter of both sexes. The nearer we drew to the widespread doors of the golden ballroom—more excessive than anything I had seen in Malin's homes—the thicker the corridor grew with people. Couples flirting, men in hushed conversation with business partners, people deciding whether to duck out early or perhaps working out a strategy before entry.

But the doorway, moderated by security officers, was kept empty to promote the flow of people. It was only filled when the concierge stopped with me, smiled one more polite time, and took a great breath from the base of his diaphragm.

"Madame Thecla Farrow, Consort of Malin Farrow, Master of the Territory Gudrune!"

At the entrance of the ballroom, I could look down across its recessed floor and see to the open glass doors on the other side. Nearly every head in the room turned at once, like several hundred owls interrupted by the arrival of a hawk. The music continued, but there was a distinct ebb in the flow of conversation. By the time most stares were rectified, one would hardly have noticed a thing if not as primed for judgment as I was.

But, as the concierge left me behind, at least one gaze had not been rectified.

Across the floor, much too dashing in one of the night's few black tuxedos, Glenn Stone waited at the bar.

Before I could deliberately snub him by turning my gaze away and taking the stairs down into the party, Parvati called to me from elsewhere on the second floor. I found her waving from the upper gallery where some guests spoke or watched the party semi-privately. A security man who had been close to Parvati's side quickly left, and I applauded their communication while the Overseer and I met halfway.

"You look *beautiful*," she said, her smile unfeigned as she put a hand on my shoulder to kiss my cheek. "I'm so happy you made it! Are you feeling better?"

Perhaps the Overseer didn't know yet. In fact—perhaps *most* of the people here didn't know what those ugly tabloids had said. It had only just been released that afternoon, after all. Nodding, I told Parvati, "Yes, much better. It was just a headache. You look lovely, yourself!"

The vibrant cerulean of her dress, when compared against the copper of her skin, made me pine to see the ocean. To see it with Malin. Oh, another wave of that endless longing. I worried my fingertips over my necklace as the Overseer thanked me for my praise and said, "I was worried when I heard you were bowing out. This is honoring *your* visit, after all! Come on—"

Her hand, which had remained upon my shoulder, turned me toward the stairs with her. "Let me introduce you to somebody who's a bit more of a…social butterfly than I am. You don't want to be bored to death talking politics with me all night, I'm sure, but I'll catch up with you later to see how you're doing!"

Her enthusiasm always seemed so genuine. There were times when I interacted with Parvati and wondered why my husband spoke of her with only the most withering disdain.

Then, when she was gone and the consequences remained, I understood him better.

In the throng of conversations that surrounded a swirling pit of dancers, Parvati knew just where she was taking me. I hesitated only long enough to pluck a glass of champagne from the tray of a passing waiter, eager as I was to lubricate my social sense more than the red wine had. With it in hand I hurried after her, making little attempt to recall names or even really parse what she said as she pointed out a few people we passed.

But it was before a gayly laughing woman that we stopped. Her face half-hidden by a fan she used to take the edge off the stifling chamber, the elegantly styled blonde looked away from her trio of conversational partners in a quick glance that turned to wide-eyed surprise.

"Madame Overseer—and the Madame Farrow! At *last*. I was wondering when I would meet you…"

Something in the cadence of her voice was familiar, but when she snapped shut the fan and turned toward me, her features were such a match for her brother's that I recognized her before the Overseer introduced us.

"Thecla, this is Kalypso Hartford of Montagne, Duke Montagne's sister."

"I didn't realize he had a sister!"

Scoffing, Kalypso tapped her shut fan against her open palm and said, "I shouldn't be surprised…my brother tends to have his *own* priorities."

As the Overseer made eye contact with somebody else, her tall height permitting her to see through the crowd, she smiled quickly and said, "Well, I'll let you two get to know each other— excuse me, Thecla, I'm so sorry—"

"It's fine," I told her, "really."

We exchanged a quick smile and Parvati was off again, leaving me in a sea of strangers.

"She never knows what to do when she's at risk of being treated like a normal human being," Kalypso told me conspiratorially, leaning in to whisper in my ear—and to examine more closely my necklace with a quick flash of blue eyes that thereafter bounced up to my tiara. "Always flees as soon as she can when she sees me in a social setting…say, what a *smashing* dress that is. Did you really have that done by a Gudrune designer?"

"Oh, yes," I lied while draining a quarter of my champagne. No real mystery why the Overseer had escaped, given what was apparently inherited overfamiliarity…but, on the other hand, I was grateful Kalypso could direct a conversation as well as her brother.

"Perhaps next time my brother summers abroad I'll come along with him…I wasn't sure there was anything worthwhile out there, but maybe I was wrong. Thecla—*may* I call you Thecla? Thank you—these are—"

She gestured between her friends, beginning with the one in a lovely gold dress matched to the ornaments of her dreadlocks. "Lenora Valquist—yes, of *the* Valquists—"

The next, a peachy-complexioned redhead who was possibly only so flushed because the glass in her hand was empty, was introduced as, "Selma Thoroughgood of Montagne, her father runs the best private schools—"

And the last, a woman whose straight black hair was pulled tightly back but adorned with the same flowers painted upon the fabric of her dress, was "Parsimony Bellefleur. Her family is European," Kalypso added with a dismissive wave that implied this was the only detail I needed.

I smiled at all three of them, of course, and they smiled and curtsied and told me it was wonderful to make my acquaintance. But was it my imagination that colored their stares so curiously? So eagerly?

Or is it just memory, projecting Kalypso's sly tone onto her more innocent friends?

"*But,*" the duke's sister resumed, "Thecla, I'm not terribly interested in them just this minute. What about *you?* It must have been a nightmare to see that article this afternoon."

My face fell a degree, or tried to. Somehow, I caught the expression before it completed. Once again, it seemed the right way to respond was the opposite of whatever I felt.

I rolled my eyes and smiled accordingly.

"If I'm to spend the rest of my life as Malin Farrow's wife, I have to expect *some* degree of nonsense from the press no matter where I am."

Lenora and Parsimony both relaxed just a little, their shoulders sliding down a degree while they exchanged a glance. Red-headed Selma alone remained tense, and I wondered if she had already managed to read the paper—if she was perhaps the source for the others.

"That *is* the unfortunate truth," agreed Kalypso, "but, come on...don't tell us *everything* was fiction."

"I don't have much of a taste for infants, if you're looking for recipes."

While Lenora laughed and loosened more, Kalypso cast her a smiling glance.

"Oh, nobody *really* believes that rot"—Selma glanced away and sipped her drink at this comment of Kalypso's, peering through the crowd—"but *that's* not what we mean." The duke's sister suddenly brightened, her face flushing as she peered over my shoulder and then all around the room. "You didn't bring him with you, did you? Eleison, that bodyguard of yours?"

"Wh—oh"—I blushed brightly, relaxing a little, myself— "no, no. He didn't want to cause a fuss. There's plenty of security here tonight, anyway."

Her lower lip protruding in a dramatic pout, Kalypso mimed wiping tears from her cheek. "But I wanted to see him in the flesh! Oh, he looks so *fine* in photos. Is it true?"

Playing dumb, I asked, "Is what true?"

With an annoyed glance toward her girlfriends, the duke's sister caught me by the wrist and dragged me close. Her friends, even Selma, pressed in, and at once we were a tight little circle in the middle of a forgotten ball.

"Is it *true*," asked Kalypso in a breathless whisper, "that your husband lets you—*use* him? That Eleison fellow?"

What a strange turn of phrase! It was another moment where I was struck by the differences in our stations, and the perception most of my peers had of my mate. How would we overcome that? "Eleison and I *are* lovers," I told them flatly, "yes—and Malin is supportive."

While the women exchanged a series of glances and excited noises—a birdlike chorus of "I knew it," "I told you," "So *lucky*"—Kalypso snapped open her fan to briskly cool her face.

"Do they—participate with one another?"

"Well…" Seeing the very real fascination in their faces, I decided that the truth was certainly better than letting a bunch of nonsense float around. If they wanted to gossip, let them have something *real* to gossip about.

"I think Eleison is still sometimes a little jealous of my husband," I said as softly as I could, "but they kissed before me just last week, so we'll see."

Kalypso produced a noise like a shriek, which muffled Lenora's gasped question of clarification. Whatever it was, I didn't catch it before Parsimony leapt in. "And Eleison—he's *altered*, isn't he? Those red eyes?"

"Oh—yes, he is."

Lenora sighed. "I've always wanted an altered man...it would never work, though. They always end up realizing they're mated to somebody else. Get ready for heartbreak."

With a light laugh for what she didn't know, I advised her, "I think I'll be all right."

Kalypso leaned closer to me, her voice almost impossibly soft to match her narrowed eyes. "What's it like when he's—you know."

I wasn't sure I did, and narrowed my eyes in return. "When he's what?"

It was like I was sitting across from the duke at breakfast all over again. Apparently, a lurid interest in profane personal details was another common family trait. Her mouth agape for but a second, Kalypso quickly regained control of her features to ask, "You mean you've never—"

In spite of the lewd topic, she actually mouthed in silence the words "had sex," and I bit back laughter.

"—while he's hybridized?"

Goodness gracious! My spine straight as a steel beam, I blushed from my temples to my decolletage. "I—I—well, that is, we—that hadn't *occurred* to me—"

Two of them, Kalypso and Lenora, looked immensely disappointed; Parsimony rolled her eyes and elbowed a relieved looking Selma, telling all her friends, "I *told* you."

"I've actually only even *seen* him in his animal form but twice," I said, clearing my throat, suddenly overwhelmed by images I couldn't banish until I remembered. First those terrible white fangs against a dark muzzle that clamped down on my arm, then the panting of a nearly dead borro as my tears dripped into his fur. My eyes flicked down to the subtle pattern of the scar before I went on to my merry inquisitors, "Anyway, trust me—he's plenty animal enough as a man."

"But"—Kalypso gasped—"isn't he both when it's terrible weather like it's been lately?"

"We've only had one event in Gudrune this month, though it was extreme…and he didn't go out in it, since we've been staying in the city." I bit my lip, reflecting back on Malin's meeting. Hadn't he mentioned something about that? The hybridization phenomenon? "I'm not sure I've ever seen him—split across both aspects like you're describing."

"Oh, *my,* well you simply must keep an eye out for an opportunity and report back to me." Fanning herself again, Kalypso said, "No wonder you told him to stay behind…if he were mine, I'd hate to think of other women looking at him too much. Thecla, dear, would you care to find a stiffer drink with me?"

Another hereditary trait. I looked at my nearly empty flute and smiled at her. "Please, yes—that would be nice."

"Anything for you, ladies?" Kalypso took her friends' orders, then slipped her arm through mine. "We'll be back—come along, Thecla, dear—"

Making our way around through the busy crowd was more effortless than I would have reckoned. I was identified—most often by men, I would add—and those who saw me tended to hurry their spouses or conversational partners out of the path down which Kalypso marched me. I peered around my guide, trying to get a glimpse of the dancers swirling over the center of the floor.

"I *hope* you don't find me crass, but the truth is we've been talking about you half the night anyway, and we're all drunk…it's *bold* of you to show up here even after that article, it really is. If only my brother had made it!"

Hopeful, I asked, "Have you heard from him?"

"Yes, yes, I stopped in and saw him from a safe distance before the party. He's *fine*...just dramatic. One small ailment and he insists on holding court like a dying king. That's what happens when you travel, though...especially if you spend as much time *slumming* as he does. Oh!"

Kalypso paused to offer another pout. "I'm sorry, I shouldn't say that. You grew up poor, didn't you?"

I wasn't sure I had ever met anyone who managed to come off as so utterly clueless with a well-meaning sentiment. Maybe it was just the *way* she said it. Managing a smile, I said only, "I'm not from a very important family, no."

"Perhaps that's why you're so easy to talk to, Thecla. You know, here I thought you'd be, oh, I don't know—stuffier, given the way Malin is. Then again, I only met him once, and I was much younger. Fourteen or fifteen. I barely remember him, though I was surprised to find him charming enough. One pictures a warlord somewhat differently."

With a quick flick of her eyes around, her mouth sloping in an ironic way, Kalypso asked in a self-consciously wry tone, "He's not *really* a dharmine, is he?"

For what felt like the thousandth time in the past week, I said, "No, he's not," and wondered why it didn't feel like the complete truth.

"I never really *thought* he was. Why would my brother be so fond of him, after all? Still, the way people *persist* in that..." Laughing, then looking at me with new, shrewd curiosity, Kalypso stepped close to me again.

"But...one thing that I've heard that *wasn't* in the article, Thecla..."

I braced myself for anything, but was still unprepared when, eyes bright, she went on.

"Is it true you have a magic mirror you use to consort with evil spirits?"

My mouth fell open.

Vividly, I remembered chastising the dharmine in the privacy of my Saalast suite—only to run almost face-first into Brea.

Brea, looking at me queerly, almost fearfully, when she left the gossip-prone duke in the game room.

And now, the duke's even less discreet sister—asking me this.

I was going to fire that girl.

"Of course not," I said with a dry laugh, daring Kalypso to challenge me. Yet, angry to have my confidence violated, and tired of these pestering questions, and frustrated by this new perception of my character, I decided to amuse myself.

"I don't need a mirror to consort with spirits." I stared into Kalypso's eyes with my best emulation of the dead-eyed, distant expression Malin adopted when he was clearly thinking about killing someone he hated. "They come to me while I weave my tapestries, you see, and I send them out on errands for me. As for the tapestries themselves…I don't envy those who cross my mind while I'm at work upon them."

I was so busy savoring Kalypso's amazed, slightly frightened expression—her calculating eyes wildly searching my face, unable to decide how serious I was or wasn't—I didn't realize someone had stopped behind me until the tap came upon my shoulder.

Torn from my satisfaction, I turned with bleak displeasure for the intrusive means of getting my attention.

And my eyes met Glenn's.

21

HIS BEARD HAD been neatened with a trim, and the dark chocolate curls of his hair had been tamed back with a comb and some product or other—but Glenn Stone could never hide the intensity of his eyes, the inviting blue warmth of a lake in summer.

"Thecla," he said while they swept openly over me, his hand extending to take the one I offered. "You look—irresistible."

Blushing, laughing despite my mixed feelings to see him, I looked back at Kalypso to find she had traded her shock for a jealous pout. "*And* you're friends with Glenn Stone?"

"I don't know." I arched a brow at him. "*Are* we friends?"

Glenn's neat white teeth flashed against his beard while he laughed. "I was going to ask for a dance," he said in good humor, releasing me, "but maybe I'd better stay back."

With a small sniff and a glance at the duke's sister, I decided between my present options without much hesitation. "No," I said quickly, "a dance would be wonderful. I'm sure I'll see you later, Kalypso. It was nice meeting you."

I almost thanked her for her insight into the indiscretion of my maid. Instead, I finished my champagne, put the empty glass in her automatically receptive (then somewhat flustered) hand, and slipped my arm around Glenn's. "Shall we?"

With a nod to Kalypso, Glenn led me through the line of people watching from the edges of the dance floor and swept me out into the waltz at the first opportunity.

Suffice it to say, I was grateful for Malin's dancing lessons. He had kept them up several times a week ever since proposing to me, just an hour or so before Charlotte's attention began to wane to other priorities than piano playing…and before Malin's attention turned from mere waltzing. But, until those moments of collapse, he had taught me to be a good dancer. Well enough that, with a swift glance down my dress under guise of investigating our movements across the floor, Glenn said, "You're light on your feet."

"And you're smoother than I would have expected."

He smiled in a self-consciously cheeky way that was painfully handsome, or would have been if not for my suspicion he had sold me out to the tabloid. "I'm just a little drunk," he admitted while I laughed. "Sorry…I should lay off, I know you're married."

"It's all right," I told him, maybe too quickly. His hand around mine, so big and warm, tightened in response, and I flushed. "I mean—that is, I wouldn't think it's my marriage that puts you off."

He scoffed. "What do you mean?"

"I mean that my—relationship with my footman, or perhaps my footman himself, seemed quite distasteful to you."

"Oh. Well…look—"

Glenn twirled me in an almost instinctive way with the beat of the song, and my heart raced to move so easily at his direction.

"For one thing, I know where I'm not wanted." He spoke when he once more had my waist in the guiding hook of his broad arm. "As for his…condition…"

The hunter lowered his voice. His head bent toward mine when half a twirl left us back to front, his arm around the lower half of my bodice. The skin beneath my exposed ear, accessible to his mouth, dimpled with pleasure.

"I don't have anything against altered as *people*, okay?"

"That isn't what I've heard."

"Yeah," he said in gruff irritation, his hot breath on my sensitive flesh provoking the goosebumps to spread down my neck, "well, you've heard wrong. The people who choose to undergo the procedure are making a mistake, but they're not bad people."

Thinking to myself that Eleison probably would have agreed with that sentiment, I said with only the slightest turn of my head, "But not everyone gets to choose."

"That's exactly my point," he said, glancing sharply away. Not at someone or something, but simply away. I had the strange intuition that he had been about to kiss my bare shoulder; then he looked back, a haunted caste to his eyes, and I wondered if he hadn't really felt the urge.

"The problem is with the procedure, with the company, with the way Gudrune funnels riftborn into it and other programs against their wills. Look—I read about your incident with Sigma

Corporation." Glenn whirled me around in another elegant turn. We once more faced each other to speak. Dizzy, I sank my fingers into his hard shoulder and tried not to marvel at his taut muscles. "I know you know they're not all they're cracked up to be. As for your boyfriend—"

"Eleison," I told him.

"Right. When he showed up, I, uh, obviously figured I was encroaching. Leaving had nothing to do with him as a person. I respect him for saving me, and I respected that he didn't want me there at that moment."

Again I was twirled, and when I was stopped we were side by side. "And it really *doesn't* bother you, does it? Are you sure?"

"No," he confessed, glancing over at the wedding band on my hand as he held it high to guide me, still dancing, from the floor, "it absolutely does bother me. It—frightens me for you, Thecla."

His expression grew pained as he consulted my face. At the very least, his eyes softened and his cheekbones and mouth went rigid in distress.

"It makes me feel like you need somebody to protect you."

"Eleison is *very* protective of me," I assured him as we slipped back into the disordered crowd.

Glenn snorted and released my hand. "I can tell. Well—don't let me keep you from the ball. Sorry if you got a bad impression of me before…have a nice night—"

"Wait."

I caught his arm before he could step away, and he looked back at me with surprise—and unapologetic desire. A new smoke filled the blue eyes that searched my face for my intentions.

"I actually hate parties," I said. "Do you want to go somewhere else with me?"

He looked around. "Where?"

I wasn't sure why, but the only peaceful place I could imagine flashed through my mind. "Go through those glass doors over there and wait for me on the edge of the patio...I'm going to get us a drink."

"Are you sure Eleison's not going to break my nose when he sees us leaving the party to take a walk?"

"He might, if he were here," I confessed with a light laugh that came off much more nervous than intended, "but I would hope he had the good taste not to...anyway, he didn't want to come. It was just—too much of a scandal."

With a fleeting look of something like sympathy, Glenn said, "That must be miserable. Sorry."

"Oh, it's torture. Anyway, go on—I'll be right there."

While Glenn headed off at one angle, I followed the wall through the crowd and let the people move around me. Soon enough, I found the bar. The bartender at the end, a tall bald man, looked at me with a smile that suddenly changed. He knew who I was, and it made him nervous.

Perfect.

"I need a bottle of wine and two glasses, if you could."

His only question was, "White or red, Madame Farrow?"

"Red, please. Don't open it, just give me a corkscrew."

"With pleasure, Madame. One moment—"

With two glasses perilously held by their stems, the opener twisted in a finger of the opposite hand, and that hand's thumb tight around the neck of the bottle, I ignored every stare on way out the back doors. The facade had been lit up to impress the guests and make things feel more comfortable, but farther away from the building, darkness fell across the perfect lawn.

At its edge stood Glenn, stroking his beard while he contemplated not the glamorous facade admired by others, but the shadows across the utilitarian garden.

"Would you help me," I said, getting his attention and earning a slight laugh of surprise. After hurrying to take a glass and the bottle from my hands, Glenn followed with his eyes but did not comment as I slid the corkscrew into his tuxedo's breast pocket.

"There, thank you...come on," I urged him, leading on into the darkness, "let's go."

"To where?"

"A preferable atmosphere."

Intrigued, Glenn looked between me and the building before stepping off the patio and upon the lawn. "People are going to get the wrong idea."

"Oh, that ship left the dock ages ago." While he laughed at the derision of my tone, I told him, "I guess you didn't see that awful tabloid that came out today...and you probably didn't talk to any journalists about me, either."

His laughter falling short, he said, "No—I didn't."

"Well, that lifts my spirits...trust me, you'll see what I'm talking about soon enough. My point, anyway, is that these idiots are going to say and think whatever they want. I'd might as well do what *I* want and damn the consequences. Trust me, being accused of an affair with you would be, if anything, a slight improvement upon my current public record."

"I'm sorry to hear you're being dragged through the mud, Thecla. I don't know you, really, but I can tell you don't deserve it."

"Thank you," I said, gratified, peering into the darkness

and re-aligning our direction. "It's funny to see you here, though—especially after meeting on the train. Did the Overseer invite you?"

"Yeah. She has some work for me, though I'm still not sure I'm ready for anything intensive yet. Frankly…between you and me, I'm tempted to retire."

"It's nice you have the option. Do you work in the countryside, or mostly in the city?"

"I go where the guild sends me," he explained. "It's mostly small places like Lescaut. Areas that have had a bad Event or are just generally overwhelmed—maybe they've lost their best local hunter in an accident, or the sheriffs think their deputies need training, or…you name it."

"I see. I suppose Valquist has infrastructure like Saalast… I've never seen such efficiency. It really feels safer living in the city—from the Rift Events, anyway."

"Until the power goes out for days on end." While I sighed and nodded, he confessed, "I don't mean to insult your homeland, but that sort of thing is why I wanted to leave Gudrune."

"I suppose the power never goes out in Valquist?"

"Oh, it does…but, I don't know. The people of Gudrune really seem more unstable somehow."

"Are you implying that's because altered are allowed to roam more or less freely there?"

"Maybe that's one of the reasons," he admitted. "People get unstable immediately after the procedure if they're not given proper care."

"Wait," I commanded, "let me guess another—oh, you're about to blame my husband somehow! I'm a mind-reader, aren't I?"

Despite himself, Glenn permitted a crooked grin through the dark. "Well, I was debating with myself whether to bring him up...but, since you did—a lot of money Malin could have put into infrastructure thirty years ago went to the military, instead."

"And whose fault was that? It was the Overseer who invaded *him* and prolonged what could have been a swift takeover of Azstoria."

"It was never going to be swift. People were dying, and there was more to Parvati's intercession than that. Malin had some dangerous ideas, and he was doing dangerous things without considering the consequences."

My nose wrinkled, I demanded in annoyance, "Do you even know what those things are?"

"Do *you*?"

"I think I have an idea. In fact, he *was* putting money into the infrastructure of Gudrune—but Parvati interfered with his efforts at energy research." I gestured over my shoulder, toward the palace and the Overseer within. "She made sure he couldn't spend any more on it by forcing him to waste his resources on a war."

""Energy research,"" repeated Glenn. "You know what kind of energy research he was doing, Thecla?"

"I don't see any reason why studying the Rift would be more harmful than accepting its consequences as a given. And if it can even *help* us, why, then—"

"We can't know that for a fact...and the risks are more complicated." Glenn squinted through the dark as the kennels and the growling, grumbling beasts within began to distinguish themselves. "I'm not sure I fully understand it, myself...you'll probably have to ask Parvati if you want details. Where are we?"

"Someplace where we can drink without anyone bothering us." Although I was tempted to stop by the cage of that darling little ertiz and pet it through the bars, I didn't want to excite the luptichs that already smelled us on the wind. Instead I stopped a few yards from the keeper's office and sat upon the grass in a plume of fabric. Glenn winced.

"Are you sure you want to sit on the ground while you're wearing that?"

"It's only grass...don't worry about the dress. Just open that bottle, please, I'm thirsty..."

Soon enough, Glenn had popped the cork and filled our glasses, then sat by my side in the dark. Together we watched the golden facade, so bright it seemed like a painting illuminated upon a dark velvet wall, until I raised my head toward the sky.

I frowned.

"You can't see a single star here."

"You can't in Saalast, either."

Shoulders sagging, I swirled my wine and agreed, "I hate it—that part of it. There's so much else to commend the city that I don't even notice it; or, when I notice, there's enough else happening that I don't seem to mind. But here...I don't know. Valquist is so lovely. It seems the sky should sparkle over it."

"I guess I can see what you mean. It must be sort of overwhelming to be in these cities after you grew up in a place like Lescaut."

"It certainly was at first...sometimes it still is." With a soft laugh, I remembered the fear that had gripped me to leave my childhood home behind. "Goodness, when I learned I was being sent to Malin, I was petrified!"

"You were *sent* to him? I wondered how you ended up together...it didn't make sense."

"What's that supposed to mean?"

"I just mean—you're obviously gorgeous and smart, but why you?"

Flushed by his easy praise, I sipped my wine to clear my thoughts. "I ask myself the same thing all the time. Malin was looking for a rarity, a—" I stumbled over my slight lie, though Glenn didn't notice. "A riftborn to bring into his service. Somehow, that person ended up being *me*."

I inhaled the bouquet, sharp and bitter black, rising from the glass. "I'm very lucky," I settled for saying, smiling to myself. "I'm lucky I was born where I was, when I was. I'm lucky that I look like I do, and that my father raised me to speak well, and that he took such care in my education. Sometimes, I lie in bed thinking about what might have happened if even one of those things were not true. If I had met Malin and not been so pleasing to him." I shuddered at the thought, saying before another, longer sip of wine, "I don't like to think about it."

"And you're really happy," he asked in a tone a vague disbelief.

"Of course! I love Malin, oh, terribly. And *terribly* really is the word. It rips at my insides when I think of him."

Now it was Glenn's turn to indulge in his wine for a second too long. "I'm not sure I'll ever be able to understand that," he said when he'd swallowed.

"What—love?"

"No, not *that*. I mean—" He hesitated, assessing me through the dark before deciding he could ask his question without consequence. "How *old* is Malin by now?"

Laughing a little, I asked, "Does his age bother you?"

"Does it bother *me* that *you're* in a relationship with a guy old enough to be your father? No. Doesn't bother me. It's none of my business."

"Yet here you are, commenting on it anyway… If you *must* know, Malin is thirty years older than me."

Glenn literally choked on his wine, leaning forward to avoid coughing stains onto his tuxedo's white shirt. "*Thirty*," he exclaimed, wiping his lips on the back of his hand.

"Yes, Glenn, I can tell it doesn't bother you in the slightest…"

"I just mean—that's pretty substantial." His eyebrows knitting before one lowered to counter the other's arch, he interrogated on, "Do you two even have anything to *talk* about?"

"Of course we do! All kinds of things." A bit offended, I snatched the bottle precariously leaning against the bell of my gown. "I'm not some brainless *nitwit*, you know. If you could talk to me about something other than my husband or my mate for five seconds, maybe you'd remember that."

Like he'd been slapped, Glenn straightened up and lowered his eyes to the glass I topped off. When I extended the bottle toward him, he said, "I know you're not a brainless nitwit, Thecla. That's why I can't figure out what you're doing with Malin—or how you can be with Malin and be happy."

"Sometimes I don't think Malin understands it, either," I confessed with a laugh. "I just hope that someday he'll believe my love completely… But, I suppose you're right, in that I do have to *prove* my love more than I think a woman his age would. At least, that's how I feel about it. Sometimes I think he's waiting for me to grow out of our relationship, or something like that."

Or he was waiting for me to discover some truth that might shake it…but nothing could, I was sure. Even when spending time with a man unaffiliated with Malin—and in fact, exactly the type of man Malin feared would whisk me away—my longing for my husband grew stronger than ever. My free hand trailed over the edges of my necklace once I set the bottle down again.

"He doesn't see himself how I see him, though. Nobody does. The whole continent has this idea of a Malin that barely exists for me—a Malin so different from the one I know that he'd might as well be a different person."

Compelled by the freedom offered in a confession to a near-stranger, I abruptly related, "When I was on my honeymoon with Malin, I even had a dream about that. I dreamt that there was a bloody chamber at the bottom of the stairs"—no point in confessing it was real—"and in the back of it was a secret door... and behind the door were more corridors than I could possibly navigate, all pitch-black. There was a second Malin there...a feral one. The dharmine everyone says he is."

Entranced by the memory, my hand slid up from my necklace to rest along the column of my neck. A smile kissed the edges of my lips while I gazed into the darkness.

"Yet, in that dream, this second Malin—he was *thrilled* to see me. He held me with such passion, such tenderness, and spoke to me as though he were on the cusp of weeping just to be near me. I was afraid—but even that more frightening Malin craved me. Craved to be near me."

My lip disappearing between my teeth, I glanced over to find Glenn watched me with those marvelous, sad eyes. "Love isn't about what people *deserve*, is it? It's like anything else in life...it happens to us, through us, regardless of whatever else is true."

"I guess so. Still—"

I raised my eyebrows at his hesitance, spurring him on to say, "If Malin were in a different position—less wealthy, less secure—would you still love him?"

"Oh yes," I said quickly, then slowing down to think it through in a critical way. "Yes. But of course, because we're ourselves, it's hard to see what else we would be in a hypothetical world like that. How would he have found me then? How would we be together? What would I be? What about him? Who knows how infinitely the variables could express themselves...but, if he were a humbler man and we had come upon one another in some way in the world, then yes. I'm sure we would still feel this passionately. Actually—"

I laughed guiltily, peering into my wine glass.

"Sometimes I *wish* he were a humbler man. It would be so much easier and safer in some ways...harder in others, of course. I'm not so far out of touch already that I don't know how hard it is, how frightening it is, to work for a living that barely seems like enough for one to exist. Like a carpet that's so small it consists of a path from your door to your bed and nowhere else in the world. But...well—"

The wine wobbled with the stinging of my eyes. Chastising myself, I stared up at the starless sky. "It's really difficult to—to just *be* when it seems like half the continent wishes your husband would die."

Glenn sighed the hefty sigh of a man who had been called out for something he couldn't deny.

"Your husband is—"

"I don't want to hear it."

"All right."

Grateful, I kept blinking away my tears. The knot in my throat wasn't sorrow, though.

It was rage.

"I don't really think I'm so bad, you know? Or, I didn't

used to—but, Glenn, I suppose I must be. Don't you think I must be?"

"I don't know, Thecla."

I looked at him in surprise, having expected some empty-headed rebuff because that was what people automatically did. But, with genuine thought, looking at me in a clear-eyed contemplation that made me somehow afraid he could see into my mind, Glenn admitted his own complex feelings on the matter.

"I'll say that life is more complicated than good and bad. But…I do think that, to really love someone, there has to be some—common thread. Some spirit that's shared between the two people involved…or three," he added with a teasing quirk of his bearded mouth. I laughed, lightly slapping him in the arm and savoring the dangerous heat of the contact while my hand bounced away. As he went on, his smile faded again.

"The way I see it, there are three possibilities…one, Malin forced you into marriage, and you're a good actress; two, you seduced Malin into marriage to enjoy a powerful life; or, three, you really do love Malin, which means you two must have something in common."

"So in other words," I summarized, a little hurt by the speculation but understanding that he barely knew me, "you think I'm either a victim, a scheming little gold-digger manipulating an aging widower, or as wicked as you all believe my husband."

He spread his hands. I scoffed, taking a great swallow of wine while ruminating upon the lessons of the dharmine. My head was floating with the alcohol by then, and my tongue wagged freely beneath the pressure of my still erotically inclined thoughts.

"If you *really* want to know what it is that Malin and I have so uniquely in common, outside of our taste in art and poetry and books and plays, and music, and *much* else besides—he likes to whip me before he makes love to me. And, oh!" My hand trailed over my heart, resting there above my breast while I sighed. "Few men have a caress as sweet as Malin's lash."

When I looked over at Glenn, I had adjusted to the darkness well enough that I swear I made out a sudden ruddy tone to the cheeks above his beard. "He whips you—and you want him to?"

"*Yes!* Oh, just talking about it! I miss him so...he's so creative. We play all kinds of bizarre games together. I don't know where he gets them, but they're always so *fun. He's* fun." I laughed to hear myself say it, adding, "Unexpectedly fun, given how much time he spends working...but maybe that's why."

Though his eyebrows had lowered from their animated height, Glenn still looked at me in a new way. "Well...I guess that *would* be something in common."

"To say the least. I don't know that Eleison cares for it, but he's starting to open himself to certain *ideas*, as it were, so we'll see...this wine is strong, isn't it?"

Serious Glenn's stony facade cracked into laughter. While his head ducked to hide the sound, I laughed, myself, and demanded, "What is it?"

"Nothing! Nothing, it's just—you have an interesting way about you. I saw you, you know. At that festival."

"Oh, *no* you didn't—"

"Yeah," he swore, "I did. It was impossible to miss you next to Malin. This was back before anybody knew you existed, so I didn't really think about it. I just saw this—this woman, like a beautiful bird, sitting there with *him*. You didn't look happy. I remember thinking, "Poor thing.""

My smile fell as I was concretely reminded of the festival.

To be reminded of Glenn's profession was one thing, but his involvement in that awful blood sport—

"I was unhappy at the time because we were in an ugly place at the behest of an ugly man, a doctor who was a substantial sponsor of the festival and had access to a private box. How you can demean yourself by participating in such vile cruelties is beyond me. It's one thing to kill an animal. Another to—"

"I know," Glenn said softly, his eyes downcast, his jaw tight. "I hate Toreas, too."

"Then why were you *part* of one?"

"Because, like I said before, when the guild assigns me someplace, I don't have a choice. That includes tasks like Torea Festivals…Winston requested me specifically."

"Winston—he runs the Gudrune chapter of the Hunter's guild, doesn't he? Malin told me about him once."

"Yeah. Called me in, gave me a place to stay…paid for my rehab out of his own pocket. Even wanted to know if I thought I'd be in fighting shape for a comeback next year."

"What did you say?"

Glenn spread his hand. "I said we'd see."

"Don't tell him *that*," I urged, bristling. "You were nearly *killed!* Since you hate it so much, tell him to find someone else! If you're as skillful as they say, it would be against their interests to force you. They'd ought to respect your wishes."

Again, annoying me, he gave a slight laugh and topped off his wine. "I can tell that's what *you* would do…I really am starting to think I had the wrong impression of you, Thecla."

"I may be an orphan, but I'm not some helpless waif—ah!"

When he extended the bottle and its last half a glass toward me, I tipped my vessel to receive it—but he, having poured with the initial position in mind, managed to splash it across my hand and over the bodice of the dharmine's mystical dress.

"Shit," Glenn hissed, scrambling to set the bottle and glass some feet away while he found his handkerchief. "Thecla, I'm sorry—"

"It's all right, don't worry—"

"If you're quick—maybe get some water, and—"

The white silk was in his hand, and hardly thinking, he blotted it against my bosom before chasing the stain down the waist of my bodice.

I caught his hand with my free one and pressed it to my heated side.

"Glenn," I whispered, "it's all right."

His eyes, their edge of panic fading, searched my face.

While his free hand raised to fit his thumb along my jaw, he tipped his head forward and kissed me.

Oh, Lord! Kissing Glenn was so different—differently wonderful from a kiss with Malin, and altogether more differently wonderful from a kiss with Eleison. A mortal man without title or exorbitant wealth, Glenn was mindful of how easily a boundary could be overstepped and never re-offered. His kiss, therefore, began with slow, tender caution, and only gained intensity when the enthusiastic trailing of my tongue pleaded to be let in past his lip.

The hand upon my waist slid around to my back. He pulled me close, his free hand plucking the wine glass from me. While his mouth turned away for a quick breath, he put it beside his, then turned toward me again.

A raw, almost pained look of passion had come upon him.

"I think you've had enough to drink," he chided me, adding, "and so have I."

"Drink doesn't have anything to do with it," I whispered back, my arms folding around his ink-stained neck, my legs contorting the dress with their operation.

When he felt my slipper, Glenn inhaled. My dress draping over his legs, I straddled his hips and reflected that, really, I sat in his lap naked at this very moment. The clothing from the Rift didn't exist. Not even the lingerie it had provided, the sole barrier between my body and Glenn's trousers, had any basis in reality.

Searching his face, gasping to feel his interest strain beneath me, I trailed my hand through his dark curls and whispered, "You didn't see that vile tabloid yet, Glenn…oh, it's terrible. It accuses me of all manner of things…witchcraft…sex magick…orgies…"

Between phrases—then, gradually, between words—I placed kisses at the corner of his beard, over his cheek, then carefully along the ridge of his ear. "By that standard, there's nothing wrong with a few fondly meant kisses from my new friend."

Glenn looked like he wanted to agree—his lips certainly parted like he was about to—but the scream interrupted us.

"Get up," he shouted, shoving me from his lap and urging me, his hands on my hips, into a standing position that had me stumbling uncertainly away.

The next ten seconds were so chaotic I could barely follow what happened at the time. Glenn shot to his feet and had turned even before something thundered at us from the dark.

A luptich, I realized, a little stunned. I even thought I recognized it.

That lock had surely been destroyed when the animal was agitated by the ertiz of Parvati's stunt. Paling, I put a hand upon Glenn's arm—to do what, I still don't know. Perhaps urge him away or alert him to the threat, as if he had not been the one to notice it. With an effortless instinct, he raised that same arm high before me, sweeping it back to shove me far behind him as he met the beast shoe-first.

While the well-aimed sole connected with the luptich's snout, someone called from a distance. A good thing we were seen. I was too stunned to shout for help and stood nearby, ready to spring away but unable to leave Glenn in case the beast truly got the better of him. The luptich stumbled back several feet, its head shaking off the blow, its ears twitching.

"Just back off," Glenn told the animal in a terse tone, as though it could listen to him.

Unfortunately, it could not.

Its senses restored after a few seconds, the luptich bared its lesser fangs and raised its head in a snarl. The rumbling ended in that infamously terrible scream of female anguish that had lured so many well-meaning hunters to their deaths. Now taking it personally, the creature lunged again.

Even unarmed, Glenn was better equipped to meet this predator than most any other hunter since the beginning of the Rift.

The tip of his shoe hooking beneath the bottle, Glenn kicked the impromptu weapon into the air and caught it before it got far. The luptich closed the distance, snarling in a fury as it did. This time it reached with one paw, as it had when it slapped the hapless ertiz.

And, much as the ertiz had then, so did the luptich howl and whine when the bottle smashed to pieces against the force of its claw. Shards cut through its thin coat of fur and left deep gashes that oozed purplish blood upon the earth while it stumbled back. Glenn dropped the jagged neck of the bottle, though I was only half-conscious of his decision to remove his jacket.

One of the whizzing carts used by the Overseer and her security grew increasingly loud. Limping a few steps back, the luptich roared—then whirled toward me, eager to vent its rage upon a more helpless target.

Glenn was quicker. Not unlike the keeper that very day, he found a vantage and waited for the luptich's lunge. At the least coiling of its muscles, the hunter sprang forward, unafraid, the fabric of his jacket a hood for the snarling animal's dangerous head. The blinded luptich flailed its limbs into space rather than at me, and its efforts to twist back or wrench itself around and slash open Glenn's belly were especially for naught: Glenn used his knees, his strangling impromptu hood, and every pound of force in his body to wrestle the lion-sized animal down to the ground before me.

By the time security parked and stumbled up with their tranquilizer guns, the bleeding beast had already admitted defeat.

T HAT BLASTED LUPTICH. Its interruption resembled the cruelly contrived manipulation of a frustrating dream, but nothing could be done. Curious about the commotion, partygoers followed the security staff who collected the animal and apologized to me. A bevvy of people gathered around Glenn to hear about the struggle. As those same people studiously avoided acknowledging me, I was now separated from him by an impassible throng.

Our eyes met. I traced the track of an imaginary tear down my cheek, then blew him a kiss and turned away.

"Thecla—"

His call above the crowd interrupted its several babbled conversations. I looked back to find him shoving his way through them with a muttered, "Excuse me," until they realized with disappointment their hero wasn't in the mood to impress them.

When he stood before me, it was with a glance down at my hand. As if resisting the impulse to touch it.

"I don't know how much longer you're here," Glenn said, now drinking in my face. "But, if you do need to talk about... anything, or if there's something I can do for you...I live on the canal, just in sight of the Hunter's Guild if you look from the alley between myself and my neighbor's house. I don't know *what* I can do for you, but—I don't know."

His words had dropped to a breathless, almost mystified sort of whisper.

"I look at you, and I see a woman I want to save. Then, I talk to you...and...."

"And?"

"And I wonder if you're not the type of woman I need saving from."

Unable to help myself, I smiled the sort of smile that made Malin look his most deliciously, playfully wicked.

"Glenn...can't you tell? Whatever I want, Malin lets me have. Just think what will happen when I tell him that I want *you*."

A small but notable shudder rushed through Glenn while his eyes flickered over me, from the hem of my dress to the stain upon my bodice to the white bosom swelling from it.

Then, again, my eyes, which he met with the tightening of his jaw against our mutual craving for a kiss.

"Good night, Thecla," he said, ducking his head to regain the will to pass me by. "Thank you for the dance."

While his hands slid into his pockets, Glenn stepped off with his head raised toward the glowing palace. I watched him go, pained somehow.

Glenn! He was a fine one to talk of deceiving first impressions. I had thought anyone involved in Torea Festivals must have been very cruel, but the truth couldn't have been further. Glenn was concerned for me in a way that was deeply touching. He saw that innocent part of me that Valquist couldn't.

And there he was, about to make his way home past scores of newsstands all plastered with my image.

My source of pleasure having gone, a dark cloud passed over me. The reality of the tabloid's existence cut into my heart.

Mouth tight, I raised my hem a few inches and made my way back into the party.

I tried to, anyway.

On the edge of the patio's sea of lights, I stopped. "It's already half-past eleven," lamented somebody who smoked with a group in a corner. "I'd better go soon, I have a meeting tomorrow…"

From there, I scanned the glass windows that revealed a ballroom aswirl with activity. All these people, talking and laughing about things in a world that was somehow apart from mine. All this activity, this community, poised to exclude me no matter my import.

About to turn away to take a long walk around the building and find another, quieter entrance by which I could slip back to my room, I paused when Parvati's familiar contralto enthused, "*There* you are— Oh, what's happened?"

Her eyes were on the stain. I spread my hands in helplessness. "You caught me…there was an accident involving a luptich. I was just going to sneak back to my room before anybody saw me in this condition."

"You're *leaving*? Already? But you've hardly been here an hour!"

"Well, this dress. And—I must admit, Parvati—"

I met her eye, letting her see just how humorless I felt. The duke was right—I didn't need anybody's permission to be angry. Not when someone like Glenn, who had no love for my husband, could see me so clearly.

He proved there was no excuse for the way I was being characterized.

"I really have been affected by that ugly article today." Parvati's face fell as I confided in her, the soft light of genuine compassion illuminating her eyes. Whatever Eleison thought of her, she was no more pleased by the tabloid's story than I was. She had not leaked the details, either. "Even at this ball you've thrown to greet me, nobody wants to talk to me unless it's for gossip. I thought the people of Valquist were supposed to be pleasant. You know—for as cruelly as everyone speaks of Gudrune and my husband, neither one has ever made me feel so *bad* about myself."

"Thecla…"

There was something new in Parvati's face when she looked at me, but I couldn't place it until a vision of my stepmother flashed before my inner eye. Pity—a strange kind of maternal pity for young women. A world-wearied remembrance of feelings long-since eliminated.

"I'm sorry your visit so far hasn't worked out the way I hoped it would," Parvati summarized. "Maybe tomorrow—"

"When will I be permitted to return home, exactly?"

"Well, the next train for Gudrune departs in three more days, but I was hoping you'd stay on for another week and let me show you a few of the surrounding territories. Doesn't sound like that's in the cards anymore?"

"I'm sorry. I have been quite disappointed, and I'd prefer to be at home with my husband."

Parvati sighed, her own disappointment visible. "I understand. *Think* about staying, anyway. But, whatever you choose to do, let me know."

"I believe I just did."

Now she managed a smile again: small and thin. Whatever she wanted to say, she reserved it for herself.

"I hope your night improves, Thecla," she told me, turning away to head inside and instantly beaming for whomever caught her eye.

Three more days.

As I released a low breath, my heart flew.

Three days! I could bear that. There was no doubt in my mind that I could grit my teeth for three more little days. Two and a half, really, depending what she meant. Why, as early as the train departed from Gudrune, it would probably be more like *two*!

Yes. I could stand that. I could stand that so well that giddy excitement overtook me, the road home suddenly clear.

Heart pumping, I slipped around the building a long way until, encountering a security guard, I was brought through a side entrance and permitted to return to my quarters on my own once I recognized the foyer to which I had been shepherded. The young concierge who had announced me recognized me, and still smiled and nodded politely as he had before; but there seemed a new sparkle in it, a new, more genuine note that made me beam back. We were both at the end of a long night and looking forward to home.

Home again! Home again in two small days.

Pity it was so soon after meeting Glenn.

What was I thinking? Forget what I was thinking. What had I *done*?

All the familiar feelings from the past year came rushing up, and so much worse this time—why, why could I not be satisfied by *three* men?—but I discovered, also, a curious new ease in bandying them away.

After all…why did I need to be satisfied with *any* number of men? Didn't most men fritter away their lives "chasing skirts," as it's been put? Hadn't my very own husband been a notorious rake throughout much of his life?

And didn't he, who kept so much from me, seem to enjoy it when I confessed infidelity to him, fictional or otherwise?

By the time I sat upon the edge of my bed, it was twenty till midnight and everything was just as the dharmine had promised. The room sat empty; and, when I slid my shoe from my foot, its partner disappeared along with the dress. It all evaporated in a violet haze, curling from my body and into the ceiling like ordinary smoke. I marveled, though as my eye followed the color of the fading radiation, my headache's persistent throb worsened. With a cringe, I looked away, picked up my pocket watch, and called my husband with my stomach tightened in fear.

"There you are! I wasn't sure you'd be up to talking today."

"Oh—Malin—"

Hearing his voice for the first time since discovering that awful newspaper was too much for me. I burst into tears, drunk and ashamed and miserable with my steady headache.

"Darling, darling—oh, no, angel. Don't cry while I'm not there."

"I'm sorry, Malin—"

"You *can* cry, I just wish—oh, Thecla."

"Did Eleison tell you about it?"

"Yes, darling, he told me all about it. Don't worry, all right? Everyone will forget it by tomorrow morning."

I thought he meant that hyperbolically—that soon the public's focus would turn to something else. Sniffing, I wiped my nose on a handkerchief I remembered too late was charcoal-stained, then went to rinse in the sink

"In three days, anyway, when I've left this blasted town—I've negotiated my release, Malin. I'm tired of it here."

"Oh!"

The singular noise emanating from my watch was so bright, so hopeful, that I smiled. While I ran the tap and soaked a washcloth, my husband said in barely contained pleasure, "Do you mean it?"

"Of course—I still don't even know why she's *brought* me to this contemptuous place, other than to be made a spectacle of, and…make my*self* a fool. Oh—Malin—"

With a miserable sigh, I pressed the washcloth to my face. "I kissed someone at the ball tonight, darling. I—I don't know what I was thinking, I don't know."

The low vibration of his hum filled the line. "You naughty girl," he remonstrated lightly, racing my heart and heating my loins. As endorphins filled me to realize he wasn't going to divorce me for *this* indiscretion, either, I whisked the device with me while snapping off the lights around the room.

"You don't hate me for it, do you, Malin?"

"Oh, no, of course not…as sexy as you are, as hot and eager in bed, I'm always surprised you don't let more fellows enjoy you. Then again, you deserve to have a high standard. Anyone I would know?"

Letting my embarrassment remain apparent in my voice, I said, "Glenn Stone."

"Oh, Eleison will love that." While I cringed at the thought of having to tell my mate—much worse, I realized, than telling Malin—my husband chuckled. "But, now, that *is* a worthy trophy for your shelf, at least so far as status is concerned. Are you going to let him fuck you, my lovely Madame Farrow?"

Shivering, I confessed as I snapped off the last light, "I—might have thought about it."

"Well…if you do, I hope you'll tell me all about it. Even if I have to thrash the details out of you."

I moaned, my hand moving over my breast. "Master, oh, I'm desperate for a stern beating! I'm desperate for you."

"Less than a week now, though! Oh, thank Heaven…I wasn't sure how I was going to survive another fortnight without you. A week, though—it's still far too long, but it will be over before we know it."

"I *love* you, Malin. Oh, Malin—"

I wanted to ask him about what Parvati had encouraged me to deduce. To ask him just why, exactly, he felt his riftborn nature, if true, was something to be kept from me.

But, when he allowed me every liberty under the sun, it didn't seem right to interrogate him.

"Promise you'll take me to bed the very second I'm home," I begged instead.

"Thecla, my darling…I can't wait to hold you. I can't wait to kiss you. My one true love, whose other loves are my joy to behold in you—I adore you. I'll count every minute. Don't worry about that evil tabloid. I may not be able to do much from a distance, but this is one area I can help us both."

I thought I knew what he meant—that he was talking

around the tabloid man Eleison had targeted. When I hung up with Malin and the time read 11:58, my focus became fully pinned to my mate.

My mate, who was out killing a man while I kissed a famously anti-alteration hunter.

How was this going to go?

The pocket watch glowed in my hand while I lay naked in bed. The little numerals of the digital face slowly shifted.

11:59

12:00

12:01

Just when I thought the dharmine had lied to me, Eleison's whistle echoed so loudly down the hall that I heard it through the shut suite door.

Breath held, I sat up in bed with the covers drawn to my breast. The lock rattled.

The door swung open to spill vibrant yellow light across the dark bed.

"Oops," said Eleison, laughing, a little too loud, "shit, baby, sorry—"

After shutting the door, he asked, "Thought I was being quiet. Did I wake you up?"

That artificial vigor behind his words—he was drunk.

No.

He was *pretending* to be drunk.

"No," I told him, actually drunk, and annoyed he thought he could lie to me, "I've been awake. Are you all right?"

How much more I wanted to ask him right that very minute! If he had been seen, if any noise had been made, if blood had been spilled—but such things were unsafe to press him on, especially before the RMS panel. So long as the dharmine was good to its word, none of that would matter.

Eleison took the question as though it were queer. "What? Sure, baby, I'm fine...just cleared my head by going out for a couple of drinks. There's some all right places here in Valquist... say..."

Having dropped his coat by the door, otherwise fully clothed including his shoes, Eleison slid upon the bed with me. He ignored my protests (despite the wonderful comfort of his weight and warmth through the covers) until they were silenced by the slide of his arms around my waist.

"I was gonna take a quick shower before bed...you want to hop in with me?"

"God, yes," I begged, desperate to be satisfied after having been teased by the dharmine's caresses, the hunter's kisses, then my husband's words. "Yes, Eleison, please—I'm in the mood to be fucked, oh, please—"

An evil grin tilted his mouth. "So you're saying I should tease you tonight."

Throwing my head back with a miserable whine as he got up, I scrambled out from under the covers and pursued in the nude. As he finished turning on the luxurious glass shower that ran along about a quarter of one of the bathroom walls, he turned and saw the state I was in.

He couldn't have looked more sober if he'd tried. There was nothing drunk about the desire that hardened his features at once; nothing loutish or silly. While he drank me in, I walked past him, my hand running along his chest, and stepped into the shower.

I slid into the warming water with a sigh. Eleison's distorted figure undressed on the other side of the glass. A chunk of black gave way to a chunk of white. That submitted quickly to the flesh of his chest. The black of his trousers slid down; the dark blue of his boxers left him, and he was all pale hues with the shadows of hair, the edges of well-defined muscles, the shape of his downright dangerous anatomy obscured by the shower.

Then, he stepped in with me, and shape and color were transmuted into perfect, hardened form.

"Oh"—I sighed as his arms slid around me—"oh, Eleison, I missed you tonight."

"I'm sorry I had to go out, Thecla. I couldn't just stay here doing nothing."

One hand slid into the small of my back while the other fit into my hair, his fingers tangling against my scalp. I slid my hands over his chest, so happy to touch him that nothing else mattered to me in that moment.

"It's all right. I understand. But...I missed you. I get into trouble without you around."

My fingers trailed a few beads of water that raced down his abdomen and along the lines of his most tantalizing muscles. As I reached his adornment, my fingers curled around it to make him inhale. Only then did I admit, "The dharmine came to me..."

His jaw tightened, eyes narrowing in alarm. "Here?"

"Yes...here." My hand working in long, loving strokes of his length while I gazed into his eyes, I told my mate, "It begged to pleasure me. It told me all sorts of interesting things...and it left only to do me a favor."

His hips slowly rocking into my caress, Eleison slipped both hands down to my rear and slowly squeezed. "What kind of favor?"

"Well...it told me a story. About a sulky boy who wanted to avenge the girl he loved. And he told it so well that I was very worried about the boy."

While understanding paled Eleison's features, I released his cock to press body on body.

"So...I asked the dharmine to look after him...to make sure nothing would be left behind, and that the story would have a happy ending."

The shock passing into anger, Eleison grit his teeth. "I didn't want you knowing about that," he said, that low growl rising from his chest. "Thecla—"

"It's all right, Eleison."

"No," he insisted, quickly, sharply, "no, it's not."

"It is, Eleison. It's perfectly all right. You were doing it for me, weren't you? Then I'd *ought* to know. Let my knowledge ease the pain for you."

"I'm not proud."

"And I'm not proud of the dharmine, or its services to me...but—you're not alone anymore, Eleison."

Hearing his own words bandied back to him, his nostrils flared and his eyes shut. I went on, my hand raising to stroke along his cheek before I reached past him to fetch the fresh soap. While I spoke, I developed a lather I applied to his chest with the caresses of my hand.

"I'm happy to take on your burdens. I love you so deeply, oh—Eleison, please, let's share everything. Let's tell each other the truth."

Despite his bleak mood, I smiled.

"Soon," I told him, "I think there really will be a day when there are no more secrets between any of us. Even between Malin and I. And, oh, Eleison…no matter how difficult the path, I can't wait for that."

Though dark and sad, his eyes opened to fix on me.

He bent over me, drawing me up into his arms and tight into his kiss.

Collapsing into his devouring caress, I ran my fingers through his damp hair and clutched his body to mine. "Thanks for making it easy to talk to you," he murmured when we parted for air. I lowered my shoulder to let the water rinse his chest as he went on, "I guess even a parasite has its benefits…sorry you didn't hear it from me, though."

"That's all right. As long as you're safe, I don't care what you need to do. Just promise you'll always come home in one piece, wherever you go."

"Always," he swore without hesitation, pressing me back against the wall to savage my mouth with another long kiss. For its duration, that kiss was all I was. The rest of my body melted away, dissolving into the golden impact of Eleison's mouth upon mine.

As his hand slid down over my rear, my teeth sank into his lip to encourage his thunderous growl.

"Watch what you're starting with that, Thecla…be careful with me tonight."

I ground against him, my stomach sliding against that terrifically turgid weapon between us. "But that's what I *want* from you, Eleison! Please, I would do just anything for you to whip me. For you to take your belt and—"

"I want to do more than that, Thecla." While I trembled beneath the pressure of his gaze, he caught my face with a mighty hand. "Those little games that Malin likes to play with you barely touch the way I feel when I look at you. Especially right now."

I bit my lip.

"Then I'm afraid to say I must confess something else to you, darling, oh—don't hate me, Eleison—"

He searched my face, one dark brow arching.

"The dharmine—it gave me the opportunity to go to the party even though Charlotte was in bed"—Eleison inhaled sharply, his eyes narrowing in an expression of dry displeasure that increased by the second—"and…Glenn Stone happened to be there…"

"If you tell me you fucked him tonight, I might be going to kill a second man."

"No," I said too quickly to ease the crimson fury growing in his eyes. "No, please, Eleison. I didn't…but I did—kiss him."

"Why?"

"Because he was kind, and— "Why?" How can I explain? I don't know. Because I missed Malin, *do* miss Malin. I just want to go home, and Glenn was— Don't be angry, please."

His brooding look had turned from me, focused into some distant space between himself and the wall. "I was trying to explain to him what Malin and I have in common, and one of those things I brought up was our games, and…I don't know, I got myself too excited, and—"

The animal within him showing in his face, his posture, his baring teeth, Eleison slammed off the water. My heart seized in pain while he slipped from the shower and bent to collect his clothes. I hurried out after him, frightened.

"Oh, darling, Eleison. No, please, wait—"

But he wasn't grabbing his clothes. Just snatching something from among them, as I discovered when he grabbed my dripping arm, then straightened with the pocketknife in his other hand.

"I don't think you understand what you're asking for when you beg *me* to be cruel to you, Thecla." While I cried out, then went still in his grip, Eleison raised the knife I was amazed he'd slipped in past security. He let the flat of the blade press along my neck while that same thumb fit to my cheek. "You don't want me at my cruelest, baby…you don't want to know the things the borro makes me think about doing to you."

Parvati's explanation of the mating dynamics still fresh in my mind, I stared into the face of my predator with a nod.

"Yes," I whispered, my body quivering with an imminent immolation. "Yes, please—I do."

Searching my face in astonishment, almost rage, Eleison released me.

I thought he was really going to let me have it this time: the lecture of the century. Instead, with the urgent look of a man who barely had himself under control, Eleison gestured the blade toward the door. "Go wait on the bed."

My heart leapt. At last! Oh, yes. Whenever Malin gave an order like that, it was like entering a second world. I inevitably knew something fun was about to happen, and that our dynamic had shifted for the duration. The same was true of Eleison. At once yielding to my instinctive, giddy fright for his power, I darted into the bedroom and let the door swing shut behind me.

But, as it clicked, a funny impulse came over me. Why make it easy for him? Once he had his hands on me, I simply had to give him my body. I could do nothing else: it was not a matter of will or intent in any way. Every pretense would collapse, and I would yield to him absolutely.

And, if I did yield, would he keep playing the games I wanted to play? No…he would see to it he had me too well-fucked to care, and next time it would be more of the same.

So, with a quick scan around the room, I found someplace to hide.

Under the desk was too obvious with the stool as the only cover, and the bed was just a little too low for me to comfortably hide beneath. Behind the curtains, well—they were floor-length and wide, but a little obvious as hiding spots.

But the walk-in closet, though obvious, had a certain breadth that made it escapable. If I hid far in the back, I might duck past him to shut myself in the bathroom again. Trying not to laugh, I snatched up my robe and tied it on while I crept to that friendly closet. The room's only other door outside the hall door and the bathroom door.

And that magical door that disappeared just like the slipper I removed from my foot.

The dharmine could sense my pleasure, of that I had no doubt. However, much to my surprise, I didn't feel its intrusive presence. My reward for having already fed it—not only with myself, but with my offering to it. The victim of Eleison's crime.

Yes…I couldn't forget that Eleison really *was* a criminal. A murderer. And here I was, teasing him. Pressed back into the guest suite closet, giggling behind a number of courtesy robes and my own carefully hung, simpler articles.

The bathroom door swung open, floorboards creaking beneath his steps.

"Thecla," he said in a tone of low warning, "I know you're still here…"

My heart raced and my stomach tightened. The pulse that raged through me throbbed most heavily between my legs.

"I thought I told you to get on the bed."

Those wandering footsteps led him to the curtains. I contained my delight and praised my instincts, though it was but a short delay. One by one he rustled them, the set of four, saying to me as he did, "Doesn't matter…this is a bad room for you to try hiding in. There's only one more place for you to be."

My respiration stopped altogether. I froze, my muscles tight and my mind rushing with solutions for escape. That night, that first night, with him—the kidnapping—the carriage. It felt like this, in a way.

The door flew open and Eleison stepped into the closet, his height and broad shoulders shrinking its scale.

"There you are," he said, covering the distance to me in a few long strides. "Come on—hey—"

Crying out with a girlish scream of half-delight, half-terror, I weaved to his right and ducked past him. Thanks to good luck I narrowly squeezed into the gap between his body and the wall. He caught my wrist but only succeeded in pulling my robe from my shoulder. Half-naked, I was propelled by inertia and tripped out the door.

I sprinted, laughing, toward the bathroom.

Before I was even halfway, Eleison burst from the closet so suddenly I screamed.

As he caught me, his hand flew over my mouth and that knife found my neck again.

"Sh," he urged, "you'll get me shot…you don't want that, do you, Thecla?"

Shaking my head rapidly against the pressure of his palm, I gasped for breath when he allowed me to and told him in a whimper, "No, Eleison, no, please—ah!"

His lips brushed my ear, then peeled away to allow his

teeth to sink into the ridge. "Then you'd better be quiet, Thecla, and take it like a good girl."

I moaned, gazing starrily into Eleison's face even as my throat tightened beneath the blade. "I swear I'll behave," I whispered. "Oh, please—"

"Are you sure about that?"

Eleison trailed the knife low, tickling it between my breasts, then guiding it slowly over the flat of my stomach. The sensation wasn't a sting, not a scratch. But, as it etched a thin pink welt into my skin, the knife made me keenly aware of its presence. My entire body tightened, and I couldn't seem to help myself but lean back against my captor with a long, slow grind along his hips.

"Please, Eleison, fuck me—"

"I thought you wanted me to play scary games with you, baby…are you too scared?" The tip of that knife disappeared into the thicket at the apex of my thighs as he commanded, "Spread your legs."

I did, letting one foot slide up his leg to further the splay while maintaining my balance. His lip brushing over my ear, Eleison used the new angle to let him trail the knife down further.

As the cool metal tip brushed against my clitoris, I gasped.

The second time, I had to cover my latest scream.

"Oh," I moaned, "Eleison—oh, be careful—"

"Don't act like you don't love this." His chin resting upon my shoulder even as my pose tired my legs to trembling, Eleison slid the blade's tip down a few centimeters. "It makes you realize what I could do to you. What I want to do to you, sometimes. Oh, baby! Thecla, I'd never hurt you…why do I want to? Why does the borro make me want to?"

"Why do I want you to," I begged to know, provoking a quick flash of his smiling teeth against my flesh.

Slowly, carefully, clearly aware of the potential for very real damage and as aroused by it as I was, Eleison pressed the knife's tip just into the center that had been denied true satisfaction all night. Not far enough to spread me—barely far enough to be felt—but oh, there it was. And it was capable of going farther. If I so much as twitched, or if my muscles fluttered with pleasure, I would have cut myself against the blade.

With a ragged breath, I held the difficult pose and prayed my muscles to withstand their strain.

"I can't believe you let that piece of shit hunter kiss you," Eleison growled into my ear, "but I guess, if you'll get this wet for a knife, I shouldn't be that surprised."

"Oh, Eleison—I wish you would fuck me with it, oh—"

"Thecla...ah, fuck—"

Overwhelmed, Eleison slipped the blade carefully from me. My relaxation was short-lived. The second it was free he pushed me forward against the bed. Catching myself upon the edge, I looked back to find him striding after me.

When something next pressed to my exposed center, it was certainly not a knife.

"You'd better think carefully the next time you kiss somebody other than me or Malin," Eleison warned, slowly pushing into me to make me moan while the tip of the knife ran along my outer thigh. "I mean it, Thecla..."

As I had predicted, the knife bounced upon the mattress, rejected practically the first second he was inside me; but I was too high on Eleison to mourn it. He gripped my hips with his newly freed hands and plunged himself to the hilt in me, gritting his teeth while I ground back against him.

"Some hunter can't understand this," insisted Eleison,

reaching down into my hair to grab a great fistful of locks. The sting enriched my every burst of pleasure until it seemed I would choke on my own enthusiasm. "He'll never know what it's like to look at his mate and be so—*consumed*. Fuck, ah—Thecla—"

His flesh slapped hard and fast against mine while he fucked me, the previous flames of the night rekindled by his rough treatment. I yelped with pleasure beneath one particularly savage thrust, slicker with desire by the second.

"If he touches you again," Eleison growled, "even with your permission, I'm going to make him regret it...so make sure you warn him. Otherwise, it's not fair."

My toes curled while I bucked against him, thrashing in protest and fighting against my body's urge to submit just long enough to try and drag myself away. He kept that grip on my hair, tugging me back effortlessly while I whimpered, "Eleison, please—you'll only harden his heart against altered."

"Against you, you mean...and you couldn't stand that. Malin's right. You really are a slut, Thecla...and it would be very hot"—his words snarled against my ear to the time of a few very carefully-aimed thrusts within me—"if the borro didn't want me to *fucking kill him.*"

Moaning while Eleison pinned me down into the bed by the nape of the neck, I struggled to catch even his arm in my periphery.

"Maybe your borro is jealous," I whispered, my face hot.

"You're fucking right, it is—"

"No," I went on, plunging into the sea of embarrassment to seek the rewards of trust between lovers. "No, Eleison, I mean— your borro is jealous of *you.*"

His pace slowing a little, Eleison draped himself over my

back and released my neck. Instead, sliding his powerful arms around my body to enfold me to his heart, he buried his mouth in my hair to ask "What do you mean, it's jealous of *me*? It *is* me."

"But it's not," I whispered, "just like whatever's in me isn't me, but is me. I can feel it sometimes, stirring in me…Eleison, oh—" His hand ran down my stomach, slid along my thigh, then trailed beneath my leg to fold it toward my chest and deepen his strokes into me. "Eleison, darling…it occurred to me today I've never even met your borro in peaceful circumstances. Don't you think it wants to meet me?"

"Thecla…you *did* meet it."

"Yes, but that's just my point. I'll do better this time." I threw in a note of girlish plea that made him growl anew; especially when I managed to look over my shoulder and into at least one fiery red eye. "Please, Eleison—oh, I promise, I'll treat it so kindly…just think. In all the years it's been in you, has anyone ever *been* kind to it? Has it ever known the kisses and caresses of a human?"

The growling lowered to a slower sort of rumble in his chest, his heavily lidded eyes searching my face in sincere contemplation as I went on to murmur, "*I* would be very kind to it…to you, Eleison…Eleison's borro, deep inside of you. Can you hear me talking to you through Eleison?"

I reached back, my hand raising to Eleison's face, and the look in his eyes grew distant and thoughtful. Unfocused—almost entranced.

If we stabilized one another, I suddenly wondered, could we also perform the opposite feat? Could I draw the animal out of him as easily as I could soothe it away? No wonder the mating bonds were dangerous…I had to take care.

"I'll be so kind to you," I whispered to the beast within my mate, the predator of my own sleeping monster. "I'll stroke your fur, and sing to you. When you're tired from keeping us safe from the Rift, you can rest your great head in my lap and go to sleep. Then, I'll protect *you*. Eleison—"

His meditation interrupted by his name, Eleison remembered he was not an animal, but a man with an animal in him. It were as though I felt his consciousness externalize into me and the present moment again.

"Maybe it is jealous," admitted Eleison. "That sounds nice. But—Thecla— What if it hurts you?"

"I don't think it will…I don't think *you* will. Please, I want to make up for the night we met. I want your every last instinct to trust me. Eleison—Eleison—oh—!"

His hand slipped beneath my hip and toyed against that jewel of lust while he found a new sense of vigor. In the delicious straitjacket of his arms, I was helpless to do anything other than brace back against him to sweeten the pressure of his strokes.

"What if it wants something else, Thecla," he asked me harshly, his teeth grit against the pleasure of taking me. "You don't want that, do you?"

"Oh, Eleison—maybe I do!" The noise he made—a sort of barely withheld gasp, or perhaps a choked laugh of delight—came with a greater definition to both the power and petrification of his weapon. I yielded to him utterly, helpless with pleasure as he fucked me, confessing to him, "Maybe I do, oh, Eleison, Eleison— it's just you, isn't it? After all—oh, it's just you—"

My brow furrowing, I turned to stroke his cheek again. To look into his eyes as the climax rose upon me, crashing into me while I cried, "My love! I would do anything for you."

"Thecla—"

With a low, shuddering exhalation, Eleison let one hand guide me through my orgasm while his other caught my jaw to hold me for his kiss. I trembled, delighting in the rigidity that overcame him within and against me.

"I'd do anything for you," he responded fiercely, tearing his lips from mine to stare into my face as his body contrived its own satisfaction. "So—I swear not to kill him—"

"Oh, Eleison, thank you, thank you—"

"But, I stand by what I said. You'd better warn him. When Malin's around, when Malin's not around, no matter what the law or anything else has to say about it—you're mine, Thecla. Say it."

I moaned, nodding in agreement, my body and heart and mind in perfect harmony. "I'm yours, Eleison," I swore, thrashing in his arms with a second, more quickly mounting iteration of pleasure, as often came upon me when my men worked me through the first climax. "Oh, yes—I'm yours, yours before I'm anyone's! Eleison—Eleison!"

"Fuck, ah—*Thecla*—"

As his passion burst within my core, his kiss pushed me over that second edge.

Together, we made a happy descent.

B ETWEEN HIS WORK and our lovemaking, Eleison dropped into a sleep so deep he barely breathed. Had acknowledging the borro soothed something in him? It certainly had earned a stay of Glenn Stone's execution, which I sensed had been a serious contemplation while Eleison's hands were still stained with the blood of his day.

But, drunk though I still slightly was, I couldn't seem to enjoy the unconsciousness that was, that very minute, claiming many attendants of the night's ball.

With one notable exception outside of myself.

At one-thirty in the morning, my uneasy quest for sleep was interrupted by the softest tapping. Disturbed, suspecting at first the dharmine, I sat halfway up from bed and looked for the source.

Another soft set of taps. The door. I let my breath blow free.

With a glance at Eleison, I snatched up my robe and pulled it tightly about myself. Covered, I crept across the floor and turned the doorknob in as close to perfect silence as I could achieve.

There stood the Overseer, her eyebrows lifting along with her smile.

"Good morning! I wasn't sure you'd be up, but now I'm glad I tried."

With a glance over my shoulder at Eleison, whose soft breathing was slightly disturbed, I slipped into the hall and closed the door behind me. "Is everything all right?"

"Fantastic," said the Overseer, her words as softly moderated as mine. She still wore the same blue gown from the party, though she had gotten rid of her jewelry and hair ornaments. "The ball was a riot! You should have stayed…but, I understand. Did your night get better when you left?"

"Much."

"Then you made the right decision." The Overseer nudged my arm. "I know it's late, but do you have time to come with me somewhere? There's something I'd love to show you."

Lips pursing, I contemplated the door that held my sleeping mate. "What is it?"

"You just have to see it," she said, waving me with her.

"I'm—not exactly dressed."

She shrugged. "Do you have to be? It's just me. Come on, you'll be fine. The weather's warm all night this time of year."

Though Charlotte's advice—to avoid separation from Eleison whenever possible—fluttered back through my head, I found myself oddly intrigued. The Overseer was a strange woman.

"Eccentric," I suppose, was the word to use when the strangeness was attached to someone of her station. She clearly operated on a level of thought that was big picture, rather than in the moment. At times, this made her seem scattered.

In other words…I could not stop myself from thinking her rather harmless.

Leaving Eleison behind, I padded after Parvati her through the front doors of the palace. In the quiet of the early morning, an autohorse and its brilliant white carriage awaited us. I hesitated again, then climbed aboard.

The car rolled into motion. Parvati said while reclining across from me, "You didn't tell me you got to see Glenn."

A guilty flush settled over me at the mention of his name, doing battle with longing. "I'd just as soon not talk about it. Oh, Eleison is very jealous."

"I have to admit I'm surprised he's not *more* jealous. Isn't he bothered by your marriage to Malin?"

My hands spread apart before refolding upon my knee. "He's welcome to ignore it or celebrate it as the mood strikes. Slowly, he's choosing the latter…but I do think there are times when he wishes he were the only man in my life."

"And Malin?"

"My husband"—whose sensual crooning mere hours prior returned to flush me with more than guilt—"is sensitive to the gulf between our ages, and my lack of life experience, and is happy for me."

While pouring herself a drink and offering one to me, (I refused), Parvati shook her laughing head. "That just blows me away. Doesn't sound like the Malin Farrow I know at all."

"That's the point I've been making since I got here," I told her, earning a brisk glance and half a little smirk.

"I guess it is. But you have to understand my perspective, Thecla…I haven't seen him in decades."

"Because you banned him from your territory."

"Because he made a public promise to flay me the next time I set foot in Gudrune," she said with a shrug and a defiant stare back at my sharp look. "It seemed like a reasonable precaution."

"*Precaution*," I repeated, annoyed by my lack of sleep and the hangover that had begun to leech the pleasure from the drunkenness. "Please. You really think my husband would have hurt you if you let him tour Valquist with me? He wouldn't be so stupid…or so crass." The pain! I felt acutely how much better the trip would have been. His hand on mine, his body—

"Maybe not this time," Parvati insisted. "But who knows what information he could absorb by being here firsthand? If he decided to launch another campaign—"

"Didn't *you* start the last one?"

"The Gudrune Expansion? *He* started that by breaking intracontinental decrees."

"His energy research, you mean?"

"Yeah—the "energy research" that required unfettered access to Azstorian dig operations. The same territory where they buried radioactive materials after the Rift made it too dangerous to maintain nuclear bombs and other equipment. Bet he hasn't mentioned his little energy project requires uranium, did he."

"No, but I trust him. Why would he mention it to me? It's not as if I'm responsible for funding."

Her scoff was uncharacteristically unsubtle. I wasn't sure whether she was drunk or trying to tempt me into inquiring, but I decided it was genuine inebriation when she lowered her glass and abruptly said, "You know, I was close friends with his ex-wife."

Finally, something that made me sit up. "Were you?"

"Yes, well—as close as one could be across the country. I used to visit Gudrune the way I do all the other territories. They came here a handful of times, but mostly I went out there." The rhythm of the wheels changed as we crossed a broad river to exit the darkened city. The Overseer paid it no mind as she talked on. "I always liked her. I never thought she was a good fit for Malin. She was charismatic, and she could strike up conversation to win anyone as her friend, but her tastes and mannerisms were very— conventional."

"I have heard they were ill-matched," I confessed, not elaborating other than to add, "and I'm glad they were, because he and I seem made to be together."

"Do you really mean that?"

"Of course."

She stared me down, her gaze sometimes wavering from mine to absorb some other feature of my face.

"I guess it would be rude of me to question your reasons for being with him," she said. "But do you ever wonder if Malin— I mean, he obviously must know about your being second-generation altered, so—"

"Please, stop."

Her mouth shut, thankfully, and I went on in a firm tone. "While I'm sure you would love nothing more than to dissuade me of my passion for my husband—"

"That's not—"

I carried right on, just as Malin did when interrupted. "—I think there's far more between us than you could possibly guess. I'll be the first to admit it's a very practical arrangement for both of us, for many reasons. But, if you'd had the decency to really look at reality and invite him here along with me, one look at us for a few seconds would show you what I alone can't. Namely, that he loves me, and I love him."

"That may be so, Thecla," Parvati admitted at last, "and it may be that you love him with all your heart, and that his love for you is honest. I won't deny that. But—the decision to act on love is a choice. And your willingness to love Malin Farrow testifies to your character."

My demeanor grew more frigid by the moment. That fire of rage flickered within me.

Against expectation, the dharmine nudged my mind.

And I realized something.

Wherever she was taking me, whatever we were doing, it was a tremendous risk to Parvati. A risk she did not even recognize.

I had told her about the dharmine, after all. But I had not told her the dharmine served me. I did not let her have any idea that it might have followed me to Valquist.

And so, here we were. Drawing toward the edge of the city, the Overseer and me.

Malin would be ecstatic.

If only I could find some way to avoid culpability.

"My love of Malin does say something about me," I agreed stonily, the rush of power intoxicating, the temptation thrilling, the self-control I exerted to push it all away something Malin must have felt every second of the day. "It says I'm willing to overlook the flaws of the person I love…and frankly, even Malin's flaws have a kind of gloss to me, but the past doesn't matter as much as present behavior. He proves himself to me all the time: with every interaction, big and small. I believe he has the best interests of Gudrune in mind. Since you haven't spoken to him in my lifetime, I wouldn't expect you to believe that…but I don't really care."

"How old are you again, Thecla?"

Taken aback by the question, I answered, "Nearly twenty-five."

"Twenty-four! Oh, Thecla…" Parvati propped her elbow against her window to rest her forehead against her sinewy fist. "You're so young," she said with a pity I found condescending. "You haven't even been a legal adult for ten whole years. And you think you can trust Malin?"

I hardly knew where to start, so I didn't answer. She shook her head and stared out her window. "I'll stop talking about it, but I'm worried for you."

"Don't be. I have faith in my husband. Where are you taking me, Parvati?"

"I just want to show you that you have a reason to trust me," she said cryptically, her eyes still on the landscape as the carriage rolled onto a ramp that curved out of the city.

We grew silent. I watched through my window for five minutes that stretched on forever. Gradually, the road to which the ramp let out grew thick with trees on either side. I recognized the forest from our arrival, though it took on a new, far more menacing character in the dark.

When we were perhaps seven miles from the city, the carriage rolled to an automated stop at the side of the road.

"Where is this," I asked as she, smiling, slid up from her seat and bent toward the opening door.

"I come here all the time." Parvati hopped down into the grass and told me, "Watch your step."

I did, peering into trees so thick they seemed a wall in the night. "Perhaps a better question is "Why are we here?""

"I wanted to see if I could inspire you, I guess. Malin's first wife and I used to come out here when he was—busy."

I snorted at the euphemism. "I don't think she knew how to handle him."

"I don't think she *wanted* to. It was an arranged marriage… and, like a lot of wealthy young women forty or fifty years ago, she was altered at a young age to make her more valuable as a bride. She must have felt very different from her husband, and very resentful."

These details had never been relayed to me. My ears twitched with them, my shock so great I hardly registered Parvati twisting her arms toward her back.

"Malin never told me she was altered," I said, earning a short laugh from the Overseer.

"Nobody wants to talk about their ex…even I can be charitable toward him about that. But, yes! Of course she was. I thought you knew! She couldn't always transform with me, of course—"

"With you?"

"—but whenever a Rift Event coincided with their visits, we would run together all night… It was so fun."

I followed the drop of the dress around her feet, then searched her brilliant eyes through the dark.

"*You're* altered," I gathered through my daze.

"Second-generation," Parvati said, nodding. "Just like you."

A warm breeze blew between us. Turning away from me, Parvati removed her bra and said with a look at the sky, "It's a lonely life. Even among altered, Thecla, we're alone."

There was so much I wanted to say, but I was so amazed that I couldn't form the words.

And, anyway, her next sentence took any semblance of thought from my brain.

"That was sort of what I liked about *her*. Even though she was first-generation, she was alone just like I was. Whenever the ventil came out, you could see how free she suddenly was. I never saw her that free as a woman."

Yes…that was all very sad.

But I had stopped listening.

I was too preoccupied by the sour twist in my stomach.

"You said she was a ventil," I asked, the words soft in my dry mouth.

Now naked, Parvati looked over her shoulder at me.

"Hm? Yes, of course Giselle was altered with ventil DNA. I really thought you told me you knew that. Didn't you?"

Whatever remained of my inebriation vanished into hard, ugly sobriety.

The world tilted around me as I whispered, "Of course I did."

She didn't seem to know what she had said. What she had just told me. Once again turning away, Parvati stretched her arms toward the still visible sliver of moon.

"I hope one day you'll come running with me, Thecla, but if you can't tonight, I understand. Feel free to take the carriage back…I won't need it."

For the first time in my life, an altered individual transformed before me. I was so preoccupied I could appreciate it but distantly. The shimmer of vibrant Rift radiation rippling purple across her flesh grew more rapid each cycle; grew brighter, too. While I averted my eyes in narrow avoidance of a spike back into my headaches, I caught the second she leaned forward to set hands upon the ground.

Once I managed to look back, she had already changed.

No wonder that ertiz had been so friendly to us. Could it recognize her as one of its own? It must have. Yet, among ertiz, there were surely none like Parvati. The brilliant gold of her fur had faded to silver tips with her age, but, like some living river, she flowed about with a grace far exceeding her domesticated cousin. All four of her ears stood at high points, and her brilliant malachite eyes reflected the light that made felines so unnerving in the dark. When she moved, she seemed to slither toward me, her body undulating against my legs in a gesture of friendly encouragement.

Then, sitting back on her haunches, her slender paws neatly arranged before her, Parvati appeared to wait.

I shook my head, barely able to order my thoughts (Giselle!) away from (not Giselle) the questions (not *my* Giselle) that rushed through me (not my mother) and stole my attention from the scene (not her).

"I'm sorry," I told her. "I really can't. I don't know how to join you. Please—don't waste the night on my account. Only a few hours left."

Even as an animal, she understood me too well for my liking. She heard the strain, the sudden distance in my tone. Her eyes narrowed with the tilt of her head.

Unable to make sense of the shift in my mood, the Overseer galloped into the forest and left me behind.

THE RIDE BACK was so long.

Over, and over, I searched for an explanation and found only a deep, screaming intuition that I *had* the explanation. I knew it.

Maybe even had known it already.

After pouring myself a very stiff drink from the carriage's bar, I considered the facts.

The first: I did not *really* know my parents. It went without saying that I did not know my mother firsthand at all, as she died at my birth. But my father—I knew him only *as* my father. At that critical age when most teenagers begin to experience their parents as not just parents but flawed and nuanced human beings, my father exhibited the ultimate flaw: mortality. He died, and took with him the answeres to all my adult questions about his past.

What did I know of him? He claimed to have previously lived in a place comparable to Lescaut. If so, how did he come to know my mother, who was altered? How had he known the taste of chocolate well enough to describe it to me? Where had he learned to so expertly engineer and repair security devices for our neighbors around town?

Then…there was my mother. My mother, whose name I could suddenly no longer bear to think. My mother, who was altered, yet was able to have me. As if she had been able to avoid government scrutiny or altogether refuse the birth control that was part and parcel with alteration.

And then there was my lifelong fiction. The lie that I was an average child, when in fact I was riftborn and naturally altered at once.

If Malin had taught me any lesson at all, it was that those who omitted one thing tended to omit many other things as a consequence.

Malin.

Malin, Malin.

I did not know how I felt about Malin just then. Somehow, I almost could *not* think of him. My thoughts turned toward him only to be paralyzed.

What was I supposed to feel? I could only think of one answer—fury—yet I somehow couldn't muster it. With a web of so many secrets between us, this felt less like shocking revelation and more the snapping in of an undeniable, somehow obvious fact.

It reminded me of Malin, talking to Eleison and me. *I do feel rather like a fool.*

No. I couldn't be angry in that particular moment. The idea was still settling in on me, in that muddy twilight state between drunk and hungover. However...I was hurt. I was *certainly* hurt, for perhaps more reasons than I could articulate. I had consented to Malin's secrets when I married him, as I confirmed during our honeymoon. Malin's true inner life was not capable of unfolding overnight, much as I longed for it to. The respect for this steady process was based in part on an unspoken trust: that his secrets would not affect me, did not pertain personally to me.

Therefore, whatever I felt was discernably not anger.

In fact, I would even describe it as a curious sort of apathy.

Who knew this disappointing truth? I sorted out everyone I knew. My stepmother? I would write to her to find out, but I had a feeling she had known. Eleison? He had been in Malin's staff ten years, and my mother had died twenty-five years ago, roughly, but it was possible, even likely, Malin had confided in him prior to bringing me to the manor. What about the villagers at home? The duke?

And all of that endless accounting was punctuated by the leitmotif of one question: Had Malin been genuinely dangerous to her?

That quickly, I just wasn't sure anything anymore.

At the palace, I finished my drink and climbed out of the carriage to find a security officer at the door. Without a word, he let me in and bade me a pleasant morning.

I glided past him, through the halls, up the stairs, and along the corridor to my room.

Before I reached my door, I passed the room of the one person I was sure *did* know about all of this.

Emboldened by drink, I stopped and knocked.

There was a delay of about twenty seconds, with a lot of shuffling and a muttered curse. When Charlotte opened the door, her eyes screwed shut against the corridor's unrelenting light. Her usually placid features showed just a hint of their age as they tightened with her squint.

"Is there an emergency, Madame? It's still half till four."

"An emergency—no, not an emergency. As you can see, I'm going to be sleeping in. However—"

I wanted to talk to her about this now, right this very second. The anger I couldn't muster for Malin suddenly boiled up in me, fighting for a release I barely prevented. Charlotte wanted to tell herself that she was on my side, I knew. She wanted to feel that she was good to me, a good mentor to me, and that she acted in my best interests. But keeping this from me had *not* been in my best interests, so far as I could see.

I wanted to tell her that.

But I looked at her, and I somehow couldn't.

Instead, I said, "When I'm up, I'd like to spend time around town. We won't be here more than a handful of days longer."

The corners of her mouth flexing with annoyance to have been woken for such a directive, she said, "Yes, Madame. Shall I wake you?"

"If I'm not up by the time you come see me around noon," I told her, departing for my room. "Sorry to bother you…I'm drunk, the time's gotten away from me…good morning, Charlotte."

"Good morning, Madame," she said, too tired and annoyed to see the strangeness of my visit outside of what she likely interpreted as inebriation. As my door opened, hers shut, and we both retired to bed.

Mine had somebody else in it.

"Should I bother to ask"—Eleison's sleep-worn voice edged to a low sort of bark—"where you've been?"

After dropping my robe, I crawled beneath the covers and

into my mate's warm arms. He drew me tight against his chest while I closed my eyes.

"The Overseer wanted me to run with her—as beasts, I mean."

Eleison's head whipped toward me. "She's altered?"

"Second-generation."

"What a hypocrite. Shit...no wonder she put restrictions on altered reproduction." My flabbergasted mouth opened even as he went on, "Malin is right. All she thinks about is maintaining her power."

"Go back," I demanded. "That was *Parvati*?"

"Oh, yeah...way back, too. It was one of the first things she did after she and Malin started to fight, I think. Her, I'm gonna say great-grandfather—the first in her family to be Overseer—created the earliest riftborn registry. That's probably where she got the idea to control altered populations...can't be too careful."

Small wonder she had such a problem with Malin, his funneling of riftborn into alteration programs aside. If she thought he might be unregistered riftborn, he must have been very threatening to her.

I shut my eyes and buried my face against Eleison's neck, murmuring, "I hate that I ever came here...oh, Eleison. Malin was right. This place is terrible."

Not wanting to admit he agreed, but neither able to truthfully rebuff my lamentation, Eleison kissed the top of my head.

"We'll be home soon," he promised.

I wasn't sure if that made me feel better or worse anymore.

When I awoke a little before noon, Eleison still sleeping soundly along with me after his own laborious night, that numb feeling remained intense. So much had changed in a night! Not even the man beside me had been untouched. Even as it pained me, I withdrew from Eleison to dress, my mind so busy with reflection it seemed the task accomplished itself.

There was something else beneath the veil of sensory deadness. A purpose that had been incapable of growing in my heart while I was still shocked. Now I had slept, and I was through the shock—at least, in part. I dressed with trembling hands in the same closet that the night before had been an accessory of sensual delights. It seemed so far away somehow, that wonderful night with Eleison.

Eleison, who was so close to Malin that I couldn't risk asking him anything—no matter how I longed to. I wished to weep and confide in him. To shout at him, too, and to rail against the cruelty of the charade in which he had participated. The illusion that Malin had loved me because of *me*. Not because of whose daughter I was.

But I realized exactly what would happen. Eleison would instinctively position himself with Malin, perhaps not even meaning to. A conversation would ensue wherein I was rationalized into releasing all my umbrage: into seeing the wisdom in accepting reality without making a fuss of it. Eleison would urge me to compromise—to compromise with my own feelings, as he once decided to when trading his liberty for a life of indentured servitude in the name of his brother.

When I emerged from the closet, my mate stirred in bed; I drew back the drapes one set at a time, letting early afternoon into the room to fill the space across from the bed with light. He grumbled. But, as I trailed back to the bedside and slid into his hot embrace from the other side of the sheets, Eleison's lips nuzzled into my hair, across my forehead, over my eye.

"Will you go out to dinner with me tonight, Thecla?"

My heart skipped a beat. He never asked such things in Saalast. Eleison was always so worried about putting up a professional boundary between himself and the eye of the public—for Malin's sake. Always for Malin's sake.

"I suppose my image here is already so tainted that it doesn't matter to you," I said with a half laugh, immediately chagrined to have spoken so pettily to him. Sensitive man that he was, he grimaced against my cheek as I quickly apologized. "I'm sorry, darling. I don't know why I said that."

"Hey, no—you're right. I've been thinking about that while we've been here. Since the train, really." Head rocking back against his pillow, Eleison rubbed his hand over his forehead, then down across the bristles of his unshaven mandible. "I need to start taking better advantage of Malin's—I don't want to say "generosity," but—"

"Yes," I found myself saying in a sharp, clipped sort of way that cut him off, "Malin is *very* generous toward us both. But I don't like to think of it as generosity in this context because—oh, it makes me feel like such a commodity. "Compromise,"" I urged, primed by my own thoughts from mere moments before. "Say "compromise.""

"All right." Eleison's tone was cautious; curious. "Is something the matter?"

"I'm a little hungover," I told Eleison honestly, pressing my face to the shade of his chest hair and marveling at the soothing effect his body had against my shut eyelids, my swiftly receding headache. "And I—I don't feel very *good* about some things right now, Eleison…but you're not one of those things."

"All right," he repeated. "Did something happen?"

"Something *else*, you mean? No, nothing. Nothing *happened.* I just feel—queer. I feel very queer, and I'd like to get out and about today. So...yes, I'd love to dine with you." My body heaved with an exasperated sigh. "I'm sorry I'm feeling so foul, darling."

"Hey, no, that's okay—aw, Thecla—"

My shoulders shook, my voice strangled out against a sob that overwhelmed me.

"I'm just so tired of *being* here! I—I think Malin was right. All that awful woman wants to do is ruin—"

A brusque knock interrupted us.

Not Charlotte's.

Exchanging a glance, both of us plagued equally by thoughts of Eleison's activities the night prior, we separated to move in absolute silence. He slipped into the bathroom to dress. I, wiping my cheeks as interruption's shock jolted me from misery, made my way to call through the door. "Who is it?"

"The Overseer's personal guard, Madame," boomed the voice on the other side. "We're here to bring you to meet Madame Parvati."

Surprised and confused, I looked at the bathroom door over my shoulder. "I don't think I have an appointment with her today—"

"This is an emergency situation; bring your man, too."

I hesitated, studying the Rift Monitoring System readout beside the door. It *was* unnervingly high, at a 70% likelihood of Rift activity—but the alarm hadn't gone off.

"Did she say what it was about?"

"You'll discuss it during your meeting."

My stomach sank lower. Why were they speaking to me as if I had done something? *Had* I? My mind raced through possibilities before settling on—the dharmine? Perhaps they had somehow detected its presence the night before. Perhaps they really had been monitoring my quarters, and had divined something from my one-sided conversation.

Perhaps I was only growing paranoid, as my own web of deception wove more thickly around me.

Pale by the time Eleison emerged, his clothes on and his expression grave, I cracked open the door and considered the three tall men arranged before me. Each wore a dark suit and a deathly serious expression.

And when we arrived at the Overseer's office, a golden rotunda overlooking the glittering lawn of the palace, the grim set of Charlotte's expression proved even sterner than theirs.

"What are you doing here," I asked, shocked to find her in the office ahead of me. The Overseer responded for her, turning from the largest window to fold her hands over her desk's tall chair.

"Wasting my time," was Parvati's answer, her tone hard. "Sit down, Thecla."

"Don't say anything." Charlotte spoke quickly, meeting my eyes as I slid into the couch across from her in the recessed meeting area. "It's all baseless."

Seeing that Parvati snatched a newspaper from her desk and brought over to us, I laughed. Thank goodness! "Oh, *that.* Yes, Parvati, come now! I thought you understood that tabloid was nonsense."

"Not a tabloid." She threw down the morning's copy of *The Imperial,* the foremost journalistic establishment in Valquist. "Real news—no, *intelligence.* Dangerous intelligence, printed in a newspaper before it ever hit my desk. I'll tell you what; I'm really learning a lot about my relationships with people this morning."

Baffled, I leaned toward the headline that had unfurled across the coffee table.

My eyes widened.

Gudrune Oks Energy Research: Farrow Pledges Fortune in Defiance of Treaty

Had Malin leaked his announcement to turn the media narrative away from me?

While I raised the article near enough to skim, the Overseer waved a hand.

"There's your precious Master Farrow," she said scornfully. "I knew something was changing when he married you. You had me thinking he'd progressed, rather than regressed...too bad."

"I know *you* don't like it, but I trust Malin's intentions." I half-skimmed the article, intrigued by its specificity and confidence. "Really, it's wonderful news."

This level of detail, the timing, the complete bypassing of Parvati: the source had to be Malin. Hadn't there been some lapdog of the Overseer's at that meeting? And she still didn't know. That man had been wiser than I might have gambled to look at him...then again, it wasn't a difficult decision. Better to betray the Overseer and live than leak Malin's information and die.

Though if looks could kill, the Overseer might just have killed *me* in that moment.

""Wonderful news,"" she repeated in disgust.

"It is. If the Rift can be used as a source of clean, renewable energy, then—"

"Energy's not the problem. It's storage, and power during Rift Events. It's why we mine lithium, why we recycle it, why *that's* where we need to be putting our research. It's why Gudrune *pretends* to do those things. Have you ever—"

The shut door to the office echoed with a brisk knock. When it flew open, the disheveled and obviously still a bit ill duke shuffled in a few steps.

"It's a regular afterparty in here, isn't it…look at all these happy faces." Cringing as the door shut heavily behind him, Aleister looked back at Parvati and asked in an arrogance few others would dare, "So just *why* have I been called out of bedrest for this? What is this little intervention about? Don't tell me it's for my drinking. Alcohol has been the only thing keeping me alive this past few days."

"I don't suppose *you* knew anything about Malin's energy grant," the Overseer asked, her tone vibrating with the kind of growl Eleison produced in dangerous moments.

Aleister's eyebrows raised. "Is the madman dusting off that old project? Even after what happened last time?"

"Apparently, he's inviting me to visit again." Parvati's words dripped with displeasure. "My military, too."

I laughed.

Every eye turned upon me, but the Overseer's blazing stare most especially struck to the depths of my soul.

By that moment, I was so absolutely beyond it all that I didn't even blink.

"You wouldn't dare," I told her, every bit as cold as she was hot. "Do you really want to be remembered as a failure, after all?"

Though her lips parted in shock, her eyes narrowed.

"Are you threatening me, Thecla?"

"Of course not. I just mean to say—well, it didn't go very

well for you last time you moved against Gudrune. What's different now? That sort of sorry conflict is the way you want history to remember the climax of your career?"

A shadow veiled Parvati's features. She studied me carefully, here eyes sweeping me from the top of my head to the toes of my red leather shoes.

"Well, I wanted to see why Malin married some girl from Lescaut, powerful heritage or no…and I think I'm starting to understand. The only question is—do you?"

The thinnest of smiles contorted my mouth. "I think we both understand that, Parvati."

Her teeth bared.

"Then let's figure out what we both understand. You can take the maid out…she's not cooperating."

A security guard moved to meet Charlotte. "And the footman, Madame Overseer?"

"Touch me," Eleison growled. "See what happens."

"I can walk myself out," Charlotte replied with equal aggression, jerking her arm from the agent who tried to take hold of her. "And I expect you can guess who I'll be calling."

"Let me know if he picks up for you," Parvati rejoined, still seething from the fruitless interrogation that had surely been unbearable against a woman as closed-lipped as Charlotte.

The door once again opened and shut. I looked over my shoulder as though at it, when in fact I assessed the number of individuals in the room.

Three security agents: two flanking the door, plus one looming about two feet behind Eleison, who stood with his hands folded and his body taut with awareness.

Upon lowering into the seat vacated by Charlotte, Aleister

reclined with a dramatic sigh and witheringly said to no one in particular, "I'm doing just fine, by the by…final verdict is food poisoning. Josko will be getting a personal complaint next time I ride the rail, I assure you…"

"*Josko*," muttered Eleison, snapping his fingers. I glanced back at him, but he banished my attention with a sharp red stare. I averted my gaze.

"I *am* glad you're feeling better," the Overseer was saying sincerely, pausing her beratement to soothe the duke's ego. "And I'm sorry to call you out of bedrest, but I think you need to hear this just like Thecla does. What do you know about the Rift and what's on its other side?"

She addressed me now. I sat up, primed by Malin's explanation. "It's a parallel universe of reverse entropy, isn't it?"

Parvati nodded. "It is—a different dimension, of sorts. I suppose he's explained a little of his vision, since you're versed?"

"Just enough for me to be sure that his energy research is a harmless endeavor."

"And how *can* you be sure of that? I'm sure I don't have to tell you what uranium, which he has spent decades telling me he's *not* digging up in Azstoria, was used for in the pre-Rift days. That's just the *known* risks. The guaranteed risks. Who knows what could happen if he uses that uranium for energy research instead of bombs? The results could be just as deadly. Worse."

I spread my hands. "Rift radiation is around us all the time, just like electromagnetic frequencies of all kinds. Why not harness it?"

"But I keep telling you, the energy isn't the issue. It's what goes *into* the energy…and what comes out."

"What exactly do you mean, Parvati?"

My tone was harsh, and I didn't care. I was tired of her dramatics and self-importance. The more time I spent with the Overseer, the less I liked her. Frankly, by the time of what Aleister had rightly called an intervention, I hated her. Just as Malin said, she had punctured the bubble of our innocent Eden. With her cleverly discerned and then disseminated truth, Parvati had stolen the time when Malin was sinless to me. At least, the time when I could hide my eyes and tell myself that he was.

Yes, there she was—the only person willing to be honest with me.

When it suited her.

Looking between the duke and I, (thereby ignoring Eleison in a manner unintentional but nonetheless very annoying to me), Parvati said, "You want to know why we can't explain the Rift? Why, in two thousand years of observing and recording the phenomenon, we can describe *what* it is, but we still have no clue *why*, or even how?"

"Just tell me," I urged, arms folding.

"Because it hasn't happened yet. The Rift is the fallout of a kind of explosion, but not an explosion across space. An explosion across time."

At my deep, staggered inhalation, Parvati's expression softened just a little.

"My fear," she said, hoping to at last get through to me, "is that, putting aside the dangers of digging up old radioactive materials, Malin's energy experiments could potentially be the cause of the Rift. It's always been my hope that perhaps, by dissuading him of his interest, we could *close* the Rift."

In a caress like a feathery kiss, so palpable I turned my head to ensure he wasn't there in the flesh, Dinon leaned against my brain.

"But," I said carefully, fixing Parvati with my stare once again, "if we are experiencing the Rift now, and it *is* what you say it is—this fourth-dimensional explosion—doesn't that mean that its cause will occur in the future no matter what we do?"

"We can't know that for sure. I refuse to live in a pre-determined universe. Surely the human will has to count for something."

I spread my hands a little, asking as if prompted by the dharmine, "Why can't the truth be a nuanced reflection of both? Why can't the inevitable wills of the individual humans involved determine destiny as easily as any god?"

"Because wills can be changed. Destiny can't be." Her eyes narrowing, she lowered herself into an arm chair between my sofa and the duke's. "Are you telling me you don't care that there's a possibility of closing the Rift?"

"Of course," I hastened to assure all present, and myself, "I do—but I'm hardly convinced Malin's project will be to blame. Do you have any evidence?"

"Increases in Rift activity and radiation signatures indicate we are at a point of high saturation. It's considered likely that, in our lifetimes—that is, within fifty years—we will come to understand the cause of the Rift. It depends on whom you ask, though…I've seen some research that indicates ten."

"In other words, you assume, based on pure circumstance, that my husband will be the one at fault?" Somehow I managed an unconvincing laugh, though I still nearly shouted, "I was there in Saalast when the power was killed by the Rift. Since I left so soon, I can't account for the death toll, but I'm certain there was a notable one with the way the heat has been. If Rift energy permits us to run air conditioning and life-saving electronics in poor weather, we must pursue it."

"At what cost, Thecla?"

My head throbbed. How I hated her and this sanctimonious, bigoted, cowardly amusement park of a city. I hated her for what she had done to my husband and his reputation.

But, in a hate deeper, rawer, blacker than all of that—I hated her because she had tried to come between us.

And as hurt as I was by Malin, still I stared the Overseer down and longed to see her as dead as I had seen Dr. Gall.

Ba'al-Dinon bent over my shoulder, his silken voice caressing neurons that produced the sound in my brain as though through my ear. "Command me to the task...my hand is yours."

The lurid tabloids.

I couldn't let them be right.

Inhaling, I stood from my seat.

"You will address me as Madame Farrow," I told Parvati, my stare hardened with a headache my fury had renewed. "And I think, Madame Overseer, that if you *do* believe the Rift Events are the unfurling of an explosion across time, you know as well as I do there is nothing you can do to stop it. It's not *causal*. What seems to be a starting boundary in our past is only the demarcation of a great mushroom cloud created at a different point in spacetime. Isn't that right?"

Her jaw tightened along with the narrowing of her eyes.

"There are therefore only two possibilities, as I can see them...that the Rift is a natural or otherwise unstoppable occurrence...or that you will fail to stop it. Perhaps even die before it's stopped."

"Is that another threat, *Madame Farrow?*"

Though not a drop of humor lay in me—though I was tired, and sick, and angry—I found room for one last girlish giggle. The noise was short and sharp, and I lowered my head to watch my own hands smooth the wrinkles of my gown for a few long seconds.

"No, Madame Overseer…you'll know when I'm threatening you. Today, I'm talking sense into you…but I'm tired now. I'm tired of this, I'm tired of— I'm through here. Good-bye."

Hardly thinking anymore, I turned on my heel and strode from the little conversation pit. Eleison followed me and I very nearly barked at him to give me a few moments of peace, but the Overseer did it on my behalf.

"You—Eleison. I'm not through with you."

"I have nothing to say to you. Thecla, wait—Thecla—!"

He had turned to follow me, extending a hand for my shoulder despite the distance already between us. This much I surmised in the glance I cast back while rushing out. Annoyance tightened his normally so tranquil features, then was gone. By the time the door closed behind me, he faced the Overseer with an expression as empty yet baleful as Charlotte's had been.

How did *I* look in that moment? I hurried along the halls of the palace, the bright marble of its artful construction stinging my eyes and provoking the pulse of my headache. In the black mat at the edge of a painting, I glimpsed my own pallid reflection and thought for a second I beheld Dinon's white face.

I needed air.

With a great gasp, I burst through the front doors and out to the lawn of the palace. Had I been running? I must have been. I was barely conscious of anything in that moment—just my own helplessness.

I didn't want to wait. I wanted to be gone. To be far away from the palace and this awful city right away.

But did I want to go *home*? Did I want to see Malin?

Yes—yes, of course. But, somehow, I couldn't stand the thought of looking at him. Rage filled me to think of how easily he might settle my nerves; how he would say a few charming things, and pet me, and console me, and kiss away my tears, and there I'd be. Docile, walked on, lied to.

Oh—the *lies*. My whole *life*! The trauma of the revelation rose up on me again, its scale unfathomable. Reeling, I strode across the lawn to the shut gate. The security men there looked at me with some surprise.

"I'm going out," I told them hoarsely. "If you would please—"

"Would you like me to order a security detail for you, Ma'am?"

"Madame Farrow," I corrected, going on, "No."

"With respect, Madame Farrow, we can't just let you out without protection. It's too much of a liability."

My face tightened with a disdain that peeled my lips back from my teeth. Hateful words boiled under my tongue.

Another guard looked behind me, his eyebrows raising. "Oh," said this other man, "there he is."

I turned, my stomach sinking just slightly. It was a terrible feeling to find myself regarding Eleison's approach with dread rather than elation. I wanted to bask in him, always: but what I needed in that moment was to think.

Yet, when Eleison slunk up, an eerie half-smile fixed across his lips, his eyes flooded me with terror—then a burst of understanding.

His irises glowed silver...but not because my love had once more fallen under the control of the Rift.

Because they were the eyes of my slave, who had taken Eleison's form.

"Sorry for the delay, Madame," Dinon said with Eleison's lips, with Eleison's voice box and face. Yet there was no disguising the breathy intonation of the words—nor that queer smile, nor the curiously empty animal stare fixed upon me. "Are you ready to go?"

I shivered as all the old stories about dharmines never coming out in good weather were summarily dismissed. "Yes, thank you, Eleison…if you please, gentlemen."

My heart raced while the guards turned away and one raised his watch to enter a gate code. Eleison's eyes crinkling, Dinon smiled widely at me, and I realized in that second one of the qualities that made him so unnerving.

He didn't *blink*. Not even while disguised as someone else.

As at last I put my finger on it, the black gate ground open to ease the anxiety I hadn't consciously perceived. Dinon waved Eleison's arm out before me in a deferent, gentlemanly gesture and I led the way, each step bearing me farther from the palace gates.

But to where?

It didn't matter. Not really. I just walked, and Dinon followed. As the gates closed behind us and reduced the likelihood that Charlotte or the real Eleison would detain me, my reasoning mind once more peered through the fog to ask questions.

How deep did the lies run? Had the citizens of Lescaut been complicit in hiding my background? While my mother was not well-known to them at the time of her death, there had to have been at least a few who understood the truth. Had the Leftners, who agreed to shelter me after my father's death, been made privy to my mother's identity? Had the Parsons, who employed me, realized the threat they faced?

"You were born into conspiracy," Dinon echoed of my

thoughts, earning a spiteful glance I could not maintain while he borrowed my mate's visage.

"You disgrace Eleison by wearing his face." I marched on, hurrying along walkways I remembered but vaguely. "And I wish you would stay out of my *thoughts*, damn you."

"That, Madame, I cannot do…but I can look like whomever you'd like me to look like. I would suggest Master, but that would get us much too much attention, don't you think?"

"I'd *prefer* you looked like yourself," I snapped, "or nothing. And right now, Dinon, right this very blasted minute, what I want is to be *alone*!"

I jerked toward him, my gaze as spiteful as my tone.

He was already gone, of course.

Somehow, I made it to one of the city's famous bridges without even realizing. The water beneath me ran low, summertime promising little relief for it or the populace.

I wondered what it would be like to jump in. Not to kill myself per se—but to float away, suspended upon the currents, drifting and drifting, on and on. The thought calmed me. In that calm, I took stock of myself.

And I didn't feel right.

Something was *wrong* with me. Something was wrong with my brain. Was it the hangover? The discovery? A Rift Event, building in the air?

I couldn't think of a time I had ever felt this way. It were as though my white matter was full of a kind of detritus that slowly built throughout my time in Valquist. It was not so much that my thoughts had grown sluggish as they had grown distant, joyless. It was a joylessness that crept down my wrists and into my very fingertips, my flesh and bone made heavy by some new kind of gravity.

I wanted for purification, by weeping or loving or screaming—but who could cure what ailed me the way my husband could?

Only Malin held the power of the truth over me. All others were blameless. In having none of the blame, these others had no power to heal me, either.

Yet, stubborn as I have always been, (Yes, Eleison, I admit it now, this once, and never again!), I could not stop myself from trying.

The Hunter's Guild appeared, familiar from the tour as few buildings were. With grim regard for the weapons upon its seal, I turned ninety degrees to study the canal.

Once more, I crossed a bridge.

My watch chimed with an incoming call as I reached the halfway point.

Charlotte.

"Where are you," she barked as I answered.

"Can't you see it on whatever tracking feature your device has tethered to mine?"

"I suppose I should ask "What do you think you're doing, going out without Eleison?" "

"Is he there?"

"Obviously."

"Please let me speak to him, Charlotte."

As I walked on, grateful the neighborhood I entered was more sparsely trafficked than the trades district had just been, the watch reverberated with passage from one hand to another.

"Thecla"—oh, there he was, *real* Eleison, sweet Eleison, his gruff tone softened by concern, by heartache—"where you going, baby? Let me pick you up."

"Eleison, darling—I love you so. I'm sorry we've had such a foul time together here—"

"It's all right, it doesn't matter. Why don't you just stay put, and—"

"Please, let me finish. There are some things I want you to hear."

He stopped dead in his proverbial tracks. "All right," he said in a tone of enforced tranquility, as one uses when bracing for bad news.

"I just want you to know—no matter what, Eleison, I'm not angry at *you*. I don't blame you for anything. And…I hope you can forgive me, but I just really do need a little while to think."

"Okay." Again, the strained neutrality. "How long?"

"I—I don't know. I really don't know, Eleison, I'm sorry. I—"

"Let me come get you, Thecla."

"No! No. Please. I want you, Eleison, but—I'm afraid that if you talk to me, I won't be able to sort things out for myself. This is—this—I—"

Stopping in my tracks, tears at last brimming over my eyes, I said the words out loud for the first time: wetly, quietly, but in a way sharpened by the grief of my humiliation and heartbreak.

"I think Malin was married to my mother."

My lips twisted into a gasp of perverse shame. I stopped where I was in the walkway, blessing its emptiness, trembling from my shoulders to my fingertips as I tried to contain my weeping.

Aside from his short intake of breath, Eleison was remarkably silent.

"I take it you knew," I whispered to him.

"Thecla," he began, "I—"

"Please, Eleison. I'm so tired of lying. Let's talk straight, now."

"Yeah," said my mate, the word heavy with guilt. "I'm sorry, Thecla. I knew."

I nodded, although he couldn't see it. "I thought as much. Thank you for telling me the truth. Would you pass the watch back to Charlotte?"

"Will you call me in an hour or two and let me know what's going on with you?"

"I will," I promised him. "I will. Eleison—"

His slight disgust for Malin's courting me early on. *Some families like their secrets.*

Yes—he had certainly known.

"I love you," I told him. "I know that, in another position, if not for your brother, you would have protected me from all of this."

"Please call me soon," Eleison urged hoarsely. "Here's Char."

Charlotte, who had been listening, took the watch from me and launched in at once.

"Thecla, you should know it wasn't my idea to keep anything from you."

"Obviously not," I told her with withering displeasure. "But why did *he* keep it a secret?"

"I can't speak to that without speculation. All I know is that, when he sent me to fetch you, he told me to let him explain your heritage. That it was possible, based on what we knew, that you hadn't been told, and that you would already be overwhelmed. He said he was going to discuss it when you arrived, but…he changed his mind."

"How long was my mother running from him before I was born?"

"Seven years," answered Charlotte without having to think.

"Then—you weren't tasked with looking for a special case at all. Not just any second-generation altered. He had midwives looking across Gudrune for my mother, didn't he?"

Charlotte hesitated a few seconds—how rare, for her hesitate over anything—before saying, "This would be so much easier to explain if you were here, Thecla."

"If you can talk about it in person, you can tell it to me on a call."

I stopped short. The red masonry of the Hunter's Guild had flashed in my peripheral vision and now was gone. Skin flush with sudden warm, I stepped back a few paces and peered down the alley, beyond the canal, and along the symmetrical passageway between nearly identical homes on the canal's other side.

There was the Guild, peeking through.

"Eleison couldn't break Malin's trust because of Kyrie," I said, my head lowering, "and I understand that, though it hurts me. But you, Charlotte—"

I couldn't come up with anything that got to the heart of the matter quite like the simple, perhaps juvenilely accusatory observation:

"I thought we were friends."

Somehow, her inhalation sounded more hurt than ever I had imagined her capable of. I willed myself not to care—she'd had ample opportunity to tell me the truth, after all—but the tang of guilt still stung me for the barb I'd launched.

Now, of course, I realize how much worse she had endured in my husband's fits of temper, and how genuine her sympathy toward my anger truly was.

"Thecla—I know you're hurt, but—"

"Yes, I am. And I need time to process my feelings before I see Malin. I don't even know what to say to him."

"You'll have plenty of time to think on the train," she advised.

For some reason, her response blistered me. "Good-bye, Charlotte," I said while hanging up.

Breath held, I hurried up the short path, through the spare garden, and across the porch of a two-story house I'd never seen.

Yet, not thirty seconds after my knock, the front door swung open—and there, his blue eyes wide with surprise, stood Glenn Stone.

WITH A QUIZZICAL blink in defiance of his eyes, the hunter looked over my shoulder, then back into my miserable face.

His brow furrowed with concern—and his lips drooped apart with something more than a simple frown of empathy.

"Thecla?"

"I'm so sorry to bother you, Glenn. May I come in and just—sit in your house to *think* for a while?"

"Of course, please! Uh—"

As I sniffled in the vestibule, Glenn looked over his shoulder and sprang from shutting the door into the motions of tidying an open concept parlor adjacent to the entry. My eyes slid over the wood paneled walls: largely bare, to my surprise. A viewing screen was arranged along one, and there were some green houseplants that broke up the monotony of color, but something was off about the room.

"You don't keep trophies?"

The question flew out of me as I noticed it. Glenn, his broad arms full of an old glass, a few documents, and—ugh, a copy of that wretched tabloid!—paused on his way to the kitchen opposite.

"Trophies...they're not really my thing. My tattoos serve that purpose, I guess..."

I nodded as he hurried on. The rest of the room was tidy, if only due to its spare decor. Then again, he had been away from home for some months. "Do you employ a housekeeper, Glenn? You keep a neat place for a bachelor."

"Uh, yeah...I have somebody come in and dust the place, water the plants, whatever. I just can't commit to doing it myself when I'm working all the time."

"But you're not back at work yet, I see."

"No...strictly speaking, I'm still recovering until two weeks from now. I just had a feeling I should respond to the Overseer's invitation quickly. Now I'm glad I did."

Appearing around the corner of the kitchen, his face tight beneath his beard, Glenn folded his arms to regard me. With his crisp white undershirt short sleeved around his bicep, I recognized for the first time just how extensive those tattoos of his were. Goodness, yes. They really *were* his trophies: the sleeve of inks provided habitat to an open-mouthed juntis leaping from the sea, a snarling borro that made me long for my mate, a ventil's floral crown blown to petals by the wind. These represented victories, I assumed. Most of the creatures depicted were quite violent animals for a man who spoke to me—who even *looked* at me—so gently. As if he were afraid looking at me might shatter me somehow.

"You don't have to talk about what's going on, obviously,"

Glenn began. He made no move to approach where I sat in the corner of his rustic couch, a stylish but simple orchestration of brown leather and exposed wood. "But, I hope you know—it's a little concerning when a woman shows up at a man's door looking as upset as you do."

"I don't mean to worry you, Glenn. I'm sorry to intrude, I—"

"You don't have to apologize, Thecla. Please." Though his lips briefly turned as though to laugh, he suppressed the instinct and said with a sweep of his eyes along me, "I'm happy you're here."

Those male thoughts. I was so used to the animal behind Eleison's stare—or the devil behind my husband's—that it seemed an altogether different experience when Glenn studied me and let his mind turn, however briefly, to impious avenues of contemplation.

Yet—they didn't seem impious. Not from him.

My heart drummed while his eyes lowered to my shoes. "Can I get you something to drink? Do you need to call anybody? Are you lost?"

Are you lost? That first question again. It coaxed a smile from me.

"No," I told him, "nothing like that. It's just—everyone I know has some...some *interest* to be accounted for. Oh, it's exhausting. I can't speak my mind to anyone without fearing for the politics of what I say...and, worse, because what I want to say today is about my husband, everyone around me has a vested interest in either pushing me toward or away from him. Even Eleison—everybody I know, no matter how concerned for me they seem, will only weaponize that concern to get more information from me. I have nobody to talk to. Even you have an opinion on my husband...not that you intend to do anything about it, but—"

"I'm sorry to hear you're feeling alone," Glenn said in patient response to my tearful ramblings, withdrawing a different, cheaper quality handkerchief than the one he had used to blot the wine stain only the night before. As he crossed the room to pass it to me, he continued, "I feel pretty isolated myself, sometimes... but I don't think I could ever fully empathize with the kinds of things you're feeling."

"Pray you can't. Oh, Glenn—I'm so confused." After wiping my cheek, I pinned the handkerchief to my throbbing temple with the heel of my palm. "I *love* my husband, I do, but— oh, you see, I've just learned something that's hurt me. I'm not sure how to take it."

"Do you want to talk about it?"

As Glenn sat in a loveseat adjacent the sofa I had selected, I lowered the handkerchief to wring in my lap. "Do you know the name "Giselle?""

His lips pursed for a few seconds in which he stared up into the space of his thoughts. "No, I don't—wait—yes! I do. That was Malin's missing wife, right?"

"She wasn't really missing, though, you see. She was on the run. Giselle was my mother...she and my father, I see now what happened—"

My heart broke to think on it; to press the kerchief to my sorrowing chest and say, "When she disappeared for such a long time, and then my birth killed her, it must have been far less taxing for Malin's name to let people think he might have executed her. The truth could have done him some social damage...the fiction, surely that's only added to the fierceness of his reputation through the years."

Realizing Glenn hadn't spoken, I looked over to find his

bushy brown brows high with shock. "I guess that would explain some things," he said, eyebrows slowly lowering back into serious place. "About, you know. "Why you." For a certain definition of explanation, anyway."

I nodded, moaning sadly to say, "And everyone knew it. Everyone in the manor, I mean. Nobody knows she went to Lescaut except for Malin and—well, our housekeeper. And Eleison knows, because he's Malin's close confidant…but I'm not sure who else has been told. Whoever else, it's been too many. I feel like such a fool, like I'm—"

My watch chimed in my pocket.

The bird of my heart battered against the bars of its cage, rattling my entire skeleton with the urgency of its protestations.

There was no need to check who was calling me.

With a pale look at Glenn, I asked, "I'm sorry—is there someplace private I could take this, or, perhaps, could you—"

"Of course," he said quickly, springing up and striding for the kitchen. "Why don't you use my office while I make you some tea."

The office was obvious: an open door, tucked below the cantilevered staircase to the narrow mezzanine of the second floor. "Yes, please, thank you. I'm sorry to be such trouble—"

"Thecla, please. I have a guest room upstairs." His eyes dropped to the pocket watch I had removed but not opened. "Stay as long as you need."

Touched—and a little guiltily excited by the invitation—I managed a small smile, thanked Glenn, then shut the office door. While hovering before a window that overlooked the canal, my face grew too numb to maintain a pleasant expression.

Somehow, my fingers answered the call.

"Oh, thank God." Malin's hewn voice such a balm—and such a pain. Like a knife in my soul, every urgent note. "Thecla, my angel, please—"

"What do you love about me, Malin?"

However he had expected me to open, that wasn't it. The effect was diminutive, however. He faltered for hardly a second before effortlessly beginning, "You're driven, and wise. Your enthusiasm for life, your curiosity for it, is so erotic to me—and besides... I've never seen a woman more beautiful in my entire life."

"Never?"

"Never, ever."

With a sharp inhalation, I turned away from the flowing waters of Valquist and sank into Glenn's leather desk chair. Thumb lowering from his bookshelf to a thread I plucked from my dress, I commanded my lying husband, "Go on."

"The way you smell, the softness of your skin, the lustre of your hair, so radiantly dark...oh, Thecla! Your body drives me mad—mad! I love the way you tolerate my games—"

"I *love* your games," I corrected him firmly, my eyes filling with new tears as they squeezed shut. "I love *you*, Malin."

"Then come home, darling. Thecla, oh—angel, please. Just come home. Let's talk."

"I—"

The idea of acknowledging what I had learned made me feel like I was going to vomit. I could speak my new knowledge to Eleison, or Charlotte, or Glenn. I could tell anyone.

But I could not speak it to Malin. Not on a call. And not just then.

"I can't yet, Malin," I told him, the words raw as my throat. "I'm not ready to see you."

"Please—"

I had never heard him like this. As his love for me stoked his temper, it also inspired a desperation that seemed unnatural in his voice.

"Please, Thecla, I love you so very much— What we have, it has nothing to do with anything else. There is nothing in the world like my love for you, Thecla."

"Malin—"

"Are you planning to stay with the Overseer?"

"Blast the Overseer, you were right about her. I hate her, I hate it here."

"Then come *home*, darling. I can call a car that will get you started right now. Slower than the train. Time to think."

"I can't." The words erupted amid a sob. I pressed Glenn's handkerchief to my eyes as if to emphasize my point while I cried, "I can't look at you. I'm so embarrassed. I'm like a cheap substitute, a—"

"*Never*. No, Thecla. Not ever. This has never been about that, and it will never be about that."

Malin's voice was tinged with anger, sharp and hard beneath the layers of his sorrow. What right had he to be angry? Clenching my teeth, I said, "Then why did you start courting me without telling me the truth about my mother?"

He began to speak, but was forced to pause as his voice broke with the first, inaudible word. My throat tightened. Was he weeping?

"I never wanted to lie to you, Thecla. I've only ever wanted to protect you. Let me shield you against those things from which I cannot protect myself."

My temple throbbed with the headache that had been

rising steadily through the day. I wanted to lie down and weep with my husband, but I obviously could not, and resentment filled my heart to think that.

"Look," I told him, "I want to talk more about this, and about my mother, and about—so much, Malin, but—"

"Then come home."

"—But you must let me—recover."

"It's not that simple. Where are you staying? Eleison and Charlotte are gravely—"

"I'm with Glenn Stone," I told my husband, coming flat out with it and adding with a furtive glance to the shut door, "and I don't know what's going to happen. I don't know how long I'll stay, or how things will…I don't know."

"Don't let him steal you from me, Thecla. Please. You're the only thing in the world that means anything to me. Do you know that?"

Shocked as I somehow was to hear the words, I found myself saying, "I'm not sure I did. Is that true? That makes me so sad, Malin."

"I keep telling you, I'm an old man…death is closer all the time. One distances oneself from worldly things as one ages. At the very least, worldly things lose their color. But when you're around, Thecla—when you walk into the room, when I think about you…sweet Heaven, when I hold you in my arms—all the color of my youth returns, and more. The world has never been so bright, so vivid. You inspire me to make it a *better* world—to give you and our children a better world to live in. Thecla, oh, Thecla…I love you."

"I love you, too. That's why I'm so hurt. Oh—I'm *so* hurt."

"I wish I could touch you right this minute."

"I do, too, but I—please, Malin. Give me time. It's the only thing I'm asking of you."

His low exhalation rattled the line. For a long handful of seconds, I wondered if the call had dropped. Then, he unbound the knot in my chest.

"All right. Yes, darling, of course, all right. But please—I hope you understand—"

His tone, though still overflowing with emotion, darkened somehow. I could hear the tension in his jaw; feel the fire in his black eyes as he said, "If you *do* think you can run from me, know that there is no place I would not go to find you—no resource I would not pool into your pursuit. My hunt for Giselle was always, at best, a background matter. The unrealized vanity project of a woman's persecution and torture. But you, Thecla, will not be able to escape me. You will be all I think about until the day I have you by my side again…and you *will* be by my side again, even if I must break the treaty by visiting Valquist, myself."

My face growing heated by his passion in spite of the pain of it all, I found myself saying in an equally low tone, "You don't need to threaten me into coming back to give you the hiding you've earned, you lying old scoundrel…you *dog*, you…libertine."

"Thecla…that's something else I love about you. You're the only woman—the only person—who could ever be my match. Come home soon, Madame."

"We'll see."

Angry he had reduced me to flirtation, I hung up on him and at once regretted it—yet reveled in it. Such treatment was the very least of what he deserved. The way I saw it, I was entitled to be rude to him.

By the time I composed myself, the kettle was near to

whistling. I edged into the kitchen, feeling more sheepish than I had in months. Glenn looked over with his eyebrows raised expectantly, politely oblivious to whatever he may have overheard through the distant door.

Tongue running over my lower lip, I asked, "Did you really mean it about your guest room?"

"Of course."

"Well, I—I think I might rest a little, if you don't mind. I'm sorry, I know you just started the kettle—"

"Thecla—" Glenn had been checking the contents of a pantry the size of a walk-in closet. He shut the door and turned to me, one hand on the knob, his blue eyes saddened by whatever he found in my face.

"You don't have to keep apologizing. I never have guests, so it's—I don't know. Pleasant. Nice knowing there's somebody around. I wouldn't mind that for a night or two."

"That's really all it will be, of course. The train leaves in a few days. I'm just so out of *sorts*. Before I can face any of them, I—I need a chance to look at the big picture. To be myself. Thank you."

Glenn had approached to snap off the kettle before it could whistle, and I dared to catch his warm hand as it lifted. He froze, his arm braced, the dark hair that ran to his tattooed wrists so much more animal than man. It was funny—to look at us both, one would have assumed *him* to be the altered person.

Almost imperceptibly, Glenn's hand tightened around my fingers. Then, releasing me with his nod, he said, "You're welcome."

"Could you tell me the address of this place? I need a few articles if I'm to sleep here."

He relayed it to me, then added, "But I'm going to run to the market for some things, so I don't know if I'll be around to answer the door while you're asleep…I'm not used to cooking for anybody but myself."

Smiling even as I turned toward the kitchen's exit, I realized, "I haven't had a man *actually* cook for me since Father died…not counting the chef Malin employs, of course."

Glenn laughed, pouring himself a mug of tea and leaving an empty cup if I changed my mind. "Well, this isn't going to be what you're used to…but I've kept myself alive this long, so it must be okay. Come on, I'll show you the guest room."

GLENN'S GUEST ROOM was cozy, to say the least. After pulling back the rustic quilt and sliding, still dressed, into the cool sheets, I reflected on the time I awoke, disoriented and wounded, in some guest suite of Malin's.

In the dim light of the shuttered bedroom, I traced the scar Eleison gave me in the gloomy dark of that nearly fatal pre-dawn accident. My fingertips trailed along the discoloration, the pale pink of scar tissue representing little gashes where my mate's teeth slid into my flesh for the first time.

I shuddered, the spot so sensitive alongside the memories that I soon found myself thinking other, altogether hotter thoughts of Eleison. Oh, Eleison…I regretted having to shun him along with Charlotte, but I needed to be firm. My two dearest friends were Malin's associates and co-conspirators; I couldn't let them influence me while I sorted out what this meant.

What to do.

What *did* I want to do? To understand. No—to believe.

That was what I wanted.

I wanted to believe that Malin truly loved *me*. Not my power, or my heritage. I reflected on his words during the call, the sincere hunger in them, and I wanted very much to accept them as I always had.

But that acceptance now had to combat a doubt never before known. When veiled in too many possibilities, my doubts (Oh, my honeymoon! So far from me then, it seemed) had been abstract. Now that the truth was mostly out, my doubt had taken a specific, newly unshakable form. And it bent over me as my restless mind tried to empty itself for blissful unconsciousness; bent over me, stared into and through me. Just as I found the dharmine doing when, accepting rest was not forthcoming, I opened my eyes.

"You're keeping me from sleep," I told it, my voice softened not by tenderness but by simple exhaustion that prevented me from showing it my usual derision. "What do you want?"

The demon was extended along my body as though we were lovers. I supposed we were. His smile widened as the thought struck me and his fingers trailed over my cheek, up along my brow and into the tangles of my hair. "I was just admiring your beauty. I love it when you're angry. Will you kiss me, Madame?"

"No, dog."

With a wretched but beautiful moan, Dinon lowered his head into the tassels of my hair and took a heaving breath. As his head turned, his lips brushed over my ear.

"You should have permitted me to destroy the Overseer for you, Madame...but I knew you wouldn't."

"Then do you also know when Charlotte will be here with my bag? I'd like a bath. I feel simply terrible."

"Charlotte won't be coming…someone else will."

I paled a little, my body tensing. Eleison, then. Well—he was going to make me feel very guilty about this, but—

Someone knocked on the door downstairs. I jumped in fright and turned my eyes upon that pantherine smile.

"How did you do that?"

"Do what, Madame?"

"How did you—lure me into conversation so I would say that just before—"

"Thecla? It's Aleister."

I sat up in surprise, so befuddled that I was halfway out of bed before I realized Dinon had disappeared. "Just a moment," I called back, not sure if my voice carried through the house as well as Aleister's. When I made it into the mezzanine, another round of knocks rang out; I hurried down to the front door, where I found myself perhaps ten seconds later.

"Thank *goodness*," said Aleister with a sigh, gesturing for the security guard he'd brought. The man at once fetched my familiar bag down from the roof of the carriage. "I was starting to worry we'd gotten the wrong house…or that you'd *really* run away. I'm not used to doing errands."

"Why *are* you here?"

His visitation so surprised me that the question may have come off a bit rude. Luckily, Aleister laughed while he let the security man pass him into the house. "I'm wondering that, myself. Malin seems to think I owe him for bringing you up here. Never realized he was the type to shoot his messengers like this."

"It's that room," I told the man, pointing to the guest room before looking back to Aleister with my arms folded and my mouth tight. "So Malin thinks you can talk sense into me?"

"Maybe. Or, maybe he thinks I'm the least threatening option... I'm sorry, dear. I know it isn't your house, and I hate to impose, but—"

He was eying the sitting area, and I nodded while letting him in. "I'm sure Glenn won't mind if you sit for a few minutes."

"Thank you, oh, good Lord...I got dressed, had a meeting and rode in a carriage, and just like that, I'm ready to go back to bed. I'm never eating fish on a train again. Never ever..."

While Aleister sank into the arm of the loveseat and pressed his handkerchief to his forehead, I cast a frown into the kitchen. The kettle was still warm enough, and the teacup from earlier waited for me. I poured a cup for Aleister as he said, "Anyway, *I* know I can't convince you not to spend a few days shacking up with *the* Glenn Stone, but let's be realistic...you understand Malin will have him killed if you two get some kind of idea, don't you?"

Mouth drawn, I handed Aleister the mug and watched him animate just a little. While he leaned forward to sip from it, I sat in the couch diagonal to his seat and told him, "That isn't what this is. I just—"

"Need time to think, yes, that's what Uncle told me. But look how his ex-wife's "thinking" turned out."

"It produced me." I waved a hand over myself and earned a curious look that slowly gained understanding. "Do you know why he was so upset about me coming here? Because he knew it was inevitable I would discover his first wife was my mother, Giselle."

First arching a brow, then narrowing his eyes and tilting his head, Aleister sat up a little. "That *is* where I know you from, isn't it! You do almost begin to resemble her...almost. I've only seen photos, of course. That was before my time... How interesting! I suppose you're not a peasant after all."

As the duke sipped his tea, I scoffed. "It doesn't—I don't know, *shock* you?"

Aleister's laugh was patronizing for the second it erupted; but, to his credit, he kept it short. Waving the cup with his shrug, he said, "Dear me, the parties I've been to? No, I suppose it doesn't really bother me. I mean—it's not real, genetic incest, is it? Why, it's barely even *legal* incest. His decision not to tell you was in poor taste, certainly, but...goodness, if I were him, I probably wouldn't want to tell you, either."

Balking at this casual confirmation of the duke's low morals, I rubbed my forefinger over the bridge of my nose. Even that seemed like it was beginning to tighten with this undying headache. "That goes to show why you two are such good friends..."

"And you, Thecla?"

When I opened my eyes, Aleister spoke to me in defiance.

"If you were the Matrix of Gudrune, if you had all this money and power and could buy any man you wanted, and then—let's say, long-lost Eleison's son comes trotting into your study, and he's just so beautiful that he steals your heart. Are you really going to crater the chemistry by saying, "Oh, you know, I was embroiled for a few years in a miserable relationship with your father.""

"Eleison and I have a wonderful relationship," I protested, although I knew that wasn't the point and was summarily rebuffed as such.

"It doesn't matter, it's just an example. You know what I mean, blast it. Malin *loves* you, Thecla. The way he tells it, he fell in love with you at nearly first sight. When was he supposed to tell you?"

"I—I don't know. Before the wedding, surely."

"Then you would have had the same problem, perhaps on a worse scale. Especially since you didn't bear some degree of obligation at the time. But now, of course, you *are* obligated to Malin...so I hope you're going to keep a level head and get on that train."

Jaw clenching, I lowered my eyes to the mug in his hand because it was easier than looking in his face. "You don't need to speak to me like I'm some sort of—unruly *child*. Furthermore... you're a very fine one to be here talking to me."

Aleister scoffed. "What's that supposed to mean?"

"I suppose you haven't seen that awful tabloid, since you've been in bed. Here." I rushed into the kitchen, where I'd seen Glenn pile it upon the edge of the dining table; a few seconds later I tossed it into Aleister's lap to let him regard it in growing shock.

"This article is full of absolute drivel, but there are details about myself and Eleison that are derived from truth. Is this where you ran off when you got off the train that day, Aleister?"

"Of course not! No, no—why would I do a thing like that? I don't need the money, certainly...nor Malin's ire."

"Then maybe I should ask your sister for more details about this magic mirror of mine." Aleister blushed furiously at my barb, and I knew I had him. "It was Brea who told you that one, wasn't it?"

"She was a *very* chatty little creature," Aleister admitted, chastened enough to fidget around in his search for a place to set his mug. "And I admit, I can never resist gossip. Perhaps—well, I didn't tell any tabloids anything, but...I do suppose it's possible I might have...confirmed some curiosity of Josko's when I was feeling comfortable aboard the train."

My hands clenching into fists, I told him darkly, "I thought Malin was your mentor. That you cared for him."

"I *do*. Of course I do. It was just, you know, a few moments of poor judgment…poorly chosen confidants…lesson learned."

Something in Aleister's tone gave me pause.

He was afraid of me. Even if only a little—only in this moment—the duke realized I had the power to destroy his relationship with Malin. End it so utterly his very life would be in danger.

I would never have done such a thing, of course.

But I *did* have that power. And we both realized it.

"Well," I told him tersely, stepping back toward the door to encourage him out of his seat, "for someone who claims to be my husband's friend, you've chosen to become very chummy with a lot of people who despise him. It's shocking to me, Aleister, that you have any love for him at all. When I hear what the Overseer thinks of him, and when I read what all the people here are willing to say of me, of us—I just think you can do much better."

I pulled open the door to reveal the security man waiting patiently outside. "I hope you'll think about that sincerely."

With the look of a whipped puppy, Aleister gazed at me from beneath lowered lids. The barest hint of a pout tugged at the corner of his mouth, and I had the distinct impression I was looking at a boy in the rough size and shape of a man. He possessed a psyche that had never progressed very far beyond the hedonism of mid-adolescence.

"I'd rather get a hundred of Malin's temper tantrums than another guilt trip like that, Thecla…good gracious. I—well, I shouldn't defend myself."

"You shouldn't."

"But I *am* sorry." He glanced at the tabloid shut in the couch. "That looks like a very ugly article, and if I had known— I'm very sorry, Thecla."

"It's fine. It doesn't matter anymore." The person who wrote it was dead. That thought's comfort settled over me with a soothing weight. Like the dharmine's embrace. "Thank you for checking in on me, but I'm really all right…I promise, I'll be on the train."

When I shut the door behind him, a great burden dropped from my mind.

There. It was done. Amazingly—blessedly—I had gotten out of that awful palace for the remainder of my stay. I would be able to process what I had learned.

What Aleister had asked me.

Brooding, I made my way back up to the mezzanine and set my hand on the guest room knob. Just as I opened the door, I recognized the sound of water running in the bathroom adjacent. My motion froze. With only a little hesitation, I made my cautious way to the shut door, knocked upon its surface, then leaned hesitantly in.

While warm water poured into the bath, Dinon hung my robe above a small heater. The reverence with which he trailed his fingers along the hem made me feel as though I had been touched, and I willed myself to feel only the same old disgust for the shadow chasing me across the continent.

"If you can move so quickly to and fro, Dinon, why did it take you so long to catch up with me?"

"I glide on your thoughts when you think of me. When you don't, or won't, I can only move as any being does. Please—allow me."

I had raised my fingers to the buttons of my gown, but Dinon swept across the dark blue mosaic of the floor to kneel before me. Even then, his head met my chest. I willed my heart to steady itself as his pale fingers moved from button to button.

"I suppose that's why you arrived so quickly when I finally thought of you…"

"Yes, that's why. I love being thought of by you. Though it's never as good as sight, or touch, or taste…" His silver eyes flickered over my bustier as he gently pushed the fabric open and helped me slide it down my body. He kept the gown from the floor as I stepped out of it, folding it over his arm and averting his eyes without my having to command him. Turning away from him all the same, I slid my underthings off as he went on to sigh, "And everything is nothing beside our congress, Madame, oh, Madame—"

"You say that as though it's a given. I can't ever imagine disgracing myself by letting you mount me, animal. I'll take Eleison's borro before I permit such a thing."

"You will," Dinon agreed, that insufferable (insufferably lovely) smile illuminating his voice as I tossed my bustier in annoyance. "But, Madame, I am patient…endlessly patient when it comes to you. May I serve you in the bath?"

"No," I told him, even though the genuine hope of his soft plea sent a bolt of red excitement running through me. "Just arrange a fresh dress for me and make yourself scarce. And no matter what happens, do not lay a finger upon Glenn. Not—not unless he's an active, present danger to my life, or to Malin's. The same is true of anyone, in fact. Take what I give you and nothing more, unless there's peril."

"As you wish, Madame."

"But—" He had been stepping toward the shared wall between the guest bedroom and the bathroom. Now he paused to look back at me, my clothes over his arm. "Mind that you listen for me, wherever you go when you're unseen. I may require you this evening."

With a bow, Dinon said, "It would be my great pleasure, Madame. Don't worry. I'm always listening for you, wherever I go."

As he stepped through the wall and left me alone, I shuddered, then cut off the water.

The tub was a far cry from the fancily outfitted and ornamented one of the Overseer's guest suite, or the clawfoots favored in Malin's homes. It was slim and simple, but it did the job. I slid into the warm water, letting my hair wet to my neck, and felt as I simply hadn't when in the bed with my eyes shut.

But my mind still struggled for a solution.

If Malin really, truly did love me for reasons apart from my heritage, then fine—that was what I wanted, all I wanted. I could live with having shared a man with my dead mother if I knew that was the case.

And I *did* know that...but that doubt, that hateful doubt! The anger. This was why I hadn't wanted to talk to Eleison or Charlotte. Even Aleister had managed to reason with me too much for my liking. He had forced me to empathize with Malin almost against my will, because he'd had something of a point amid all his flippant responses. It was impossible to know when to reveal the truth to someone who had spent their whole life bundled in lies.

But, my God—Malin hadn't even *tried* to be honest! I couldn't fathom ever being in his position and not looking for every last opportunity to reveal the truth.

And, yet—

It *would* have changed us, wouldn't it? As sensitive and uncertain as I was when Malin first courted me, that knowledge would have shocked me out of our developing romance.

Now, of course…something in me had changed. The deaths of Gall and Vivian saw to that. I was still shocked, and pained; but, as the dharmine observed, it was possible to hold two conflicting notions simultaneously. There were two hands involved. On the one, Malin was my romantic partner, my husband, my lover and friend; on the other hand, separately, he was also my mother's legal husband until her death, and shared with her an antagonistic emotional history that had been hidden from me.

These two states, objectively speaking, didn't *need* to affect one another. They existed in different spheres of time, and in the gap between, Malin had surely grown into a different person. Yet, I couldn't keep them from collaborating in some perverse superposition in my mind. It was like the Rift dimension brushing against ours. Sometimes, impact was impossible to avoid.

A sort of understanding struck me. My head sagged back against the rim of the tub. The blank canvas of the ceiling seemed to contort with the aura of my migraine.

"It's Rift weather," I said softly.

"There will be an Event," Dinon agreed in my mind's ear.

Downstairs, the front door slammed shut.

My nerves crackled with Glenn's presence in the house. It were as though I had somehow managed to forget where I was, or what he had to do with it. Now, his every step echoed in the center of my body. I laid my hand upon my heart and braced myself against the sudden surge of greedy thoughts half-formed by his nearness. His heavy boots trekked into the kitchen, where something was deposited upon the counter; then, step by step, they eased toward the staircase.

The house creaked with his ascent.

My pulse sped. Had I locked the door? He was a respectful man, but I suddenly felt so exposed—

Yet so excited.

Glenn stopped a few steps from the door.

"You in there, Thecla?"

"Yes, I—I'll just be a minute—"

"It's fine, take your time. I'm getting dinner started. Just thought I'd let you know it takes a couple of hours."

"Then I'll spend them with you, starting in a few moments. It's kind of you to make me dinner."

"It's my pleasure. Really."

The sincerity of his tone was so touching…and saddening. The loneliness and hopelessness of it! I wanted to draw him into my arms and simply hold him.

But, of course, that wouldn't be the end of things.

Perhaps that was how Malin felt toward me, in a way.

What *was* I doing? My mood had settled just enough for me to critically examine myself. I had three men, if I included the demon whose persistent overtures were by now undeniable— what did I need of four? Why, that blasted fortune teller had only accounted for *three* men, for starters!

Hadn't he? Well—how had he said it? I rubbed my forehead, struggling to remember the precise wording used. My brain presented me with images of Eleison, and the panic of the Rift after. Only then did I successfully evoke the sound of the old man's voice.

Two…no…three. But…the other is only a man as much

as a shadow is a man...as much as a male beast may be called a man.

Something like that. But had he meant "the other" as in "the third man," or had he meant "the other" as in "another being, apart from the men?"

Had I not understood?

Parvati, arguing about free will to me, didn't seem to realize there was no reason free will and predestination had to be mutually exclusive. What choices could we make, after all, but our own? What might we perform in this life but that which our souls have already scripted in the annals of Eternity?

How could anyone believe depriving humanity of technological advancement would stop the Rift?

Emotionally drained, I lay in my watery cocoon another twenty minutes before crawling out with a shiver for the comparatively cold room. The dharmine had the foresight to leave my brush upon the sink's edge, and I quietly contemplated the vague colors making up my steamed reflection while I detangled my hair. Satisfied, I fetched my warmed robe, enjoyed the embrace of its paisley silk, and slipped out into the hall.

I headed toward my guest room to dress, but Glenn stepped out of the kitchen, so I paused to smile at him. "Oh," he said quickly at the same time, seeing me in my robe and stepping back from sight with a muttered, "Sorry, excuse me."

Laughing, I leaned against the mezzanine's banister to bend over it just so. "It's all right, Glenn, you can't *really* see anything. I'll prove it."

While he reluctantly stepped back into sight and allowed himself to appreciate the look of me, I felt that developing strain of boldness express itself in me again. Why dress at all? I decided to skip it altogether and made my way down the stairs with a smile, twirling as I reached the bottom. "See?" The hem of the green robe fell around my knees while I assured him, "It's even almost modest."

"Almost," he agreed with a wry laugh. "You want a little wine?"

Moments later, there we were, chatting as if we'd known one another for decades. While I leaned against the partition along the back of the kitchen counter and the busy stove, Glenn cooked and drank and refilled my glass from the other side. "It just amazes me," I said, mesmerized by the deft motions of his hands along vegetables and a side of ferato meat. "You're nothing at all like I had imagined you, Glenn."

"Care to elaborate?"

"Oh, I don't know...there are a lot of men who think they're above cooking. Or"—I added with a sidelong look at him from behind my glass—"they do just enough of it to lure in a wife, then stop."

His teeth flashing in a brilliant arc of white beneath his beard, Glenn jostled a layer of sizzling onions along the bottom of the pot. "That's probably true...nobody else is going to feed me if I don't cook right now, after all. But—I don't know. I've found that I really enjoy cooking. Especially if I've hunted the meat myself. It's a time where I don't have to think about anything...I'm just present."

"That's how I feel about my weaving. Ugh!" Suddenly miserable at the thought of my loom, I draped my arm across the partition and let my head sag upon it. "I've missed my work terribly on this trip. Oh, blast—I hope Charlotte is careful when she packs my new design."

While I nibbled on the edge of my thumb and wondered if I'd oughtn't to call her, my host looked up at me with interest. "I didn't know you were a weaver."

"Yes, well, they managed to omit that from the tabloid article, funnily enough…" He cringed guiltily while I swirled my wine. "I must admit I was the *tiniest* bit disappointed to see you with a copy of that trash."

"Thecla—I'm sorry. I just—"

"No, it's all right, I understand."

"The picture of you on the cover," he blurted, his eyes skipping over me. My mouth opened in silent surprise as he went on. "I know I invited you to come by, but I didn't expect— When I woke up this morning, my first thought was that I'd never see you again. I didn't want to forget your face."

As brightly as this sweet notion speckled my cheeks and throat, I couldn't help but pout. "That awful picture? But that's not how I look—"

"It's a beautiful picture," he insisted, referring to the one snapped while my expression seemed grim. "And it *is* how you look."

"You know, I've heard men sometimes insult women as a form of flirtation…it doesn't work, Glenn."

While I hid my smile, he laughed and protested on. "I'm being *serious*. You're sexy, of course. And—fresh, somehow." He added this with a quick glance into my face, then into the pot where he slid the seasoned meat. "As if you're young, but…if you don't mind telling, how old are you?"

"Nearly twenty-five."

"You *are* young," he observed while I scoffed with displeasure. "I don't know why I thought you were older than that. Maybe it's just how you move, or speak. There's something about you that's—stern."

Now he described Malin…and I wasn't sure I could argue with him. "Most people would say that's a bad quality," I said into my wine glass nonetheless.

Almost too quickly, Glenn assured me, "I wouldn't," then stopped himself with a look away as if in assessment of his ingredients.

Something changed in the air—in my understanding of Glenn.

"I suppose"—I set the glass upon the bar to rotate its base beneath both sets of pointers and thumbs—"there are those rare men secure enough as not to feel threatened when a woman takes a firm hand with them. I'll have to keep it mind. Did your mother teach you to cook, Glenn?"

Was it my imagination, or did new color shine in his face? Did his eye more boldly appreciate the column of my throat, the shade of my cleavage?

"My grandmother," he said, relieved my change of subject allowed more innocent discourse. "She ran a tavern where I grew up."

"And where was that?"

And on we talked…although now, as predatory fish respond to blood in the water, I was charged with increased interest in what Glenn could provide me. Not to mention—I was embarrassingly preoccupied by his assessment of my character, however erotically weighted it had been. Although I didn't want to think of myself in such a way, I really was becoming increasingly stern. With the dharmine, with the help; even Charlotte.

Everyone but Malin and Eleison, really…and why were they exempt? Because they made me feel soft-hearted to look or think upon? Because they were men who made me feel existence itself were an erotic delight, and that submission to them was as natural as the contortion of water to the shape of its container?

Why did I feel this compulsion to be agreeable? This shame to assert reasonable boundaries?

At least I knew the guilt of that evening was largely because of Glenn. The temptation he represented was one I never would have expected to feel. But—outside of some latent longings that Malin's libertine lessons had primed me to sense, Glenn was just so *normal*. Luridly normal. After nearly a year of two exceptional men, both of whom had ample reason to love me from the start of our acquaintance, here was a man who was attracted to me—maybe even capable of falling in love with me—and who was not compelled to do so by either biology or history. Here was a man, I imagined, who would make any woman very happy, in a peaceful, comfortable sort of loving quite different from Malin's ownership or Eleison's immolation.

And, as dinner wore on, somehow all I could think was how jealous I was of that theoretical woman of Glenn's. In fact—a part of me began to hate him, almost despise him, knowing he could never be mine. A man so normal could never be satisfied with the kind of lifestyle I and my lovers enjoyed.

Especially not a man who hated my husband.

My other relationships loomed large but silent in the room. We talked about everything else. I explained the process of weaving to him, since he seemed interested, and I went on to describe in enthusiastic, drunken detail the story of the play I adapted to tapestry. From there, we got to talking about books. I told him about the Leftners, whose small in-house bookshop Glenn did in fact visit one day during his time in Lescaut. In return, he traded his own small-town stories with me, and by the time dinner was over and we were into the second bottle, four hours had passed with hardly a lag in conversation.

"Now that I'm no longer there"—I sighed contentedly as I reclined in the couch beside his loveseat—"I'm glad I grew up where I did...but, at the time, it was *miserable*. That little girl I used to be! Oh, the things I could tell her now."

My laughing lips closed into a lingering smile. I ran my fingers around the rim of the glass balanced on my thigh. A strange impulse came over me, and I said to Glenn, "About the only interesting thing that ever happened was when the circus came to town."

"Oh, really? I've never been."

"No! Not once? Goodness, I wish I could take you!" The idea of beholding someone's first trip through such a spectacle—being responsible for it, no less!—filled me with sympathetic delight. As he laughed, I went on, "It's *very* fun. There are rides and exciting amusements—tattooed ladies, you might like them. Bearded ones, too. And, oh, cheap games...but they're all frauds, all of them. Except! One time, when my sister was very young, I won a—a little fish... Now, *that* was a very fun year. It lived quite a while! Three years, almost four...hm."

I smiled to think of that well-kept, merry goldfish, and pined for my sister, Sable. What a simple time! A father to watch over us, and a village that was full of love and comfort.

A village where everyone must have known the truth about me, and had quietly protected me until some stranger from out-of-town broke trust without knowing better.

Not so simple at all.

Suddenly, I was tired of wine. My drunken pleasure turning to melancholia, I leaned forward to set my glass upon the coffee table. My robe fell from my thigh and Glenn' eye dropped to the limb, then struggled back to my face by a scenic route. I made no effort to fix my dishevelment while I went on.

"One year—the last year it was *really* fun—I met this…old fortune teller." I crossed my legs and let the fabric fall away from the other as well. Glenn's view was hampered only by the arms I crossed over my closed thighs as I sat forward in the telling. Now sure he was invited, the hunter looked.

"He seemed like a normal con man—"

"I like how you know the standard for that," he teased while I took my turn to laugh.

"*Well!* You do get to know the type when you visit the circus…and I didn't grow up in the *finest* parts of Lescaut, now, but that's another story. Anyway—he told me that he was riftborn. And when I didn't believe him, he proved it to me."

The tone changed a little. I became more introspective, looking down at the diamond of shadows where the edges of my robe split apart against my thigh. "I didn't understand what he was telling me, but he showed me—Eleison. And he told me how many men would come to love me."

"How many?"

"That's for me to know," I rejoined Glenn coyly, allowing myself to admire the swell of his broad chest beneath the dark blue fabric of the buttoned shirt he'd pulled on before dinner. "And for the men in my life to wonder about until the dust has settled into a constellation that pleases every star…oh, Glenn—"

I sighed, settling back into his couch, my hand sliding over my throat as I admired him.

"It's a pity you live so far away, out here, in such an inhospitable place."

"Maybe it's for the best...I don't know how well I'd get along with your husband."

"You've never even *met* him. I'm sure you would get along with him just fine—he'd probably even like you, if only because I do. Why does everyone think he's a monster?"

"Well, the war aside...people are suspicious of Giselle's disappearance."

"Exactly." My arms folded over my ribs as I spoke with withering displeasure. "All these books claiming he murdered her—utter nonsense, the foulest libel."

"He never did anything to dissuade people of the idea he had her executed, though, Thecla. What was the world supposed to think when his wife disappeared?"

My throat tightened to remind myself of the reality: that this *was* my reality, the very genesis of it. "I suppose that's true. But—well—don't you suppose he had a good reason not to tell the world about...everything?"

Looking at me for a long time, Glenn finished his wine before saying, "Yeah. I guess he did."

"How you hate a man you've never met!"

"Well? I'm sorry, Thecla. I know this will upset you, but I think it's pretty awful that he groomed you—"

"*Groomed!*"

"—without your knowledge, might I add, into a marriage that's, well—incestuous."

Funny to think the duke had earlier sat in that same seat, arguing the absolute opposite point! "You're using such strong language," I protested. "I'm an adult. He didn't *groom* me, he seduced me. It's not as if Malin's really my stepfather."

That earned a look from beneath Glenn's arched brow.

"Were they ever divorced?"

My hand shot forward to collect my wine from the coffee table again.

"I *suppose*," I sputtered while Glenn stroked his beard to physically withhold a laugh, "on the most *absolute and technical* level, then, well, then *yes*, he *was*, one might argue, my stepfather in a very—*limited, legal* sense, *strictly!* But then my mother died, and Malin didn't adopt me. I didn't even meet him until this year! We have known one another only as adults, and my relationship with him is adult, period. And what are you laughing at, you scoundrel?"

"I'm so sorry"—Glenn's eyes crinkled with delight while I scowled, his hand dropping into a shrug with its fellow—"it's just, your face is so red. It's awful to laugh at—"

"*No*," I said with a sigh, admitting, "this whole thing feels like a classic farce. Before you know it, someone's nefarious schemes will be discovered while someone else is hiding in a closet…anyway, my point is that my mother's life overlapped with mine for but a handful of hours once I was born. And I'm sure, if Malin *had* taken me as his ward when my father died, he would have been a stellar stepparent, and in those circumstances I would regard him in a paternal manner. But—I simply can't imagine that now."

My high-growing headache's throb swiftly outpacing the wine's ability to numb it, I rubbed my hand over my brow. "I need this time to think because, intellectually, I *know* I should be revolted and betrayed…and emotionally, I am those things, of course. But—"

That hand slid from my face to my throat, which strained with sorrow.

"—the love is so much greater. It's pathetic to admit—airheaded, maybe—but he was right. It's not what I've learned that upsets me most…it's that I've learned it at all. The first and purest season of our love has been ended in favor of a new one."

A new one—but perhaps a deeper one, if I could ever stand to forgive him. That would all depend on what he had to say, and how sincerely he meant it, and how I felt when I finally had more time between myself and the revelation.

And whether or not that was the end of his secrets.

"You must have hundreds of women at your beck and call," I chastised Glenn for his wince as I pined for Malin. "Why do you look so sad when you hear that I love my husband, or Eleison?"

"It's hard not to when we've just been sitting here talking about—Lescaut, a simple life, all of this. I can see how open and sensitive your heart is, and it makes me worry that you're…being taken advantage of. If you want to know the whole truth, I feel bad that you've fallen so passionately in love with somebody who's dishonest."

"And you would be honest. Wouldn't you, Glenn."

"Yes," he said unflinchingly. "People who love each other shouldn't keep important secrets from each other."

"You're such a rare breed! I believe you when you say that."

"Moral people aren't as rare as you seem to think they are," Glenn told me, adding, "but I understand why you'd get that impression, moving out of Lescaut and into Malin's life."

"Goodness…" Sighing, I tossed back the remainder of my glass and set the empty thing aside. "For one of his detractors, you certainly do bring him up a lot."

"Sorry. It bothers me."

"I can tell…oh, but Malin's done so much good for me. He's

clothed me and fed me things I never would have had otherwise, and made love to me—and *taught* me the art of love. And its variations.”

My hand, upon my throat again, trailed down the swell of my bosom. “Have you ever let a woman whip you, Glenn?”

Though his nostrils flared and male hunger darkened his features, he only followed the trailing of my fingers for a second or two.

“I can’t say that I have.” His breath escaped him in a near-gasp as I drew the edge of the robe back from my breast. “Thecla—”

“It’s the sweetest ecstasy, being whipped by one’s beloved. Caned or spanked or birched—oh, my favorite, birching. It’s got a delicious sting.”

My nipple beaded with exposure to his eye. I ran my fingertips along its nerves before steadily undoing the knot at my waist.

“Thecla,” Glenn murmured, unable to help but watch as I untied the robe, “you’re drunk.”

“I’m Madame Farrow of Gudrune. If I want you to look at me, you’ll look.”

Breathless, Glenn searched my face, then followed the motion of falling silk. “Okay. I’m sorry.”

“That’s all right, darling…I know you didn’t mean it. I know you want to look at me. You just don’t want to let yourself. But that’s the good news. You don’t have to let yourself do anything. I’m *telling* you to do it.”

Free of the robe, I rose.

How his avid gaze kindled a furnace in me! Turning with all the grace I could muster in my drunken state, I ran my hands over myself and begged to know, "Don't you think I'm fuckable?"

As unprepared to hear the word from my lips as I had been to hear any such thing from Malin the first time, the hunter grew powerless beneath me. "Very," he whispered. "God, yes. You're gorgeous—oh, Thecla, but—"

I pouted, my lower lip protruding to comedic extent. "But you don't want to fuck me, because I'm Malin's wife."

"No," Glenn said quickly. "No, no, that's not it. It's just, you're very drunk"—he inhaled as his cursory effort to stand was ended by my hand upon his shoulder and the straddling of my thighs over his lap—"and I don't want you to…regret anything."

"I don't think I will," I told him, taking his face in my hands. His beard was so much softer than it looked. My pulse thudding in my very fingertips, I bent my head until our noses brushed through the screen of my hair. "Please, Glenn…oh…"

I whined, suddenly aware with alarm of the rising pressure inside me. My body felt dense, as though the headache had extended itself over me. Sensitized me. All I wanted was to lie in bed while the men—*my* men—made love to me to ease my terrible suffering.

Another heat, I realized…and there I was, Glenn the only man in reach.

Once our lips had brushed and my tongue had barely been permitted to snake into his mouth, Glenn told me in that soft, so very patient tone, "If you really want to now, you'll really want to tomorrow…when you're sober."

Another, more pathetic whimper arose from my throat. How could I tell him that, if the Event ahead was as severe as my forecasting headache hinted it would be, I wouldn't be sober for some days? How could I explain without revealing my nature that, with the fever I was about to endure, the question was not one of want, but of need?

"Fine," I told him in a husky murmur, turning around to sit in his lap with my legs splayed. "Then hold me, and endure your torture without relief…ah—"

As Glenn realized with a low intake of breath that the hand I caressed along my thigh was doing more than trying to entice him, he once again murmured my name.

"Keep saying it," I begged him in a whisper. "Keep saying my name…oh, Glenn!"

How it had excited me to exhibit myself to him! The resulting slick between my thighs made me so unbearably sensitive that I marveled. I'd hardly realized the effect teasing him had upon me—and I was far from alone. Now that I was against him, the heat of his body warm against my back and arms, I could feel, too, the protrusion in his lap.

"Touch my body, at least," I commanded while I built my own pleasure in the valley of my thighs, shocked by how sensitive I was to even my own caress. "Kiss me, Glenn—oh, Glenn—"

That, he could do, and his great hand cupped my cheek to turn my face toward his. Panting into his mouth, I thrust my tongue into this still unfamiliar territory and pleaded with him to follow along into mine. Tentatively, then with irresistible vigor, he probed past the warm cave of my lips, and the hand that had lain upon my cheek trailed down to the very edge of my bosom. My free hand caught his, and though he wouldn't let me guide it to where my other worked me to ecstasy, he let me press his palm to the flesh of my stomach, the tensing muscles of my abdomen, the curve of my rocking hip.

"I thought," he breathed hotly, his fingers sinking deeply into my stimulated skin and absorbing every twitch, every flutter and spasm, "that you needed protection from other people. But I'm starting to think you're the kind of woman who needs protecting from herself, Thecla."

"What a strange thing to say…oh, Glenn—"

"It's not, though. You run so hot…your heart is so—ah, so open—"

His hand had crossed from the right breast to the left, which he held and sweetly caressed while his mouth swooped toward my neck. I moaned, gasping in delight, sometimes tickled by the brushes of his beard as his lips and tongue collected little tastes of me. The hunter's weapon was stiff against my rump, and as I ground against him in my pleasure, I swore I felt it twitch. My bliss was all the sweeter for it. I found myself once more urging his unoccupied hand toward my busy one.

"Thecla," he began again, but I gasped in desperation as he raised his head to look into my eyes.

"Please, Glenn—don't be frightened of me just because I'm—"

A fire leaping in his eyes, he leapt, too. Glenn lunged down against my mouth to keep me from saying it. I moaned into his kiss, thrashing, then thrilling. His great hand, warmer and so much more calloused than the hands to which I was accustomed, slid over my working one of its own accord.

We moaned together, me at his small allowance and him at the ardent workings of my fingertips between my labia. It was still an unbearable tease, for he only shadowed my fingers and directly brushed my vulva or clitoris in torturous glances. My toes curled and I found my knees sagging apart just a little more, my pelvis arching to steal a direct brush of his finger or thumb against shimmering flesh.

How the embrace of his hand on mine intensified my pleasure, even without those stolen caresses—those whispers of contact whose escalation he somehow managed to resist! Arousal poured from me, and the fingertips that mimicked mine as they swept down to take advantage of it only increased the deluge. He deviated when I crooked a pair of fingers inside myself, the pads of his middle and third finger drawing back along my knuckles to resist my entreaty; but he gasped softly, or so I swore, and when I opened my eyes from the half-dreaming state into which they'd slid, he was looking down into my lap with an expression of wonder.

Then, at last unable to resist, it happened. Those deviating fingers slid aside from my hand and, with tentative care, caressed me.

Overwhelmed, I cried his name in shock and delight. He said nothing, though his soulful eyes raised to study my face as his fingertips tickled the mound of my clitoris. By the third such trailing around and over the nearly deadly nerve, I was so faint with pleasure that I drew my fingers from myself to extend the moment.

Feeling the shift, Glenn delivered a slow, passionate kiss that seemed synchronized to the slide of his fingers just barely inside me.

I sank my teeth into his lower lip and twisted my head to cry his name. He slowly, tenderly worked his digits within my boundary, barely even spreading me with their penetration—yet, in that moment, I was so primed, so desperate to be filled, that anything was better than nothing.

Though there was no substitute for the firm, pleasantly sized prick I reached back to paw through Glenn's trousers.

"Don't," he commanded even as he pleasured me, the word a growl. "Don't do that, Thecla."

"Oh, but Glenn, why does it matter now?"

"Some heavy petting is one thing...*fucking*, as you put it, is another." I moaned sharply at his word choice; more sharply still as his fingers sank deeper into the mossy bed of my soul. With reluctance, I withdrew my hand and raised it to tangle with his beard. He kissed my ear, his words pouring hotly into it. "And it's getting harder to resist you by the second...you really like to get fucked, huh, Thecla..."

"Oh, yes, oh, *heavens*, yes, it's my favorite way to pass the time, there are some days it's all I think about—oh, God, oh, Glenn—Glenn!"

His fingers hastened, their experimental crooking soon, with the help of my gasp, uncovering the right angle by which to coax me to powerful completion. "I promise you," I whispered to him, my breathing rapid as my heart, "I want you to take me—I want your prick inside of me, oh, fuck, Glenn—"

While he groaned, his hand upon my breast slid down to replace my work at my clitoris. I nearly screamed, relenting to his control of my body, and kissed his cheek and beard and firm-set mouth while he drove me to a point of no return.

"If you really want it, you'll still want it tomorrow...won't you, Thecla..."

"Oh, no! You evil man, no—I'll refuse you just to spite you! Oh, sweet fuck. I'll pleasure myself all day and make you listen."

"You might have me breaking down the door," he admitted, his expression changing as he identified the glassiness in mine. His fingers worked expertly within and without me, the musician playing on a new instrument to test its tune. "Are you going to cum for me, Thecla? Go on"—he smiled as I groaned with deep pleasure at his question—"let me see it. You've got the most beautiful face! Thecla—"

"Oh, Glenn!"

My entire body rippled with a singular tightening. I arched my hips, gripping him with one hand and the loveseat with the other. As I managed to let go of his beard, my throbbing body pulsed wet, hot love around his fingers. He gasped in soft wonder, his fingers remaining sheathed until I was through.

Then, gingerly, they slid away.

"We should probably get to bed," he said.

Though I nodded weakly, he caught my cheek.

"I mean it, Thecla…if you still want to—"

"I will."

"Then we can. As long as you want it, and you don't get too drunk."

As he tacked on that last part, I laughed a little: but, now that I think of it, getting drunk might have made the next day— the next afternoon, anyway—a mite easier.

EXHAUSTION HAD RUINED me; yet I could not sleep. I was drunk, I had not rested well since falling asleep in the cinema, and my brain pulsed so urgently within the case of my skull that I felt my head really was going to burst this time. All I wanted was sleep; yet there I was, tossing and turning, nursing my deception. My rejection.

Damn Glenn and his gentlemanly ways! Malin would have—

Malin would have taken me unhesitatingly, appreciative of my amorous nature when it was exposed by libations.

I shivered, able to see the trouble at once. The trouble was not Malin's nature. It did not upset me, because I knew it before I ever met him. I knew him to be a liar, a fiend, a rake. To ask him to be anything but those things was to desire a wholly different person.

And that was my problem. Because, oh—even as his lies hurt me, the mere thought of him taking advantage of me set my body endlessly aflame. Tears filled my eyes to become fully aware of the empty bed where I lay, my pocket watch so near.

What was wrong with me? Why did I crave Malin's evil treatment as deeply as I craved his tender favors, his kind regard?

Why, in my drunken state exacerbated by the rising Rift, did I find my excitement for him deepened by the true nature of our relationship?

"Because"—Dinon rose out of the bedspread beside me, his body naked beneath the covers and his head propped against one marble fist—"now you know he would never give you up, no matter what you did."

"Shut up. You want me to ruin my relationship with him, I'm sure."

"I would never betray you in such a way, Madame…nor would I dare disobey Master." Dinon's long silver eyes slid over my throat and down to the sheet he gradually pulled from my body. "His love for you is as plain to observe as the effects of a wildfire. Ah—Madame—"

He sighed in pleasure at the sight of my breasts. His head bent over one sensitive nipple, torrents of brilliant white hair flowing down his back and free to hang around his face. Between the brushes of lips that made me sigh and arch my back into his mouth, the dharmine murmured, "Your headache is marvelous tonight…I love it when you're sick."

"You hateful beast—ah—stop!"

Something sharp brushed the edge of a nipple that had been stroked to a peak by his tongue. The demon jerked back from me at the command, and while I recoiled, his smile widened to display the fine points of two extended cuspids.

"Excuse me, Madame…I forgot myself."

I sat upright, throwing on the light to ensure I hadn't actually been bitten. Wouldn't Eleison have a few choice things to say to me then!

Oh—Eleison.

Though my plans to command the dharmine to produce a whip for his own beating dissolved instead into more pensive ruminations of my beloved, my mood could not long take its sulky turn.

Before I even demanded the dharmine leave me, the RMS alarm clanged through the house.

I shut my eyes, my hand pressing into my brow.

"Extreme Rift Event Advisory," the machine intoned throughout the little house, the message and even the voice different in this foreign territory. "Please operate with caution during the next forty-eight to seventy-two hours. Avoid leaving the domicile for unnecessary reasons, especially at night. If you require emergency supplies—"

Glenn knocked on my guest room door without opening it, no doubt noting my light and not wanting to put himself in the position of seeing me nude before he was prepared to relent. "Thecla? Can you hear that?"

"Yes, I can. I certainly picked a bad time to bother you, didn't I?"

"What? No—I didn't mean that. But the train won't be able to depart in an Extreme Rift Event. It's just not safe. Everything's going to be shut down."

My lip slid back between my teeth. "I hadn't thought of that."

The comingling of frustration and relief was a strange one, but undeniable. I wanted at once to be home, yet to have more space and time. With a multi-day Rift Event about to begin, the decision was taken out of my hands. Circumstance was now the true culprit forcing me to stay with Glenn.

I released a low sigh of absolution. "*Will* I be a bother if I stay with you a few extra days?"

"No. No, of course you won't."

His tone. That first 'no' had the barest edge of something like a laugh in it, as though the idea were ridiculous.

The rest had been reminiscent of a plea.

My heart melted as if made of candlewax, the old turn of phrase given new meaning to me by Glenn's sensitive nature.

He was so different from the other men, and so wonderful in his way. Oddly, I wanted to protect *him*. I wanted to shield his mind and spirit from all the woes of my strange, dark little world.

Yet, far more urgently, I longed to drag him into it.

The shutters lowered and Glenn returned to bed, leaving me alone with my thoughts. About fifteen minutes into the official start of the Rift Event, my pocket watch blinked with a message. I rubbed my weary brow and sat upright to open the device, then winced at the cold light that shocked my aching frontal lobe through the dark.

From Eleison. *Let me come get you.*

My throat tightened. It was tugged sharply, perhaps, by the descent of my heart down into my stomach. Every molecule of my body screamed with desire for Eleison, and I do not exaggerate when I say that I was overwhelmed by a tremor as I wove my fingers through the projected keyboard in my struggle to construct a response.

Please don't worry. I'm perfectly safe.

He began typing at once and I cringed, watching the accusatory little icon until it disappeared in favor of his next message.

Not during a Rift Event, you're not.
What if this time is the first time you change?
Glenn's a hunter.
And I'm your mate.

Fire erupted along my arm from the little watch sitting in my hand. His forceful nature! His mouth, his body, the blazing borro eyes looking out from his celestial visage. Strange waves of sensation rippled from the scar of his animal bite.

All I want is to lie in a bed
with you for three days, Eleison,
but you can't imagine
what I'm going through.

Help me imagine. Talk to me.

Before I could respond, another message came in. This, with a hint of sullen accusation flavoring its letters.

Don't punish me because you're angry at Malin.

Sighing in exasperation, I rose to Eleison's bait. I called him. He picked up before it even rang, somehow.

"Eleison, darling, please—I'm not punishing you. *Or* Malin, for that matter."

"Try telling him that. He's sick over this."

"Well." I spread my free hand as though we spoke face-to-face, saying into the open air, "Don't you think he deserves to be, a little?"

"Sure. But he also deserves the chance to properly apologize."

"If *I* say he deserves one." Eleison didn't argue with me, and I went on after regaining some patience. "Malin will have a chance to apologize when we're home. But, why, this Rift Event—it's like a sign, isn't it?"

"What do you mean?"

"If the trains can't safely operate during the peak days of the Event, we'll be delayed in coming home anyway. I needed time and space and it's been *given* to me. You see?"

I had only been smilingly about to suggest it was heaven-sent, but something dark caught my eye. Dinon, now dressed in his trousers and cloak, leaned back against the corner of the room to watch with that leonine amusement.

Turning my face away, I could only bring myself to say softly, "It's like a gift."

"But why does space from Malin mean space from me?"

"Eleison, in this short conversation you've *already* tried to reason with me on his behalf."

"No, I— Well—"

"You *have*, and I know you mean well. I know you love him." Silence filled the line, and I went on softly, "I do, too, obviously. All I've done since coming here is think about him. I love you both and I just—I want things to be normal. Perfectly normal."

"Then let them be normal."

"I want them to be. I believe really and truly that they will be. But—"

Inhaling, I bent my leg at the knee and leaned to rest my forehead upon the joint.

"If I speak to him too soon, and I don't feel we've fully reconciled in our hearts, I hardly see how things can ever be normal. My emotions are so—so high, Eleison. And when my emotions are high, *you* want them to be evened out, so you do everything you can to make me forget my worries. But I can't forget these worries. I can scarcely think of anything other than all this until I've sorted out—what it means for me."

"Are you thinking about trying to leave Malin altogether?"

"No," I told Eleison quickly, sharply, frightened of the mere idea. "I could never do that. I love him. He's my husband now, whatever he is or was. And, anyway, I—I couldn't stand to leave either of you. Oh, how could I live? No—never, ever. But, Eleison—oh, darling—"

My eyes filled with tears as my headache crested to a new, greater height. As my hand pressed to one side of my face, I listed toward the watch and said through trembling lips, "I feel so ashamed."

"There's no reason to. It isn't your fault. Malin owed it to you to explain things, and he didn't. That's not on you, baby."

"That's not why I'm ashamed. I'm ashamed because—oh, God! Because my father would be ashamed of me."

"Thecla…"

My shoulders trembling at the sound of my name—the only familiar thing about myself by then, I reflected in that self-indulgent second—I burst into tears. I wept at the pain of the headache, and the heartbreak of Malin's deception. But mostly, I wept for my father. My heart filled with pleas that, wherever he was, he might forgive me for the person I could not stop myself from becoming.

No—the person I *wanted* to become.

"The basic problem, you see, Eleison"—I sniffled, indelicately blotting my cheek on the hem of Glenn's sheet—"is that I love you and Malin both far more than I care about being a good person. And that's changing me."

"Everybody's always changing all the time, Thecla."

"Yes, but...so much?" I clenched my teeth and took a breath to steady myself before going on wetly, "Sometimes I have thoughts and I don't recognize them. They're *mine*, but they're— foreign to me. They frighten me."

The slate of his voice was smoothed by love to a soothing pillow talk reverberation when, after short delay, Eleison said, "I know exactly what you mean."

"I know you do. That's one of the things that frightens me."

"Thanks."

I laughed, and I thought I heard him produce a scoff of a chuckle, too. "You can't blame me. You've been so *affected* by life, Eleison. I look at you when you talk about your brother, or when we were at the cinema, say, and—that's you. The real you: that innocent and incorruptible heart of you that was brought into the world. And I love that man. I love to be with that man. I feel so close to him, so safe with him. But—

"The man in you that most excites me is the one I'm afraid of. It's the one that life has shaped you to be. That Malin has shaped you to be. And when I feel myself responding to that version of you, Eleison, it's like I can also feel myself changing to suit that version."

"Don't misunderstand—I don't want you to feel you have to change for me."

"But I've already had to, darling. Oh, Eleison, darling—don't *you* understand?"

He did understand. I didn't have to say anything because I'm sure he knew that, on some level, I needed to process the thought that Eleison had killed for me—and would, I was certain, do it again—just as I needed to process Malin's betrayal.

Eleison's breath hitched like the guilty lump in my throat. "I'm sorry," he said softly. "I wish I were a better man for you, Thecla."

"You're a *wonderful* man. Don't say that."

"I'm not, baby. I'm not at all."

Before I could offer my next adamant denial—and I do mean 'denial'—Eleison went on in a firmer tone.

"I'm giving you twelve hours to come to your senses and call me to come get you."

"Eleison—"

"Charlotte has the address. I know where he lives. If you don't meet me at the door with your bag, then you'd better kiss those clothes good-bye, because you're coming back to the Overseer's palace with or without them."

"I want nothing to do with that spiteful old hag. Never again."

"Don't worry. Once I get you back here, I'm not letting you leave your room until it's time for our train to depart. Send me a message when you're ready to go."

The line went dead while I balked, speechless, at his audacity.

What was going to happen now? The mere idea of seeing Eleison flooded my body with a fever of anticipation. The throb of the headache was a hammer beat that kept my eyes forced shut against my thoughts. Oh, Eleison! My mate.

Yes...he *was* my mate, and though I knew precious little about the matter, his command over me was as natural as it was erotic—and infuriating. I was Madame Thecla of Gudrune, the consort of Malin Farrow. None but my husband or the Overseer had any right to command me whatever the cause, unless ordained by one of those two.

And Eleison *was* ordained in that sense, it was true. But we both understood, without the need for discussion, the straightforward truth. The animal in him craved to hunt the animal in me. I was, though not subservient, somehow yielding in his presence. When he commanded me, when he expected something of me, it was natural—more natural, even, than Malin's legally imbued command.

So, I dreaded Eleison's arrival. As maddened as I was by him on a normal day, I was afraid of what would happen when my body was in the state of sensitivity into which this particular Rift Event seemed to be plunging me.

I was even afraid to be around Glenn. I wanted him more badly than ever, and as I used the shower in the bathroom between us at four in the morning, I swore I perceived him listening to me. Even through a wall, his attention was as hot on my skin as the water that sluiced along my aching face and body. How I longed to slip in through his door and into bed with him; to beg him again for the attention I knew he'd give me at last!

But say that I did, and he discovered me insatiable for the duration of the Rift Event? Would he recognize I was altered?

Would that change the friendship developing between us? The warmth, the natural warmth, and all the real, human attraction?

Would that mean he could never love me?

I must have been insane to care about such things. But, as pathetic as it was, some part of me seemed to feel that, if I could be loved by a man like Glenn—a man of whom my father would have approved—perhaps I was *truly* not all that bad person. The dharmine's word games of dialectical redefinition could be used to justify Malin's hypocrisy or Eleison's homicide, but when it came to the state of my own soul, the only proof that mattered was Glenn's opinion.

Frightened to spoil things, I committed to riding out the day (the worst day of the heat, when measuring in lowered inhibitions and heightened sexual thoughts) in my guest room for as long as I could. I'd have to write Glenn a note to warn him about Eleison's intentions: seeing my handsome host in person to even say that much would have been disastrous to my will. To make that idea all the more tempting, I was looking at many hours of boredom. I longed for my loom, but recalled the small library in his office and knew I could find a book to read once I had jotted my advisement to him. Moving softly as I could to avoid disturbing my host more than the water pipes already had, I stepped into his open office.

Though the light made me cringe when I flipped it on, I knew from my experience during Malin's captivity that this was far from the worst my headaches could get. I could still see, for instance, auras not being a common feature if I was not exposed to the Rift Event directly.

But I was still alarmed as my eyes adjusted. Considering I had not been outside, this headache was exceptionally bad. Just what was going on? Had my allergy escalated, perhaps due to that period of prolonged Rift exposure? Or was this all because of separation from my mate?

As my half-blurred vision swept over the bookshelf, intent on the desk, my attention was seized by a familiar arrangement of letters amid many that had fused or doubled with the pain. Even once used to the light, I struggled to see through the headache—but my vision was not so poor I could not recognize my husband's name.

Unprovable: A Biography of Malin Farrow

My hands prickling, I slid the book from its place. The heavy tome, hardbound, lacked a fancy cover but made up for it with a handsome black-and-white image of Malin, my darling, glowering into the camera as a defiant, deadly looking young nobleman. Wind had buffeted his collar at just the right moment, and the harpro perched upon his great leather glove (must have been hunting, as I'd never known him to do!) twisted its narrow head toward the breeze.

Filled with unbearable longing, I locked myself behind the guest room door and, negotiating slowly owing to my ailment, read about my husband.

I confess I was shocked by some of the accusations regarding his youth, which I do not think I had ought to detail here lest I seem to endorse them. Not having been there for Malin's early life, I cannot account for it; nor can I act as authority on the middle years which remained notoriously rife with scandals involving someone else's consort, or betrothed son, or any number of coldly used maids. The title of the biography, I suppose, was a double entendre alluding to the unprovability of these claims...and to a pattern that emerged during the war.

Somehow, perhaps because I wished to think the best of

him, I had not spared much time thinking about the Expansion in detail. The war that earned Gudrune's power and reputation had always been something abstract to me. Not having seen any military conflict in my lifetime outside from, very occasionally, newspapers reflecting the tribulations of continents far from mine, I had lived a privileged, downright blessed existence away from the realities of violence.

Not Malin. Malin had been young and ambitious, and, I confirmed, annexed Azstoria before the Expansion was ever formally recognized by other territories. The stated goal had been lithium. Everyone knew he was actually interested in the radioactive materials that had long ago been disposed of in the Azstorian deserts, though the general opinion was split as to why. As if to prove his interests were not in building and using a bomb, my husband beckoned war with the Overseer by flaunting the controversial energy program that went into motion with Gudrune's sudden opening of Azstorian dig sites once strictly forbidden for archaeological research…though I was sure the actual timing of the Overseer's intervention had more to do with the disappearance of my mother than it did the research, or even the famine orchestrated to squelch Azstorian resistance.

I have never had a head for non-fiction detailing the ponderous stratagems of history's great generals, but I found myself intrigued as I read about my husband. Then so young, my age, (somehow illicit to think on, as though Malin's present love had already aged me ten years past my peers), he was time and again faced with slim odds from which he emerged victorious. The pattern that developed was one some considered underhanded and many considered a war crime. I confess I was a bit shocked, myself.

Malin's legions did their best work, it would seem, during

Rift Events. It was widely regarded across continents and cultures that such a thing was indecent. In fact, there were a few famous historical instances of conflicting sides joining forces to withstand a particularly violent Rift Event and all the creatures it brought along. When the weather cleared, combatants would regroup and do battle another day.

But my husband did not flinch from utilizing the Rift any more than he utilized terrain or famine. He took advantage of Events, in fact, to lay siege on Overseer-occupied Azstorian towns or target the buildings that housed Parvati's units. He crippled supply lines and prevented emergency workers from reaching areas badly afflicted by Events.

And when a long skirmish seemed impossible for Gudrune's forces to overcome, Malin would command them to hold out however long it took for the weather to go bad. Inevitably, within two days of the Rift Event, the victory would go to Gudrune, and the Overseer's campaign to liberate Azstoria would be pushed farther back.

This was what the title, *Unprovable*, referred to in the context of my husband's life. The biography drew the same controversial conclusion toward which the Overseer had shepherded me. This particularly insightful biographer's thesis was simple: that Malin Farrow was not a dharmine as gossip held, but riftborn, and gifted with the exceedingly rare and dangerous power of "communing with the Rift beasts," as Mr. R. J. Lankin put it in his dry textbook style.

Political opponents who had fallen out of windows with harpros' talons having gouged great chunks of their scalps. Impossible battles that became decisive only when Rift Events unleashed a wave of reinforcements for Malin's manipulation.

Would-be accusers of his allegedly low morals, who sometimes simply disappeared. In as close to a climax as a biography could have when written for a living man, the book deftly wove its evidence so as to conclude to its reader, (who did not know Malin as intimately as *my* reader, and therefore needed more persuading), that the Master of Gudrune was by no means an ordinary human.

But I did not require so much proof. I reached the end of my skipped and skimmed readthrough of the book, raised my hand to the bridge of my nose, and groaned to press my cool palm against my throbbing forehead. The sweet ultra-darkness of that double shade made me sigh. I reclined back upon the bed to lay the book in a friendly tent across my face.

My muscles unwound. At long last, sleep was upon me. I sank into the delicious darkness, my tense cheekbones relaxing, my jaw falling loose from my top row of teeth.

Yet, as my eyes rolled down with the onset of REM, I caught sight of my own body. Somehow, I was standing. I raised my hand before my face to find my closed eyes could see.

I had no awareness of my headache. I had awareness, in fact, of nothing but the space around me: an endless expanse I gradually realized I had seen before.

Just as I had seen the black loom that once again stood before me, waiting to be used.

Last time, it had been untouched. Now it had been prepared with threads of fuligin so much darker than the black of the void that I somehow could not set my eye on them. Instead, while sliding into the seat before the loom, I found my gaze settling in the space between myself and the threads.

And, as I emptily gazed, a template—*the* template—illustrated itself with such perfect clarity I did not hesitate.

I took up the shuttle waiting for me, and I wove.

When I stirred around eleven in the morning with the somewhat panicked knowledge I had forgotten to write a note about Eleison, it was to the distant sound of Glenn's voice.

"Yeah," he said, "I'm back."

The call to his watch must have awoken me. I sat up, rubbing my eyes, glad to find the nap had reduced the headache just enough to make it manageable; though, as Glenn made his way down the stairs, I found my body just as activated by his proximity as it had been earlier.

"I saw that," he said around the time he reached the bottom of the stairs.

There was a delay, a period during which Glenn produced a scoff before listening on.

"Look," he said at last, "I know you're upset. I am, too, but—I'm still not interested. In fact...I'm less interested than ever."

This delay was shorter. I had been half-paying attention before, but as I rose to shed my robe and pull my on shift, his sudden change of tone drew my interest.

"No—*no*, that doesn't make me a— That's insane. Will you listen to yourself? Look—"

Glenn's heavy footsteps, which had paced toward the kitchen, now turned to thunder in the office. The door shut heavily and I shook my head, too focused on my own problems to care. How was I to warn Glenn without revealing my nature, either by way of explanation or by total accident? Just clapping eyes on him ten minutes later, as he sat drinking coffee in his living room and looked up to see me, I wanted to leap over the banister and fly across the room into his arms.

My knuckles whitened as my hands tightened into fists. The

lightening effects of joy upon his face incensed me. As it had been with Eleison, the repression of any hint of my desire for Glenn seemed to leave the only alternative as a kind of simmering rage.

"I'm sorry, Glenn—I don't think I should stay here any longer."

My headache seemed to worsen as his face fell. While my heart ached for him, he asked, "Has something happened?"

"I've thought things over. You were right to deny me last night. It will make things less dangerous when—" I had to just say it and took a great breath. "Eleison is coming here."

The alertness of Glenn's posture changed. Hardened, somehow, along with a glance toward the door. "When?"

"He said he would give me until around noon, but I wouldn't count on that."

"Anytime, in other words. Why didn't you tell me this sooner?"

His justified anger made me cringe. "I'm sorry, I—" My hand pressed to the side of my forehead. "I have a Rift allergy, you see, and—"

"A Rift *allergy*? I've never heard of that."

"I've never heard of it, either, but I've been this way my whole life. I experience terrible headaches anytime I step into the Rift, but it's different this time. I've been indoors this whole time and I feel positively wretched, oh—"

"Thecla…"

"I'm riftborn, you know. I don't know if that has anything to do with it, but I also don't even know if I have any tangible power of any kind, so it's all very—" I struggled for a word against a sudden wave of pain and rubbed my brow, finding at last, "Cryptic."

When the couch was jostled by his sudden movement up to his feet, the simple squeak of a wooden leg against a centimeter of floor seemed to fracture my skull. "If this is how bad you are while staying inside, should you be going outside for even the length of time it will take to return to the palace?"

"I—I don't think anything *cataclysmic* will happen if I spend a few seconds passing through it to get into a car or walk into the palace, but to be frank, Glenn, it's usually not so bad indoors, and—I'm a bit frightened."

Lips trembling and eyes shutting, I said with a soft gasp, "Between you and me, I don't want to go—"

"Then don't."

"—but it's not so *simple*! Eleison is jealous. I don't want him to hurt you."

His jaw tightening within the grove of his beard, Glenn strode for the stairs. Eleison's early plight rushed in with new empathy. I found myself bolting back, terrified to be touched, afraid to discover what Glenn's mere hand upon mine would do to me in my pliant condition. By the time he was at the top of the stairs, I had recoiled within the guest room and set my hand upon the edge of the door.

"Thecla"—he said my name so carefully as he appeared on the other side of the doorway, his eyes pained to see the wild, easily misinterpreted fear in mine—"if you don't want to go back, I won't let him take you."

"Of *course* I don't want to go back to the palace. The Overseer—"

"I don't mean the palace."

My stomach tightened in a jolt of offense; but some part of my abused, aching brain, until that second crippled by the hopelessness of a cornered animal, raised its head to listen.

"You deserve better than this life, Thecla—living as the ornament of one of the evilest men in the world."

"My husband isn't—"

My mouth hung mutely open for a few long seconds before I shut it. Glenn's eyes slid over the book on the nightstand behind me.

"He doesn't treat me as an ornament," I corrected. "He's—mentoring me."

"To make sure you raise his heirs correctly when he dies before you, I'm sure. Thecla—"

"No, please—"

In a quick, natural impulse for which I didn't fault him, Glenn stepped into the room to catch my shoulders in hands that felt so massive and hot I was sure I would collapse into ashes in his grip. In my futile effort to wince away, I had raised my hands, and to grab hold of me he had stepped against them. Now I swore I could detect the steady rhythm of his thudding heart beneath my right palm, the taut pectoral of his chest a drum pounding with life.

"If you want me to protect you, I will. Just say it."

"I—I want to go *home*, eventually, but…I do wish I could stay just a few more days." Overwhelmed by frustrated tears, I rolled my eyes away from him before daring to look into his face. What an awful mistake! I couldn't help but raise my hands to his beard; to the copper brown curls that crowned his apollonian beauty. "Glenn—oh, I want more than that. I want you to live in Gudrune. I want to see you. Come stay with us some season! Please, let's not wonder what could have been. There's no reason to hold back. I'm sure—I'm sure Malin would—"

"I won't have anything to do with him," Glenn said darkly. "Even if he didn't really kill his wife, that doesn't change the rest of it. And it doesn't change what he intends to do—like restarting his energy program."

My teeth grit. "Don't tell me you *also* think he's going to be the reason the Rift opens someday…you and the Overseer give him much too much power. It's no wonder everyone thinks he's a blasted dharmine—"

Before I completed the word, the front door of Glenn's domicile rattled with a demanding fist.

Glenn looked sharply toward the noises, then at me.

"Just stay here. Let me talk to him."

"Oh, Glenn, no—wait—"

But he knew what I wanted; what I was too afraid to ask of him. He had already left me there on the edge of the guest room, and by the time I rushed out to the mezzanine's edge, he was already at the bottom of the stairs en route to answer the door.

And there I stood, paralyzed, as he set his hand against the RMS panel to sink his thumb into the intercom button.

"Who is it?"

"Tell Thecla that Eleison's here."

Glenn peered over his shoulder with a look that I'm sure was meant to send me back into the room. But—I couldn't. My heart hammered in my chest. It were as though I felt Eleison: felt him already upon me, within me, even before that door was opened.

Satisfied the knob was locked, Glenn slid his now free other hand up the frame of the door and rested it there. Eschewing the intercom, he leaned toward the great oak door to both call and listen through the metal shutters that barred entry all the further.

"She's not feeling well—she says she's allergic to the Rift."

"Then you need to let me in, don't you?"

"So you can take her out of here against her will? She's not ready to leave."

"I'm not leaving it up to her."

Glenn looked up at me in some small measure of disbelief. "Do you think that's reasonable? I thought you two were in love."

"Love is showing up to drag somebody back where they belong when it's dangerous for them to be out on their own."

"She's not on her own. I'm here with her."

Eleison's laughter was low and dark, and short. "Okay."

After a few seconds of silence, the shutter produced a vicious rattle beneath my mate's hand. "Thecla," he barked, "say something."

My trembling fingers having nearly twisted off one of the buttons down the bodice of my gown, I forced my hand to the banister and called, "I'm here, Eleison," in a voice that echoed through the house but did not seem to reach him.

"Thecla," he called again, with another rattle of the shutter. "Don't make me do this."

"Get out of here before the cops find you and think you've converted to serve the Rift," called Glenn with derision.

A noise—a terrible borro growl, the noise of an animal prepared to kill—rolled through the door and the metal shutter. My heart palpitating, I hurried down the stairs.

"Eleison," I called against his growling, "darling, please, just calm down—"

The shutter rattled again, now more furiously.

Now, it did not stop. By the time I had rushed beside Glenn, ignoring his warnings, the rattle gave way to an ominous groan.

On the wall beside the door, the house's primary RMS panel emitted a beep of warning.

"Shutter failure at Entry 1," the little voice announced to chill our blood. With his eyes wide, Glenn whipped his head toward the panel to watch the security footage promptly displayed.

Air sucked past my lips to see Eleison on the other side. Somehow—owing, I would find much later, to the extreme nature of the Event—he had strength enough to jam his fingers quite literally through the metal at the base of the electrical shutter. I have always heard external shutters were better, since they do not allow the windows and doors to be exposed, but I confess that ever since this incident I have maintained a personal preference for the internally installed models. If Eleison could tear through it with his hand, surely the strongest metals couldn't withstand the most dangerous Rift beasts in their purest forms.

Yet, as I looked—as, gritting his teeth, he forced the shutter back up its track in spite of the mechanism's futile protests—I realized it was not just Eleison who was at work pushing high that slab of metal. By the second, the shape of his hand, buried deep in that shutter, contorted and extended. When he tore himself free with a snarl, it had grown into the black claw of a borro. The muscles of that same arm, already accentuated by the strain of his task, burst from the fabric of his dark suit along with a layer of dark fur.

It were as though the dark scar, that mark of the borro within him permanent upon his left shoulder, expanded to the very tips of his fingers.

The mechanism submitted when the shutter's ruined base leveled with Eleison's jaw. A gear snapped, and thereafter the sheet of metal rolled effortlessly up out of the way.

I was so shocked—so frightened, so excited—that I didn't even remember I was standing against the door. As Eleison drew back to raise a foot, Glenn had to cry out and jerk me back.

The door burst inward on its hinges just as I was pulled clear.

His red eyes aglow with animal fury, Eleison stepped into Glenn's house and let the ruined front entry bounce closed behind him.

28

WHILE ELEISON ADVANCED, Glenn pushed me back and stepped between us. I recognized the mistake and cried out even before, growling all the more maliciously, Eleison closed the distance and got into Glenn's face. Glenn was shorter than him by no more than an inch or two. He barely had to shift to level their gazes, which he did unflinchingly.

"You're embarrassing yourself in front of the lady," Glenn said, earning a dark laugh from Eleison. While my mate raised his black claw to catch Glenn by the front of his shirt, I released an involuntary shriek.

"What's embarrassing is you. You have no idea what you're doing, getting between the two of us. She needs me."

"What she needs is to be treated with dignity," said Glenn, his tone level in his efforts to defuse the situation and loosen the claw around his shirt. "If Thecla needs space, you should give her space."

"That was before the weather changed." Every word Eleison spoke was laced with the smoke of the borro growl, that thunder weaving through his syllables and peeling his lips from his teeth. "I don't trust you to look after her—and it seems like I'm right not to. Your shutter's broken. Front door, too. In an Event like this, that's just not safe."

"Eleison, *please*"—the sharp turn of his eye upon me kept me from approaching, so I simply listed forward with my fist over my heart—"darling, I really am perfectly safe—"

"What happened to your allergy?"

The chaos of his arrival and all its distractions aside, my headache *had* eased with his presence—barely. I stepped toward him, extending my hand. "Your nearness is healing it. Now, please...don't hurt Glenn—"

"Thecla...don't you remember what we talked about?"

While my innards chilled, I looked helplessly between the men. Eleison's eyes shut.

"You didn't warn him like I told you to? Well—that's too bad for him."

"Glenn," I screamed while Eleison raised his still human fist, "watch out!"

His expression contorting with the sudden reality of a fight, Glenn caught hold of Eleison's black claw and ducked from the punch with a great tearing of fabric. While his shirt ripped down the front, its tatters still clutched in Eleison's fist, the hunter sprang up and volleyed a punch of his own.

His landed, but while he managed to ring Eleison's bell, all he did was enrage my beastly beloved. Eleison jerked his head back from the blow and raised his clawed left hand to the side of his face, snarling all the while. When Glenn threw his next punch, the hand Eleison used to catch it was already transforming to match its more easily provoked partner.

As the hand around his fist contorted into a matching claw, Glenn released a cry of agony. I shouted his name, then Eleison's, then stepped forward—but the transformation, which now extended to my mate's handsome features, stayed me.

"I should have let you die in Pont," growled Eleison through his transforming mouth. It, like all his flesh, rippled with purple waves of the same Rift radiation aglow outside. "You're turning out to be a real pain in my ass, Stone."

As though throwing a ragdoll, Eleison hurled my friend into the loveseat. It toppled and groaned along with Glenn's cry. Screaming, I darted over to find the hunter struggling to push himself from the shattered wood and broken springs of the frame. The task was made harder, as he kept one arm across the only recently healed injury over his ribs. I helped him, but was caught by the wrist.

"Eleison," I begged, whirling to face my beloved, "oh, darling, please! Stop, just stop. Glenn's treated me with such kindness—can't you see that he's a good man?"

"He thinks the world is better off without us, Thecla."

While I bit my lip in hopes that Glenn was too dazed to take Eleison's meaning, I pleaded on, "But don't you see, that's just not true. The way the media has treated me here, demonizing me—it's the same thing that's happened to Glenn."

Eleison was unrecognizable, yet alarmingly familiar somehow. He stood before us in the rarest state of alteration, that hybridization I had heard about: a fusion between the host and the Rift beast, provoked during Extreme Rift Events, or when an average one intersected with a moment of great personal trauma.

Oh, he was terrifying! Truly a beast in that moment, his height having grown in accordance with the changes to his anatomy. His legs bore more resemblance to the borro's powerful limbs than to a man's, and although his front claws and arms maintained the general form of a human, (and, comically, he still wore the tatters of his suit, split beyond repair down his powerful legs, his expanded chest, and the back that hunched to regard me from his new eight foot plus height), nothing of a man remained in his face. The visage Eleison wore was all the borro, whose jackal features and red panther eyes regarded me severely through the black fur bristling over his muzzle, cheeks, and vigilant ears.

"I've spent time with Glenn," I told Eleison gently, astonished I could stand to look upon my brutish mate then, let alone to step toward him—or to, most mysteriously of all, find him as appealing as ever, the increasing proximity of his body echoing through me like a bell that called me to church. "I've talked to him. If he were as hateful as people say, I'd be able to tell."

"You can't know that so quickly."

"I *trust* him, Eleison—and I trust you." While his tails thrashed uneasily, all three of them flicking with somehow feline displeasure from the split in the seam of his trousers, I rested my hands upon his chest—raising them to do so—and couldn't stop my gasp. "Oh," I cried to feel him, the remnants of my pain surging out of my face to leave only bliss, "Eleison—"

"Thecla..."

The snarl of the borro's voice was even with his now: no longer mere shadow, but the very essence of his speech. And both those tones were rich with longing. Eleison bent, his red eyes fixed upon my face.

While his animalized pupils expanded in their crimson thrones, his black nose twitched. It happened again; then again. Was he…smelling me?

I paled, realizing what an error I'd made, and tried to step back.

Eleison wouldn't let me; with a sudden gasp of understanding for whatever he scented on my body, he snatched my forearm to keep me against his chest. He groaned, his head lowering, his cold nose thrusting into my hair and neck to make me gasp, "Fuck, Thecla—baby—"

"Don't, oh, Eleison! Please, let me go now—"

"You're in heat, aren't you?" Eleison's great maw opened, his tongue unfurling along my throat. I moaned, electrical pleasure shooting through me at the warmth of his breath. "You taste so good…"

"Darling"—my voice was a whimper, the words tremoring like my frame while Eleison's fangs scraped and nibbled my neck—"now's not the time, please. Let's all just come to our senses and—ah!"

His muzzle clamped along the curve of my neck into my shoulder. I screamed, certain he had broken the skin but quickly amazed to recognize by the sustained pressure that he hadn't— even if he snarled like he wanted to. Now that I was captive, those frightful claws released me, but only to caress me; and, as he pressed my body more thoroughly against his, Eleison grew so preoccupied that he completely missed Glenn sneaking up to wield the nearby floor lamp.

As he swung it down upon Eleison's back, the bulb burst. Sparks singed my beloved's fur as I screamed. He snarled, releasing me to wheel about with one claw sweeping through the air. It caught Glenn along the side of his face and threw him back into the kitchen table, which shattered to leave him in the ruins of it and an unlucky chair. His head raised along with some futile attempt at movement on the part of his body. Then, too quickly for my liking, he gave up and let his head drop back.

Fangs bared, Eleison advanced.

Another cry edging from my throat, I grasped the ruins of the suit across his rippling back. The lamp, I was relieved, had done little damage, but all the same he winced and turned on me in a replaying of our first meeting. Chilled by the memory, I winced.

This time, however, he didn't bite.

This time, it was I who took the prey.

I could not overwhelm Eleison with strength, nor could I persuade him with logic when he was literally half a monster.

But I could throw my arms around the mane of his great, beastly neck and press my desperate lips to his hot muzzle.

Those deadly jaws fell open in a gasp, then shut with a growl as he allowed my kisses along his mandible. "You think you can distract me," he murmured, the words rolling out from his chest and between his clenched teeth.

"No, Eleison, please—I want you, I need you, I need you so badly—" My hand slid over his chest before dropping to his groin. I gasped to feel the protrusion barely restrained by the vestiges of his trousers. "Oh, darling—it's so big. It's always so big, but it's—ah—"

As heat flooded up across my face, I tried to lift my hand but couldn't make myself. I kept stroking, and Eleison produced a noise like a choking gasp, a breathless hum. One of his claws fit along the back of my head, the other wrapping around my waist to keep me against him. And I do mean 'around,' frightfully: with one great claw, Eleison could have picked me up by the waist and carried me as effortlessly as a child carries a doll.

"Your little boyfriend over there isn't doing the job you need, is he." Eleison's ears pinned back with his glance over his shoulder. I somehow forced myself to slide my hand up high enough to grasp his tie, which drew his attention back to me while I gave it a tug.

"He hasn't made love to me, Eleison—he wouldn't, even when I tried. I made every effort, trust me. I made him look at me; I even got him to touch me just a little. But…"

The rhythm of Eleison's breathing was disrupted by a new growl. With both hands, I reached up to stroke his muzzle.

"Yes, darling," I told him while he backed me toward the ruins of the loveseat, "oh, Eleison, yes, that's it—*I'm* the one who deserves your anger. Sweetheart—"

"I'm going to make him watch while I fuck you," Eleison growled, his blazing eyes fixed upon my face, "and then you get to watch while I kill him."

"Please, don't! He thought you were hurting me. Can't you see he's trying to protect me? Just like— ah! Oh—"

My ankle hit the remains of the furniture sooner than expected. I tilted backward, my arms flailing for balance until, effortlessly, Eleison caught me around the ribs and hefted me into his arms. With the new, uncanny length of his stride, he stepped over the pile of wood and upholstery to lay me upon the sofa visible from where Glenn lay. Then, his great tenderness belying both his terrible form and all the violence of his anger, Eleison leaned down to nuzzle his face and head against mine. The tip of his nose probed into my hair. I moaned, stroking his chest and stomach while his tongue resumed its explorations from but a moment ago. As it curled around my ear, I worked free his zipper and slid my hand into the hot forest of fur.

Oh! Not just longer, but broader. I moaned, my hand tightening around it, him, while he growled hotly against my ear, then tilted his deadly mouth away.

"Let me use my mouth. I want you, but I don't want to hurt you." A whine trailed from his words, the faint protest of a beaten borro, even as the hunger in them grew by the second.

"Then don't." My hands slid into the thick fur of his neck. "Give me the control, Eleison. Just be still, darling…roll over…"

"But—"

"Oh"—I tugged his muzzle toward me, unflinching at the brush of his fangs as I directed his gaze away from Glenn—"please, Eleison! You're in such a state. I've never seen you like this. You're so wild. Let me soothe you, darling. Please."

Shuddering as I stroked a hand along his muzzle, Eleison shut his eyes and opened his jaws as he might have parted his human lips identically beneath my caress. He leaned into my palm just the same. Then, his nose tucking down against the ticklish flesh of my inner forearm, Eleison rolled slowly upon the floor beside the couch and pushed aside the coffee table to give himself room.

Unspeaking, I slid atop his massive form and once more took his jackal-face into my hands. Somehow, all I could see was Eleison! It was so strange, still is strange sometimes when I think heavily on it. The gossips at the party were so luridly eager for details just like these. They wanted something profane: something very exotic and taboo about which they could harmlessly fantasize during another mercifully short stupor beneath some grunting arranged spouse.

But there was nothing profane about this to me—to us. It was an act of pure trust. A demonstration of absolute understanding and belief in our love, and, in particular, in Eleison's love for me. It was miraculous, in fact, how purifying that love proved to be. Through its gaze, I could press my lips against his monstrous muzzle and all the fangs within with perfect impunity, or enjoy an intimate thrill at the lash of his (far larger, more pointed, and quite dexterous) tongue, or writhe with bliss at the caress of his awful paws over my body, down beneath the hem of my dress, back up over my thighs. I raised my hands away from him to strip away my gown and undergarments, and while his red eyes swallowed me whole, I stood to divest myself of the final scraps.

When the underwear had glided down my legs and I'd managed to get one ankle out of them, Eleison's massive hand caught my thigh as simply as he might normally grab my bicep. I cried out, unbalanced, one foot on the ground and the other flailing a little in the grip he used to spread apart my legs.

Before I knew what was happening, his head lunged up at me.

I screamed, hot and wet, unrivaled bliss sliding along the valley of my pleasure while Eleison's transformed tongue went to work. Amid the fiery breath of animal panting and the inevitable grazing of fangs along my flesh, he kept me still with one hand while using the other to support my backside and subtly increase his pressure against me. I drowned in sensation, my one stable leg trembling at the knee while the other helplessly thrashed within the pleasurable confines of his grip.

"Thecla!" He nearly howled, his tongue receding to allow his muzzle to probe along my labia. I moaned and shuddered, somehow only then fully feeling the reality of his animal state, but

I couldn't bring myself to care. If anything, as with the terrible thoughts I had of Malin, I was more excited than ever. I slid my hand along the back of Eleison's head while he growled on, "You smell so good, baby. You smell like you want me to fuck you. Like ,"you want me to lock you up in a room and tie you to the bed for a few days"-kind of fuck you..."

"Oh, Eleison! Yes, yes, please—hm, ah!"

That muzzle parted against me again, but this time, when Eleison's tongue slithered to work, it probed against the brink of the grotto that had been eager since hearing his voice the night before. Vaguely, I was aware of Glenn's labored breathing. Poor, wounded, scandalized Glenn, half-conscious at best, his scant waking visions filled with this.

That notion, I'm ashamed to say, only excited me as Eleison's tongue plunged up into the heart of my euphoria.

With his name rising from my lips, I sank my fingers into the fur at the back of his head while I whimpered and writhed along with him. The dharmine's tongue had been unnaturally talented in such manners, too—but the intimacy and ecstasy of being so tasted by Eleison was truly second to none. Too aroused to find shame anything but a promoter of pleasure, I basked in every second of his great, hot tongue's fucks into me. Drool flecked the edges of his muzzle and the terrible blades of his teeth sank against my most sensitive flesh, daring me to buck too sharply and thrill him with the flavors of my blood. Would he come to his senses then, as he had the first time, or was he so far gone that such an experience would only incite his attack upon me? I shivered, biting my tongue to contain myself; by the time he slid his free, I panted as savagely as him, and the channel he had left behind was positively drenched with desire.

"Lie down, darling, oh, Eleison—lie back down, let me enjoy you—"

His ears pinned back even as my hands fumbled to tear away the remains of his ruined clothes. "Let me take you back and calm down a little first, baby…I don't want to hurt you…ah…"

The three tails that worked in perfect synch all shuddered as my fingers plunged through the fur of his stomach. I lowered my head to breathe the intense, hot animal aroma (clean fur; Eleison's body; a coppery tang that may have been his arousal or Glenn's blood upon his nearby paw, or both) that left me almost drunk. In fact, I moaned, so excited by the feral scent—by the nearness of his cock, beside which I slid my hands while stroking his fur to tease him—that I spread my thighs all the wider in hopes the sight of me would convince him.

"Please…I want you, Eleison. You're as beautiful as ever to me. And oh…you're right. I want you to take me, savagely. With this." The black borro-flesh of his prick twitched against the bed of fur along his stomach. I regarded it with a shudder, my blood running hot as I slowly eased a hand along the straining shaft.

Eleison snarled as though I'd struck him. I shushed him, a moan of pleasure soon thereafter erupting from my lips just to caress him. The hypersensitive heat of my body responded to the mere opportunity to run my hand over his throbbing tool, a flood coming upon me while I lowered my head to kiss and taste him.

"Thecla…ah—Thecla—"

The growls that rolled from him were intense, sometimes increasing in volume or ferocity as my lips parted and my slithering tongue delivered an especially appreciable strike of pleasure through him. Amazing how, even as a beast, he simply tasted of Eleison! How, even in this form, knotted at the bottom and curved upward at the head, my mate and his increasing pleasure so excited me that I couldn't help myself but to sit upright and align myself to him. I was desperate to mark my territory and, in turn, be marked as his. One great claw caressed my cheek. Guiding his pillar with two hands, I teased him along an entrance that seemed too small but was, to compensate, absolutely soaked by the thrill provided by my out-of-control mate. By the danger, and by my own readiness to give myself completely to him.

By poor Glenn, forced to listen to it all.

Moaning Eleison's name, I slowly eased myself down the quivering tension of his transfigured shaft.

The pleasure struck us both as nearly painful. Aside from the intensity of the way he filled me, his flared head stretching me wide from the start, the heat into which I'd plunged had made me desperate for exactly this. Perhaps there was an ache of initial discomfort, oh, yes—he really was far, far larger than normal— but that first sting passed. The deeper I impaled myself upon him, the more my body seemed to relax to accommodate him. Some trick of the mating bond, or a simple sign of my desire in that moment: all I knew was a satisfaction so staggering my mouth fell mutely open, then emitted a long, low scream while my hips and thighs found the proper rhythm.

"Oh," I cried, "yes! Eleison, you see, I told you I wanted you."

"Ah, fuck...you did, you did tell me. Be careful, baby. I meant it. I don't want to hurt you—"

"Yes, please! Eleison, darling, oh, *hurt* me with it!" Gasping to viscerally feel him twitch inside me, I worked myself as far down his length as I could—about three-quarters of the way, for his shaft thickened again at the base and made me whimper with want of practice. Forced to stop early for now, I settled for grinding back and forth to enjoy the pressure of his hard head inside me before the next self-impalement. My fingers sinking into his fur, I tightened my legs against his haunches and gasped, "Use me, mark me, oh, yes! You just need to let Glenn know who owns my body! That's right, then you'll feel better, won't you—ah!"

My eyelids fluttered. I had never felt so full yet in want of more. The Rift's control of my body was so powerful that I never could have been pleased. I wanted to be run through by Eleison: to be used by him until there was absolutely nothing left, until I was a broken and trembling bundle of sex made to be dragged back to some den and used again on my recovery.

By the second, he seemed tempted to do just that. His claw slid around to my rump and tightened, holding me down while he pounded up into me; I gasped out his name, the pleasure overwhelming, my eyes shutting against it.

"Oh, Eleison, I'm sorry, darling. I don't mean to punish you—"

"Of course you do, you fucking brat…"

With a rough grip of my ass, Eleison pushed me off him before shoving me back into the couch to take control. And take control, he did. I moaned with excitement and scrambled upright as though to escape, though in truth I hardly so much as extended a foot before he was atop me. His great paws pressed upon my inner thighs to force wide my legs.

There he was again: this time, sliding into the core of me in a hard thrust that made me cry his name. The heat of his body above and against me thrilled, frightened me like the moist panting of his breath through his fangs. The only means I had of keeping him even near to docile was my body: my nakedness, our pleasure, this love so hot between us. This absolute trust. With me exposed to him, held there for him to admire, Eleison took to pounding so roughly into me that I swore novel colors bloomed bright across my eyes. My mouth opened and my brow furrowed, gaze fixed upon the stunning sight of his bare cock thrusting in and out of me. I arched against him, so overcome with my own bliss that I swore I felt it pulse within me.

"You think I'm on Malin's side," Eleison growled, studying my face, "so you want to punish me along with him...but you get second thoughts when I fuck you like this, don't you, baby?"

"Yes, yes, oh, Eleison, oh—I don't want to punish you, but—oh, I wish I could have you, could have you and have peace to think, but oh, Eleison, Eleison—!"

He released one of my thighs to catch my cheek and hold my face for his frightful kiss. That great muzzle snapped open, his teeth scraping along my cheek and jaw. His tongue plunged into my mouth so deeply I groaned. It seemed Eleison fucked my throat with his kiss, it was so hungry and intense, and when at last he pulled away, I was enough in want of air that I gasped.

"When you fuck your boyfriend, I want you to ask yourself if there's a chance it will ever be half as good as this. You think he can make you cum like I can?"

"Eleison, oh, no one can—"

"That's right...I know you need me, baby...I know you're just hurting right now."

His eyes shut. When they opened again, and I once more saw into those vast, red depths, they had grown somehow gentler. His thrusts adopted a smoother, less savage rhythm of lovemaking. More a man's than an animal's, no matter how low the snarl of his voice.

"I don't want to worry about you."

"I'll be safe," I whispered, stroking over his face and up past his ears to guide his kiss back to mine. "I swear, Eleison. I'll be safe, and I'll come home."

He kissed me. Slowly, steadily, Eleison pounded up and into me, and each hammer of my flesh tightened the coils of my pleasure. I gasped, clutching at him, my legs and arms tightening around him while his clawed hands slipped beneath my rear. Drawing my pelvis up and using this new leverage to pound me deeper, Eleison worked us both to orgasm while raising his head to look into my eyes.

"Think of Malin," Eleison implored me. "Fuck, ah— Thecla—he loves you—"

"And I love him—and I love you, Eleison!"

"Thecla, Thecla...let me take you home."

"Eleison! Soon! Soon, I swear, oh, darling, oh, Eleison, darling, darling!"

"Thecla—"

His kiss plunged down against mine, our bodies breaking together. All around us, reality dissolved. Eleison's body rippled with purple Rift radiation, the transformation reversing.

Far away in Gudrune, Malin spent a sleepless night alone.

HIS HUMAN SENSES recovering, even if mine were all the more incensed for the heat of his essence within me, Eleison stared into my face with the increasing clarity of a man woken from a jealous dream into a less emotional, more comprehensible reality.

"Thecla"—his normal, natural hand stroked across my brow, inspiring tears to prick the backs of my eyes when I realized how he had healed me while I tamed him—"please listen to me. It's not safe for you here."

"Everywhere I go is safe for me now, Eleison." The words were a somehow hysterical whisper. Certainly a desperate one. Yes: desperate to make him believe; desperate to believe, myself. My heart hammered in my breast while Dinon's presence renewed in me, a shroud draping across my right hemisphere. "I'm in no danger. Not even the monsters of an Event like this one can touch me…not even with a blasted door hanging from its hinges."

His jaw tightened as he glanced toward it. Then, kissing the edge of my mouth, he separated from me as gently as he could stand to.

Eleison's eyes narrowed at the door again.

"I shouldn't let you stay here."

"But you're considering it."

"Just let me think, all right?"

With a wry look at his snappish response, I sat up to stroke his powerful thigh through his ruined trousers. "That's all I've wanted, myself…to think."

Nostrils flaring, Eleison studied me from the corner of his eye with a look that was still undeniably displeased. Weaker to his disapproval than I would have preferred, I wilted forward to lean my head against his hip.

He sighed at the contact. While his hand raised to stroke the back of my hair, I turned my gaze up at him and, I confess, went out of my way to look a little wretched with the disturbance of my soul by Malin's truth.

"Go on, then, Eleison. Decide what to do, and I'll do it. As it concerns my welfare, you have control over me. I can't call on any legal commandment to stop you. I can only ask you to think the situation all the way through."

My voice dropped to a whisper, barely a breath; but his altered senses, going by his glance, took in what Glenn had no hope of hearing.

"Wherever I'm invited, Dinon is invited, too."

Eleison's handsome mouth curled with a sneer as he realized my meaning. "So now it's "Dinon,"" he murmured back, glancing away.

My heart fell. Now he would tell me to get on my clothes and come with him to the carriage. That would be that.

And what would become of Glenn?

"I'm going to spend the Event patrolling this area," said Eleison in a tone of reluctant assent. As I gasped, sitting straight up, my mate looked at me in a manner far sterner than infamous Malin ever did. "If I get the feeling that I need to take you away—"

"I understand! Oh, darling, thank you."

"A notice went out that the train is officially delayed for three days. When it's all said and done, you're coming home. No arguments."

"Of course. Yes, Eleison, of course. I just need some time."

The tatter of his split sleeve sagged from his forearm as he caressed my cheek.

"I don't blame you," he told me softly. "I love you, Thecla. I'm sorry about all this. I'm sorry for the part I played in your ignorance."

"I understand, Eleison…you have to protect your brother."

"That doesn't matter. It wasn't right of me, and I knew it wasn't right of me. I wish there were something I could say to make it better."

"If there were, I'm not sure I would want you to say it. I have to accept what I'm feeling, Eleison. And so do all of you… especially Malin. He makes me feel so many wonderful, good, dreamlike things. He makes me so happy. And those are real feelings, but—I have to admit to myself that these other feelings, these other things about him, are also real. I'm sure you can relate."

"Yeah," said Eleison softly. "I can."

My muscles uncoiling with relief, I gazed gratefully into his face as he knelt to take my hands in his.

"Whatever you need, whether it's here, or with Malin—tell me. Okay?"

I nodded, managing a true if small smile while he leaned forward to kiss the corner of my mouth, then the fullness of my lips. I sighed, opening myself to the complete depth of his kiss. The mingling of his breath with mine was an incomparable bliss. The slow, controlling encroach of his tongue; the scrape of his teeth over my lip.

That sad drawing away, and the slight look of anguish that quickly closed into hard, jealous displeasure he directed like a knife at Glenn.

"And let me know if your boyfriend needs to go to the hospital…I guess it's not beneath me to save his life a second time. See you in a couple of days, baby. I'll text you when it's time to leave."

The simple manner in which he uttered his commands had a way of resparking my hyper-excitement, but before I could even dream of begging him for more attention, Eleison crossed around the destroyed loveseat he observed with disgust—as though he himself had not been the cause. He stopped on its other side, standing between it and the hunter who remained supine but evidently still conscious in the ruins of the table. There, in the middle of the vestibule between kitchen and parlor, Eleison fished out a mostly crumpled pack of cigarettes from which he managed to find a whole cylinder. He bent his head to light it, his eyes fixing upon Glenn when he lowered the lighter and raised his chin in one smooth motion.

"You can fuck her now," Eleison said, blue-tinted smoke curling around his lips. "Doesn't bother me anymore."

Turning to fix me with his stare, he said, "I love you," and didn't wait for my response before striding through the piteously easy-to-open door. While I called out, it shut weakly behind him, and the shutter rattled as he jerked it down into place.

Trembling, I sprang from the sofa and dashed through the wreckage to kneel by Glenn's side. "Oh, Glenn—darling—"

I set a hand upon his chest and elicited a reflexive wince: one that deepened while blood wept from the claw marks Eleison had raked into his cheek.

"Maybe you *should* go to the hospital," I began with a reluctant glance to the door.

"No," groaned Glenn, clutching my wrist. "No more hospitals."

"But—"

"Just help me up, please. Just—ah—"

Grimacing, I slipped my hand beneath his shoulder and hooked the other under his arm. Even this seemed to cause him great pain, and my heart wrenched at the breathless moan with which he announced the working of bruised muscle.

Together, we got him to his feet. I kept a careful eye on the wreckage while, in my bare feet and his house slippers, I eased him to the stairs. He had to pause to catch his breath three times. I worried his old injury had torn open, or that Eleison had cracked his ribs by throwing him into the table. Maybe Glenn would at least let me call the doctor for a house call! Surely, he would agree he didn't have a choice.

"I'm fine," panted Glenn when I pressed him on this point at the top of the stairs. "Just—in a lot of pain."

"That's a sign that you need to see a doctor," I insisted, guiding him to his bedroom door.

Uneasily turning his head just to fix me with a bleary but dark look, he asked, "And what? Give the tabloids more to say about you? Let the doctors report the assault to the cops so your footman winds up in jail? I'm not going to let that happen, Thecla. Just help me into bed. I'll manage."

"That's all very sweet, but surely you can't mean to die on my account, Glenn."

"I'm not going to die, for God's sake, Thecla…and, anyway, think of the political consequences."

My lower lip disappeared between my teeth. He was right, of course. It was still hard for me to remember that everything I did had a broader implication now. When my mate from Gudrune assaulted the most beloved hunter in Valquist, (possibly the continent!), ripples were sure to emanate.

"I'm sorry," I whispered. "I should have told you earlier."

"No, you shouldn't have." While I pushed open the door and squeezed in through the frame with him, a rich cloud of oak and coffee and Glenn's warm body welcomed me. "It would have been worse…I would have had time to get a gun. Ah—"

While he eased down upon the faded quilt over the bed, his brow deepened its furrows.

"Just relax there, Glenn. Do you have medical supplies?"

"In the bathroom, the top shelf of the cabinet. You don't have to worry about it, Thecla, let me—"

"No, Glenn. Please." How it saddened me to focus on his beautiful, bloodied face and know I'd played a part in it. "I feel so ashamed that this happened to you. It's all my fault. If I hadn't come here, I never would have exposed you to danger."

Even through his pain, Glenn looked at me like I was mad. "What are you talking about? You didn't ask for him to act like that. Don't blame yourself…you're not responsible for what either one of them does."

A chill settled over his eyes, which turned from me. "The only thing you're responsible for is choosing to stay with them despite knowing what they do," he concluded in a simple, clearcut remonstration.

Unable to look at him just then, I stepped from his bedside. "I envy you, Glenn. It's very difficult to fall in love with an evil person. You've never had to experience it that's like."

My hand dropped upon the knob while Glenn's slippers hit the floor.

"I wouldn't be so sure about that, Thecla."

Heart throbbing in hope and shame, I slipped from the room without looking back and surveyed the ruins of my friend's house from a new, more accusatory angle. Between the splintered loveseat, the shattered lamp and, of course, the pile of firewood once making up the kitchen table, the devastation made me wince worse than Glenn's injuries.

Dinon stepped out from the kitchen, his inexorable slide into visibility startling even as I grew more accustomed to his coming and going.

He showed his teeth as he smiled at me, his silver eyes trailing over my breasts and down along my hips as my hand pressed to my hammering heart. Scowling, I turned away and stepped into Glenn's bathroom. I wrapped myself in my host's soft navy robe and fetched the medical kit, which was, I was happy to find, substantial.

Covered, I returned to the mezzanine to find the house in impeccable order. So neat even Malin would have approved. Dinon now stood in the center of the refurnished parlor, from which he gazed reverently up at me. He bowed to theatrical depth while I inclined my chin and walked on to Glenn's bedroom.

"I'm going to have new furniture delivered for you later today, Rift Event be damned—please don't argue." His opening mouth shut without sound. "If you won't let me pay for a doctor, at least let me replace your furniture."

"That's very decent of you. Thank you."

"The door, too—I'll have something done about it by tonight. I'm sure the city repairmen are used to emergency situations during weather like this. As long as calls are still going through, anyway...it seems terrible out there."

"How's your head?"

There he was, in the sorriest state I'd seen a man since I nursed my dying father, and he was worried about *me*. Tutting, I soaked a cloth with distilled water and cleaned his wincing cheek. "My head doesn't matter, Glenn," I told him gently, not wanting to say that Eleison's arrival had at least temporarily abated my suffering. "Don't speak just yet...let me take a look at your cheek and decide if I'm really going to accept your decision to turn down medical care."

Gradually, as I rinsed and daubed the blood away, I was relieved to discover the cuts were not as deep as I had feared. I released a slow, steady breath once I leaned back from him, my hand dipping back into the medical kit for a brown glass bottle.

"I'm sorry to say this is going to sting," I warned, fishing out a cotton pad I soaked with the antibacterial fluid, "so close your eyes and try to breathe."

He didn't close his eyes, but he clenched his jaw while I carefully pressed the soaked pad along his wound. Three distinct cuts of varying size arced around his orbital socket and across his cheekbone, while a smaller claw that had failed to hook in had simply sheared into his beard to leave a more superficial scratch. While, shielding his eye with the cup of my hand, I splashed a bit of the antiseptic directly in the wound, his nostrils flared. He stared rigidly into space but, firm in his commitment to his dignity, uttered no sound.

When at last I applied gauze and a bandage that had to be trimmed to compensate for his beard, I sat back with a sigh—and a cringe I couldn't help. My eyes had dropped to his colorfully tattooed chest, bared from the tear in his shirt. Along the bloodied obliques that peered through the fabric, the cruel purple of a dark bruise was already expanding toward the still new scar tissue of not just the Torea Festival but some subsequent surgery, perhaps to repair his lung.

Guiltier than ever, I said, "Let me see your bruises, please, darling…I should freeze some towels for you to ice them with, oh! Poor Glenn—"

As I spoke, I shifted the shirt back from his shoulder with his limp cooperation. This involved him turning slightly upon one side to slide the vibrantly colored, statuesque muscles of his arm from its sheath of torn cloth. Oh, Glenn! If the assailant had been any other man or beast, this specimen of a hunter would have dispatched them effortlessly: of that, I had no doubt. But Eleison, fighting for me—that was a danger truly deadly to provoke.

With him free of his shirt, I took a full catalogue of his injuries. Through the snarling maws of Rift beasts, purple bruises stretched like the cruel fingerprints of some great giant across Glenn's back. Blotches spread from his right shoulder blade down, with another arching along his lower back not far from his tailbone. "Are you sure you haven't broken something?"

"Let's wait and make that call tonight…I'm so sore right now. I don't think it's worth trying to ask that until the swelling has gone down."

"Then I'll freeze those towels. Do you have any ice?" At his nod, I closed the lid of the medical kit and shifted to set it aside.

Before my weight left his bedside, Glenn caught my wrist.

"Thank you, Thecla."

"Oh, please…it's the least I can do."

Our eyes met, the pain in his finding the pain in mine.

The fronds of my hair tumbled around his face as I bent to kiss him. Glenn gasped and shut his eyes. His lips parted to receive me, his tongue surprised, receptive, inquisitive, in that order. While his hand raised to slide along my arm, however, his lips twitched in a wince.

I tilted my mouth away, shifting my arm back to urge his hand down.

"Please, Glenn—let me take care of you."

While my fingers trailed back up the firm muscles of that wonderful arm, he searched my face. The barest hint of self-deprecating mirth crooked the corner of his mouth.

"I should have taken my opportunity last night."

"There's another right before us."

"While I'm here like an invalid… All I could think about last night was you, Thecla. I kept thinking I'd made a mistake. But the right thing can never be a mistake, can it?"

"It is when a giant borro-man is determined to break your nose one way or another…if that's the case, don't you suppose you'd ought to let go and live a little?"

Softly with respect to his injuries, he laughed. I laughed, too, even as I untied the belt of the robe I let fall from my shoulders.

His laughter faded, but the sparkle in his eyes remained beautiful and bright.

"You're a bad influence, Thecla."

Pouting, I ran my fingertips down the undamaged muscles of his chest and stomach. So firm and packed with power! Built to an even greater extent than Eleison's. "A bad influence, me? Just because, if it had been you drunk and pliant, I would have taken full advantage?"

My nails tickled down toward his waistline. He inhaled, his eyes searching mine as though for honesty while I plunged into his kiss once more. As my tongue instructed his on the intimate liberties he was to be permitted, my fingers slipped open the latch of his denim trousers.

"I confess, though, Glenn…I like the thought of you being helpless to resist me even now. You're not lying there like an invalid…you're lying there like my victim."

His sigh—my name—sweetened my lust, and excitement quivered through me to think of taking him into me so soon after Eleison. I pushed away the fabric of his boxers along with his jeans, and the stiff rod that brushed my hand made me sigh.

"Oh, my… That's what you want, too, isn't it? To be helpless to stop me."

While my fingers wrapped around the admired staff that throbbed at the contact, Glenn gasped in pleasure as he simply hadn't at pain. I tugged him gently, savoring the flickering shut of his eyes.

"You should count your stars Eleison gave you your thrashing already…if I'd been the one to give it to you, you'd be *really* sorry. Though, I'm still tempted to punish you for disobeying me last night. And don't you think you deserve to be punished? I know you do…say "Yes, Madame Farrow." Go on."

At the stroke of my hand in time with the command, the words I wanted erotically profane to him, he twitched in my grip to say, "Yes, Madame Farrow."

"That's a good boy…oh, Glenn…you poor, sweet man… it must torture you to know you want so badly to fuck Malin Farrow's consort…"

"I want more than that," he murmured earnestly, seeking something in the depths of my eyes while I straddled his hips with careful intent. I refused to set my weight on him and cause him discomfort. Instead I balanced myself upon my hands, my fingers sinking into the feather pillow on either side of his head while my sex found his. A haggard moan rushed past his lips to feel how wet I was, then sharpened as I drew him back and forth along my nerves to tease us both. He tried to glance down, but I caught his jaw with a finger that plunged against his beard and craned high his chin.

"Now, darling, don't strain yourself...just let me enjoy you...oh, Glenn! You're so unbelievably hard—"

At every slow, slick stroke along his length, the sensation grew all the sweeter. When no longer able to resist, I reached down and steadied his position to take him into me. Our breaths had raised to a mutual pant.

"It's sweet you're so happy to fuck your mistress, even with her pussy still wet from Eleison's cum...oh! Fuck—"

Glenn groaned at my bedroom banter, then again as at last I mounted the deliciously curved rod that throbbed for my greater pleasure. "Yes, yes, what a good boy—oh, Glenn!"

The need for protection of some kind occurred to me, but the mere thought that his naked prick was at that second thrust deep within me was so sweet. I didn't want to spoil it in any way. Besides—it didn't seem necessary. Malin and I had been hoping for a pregnancy for several months, but so far, nothing had taken. I couldn't imagine one night with Glenn was much of a risk.

Though what risk there was made each rock of my hips in his lap so much the sweeter.

"Can you feel him still inside me? If he hadn't hurt your

precious face, I would have commanded you to lick me clean before I let you enjoy me…it's what my husband does. Mm—ah!"

Clenching his teeth against the pain, Glenn reached up to grab my bicep and tugged me against his chest. More easily able to catch hold of my face and hair while I lay upon him, Glenn kissed my mouth and held me close while his hips pounded up against my lust. I gasped, crying his name into his lips, my brow furrowing with the sudden force he exhibited against all advisory. How sweetly he filled me! How each stroke seemed to reverberate up into my ribs and beyond, to the very tissue of my heart!

"I want to save you from all this, Thecla," he whispered to me as our lips parted. "I want to take you away from this life."

"Glenn…"

"You deserve better. You deserve somebody good—to have the opportunity to be good."

My lips trembled at that, but I managed to contort the expression into a smile and regain my balance along with my control. As I met his strokes into me with equal force, each thrust grew so jarring with pleasure that already my body coiled toward orgasm.

"Life is more complex than good and bad, Glenn…for instance, my wickedness, and even the wickedness of my husband, excites you. Isn't the pleasure that excitement brings so intensely sweet? Isn't it good?"

"It seems that way now, but—ah—Thecla—"

I bore down heavily against him, the pressure overwhelming. Now I was less afraid of hurting him than I was desperate to savor the cresting of my pleasure. While his hands fit around my rear, his fingers sinking into my flesh, I arched my back and ground against his body with that full, wonderful length within me.

"Glenn! Glenn, oh—you sweet man. No wonder my husband takes such joy in corrupting me...all I want to do is ruin you."

Throatily, Glenn gasped, and the hand that had been sliding along my thigh braced up against me. "Watch out," he said, or began to say.

But then, he seemed to really see me—there above him on the edge of my own ecstasy, my face contorted in the expression of pleasure-pain that men, Malin particularly, found so alluring—and the warning failed halfway through. As though to signal his half-heartedness behind it.

I did not even halfheartedly want to stop. I wanted him, this good man, inside of me as I burst into flames; and I wanted him to linger.

My hips working fast and hard as I rode him to our pleasure, I swooped down upon him and caught him by the hair on the unwounded side of his head. His stomach tightened beneath mine as we kissed, his every inch more rigid within me by the second. I cried into his mouth, the convulsions of ecstasy rising to an earthquake within me.

"Oh, Glenn! If you don't follow me to Gudrune, I'll have you brought there and lain at my feet! I'll whip you in public for your impudence, the audacity to think you can deny me your heart—but, then, you want me to beat you, don't you, Glenn? Admit it."

And, to my gasping delight, his every word sweetening the hot tremors of my orgasm as well as inciting his own, he did.

"Yes, Madame Farrow—I want to be beaten by you." While I tightened around him with a cry of dissolution, he groaned and arched his hips into me. "I would let you do anything—anything you wanted to do to me."

"Be careful…oh, Glenn…there's so much I could dream to do. Oh! Glenn—I'll make you my slave."

The breath caught in his throat, his mouth open and strangled by pleasure. While his urgent, somehow shocked eyes found mine, I held his face to kiss him, murmuring, "Yes, yes, oh, yes—Glenn, yes, give it to me, I want to know you've been inside me—"

He panted desperately, bucking up against me. As Glenn's mouth fell back from my kiss, he struggled to catch his breath amid the delicious twitches that released bolts of pleasure within me. My own quivering continued on, extended by his climax, and I moaned his name softly against his throat before kissing his ink-stained heart.

Slowly, his breathing eased. So did mine. His hand slid into the small of my back.

"I'm sorry," he said quickly, "I don't know what I was thinking."

"What do you mean?"

"I mean, I shouldn't have—I don't have an excuse."

"Oh! Glenn—darling." I laughed gently, my lips nuzzling his. "I wanted you to do it."

"But—what if something happens?"

"Nothing's going to *happen*." Smiling, I tilted my head back to kiss the tip of his nose. "Once won't hurt."

Glenn looked at me with great skepticism, but said nothing. He only raised his head to kiss me. Then, he let it collapse back upon the pillow with a soft sigh.

"I was going to go down and fix that door, but…maybe if you would call a repairman for me, it would be a big help after all."

I was glad to agree.

ALONE, WITH PLEASURE ebbing from me and Dinon the only waking witness of my guilty conscience, I expected to be overwhelmed with shame for what I had just allowed. Yet much to my amazement, and a somehow greater shame, I was not sorry at all.

A part of me—more than a part of me, too much of me—wanted to hurt Malin terribly. In an abstract, somehow distant way, I enjoyed the thought of him being upset. He got away so easily, after all! He was the worst sort of cad, a devious and cunning liar, murderer, more—yet he lived a life any human would envy. His twenties had been filled with war, and, I knew now, the pursuit of my mother; his thirties had been full of wine and pretty men and women, whether they were interested or not. Only in his forties did it seem he retired to a less scandalous existence, his sins restrained to monetized entertainment among the staff until I arrived.

But *why* had he withdrawn? What had made him so abruptly reject all those more hedonistic indulgences he once held dear?

From where I sat with my temporarily clear head poised against the tips of my fingers, I studied Dinon. While I brooded in the couch, the dharmine had watched me from the center of the parlor. Now, as the neurons of my brain brightened with my intent to address him, he genuflected at my feet and gazed up into me with those fathomless silver eyes.

"Is Glenn asleep?"

"Yes, Madame."

"Help him dream sweet dreams, please—and let him hear in it the sounds of busy men, and hammering, and furniture being moved."

"With great pleasure. Shall I get the door, Madame?"

I thought he was asking whether he should fix the door, to which I replied, "I thought you already did," but I quickly understood his true meaning when the RMS system released the chime of a digitized doorbell.

While I sat up with a quick look to the panel, then to the servant at my feet, I asked, "Who is it?"

"Not one of my kind, if that idea frightens you."

My tongue darting across my dry lips, I eased up from my seat to peer into the security footage.

Based on the black body armor, an armed delivery person: a mercenary who stood with hands folded and a white carriage parked on the street behind him.

"Can I help you," I asked through the speaker, animating the man as though from paralysis and causing him to lean forward with a slight adjustment of his hat.

"I've been sent to this address on behalf of a party who requested discretion"—Malin, in other words—"to help deliver flowers for you"—definitely Malin—"if you feel comfortable getting the door. Would you prefer to see the paperwork first, Ma'am?"

Biting my lip with another glance toward Dinon, who I discovered was no longer visible, I said to the speaker, "No, that won't be necessary—would you give me a moment, please?"

I collected the abandoned dress and shift, pulling them on to make myself decent before deactivating the front door's security shutter. The deliveryman, who was by now conversing with a partner, turned to me with a nod.

"If you'll please step back, Ma'am. We were advised to make it quick because of your allergy. Oh—"

The other deliveryman was on his way back to the carriage, out of which a flustered but high-spirited looking florist stepped with a vase of what must have been fifty roses. Alone with me, the speaker gestured to the porch, then bent to pick up an envelope that had been lodged under Glenn's mat.

"This was here when we arrived."

"Thank you." I produced a flustered smile for the gentle-looking lady who scurried past for a place to set the vase. "Oh, uh—how about over there—"

I had gestured to the kitchen table, optimistic that would be it. Then I turned. The second deliveryman was stepping past the threshold with another, equally overflowing vase. Meanwhile, the first deliveryman had already retreated to the carriage to take a display of his own.

After a surprisingly efficient three minutes, Glenn's house had been transformed into a botanical garden. The florist's mystery caller had purchased every rose in the shop, and every lily, too; the dark red petals were intensified by the white accents occasionally slipped into the edges of the sumptuous bouquets that cluttered the coffee table, the desk in the office, the display shelves of the living room, even the bar along the back of the kitchen counter. By the time the slip was signed for proof of delivery and the very happy florist insisted on refusing my tip, I couldn't make out a single detail of the room outside of the flowers.

And, as the shutter rolled down into place behind them, I found myself almost angry about this beautiful gift. Angry and sad. Sad, because I could not be happy; angry, because it seemed Malin found me very simple.

Did he really believe this was all it would take? That all he needed was to spend enough money to persuade some people out in a Rift Event, and I would forgive him?

I frowned, my fingers trailing over the silken petals of a rose.

Before I could sink too deeply into bitter thoughts, my pocket watch buzzed with the call of the man in question.

"The delivery people just left," I told Malin, staring into the faces of the flowers.

"How are they? Do you like them?"

Bowing my forehead against the face of the rose I had just been contemplating, I squeezed my eyes shut and told him, "Of course I like them. That isn't the point."

"I know it's not, Thecla. I know it's not, but—oh—"

The line crackled with the unreliability of the Rift Event outside. It had to be that. If it wasn't that, Malin's voice was breaking into silence with the strain of tears. The very thought provoked some of my own.

"I love you, Thecla. I adore you, I worship you, I—I *need* you, Thecla, darling. Madame Farrow."

"Please, Malin—"

"That's why I've decided I can't wait a second longer." With a deep breath that steadied him, Malin banished the emotion from his voice and told me firmly, "Parvati be damned, the treaty, all of it. If you can't stand to come home, I'm coming there."

Blood draining from my face, I gripped the counter for support. "What? To Valquist? But—"

"I'd like to see her do something about it." His words were a snarl that jolted through me, catapulting me back to his fit at our dinner with Aleister. Would that I were there to touch him! To soothe him. I cursed the impulse, my teeth clenching as he went on darkly, "I don't care what she wants, nor what power she thinks she has over me."

"But—but you just made the energy program *public*, darling. Don't you think she has political pull if she *does* want to do something to you right now?"

"I'm so glad to hear you still care about me, Thecla."

Tears erupted from me, and I only barely stopped myself from turning, "Of course I still care about you, I love you," into a scream. My cheeks puffed with a few hyperventilated breaths before, briskly wiping my hand across my face, I told him in a tightly restrained voice, "I wish you would understand. I know you don't think like a normal man, so I'll say this as plainly as I can. You've hurt me as badly as you have *because* I love you. Because I can't do anything about my love for you. Not a damn thing! It would be so *easy* to just stop caring for you—to run away from you like my mother did. But—Malin—please, if something happens to you—"

"Don't finish the thought. Don't finish it, Thecla, please."

"Don't come here."

"I have to," he told me simply. "I can make it there faster than you can make it home at this point; the weather out *here* is fine. Thecla—are you crying, darling?"

"Malin—please. I don't want something to happen to you."

"I would take this risk a thousand times to see you even once. Just wait for me, angel. I'll come to you. I'll book us the finest hotel in Valquist—or, if they won't have me, Aleister's duchy will serve us. Yes, that's a capital idea! You know—"

"Malin—"

"—why don't we go enjoy the shore together a little while?"

"Please, Malin—"

"We can bring Eleison and have some peace and quiet. We can talk. We can make love. You can let me apologize and you can forgive me, or not. Whatever you want, whatever you need. But I must have you. Do you understand?"

The pulse of my heart thrummed through my tongue, the dark intensity of his tone leaving me dizzy. "I understand that I'm your wife, of course, but—can't you just trust me, trust I'll be home in a week? That I'll leave the moment the train can?"

"I do trust you. But if I leave now, it *won't* be a week. You'll have an extra day or two with your friend, then I'll whisk you away and—Thecla!—I'll have you in my arms again, my darling, my radiant darling, please—"

Those terrible cracks in his powerful voice! He was normally so calm, even when displeased; yet, as it concerned me, he seemed to be at the mercy of the same possessing emotions that kept me from easily forgiving.

"Malin—I know I can't stop you—"

"You can, of course. You know what to tell me if you really want me to stop. If you really want to pull out my heart and spit on it, as I deserve, then say it to me. I won't come. I'll wait here like a dog, like an idiot, and wither and die when you never come home."

My shoulders sagged. "Don't do this to me, Malin."

"Go on. All you have to do is say "Lescaut.""

"Don't make it my choice."

"It's *always* your choice, Thecla." The slightly hostile edge to his tone excited me more than it frightened me, and I inhaled while my hand raised to tinker with the buttons of my dress. "Never forget it," Malin continued. "Never forget you have the power to leave me at any time. But—you know it won't be a game anymore then, will it, precious?"

My breathing shallow, I couldn't seem to stop myself from saying, "Yes, sir."

His breath hitched and my eyes squeezed shut. If I had been in any way inclined to use the safeword to control Malin's behavior—to stop him from risking his life to come to me while also forcing him to respect my space—that would have been the moment to say it.

Instead I succumbed to a hot thrill, so awful in that moment, as I recognized I would never escape Malin. Not ever. My mother had; but I was not my mother, and he, not the boy he was when, between warfare and governance, he scoured the Gudrune countryside for my traitorous parents.

"Did you mean to kill them when you found them?"

He didn't reply for a long enough time that I already knew the answer when he instead said, "Let's wait to speak until I can hold you, and kiss you, and look into your eyes to let you feel the sincerity of my regret."

"I wish you would let me come home to you. That you would just wait."

"I'm sorry, darling. I know you want space, but—oh, Thecla, don't you know? You're my heart. Space is the one thing I can't give you. I'm going now. Don't feel obligated to say it back, but—I love you."

"But I do love you. I love you so much. Malin...I should tell you, Glenn and I—"

"I'm not naive, Thecla. I don't care. I don't care at all, as long as you're not in danger."

"Okay. Okay. I'm—I'm sorry."

"What have I told you before? You should be enjoying your body... As long as it still responds so sweetly to mine, I'm happy. You make me happy, Thecla. You do know that, don't you?"

"Yes, Malin. I know that."

"Good. I'm glad. I'd better go—see you soon, I love you, I love you—"

The line went dead while I cried it back. At the sudden silence, I collapsed into tears. I folded my arms and rested my face upon the same bar where just a night before I'd such fun laughing and chatting with Glenn. Glenn, who had only cared about my security and comfort.

A cool, powerful hand slid up my spine and fit to the nape of my neck.

"Don't be sad, Madame...your sorrow is so tender, so delicious, but don't you think these flowers are lovely?"

"There's too many of them," I wailed pitifully, sliding down to sit on the floor like the helpless child my emotions forced me to be. "I can barely walk through this blasted house...they're everywhere I look, it's too much. Do something about them, would you—"

"Of course, Madame."

Bowing, Dinon gestured with one moon-white hand while raking his gaze across the room. My heart broke to watch the flowers in their lovely vases all disappear; yet, when I pulled myself to my feet to mourn and marvel over his handiwork, I turned to find the arrangement upon the counter had multiplied in size and scale. What had been a bunch of fifty roses now was a display that numbered in the hundreds, an unfathomable planet of crimson petals broken only occasionally by the alien fronds of a lily's open mouth.

"Thank you," I said with a wretched sniff, trailing my fingertips along the great rose sphere. "Thank you, that's much more manageable…oh, Dinon—Dinon—I'm afraid to *see* him, I—"

"Because you know you'll find him the same as he was when you left, and you'll love him just as much. I feel your courage fail every time you speak to him."

"Should I run?"

"Not if you value the hunter's life, Madame."

With a wet, shallow sigh, I ground my teeth to peer at Glenn's shut bedroom. "Of course I value his life," I whispered. "Of course."

"Then neither flee with him, nor leave him while you board a train to anywhere but Gudrune. That is the advice I give you based on the question you have asked—but, Madame, I would also not pay my advice much mind. It will not matter."

"Do not speak to me of the future when I do not ask for it," I told him harshly, earning an enchanted little smile.

"Of course, Madame. My apologies."

"I'm going to rest with Glenn awhile. Can you tell if he's had a concussion, or a broken rib?"

"He has neither, Madame. No fractures at all."

I nodded, then stopped and looked at him.

Dinon smiled back at me, waiting.

"Are you actually a dharmine, Dinon?"

"You called me that, Madame," he answered. "But I am the prototype of the creatures called dharmines; so, it is appropriate to call me that, as well."

The prototype…I couldn't imagine what that meant, and shuddered to think on it too long.

"Watch over the house, then, whatever you are, and don't let us be disturbed until I call for you. If my husband is coming here, then so be it…I'll consider this Rift Event all the more a blessing, the peace I requested."

With another bow, Dinon said, "Of course, Madame. With pleasure."

The entity disappeared. There I was, alone in Glenn's house with Malin's rearranged roses.

Too tired to cry anymore, I fought the weight of gravity to climb the stairs and slump into Glenn's bedroom. My heart seized. He looked so peaceful despite the multicolored bruises crisscrossing his back, displayed as he slept on his side while half-curled toward the wall. Guilt shot through me to remember my intent to freeze some towels; yet, with a soothing kiss Dinon pressed upon my cerebellum, I felt certain I would find some when they were required. Instead of worrying, I undressed in silence, slid into bed between Glenn and the wall, and smiled to myself as his half-sleeping limbs contorted against me.

"Everything okay," he grunted, as much of a question as he could manage while I settled back against his chest.

"Everything's fine, Glenn. It's all fixed. We're perfectly safe.

Let's just enjoy being together for now…we can always talk more later."

Satisfied, Glenn nuzzled his unharmed cheek and forehead into the pillow of my hair, where he fell asleep without another word.

Lulled by his steady half-snores, I finally found substantial sleep of my own.

OR TWO DAYS, I felt as though I were on a pleasant little vacation. There I was, trembling, hot to the touch, skittish and aching to be kissed; and, somehow so much more innocent than my husband or my mate, there was sweet Glenn, before whom I had to contain my libido to something approaching a normal human pattern.

But I couldn't hide all my needs from him. I awoke that evening ravenous, abruptly aware I had not eaten since Glenn's dinner the night before. Exhausted as he was, he showed no signs of waking as I turned, and even slept heavily into the kiss with which I crowned his brow once I frowned at the bandage's stains. Yet, as I slid up in his embrace, he snapped awake enough to tighten his arms around me.

"I didn't dream it," he mumbled, the words a sleep-heavy gurgle in the base of his chest. I stroked curls from his brow and resisted the urge to sink back to sleep in his wonderful warm embrace.

"Not all of it," I said cheekily, my lips quirking in a slight smile as I went on. "Your furniture is all replaced, and the door fixed, too…"

"I thought I heard something"—he raised the hair-covered back of one great hand before his mouth as, grimacing through it, he succumbed to a yawn I feared might tear his scratches—"while I was sleeping, but I just couldn't seem to make myself wake up to go help."

His words collapsed into a slight hiss as he tried sitting up. My brow furrowing, I pressed his shoulder back into the soft embrace of the mattress.

"Please, Glenn, don't strain yourself. You should stay in bed. Let me get you that ice I owe you."

"I can't sit around here doing nothing."

It seemed my odds of keeping him in bed were as high as my odds of getting him to see a doctor. Sighing, I slid my hand away from him and permitted him to rise without resistance. After rolling toward the edge of the mattress and gingerly pushing himself upright with both arms, Glenn's wincing negotiation to his feet made me gasp aloud.

"Oh, Glenn…darling—"

In the worst areas, the bruises had now had time to deepen to an ugly purple so intense it was nearly black. Mixed into this was red and yellow, great blotches that were a fright to look upon and slowed his stride to a limp. Yet stubbornly on he went, asking, "Do you feel like eating? I'm starving."

"You ridiculous beast of a man! Are you trying to impress me? If that's your aim, it's really just annoying."

Laughing in surprise while I slid up from the bed, Glenn turned to slide his eyes along my body before it was concealed beneath my shift. "The honeymoon's already over, huh?"

"Don't pretend my sharp tongue doesn't excite you, hunter...go on. If you won't convalesce, at least stand under a cold shower for a few seconds. That bruise looks terrible, I'm so worried."

His slight laugh reduced to a faint smile. "You don't have to be worried about me, Thecla."

"Well *somebody* has to be, blast it. Go on! Let me cook for us both. You need to be looked after for the next few nights. Especially since—oh, I'm so sorry for what happened today, Glenn."

That wistful smile flattened out into a serious, distant sort of mien. "I am, too, Thecla. I'm sorry for you...but I'm not sorry about what happened."

His sharp sapphire eye caught mine and held it fast.

"Not about anything."

While Glenn limped off, I exhaled in relief to think his pride unwounded by the assault. Was it possible he could have endured such a thing, yet harbored no ill will? It didn't seem natural—but, perhaps that was Glenn's way. He was such a quiet man. "Introverted," to use a term by which Charlotte once described me.

Guilt lapped at my feet as I made my way down to investigate the kitchen. Halfway there, I was arrested by the half-forgotten cloud of roses. Each, perfectly arranged by Dinon's mystical will.

I am the prototype of the creatures called dharmines.

I shuddered, the memories of the afternoon belatedly reaching me through the thickness of sleep—and the slowly rising headache once more ebbing against my frontal lobe.

What had Dinon meant by that? Just what was he, exactly? I had heard of dharmines possessing great powers, but...producing that dress? Repairing the furniture?

"Would you like me to cook, Madame?"

"No," I told my intrusive servant sharply, not sure whence his voice emanated but nevertheless fast to respond aloud. "No, Dinon, I certainly don't trust you with food. But there was a phonograph in the office. Would you—"

Before I had finished my thought, the sound of chamber music sent me wheeling left. There the phonograph already sat upon Glenn's coffee table, the device piping out music so old I believed it three or four hundred years pre-Rift.

I smiled in pleasure to turn back toward the kitchen.

And Dinon stood before me.

"I've done so much for you this past day, Madame," he said in the innocent tone of expectation with which hotel bellhops, I would find over the years, might discuss the tip I or my husband had doled out the last time we came to stay in such-and-such locale's most solitary suite. "It's wearying work, enchanting men's dreams and fixing up the furniture."

"Even more wearying, I would think, to tweak the pieces to abate his suspicion," I said with a glance at the kitchen table behind him, now no longer a construction but a rustic piece carved from the great, beautiful cross section of one single mighty tree. The loveseat, though reminiscent of the shattered one so as to flow with the now widowed couch, bore the country-living hallmarks of Glenn's taste but with a sharper, more stylish pattern of silver and black stripes embroidered into its cushions. The cushions upon the old sofa, I noticed, had even been altered to match the aesthetic.

It was difficult to avoid being impressed, though this was by the hand of a demon.

"Well"—sighing, I braced my hips and shut my eyes to

retain an air of tranquility, refusing to admit to the erotic pleasure the demon's slavish nature inspired—"I suppose, hard as you've worked, you deserve to eat just as we do...what do you want, dog? Name it."

"A kiss, Madame. Just one."

Flush faced, I leaned back against the new loveseat and was half-surprised it did not dissolve in a flicker of light and Rift radiation. "Not unreasonable," I said as, upstairs, the groan of pipes signaled the start of Glenn's shower. "Make it quick...I need to start cooking."

His unnatural smile fixed upon me, Dinon closed the distance. As he stooped to meet me, the palm of one artful hand raised to caress my cheek. My eyelids fell closed as my mouth opened in allowance to his, a soft part of my lips that he spread considerably. Breath hitching, the demon in this beautiful, male form plunged into my mouth, feasting upon my gasps and soft, shocked moans. He crushed me against his body to once more thrill us both with that virile ornament's proximity, the leather of his trousers and the soft cotton of my shift the only things standing between his anatomy and mine.

What would it be like to let him fuck me? The thought flashed across my mind and Dinon's hand dropped to knead the flesh of my ass, the passion of his kiss growing to a kind of savage frenzy. His tongue claimed the depths of my mouth to the very the top of my throat, and I moaned to suckle upon him; trembled at the scrape of more than mortal teeth against my lip. The heat that already surged through my body intensified beyond all comprehension, and I raised my hands to tangle my fingers in the demon's silver-white hair.

Dinon released me.

"I don't mean to keep you, Madame," he murmured against my lips when his tongue retracted. "I know you're very busy…but I was famished. Thank you."

The evil creature nuzzled against my hot cheek, then back into my hair. There, his breath upon my ear sent shudders down my spine. "Call me if you need me, as always…"

"You seem to arrive *before* I call."

"When I'm near, and can, I will every time…and does that not make me the ideal servant?"

With a cheeky sort of grin, the so-called dharmine vanished. I was left alone, dizzy and distracted. And now I was to cook in this state, was I?

Though I had second thoughts about allowing Dinon to produce food for us, I was quickly glad to have something to occupy my mind—for, in the demon's absence, how quickly every thought turned to Malin! It was those flowers, as had certainly been his intent. Each time I caught a scarlet flash in the corner of my eye, my mind whirled down a chain of association that inevitably ended in him. Malin. On his way to me while I stood in Glenn's kitchen, flour up to my wrists while I kneaded a quick-rising bread dough and enjoyed some music my husband surely would have enjoyed with me.

But, then—unless we were out on a trip together, as we'd been on our honeymoon, Malin wouldn't let me sully my hands with work more involved than weaving. He enjoyed my cooking, but was convinced my time and energy had better applications, and he was right, of course…however, I *missed* cooking occasionally. Perhaps I would put my foot down and start using the kitchen in his apartments more often, just for fun.

Quickly, I caught myself. Was I really already planning

what I'd do when I settled back into Malin's comfortable little nest, the hawk's prize returned for good? I frowned while brushing my forearm along my brow and leaving the dough to rise.

Of course, I *wanted* to resume that peaceful, loving life... but it wasn't peaceful at all, I reflected while settling on an ypron shoulder that seemed like a fine enough roast. It was, in fact, a very busy, very regimented existence that we lived in Gudrune; and though it was undeniably full of great pleasure and truly rare liberties, I was also growing conscious that we were perpetually in a low level of danger.

How strange! Even though I knew that, there were still times I imagined having a pair of lovely children with Malin and enjoying—with Eleison's comforting background presence—a cozy, domestic dream. In the way a child imagines adult life as some overblown extension of the activities young people most covet, (staying up late, eating sweets, playing while chores go unfinished), I inevitably struggled to stay cognizant of what parenting with Malin would *really* be like. How much time could I ever expect him to spend with the children? Was quality time even relevant to him when it came to heirs, or would he be satisfied enough to know they existed while neglecting that existence in favor of his duties and his interest in me?

Somehow, I couldn't imagine that. If anything, I knew unwaveringly that Malin would be a devoted, generous, truly interested father. That made it so much more painful to think the aristocratic class to which he belonged upheld a more formally structured environment of child-rearing.

I didn't want governesses and nursemaids—at least, caught in my dream with Glenn, I thought I didn't. It would be much lovelier to raise children as I was raised. In a quiet, country life, comfortable and safe...even if a little boring. But how warm! How sweet! Imagine me, a mother, cozy before the warm stove every night while an adorable boy teased and chased and tickled an equally adorable girl. Imagine the fading of sunlight and the velvet anticipation of togetherness with the end of a long day. Imagine the heavy footsteps of familiar love, and the happy gasps of the little ones, and the cracking open of a door—

"That smells delicious."

Glenn's voice startled me. Between the music and my work, I hadn't heard his shower end or his footsteps down the stairs. He appeared around the corner, dressed in a checkered shirt with the wound upon his cheek freshly bandaged. Perked to see him, I drummed the spoon against the edge of a pan before turning quickly to the icebox.

"It's my pleasure," I told him while removing a few frozen towels from inside. "Lean back on these when you sit, please—not on your bare skin, of course—"

"Thank you." He nodded, accepting them, then cast a sidelong glance at the ostentatious bouquet I'd moved to the kitchen table. "Those are from, uh, Malin, I assume?"

"Yes. About that, Glenn—"

My lips tucked back between my teeth.

"He's coming to Valquist," I heard myself saying from a kind of distance. "So we'll have an extra day, in a sense, but—"

A look of shock passed through Glenn's features, which tightened.

"Malin is coming *here*? To get you?"

"So it would seem. He's really very upset...oh—"

"Do you *want* him coming here?"

"I—I don't know how to answer that in a way that would make sense to you, Glenn." I tried to laugh, but the noise caught in my throat. I simply worried my thumb along my brow. "I feel better about the idea today than I would have yesterday, I can tell you that…and perhaps tomorrow, I'll feel even better about it. But I am very afraid to discuss the things we most need to discuss."

"Do you think he'll be angry? Do you need me to be there?"

Moved by Glenn's sincere concern, I told him, "Please, don't be worried…I expect Malin will be a bit cross with me for making him come out to Valquist, if he is feeling honest. But, no. I think he's as contrite as he's capable of being. You see—"

I managed to laugh a little. As I did, I shook my head to recall Aleister's now ominous assessment of my character.

"I'm not afraid of Malin. I'm afraid of *myself*. My own anger."

"I'd say it's normal to be angry in your situation."

"Who knows the normal reaction to abnormality? But you are right…and it's not like my anger is a surprise to him. Yet—I'm afraid of what could happen when I'm angry. I'm afraid of—of what I might say, and of how what I might say will carry into the future. The consequences of my anger." I scoffed. "It hardly seems fair that my anger *should* have any consequences when I've been so wronged, does it?"

"Thecla…"

A tear escaped the corner of my eye. I turned to banish it with a hasty wrist. "I'm so sick of crying! I've been maudlin the whole time you've known me…you haven't met the person I really am, Glenn."

"No," he agreed, "but I can see her in there. And she's beautiful."

His footsteps bore him to my side, and as I turned to face him, his hand slid along the back of my shoulder.

"I just want him to love me," I whispered, leaning my cheek upon Glenn's heart and gripping his shirt rather than wrapping my arms around his injured back. "*Me*, and not some memory. And I'm so afraid that might be the case that I'd rather stay suspended in this purgatory than discover something so crushing."

"It's just amazing to me that Malin Farrow can love in the first place. But, if any woman can make him do it, it's you."

My thumb dashed across the corner of my eye while I told him, "You say such sweet things. You truly are a gentleman, you know; a gallant."

"Not always," he admitted introspectively, releasing me to let me return to my cooking. As he turned away, Glenn scanned the counter in study of my ingredients—then noted the bar. "That from him, too?"

"Mm? Oh—" I shook my head, waving a hand at the envelope that had drawn his attention. "No, that must be yours...one of the deliverymen brought it in with the, uh—with the furniture."

Why did I lie? I cringed for having said it, but it wasn't as motiveless a fabrication as it may have seemed. I wanted to be sure he was sold on the existence of the fast-moving furniture dealers, and on the terrestrial nature of my ability to fix up his house at the snap of my fingers.

Because, while I was frightened enough of letting Glenn discover I was altered, I truly didn't want to experience the consequences of revealing to him that a dharmine had followed me into his house.

Thinking not near so much of the moment as I did, Glenn slipped the envelope from the bar, tore open its seal without much of a glance, then quickly read through the note. He snorted and snapped the letter shut.

Then he froze, jerked by a thought I caught from the corner of my eye.

"Is everything all right?"

"Yes," he said quickly, stuffing it back into its envelope. "Yeah, of course. Just, uh, some people from the guild were planning a, uh, poker game to celebrate me being back in town. They're not taking the Rift Event for an excuse to cancel."

I laughed a little. "I wouldn't expect hunters to pay it any mind. That reminds me of my old friends from Lescaut…oh, I wonder how they are now?" Smiling, staring into the space of memory, I said fondly, "Every once in a while—perhaps once a month or twice—they would catch me on the street and force me to some occasion, or arrive at my apartment over the bookbinder and drag me out for fresh air."

"Were these other weavers?"

"Oh, one of them, but also a few of the children of father's friends—nursery mates of mine, really—and just the odd person around my age I knew from town. All such nice people…I do miss them."

My face fell from its enchanted dream smile to a slight frown.

"I really should write my sister while I'm abroad without my loom." The black loom flickered like a moth across my vision even as I went on. "Especially since the mail runs during Rift Events here…"

"Yeah, sometimes…" With a glance over at the phonograph I hoped he didn't mind being moved, he tapped the letter's edge against his open palm and said, "Would you excuse me a moment? I have to make a call."

"Please don't cancel your game on my account, Glenn. Did you mean to hold it here? I can make myself scarce."

Glenn's mouth tightened, the bandage along his cheek shifting with the contortion. "You're not the problem…although, yeah, it was meant to be here, and I'm not sure how wild I am about everybody knowing Thecla Farrow is staying in my house." Without even seeing the bite of my lip, he realized the easy misinterpretation of his words and glanced quickly at me. "Not for any reason other than your safety. If it were safe, if it were up to me—I'd forget everything about my reputation, my life, and I'd follow you home."

Color sweeping across my cheeks, I gasped his name. By then, his eyes had already averted while he hastened into his office; out of my sight, he shut the door, unable to bear any possible reply.

Nibbling on the edge of my thumb, unable to help my silly smile, I whispered in that shut door's direction, "I wish things were different."

What things? My ease of access to him, for one. I wished Glenn *were* closer to Gudrune. I wished he would show more compassion toward Malin, or more tolerance, at least. I wished Eleison hadn't given Glenn ample reason to dislike him on a personal level.

I wished and wished, and then I wished some more.

But the one thing I never wished for—never, not for one second—was to be free of Malin so as to pursue Glenn. It was simply not an option I could ever fathom.

Dinner was marvelous, if I say so myself, and my host seemed to agree. After helping me clean up, Glenn pressed me back against the counter and caught me in a kiss I hadn't expected. Gasping into his mouth, I melted in the embrace of his heavy hands, my whole body suddenly at ease as it hadn't been since the tension of the Rift Event. When his face raised from mine, the look in his eyes was one of incalculable desire—of dreams and heartache that signaled he was still thinking about what he had said earlier, just as I was.

Unspeaking, he knelt before me and pushed my shift up around my thighs.

"Glenn—be careful, your bandage—"

"You've taken better care of me in one day than anybody has in years, Thecla…" His hand ascended the length of my thigh, then higher, past the lacy hem. Then came his low gasp, a groan as he pushed the fabric higher to admire my exposed apex.

"Don't lose your balance," Glenn advised before leaning in to plant the first kiss.

Sparks leapt through me, into my brain and out beyond my limbs. The rough edges of his beard tickled so that I actually giggled a bit at first; but, very slowly, the kisses of his smiling mouth discovered that firm pressure and the slight application of tongue banished tickling for an altogether more pleasing sensation. Moaning, I gripped the counter behind me and widened the stance of my legs just so; as I did, the fleeting contacts of his tongue developed into loving, languid strokes, his fingers gently shifting to spread me for his ease of exploration.

The roughness of Glenn's fingers, such a counterpoint to his tongue, made me bolt with an overwhelming surge of pleasure. I took on the task of raising my hem before, aggravated, I stripped the shift over my head and let him enjoy my nudity above him there in the kitchen. While his tongue's lashing of my center discovered the sensitive heart of my lust, I cried his name and ground eagerly against him.

He was talented, but patient. More interested, I sensed,

in exploring the peaks and valleys of my flesh for his own memorization. My fingers slid into the dark curls at the back of his head, which I could bear to press to me only very gingerly, as I didn't want to hurt him. That restraint was torture! I clenched my teeth and sank the fingers of my free hand as tightly into the counter as I wished to sink them into his scalp. Unable to drape around his shoulder as was preferable, my left leg extended up to brace against the ice box. He responded promptly, his fingertips trailing along to the mouth of a raging river. One calloused pad probed gently into me, sliding deeper with the confident rhythm of his tongue's hot strokes.

I gripped him tighter, my brows knitting and my mouth open in the terrific agony of lust.

"Glenn! Glenn—please, faster, use me roughly—ah!"

I had been worried he wouldn't bring himself to it, but to my delight, Glenn obliged me at once. I moaned when a second finger joined the first, their strokes within me demanding foreshadows of what was to come. My back arched as I rocked down against him, desperate for every increase of pressure I could contrive. As the pressure increased, so did his speed. As his speed increased, so did my cries.

And then, across my mind and along the back of my neck as though he embraced me, I felt the closely caressing observation of Dinon. My pleasure erupted in an ecstatic scream and the fast fluttering of my pining body around Glenn's fingers.

"Oh," he murmured against me while he slowed, as I found men did until I had the chance to train them to keep up their pace until my swoon had ended; but I didn't mind it, didn't mind it at all, because I was so unbalanced by my orgasm that my leg had to drop back to the floor. Moving quickly despite his injuries, Glenn rose to catch me in his arms for a passionate, pulsating kiss he poured into the back of my mouth.

"You're so beautiful, Thecla," he murmured, almost growling the words against my lips while, drunk on his love, I let my head roll against his shoulder. "Will you spend the night with me again?"

"Yes," I murmured, "yes, I'll condescend to amuse myself with you, Hunter…I'll even let you walk to the bedroom on your own two feet, since you just spent so much time kneeling before me. I'll save crawling for later. Glenn! Oh…"

Teeth grit, I tightened my hand in the fabric of his shirt and marveled to find myself angered by my desire for him. The past few months had left me irrevocably spoiled. I was growing accustomed to getting whatever I wanted—if not when I wanted it, then as soon as Malin could obtain it for me.

And Glenn was just not like that, was he? I could want him and want him, and it would do me no good.

"I want to lock you up in a gilded cage like a pretty bird," I told Glenn madly, my hand sliding along the front of his trousers and then, unable to resist, within. "I'd teach you to sleep at my feet like my pet. Glenn! If you don't come to Gudrune"—my hand filled with the heat of his desire, so hard and heavy and promising, and his breath hitched beneath my words—"if you don't present yourself to me, Glenn, I'll demand my husband kidnap you and give you to me as a gift."

"Ah—"

"I'll keep you locked up for use as my love-slave. We'll let the whole world think you've retired—oh, yes, yes! This cock, oh—"

I couldn't wait another moment. I pushed his trousers down

and drew him close, sliding up against the edge of the gleaming counter where he helped me brace without hesitation. While Glenn's hand fit to the back of my head and the other supported my thigh, I guided him home just to trap him on the threshold.

"Hm, Glenn—you *want* to be my love-slave, don't you, darling, oh—"

"Yes," he whispered, his voice dark with shame, his finely carved prick pulsing with agreement in my hand.

Moaning, I commanded, "Say it louder."

"Yes," Glenn barked, his voice louder, harder.

"Yes, what?"

"Yes—yes, Madame, ah, fuck—I want you to use me. I want you to keep me for your satisfaction—"

Twisting to brush my lips over his brow, I drew him into me and basked in the low shadow of his groan. With a gasp of my own, I whispered in his ear, "Then don't act affronted when it really happens, Glenn. Oh, yes! When you awaken in my dungeon someday, darling—my beautiful, finely fucking hunter—blame and thank yourself. Thank only yourself."

"Thecla—"

I heard it in his voice. The concern. The warning. The plea. I moaned, all my body dancing with the pleasure of his cock. "Let me feel it, Glenn—I *want* your cum in me. Oh, darling, give Madame what she wants."

"Madame—oh, Thecla—"

He had almost seemed poised to argue; then, he raised his head and met my eye, and seemed at once so absolutely, fully present there with me that being naked felt more exhibitionistic than it ever had before. I shuddered, his name rising from me in a coo, while I wove my arms around the back of his neck.

Then, as if having made a decision, his body took action against mine, and I threw back my head in a scream of love's victory.

I AM SO tired of this.

No doubt, reader, you are, too. You feel with me how tired I was of being in Valquist. How tired I was of heavy revelations and disappointing betrayals.

And, like I did, you may even find yourself pining for Malin: for he is, I should say, the heart of my story, in that without his love for me there would be no story to tell you. Nothing would ever, could ever have happened as it did, and I would not be here, overlooking a city I once detested from the suite whence I rule it. Yet, curiously, though these memoirs revolve so heavily around our love and its consequences, there are two great gaps in the history of our romance which must be recorded if the chronicle is to be delivered truthfully, understandably, and in a manner that may perhaps even earn me empathy from my reader...however little I am due.

Therefore, my friend, be not agitated with my telling. Understand I am as burdened by these ugly memories as you are. Where once my pen flew, it has now crawled for a month. I have felt myself mired in an endless hell, all recollections of that unhappy time so crisp it seems I am still within them as I write them down. Still freshly living each sorrow and mistake.

But, each joy, too; and the greater joys lie yet on the horizon. Soon you will be through to less difficult periods of my life, and I will have a break in my narrative as will suit my sanity—at the time recorded as well as now, as I relate these things to you. For a few days, I will pass the pen to my husband. He has kindly agreed to inform you on the duration I cannot properly recall; for, as you will see, I was simply not myself. When he has finished his section, I will read it through, (and suffer greatly to think of his plight during this time), and decide exactly how I will proceed. I can only hope the space will have made the final leg of this particular epoch flow out somewhat easier.

But, for now, it is left to me to bring my time in Valquist to an end; and I will tell you what I can of that fatal final night, as truthfully as I can stand to.

Glenn held me through the night despite my concerns about his injuries. Though I slept soundly in his embrace, I awoke with the early morning pounding of a renewed, staggering migraine. I sat up and grimaced, my right eye cringing shut against the pain that streaked from it and up across my temple. Glenn stirred beside me, having slipped away from me in the night to sleep on his stomach. I assured him everything was fine, claiming I was only getting up to get a bit of reading in.

"This early?"

It wasn't early, not for me; not really. I kept that to myself and kissed his brow until he dozed again, at which point I crept from his bedroom and returned to mine to dress.

From what was packed for Valquist, Charlotte had selected only a small number of items: only what I could easily don myself, and then, a selection limited so as to encourage me back to her as soon as possible. From among their number, I selected a neutrally colored day dress with a cream bow that accented the bust. For the first time, it consciously struck me that this had been my mother's.

Exhaling shakily, I sat upon the edge of the bed.

The book about Malin stared at me.

It took a bit of doing through the staggering pain of my headache—even more than it had the day before—but I managed to squint through the small text of the appendix long enough to find a list of references to Giselle. Heart aching, I whirled through the indicated pages and found almost nothing of interest. Rumors and hearsay. Nothing of value but a single blurred photograph. Apparently taken during one of those early visits to Valquist before they came to their abrupt end, the image showed Malin: young, crushingly handsome, the hawkishness of his features not yet so defined but still present. They loaned distinction enough to enchant him with the look of a wicked prince, inwardly scornful of a world upon which he turned a forced little smile. He sat just left of center, his dark eyes fixed on the blurred foreground. There, Parvati said something at the right while, to the left, my mother had been captured laughing in profile.

She did look like me, somewhat. Her features were rather more severe than mine, and her hair seemed to be lighter than I recalled—though, it was hard to tell in black-and-white. I even recognized her dress from my closet, though I hadn't worn it yet and now was sure I never would.

How happy she looked in that second! Yet that single image, taken at some long-forgotten garden party hosted to honor Gudrune's visit, seemed to express so much. Whatever was being said, Malin was completely disconnected from it all. The Master of Gudrune, eternally slumped in his chair, his hands folded over his ribs with an air of bored impatience.

I looked at the date and found the photograph was from barely a year after their marriage. Had they had problems so early on? He looked so young to be so disengaged.

Or, perhaps I should write, to be so engaged.

Twenty-four had been young to marry, at least to me personally, but to many it was old. In looking back through the facts of the book, I realized with a start that Malin had taken his first wife when he was *nineteen*, and she twenty—unfathomably young, no matter how many friends I watched marry themselves off between the ages of eighteen and twenty-one.

And that was but the superficial problem. When I think of all the ways those two were set for heartbreak! It was terrible; I was not surprised to know things ended as they did. The story heavy on my aching mind, I made my way downstairs and sat on the couch produced by Dinon.

Miles away, I swore I could feel Malin, restless aboard the train that bore him to me.

How would he appear in photographs with me someday? Not many existed yet. We had taken an official portrait that was very lovely and that I cherish even now, but, owing to his preference for privacy, candid shots of us were rare. No one in Gudrune dared act as the tabloids had in Valquist; though, reflecting on it, I was a little sorry for that.

After a period of sitting with my forehead braced in my

shading hand, my headache reduced enough to cook. By seven-thirty, just after I finished and Glenn had crawled out of bed to join me, the power failed. He looked up with a soft curse while I, sipping on my tea to hide my expression, glanced sidelong in the vague direction of the palace. Yes, Parvati...that was some exceptional infrastructure, wasn't it.

In spite of the subsequent heat, the shuttered windows baking us with terrible humidity to boot, that day was pleasant. Now, colored as it is by so much knowledge of the events around it, I regard it grimly; but, at the time, it was a tranquil, very lovely day. He insisted on cleaning up, then rooted around in some utility closet in the back of the house before dragging out a generator that ran on impractically large solar batteries. In a matter of minutes, the entire house jolted with a pop and a groan of the air conditioning.

Unable to stop myself, I smiled. "You really do remind me of my father, Glenn. Just a little. At least, I'm sure he would have liked you."

"I hope that's a good thing."

"Of course, it is. My father was a very kind man, warm-hearted and wise."

How wise was it, really, to run from Malin Farrow? I chastised myself for the question and went on, studying the roses distantly while Glenn ensured the icebox was running. "I don't think I ever worried about a Rift Event while he was alive...well, no—there was one, one that was frightening, but he saved me from that one, too." Smiling a little to think of Rigel—allowing myself to smile, at least, as I seldom did when he crossed my mind in those days—I told Glenn, "He always seemed to know what to do."

Now, of course, I could see he had no more idea than I.

"That's how I felt about my mother," said Glenn with a chuckle, adding as though reading my thoughts, "but now I know better."

"Isn't it funny? A good parent always seems so omnipotent. And then—they're not anymore."

At my sad laugh while I extended in the loveseat, he asked, "What happened to your father?"

"Blood poisoning…no one ever saw the dharmine except for him, and he never regained consciousness enough to tell me about it."

Brow furrowed, Glenn stood behind the loveseat and stroked a knuckle along my cheek. "I'm sorry. That must have been awful."

"It was, but—well." I laughed again, darkly now, and fidgeted with the bow decorating my waist. "These days, when I look at the way my life has progressed, I can't help but be glad Father died when he did. It sounds terrible, I know—I'm shocked to have thoughts like these, let alone hear myself speak them aloud—but I can't help it."

"Why do you feel that way?"

It was a neutral question. Interested, not judgmental. After shrugging, I folded my hands over my ribs in an incidental imitation of Malin's contemplative pose. "Don't you think any father would be shocked to find his daughter on a trajectory like mine?"

"I suppose so."

"There's no avoiding it…children have ways of living contrary to the interests and intentions of their parents."

"That's true. My mother never liked my choice of career… but—do you ever think your father may have had a point?"

"All the time. That's why I'm glad he's dead…I'll never have to hear it. What he really thinks of Malin."

Glenn's lips pressed thinly together. They relaxed only when he stooped to kiss me, a caress occurring in synch with a brush of his fingertips along my brow. The throb of the headache increased and I winced, my eyes shutting as he pulled away.

"Are you okay?"

"Oh, yes, this headache…"

"It's back again?"

"I'm afraid so…perhaps your shutters are leaking."

"I'll check. Maybe I'll cancel that game, after all. I was just going to talk to you about it, but—"

"No! No, darling, please. Don't cancel your affair because I'll be lying in a dark, cool room." My hand raising to fit against his chest, I told him, "That's very kind to offer. But if your friends are willing to come out in the Rift to see you, don't let me be the reason they can't."

His jaw tightened, those eyes of his searching every corner of my face. "I don't want to increase your suffering. They'll be rowdy."

"That won't be a problem when I'm up there in a bedroom. Though I'd ought to come play the diplomat for a while, if you don't mind being the subject of some fun gossip once I'm gone."

These last words pained us both, thrusting upon us sudden awareness of our time limit. While his hand slid over mine, he said, "I don't know about gossip, but—I admit, I'm a little overwhelmed at the thought of hosting people so soon after recovering. You don't have to cook or anything, but—"

"Oh, please, I'd be *glad* to. That sounds like fun."

"That wasn't a hint." He laughed, his smile crooking past

the point of a cuspid to make him look somehow canine. "If you really don't mind, though, I'm not polite enough to turn you down. I'd just as soon they didn't know you're here, but—"

"It won't be any problem, Glenn, please. One of the things I miss most about living in Lescaut is just—being around people. *People*, normal people. The staff is lovely but they're always putting on airs, of course; and then there are the courtiers and others of their ilk, and you can't expect me to talk to them. It sounds fun to make some food and have a drink with your friends before retiring to let you all have your fun as I'm sure would be preferred…that is, without Madame Farrow around to make things civil."

Though he chuckled very dryly, his expression was firmed as if by a plan. His eyes slid down to my mouth.

At the slight part of my smile, he stooped over me for a passionate, thorough kiss. It had in it a sense of purpose—perhaps confidence—that his previous kisses had lacked.

And that was it. He moved on, and I moved on, and we had an extremely benign day. I tried to read until the effort exhausted me; I rested; I bathed; in the early afternoon, I sent Eleison a message letting him know about the party, and although he wasn't thrilled by the notion, he was comfortable enough with his surveillance to sign off on my involvement; Glenn and I enjoyed a late lunch, then made love and slept some more; then, around seven at night, I roused myself to cook a smattering of hors d'oeuvres for the guests. Helping my friend seemed the least I could do in exchange for hosting me without warning or complaint.

Now, I wish I had spit in the food. I wish I had looked under the kitchen sink for refills of the poison blocks used in rodi traps, tiny cages hung up under eaves to lure the little disease-spreading pests to their doom. I wish I had waited until Glenn was sleeping, then arranged for Eleison to slip into the house and hide himself somewhere for a pre-emptive slaughter.

Anything would have been better than the way it actually happened when, long after the purple atmosphere of the Rift deepened to its ultra-night, Glenn's guests arrived.

They were a rough bunch, but friendly with one another as well as with Glenn. Even before the door opened, they could be heard making merry on the porch, cavorting around as though the weather were perfectly clear and the streets not overrun with monsters after so many hours under the Event. From the kitchen where I worked, I stepped out with a pleasant smile and gladness in my heart to see the boisterous way Glenn's friends welcomed him back.

Then, he introduced them to me. Universally, their reactions were not right.

"This is Madame Farrow," he said after giving me their names.

What *were* their names? I could look up some record and discover them, but I frankly don't care to. I don't want to see their faces again, or to think of the barely contained hate that burned in a few of their blazing stares and knitted brows when they looked on me long enough to nod. It was only ever a second. As soon as possible, they'd look away in search of someone known to them, and there was always a sense of mutual relief. They all looked like nice enough people, with interesting stories, (there were even a few women and an altered man among their numbers, much to my pleasant surprise), but I knew from the first moment they began trickling in that I would never get the chance to learn the first thing about them.

This was what I had been concerned about in hosting with Glenn, but also why hosting with him had been important to me.

Every person in the room was a member of The Hunters' Guild. Like Glenn, they were likely to be more politically conservative and opposed to my husband's pet causes. As citizens of Valquist, they had surely seen my face on the tabloids well enough to at least absorb the headlines—assuming they hadn't heard it all thirdhand from their friends or relations.

But, as hunters, these were also individuals who had a great deal of influence on their community, and who, as my dear Glenn had explained, could feasibly be dispatched anywhere across the continent if their guild took up a task requiring their skillsets. I even heard several of them discuss recent meetings with Winston, who ran the Gudrune chapter. Wherever they went, especially to my own home territory, they would take their opinions of my husband and me with them.

Therefore—perhaps, just perhaps, if I greeted them warmly, and gave them good food, and laughed at a few of their jokes before retiring without incident, they, in turn, would see the softness in me. The human in me. Perhaps, if I was simply myself, they would treat me not as the tabloids depicted me, but as I really was.

The guests were all there. Eight or nine. No—it must have been eight guests, plus Glenn. I naively found myself wondering when the poker table would be brought out, and eventually decided they would just cluster together in the sitting area. The room smelled like cheap old cigarette smoke unsoftened by the flavors that sweetened Eleison's tobacco. Soon a beer spilled, and it took to smelling like that, too. There *was* laughter, and everyone seemed to get along very well.

But there was a tension in the air, too. An anticipation, as one felt for the surprise birthday party arranged against the wishes of a very private, more old-fashioned sort of person.

Once I had disseminated the little tarts and tea biscuits and other little noshes, (hello, darling, your words are always erupting from my mouth and pen and mind), I removed the apron meant for the twice monthly housekeeper and perched closely beside Glenn upon the ottoman in the corner. The tension increased substantially. A few of the conversations died slightly, or ebbed into others.

Feeling more like a wallflower than ever in my life—and that's saying something, given my solitary tendencies—I smiled silently along while Glenn, pleasant but still so very on-edge, did his level best to include me in a conversation that was about something so absolutely, painfully disinteresting to me I cannot remember to this day just what it was about. It may have been, for all I know, about the properties of different types of wood, or the various styles of guns, (everyone, I noticed shortly after sitting down, wore an arm on their hip or had unstrapped it from their back to rest it beside or behind them, the weapons so natural with the Rift Event ongoing that I felt as though I hadn't even seen them until that moment), or the troubles and virtues of the various types of public transportation in Valquist. Glenn was always very interesting in thought and pleasant in manner, but he had a way, perhaps because he was so pleasant, of getting embroiled in the must nauseatingly dull conversations if no one was there to help him.

He needed a Malin. I needed *my* Malin. I was terrible at parties, really, and unskilled at making good impressions, and as I sat with my headache, I felt like a fool for even having tried. By the minute, my smiles became harder to maintain, my exhaustion gripping me with such an unrelenting hold that my every neutral, "Very interesting" or "Oh, goodness" or "That's too bad" began to take on a sluggish, impatient quality. Increasingly, I eyed the guest room to telegraph to Glenn my imminent departure.

Then, one of the hunters filling the loveseat caught Glenn's attention.

Ending his own conversation, Glenn looked at this mustached fellow.

"So—are we going to talk about it, or not?"

Glenn didn't answer. He frowned, swirled the contents of his glass, then leaned forward to put it upon the edge of the coffee table.

I got a very sinking, empty feeling and looked into my glass. It seemed I had not extricated myself soon enough.

"Thecla," said Glenn, looking, to his credit, like a slippered mutt, "I lied to you."

My mouth, hidden by the dip of my head, expanded into a smile along with my bitter laugh.

"Yes, dear." I leaned back to take a big swig of the wine I then rested upon my crossed knee. "You and every other man I've ever cared about. All right."

I tossed my undone hair back over my shoulder and sat straighter while regarding, with imperious expectation, the room at large—but especially the speaker who had undone the tranquility with that fatal question.

"Go on, then. This isn't really about cards, I see. Coming out during a Rift Event for a blasted game…love makes it so easy to believe a lie, doesn't it?"

Wincing, Glenn set a hand on me. My name was soft on his lips even as I jerked my arm away from his touch.

"Please don't, Glenn. You want to talk some business, apparently, so let's be businesslike. Tell me what this is about. I'm tired, so please do make it quick."

"Listen to this bitch." The previous speaker scoffed, raising my hackles as well as a general murmur of agreement (and some mocking laughs) throughout the room. Glenn's suggestion that he watch his mouth went unheard as the fellow went on, "Married to Gudrune for a few months, and she already thinks she's better than everyone here."

I didn't have to be married to Malin to think that, but I kept that opinion to myself. "Whatever you think of me, I haven't stooped to calling ugly names...I've only shown you courtesy."

"Now"—Glenn leaned forward as though in lieu of putting himself physically between us—"Thecla, maybe first we should all—"

But they were in no mood to listen to their host. A graying old hunter with an artificial arm was busy sneering at my reprimand, his bloodshot eyes narrowed with anger beneath his knitting gray brow. "A lot of fucking courtesy Gudrune showed me when his men took my arm during the Battle of Azstor. Baldanders over there"—I remember that name because it suited a man with a steel plate curving between a set of scars in his patchy hair—"barely survived. We grew up there, and your husband laid waste to it. Annexed it. All to build some blasted bombs."

I smoothed my dress with one hand while raising my glass with the other. "Malin is not building nuclear bombs, despite the Overseer's overwhelming paranoia on the subject."

Glenn inserted himself back into the argument. "I agree, it's not likely he's building bombs. If he can find a way to weaponize the Rift, he doesn't have to."

"Glenn, please—"

"It's true, Thecla."

"I'm just so tired of this, damn it. You know...I really thought you were different."

My head! Oh, my head was throbbing. I squeezed shut my eyes, fighting back a glaze of frustrated tears, covering my eyelids with the cooling dark of my palm while I sat in the middle of it all and let the hunters (hunters of what?) speak at me.

"It must hurt to know I lied to you, Thecla, and I'm sorry. You can't imagine how sorry I am. I don't think I ever would have done this if not for—" Glenn waved a hand to his bandaged cheek, and though I was grateful he spared details before present company, I bristled to have Eleison blamed even in the abstract. "Then, I realized how important it was that I reach you, and everybody here wanted to meet about the energy project coming out in the news, and I just—I saw an opportunity. But…I couldn't think of an honest way to get you in the room with us. To listen to us."

"I have kids," said one man, one of the younger ones. "When I think of Rift Events only getting worse all the time, I wonder if I was even right to have them. If you add on top of that war, or—"

"Though I can assure you my husband has no plans to start one, the sad fact of history is there will *always* be some war, somewhere, eventually." My tone was taut with impatience as I lowered my hand. "And the Rift is always going to be with us, too; at least, for a time so long it had might as well *be* forever. You can't seriously suggest we halt all technological development and refrain from important research. That isn't a feasible request for human society."

"But the research Malin wants to do points to other goals than the stated ones," Glenn argued. "Look, Thecla: energy isn't the problem—"

"It's *storage*, I know, for God's sake, I've heard it."

"I mean to say, if there really is another dimension on the other side of the Rift—a perceptible world where these creatures normally live—and if it really is a world of reverse entropy…there might be metals, gases, various elements in that world that *could* solve all problems of energy storage and production, forever."

My mouth dried up just a little.

"That sounds like a worthy subject of exploration, from where I'm sitting," I stubbornly carried on no matter my reservations.

"Except—who could brave the Rift to get it? And, if they did? If they brought that metal *back?* If you bring an object that defies the known laws of physics into this world, what happens then?"

A shadow prowled from the depths of the kitchen. As Dinon, unseen by any but me, made his smooth way around the counter and down the utility corridor, Glenn pressed on, "What could happen if a metal from this reverse entropy universe interacts with one from ours?"

"The value of science, you see," I told him in cold response, "is it endeavors to ask those questions, *and* to answer them."

While Glenn's expression hardened against me just a little, the one-armed man picked up the argument. "But some questions shouldn't be answered—shouldn't even be asked. Why did the atom bomb need to be invented in the first place? What about biological warfare? There are some things the world doesn't need."

"And you sincerely don't believe that infinitely renewable, nigh-infinitely storable energy is something the world needs?"

"Don't act so obtuse, "Madame Farrow." Glenn's already assured us you're plenty smart."

"I'm not acting like anything. I'm telling you, I know my husband, and I believe in his intentions, and—"

"I thought you said she'd be open to persuasion, Glenn," snapped the altered hunter, his jaw tight beneath his poorly kept beard. "That they were on the outs."

"I said they're fighting, but—"

My voice raised as I demanded of Glenn, "What business of yours is that to share? What business of yours is *any* of this, damn you? Is this some kind of *intervention*? Why am I here?"

"Because—because I did think you would be more open to persuasion." With an almost guilty glance askance, Glenn folded his hands to avoid touching me. "I was hoping you might see the importance of stopping Malin, and the opportunity we have to do that now."

Dumbly, I'm afraid, my mouth opened and closed. ""Stopping" him—like he's a villain in a children's book. What are you blathering on about?"

"This is a waste of time," muttered one of the women.

The rest of the room murmured in general agreement.

Barely glancing at them, Glenn took a breath and at last explained.

"We believe that Malin is using his energy program as a cover to learn how to enter, move through, and exit the Rift. To develop and militarize interdimensional transport that would allow him to crush all opposition to a swift takeover of the continent, and that might even allow him to open the Rift at will."

After a few long seconds, the weight of it all settled in on me.

"Oh, how ridiculous—what a story that is, Glenn, what an imagination! Give me a break. If the flow of entropy in this other dimension is backwards, then its time is backwards-flowing with respect to ours. What you're proposing is time travel. You're accusing my husband of a fictional cliche!"

"Absolutely pointless," mumbled the one-armed man, his metal fingers drumming impatiently upon his knee.

"Malin is a danger to the world," Glenn insisted, a cold edge to his words. "His ambition has already ruined countless lives. I should think you of anybody can see that, Thecla."

Grinding my teeth at his invocation of my mother's flight, I told him in an equally chilled manner, "There is no doubt his ambition has led others to ruin. The leaders of many states throughout history have had that misfortune."

"And they're usually called "dictators" or "tyrants." Thecla—please, just look at me."

Reluctantly, the weight of my anger pressing upon me like the nauseating headache that made a vein throb in the side of my head, I turned to face Glenn. A quadrant of his face was obscured by a blind spot. As the halo of the associated aura inexorably expanded out to the periphery of my left eye, Glenn told me earnestly, "This is personal for me, too, I'll be the first to admit. My father died in the Expansion."

Lips pursing, I said, "I didn't know that. I'm sorry."

It was in as earnest a tone as I could manage given the amount of pain I was in, physically and spiritually; but it never could have been earnest enough. I *was* sorry. I was sorry that Glenn had lost his father because of the Overseer's war with my husband. I was sorry, too, that I hadn't been told this sooner. I was sorry everything seemed to be happening the way it was.

I stood. "I'd like to speak more about it later, when everyone has gone. For now, I believe I'm going to excuse my—"

"Sit down, Farrow." The one-armed man stood so quickly he startled me, the holstered gun at his hip slamming into his thigh as if in emphasis. "Your cooperation isn't an *option*."

"It could have been," said Glenn softly, evading the eye contact I whirled wildly upon him. "I meant what I said, Thecla—everything I ever—"

Barely, I resisted striking him. "Shut up."

He nodded. "Okay."

"Word is"—the one-armed man stepped close, and his hideously wrinkled visage left me thinking not all men marched into age as well as Malin—"your devil bastard of a husband is coming here to Valquist in a few days. There's laws against it, for Valquist's security and for his. In other words…what we have is a cherished opportunity, and we aim to take it."

The blood drained from my face. "You're saying you want to kill my husband."

"I'm saying we *will* kill your husband," the amputee informed me in a snarl, his robotic appendage tightening as though around some imagined neck. "And you can help us in the aftermath, or you can die, too."

"Now"—Glenn stood sharply, the only unarmed man in the room, yet the most commanding for the rarity of his stern tone—"I thought I made it clear—"

Before I could stop myself, I was overwhelmed with laughter.

At last, the first truly credible threat to my life settled in. Oh, yes…I had been at *risk* before, and certainly that appalling scientist had threatened Malin and Eleison. But to imagine anyone would have the audacity to threaten *me* was, until it happened in that moment, somehow unfathomable; and, with its fathoming, I was left so incredulous that it pitched me into hysterics.

"I'm sorry!" I couldn't stop laughing and raised my hand over my mouth, looking at Glenn and then at the one-armed man.

The others in the room regarded me with a new wariness. "Oh, I'm sorry—"

The veteran with whom I'd been arguing bared his yellowed teeth. "What's so funny?"

"Aha—ahaha, oh, mercy—"

"You didn't hear me, bitch?"

He lunged toward me.

I am going to tell you what happened as honestly as I can explain it, but it is impossible to adequately unfold the complex structure of what the mind can perceive in a simultaneous second. There was no time to think. All I had to act on was instinct, and pure muscle memory.

There I was, back in training with Eleison.

This fellow with cybernetic reflexes barked, "I said, if you don't help us, I'm going to—"

Glenn cried out while I yanked the man's gun from his holster.

Half the hunters in the room flinched while the remainders went for their own weapons. The wine fell from my hand in a bloody arc.

As the glass shattered upon the floor, a gun discharged.

One of the men (not Glenn, thankfully) screamed.

Gunpowder burned my sinuses while, with an audible groan, the generator in the house stopped working and the electricity died.

The one-armed man, a shocked look on his face, made a new grab for me, fumbling through the abrupt dark and directly into the trio of bullets some friend of his had intended to leave in my skull.

While a general cry went up and Glenn watched his fellow hunter fall with an inhalation of shock, I caught him by the shirt and shoved him down upon the floor with the body. "Stay down," I warned him.

Incredulous, Glenn caught me by the forearm and opened his mouth as if to talk sense into me, or to warn me, or to otherwise utter some needless command.

The cellar door at the end of the utility hall hammered open so hard it sounded like it broke. As the security shutters released a single siren of failure, locked in place but no longer operable by the RMS system, madness descended upon the room.

The guns that had been about to fire on me instead fired on Dinon in a bleak replication of that violent night in the Saalast warehouse, with one key difference. I had been trained in weaponry; not long, but long enough that, with muzzle flashes and some good luck despite my blinding headache, I killed a man in the dark and stumbled up to avoid the rifle-bash of a hunter whose blood thereafter sprayed across my gown from a pulsing well mined by Dinon's hand.

Glenn shouted as the fellow dropped and I recognized him. The altered man. A pity, somehow. The purplish light of Rift Radiation, bursting as he fell, ended too soon for him to complete his final transformation, but the flash of it bouncing off the darkened walls was so blinding to my sensitive headache for even that brief handful of seconds that I cried out and dropped the gun in the growing pool of blood. Glenn's next cry was my name, rising up in the chaos. He bent over me, a gun suddenly in his hand.

Dinon, a blur of black and white, lurched toward him until I screamed.

"Not him, damn you! I told you, not him! Ah!"

A terrible twitching of muscle sealed shut my right eye as the pain spiked down from my brain and, I swore, into the central column of my spine. It was so great I screamed again, my body involuntarily doubling itself while I sank to my knees in the blood. Dinon whirled past Glenn, my friend's dark curls barely moving as the dharmine went on to the final hunter, who had rushed to the door. It stood wide, and, because the electricity was out, the delayed man was forced to raise the security shutter manually. He released a lever.

Eleison, fully a borro and snarling with rage after hearing all the gunfire, tore out the hunter's belly before scrambling under the opening security shutter to reach me.

I believe setting eye on him is the only reason I remember the sudden, awful *snap* of bone from within my own skull, or the surge of pain that rocked me so powerfully I couldn't even scream. I keeled forward, barely catching myself on my hands, then collapsed upon my belly while Glenn dropped his weapon to bend over me with a cry. My eyes rolled in my skull, twitching without my control before I lost my vision altogether.

When the first bloody antler burst from my right temple, (a vulgar sensation that came with uncontrollable chills, as though three and a half feet of gauze packed in the sinus cavities of my forehead had been suddenly, violently yanked free), the headache on that side disappeared, and Eleison rushed up to nuzzle and kiss my face. It should have been an instant of happy relief: but it did not matter what he did, or what I experienced, for, as the other antler burst forth to end my headaches for good, I was simply no longer myself.

And now, I will pass the pen to my husband for a spell.

THECLA, MY LOVE, you must forgive me if my contribution alters, in part or perhaps even in whole, the tone of your developing manuscript. You write to your reader: to the unflinching and immortal eye of Time now looking back on us, completed, even as we unfold the narrative at our writing desks. I can only write to you, or perhaps to our dear Eleison; but, as it concerns conscious thought, he was well aware of events during that agonizing five and a half months spent waiting for you. You, my dear, were not.

Let me start with what I knew.

By the time the train pulled in to Valquist, all that was civilized about me was hanging by a thread. I hadn't slept in days (not since you left, certainly, angel!) and, when I did, a few of the staff had found me sleepwalking my way to the autocarriages as though unconsciously intent on reaching you. Things were better on the train, when I was doing what I could to exhibit some control over a situation that was, to put it mildly, my nightmare.

Thecla, my angel, oh, my darling…I was so angry with you that, contemplating it now, my soul is lapped by that great blaze all over again. When you tell me what you want tonight, you had better be careful what you wish for. I'll punish you now as I couldn't bring myself to punish you then, when things still seemed so tentative and I knew how I had wronged you.

That was always where my thoughts returned, no matter how I raged and deflected helpful staff members with hard looks or dead silences. No matter how angry I was, no matter how hurt or afraid—I rather deserved this, didn't I? My offense against you, the omission of our historical connection, was cruel and selfish of me.

And because I could never imagine being anything but cruel and selfish in that way, (there never was a world where I told you the truth, my love; never a world I valued honesty more than your hand), I had to accept that I was due a punishment. Sinful deeds come with costs—that is what a punishment is, really—and loving you was a deed duly punished. Mind, the sin was not in loving you; it was in the lie that earned me that love.

So, less furious than I was riddled with desperation to again hold your tender body no matter how you spat and clawed, you may imagine news of Valquist losing power did me no favors; and, when I arrived in the aftermath of the Rift Event with only Charlotte there to greet me, it is possible I overreacted.

I admit it. It was poor taste that my first moments in Valquist after thirty years were spent beating a reporter whose camera flash interrupted Charlotte's delivery of the sickening news. The ensuing photographic negative never made it out of the camera, which I shattered with the same walking stick I used to hobble the interloping troglodyte; however, I am sure I do not need to remind you numerous snapshots exist of the beating. They are some of the few souvenirs of that period that, I confess, provoke from me a smile.

When Ignatius (it's been so long, I had forgotten his name! It warmed my heart to recall him during your first volume, angel) proved the only security agent with the stones to peel me away before I could kill the man, I regained my sense of decorum enough to look the rest of the reporters, sequestered like a bunch of sheep in their velvet pen, straight in their blinding flashbulbs.

"That pales in comparison to the way your city has treated my consort."

On I went, deaf to their eager cries as staff and Charlotte surrounded me to keep me from the camera's lenses.

"I want you to repeat that for me," I told Charlotte as we made our brisk way through the train station, full of people obviously unprepared for my arrival and very eager to make way when they recognized me. "I haven't had much sleep, you see, and I think I might be starting to hear things. You said—she's run away, you said?"

"Perhaps we should wait until we're in the car—"

"*No*, damn you, Charlotte—"

I stopped dead in my tracks, whirling on her with no satisfaction for the steady paling of her countenance.

"You'll tell me what I want to know when I want to know it. Where is my *wife*?"

"I don't know, sir."

My free hand raised in a claw I used to grip my own face. While the floor seemed to drop away into a yawning black pit beneath me, I asked, "Is the hunter with her?"

"I don't know."

"Well what *do* you know, damn it?" Even in the busy clamor of the station, my shout had an echo, and Charlotte, bless her, hid her flinch with an elegant crane of her chin.

"That's why I would prefer to wait until the car, sir. What I do know is privileged."

Nostrils flaring like a bull's, I marched on. Charlotte flowed with me in perfect silence. Somehow, we reached the private carriage that had been arranged for me. Somehow, I ended up inside it, Charlotte perched on the seat across from mine.

"Now tell me something useful," I commanded her, "or you'll be walking behind the carriage while I go wring Parvati's neck."

That typically amused expression tweaking her lips even as she fought it back, Charlotte asked, "May I suggest a stop, first?"

Twenty minutes later I stood in the doorway of your hunter's mock cabin, the internal fiction of its identity—some cozy cabin mislaid from its woods—as at odds with the city as was your little game of House with your opposing natures.

"How many bodies were there, Charlotte?"

"Eight."

"All registered hunters?"

"Yes."

The scene was a mess, with the floors still stained heavily by blood around the furniture of the sitting area. Since the bodies had, of course, been removed prior to my arrival, I had only these discolorations to guide me, but they told the story clearly enough.

"How was this found so quickly? The Event ended just this morning, didn't it?"

"Yes, right around four. However, a Valquist officer on patrol during the Rift Event responded to a series of gunshots and what sounded like a monster getting in through a shutter. They followed up in time to see a ventil with fresh antlers scrambling out of the house, pursued by a borro."

My heart fluttered. Relief, or outrage? I couldn't tell. "Eleison is with her?"

"So it would seem."

"Then she must have *some* control of her faculties. Where did they go? Where are they now?"

Charlotte's impeccable mask, always so artfully even-keeled to avoid setting me off before she was prepared for my fallout, tightened grimly. My mouth opened in shock.

"You mean no one's *looking* for her?"

My ears rang with the incompetence while Charlotte explained, "When I called Eleison after the weather cleared and received no response, I hurried over to find the police...and the coroner. Nobody's sure just yet what happened, but they have some ideas."

"Like?"

"An officer pulled me aside and tried a line of questioning designed to unearth information about Madame Farrow's relationship with the hunter, Glenn Stone."

"And you said?"

"Nothing helpful, of course. But it was made obvious to me they believe those two ran off together."

Given pause, my eye raking around the room, I asked, "The hunter wasn't among the dead?"

"No. It seems like, by the time the responding officer's back-up arrived, Stone was nowhere to be found."

"And missing with him is the full story of what happened to my wife," I said blackly, eyeing the sideboard that had been emptied of guns so hastily it remained open. "Very well. Let him hide from me. He's wise to do it, but I don't really care about him. I want every resource you can possibly obtain, Charlotte, to scour the countryside for her. Talk to the officer who saw the ventil and find out what direction she was heading."

"On it, Master."

"I'm not finished yet—we'll need a team, vehicles for a caravan, and we'd better see if it's possible to obtain Stabilify in this contemptible city."

"I'll do what I can."

"Charlotte—"

She had been turning toward the door, her hand already fishing her pocket watch from her skirts, when she paused to regard me with infinite, somehow maternal patience that seemed ageless in spite of our being chronological peers at that time. That patience brought out what in me was long-gone: boyish sorrow, and bleak, empty fear that you, Thecla, my delight, really and truly were gone forever. That I was doomed to be left with only my rotten, empty, stunted kingdom until I died, and was nothing.

Charlotte saw that fear in my eyes, and her brows almost knit.

"Do you think she still loves me, Charlotte?"

"I don't think the kind of love she has for you just disappears...not even when you find out that person has hurt you."

Numb in my cheeks and fingertips, I nodded, then turned my study to the vase of wilting roses. It was an admirable display—impossible, really, to imagine the effort and patience it would take to construct a thing like it in a day, let alone in the rushed hours the florist had enjoyed once I located someone taking calls during the Rift Event.

Yet one hundred thousand roses could not rival your beauty—my Thecla's beauty. They were nothing to me by any measure, except for being hers, and that tempted me to take them; but they were also a trophy of my shame, so I left the arrangement behind and stepped out of the house.

And whom should I see trundling down the street but the Overseer herself, her white and gold carriage resplendently gleaming in the sunlight.

I turned my head to spit upon the hunter's mat before striding down the walkway. Ignoring the hand Charlotte extended to keep me from progressing, I blew right past her, catching by her tone that she was in the middle of a call too important to abort. When Ignatius opened the door of my own rented auto, I took a sharp left and waited in the middle of the path.

Parvati's carriage rolled to a stop. Her flesh-and-blood steeds responded to whatever electromagnetic rage rolled off me by pawing at the cobblestones and shifting, ill-at-ease.

The guard beside the driver got down and opened the door.

It had been decades since I had seen Parvati, and it was true to say that between the two of us, I had done the worse job of aging; yet I still found myself shocked by her appearance. Maybe I was just shocked to see her in person again, considering I had vowed never to do it. Never to come to Valquist; never to threaten her wellbeing with the simple existence of my own.

Yet, all the same, there we were. And she, more haughty than ever, her mannerisms informed by years of high society, inclined her chin to look angularly through her lashes as though I were her servant.

"Malin. This visit is a surprise."

"Why should it be? I'm sure you've heard the news yourself—and failed to act on it."

"I wasn't aware the whereabouts of your wife were our responsibility," was her snide rejoinder. "Besides, she hadn't been staying at the palace in some days. I've had no influence over where she goes."

"That's no excuse for not rounding up a helicopter, a few autos, *any* resources to find her—"

"What makes you think she needs to be found?"

"She's wandering the wilderness, trapped in the form of a ventil. And if Eleison *is* with her, then he is similarly stuck. He won't be able to risk turning back to a man if he can't guarantee his own safety—and that's to say nothing of hers."

"She's second-generation. She should have no problem turning back to herself whenever she wants."

My hand clenched along with my teeth while, feeling too confident now, Parvati closed the distance between us. "Did you really think I wouldn't recognize Giselle's daughter? Especially once I figured out she's mated to your footman. Poor Malin… nobody's ever satisfied just being yours, are they?"

"You're a fine one to talk, you frigid old spinster." She hid her shock well, but it flashed quickly through her face and then away. I dug in and met her stride for stride, practically feeling her muscles tense with the self-control it required to continue approaching me. "Whatever your puritanical ideals of hetero-monogamy have led you to think of Thecla—"

"I actually like Thecla well enough."

"—she's still going to save me from having to beg you to ratify an unrelated successor, you barren, unlovable, interloping bitch."

Her nostrils flared and her pupils shrank, and I was sure she wanted to kill me. "You're reverting to schoolyard insults, old man. It's too bad…I always thought there was a chance you'd age gracefully."

""Graceful." I showed one of your reporters how blasted graceful I am…"

"I heard that. And I came to speak reason to you, but it seems you're not in a reasonable mood."

"Because my *wife*"—I screamed the word while plucking at my travel rumpled shirt with one hand, my other extending out in a wave off to the distance—"is *lost*, do you understand? I'm sure it's impossible, since you've never cared about anybody—"

"You're incredible to say something like that to me."

"—but if anything happens to Thecla—if she vanishes into the wilderness—if she—"

I couldn't produce the word and simply said, my breast heaving with a choking gasp, "I'll *die*, Parvati. Do you understand *that*?"

Her lips pursing in sympathy I found at the time to be, at best, intensely patronizing, Parvati tilted her head. "I thought at first you must have asked her to try and hide her heritage from me…but she just didn't know about you and Giselle, did she?"

I said nothing. Parvati's arms folded over her diaphragm, the copper of her skin against her silver gown still tight with muscle. Her men were ready to shoot me dead for the least wrong move, with at least three visible around the carriage and more probably posted on nearby roofs.

And still—oh, still!—if I could have strangled her to death there in the street, I gladly would have.

"Why the hell did you bring her here in the first place,

Parvati? So you could take something else I love? To remind me you're always there, peering over my shoulder, scrutinizing every blasted stroke of my pen?" I struck my own forehead in frustration. "You may be the continent's Overseer, but you have no business nosing into my marriage. You never have."

"I cared about Giselle enough to see she was withering in your house…and, at the time, I cared about *you* enough that I could tell you hated every second of being with her just as much."

"Whether I loved her, whether I hated her: that was never, ever your business. And neither is what transpires between myself and Thecla, or Thecla and our footman, or Thecla and her damned fool of a hunter—who is lucky, I should say, that he is absent from this scene. None of that is, in any way, your affair. You humiliated me, Parvati." I pinned her in place with my stare, my scorn flicking from her heeled shoes to the graying curls I once, a long time ago, found very lovely. Now I wanted to see them seared from her scalp, and her scalp from her skull, and her brains boiled alive in their devious case while a bonfire raged around her like the witch she was. "You humiliated me in love—"

"That wasn't what I was trying to do when I told Giselle to follow her heart."

"—so I humiliated you in war. But this time—this time, Parvati, you humiliated Thecla."

My entire being blazing with hatred. I lowered my head near enough for her to hear my unsound little whisper.

"When you humiliate Thecla, you do far worse than humiliate me. I can't let it stand."

"Are you threatening me, Malin?"

Her posture was rigid and her gaze unflinching, but her fright had a way of filling up the air. For a few long seconds,

I enjoyed the tension lines flanking her mouth before I focused again on the specks of her pupils.

"The average Rift Event releases 60 monsters in a 10-mile radius during the course of its average eight-hour storm, including rodis and harpros and other smaller creatures individually. An Extreme Rift Event emits more in the order of 100 in the same time frame, often producing more violent, larger, or rare animals. How long was the one you just had here, Madame Overseer? Two and a half days? Valquist is 70 square miles, give or take. So, somewhat over 700 monsters, every eight hours, for a 54-hour Event—that's almost, what, 5000 Rift monsters infesting Valquist as a consequence of your most recent storm."

"And, over the course of the storm, we have confirmed the extermination of several thousand by city police alone."

"Only a few thousand left, then!"

"If citizens and freelance hunters haven't taken them in-hand—" Catching herself entertaining a separate argument altogether, Parvati shook the thought off with a frown and a knitting brow. "What is your point, exactly?"

"My point," I told her, staring hard into her face, "is that it only takes one."

She returned my stare, as silent as the street in which we stood.

Not daring to turn away until she had sufficient space, Parvati slowly backed toward her carriage.

"If you don't get out of my city," she said, her calm tone as affected as mine, but for different reasons, "I'll have no choice but to issue a warrant for your arrest."

Laughing, I remained where I was to watch her go. "I'd say I'd like to see you try, but fortunately for you, I won't be staying. There are more important things to do than start a new war, wouldn't you agree?"

Saying nothing, Parvati turned on her heel and hurried to her carriage. I remained where I was. Somewhere behind the door of my own rented car, Charlotte spoke hastily into her watch.

The Overseer's white carriage lurched into motion, rolling off down the street with Parvati's grim expression like a phantom in the small glass window passing by.

My shoulders sagged with an exhaustion like I have never felt before or since. Somehow, seeing Parvati threw my age in my face. Nothing had changed, and everything had changed; the world had changed, and I had changed.

But—had I changed enough? With the acidic words of a younger man still like bile in my mouth, I wasn't sure I had.

Drained, I made my way back to the carriage and patted Ignatius's arm as I passed through the door he held for me. With a glance my way, Charlotte wrapped her call and lowered her watch.

"I've just talked to Aleister. He says his sister owns a cabana he can talk us into. It's situated just outside Valquist Forest. He'll meet us there in two hours, it's not far."

"I don't want to go to some infernal *cabana*," I said tersely, my elbow perching against the window's edge to allow my hand to shield my face. "Nobody has any idea where she *is*, Charlotte. Do you realize that? Fully?"

"I am very aware. But it is obvious to me that you have not rested—"

"How *can* I rest," I shouted, dropping my hand into a fist against the carriage door.

Barely blinking, (although, I noted, inhaling with the sharp impatience of damaged pride), Charlotte went on, "—and there are more people involved in this than you alone, Master. If we're going to search for her, we need a base of operations…and you need to organize your thoughts."

A shudder wracked me. She was right, of course. I *was* exhausted. Feeling every bit my age and then some, not to mention becoming insane with the thought of Thecla in danger.

Of Thecla, disappeared.

"Oh! Mother of Mercy—"

A strange noise flooded up from me, almost like a laugh, or a cough. I pressed my fist to my mouth and looked through the window, saying sharply, "Just get us there—drive on."

"We'll find her," Charlotte swore.

I squeezed shut my eyes, my skin two sizes too tight and all aflame with agony while the carriage lurched into motion.

Please don't be too moved to know I cried in front of the housekeeper, darling…I'm chagrined enough without your pity.

34

YOU KNOW, ANGEL, this memoir business is more fun than all your moping for the last month made it out to be. I suppose you had blazes of fun through the first volume… but remorse, understandably, has a way of wringing some of the pleasure out.

At the time, remorse was all I had. The trip to Kalypso's cabana seemed endless, the humidity of the day stifling and evil despite the climate-controlled rental auto. When we did arrive, we had to wait for Montagne to catch up, which he did an hour later than estimated—and without, might I add, much more than a sheepish smile by way of apology. Maybe it was I who owed him an apology for the use of the little house along the very same rushing river that ploughed through Valquist; for the inconvenience of calling him so far out of town on business that wasn't really his.

But, so far as I could see, he was at least partially responsible for Thecla's coming there in the first place, and he had very clearly done nothing to ease her suffering (*your* suffering, my pet!) when Valquist's propagandists took such glee in the public assassination of her character. I therefore had very little guilt. While he passed the key over, my enchantress's tears, hiccupped over that dreadful call, returned to me like arrows through my heart: and that heart died against Aleister. He had failed to persuade her back to the Overseer's palace when it mattered, just as he had failed to side with me and return empty-handed to Valquist.

The cabana, then, truly was the least he could do, and I was glad he showed no sign of obvious displeasure when I politely suggested he should turn around and enjoy the two-hour drive back to Valquist before it got dark. Aleister disappeared, and while Charlotte opened the house around me, I sat in silence by an empty hearth with one hand over my mouth and my thoughts unable to order themselves.

What to do first? The responding officer, of course; he might be bribed to—"Pen and paper, please, someone!"—give up available security footage from storefronts around the area, if any cameras of relevance happened to be working at the time (unlikely)—"Hurry up, now—*thank* you"—or at least give us access to mercenaries who could be employed to serve in the search party. For fairly obvious reasons, I found myself distrustful of hunters and completely wrote off the possibility of appealing to the Guild, a decision for which I am glad.

Then, it was a matter of actual organization. How quickly could things be arranged? No matter what kind of pressure I put, what money I threw down, whatever I did, I could not realistically see everything organizing itself to my satisfaction in fewer than thirty-six, maybe even forty-eight hours. That was up to two additional days while my wife was going—

Where?

I rubbed my brow and tried to think. Did she even know where she was going? It was surely very easy for Parvati, who had been living with an animal inside of her for something like fifty years, to say that Thecla could transform back anytime she wished—but I wasn't so sure. While I had heard it whispered that second-generation altered did not require a mate to maintain human consciousness in their animal form, I was also not sure if Thecla would even understand what was happening to her that first time around. It seemed it would be very easy for someone in her mental state to be overwhelmed by her animal. To be driven by its instincts rather than her own cognitive reasoning.

Therefore, I had to assume my wife could not help herself, and had no strategic plan until proven otherwise.

Eleison, however—

My heart skipped a beat every time I thought of him with her. Oh, my loyal servant—be on my side! *Remain* loyal. Care for and shepherd Thecla.

Don't contribute to her flight from me. Anything but that.

When night had fallen and I had covered three sheets of paper front and back with notes, disjointed intuitions, and a rough plan of action, the house smelled like food I didn't want. My stomach was raw with hunger, but the thought of eating was as appealing as stuffing fistfuls of fireplace soot in my mouth and choking it down without water. I left behind my notes and fled the parlor, navigating smoothly down the hall where I assumed I would find the master suite. I did, and let myself in with a breath of relief to be alone in a room the air conditioning had succeeded in chilling behind the shut door.

Before I could close it behind me, I froze.

While I worked and the house was opened, the luggage had been brought from the second carriage via the cabana's back door. I hadn't been paying attention, nor had Charlotte; nobody had been there to point and say, "No, not that one—put that bag anywhere but Master Farrow's bedroom."

But there it was, its red suede distinct against the black fabric of mine.

Heart lurching, I pulled my Thecla's overnight bag from the row of luggage and slowly sat upon the floor with it. Then, arranging it down before me like a casket, I slid it open and nearly sobbed.

How it smelled like you, Thecla! Rich and sweet, like the dewy petals of fresh-cut spring flowers, and fragrant vanilla, and flesh. I sobbed, drawing out a mass of chiffon so soft I could not help but bury my face in it and sit there, miserable, my mind empty of anything that had any meaning.

I will admit, of course, that I had practical reasons for loving you, Thecla. There is no denying there was a rational side to the decision for our marriage. But, oh—how quickly that practical interest escalated to passion! How quickly I adapted to complete and utter reliance upon your embrace, your body, your mouth. The pure light of love in your eyes as you begged me for kisses. That light that's still there even now, darling; even, impossibly, now!

Perhaps one day, later on in your chronicle, you'll permit me to contribute some other section. Something that lets me present you as I see you in the flesh, rather than in the absence. For, oh...I have noticed how you perceive yourself, at least as regards the early chapters of your tale. And I'm afraid to say it, but Aleister was right about you. I find it endlessly hilarious that you perceive yourself as so naive, so innocent! Once you grew confident enough to relax in my presence—once you began letting me make love to you, Thecla—I got to know the *real* you, and it is that real you that smolders my soul with an endless, unshakeable love. Those shy pretenses disappeared and you became, so far as I have always seen, far more a luptich than a ventil where personality is concerned.

So: there was no doubt in my mind that this flight was a punishment for me, at least unconsciously. And I may have deserved it, but I could hardly bear it. The uncertainty—the endless horrors of worlds without my beloved—was too much for me. When Charlotte found me twenty minutes later, supine on the floor with the dress pressed to my heart and tears still staining my unshaven cheeks, I must have looked like a broken man.

"How did that get in here," was all she very casually said, moving toward the red bag as though having taken no notice of me at all.

"Leave it," I told her wetly.

She stopped, hands folding before her. "Please get up and eat, sir."

"I'll eat tomorrow, if I can stand to. Did you see my notes out there?"

"I did."

"Get the ball rolling on the list on the third page as soon as possible. I know it's late, but tonight, if you can. And write a thank-you note to Aleister's sister for me. I'll sign it in the morning before it's sent out, if you'll remind me."

"As you wish. Shall I draw you a bath?"

"No. Leave me alone until tomorrow. I don't want to see anybody unless they know where Thecla is."

"Very well. Please reconsider eating at some point."

"Good night, Charlotte."

"Good night, Master."

The door shut behind her. Eyes shutting, I draped my sweet Thecla's dress across my face and fell asleep dreaming it was my shroud.

Tomorrow came. The next tomorrow, too. By the third day, the search party was in full swing, although I'd hardly call it a merry fete. For the first time in decades, I was back at war, or lived like I was, even sleeping upright in an extremely old-fashioned open topped buggy that, despite having no horse and a relatively short range before its battery required a charge, was favored by hunters or those on military excursions for being easy to escape. I coordinated with team leaders periodically throughout the day, with each unit they represented assigned a different area of the countryside around Valquist: primarily the southwest. This was the rough area our intelligence indicated she'd been headed, but I couldn't trust the information wholly and, for my own peace of mind, also had a few groups established to the north and the east.

We were at it for two and a half weeks, nearly three. Certain dispositions had begun to shift in the men with whom I interacted: a change in tone, as the sick man feels when his ailment proves too mysterious for the subpar skills of the smalltown doctors that begin to imply he is suffering from a nervous condition rather than a diagnosable physical one. What had once been driven was transforming into a lighthearted camping trip with the boys, the atmosphere of which shifted whenever Master Farrow happened to come driving by. I didn't like the placation behind certain turns of phrase. I fired at least one fellow right on the spot, promoting somebody else at random and commanding them to give the idiot a bedroll and a handgun so he could walk to Valquist—vehicles and horses being far too precious to waste on ferrying an unemployed mercenary to town for no recompense. There were fewer issues of attitude after that, although I still got the sense that the general mood was one of tomfoolery and skepticism.

Three weeks. Three weeks of sleeping in a camper van, a lumbering sort of vehicle as antiquated as the jeeps. Three weeks of waking up at midnight wondering, and fearing, and coming to God with my palms open and my mouth contorted in pleas that also begged Him to ignore not just my past, but my future.

Then, day twenty came. The radio awoke me. Alarmed by the discordant noise, I bolted upright, then leapt from my narrow cot and snatched the device from its cradle.

"Sir"—it was a certain lieutenant who had maintained the right attitude and thus had come into close service with me, leaving me all the more sure that something of note had occurred—"Unit N2 is reporting they were approached by a borro last night?"

My spine bolted straight as an arrow, the channel through which pure, golden celebration rushed up and down and out to all my limbs. "Oh, yes! Yes, how did it look? Did they see a scar?"

"Hard to say through NVGs. They said it approached the edge of camp at night and seemed to consider coming closer before retreating out of view again."

I nearly choked. "And no one followed?"

"Not that I'm aware of, sir."

"Light them up for it so they're not shocked when I do it again in a few hours. Oh—this is good news."

"You think that was your guy?"

I was positive. I couldn't explain to him, really, without sounding like a loon or perhaps revealing a bit too much about our developing relationship with Eleison. But I knew without even having to see the borro myself that it was no mere animal left over from the latest Rift Event. This animal sounded too intelligent—not desperate enough. It sounded like it had been looking for something, or someone, before deciding against an approach.

It sounded like, if we were going to make meaningful contact with Eleison and discover where Thecla had gone, I would have to go up there myself...and I was glad to do it. That same morning, I rushed north, and after dismissing unit N2 altogether, I and my own, smaller team established camp at the approximate location of the encounter.

One night passed; a day, too. On the second night, Ignatius—who had, among his more typical duties as my security, come along to serve as liaison between myself and remotely working Charlotte—expressed his first inklings of skepticism before heading to his tent, stationed far from the camper and the lamps illuminating it.

"Maybe he's trying at another unit now...or, maybe it wasn't him."

I knew it was him, damn it. I felt it. The unit, arranged around the distant fire, looked laid back about the whole thing. Uncommitted to either success or failure. My most loyal servants were beginning to doubt me and these newly hired ones were never any real good in the first place.

I was the only person who cared why we were there. I was the *reason* we were there—the reason my Thecla, my radiant angel, fled the world of humans for the wilds around Valquist.

Whereas I, unable to escape or in any way absolve myself of shame, could only fight to make things right with my human will.

Unarmed, at the end of my rope, alone as Ignatius retired for the night, I strode straight through the camp and into the dark. A few of the men looked at me oddly, but most paid me no mind while I marched through. Unlike Ignatius, they had no stake in my wellbeing aside from their next paycheck, which was contractually guaranteed prorated to them if I died prematurely by, say, a freak heart attack (or a fatal heart break) while they were on this job. They assumed whatever I did was none of their business, and they were right.

Nobody stopped me as I walked hundreds of yards down the sloping green knoll upon whose peak the camp had been situated—but they did pay attention as I cupped my hands around my mouth to bellow into the night.

"Eleison!"

My voice echoed through the humid heat of the dark. That thick, poisonous night. Would the murky air somehow deaden my call? I took a great breath and shouted again, nearly a scream.

"*Eleison!*"

My throat was already raw. I thought of calling a third time, but—if he had not heard those, he would not hear the next.

Lowering my hands, I stood unsteadily and waited.

In my chest, my ribs were the anvil beaten sore by my heart.

The night was just so quiet.

After perhaps five eternal minutes—just as I truly gave up for the night and began the trek up the hill—the thunder of animal footfalls pounded through the darkness. My ears, which had been tuning back in on the distant sounds of camp, became hyper-focused on that rapid beat. I stopped, whipping toward it. Around the same time, someone let out a cry from the unit. A spotlight soon flooded me, and the ground before me—

And the borro, the white stripe of his shoulder scar flashing as, with a ripple of purple Rift radiation, he collapsed across the grass as an exhausted man.

"Oh! Eleison—"

I knelt beside him while, on the hill above me, the camp erupted in a mad scramble for radios, medics, a stretcher, a blanket. Eleison, meanwhile, panted with exhaustion from the galloping pace that had brought him to me. He raised his face, then emitted a groan of relief to rest his cheek back down upon the grass.

"Oh my God." He laughed a little, rolling upon his back without the least thought for his nudity. "Oh, man—I haven't been human in weeks, have I?"

"Where's Thecla?"

"She's safe. But, Malin—I saw the hunter around once or twice. Trying to get to her. Why, I don't know."

"Let's not find out. You ran him off?"

"Of course."

"Good man. Do you know where she is? Have you been with her?"

"I haven't left her side except to hunt, but she's not herself. She won't change back—won't follow me back to the capital, or any civilization at all. I've tried."

"Then she's been avoiding us."

Nodding, Eleison began to sit up before falling back, dizzy. "I think I'm dehydrated," he commented, his tone weak, his eyes rolling toward the first rush of assistance. Medics swarmed us, checking Eleison's pulse and sliding him onto the stretcher.

"There's something else, sir," he began.

Words enough to sink my heart, whatever they heralded. Though it was difficult, I smiled.

"Let's not talk about it now. I'm so happy to see you, Eleison, I—"

I caught his limp hand and pressed it to my heart. "I'm so grateful to you for trying to guide her back to me. For being there for her, and loving her. Thank you, my friend."

"Of course, Malin." He had a look in his tired red eyes, a visible craving to say much more, but instead he lowered his hand back to his diaphragm upon release. "It's good to see you."

"My God, Eleison, and you. It's *very*, very good to see you."

While he was hauled off, I grabbed the first man I saw and discovered with relief it was the useful lieutenant. "Find out from him where the ventil is and put a surveillance team on her as soon as you can, before she can get far—I don't want to lose her again."

While the fellow marched up the hill to obey, I remained there, stunned, in the dark.

Thecla was out here. Out there *alone* now, in the darkness, without her senses.

Oh, my darling! Why wouldn't she, you, turn back? I cannot write to the reader; I can only, ultimately, write to you. And I know now, as I knew then, how deeply I damaged your trust…but oh, how I selfishly wish you had mustered some for my unworthy soul. How I wish you had come back to me and trusted I would care for you, no matter your condition, or the how and the why and the when and the whom. Would I have been upset? Of course; but I was upset anyway. Would I have been affronted, disappointed? Oh, maybe a little, just a little bit. I can't deny that. I'm only a man.

But would I have rejected you? Would I have punished you? Would I have done anything at all but celebrated your return to me, your body in my arms? All my joy brought back to me, and more?

I know they were not entirely your fault, those wild months of yours. The ventil controlled you. Yes: I know that, of course.

But...I also wonder if you did not pass your pen to me to *avoid* answering that question—the question of your will against the beast's.

In the dark, watching fireflies, listening to crickets, I permitted the passage of half an hour. To fill the time I tracked the progress of a stealthy party of horseback riders into the night. When they disappeared from view, concealed by the outcropping of another, more jagged hillock, I made my way up to the tent where Eleison had been brought to convalesce.

"The central medical tent in the southwest has our stock of Stabilify," I told him. "They should be here with it soon."

He waved his free hand before dropping it back down upon the thin blanket arranged over his waist. "I'm fine," Eleison insisted, pointing to the IV bag above his head. "I just needed some fluids...Thecla kept me myself the whole time. Every second I was near her, I was lucid. I just couldn't risk turning back unless I felt a Rift Event was imminent, and one's been coming on for a couple of days, so I'm glad we found each other when we did."

"Impressive," I said, checking the readout on my watch before tucking it back into my pocket. "85%."

"Having a Rift beast inside you is better than any weather report, baby..."

While I chuckled, Eleison's slight smile fell.

"I wish I could tell you what she's thinking," he said carefully, "but I can't, so please understand that I'm just making judgments based on what I've observed."

"I understand. Can you tell her moods, at least?"

"She's very pensive. Sometimes, when I can cajole her, she's playful and likes to get up and run a little, or chase after me. It's late in the season, so when she finds flowers, I can tell she's happy. But—I think, over all, she's very troubled. Something's not right with her."

"Now that is an understatement," I told him dryly.

"I'm not trying to be a wise-ass for once, sir. I'm trying to be delicate."

"You know I hate that."

"Yeah, I do know. So *you* know what I'm trying to tell you is…a big deal. Malin—"

"Oh, Lord—"

I turned away from him too late. The onrush of emotion was already warping my field of vision. Strangled, I covered my eyes with one hand.

"I know what you're going to say. God damn it. God damn it, I know it. Don't say it."

He allowed me to compose myself in the silence. Our noble friend spoke again only when I lowered my hand to ask without looking, "How far along do you suppose she is?"

"I don't know. Not far, but further as a ventil than she would be as a human. Probably the only reason I can tell. I can smell it on her."

"Do you think she knows?"

"Yeah. I think so."

My thumb and forefinger rubbed together before my hand flattened, each individual nail upon each of my fingers its own target for scrutiny as I sought to ground myself in simple, physical, unbiased reality. "And I don't suppose there's any chance it's yours?"

"No, sir...I'm all up to date on my shots."

Inhaling sharply, nodding, drumming my thumb rapidly along the tips of each of my fingers in rapid succession, I said, "All right. Well...all right."

"I'm sorry, sir."

"You're supposed to say 'congratulations' when a man's wife is having a baby, Eleison; and I wish you'd stop calling me 'sir' when you're giving bad news."

"Sorry, Malin."

"Stop apologizing."

"Then...congratulations."

"Thank you."

Against all reason, that final three-word exchange had a kind of magic effect on me; the ritual of exchanging thanks for congratulations permitted some trick of my animal brain. The timing wasn't right. It didn't make sense.

But it didn't matter. It was Thecla's baby. That made it mine, too, no matter who engendered it.

"You're very sure about this, Eleison?"

He nodded. "I think it's why she's not turning back—or why the ventil won't let her turn back, anyway."

I nodded, too, and found myself steadier as I next set eye on him.

With a clear sense of purpose for the first time in a month, I smoothed my hand over my shirt and felt far more myself in an instant.

"All right," I began. "Then here is what we are going to do."

THE STANDARD GESTATION period of a ventil, observed in a terrestrial environment, has been reported as five and a half months. As it was safest to presume that three weeks had elapsed since conception, we had just under five months to herd you, my poor wild love, to a semi-controlled environment—and figure out how to keep you there in the least offensive manner.

I suspect this will be my final contribution to this particular leg of your histories, for they are yours, of course, not mine. However, I can think of one anecdote that might illustrate the passage of time and longing while also being related in a fashion in keeping with your style. And, if you don't see what I mean by that…you will in a moment.

The very first thing I insisted Eleison do the next morning was take me out to see you, which he did very gladly. For the first time in weeks, I shaved and buttoned my shirt. I was a new man. The compass of my life pointed in a clear direction. As the electric buggy cruised the hilly landscape to a vantage from which Eleison felt sure my beloved might be spotted, he related to me a few anecdotes.

"I thought at first that she, or the ventil, or whatever, believed I was hunting her—but when I got in front of her somewhere around the edge of Valquist, I knew something about her recognized me, and loved me. It wasn't that. She just wanted to be alone."

"I'm grateful that you didn't let her be," I told him gravely, defunct possibilities not done haunting me.

"Yeah, well...I try my best to give her space when she's in her pensive moods, but that's sort of the rub. I can't give her too much space, or I start to think more like an animal. Too long without her, especially during an Event, and—I just know I have to get back to her, quick."

Beneath Eleison's hand, the vehicle glided to a stop. I clambered out immediately, shielding my brow with one hand while my naked eye swept the lightly treed valley not far from unit N2's station.

"Have you two been in this area long?"

"Nah...I've tried to keep her around Valquist, though, and for the most part she goes where I guide her. She doesn't like me hanging out all the time, but she doesn't want us to be separated, either, I can tell..." Through binoculars, Eleison scanned the area with a loving mate's near-telepathic understanding. Soon enough, he stopped. "There she is," he said.

"Oh, where—let me see—"

"The view's not as good as I'd hoped from here, she's under that tree. Let's take this slope by foot."

Delays, delays! My heart throbbed as I hurried down the hillside as quietly and smoothly as I could manage. The tree Eleison had indicated lay several hundred yards from us, yet one errant breeze would be all it took to give me away. I cursed myself for shaving. Would the scent alarm her?

Would she run from me again?

"Okay," said Eleison softly, "stop here."

I paused with him. Breathless, I stepped just behind the edge of the moss-covered tree that, along with the fronds of some overgrown shrub at its base, offered scant camouflage.

"You see that oak over there? Just beneath it—look down."

He gave me the binoculars. I could barely feel my face, let alone the hand that gripped them. Bless those precious lenses; bless Eleison! Bless every single man involved in the hunt for my absent wife—even the one I fired.

Everything and everyone was instrumental in that moment when at last, after a month of pining—a *month* since you had left for Valquist, oh, it felt like a lifetime!—I set eyes on you again, Thecla.

Oh, Thecla! It was not you yourself I beheld in those binoculars, of course. It was some wonderful, spiritual part of you, externalized. Made so unspeakably beautiful to me.

The doe was resting, the pale tan of her snout appearing at first like some great root. Then, gradually, I took in the vast black orb of a studious yet somehow dreamy iris; and, above that, an extraordinary rack of antlers ornamented, as in all female ventils, with a panoply of exotic Rift flowers still somewhat in bloom.

They were actually a fungal parasite in symbiotic relation with the ventil, and they wreaked havoc on the environment in our terrestrial plane; but oh, my darling! The tender deer of your heart was such a gentle, lovely creature. I could not imagine any man, be he conservationist or hunter, would ever have denied it these artful accessories of femininity.

"Even now, she's the most beautiful creature in the world. Oh—Thecla—"

I tore the binoculars from my eyes with a sob. "I only saw Giselle this way once, the one time. How strange that they should look so unalike. Her mother's ventil was so much darker, and her antlers weren't in bloom…and she was so full of hatred, just the—awful madness in her eyes. The way she looked at me."

"Did you deserve it?"

"I suppose I did." I hesitated before confessing more surely, "Yes, I did. I said terrible things to her. But I didn't deserve this." I touched the scar on my face. It had been so hateful to me before my Thecla's fingers showed fondness for caressing it, and her lips predilection for laying sensual kisses along it. "Perhaps, if Giselle had not done violence against me, I would not have felt so maliciously toward her. If not for this final spiteful cruelty after a short, ugly, pitiless marriage in which I restrained my own violent urges and let her say whatever unpleasant things she liked, I wouldn't have looked for her, or cared."

"And you wouldn't have Thecla, either."

"Do you think I still do?"

He looked at me in surprise. "What do you think she's so heartbroken about? You don't wind up this miserable if you aren't deeply in love with somebody…take it from me."

"You can say that again…"

Once more, I raised the binoculars, my heart hot with impossible dreams.

I had the thought just as Eleison expressed it aloud.

"Maybe you should go over there and try to talk to her."

"I— God, I want to—"

But—the thought of approaching this beautiful creature, only for it to clamber up and run from me again, was too crushing to be endured. Worse, if it attacked me like its mother—

"I can't," I murmured, my breath a shudder in my lungs. "I can't, Eleison. I want her to be ready to come to *me*. And I have an idea."

So it was that, beginning with the imminent Rift Event that permitted long-suffering Eleison to resume his duties as beastly guardian, I and the units formerly employed to search for you, Thecla, now herded you across the continent. Eleison guided you westward, chasing you across rivers and gradually coaxing you ever farther across land; and when you did not want to go his ways, the scents or even sometimes sights of units you perceived to be hunters steered you back on course. Before each Rift Event, Eleison would return to the nearest unit for a few hours to check in about your health, the quality of food in the area, and whatever other needs came to mind. When the summer broke fully into autumn and I began to fret, he was good enough to collaborate with me on a series of caches where my teams hid sweet fruits and bushels of berries, and rich green vegetables your well-fed ventil never seemed to question.

(I do always wonder, Thecla: Is it like having a dream? Like being sealed in a coma and listening to one's family make solemn plans? I cannot fathom what it is to have one's psyche so displaced; with the displacement of mine, I was just made more myself.)

Dedicated to my plans and forced to reorganize my life if I was to fulfill them, I again took up my duties as territory master, now from the road. Charlotte, I sent to the property at Azstoria Game Preserve so she might apply her feminine knowledge to the matter of your human spaces…and to accustom the preserve to my specific expectations.

As to the game preserve—which owed me, so far as I could tell, an incalculable amount of courtesy, given I owned property on their land and granted the tenuous permission to operate in the first place—they canceled many millions' worth of hunting reservations. The owner's pain was audible through his smiling voice as we discussed this on the call. I didn't care. The preserve was the only expanse of ventil-friendly habitat that was enclosed, within Gudrune, and under my thumb. It was enough trouble keeping an eye on natural and alien predators interested in ventil meat, and occasionally responding to rumors that a human figure had been seen observing my beloved from a distance at night; the last thing I needed was some irresponsible bastard, caught up in playing curated safari games, to put a bullet in my darling's head.

In the end, having kept up a leisurely pace both to allay your suspicions and prevent harm to the baby, the journey from Valquist to the preserve—located at the extreme eastern edge of the territory, to promote tourism—took about three months. By the time we arrived, I had lost fifteen pounds; was, if I was not mistaken, a fair bit grayer than when last I held you in my arms; and had not taken a day off throughout the entire ordeal. No one could convince me to, either. The way I saw it, if my wife was hyper-alert as a ventil, I owed it to her to remain in a comparable state, and to look after her as much as I could.

The only person who could persuade me to relax was Eleison.

As soon as we arrived at our destination, he showed no compunctions about resuming uninterrupted human life for the first time in four months. I gave him the first week off, expecting him to refuse it and to be eager to return to your side. When I remarked on this, however, he shrugged.

"She's doing fine. Are you kidding? She's a princess out there. The regular deer stare at her like she's some kind of goddess, and she's got all the food she needs. I'm interfering with her... uh, presence of mind, I guess. Next Rift Event, I'll check up on her. Otherwise, I'm content to watch from afar, with thumbs, and climate control."

"Do you think she understands where she is?"

"I think the ventil recognized the human building as an unnatural object, but I also think having the normal deer populations around are signaling to it that the area is safe."

The property, a tower, in essence, was a semi-subterranean building installed in the side of a sharp cliff to overlook the northern edge of the preserve. It was a sight to behold, a tall glass structure that allowed an outsider to look in as though at the innards of a dollhouse; at six stories, it was somewhat shorter than the Saalast home, but it receded back into the hillside at an impressive depth and provided, in my estimate, more than sufficient space to excuse what I was going to do.

Privacy was not a concern to me. With all the reservations canceled, the only humans on the preserve aside from myself and my staff were the game wardens who appeared at discreet distances to do headcounts of the animals from time to time. Splendid redwoods of phenomenal expanse towered to the left and right of the building, with those and other trees scattered around and up the hillside into a thickened forest that marked the end of the park. Between them, the view into the manicured terrain was stunning, and I could watch from my penthouse the ventil, who commonly spent time in the area.

Yet I remained terribly anxious that something might still happen. I pressed Eleison, "You're really sure she doesn't want you with her?"

"I don't think it's me she wants to hear from…but, having said that, Malin—maybe you need to relax." His hand landed upon the back of my shoulder, heavy and comforting, the touch of a human welcome when I was so psychologically isolated. "She's safe," he told me, gesturing out to the park with his other hand. "She's absolutely safe, healthy, the park is enclosed, the animals are even vaccinated—"

"I'm just so worried about the baby."

"Don't be. Thecla looks beautiful. Her fur is glossier than it has any right to be. Her flowers have wilted for the season, but the leaves still look vibrant. They haven't even started to turn color. If the baby needed extra medical attention, we'd be able to tell something was wrong."

I nodded, rubbing my brow. "Yes, you're right, of course. You know it's not like me to *fret* like this, Eleison, it's just—"

"I understand…trust me, I get it. You don't think I'm worried, at least a little? But…I guess I'm more confident than concerned. Plus—" He smacked me heavily upon the back, grinning at my dry sidelong look for his jocular affectation. "I have faith in you…you've taken care of her so far. As long as you're around, you'll have her covered."

My eyes fixed through the window again, I nodded. He turned to leave me, already removing his tie in anticipation of his time off, and I felt a pitiful tug of disappointment. I hadn't even realized how lonely I had become until we reached the building and Charlotte was suddenly around to see to small needs—but her pleasant conversation and valuable insights couldn't fill the hole in my spirit.

Eleison couldn't, either...but his heartache, I knew, was similar to mine, and our shared love had turned my fondness for him into something that was just a bit more. At least, it seemed as such when he stopped by the door. "Maybe I'd better come up for a drink to make sure you actually take time off."

"That would be fine," I told him, disguising my interest with a glance into the face of my pocket watch. "I'm sure you could use an hour or two of human conversation."

"Or sixteen...or twenty..."

We laughed together, then he stepped from my suite and was gone.

It had been, by that point, a cruel hundred and twenty days since I'd last had sex of any kind. Though it was true my promiscuous wife was uncharacteristically celibate during the same span, I was also not sure ventils had anything of the conscious drives normally remarked upon in humans. Thecla's needs, in other words, were being met, but I willfully refrained from meeting mine out of respect for my relationship. I had already agreed to accept Thecla's nature, her youthful cravings and impulses, in exchange for her love, and I had further agreed to do for her what I had not done for Giselle: to eschew other women in all their forms, and, though it was not explicitly stated, unattached men.

Yet she had, before her trip to Valquist, made one encouraging comment in passing, even if we had not had time to discuss the concept in detail. And oh, I confess that Eleison, who has always been simply gorgeous, was especially so when I was so long in a loveless desert. Never had I been above admiring my loyal footman, (I am shallow but honest enough to admit that his good looks contributed to his successful petition on behalf of his brother), but, much to the shock of certain crude biographers whose research methods lay in question, I had never before received from Eleison the sense of anything but friendly interest in my wellbeing, and I was not interested in forcing the issue.

Then, fair Thecla arrived. And the entire structure of life changed for me, for my house—and for Eleison, too. We had been brought together by her, and the crackling attraction I felt for my footman could no longer be denied. Especially not when she brought him into our bedroom first as a figure of fantasy, then as my peer in her love. That marvelous first time seeing them together, I at last sensed Eleison's curiosity toward me...and I had been rather obsessed with it since. It had become a game for me. How long would it take to tempt him into fully committing to the both of us? How long before he accepted that this was not a simple matter of two separate loves, but a nested chain, a spiral, a whirlpool?

Accordingly, with my darling absent from the picture and Eleison's curiosity now left to stand alone, I wondered if I had not been going about my game the wrong way. Why, it only then occurred to me how intimidating it must have been for Eleison to think of his first homosexual experience being fetishized by Thecla's observation. When I looked at it critically, I got the sense that I had been crass; arrogant, as I had not been in years.

What on Earth had made me think that Eleison did not need—no, deserve—to be seduced as much as Thecla had? Why had I assumed our existing relationship would provide evidence of my love for him, above and beyond anything a fond employer felt for his best employee?

How had Thecla so hypnotized me that I had not fully considered, until the day I spent anticipating Eleison's visit, that my relationship with Eleison was separate from, yet contingent upon, my relationship with her? She had told me that herself. Her encouragement had sexual allusions, but, as I recalled, she had urged me to cultivate a *romantic* connection with Eleison. How much more clearly she had seen the situation!

Just as I had been rejuvenated to finally make contact and confirm Thecla's wellbeing, I felt my spirit further restored by the promised pleasure of a conquest that was, I reasoned, not at all illicit within the context of our marriage. If anything, it would benefit our union later on, and would continue to ensure her mate's interests in me were sincere.

The trick with a man like Eleison was not coming on too strong. Too much affection too early, and he would recoil in self-conscious awareness of his own social persona as a heterosexual man. Yet, if I played too distant, he wouldn't sense the opportunity—nor would he feel the all-important hint of magnetism which I felt between us, but which he may not have been able or willing to recognize outside certain contexts.

Therefore, when he arrived in my lair in the evening, with the sun receding to a beautiful red velvet veil across the preserve, I greeted him with a smile and a friend's half-embrace handshake; but I also, before he pulled away, dashed across his cheek the kind of ambiguous kiss one might interpret as either aristocratic greeting or flirtatious affection, depending upon what was on one's own mind. As I released his hand to step back, the embers of his eyes burned heavily enough upon me that I knew how he had perceived it.

"I brought up some scotch," he said, hefting the bottle. "Had the park people bring it over from their store...I know you're normally a wine man, but—"

"No, please, that sounds very fine. Come sit, I'll pour... My word. I'm just not over the novelty of seeing you around again, Eleison."

He laughed, making himself at ease by unfolding his powerful body in the corner of the couch that, oddly shaped to run flush with the curved conversation pit in the center of the living area, permitted him to watch me at the bar. "I'm glad to see you, too, Malin...I've missed you. And cooked food. And doors. Bathrooms. Baths. Beds."

He sighed at the pouring ribbon of amber liquid, adding, "Alcohol," behind a hand that covered half his face.

"I'm surprised you didn't stumble up here already fairly well lit, I admit."

"Oh, I had a couple of beers with lunch, but mostly I've been reading and listening to music. Just trying to make myself feel human."

"I'm sure inundating yourself in art will go a long way to helping with that...ah, you know"—I crossed to hand him one glass from behind the low couch, then strolled on toward the windows that were quickly taking on reflective qualities with nightfall—"when Thecla is well again and things are stable—when she can bear to be away from the baby—you should come with us to an opera as our *guest* rather than our servant, Eleison."

He made the exact noise I knew he'd make, an intake of breath mingled with a noise of playful disgust. "I don't know..."

"Oh, they're good fun if you don't go in determined to be bored. We'll take you to a comedy—*Il barbiere*, perhaps. That one will remind you of the early days of our relationship…except, of course, that the handsome young swain there to sweep the girl off her feet is a count, with holdings and a title and so on…"

"Well," he relented as an excellent idea settled upon me, "maybe sometime. If it wasn't an intrusion—"

"Perish the thought, Eleison! Please."

My wandering had brought me back anyway, so I didn't hesitate to sit closely beside him. As I did, my arm fell as if to brace along the back of the couch past his shoulders. Imperceptibly, he stiffened; then, with the passing of a second and the continued sound of my voice, relaxed.

"I care about you as a friend," I told him. "And as more than a friend. We hold very different social positions, but Thecla's love makes us peers—and my love for you, Eleison, apart from that, elevates you the same way it elevated her. You're never intruding on anything."

"Okay." He searched my face while his glass raised to smirking lips. "I'm not used to this."

"Not used to what?"

With a brisk swallow, he leaned forward to set the empty tumbler upon a coaster on the coffee table. "This, uh—form of your attention."

I raised my own glass to let a mouthful of the shallow pour roll over my palate. Sharp, heavy, burning. Had a way of focusing one in the present. "Does it bother you?"

He answered after some consideration, "Not as such. But—I guess I don't know what to do with it. You know what the problem really is…"

Eleison settled against the arm of the couch to face me properly, his scarlet eye beneath a messily falling dark lock bright with tigerish mischief. "I'm not used to being seduced…much more used to doing the seducing."

Oh, that rogue. He was irresistible, and it was clear he knew he was irresistible from the way he cocked his head to look at me.

"I wouldn't be so sure you're absolved of your own designs," I told him, gesturing with the glass I set aside. "Don't think I don't notice you wore a suit for me."

"And you decided to go casual," he said, eyeing the sleeves rolled to my elbows while he smoothed his own fresh black tie. "I feel sort of touched that you'd think about what appeals to me."

"Of course. You know I find you very attractive, don't you, Eleison?"

Struck by the well-timed bullet of a pointed remark, (my favorite tactic going some ways back), Eleison smiled in a crooked, fiendishly handsome way that gave his powerful features the barest hint of boyish appeal.

"Shucks, I'm blushing. But, yeah...I know I'm your type. I always expected you to hit on me, but you never did."

"Oh, I made a pass once or twice when you started with me, but it went over your head, so I dropped it...and I'm glad I did, because it wouldn't have meant anything before Thecla."

"No," he agreed, "it wouldn't have. And...I don't know if I could have let myself see you that way."

"And now?"

"And now..." Eleison looked at me steadily until, laughing a little, he couldn't hold my stare a second longer. "Malin—"

"You don't have to be scared, Eleison."

"I'm not. Well, not *really* scared. Not like that. But..." With a sidelong glance to his empty glass, he slid up from the couch to pour himself another finger or three. "I guess it's a kind of identity shift."

"Why is that?"

"Well, uh, I've always considered myself strictly heterosexual, for starters…you want any more?" Waving the bottle.

"Oh, maybe a little." As he stalked back with the scotch in one hand and his glass in the other, I weighed his loping gait, his pleasant tone, the slight smile that warmed his perpetually brooding expression. All these in mind, I felt it safe to probe, "Does having one male lover really make you *less* heterosexual? Does it take away from your attraction to women, I mean."

"Well, no. It's not like it's a budget."

"Very well. And are you attracted to good-looking men generally?"

"I really can't say that I am. But—I don't know."

"What?" He bent past me to pour the scotch. I drank in his profile instead, the flick of his eyes into his periphery and upon me brief but intense. "Tell me, Eleison."

"You and I spend so much time together…that's all. I've gotten to know you over the past decade. We work well, we get along. I do feel chemistry with you. But isn't that just your political charisma?"

"Perhaps…or, perhaps I represent something you need. Something you'd like."

Sliding back into the couch again, this time to my left, Eleison asked, "What's that?"

"The freedom to explore yourself, and to enjoy types of pleasure you find taboo." He snorted a little at that, but I nursed my glass while telling him, "I'm serious."

"I don't find homosexuality to be taboo."

"But you just got through telling me you don't think of yourself as homosexual." I set the glass aside again, settling into the embrace of the couch while basking in the warmth of this gorgeous man on whom I'd long ago given up. Now I reached out to straighten his tie, smoothing my hand along its length to enjoy his inhalation as I said, "And I have no doubt at all that you are heterosexual. But it is possible to be attracted to a person in defiance of that nature, Eleison...and isn't that where the excitement comes in, at least in part? The novelty..."

The gaunt edge to his features spoke of a desire repressed too long. "I don't think of what I want to experience with you as some one-off novelty, Malin."

There was no suppressing my smile as I leaned in to him, my fingers still pinching the tip of his tie, my eyes on his until we were too close to focus, and they closed. "Good," I murmured all the while. "I don't, either."

My mouth brushed his, and he stiffened beside me, his body tensing before releasing into acceptance of the affection. As his lips parted, his tongue greeted mine, slipped past it, retreated. He chuckled, his mouth twisting away, his red eyes opening again while my hand lowered to his belt buckle.

"Malin—"

"Just trust me. Don't dwell in the fear or it'll stop you. Let me—"

"Damn it, Malin!"

I had kissed my way along the line of his jaw to the edge of his broad throat. In fact, my lips were descending to his Adam's apple and the belt was already free of his waist by the time he pushed me back, a hand upon my jaw. His lips contorted in a snarl that, when paired with his glowing demon's eyes, excited me far more than it deterred me.

There are few items in existing biographies that correspond with actual truth about my sexual life, though I remember reading once the sentence, "Farrow's appetites are no more limited by matrimony or manners than they are by the natural romantic dispositions of his intended victim," and thinking that, despite its florid prose, it did offer an insightful encapsulation of my interest in a certain kind of man. Eleison's kind of man…you know. The "straight" man, who only suffers from such a personality defect because nobody has taught him how to have fun. With these types, a certain amount of straightforward, sometimes intimidating flirtation was required.

Therefore, smiling on in the face of his animal snarl, barely glancing down at his hand along my cheek, I asked, "What's the matter, Eleison? Am I moving too fast for you?"

"It's not that," he said, to my pleasure.

"Then what?"

"I haven't forgiven you for lying to Thecla. For forcing *me* to lie to Thecla."

Inhaling sharply, I twisted my face from his hand. Like a sullen child, I glowered at the glass upon the coffee table, willing it to shatter and change the subject. "I think I'm steeped in guilt enough already, Eleison. Need you add to it?"

"You *deserve* to be, damn it! She's an orphan. you know—"

With an impassioned wave of his hand, Eleison fell against the support of the couch, but not away from me. "I at least knew my mother and my father. My father died when I was nine or so, but my mother—she lived until I was in my late teens. I knew them both…and I would still do anything to sit down with the people who knew my father on the intimate terms that you knew Thecla's mother."

"You don't understand." Guiltily taking up the drink again, I sulked over the fluid that matched the amber radiance at the edges of Eleison's crimson irises. "Thecla's mother was nothing like Thecla. I hated Giselle. I can't speak of her without soon veering into unkindness."

"So you should have *told* Thecla that. You owed the information to her—certainly owed the information that you were her stepfather. Or are you still? I'm not really sure."

With a sidelong look at him, I took a mouthful of scotch before replying, "We massaged her birth records while submitting the marriage and riftborn registration to the Overseer. I kept Rigel's name because there wasn't a chance in hell Parvati knew or remembered it after all these years, but she would certainly realize right away it was *my* Giselle, so I had her stepmother penciled in. Not that it mattered…it sounds like Parvati recognized her almost right away all the same."

"Right. So what you're saying is, the paperwork no longer reflects any legal connection between you two, therefore, it's okay you lied to her?"

My thumb and forefinger massaged the bridge of my nose. "My goodness. Nobody warned me that when your wife doesn't nag you, her mate will…"

"You'd just better be grateful I'm giving you the chance to get comments like that out of your system, old man. They're not going to go down as well with Thecla when she knows she can just turn into a ventil and gallop—"

"*Don't* say that."

Eleison stiffened as I whipped around to face him, my shout accidental but unsoftened by apology. The breath leaving me in a great shudder, I searched my friend's face until I turned away again, my elbows resting upon my knees. "You can say whatever else you want," I told him, my throat hoarse before I took the last pull of scotch. "You can call me an old man; I don't mind. I am. You can have your own feelings, you can think whatever you want. But I am fatally superstitious these days, Eleison. I beg you, do not speak her parting from us into existence. Never again. I never want to be separated from her again."

The futile longing. I caught up the bottle and covered the bottom of the glass, then added a splash more. "I know it's not possible to never spend time apart," I said. "I know it's not healthy, either. But—these past months, Eleison—all I've longed for is her. To give the time I have to her. Every day of it."

Just so, his expression softened. "I know."

"And I'm sure that you're bitter, that you feel a bit cheated—and you have a right to be, I believe, so no need to deny it. Your loyalty cost you her undivided love. If you had just yielded to your nature and told her the truth about me *and* about you two being mates, she wouldn't have had a second of hesitation about leaping into your arms and begging to be taken away."

"You can't know that. How could I have done that if she had, Malin? No—I don't believe it. She wouldn't have. I know she's loved you since way back."

""Way back."" I laughed a little, astonished to find myself saying, "I've known her a full year. That's this month. One year... I'm fifty-five now. One year shouldn't be anything to me anymore. And this year, this year with her and without her, feels like a dream, it's true...but it feels like eternity, too. Every second we're together, I just feel so—so absolutely *alive*, so vivid. The world feels real in a way it doesn't when she isn't around me."

"I get what you mean."

"I know that you do. And I know that you're her mate...

and I know I've offended you, both by offending her and by compelling you to offend her. And I am terribly sorry, Eleison. You deserve better...she deserves better."

A kind of sympathy passed between us. I seemed to hear Eleison calculating all the immoral things he would have gladly done if it had meant a chance to earn Thecla's love. The immoral things he *had* done because of it.

"You're right," he said coolly, his gaze lowering to the belt he picked up from the cushion between us. "But, instead of someone better...she married you, Malin."

While he casually assessed the belt, then doubled it over in an experiment that incited my blood back to a hopeful simmer, I agreed, "Yes, she did. Against all recommendation."

"Don't you think you owe her a penance when you fall short of what she deserves?"

Mouth dry, I spoke in half a whisper. "Of course."

"Then I'll be sure to tell her all about this when she's feeling more like herself. You can, too, if you'd like, but I'm sure it'll be embarrassing to admit you enjoyed it."

"Hedonist though I am, Eleison, I'm sure you can make it count."

"Bend over the arm of that chair."

I set my glass upon the coffee table that Eleison pushed aside with his shin. After following me, he watched me arrange myself with an expression of nearly bleak intensity. True frustration, heartache—and that flame of whispered desire, withheld, surreal. One hand braced against the back of the chair, I made myself comfortable as I could.

He raised his arm and cracked down the belt without warning. Despite years of adaptation, I jerked at the surprise of the early lash. "You'll have to strike harder if you want to punish me," I coached him, regretting my words when the next snap once again came early. I gasped, my jaw tightening, an endorphin-tinted wave of lust rushing through me along with the sadistic satisfaction I took to permit my hiding at Eleison's hands.

I confess, it was his turmoil that contributed most to my pleasure. The knowledge that his frustration was not just for you, Thecla, or for me, but for himself: for his own mind and body and perception. He wasn't fully comfortable with the idea of kissing a man, let alone bedding one. Yet there he was, the throbbing lash of his belt cracking against my trousers while I took each strike after the second with the half-silent satisfaction of an occasional, pleasurable gasp.

"Poor Thecla. You're holding out on her…ah, Eleison"—he sneered while I sighed at number six—"all she wants is for you to treat her cruelly."

"And for you to treat her decently." The next crack inspired a flinch, but I produced no noise as he went on chiding, "Yet you can't seem to do that in the ways that matter."

"Not so—oh! Hell, Eleison—"

"You think her dead mother's clothes are good enough for her? You think *lies* are good enough for her, Malin?"

"Of course not. Of course not, Eleison, darling, but—aha—"

They were harder now, and faster, the whipping enhanced by his rage and inspiring another pulse of pleasure through me. Ah…I wanted badly to fuck him, but that would be too much for his first time.

There were solutions to that, though.

"You know better." He withheld the lash for an interval

in which I pressed my cheek to the upholstery of the chair, my breath quickened. The sudden break in the building crucible of pain proved both a relief and an amplification of the next stroke, which landed as he said, "But you do these things anyway."

"It was complicated, Eleison. I couldn't just—"

"Shut up. Save your excuses for Thecla. When she can speak. When she's not a fucking ventil because of you."

The newest blitz was so intense that, my tongue swollen in my throat, I found I could no longer respond. I could only shut my eyes and ride out this carmine wave of red-hot agony while Eleison, increasingly agitated, gave vent to his justified outrage.

"If you had told her the truth, even if you waited until you were married, none of this would have happened the way it did. I know it—I don't have to ask her to know it. If you had prepared her for what she was walking into, for your real relationship with the Overseer and her mother—"

"But I didn't." I spoke thoughtlessly, dizzied by the blows that, at their crescendo, blended into a unified wall of pain so vast I felt nothing but a rare, delicious euphoria. At least, rare to me. In sexual interaction, I find there are two types of passion; yielding and commanding. Not every person exhibits both, but I am lucky enough and have always been lucky enough to experience the full spectrum of pleasure—albeit, with a preference toward commanding my lovers, rather than indulging someone else's control. It was infrequent that I found someone, a man especially, who inspired in me the pleasure of submission…but, of course, even in Eleison's case, I enjoyed the cruelty of seducing him out of his comfort zone far more than any masochistic thrill of my own.

Therefore, beaten by my wife's furious mate, I gladly confessed my sins.

"You're right, Eleison. I knew what I needed to do, and I didn't do it. And there is no excuse. I know there isn't."

"And you made *me* lie to her, you bastard. Tell me you're a bastard."

"I'm a bastard—"

"Louder," he snapped along with the belt.

"I'm a bastard, Eleison," I confessed, crying the words against the pain of his strike. "I'm a pig, a craven liar! The truth was too difficult to navigate around, so I lied. I did what I thought was the easy thing and deceived my wife into loving me!"

My breath was short and staggered. I braced myself for the next lash, the next heavy slap of the leather against my ass beneath the powerful arc of Eleison's arm. But nothing came.

With a few long strides to my side, Eleison grabbed me by the back of the shirt and the front of my collar. He released the former when he had me on my feet and could stare into my eyes, his own ablaze with animal rage.

"And because you lied, we *both* nearly lost her. Do you fucking understand?"

Cold terror lodged deep in my heart at the words. I nodded. "I do," I whispered to Eleison. "Of course, Eleison, darling. I do."

""Darling."" He snorted, his stare faltering before narrowing back at me. "Pretty bold to assume you get to fuck me now that I'm so pissed off, Malin."

"And let this go to waste?"

His expression—his entire body—stiffened when I slid my hand along the front of his trousers. For my part, I gasped to feel what I had barely glimpsed as he pulled me upright. I couldn't risk letting him pull away and quickly took hold of the friendly button that popped open under my fingers. An animal growl rolled from him. Still holding my collar, he began, "I don't know—"

"And anyway," I cut him off, knowing all his protests before he made them, "who said anything about me fucking *you*, old boy?"

His breath hitched as my hand dipped down past his waistline to catch him through his boxers. While, against his better judgement and his own self-perception, Eleison rocked gradually into the well of my palm, I bent my head and let my nose brush his.

"I know how difficult it can be to try new things…so, why rush? Of course"—with the hardening of Eleison's cock, my caress transfigured into a slow and devious stroke that parted his lips for an astonished inhalation—"some happy time in the future, I hope you'll forgive me…trust me…love me, Eleison…well enough to submit to me. But…ah. You're an animal, aren't you?"

While he strained, I forced myself to release him if for no other reason than to savor his flinch of disappointment. It eased at once when, invading his boxers next, I took in hand the throbbing heat of his conflicted cock and tugged pleasure from him while our mouths just brushed.

"A wild beast," I went on, reminding us both. "Full of base urges and primitive associations. I'm sure the last thing the animal heart of you wants is to accept my dominance over you by such instinctive means. I'll tame you yet, just as I have Thecla, and perhaps sooner than you'd expect. For now"—I squeezed again, gasping at the sheer size of the prick I loved to see hammering home inside my wife—"I'm more than content to take this big, gorgeous cock of yours, Eleison. Punish me with it. Spare me nothing; use me as you like. I want you to fuck me."

"Ah, Malin—hah—" Between his breathless wheezes of pleasure, he endeavored to laugh. "I never know what to expect from you."

My mouth seized fully upon his. Appropriately unprepared, he released a muted groan into my mouth. My free hand raised to the nape of his neck. Emboldened, his tongue forced mine back across previously gained ground, then broke through to the vault of my mouth. While the dexterous organ stabbed into me, he dropped the belt and raised both hands to my face.

Thecla, darling! Even with your soul exposed and your mind an eternity away, I felt so close to you beneath the hands of your mate. It was something I shared with you: an experience that bonded us across time and space. The pressure of his kiss forced me back against the arm of the chair, where the welts across my backside elicited a low rumble of desire from the base of my throat. I withdrew my hand from him and still he drove on, his body pressing close to me and his next exhalation, as he felt the protrusion of my own intense lust, nearer an animal snarl than a lover's sigh.

At last, as his hand tightened in my hair and against my scalp, I succeeded in pushing against his chest firmly enough to extricate myself from the kiss.

"The bedroom," I urged. "It's more comfortable there."

Eleison absorbed my face in one long, scrupulous study before stepping back and turning without comment. His belt abandoned upon the floor, he stalked across the living room and disappeared quickly down the hall.

Breathless, I caught up that sacred strap, kissed its happy leather, and followed him.

Beside the low-set, abstractedly generic bed that had been furnished in accordance with the sleek architecture, Eleison looked somehow out of place. An ancient statue, too intricate and beautiful for his bland museum space. I rested his belt upon the vanity and, finding him already halfway through unbuttoning his shirt, stepped up to help him.

"Why don't you sit down," I implored him, my stare unflagging while I stripped him of his shirt. "Let me earn your love, Eleison. Oh, gorgeous—"

The finely cut abdominal muscles rippling down beneath the undershirt I raised made me gasp. Eleison's beauty is unmatched in the male sex, so far I am concerned. "Adonis" would have been a better name for him…and "Venus" for you, my darling, my angel, my radiant Thecla, for whose gaze I longed as, kissing Eleison's mouth and then his jaw, I made my way to the lap my expertly working hands had exposed.

The heat of his flesh seemed to increase every inch south that I kissed. By the time I reached his navel, that crater in its halo of the same dark hair that trailed down, down, down, I swore he would burn me. But, if so, I was eager to be branded, and did not hesitate to stage a trail of kisses along the shaft of his admirable scepter.

"Fuck." He gasped as my mouth engulfed him, the bobbing of my head down his length inspiring a jolt of pleasure, a few more degrees of arousal, in my own tortured body. "Fuck, oh, Malin—you're really good at that…"

"Maybe sometime I'll help Thecla practice on you," I told him, stroking him by hand when my mouth raised to permit speech. "Not that she's lacking in talent, of course…but, I do think of myself as her mentor."

Again, I dove, and now it was Eleison who choked. Oh, the radiant heat of that full, gloriously hard prick! There is no tiring of it, is there? No more than I could tire of my Thecla's body, ripe and wild, dancing through my head to incite my longing and spark my tenderness as I stoked the willingness of her mate to take me as he might her. While I pushed on against the resistance of his girth to take him ever deeper down my throat, my hand slid beneath the tightening sac of his testicles and coaxed from him another low, wondrous gasp.

"Fuck—sir—I mean, Malin—"

"You can call me whatever you like," I assured him, my head lifting again to allow my tongue to run along his length. "Whatever you want, Eleison. As long as you promise to give me the good, hard fucking I deserve."

"Then you'd better knock that off—ah, sir, please—"

"Oh, Eleison…you're even more gorgeous when you plead with me. Fine…but one of these times"—I released him—"not stopping will be the point. Especially since it was so cute to hear you begging just now…"

Scoffing as I raised my head to kiss him, Eleison growled at the taste of his own body on my mouth. "Did you really just call me "cute?""

"You are, of course. The distance between your age and mine isn't much different than the one between Thecla's and mine. There's no doubt you're exceptional, virile, an absolute stud…but there's something charming about you, too, just as there is about Thecla. You're even blushing."

"Shut up and take off your clothes," he muttered while I laughed. "Where's the lube?"

"The drawer there," I told him, quickly unbuttoning my shirt and divesting myself of the one beneath. By the time he had the bottle out, in fact, I was half-undressed; and to my delight, he caught my hands, which he pushed away so as to remove my trousers and underwear himself.

Then, he glanced down, and hesitated. I caught him by the back of the neck, my thumb fitting along his powerful jaw to crane his attention back up. "You don't even have to think about me," I murmured, consoling him with a kiss upon the corner of the mouth.

But Eleison was just as capable of surprising me as I was of surprising him. As I kissed him, the warmth of tender human flesh brushed my cock for the first time in months. I gasped his name into his mouth, my own forming into a smile. Gradually, against the other side, his fingers and palm trailed along my shaft, then took me firmly in-hand to press me along his own length.

"It's nothing like that. I was just thinking I've never touched another man's cock before."

His pupils, large with abandon as he studied the pairing of our bodies, made his eyes look somehow mad. Though I knew him of a certain disposition, I simply couldn't imagine a life so closed to experiment and still found myself marveling, "Really, never? Not ever? My...you and Thecla both managed to find your ways to my bed having touched only one prick. I'm honored. Maybe next *you'll* be the one getting in certain other types of practice..."

"Don't go crazy," he said in a warning tone that yet had a certain accessibility, a certain consent to be pushed out of confining comforts and into self-expansion. While I chuckled, he kissed me, and it had that same, overwhelming power he'd shown in the sitting area. I moaned a little, breathing an expression like an "Ah!" of surprise between his lips, and as his ferocity grew, he caught me by the back of the neck as I had him. Then, grasping my arm with his other hand, Eleison exerted force to turn me to face the bed.

His strength inspired a shock of longing in me. I twisted back and down beneath his arms with a maddeningly sharp impulse to fight him, to aggravate him, and thereby be the recipient of that strength to an even greater degree. Yet, as I reminded myself, it was his first time, and I didn't want to initiate any games that might have been past his purview. At his insistent push, I therefore stretched myself along the mattress and maintained my comportment but for the hitch of my breath as he removed the crystal stopper of the bottle and liberally applied its contents to us both.

"I can tell I don't need to ask if you've sodomized anyone before… Have you fucked Thecla's adorable little ass, though?"

"Not yet," he said with a bit of longing, and a hint of relief that I was not above evoking our conjoining puzzle piece. "I wasn't sure how she'd take the idea…but I love fucking her from behind and getting a chance to watch it."

"Isn't she a sight. I've been thinking of installing a mirror over the bed in the Saalast house when we're back. Once I have her, I never want to stop looking at her. Never—ah—oh, Eleison—"

While he pressed against me, I glanced back to find his head bowing over mine. Amid a rough nuzzle of his lips along my ear, he asked, "Are you ready, sir?"

"Oh, Eleison—yes, darling. Go on, let me have it. Let me feel—oh! Eleison, ah, yes—"

With a thunderous growl from the animal within, Eleison eased into me and left me breathless from the first, thrilling penetration. "Is that what you've wanted," he asked once his teeth raked my neck and his tongue lashed flesh already beading with sweat.

"Fuck, oh, yes—what a fine, big prick you have! I don't know how Thecla can stand to take it—ah, Eleison, ah, yes, and so hard—"

My cock throbbed while his slid home into me, his descent into my body unyielding as it was sweet. By then it had been some years since I had last been buggered by a male lover; yet even before that gap in experience, I could not recall finding a man so well-shaped. I have heard you say he was made for you, Thecla… but I suspect that cock was crafted for both of us, just as you (your body, your soul, your devious mind!) belong in equal measure to Eleison and to me.

One arm of coiled muscle slid around me and pressed my back to his chest while we rolled to the side. He found his rhythm, each steady beat into me pulsing up beyond me in a wave of euphoria I felt as far as my face. With his arm still folded around me, his palm flattened against my heart. I grasped it with the same hand banded by my wedding ring.

His mouth pressed to the nape of my neck, the center of my shoulders. I twisted around to trail my fingers along his scalp, to grasp at his arm; to stretch back and pull his hips closer, his body deeper, his essence and existence and very form the shadow that proved the existence of your absent matter, Thecla! Oh, Thecla, my darling, how I longed for you then. The arm I clutched across my diaphragm, in my mind, became your supple body, and the hand I worked along myself was the sweet heart of you, the heat of you, the belly inaccessible to me while you buried yourself in the secretive skin of some wild animal.

I could have forced you to change back.

I could have gone out and called you by your name, and commanded you to return to your senses.

And I was certain you would have obeyed me, as all Rift animals do.

But I did not do that. I could not do that, because when you were no longer an animal, my jewel, you would have hated me more than I feared you already did. The one thing I could not, would not do to you, was take your will away.

I had done enough damage in that regard already.

The hand Eleison rested upon my heart slid down, pushing mine away to envelop me. I shuddered, half-turning, my mouth opening to assure him he didn't need to exert himself for my sake; but he kissed me before I could speak, and after leaving impressions of his teeth at the edge of my underlip, he said in a gruffly affectionate way, "You're very important to me, Malin."

"Oh, Eleison…" I smiled, rocking back against him, offering my mouth again. "You know you're more to me than just a footman."

"I know that. I want—I want things to be different between us when life's back to normal." The delicious, shattering stiffness of his erection grew all the harder at the implication of his words. I gasped, the weapon within me and the deft hand around me driving me onward into glory.

"Don't worry, Eleison…no doubt, they will be. Oh—sweet fuck, that's just right, good man, oh, fuck, just like that, like that—"

While his face, teeth bared, pressed against my neck, I at once arched back upon him and up into his grip. The tension of both our cocks was replicated with increasing accuracy in our bodies, which tightened against one another. My hips arched back to permit the fast working of his hand in time with his strokes, his words intensifying the hazy throb of it all.

"Maybe, when Thecla's behaving herself again, we should let her watch this." His breath as he spoke was as ragged as mine was while I wheezed out a low laugh.

"And if she's not inclined to behave herself?"

"Then we'll tie her up and blindfold her so she can only listen."

"What a thought! Can you imagine the whining? Maybe we should try that anyway. Ah, what a girl she is…Eleison, Lord, ah—yes, keep going just like that, oh, sweet fuck, Eleison! We can't keep her tied up that way without enjoying her a little ourselves, though…ah, you dog, what a fine idea you've given me."

"As long as I get a turn," he managed to chuckle out, on the audible edge of ecstasy while I gasped toward my own.

"Eleison, please! Of course. Fuck her in front of me any time…and perhaps while you do, I'll show you what this feels like."

A noise choked up from him. He caught me in a pattern of steady, supportive pressure that so perfectly flowed with the pace of his hand I cracked, groaning into the height of a climax made more satisfying by the invocation of our dearest ghost. His hand drew away almost at once. I thought he recoiled, but I realized it was to avoid hurting me when he gripped the sheet so tightly the fabric produced the warning sound of some small tear. In me, against me, he surrendered to the ecstasy of what, I daresay, was lovemaking even then, and I found myself gasping his name as he let himself go in me. Through my own spacetime-distorting platinum mist, I stroked his hair and slowly emerged from these rhapsodic coils to find the world a little different. A little brighter.

And my mind—oh, infinitely clearer.

Not ten minutes later, after we had cleaned up and I had convinced him to recline in bed for another drink with me, (having agreed, albeit reluctantly, to allow him to smoke…I would have to whip that habit out of him sooner rather than later), I pondered his profile for a long moment in which he pretended not to notice. When sure he wasn't going to ask, I broke the silence by voicing my unbidden thought aloud.

"I'm trying to decide what title we're going to give you, but as concerns your official position in my court, I think you'll object to everything I'm coming up with."

He produced a cough of surprise, ignoring my paternal tut of disapproval as he repeated, "What *title*? What the hell, Malin."

While he followed this up with a soft laugh, I raised my eyebrows. "What's the matter, darling?"

"And you're still calling me "darling.""

"Well…we're lovers now, just as much as you and Thecla are lovers. And to know each other so intimately, bonded as we are not just by her but by our years together? I can't help but speak to you with great affection. You're family to me. Now more than ever."

Smoke barreling from his nostrils, Eleison lowered his eyes and let his left hand fall to rest upon my nearby right one. While he permitted my fingers to wind through his, he said, "You're family to me, too, Malin."

"Then it's settled…you simply can no longer be considered my footman. I would appreciate it if you would remain functionally the same as concerns guarding the lives of Thecla and myself, but let's promote someone else to head of security; and if anybody tries to give you an order, even Charlotte now, ignore them."

"Oh…was I not supposed to be doing that already?" While I smirked, leaning over to swat him in the pectoral with the back of my hand, Eleison laughed and said, "Well, sir…I won't say I don't appreciate the gesture, but—"

"I haven't thought it all the way through, now, don't stop me… Would you have an objection to being formally declared cavalier servente of Gudrune?"

For not the first time that night, dear Eleison blushed like a ruffled schoolboy. "Uh—well—not as such, but…it's pretty telling about the nature of our relationship. And, anyway, I'm not even involved in the peerage system. Don't you think it's going to look a little, I don't know, scrubby?"

"I've been thinking about that, too. You'll need—"

"Malin."

"No, really. Let me finish, please. You'll need land of your own if you're not going to be completely dependent upon Thecla when—circumstances inevitably change." His expression grew grim, but I could see in his tranquilized yet still shrewd eyes that he had experienced this or some variation of this thought at least once before. I sat up to face him and tried not to take too much gratification in the irresistible flight of his eyes down to what the sheet revealed, then back up to my adamant expression.

"Let me award you an estate and a courtesy title. Lord or somesuch. Call it, for services to the territory. Since I would expect you'll spend most seasons with us fulfilling your new position in my court, perhaps your brother could manage your holding for you...or you could let him go elsewhere, since I can't see any reason to keep you indebted to me anymore."

Eleison's breath seized in full understanding. It were as though such a possibility had never occurred to him before, and his eyes went uncharacteristically wide. Shocked—moved—though he was, he knew better than to go through the usual motions of mock protest.

"Thank you."

"I truly do love you, Eleison—and I will no matter what. I hope you'll remember that."

"Of course, I will."

Who knew what the future would hold for Eleison's perception of me. Things were going to change. How soon they would change, I did not then know; but I had some idea that a seismic shift was on the horizon for me, and I would have to suffer to earn back what was mine.

And I do not just mean you, Thecla.

With the change in Eleison's title and caste there came, I would say, a definite change in his countenance. There was a lightness to his steps and manner that had not been there before, and I was a little ashamed to see clearly how his debt to me had weighed him down. Yet, I could not feel too guilty for that debt; no more than I could feel truly guilty for lying to you, Thecla.

When I look back on our lives thus far, all my mistakes have seemed but the calculated devices of a greater script in which I am but another blind, oblivious player.

I tried to see you six times over the coming weeks. Though I remained afraid, making love with Eleison had broken open such a longing for my missing bride that I thereafter daily rode out upon one of the park's stallions to watch you idle in the grass.

Six times, I approached you. Six times, when drawing near, some sound would give me away, and the startling deer would startle you, and all would retreat; or the wind would pick up, and only *your* eyes, my dearest, would widen in fright, and the ventil with its enormous belly and winter-bared antlers would trundle off into the trees at a pace brisk enough to break my heart; and, just once, you saw me coming, and you did not recognize me, (or worse, you did), and you galloped away while I sank upon the flat of a nearby stone to bury my face in my empty hand.

Then, not long after that sixth time, the Rift Event came. And somehow—as though I could feel your body calling out to mine, my heart!—I knew what would happen even before Eleison came running back to the tower an unexpected three hours in. I had been pondering the weather and the headache it would be, as security team members would be forced to work with rangers in sorting out which animals belonged to the park, and which were new arrivals in need of vaccination and processing—or euthanization to preserve the safety of everyone, my wife most especially. Through the window, the borro's lank body was unmistakable; and by the time nude Eleison had grabbed hold of a security guard at the base of the tower, I'd already yanked on my coat.

My watch rang out a chime, a beautiful, merry chime, forty seconds later.

The memory moves me so intensely! But I return your pen, my darling, for the final stretch of this second, most agonizing episode in our love. How sweet a victory, our true reunion!

Now, as then, I must leave all that to you.

I HAD BEEN partially aware of my surroundings while the ventil shielded me within her sorrel hide. As in a dream had during illness, my memories of those months are a disjointed tapestry of sleeping and waking; of black, heavy slumber with no dreams, and vibrant Rift radiation curling around me like the smoke of another world. All these splinters, interspersed with vague half-memories from before. Before, and during. The ventil's sudden yielding to the ground. That rapid heartbeat: hers, not mine. The friendly borro charging off into the violet night.

And then, with the most brilliant clarity of all, I was upon my back for the first time in months.

I *was* for the first time in months.

I. Me. I was Thecla.

Thecla, surrounded by the clamor of people and idling vehicles and urgency, and a baby screaming, and Malin's tearstained face, so close to mine, his kisses upon me while he whispered, "Thecla! At last—I love you, oh, my darling, my life! Can you hear me? I'm with you—"

The heavy cloak of darkness again. Richer this time. Restful, instead of empty.

Before I was truly, consciously myself, the black loom stood in the center of my sleeping mind.

The atmosphere lacked the pressure of Dinon's invisible presence. Where was he? Could he still locate me after all the time I spent outside myself? Even though the thought occurred to me in sleep, the environment altered at once. The dream, my mind, my dream-mind-body, shifted and warped with his sudden, albeit distant animation.

That quickly, the dharmine was on his way, coming ever closer. A rising siren that lifted in the distance. Violet Rift radiation dulled the darkness, obscuring even the loom; even my hands. The siren grew louder: an alarm.

No.

A newborn.

I shot up out of bed, knowledge flooding me despite the leave of absence I had taken from Earth for five and a half months. During that time, I had been pregnant. Or...the ventil had been pregnant. It—I—we had given birth.

And I was a mother.

Across an unfamiliar room, a woman bent over a cradle, her dark red hair imbued with a copper shimmer by the angle of the low light. I pushed myself up out of bed, delirious enough that I made it three steps before I realized how amazed I ought to have been. My body felt not at all like I'd just given birth, but rather like I'd had a substantial (if disorienting) brand of sleep.

"Charlotte?"

Her back straightening sharply, the housekeeper turned with the crying babe in her arms. "Madame," she began in astonishment, all the more shocked when I rushed to intervene.

"Don't touch my child." My tone was sharp as I swept the sobbing bundle from her arms. "I won't have it. You've betrayed me worse than anyone."

"Thecla...please—"

"The men lying to me—their motives are obvious. But you're a woman just like I am, Charlotte. Moreover, a woman who has been a model to me...and you've been no different from them all this time."

I clutched the baby to my breast. Tears shimmered in my eyes while I stared down at the red-faced, wailing infant with an intense sensation of rising helplessness.

By my reckoning, just yesterday I had been childless, in Glenn's apartment—

Betrayed again, and fighting for my life.

Now this. A baby. A living, breathing, screaming baby for whom I and my body were helplessly unprepared. As I crushed her to my bosom I could tell without even having to check that my breasts were milkless. The ventil had been equipped to care for its offspring, but I, absent during the same timeframe, was not.

Before I succumbed to crying along with the child, the door that stood roughly six feet from the cradle flew open. I flinched back a frightened step.

Then, somehow shocked, I froze in the center of the room.

"Thecla."

Finely polished shoes paused for but a second before they echoed across the white floor, inexorably closing the distance. I could not move an inch; could not even think to, somehow. The knot in my throat was too thick to permit me to do anything but measure my breaths. His dark eyes, as intense as ever, were softened by love, and joy. His hair had silvered since last I'd seen him, and the lines of his features were just a little deeper.

But, like he had never stopped, Malin slid his arm in the small of my back and stood close to me. His body pressed to mine while his gaze fixed on the sobbing infant. "Isn't she beautiful," my husband remarked, squeezing my shoulder while I looked up at him in shame and terror. "I'm so proud of you, darling."

Tears flowing down my cheeks, I studied the baby (a girl!) and confirmed what I already knew. The dark curls of hair just beneath the edge of her white cap; the flash of blue behind her watering, tightly squeezed eyes as she cried and cried for what I couldn't provide.

"You shouldn't be proud of me, Malin," I told him, lips trembling. "I'm terrible. I'm a fool. I— She's—"

His big hand, so warm and familiar that its contact through my nightgown was enough to release sorely needed endorphins, stroked my back while he hushed me.

"Sh. I don't care. It doesn't matter to me. She's my child. All right?"

"But—Malin—"

"Unless, of course, you don't want me to be involved with her...which, I suppose I understand."

"No!" Quickly, leaning against him—and cursing my joy at the natural way his arm tightened around me—I searched his face and begged, "Of course, I want that. But how can I ask that of you?"

"You don't have to ask it of me. I'm your husband: I'm the father of all your children, no matter who sired them." His free hand fit to my cheek, the tip of his thumb sliding across a tear track he smeared toward my ear. "All right?"

Overwrought, I looked mutely into his face for five long seconds before dissolving into sobs of my own.

"Oh," he murmured, "Thecla…oh, Thecla, darling…let Charlotte hold her for a moment, would you? Sit down—you shouldn't be up, anyway."

"I'm fine," I gagged through my tears; though, submitting in the name of my own sanity, I did allow Charlotte to take the baby from my arms. Upon sliding into the vacant chair beside the cradle, I buried my face in my hands and sobbed on. "I can walk, I could even run if I wanted—but I can't feed my child. How can I take care of this baby?"

"We spent the final months of your pregnancy arranging for a wetnurse, since we already suspected something of the sort might be a possibility…don't worry. Charlotte was just taking the baby to her. I suppose that was what woke you up, since, with few exceptions, we've been bringing the nurse in here."

My trembling hand pressed across my damp eyes, I asked, "How long have I been here? Since her birth?"

"Three days…and I've counted them with bated breath. Thecla—my love—"

"Please—" Bending over entirely now, my forehead to my knees, I begged him, "Please, don't speak to me with such tenderness."

"But that's all I feel for you, angel. Now, more than ever."

Slowly, I shook my head against my lap, then straightened while the door shut to mute the baby's wails. "I don't know *what* you feel for me. If what you feel is for *me* at all."

Malin's mouth tightened.

"I have spent every day of the past five and a half months"—five and a half months! I was so shocked by the number I barely comprehended it as he went calmly on—"waiting, wishing, praying for this opportunity to see you, and speak to you, and beg your forgiveness...and I still barely know how to proceed now that we're here."

"You've had more time than my pregnancy to figure it out," I reminded him, unable to help my sharp tongue despite the longing his presence sparked in my soul. While his head lowered, I wiped my hand against the back of my cheek, then looked down at my nightgown with a sense of helplessness. "I'm so overwhelmed, I can't even think right now."

"That's all right, darling. So am I. Oh—Thecla—"

He took a step toward me. Hesitated. His hands raised to his mouth, then lowered as fists.

"May I kiss you," he whispered.

I sobbed.

"I wish I could tell you "yes," but I—oh, please—"

Malin's cheekbones tightened along with his jaw. "I understand." His voice was rough with injury, but he didn't press. He looked away from me, striding to the bed and the floor-to-ceiling curtain that formed the wall behind its headboard. "It's a beautiful day, you know. Let's open these curtains now that you're awake. Won't that be nice?"

I sat still, unspeaking, unmoving, my thoughts an inundation of sensory and factual information (I was a *mother*!) as well as the rapid slide into the complex feelings related to that information. Taking after the men who loved me, I brooded in silence. Malin waited for my answer, then simply drew the curtains by walking them across the room one vast wing at a time.

The entire wall was a great window. My eyes squeezed shut against the sudden surge of light following a three-day coma. Having spent my last week as a sentient human with a constant headache, I expected a throb in my skull, or a terrible shot of nausea in my gut. Nothing came. While my eyes adjusted, my husband's dark silhouette suggested, "Perhaps, if you feel up to it—tomorrow, when you've had time to sort out your thoughts— you might take a walk with me outside. Like we used to, darling."

"Like we *always* do," I corrected him. "Oh…just last week—before I left Gudrune—"

My eyes widened. I remembered not last week, but yesterday. Trembling, I stared down at hands that had just been holding a gun. Hands that had just been bloody with the dharmine's kills while Glenn struggled with whether to protect me or detain me.

I leapt from the chair so quickly that Malin emitted a cry.

"Be careful, Thecla," he urged me, rushing forward to support me with a hand upon my forearm. But what I had remembered was too vital to withhold, and at any rate his concern was needless. I felt just fine, in perfect health.

So I was, on the inrush of memories, not worried about myself, or our fight, or any such thing. I was only worried about Malin.

"I don't know what you must do—I don't know what you *can* do"—I clutched the lapels of his suitcoat while he wrapped me in his arms with a hopeful, low gasp—"but please, Malin, you must do something. The Hunter's Guild wants you dead."

His arms froze around me, those black eyes carefully narrowing in their search of my face. "What makes you say that?"

"Last—my last night in Valquist." My expression grew grim to recall it, and grimmer still to think on my naivete. Nevertheless, I explained in brief the poker game that had turned out to be an unexpected meeting of a terrorist cell. "Gradually," I went on, "it grew apparent the meeting's purpose was to persuade me, or perhaps threaten me, to cooperate with an assassination attempt against you when you arrived."

"And what happened, angel?"

I bared my teeth, staring Malin straight in the eyes.

"I killed them—one of them, at least. The rest, I fed to the dharmine."

"Oh, Thecla..." His face filling with unspeakable love, Malin caressed down my arms to take my hands in his. "You would once more bloody these innocent hands for me?"

My stomach wrenched at his love: the love I wanted so badly to receive. Yes, fawn over me! Lull me into complacency, suck the outrage from me with your kisses!

That was what I wanted to say. Then I remembered his lie. The nature of his lie. His nature, and mine. Inhaling sharply against my love, I told him, "Please, I'm so concerned. It sounded like more of them than just Glenn were chummy with that fellow from the games. The one who runs the Gudrune chapter of the guild...Winston. That was it. If that's so—"

"I can certainly see your concern," he said, raising my hands to his lips and pressing there the kiss I couldn't let him plant upon my mouth. "Perhaps you're right...it's high time Gudrune enters a new era. The Guild is a relic of the past, after all...with police presence improving all the time and small towns largely self-sufficient thanks to RMS community monitoring programs, I don't know if the old "wandering hunter" model is worth supporting anymore."

One hand raising to my cheek again, Malin searched deeply into my eyes. "Thank you. Thank you, Thecla. I'm grateful to know you still care about me."

"I feel like I've failed you," I mourned, glancing toward the empty cradle as he shook his head. "No, Malin, I have, I—"

"You haven't at all. I just told you how proud I am of you. I mean it. You've given us a beautiful baby."

"Why must you be so *kind* to me, damn you?"

"Because I love you, darling…and I love our child. Ah! I'm just so happy, I—"

Unable to help himself, he bent to kiss me; but, snapping to awareness halfway, instead he dragged me to his chest and smothered me against his heart. As his chin lowered atop my head, the only sound was the rushing thud of his celebrating pulse and the half-sob of his relieved words.

"Every day, every night, you've been all I've longed for, angel…I'm so sorry for what I've done to you."

Squeezing my eyes shut against the prickling of more tears, I whispered hoarsely, "I suppose Glenn was among those hunters killed by the dharmine, in the end?"

"Your friend has been unaccounted for since that incident, actually." Malin's tone was so casual he may for all the world have been speaking of Charlotte and not the father of my unexpected child. I exhaled, one of the many worries in my heart untangling while my husband went on to ask in a light tone, "Do you reckon him in love with you?"

"I—I'm really not sure, Malin."

"Are you falling in love with him?"

My lips pursed. "He was kind to me, and generous…but,

the way he hates you—I don't want to think anything of him at all anymore."

"Of course, you don't want to…but you still will."

While I lowered my eyes, shamed, Malin stroked my arm.

"That's all right, Thecla. I keep telling you, it's all right. Why would I deny you love, happiness, pleasure? Why would I chide you for creating and carrying a brand-new little human?"

"A brand-new little ventil," I said, bitterness to my tone. "I feel so strange about this. I—I'm so overwhelmed."

"I'm sure that you are. Take your time. You have your own staff committed to this floor. Whatever you need, whatever you want, you'll have it. Everything here is arranged with you in mind. Charlotte and Brea are—"

My expression sharpened. I stepped back from him and blotted my face on the edge of my sleeve. "There's two names I long to hear less than even Glenn's. Charlotte, I understand if you must keep—but *please* swear to me you'll fire Brea, that wheedling little gossip!"

Though his scar twitched with long-practiced resistance to expressions of surprise, he certainly held a grave curiosity in his tone. "Is there something I'd ought to know about?"

"She overheard me speaking to the dharmine and, by the time the rumor passed through Aleister and on to his sister, lo, I was a witch with a magic mirror and a bevy of bad spirits."

Malin's features hardened. "I'll have her employment terminated at once." His eyes lowered to my hands, telegraphing his longing to touch me and sparking my own longing to be touched; then, once again, I looked at him and remembered everything he had kept from me. The longing deflated.

Recoiling farther, I told him, "And I would like new clothes immediately. As soon as they may be provided, here and in all our houses."

He nodded. "Is there anything else I can do for you now, right this very moment?"

"Please—just leave me alone."

Having adopted a more purposeful, professional demeanor at my insistence he fire Brea, Malin withstood my request without too great an outward show of pain. Even so, he hesitated to turn away. His eyes swallowed me up as he asked, "Would you like me to send Eleison in for you?"

In addition to my—to me, very recent—memories of having narrowly persuaded Eleison not to murder Glenn, I had the sense that my mate and I had spent a lot of time together during my sabbatical. "No, thank you. I just want to take a bath and…order things properly in my mind."

Malin nodded once, then paused at the door and slid his hand into his pocket.

"I retrieved this from the investigators in Valquist," he said, setting something small and metallic upon the edge of the changing table. "You don't have to wear it if you'd prefer not to, of course, but…perhaps, if you would feel up to joining me for dinner—"

My diaphragm tightened with the kind of anticipatory hope I once felt whenever I was to see Malin at the country house, though now it was mingled with something else. "Maybe not tonight, but— What floor is it?"

"You have your own dining room here…I'll come and join you, if you send word that you're willing to see me. Maybe, if things go well, I can take you up to my floor for a glass of wine… or we could just have that walk, and talk a little…"

After small delay for mental processing, something became apparent to me. "You're *keeping* me here."

Malin's eyes averted to the wedding band he had set down for my consideration.

"You should start thinking up names for our baby, darling...I can't withhold the announcement much longer if her actual birthday is to be the public holiday, don't you think?"

Inhaling wetly, I begged, "Where are we, Malin? How long are we staying here?"

"I can't bear to have you run away again, Thecla." His words were sharp, his breath sharper. Turning quickly from me before he lost all composure, he said, "I'm sorry, darling. We'll be staying here until I've had a chance to earn your forgiveness."

While I cried his name in dismay, he hurried from the nursery and shut the door behind him.

A low groan—half a scream, in truth—tore free from my throat while I stood alone in that room. My hand slid over my face, over my eyes, and I sank into the chair I soon realized was meant to be rocked. Gradually, I found a rhythm of rocking to match the rhythm of my breathing; and, as though I were as in need of comfort as the infant, I let the steady pace ease my sorrow to calm.

I was overwhelmed, that was certain; but, for having two of my concerns already addressed, I could sort other matters with greater ease. Knowing Brea was gone and Glenn was still alive left me focused on the baby, on my relationship with Malin—

And on the dharmine.

The throb of Dinon's presence in my dream had seemed to come from a great distance. Had he truly been unable to follow me while I was an animal? Perhaps not; the consciousness of an animal was not like the consciousness of a human, structured around narratives and timekeeping. It may not have provided the kind of sustenance Dinon required. The ventil had been worried only about surviving: a task made easier by the borro that, defying logic, had accompanied her as friend and guardian rather than taking her for a meal.

I changed my mind about not seeing Eleison and sprang up, suddenly desperate to see him—but the door to the room cracked open with a soft knock. My baby in her arms, a smiling young woman I'd never seen stepped into the room.

"Good morning, Madame! Look here, baby, Mommy's awake, isn't she lovely? I'm Nellie."

"It's nice to meet you." I glanced from the baby's far more tranquil expression to the slight dishevelment of the bow at the front of the maid's dress. "You're the wetnurse?"

"Yes, Madame, that's me." She was a pretty girl, her big smile bright against her pigmented features as she stepped up to me to offer the baby. "And here's your little girl. Would you like to hold her?"

My face and throat and eyes all straining against tears, I opened my arms for her to slide the infant into my embrace. "There you go," Nellie said, smiling on softly, the baby fussing just slightly to be shifted from her arms to mine. Then, relaxing against me with a soft noise that inspired a great stab of love through my heart, she quieted altogether. My child peered hazily up at me through those pretty, unfocused blue eyes.

"She's so small," I marveled, leaning her against my breast while folding my thumb and forefinger around the entirety of her palm. How strange to imagine that every human I had ever seen was once such a size! Even Malin; even me. While her impossibly soft hand tightened in some unconscious reflex, I tore my gaze away from her to look instead at Nellie. "You must have children of your own," I observed. "Are they here with you?"

"Yes, Madame, I have a little son who's just turned three months. Hector; he's sleeping now, but I'd be glad to introduce you to him later."

"Has the staff treated you well? My husband?"

"Yes! Yes, and—it is crass to talk about money, Madame, but I am very grateful for the wages I'm being paid to stay here."

Nodding, I patted the baby's back while I assured the nurse, "I'm grateful for *you*. I suppose, given my condition, there's been no need for a monthly nurse. Are you the only childcare staff?"

She shook her head. "For now, but Master Farrow assured me he will be helping you interview for a nanny when we have returned to Saalast, and that the housekeeper's services are at your full disposal until then—along with the rest of the staff on the floor, of course."

The idea of interacting with Charlotte after she had disappointed me like everyone else struck me with displeasure. "Please, if Charlotte is too busy and the task becomes too much between your child and mine, let me know. I'll gladly press my husband into hiring a nanny sooner."

Her smile widening, Nellie curtsied and assured me, "That's all right, Madame! Your baby has been very easy so far... Fate willing, she'll stay that way! Would you like to be left with her awhile? There's a lot I think I'd better teach you, but, given everything, maybe you'd just like to sit with her while her needs have been recently seen to."

"Yes, please. And—perhaps, if you could send someone word for me—"

Ten minutes later, while I rocked the slowly drifting child and wondered idly over names, Eleison's knock at the door gave only a few seconds of warning before he hurried in. A look of wild excitement brightened his face as I'd hardly ever seen it, and my own countenance at once reflected the joy in his.

"Thecla," he said, lowering his voice when I hushed him at the baby's wince. "I'm so glad to see you—"

Unlike Malin, Eleison didn't wait, or ask. Making short work of the distance, he strode over to me and took my face in his hands for a plunging, celebratory kiss that stole my senses. When they returned, it was only because he had pulled himself away and knelt beside us with a devoted smile of golden warmth.

"What a sweetheart," he said, peering into the baby's face while his hand fit to the back of my shoulder. "I think she's happy you're up. This is the first time I've seen her that she doesn't look like she's scowling."

I laughed. "I hope she's not going to be disappointed in me...goodness knows, I barely have any idea what I'm doing as a parent."

"No parent does. Lucky for you, you've got more help than most." Excitedly, with a kind of animated warmth, Eleison asked, "Can I hold her?"

"Do you want to?"

"Of course! She's your baby...hey"—his conversation turned to her as I slid her into his arms—"hi, kiddo—"

In my vague notions of what motherhood would mean to me when Malin and I eventually conceived, this—the sight of my child in Eleison's or even Malin's arms—had somehow not occurred to me as an inevitability. I was therefore not prepared for how moved I would be...or how oddly stirred I was by the unhesitating avuncular—perhaps even paternal—love my mate already showed for my daughter. While I watched with my lip bitten, Eleison fell back against the wall to sit there on the floor, the infant cradled gently against the fabric of his collared shirt and the tie loosened in the hallmark of a day off. He was so maddeningly handsome—and, in that moment, so gentle and loving—that he made me forget for an instant his violence against Glenn, or the killing he had done on my behalf.

Which reminded me of the killing I had done on Malin's behalf.

After cooing over the baby, Eleison looked up to me and saw the distant expression upon my perhaps too serious face. "How are you, Thecla? I've missed you. Well…talking to you, at least."

"I'm so grateful you were with me." My hand rested upon his head and slid back through his black hair. "Without you—I don't know what I would have done."

"Malin was with you, too; for nearly as long as I was." When my hand lifted away in surprise, he arched his brow at me. "Where do you think all those caches of fruit and vegetables came from? How do you think you ended up here?"

"I—I don't even know where 'here' is."

Brow knit in sympathy, Eleison glanced down at the baby he joggled very gently against his heart. "It's a game reserve on the eastern edge of Gudrune, in Azstoria. About a day and a half to Saalast by train. Man! She reminds me of when Kyrie was born, he was such a tiny baby…hi, kiddo. For somebody who's so sleepy-looking, she sure can stare…"

"It's because she can see how handsome you are." Laughing a little, then sighing, I rested the temple of my forehead against the tips of my fingers. "I don't even know how I'm going to explain her family to her…will you be her uncle? Her daddy?"

"Oh, I know Malin's just dying to be her father, so I won't steal his thunder. Uncles are more fun than dads, anyway."

"Very well. Then that's your Uncle Eleison…and, Uncle Eleison, here is—Baby."

We laughed again. The child frowned in annoyance at our mirth, more than ready to nap by this point. "I don't even know what to *name* her," I said, sighing hopelessly.

"You'll figure it out…most people have nine months to think of names. Nobody's going to blame you if you take a few more days."

"I suppose." Malin's comment drifted through my mind. Sighing heavily, I accepted the infant back into my arms once Eleison clambered carefully to his feet with her. "Does Malin really intend to keep me here until I've forgiven him?"

His mouth contorting a little, Eleison said, "I think he just wants to be sure you're not going to go right back to being a ventil. Once he's said his piece and he doesn't think you're as much of a flight risk, I'm sure he'll get us moved back to Saalast."

Sighing, I gazed down at the little lamb—the little deer!—tucked in my arms. My finger found its way to the pretty rosebud of her cheek as if by its own accord. As rosy as the bouquet that had been the only remaining witness to the violence.

To my violence.

""Rosina."" I smiled as her lips contorted to show her naked gums. "Yes, princess, we like that, don't we…"

"This kid is going to end up so horribly spoiled."

While Eleison laughed at me, I pouted. "And why shouldn't she be! Look at how adorable she is…besides—"

My stomach tensed as I regarded her, the rocking in which I'd engaged unconsciously coming to a sudden stop.

"Even though she'll have you and Malin—and you're both being so ingratiating, so generous of heart and spirit—I—"

Mouth opening and shutting, I lowered my eyes from Eleison's expectant ones to study the baby instead. "It's just a terrible pity she might not have the opportunity to know her actual sire," I found strength enough to confess.

"Yeah," agreed Eleison, grudgingly. "I guess."

"But it's just as well." I sat up a bit straighter and covered the child's ear with my hand, as though she could already understand. "He, Glenn—he wants Malin dead, Eleison. They all do in the Hunter's Guild, I think. At least, they seem to have a network of extremists among them."

"That doesn't surprise me. Malin allowing alteration and permitting riftborn to live in the territory with proper registration protocols have always been two policy decisions that never sat right with conservatives."

"And now that his energy program is reestablished…oh, my goodness, I suppose it must have progressed so much since— *Sable*!"

With great dismay, I realized it had been close to six months since I had written my family, including my poor sister; that I had missed several holidays; and that even my own birthday had come and gone, leaving me twenty-five, and so different I might as well have been an entirely different person than the year prior.

I was certainly living an evolving life, I reflected as Rosina's eyes blinked shut with greater success.

"I must write my sister at once," I said softly. "And my weaving—oh, I want everything to be normal. I'm sorry, Eleison.

I'm so sorry I've caused you such problems. Not even Malin deserved—"

"Hey…Thecla, baby…it's okay."

His tone warm and soothing, Eleison drew me against his chest while bending over to cover my brow in kisses. I fought back another wave of tears to avoid disturbing Rosina.

"If you wanted to live a hundred years as animals," he told me, speaking against the top of my head, "I wouldn't be thrilled, but I'd do it for you."

"Stop being so devoted to me, Eleison. I'm too cruel, I don't deserve it—"

"Never…I'll never stop. And you definitely do deserve it, Thecla."

His fingers weaving back into my hair, the caress of his fingertips along my scalp so soothing it felt as though sparks of pure bliss trickled through my brain and down my neck, Eleison gently guided me back to let him look into my eyes.

"I of all people understand you couldn't help it." He looked between us with the intensity of a deep secret; something too unspeakably intimate to ever share with anyone else. "Okay?"

"Okay," I whispered back.

That mouth! It smiled as he bent to kiss me, and my heart raced. Though my mind was disoriented, my body knew how long it had been since I'd felt the touch of love. I was absolutely starved for it. I pressed up against him, flush with desire, but not long after sank my teeth into his lip and I turned my face from his. "I have a few matters to contend with now, Eleison…and I'm sorry, but I don't think I can have dinner with Malin tonight. Will you tell him?"

"That's all right, baby…I'll let him know." His tone

brightening, Eleison smiled down at the child and told her, "See you later, Rosina! That's a cute name...I'll let you share it with Malin when you're ready, don't worry. Secret's safe with me."

"Thank you. Will you come see me tomorrow? Do you have the time?"

"Oh, sure, I have the time...Malin fired me. Or promoted me. Sort of depends on how you look at it."

I balked. "What do you mean?"

"He gave me the country house," he explained with a doggish grin while my mouth widened all the more, "in Karrisregion. You're now looking at Lord Eleison of Karris. But how about we discuss it once you've had a chance to speak to Malin."

"Yes, I'd love to—oh, Eleison! Congratulations! And your debt—?"

"All gone," he said, touching his hand to his forehead and letting his fingers float away while his eyes raised to the ceiling. "Bless Malin Farrow...he saved my brother's life, and brought you into my world, and now he's made me a lord, and a property owner...he's the best man I've ever known, even for the worst of his flaws."

As Eleison left me with Rosina, I hated to admit I felt the same.

IN SOME WAYS, that first day with Rosina felt like a strange recreation of the first day I spent awake in Malin's (former) country home. Still in shock, I convalesced with my dozing daughter and brooded endlessly over the months I had lost forever. When her needs interrupted me, I found Nellie and let her contend with the details for which she'd been hired.

What a relief, that wetnurse! I, who had never so much as read a book on child-rearing, (who had never even known myself to be pregnant!), was perhaps as ill-equipped to care for an infant as anyone I have ever known. In the matters of cuddling her, singing to her, loving her, I was natural, as would have been anyone with the least bit of heart. But when it came to changing diapers, feeding, burping? I confess I was lost, to the point that I was even frightened to lay the child in her cot for fear I would do so the wrong way. The patient and kindly bastard daughter of one of Malin's colleagues, Nellie—who, I would learn, had assisted in raising the remarkable seven brothers and sisters to whom she sent a large portion of her paychecks—had absolutely no trouble at all, and was more than happy to demonstrate for my benefit those small details of having a newborn baby.

I had a newborn *baby*. It was dizzying, and so strange. And the strangest part of all was that, as frightened as I had been to awaken and know at once she was not Malin's—I had the very distinct sense that this baby was already bringing Malin and Eleison and I closer together than ever before.

If only I could allow myself to truly experience that closeness.

The first few days of my being awake were difficult on a mental level I have not experienced since. With my feelings about Malin unresolved and Glenn absent, the only sense of stability I had was given to me by Eleison. And no doubt, when Eleison came by for the mid-morning visits that quickly grew to be a pattern, my mate was at his best. He spoke to me with absolute normalcy, asking questions about Rosina or my experience with babies and, with increasing frequency, was spurred to reflect on his own childhood, or Kyrie's. When my emotions became overwhelming, kind Eleison would slide an arm around me and let me cry myself into a doze against his chest—all while his other arm supported the baby that slept in my embrace. He was generous enough to let me say anything at all: things not worth recording because they were spiteful and angry, mere passing emotions about Malin that expressed themselves over and over again in search of validation. And, with each amply provided validation from Eleison, the expression of those heated feelings seemed more and more pointless. By the day, my anger deflated.

But my sorrow grew.

Each time he left to give me time alone, Eleison would pause by the elevator and ask, "Would you like to have dinner with Malin tonight?"

Three times in a row, he asked that question. Three times, I couldn't bring myself to accept.

The fourth time—the fifth day of waking, of confinement, of motherhood—not more than twenty minutes after I had sent Eleison down the elevator, the car came back up. Expecting a maid with a load of laundry, I made no move to rise from the central parlor where I sang to the child in my arms.

Then the door opened, and Malin stepped out. My face flooded with color, the latest note freezing on my tongue.

Not having expected me there, he took a step toward me, then forced himself to stop with that look of true pain. "Don't let me interrupt you," he begged me.

Mouth dry, my body aching for his embrace, I lowered my eyes to Rosina. "What is it? Am I finally allowed to leave this floor?"

"I just need to be near you, Thecla. Please." He gestured, waving the book in his hand while saying hoarsely, "Let me sit with you. Read near you. I'll be absolutely silent. You'll forget I'm here."

"I feel your presence much too acutely for that, Malin."

His dark eyes glittered with hope, but he said nothing. Cheeks puffing with a low, long sigh, I shut my eyes. "Very well."

A hitch in his breath, Malin said, "Thank you."

Then, with a loving look at me, my husband took a seat in the sofa arranged symmetrically to the one where I sat with the child. One ankle resting upon his knee, he settled back into the embrace of the couch and, true to his word, took to reading. The only sound he made was the flip of a page, and his eyes never raised—though I sensed they strained to.

Wishing to punish him, I took Rosina to bed, then crossed to the wing opposite. The loom waited, naked with promise. I left the door ajar so Malin might hear I would be busy. If he expected me to capitulate, to forgive him simply because he deigned to appear in my prison, he would be sorely mistaken. For hours, I threw myself into preparing the loom and beginning the very first portions of the tapestry I worked out in Valquist. I worked endlessly, certain if I did I would succeed in chasing him away.

Supper came. One of the servant girls interrupted me with audible unease to do so, asking in a nervous tone, "Shall I set a second place at the table, Madame?"

I took that to mean Malin had not gone as I'd hoped. "I'll take supper in here tonight," I said, turning my gaze back to my work. "Don't mind Master Farrow. Just pretend he isn't here."

By no means anxious to obey me in that particular directive, the girl hurried off.

Guilt filled me to make my point, but I made it. I ate in my workroom and then I worked some more. When eventually my body was too sore to allow me to work on without consciousness of every little ache, I got up.

And he was still there. Still patiently reading. He had spent hours there, and had missed dinner.

He looked up at me.

Teeth grit, I hurried on to check in with Nellie, then put myself to bed without telling my husband good night.

This pattern repeated itself two more days. First Eleison, then Malin; Malin, who did not complain or demand anything of me when I went out of my way to neglect him. He missed dinner two nights in a row and said nothing of it while I ate in my workroom. We exchanged not a word with one another. I hardly looked at him.

And he just kept reading, uncomplaining, making no effort to interrupt my work or insert himself into the child's care or follow me to bed.

On I wove and wove and wove, empty work to fill the air. How hollow it felt! How outside of it I felt, knowing Malin was listening to me, and I could not listen to him. Somehow, without being able to put my full heart of love into the threads I wove, I felt so listless and drained by the work that I'd might as well have been back in Lescaut, mass producing rugs and curtains at the textile factory.

By the second day, my resolve flagged and my pace slowed. I longed to sit beside him. To touch his hand, and be touched by him, and speak my mind to him and be spoken to by him. Without accepting his offered intimacy—without extending to him the opportunity for forgiveness—my hands were empty when they were full, and my mind rejected any thought that was not linked to him.

When, on the fourth day, the elevator doors slid open to permit Malin into my floor once again, I began to wonder if I wasn't hurting myself just as much as I was hurting him. I still got up and let Nellie care for the baby while I worked, but I was more aware than ever of every breath, every sigh, every flipped page from the adjacent room. I got little work done and spent close to an hour staring blankly out the window, amazed to think I had wandered this same park as an animal.

And the whole time, my husband waited for me.

I succumbed when the light signaled late afternoon.

Any sane man would have long since given up—would have given up on me months before. I ceased my passive aggressive clatter and emerged, and there was my insane husband. Four days on, yet another book. Still he read and waited, undaunted, this new volume in his hands nearly finished, his position only having shifted throughout the hours of that day to allow him to recline against the sofa's arm. My unanticipated footfall drew him from his thoughts—or the posturing of his thoughts, for he had no doubt at least somewhat readied himself for the possibility of my arrival since my loom had fallen silent.

But whatever he had thought or not thought, he was not ready for me to cross around the couch and sit beside him.

The flare of his nostrils along with the slow, leonine pursuit of his gaze telegraphed his desire to touch me, but he didn't try. He merely sat up, continuing to read, the hand with the book propped against the couch's arm. His other hand rested upon his knee, ready to turn the page any second.

Here he was. Just as he'd said. Just as he'd been the whole time.

Present. Silent. Waiting for me. For *me*—when he could have snapped his fingers and had a hundred women lining up to play the part of Madame Gudrune the first time I denied him anything.

Heart throbbing with his nearness, I let him turn the next page, then sild my hand into his. His chest expanded with a sharp inhalation that matched the instant squeeze of his fingers through mine. The weaving of our flesh was sufficient to bring a mist to my eyes.

Dedicated to passing what he felt to be (and what I suppose

was) some test, he did not look away from his book until he had finished the final page. He had a chapter and a half left. I did not interrupt him and was in fact content to sit in silence: to bask in the nearness of his presence, allowing the circuit of love flowing between our hands to fill me with new life. Then, balancing the finished tome upon the knee opposite the one where we held hands, he looked expectantly over at me.

"Would you dine with me tonight," I asked him sheepishly.

Unhesitating, Malin raised his now free left hand to fit against my cheek. His forehead bowed against mine as my pulse thudded in my tongue.

"I'll go get ready right now," he told me, nose brushing mine in lieu of the kiss we both wanted. Instead, he bent to kiss my hand, slid free from my grip of him, and departed by the elevator with a subtle but hopeful smile.

What was going to happen at dinner, or after? I cringed at the conversation ahead of us. Despite my disappearance and my immediate rejection of his olive branch, Malin had yet to express any anger; only relief to have me back. Yet that dinner with Aleister flashed back through my mind, rushing along with my own distorting rage.

It was entirely possible this would be a difficult conversation for both of us.

At a quarter to five, when I had spent a few hours with Rosina, I had a bath drawn and sank into the glorious embrace of the scalding water. I had never felt so strange to feel like myself. Everything, every last detail, was as it had been before the ventil took over to act as my surrogate; yet, inside, I was so changed. After stewing a time, I dressed in a gown that, shoulderless, was dark but for a splash of color across the left hip, breast, and down along the bustle. I managed my hair by myself, sweeping it back from my face in a wild pseudo-chignon that hung in a bundle at the nape of my neck. The jewels I found in the dressing room of the floor's boudoir were new. I recognized only the necklace Malin gave me when we married, and I selected it above all the other gorgeous pieces from which I could pick, but did not.

When I stepped out of the room fully dressed, he was already there to meet me.

In a pressed suit of dark copper that enriched the remaining color of his hair, Malin spoke with Nellie and Charlotte just outside the baby's door. Seeing me, Charlotte excused herself from the conversation and left at once, which I appreciated, but which struck me through with a new bolt of guilt. How absurd... *She* was the one who ought to have felt guilty. Wasn't she?

"Thecla." Malin's attention snapped to me at the housekeeper's departure. He extended one hand toward me, then slid it instead into the pocket of his trousers. "You look stunning."

As, smiling at us, Nellie also excused herself, I felt at a loss for what to do. My body and heart longed to cross into his embrace: to kiss him, to forget about everything and live as we had before. To let the truth exist as but an unspoken whisper between us.

But I could not. The sheer weight of that truth had altered our relationship in a manner that needed to be addressed, lest it destroy us.

Unable to approach but incapable of staying where I was, I gestured toward the nursery. "Would you like to see your daughter?"

The light, the hope—the shine that all came rising into his dark eyes inspired the same in my heart. "May I? The nurse said she's sleeping."

"We can do it quietly…come on."

Stepping up by him, my arm itching to at least brush against his, I clicked open the door as softly as I could and slipped through to the darkened room on its other side. The bed in which I'd awoken had been remade and was now decorated with a few charming stuffed creatures, including a cheerful little ventil with hand-sewn silk flowers in its antlers. I smiled at it, and when I turned, I found Malin stood in silence at the edge of the crib where the cherub, open-mouthed and drooling, dreamed of her bright future.

"I've decided to name her "Rosina,"" I told him in a whisper. "After the flowers you gave me in Valquist."

"Flowers, what—oh!" With a soft laugh, Malin turned his merrily crinkling eyes upon me. "That was so long ago. I'd already forgotten…I've been so preoccupied. "Rosina," eh…"

There was something so gentle about the slight crook of his smile; a little distant, a little mystified. How I wished my first child had been his! But—she *was* his.

And he was mine.

"Would you like to hold her?"

"Don't bother her," he implored, good naturedly tutting as I reached into the cot and gently drew her out anyway. Though she stirred, her little limbs giving a wriggle in protest, when I slid her into Malin's arms, she calmed.

"You've held her before," I observed, earning a quick flick of his eyes from the baby he gently supported.

"During your coma."

"I'm glad. I've felt terrible to think I wasn't conscious for her first days of life. Nellie is a very nice girl, just wonderful with her, but it matters to me far more that Rosina was held in those first days by someone who loves her. By her papa."

Something in his expression lightened just so—the effect of some set of muscles ironed by hope. "That was my thought," Malin murmured, his eyes on her face. "While you were asleep, I was visiting you both, oh, six, seven times a day, sometimes hours at a time...I hardly left this floor at all until you awoke. Not since we got you both back here. Oh! Rosina. Thecla...you are terribly generous to permit me the honor of parenting with you. Thank you."

I wanted to tell him I loved him, and to remind him he was my husband eternally, but I could not yet voice the words. Instead, as he bent to lay Rosina back in her cot, I took the wedding ring from the changing table.

"Will you put it on me again," I asked him, handing it over.

Moved, Malin studied the ring, then took my left hand in his very gently. While I melted beneath the pressure of his stare, he slid the gold band around my third finger. I exhaled at the already so familiar, so necessary, feeling of the metal. We had been married ten months, and I had been conscious for four of them.

Yet, in that time, I had come to feel as if we had been together forever.

Dinner was delicious terrestrial pheasant. Not having had meat in months, I savored every last bite while Malin explained the details of what he had done in my absence: how he found me, herded me, and cared for me. I marveled at his ingenuity, feeling more than a bit guilty as he explained the lengths to which he had gone—and his dedication to finding and caring for me, already lightly illustrated for me by Eleison, made me wonder if I had a right to be angry about the distant past.

Then, I would look at Malin more closely, and how I was

looking at him would change while I imagined him married to my mother. And the process would start over again, this terrible conflict cycling endlessly through my head: the love, the betrayal, the rationalization, the love, the betrayal again. How desperate I was for some catharsis!

After dinner, he invited me up to his suite for a drink. "I'm sure we can drink down here," I told him, earning a look of disappointment—and challenge. Agreeing, he called for more wine, and soon we were comfortable in the glass sitting area overlooking the park. The sofa in which he arranged himself faced the view, which I suppose was meant to encourage me to sit beside him. Instead, I filled the solitary armchair across from him, my wine balanced uneasily upon my knee while my husband studied me with an expression more feral than any of Eleison's.

"In five months, you only managed to grow more beautiful."

His smooth flirtation; the erotic electricity he evoked in me with a look, a word. I wasn't prepared to succumb. Aggrieved by his sensual power over me, I straightened up to raise the glass to my lips.

It was time to shatter the ceasefire that had, like an agonizingly tense note at an aria's climax, been sustained between us since my waking.

"Do I look like her to you?"

Malin's slim smile tightened. His eyes lowered to the glass whose stem he rolled between his fingers.

"I suppose," he admitted, "from certain angles, there is a vague resemblance...but, you said so yourself. You take after Rigel."

"The Overseer seemed to recognize me...at least, well enough to assume I already knew the truth."

"Her mistake was corrected."

My breath hitched. "You saw her?"

"Yes." He left the details of their interaction unspoken, instead studying his glass for a long moment before raising its contents to his lips. "She and your mother used to be friends."

"I gathered."

"And so were Parvati and I, if for no other reason than because it was the done thing. Giselle and I traveled to Valquist, oh, it seemed like every three or four months of the period in which she lived with me. Hm..."

His free hand, its elbow poised against the back of the couch, rested its index finger parallel along his lips. "I'm not sure I've ever spoken aloud of these times...or of her. Perhaps once or twice, or in passing, to give context to some thought. But—I have worked so hard to isolate my past from my present that I have also isolated myself."

"You don't have to be isolated." I sat forward. "In Valquist, Eleison grew very frustrated with me, and he told me, "You're not alone anymore." And he was right. None of us are alone anymore. Certainly not now—and never again, if I can help it."

He contemplated me very intently then, his hand still bracing his mouth, his dark eyes hooded as though to restrain his dreams. "I feel the need to carry these things to protect you, Thecla. Some of them, anyway."

"But other pieces of information, you kept to yourself because you knew they would interfere with your—conquest."

"Yes," he admitted. "I couldn't let you know the truth. Of course not. I took one look at you and that was all there was for me. First, I thought you would make just another pretty playmate, but oh, Thecla, my darling...won't you sit beside me, please?"

Though my cheeks and throat warmed with the desire in his voice, I shook my head. Malin's dark eyes narrowing, he said, "Very well," finished his glass, then got out of his seat to cross to me.

There, his hands resting upon my chair, he genuflected, then shifted the position of his arms to fold his fingers over my knee as though in prayer while we spoke. I frowned, insisting, "You'll hurt your joints, darling, don't," while he chuckled guiltily.

"Listen to you, allocating attention to my old man's concerns. You should command me to kneel before you round the clock. I deserve this penance, and worse; far worse."

While my hand slid over his, he leaned forward to kiss my palm, then my knee.

"What do you want to know about—everything?" His eyes raised to my face, boring there intently.

"I don't know. Did you intend to seduce me before you brought me to your home?"

"No."

"Did you ask Charlotte to keep the information from me?"

"Yes. Please, darling, don't blame her. She's just shattered over this."

Unable to help myself, I inhaled a little sharply and assured him, "She had ample reason and opportunity to defy your order, if only because sharing the truth with me was a moral necessity… and that goes for Eleison as well. I can forgive him more easily because he has his brother to mind. But Charlotte? With no one but herself to care for—and a woman, besides! She owed me the truth; had a sisterly duty to extend it, if nothing else."

"Unless she believed that withholding the truth would provide you with a better outcome."

"But that's for me to decide once I *have* the truth. It's my responsibility to choose my own outcome in life... And for all you know, even with that information, I still might have made the same choices."

"I suppose that is true. But...it would have been different." His thumb working tenderly over the well of my palm, Malin said while studying the contours of my flesh, "There would have been seedy undertones. A taboo shadow that, while a fun enough novelty in the bedroom, would only fetishize our love. Our wonderful love, which is—to me, anyway—so pure an experience. The purest experience of my life. Sex has never felt as sinless as it does with you, Thecla. How could I ever bear to taint that?"

Exhaling slowly, my eyes shutting, I bent my head and folded my body in half to press my forehead against Malin's.

"Did you love her?"

"No."

"Then why did you pursue her when she ran away?"

"Because I wanted to kill her." His words were unflinching as he stared back into my eyes. Slowly, my gaze remaining fixed on his, I straightened up into the embrace of the chair. "And your father, too. They deserved to die for humiliating me—and she most especially deserved to die for this." He touched his scar. I gasped slightly, not having realized, owing to his crafty conversational redirections, where it had come from. "That was the original idea, anyway. But...a year or two after, when I still hadn't found them, I had a much better idea. After all—why would I kill them and end their suffering? I could do something much worse."

Barely comprehending, I stared into the black eyes of my husband as his story wound steadily on.

"I sniffed around for midwives to hire," he explained.

"Those without scruples, or so I thought. Of course…the one that found you had scruples enough to refuse the duty for which she'd been paid. And I am more grateful for it now than I ever have been before."

My mouth opened in a numb shock. "Charlotte was supposed to kill me?"

"But she couldn't…of course, she couldn't. I was incensed. Sick with anger. All this time of planning, waiting, looking, wasting: here was the moment. And she couldn't do it. I took an auto to Lescaut as soon as the Event cleared, and waiting for me there was Charlotte, helping Rigel look after this…quiet baby. Giselle was already buried. And, rather than my enemy—"

His breast heaved. Malin glanced away, his hands tightening around mine.

"I saw Rigel as nothing but a wretched man who had lost his wife and had this one single reminder of her. And I decided… well…it seemed foolish to kill the infant then, when he hadn't attached to her yet. It wouldn't have been painful enough. So…I made a deal with him. In exchange for funding his daughter's care, I would take her from him when she was at the peak of life. When he had enjoyed raising her, and grown attached to her and her future—that was when I would steal her from him. What I would do with her, I didn't know…but I had no doubt you would be valuable."

His gaze somehow mystically softening in the center of his dark confession, Malin assured me, "I just had no idea *how* valuable."

The world tilted around me—yet his story brought me a sincere, albeit perverse kind of relief. Malin really *had* hated Giselle. At the very least, she had so offended him that any affection he felt had been mitigated. Lost in the annals of time.

And, if not for Charlotte, I might have been destroyed by that hatred.

Perhaps his love for me was not some echo after all.

"I've been terrible to her," I murmured softly, drawing Malin from a momentary spate of brooding into which he had lapsed with the completion of his tale.

"No. She understands. You are right, Thecla...we all owed you the truth, and we failed you. But I hope you see now why it was so difficult to share. How my own lust for revenge shames me! Especially now, with little Rosina sleeping in the nursery—to think I ever would have been gladdened by your destruction—"

A shudder wracked Malin's frame before he went on. "I owe Charlotte more than I could ever provide her. Though I know you've been terribly betrayed by her, and would like her to be fired—"

"No! No—" Dialing down the urgency in my tone as much as possible, I bit my lip and told him, "You must think *I'm* vengeful. I suppose I can't blame you for thinking that after the way things have happened."

Hands tightening around mine, his head lowering so his lips could brush kisses over my knee, Malin said, "I would endure the cruelest, most spiteful treatment if it meant keeping you with me, Thecla. To have the tender moments of your love, I'll pay any price."

"Please," I begged, "don't think of me as spiteful, don't—"

My eyes filled with tears. Wretched, I pulled my hand from his grip to cover my face in both my palms. Malin gasped my name and rose to take me in his arms, already consoling me, but I whimpered on.

"I wish I hadn't done that. I wish the ventil hadn't taken

me away, but, oh, Malin…who could understand? I was so sick with my headache, and all I knew was how *alone* I felt, and how afraid, and—and everything was so violent, so terrible—"

"It's all right," Malin murmured, kissing the top of my head and rocking me as gently as he had Rosina. "It's all right, Thecla. I know you had no control…I know, if you could have helped yourself, you would have at the very least turned back to a woman."

Shoulders trembling, I took a great breath of his chest. The rich, woody scent of him reinforced the reality of his presence. He *was* there with me. He *was* still in love with me. He *did* forgive me.

"I won't touch you if you don't want me to," Malin whispered against me, his lips and nose nuzzling ever-deeper into my hair, "but—would it be too much to ask that you lie down with me?"

Weakly, I asked, "Can you really resist touching me, even if I tell you not to?"

"Well—Thecla, darling, I…please."

Raising his head to tilt mine back, Malin gazed into my very soul. I felt him tugging at it in the nerves of my fingertips; in the front of my skull.

"You're right," he murmured, "I can't resist holding you, or touching you, or sometimes even kissing you…but you know I'll never take you if you don't really want it. You'll come to me when you're ready, I'm sure. Just rest with me, please. I've slept without you for so long!"

My lips trembled. "And I've slept without you. Without even understanding I was sleeping. Oh, Malin—please, yes…I want you to hold me."

Brilliant esperance once more glowing in his eyes, Malin enfolded my face in his hands and seemed about to kiss me. Freezing, his jaw clenching, he drew back altogether and made his way to my suite without waiting to see if I followed.

There it was I found him, his shoes off, his suitcoat in his hand. He hung it over the edge of the chaise near the darkened room's window before stretching out, still in his waistcoat, upon the bedspread.

My teeth dug into my lip. I stepped from my shoes and quietly regarded my husband, his eyes full of gentle sorrow, and love, and strangled desire. He reclined on one hip, his arms poised to take me in the second I stretched beside him. How beautiful he was in that moment! How tender.

How loving.

For he *did* love me. He loved me in a way that clamped me tight and shook me, his love the muzzle of a great beast that crushed the rabbit of my heart. It was a love so immense and so complete it took no quarter. It was a love that was willing to hurt me, to lie to me—to hold me captive, if that was what it took for me to accept it.

It was a love that swallowed me whole and left me trembling as I sank slowly into Malin's arms, my head beside his upon the pillow, my body pressing flush to his through the layers of our clothing.

"Oh"—his gasp was one of mournful, spiritual bliss—"Thecla—"

Silent, I fit my hand to his cheek. His eyes shut as if he were in terrible pain, with one hand raising from me to keep my palm still while he planted a kiss in it. I savored the warm caresses of his lips, then slowly pressed his cheek to turn his face toward mine.

"Are you really riftborn," I whispered to him, my thumb trailing around the edge of his orbital socket and up along his undamaged temple.

"Yes, angel…if you bring that dharmine around me, I'll prove it."

Pleasure flushed color through my cheeks. "Will you give him to me?"

"Of course. I'll give you anything. Ah…hm…" His hand, having slid up my bare arm and over my shoulder, came to rest so the tips of his fingers could barely slide into the back of my dress. "You're right…this is more difficult than I thought it was going to be."

My indulgent laughter inspired the smallest quirk of his serious lips. "I told you…"

"What a dog I am."

My laughter fading into a slight smile, I searched his eyes while saying, "No—you just love me. And I love you, Malin. And I—I want to make love to you so badly—"

His lips parted while, shutting my eyes against my own admission, I whispered on.

"But I feel so—rotten, so ashamed."

"Don't feel ashamed because of something I hid from you, darling. It hardly even matters. From a legal sense—"

"I'm not talking about that. I'm talking about—what I did to *you*."

"Oh! Thecla—"

My eyes batting, I said through the strain of new tears, "I've been horrible to you, Malin. Here I am, running around, kissing all the boys and taking everything you give me, all while getting cross with *you* when you show the least sign of—of being human. And then, while I was—absent, there you were, tortured by me—"

"I was just glad you were alive, darling."

"—all the while taking *care* of me, Malin…oh—"

Sobbing, I forced open my eyes to find his glazed with tears that deepened my sorrow.

"I love you more than I care about any way you've ever hurt me," I told him. "You didn't deserve—"

"Yes, I did."

"No! Stop, please. You didn't. I just—I was so betrayed, I felt so betrayed by everyone, everyone. Like there was no one I could trust. But I could have looked at the roses on that table and seen your love for me, and believed in it. I could have just believed in *you*, Malin. I'm sorry I didn't. I—I was angry, and hurt, and…I wanted to hurt you. And I'm so sorry I did, oh, please, forgive me—"

"I forgive you," he whispered hotly, his hands enfolding my face and drawing me closer, closer, until our noses brushed and there was hardly space to move without our brows or jaws or lips colliding. His arms rewound more tightly around me, one hand sliding up and down my back to stroke along with my half-contained sobs. The intensity of his voice lowered to a comforting murmur. "Of course, I forgive you. Sh…just look at me, Thecla."

Trembling a little, I did. Once the eclipse of his thumb stole away a fresh tear and disappeared, there was nothing in the world but the pitch of Malin's eyes.

"Thecla…I am going to reiterate the things I have kept from you…and I am going to try to speak around the final one, one I cannot—"

"Malin," I began, my tone a plea he stopped with the same kind thumb that then pressed across my lips.

"Please. This is a secret that *is* mine to hold. You have every other now. That your husband is himself an unregistered riftborn, and a hypocrite, and a liar; that he was also, for approximately six hours of Giselle's malingering and only in the most purely legal of senses, your stepfather, a role to which he has never esteemed so far as you are concerned; and, oh—hm, I should probably add now, darling..."

A certain coy, almost humorously self-effacing look unexpectedly changed his contemplative expression to something more impish.

"Eleison and I ended up in bed together while you were off roaming the park. I hope you aren't upset by the idea. It's not something we've talked about in any great detail, as such..."

The information dropped upon me in a pleasant shock that reddened my cheeks and stirred my loins. My intrigue and excitement immediately drew me into a more typical state of consciousness—and, accordingly, a more typical strain of banter with Malin, which gave me great joy and hope that this, our first argument, (and, in truth, really only notable one, if I can write such a thing without cursing us), would be overcome until it was but a blip in the long annals of our time together.

"You're *joking*—oh, Malin, darling..."

My hands slid over Malin's chest. His rum dark eyes lowered toward them, a low hum of pure male need rumbling from his half-parted lips as I begged to know more. "What happened? Was it fun? Oh...tell me about it! I wish I had been there..."

While one hand tightened in the depths of my hair in concert with his heavy sigh, the other flowed down my body to settle over my rear. When I didn't protest—could in fact not even hide the way pleasure sped my breath at his caress—he patted me gently, then far more firmly sank his fingers into the plush flesh by which he pressed me closer. While my stomach gave a jerk of pleasure to feel more clearly what my proximity had done to him, he intensified the effect by rocking my body back a few degrees to allow me to feel a hint of his weight. The pressure of love. How hot my face was! And he'd hardly more than patted me.

"I was so glad to see him when we were back here, and so alone without you…and grateful to him for looking after you. Of course, I wish you had been there, too….but, it was better that you weren't, in a sense. It was his first time fucking a man, he would have—"

"*He* fucked *you?*" Jaw agape all the wider, I gasped, then slowly released a noise like a giddy scream while shaking my devilishly laughing husband by his fine waistcoat. "*Malin!* And I missed it. Oh, you're right, it probably was for the best…but isn't his prick so big, so wonderful?"

My husband chuckled, as momentarily transported from our troubles as I was, his lustfully hooded gaze augmented by the crinkling lines of his teasing half-smile. "I told him it's amazing you can take it…but, then again, you get so hot for him, I shouldn't be surprised. Speaking of your special friends, though…did you have a good time with your boyfriend before he disappointed you?"

My countenance fell a little as I admitted, "Yes, but I think I spent the entire time feeling too badly about it to really enjoy his company."

His slight smile softened as, nostrils flaring, Malin glanced down my decolletage and said, "That's such a pity…I'm sorry to hear that."

"The devil you are!"

Though I laughed and teased him, he looked back up at

me very seriously. "No," he said, "I don't want you to feel guilty about it. Not about anything, darling."

My faded laughter left my face placid, but no longer joyless. "I can't help it. I feel like I've been cruel to you when you've only treated me kindly. Lovingly, whatever you once intended."

"Yes…that should be added to the list of what I kept from you. That, while he *was* your stepfather, your husband intended to kill you, then decided to use you more sadistically, before finally setting eyes on a lovely, funny, intelligent young woman who made him fall in love."

Still as a wax figure in his arms, I found myself studying Malin's perfect mouth. His lips were thinner than Eleison's semi-permanent pout, but so impossibly soft to kiss and oh, so talented at the art.

"I love you, Thecla. I love you. I'll give you anything you want. Kiss all the boys you like…all the girls, while you're at it. Turn into a deer and run away from me, and I'll spend the budget of a military skirmish on keeping you safe and well-fed and left to your own devices for as long as you like. Who you want fired, I'll fire. Who you want me to love, I'll love. Whatever child you bring me, whatever friend you want to keep, I'll—oh, darling, Thecla, please don't cry—"

"I don't deserve you." My words were a ragged whisper. He tutted and kissed my brow, then pressed his lips to my ear.

"Never say that," he told me, stroking my haunch down the length of my thigh and back up, gradually encouraging me to drape my leg over his hip. "You do deserve me. And I'm going to tell you why. But you must do me a favor, darling, and swear you will never tell anyone what I have told you. You must never tell

Eleison, or Rosina, or anyone. By the time the secret is out and everyone knows, it won't matter anymore."

"Is this your last secret?"

"Yes." His voice strangled. Malin drew back, his head resting upon the pillow with mine again. "And I cannot tell you all of it...because, as I said, it concerns something that is *mine*. The only thing that belongs to me, or any man. But...Thecla, I want you to know that, no matter what happens, you should never, ever be afraid...never. You are worthy of me—worthiest of all."

His hand came to rest upon my rear again.

"I'm going to live forever," he said simply, his tone the whisper of a true, wholeheartedly believed secret. "And it will be thanks to you."

My eyes widened in shock at the earnestly delivered absurdity. On seeing no trace of humor in his face, I pressed, "How is that possible? How could you know such a thing?"

"A little birdie told me, oh, almost ten years ago."

Could it be? "A fortune teller, perhaps?"

But he chuckled. "No...someone, something, else."

Some*thing*. While my lips pursed to reflect on Dinon's penchant for sharing the secrets of the future, Malin went on.

"What I have said is all I can say; but it is what I want you to know, my treasure, my beautiful jewel. Even if what has been promised to me is, against my expectation, denied to me, I will have spent my final years in your arms as the blessed recipient of your love. But...based on the source of this information, there is a strong probability that what I have told you is the truth. And it makes me all the more inclined to find you sinless. To love you furiously, blindly, with true unconditional passion. Thecla— Thecla."

Pained desperation had worked itself into his features, tightening his jaw and eyes and cheekbones.

Crying out, moved by the romance of the jarring claim, I clasped his face in my desperate hands and at long last pressed my mouth to his.

The gasp Malin choked on was one of disbelief as much as absolute ecstasy; pure celebration. He tightened the fist in my hair, then relaxed it to flatten his hand along the back of my neck. While his tongue urgently leapt to meet with mine and carried the low groans of his voice into my throat, I scratched through his scalp, the back of his neck, the elegant column of his spine beneath the silk of his waistcoat.

"Darling"—he gasped with joy as I twisted my head away— "oh, Thecla! Let me kiss you again—"

But, avoiding his lips, I lowered my chin to let my brow contact his jaw. "I want your kisses, Malin—I want to believe what you've said. But...how *can* I deserve your love after all this? After what I've done?"

A low noise of frustration, a kind of grumble, revved through his body. "You deserve it because I say you deserve it... but, then again...maybe you know best. Maybe you don't deserve it yet."

His tone changed. He looked at me very curiously. "After all," Malin continued in that low, smooth tone that, through prior association, fired my blood with crippling desire, "if you feel like a wicked girl...a dirty girl...then you can't appreciate anything I do for you. You're not ready to receive my love without penance, are you, precious."

My raging heat was amplified by the teasing with which he tested the waters of my interest. "I do feel wicked," I agreed, the pain in my face and whispering voice genuine as I looked to Malin for help. "And I have so many strange and wicked thoughts about this, all of this. About your relationship with me."

He once more patted my rear, each slow, gentle strike of his palm against my covered flesh promising something so much harder on the horizon.

"I think I've been looking at this all wrong," he suddenly said, so matter-of-factly I was taken aback and worried I had just upset him.

I frowned. "How so?"

"If you really didn't want me to kiss you, to hold you—to fuck you—you would tell me the safeword, wouldn't you."

My breath froze in my throat, each one of my fingertips growing numb in response.

After staring into me with that metaphysically measuring look, Malin lowered his eyes and sat up.

"I'm going to whip you, Thecla, but I'd prefer to do it in my bedroom upstairs…if you would be so good as to come with me."

My throat too dry to speak, I nodded. With a tightening of his cheeks as though he fought back a smile, Malin extended his hand to help me from the bed.

Though the elevator only had two floors to travel, at the shutting of the doors he caught me by the back of the neck and held me for the pressure of his savage kiss. I groaned, nearly choking back a sob at the ferocity of it, and could place my hands upon his chest but could not convince him, by pushing or squirming, to release me.

And, with the passing of each second, I wanted him to all the less.

"How are you physically," he asked with gruff concern, his eyes searching mine for any final expressions of true resistance.

I had none. I could not resist him. "I'm just like I was last week," I told him, my voice a quivering whisper. "When I was in Valquist."

"When you were killing men in Valquist, you sinful girl; you murderous slut. Is your dog around?"

As the doors opened, Malin pushed me into the stern penthouse suite of the property. For its central sitting area and the two wings extending on either side of a vast overlook of glass, it seemed like the web of a spider. Vaguely understanding he referred to the dharmine, I told him, "No—it hasn't found me since I awoke. It wants me. It's reaching for me. But it needs me to…*call* to it if it's to reach me in any degree of haste. That, and—"

I colored about the cheekbones, but, his hand sliding around the base of my neck as he walked me to the bedroom, Malin pressed with interest, "What is it?"

"That appetite it has. Those men, it killed them five months ago. It must be starving by now."

"Oh, I'm sure it's gotten by…how sweet you are to worry about it." While I scoffed and protested, Malin stopped me in the doorway of the sprawling bedroom to brush his nose against mine. "Well? Don't you?"

"It repulses me…I despise it, yet it serves me so well. Unquestioningly."

"Nonsense. It's fiddling about, playing games with you. Using you as is inappropriate for a true servant. But…don't worry, my pet. Just like I promised, I'll make it another gift to you."

My heart seized at the idea. "Will it really be so easy?"

"Never doubt my way with animals, my trembling doe. Are you afraid? You should be…you've been an awful brat. The most ungrateful little harlot I've ever met. The only reason I should have told you the truth of our prior relation was to take up the task of tanning your hide, but it became my duty as your husband, anyway. Go take off your dress…I'll be back."

While he disappeared into the adjoining bathroom and, blindsided, trembling, scarlet with arousal, I contorted to loosen the laces of my bodice, my imagination drank in the room. Was this where Eleison and Malin consoled one another in my absence? Had it been fierce, or tender? I longed to watch and, ruminating on it, fell into a sort of trance while I pushed away the fabric and stepped out of the gown. As a consequence of my slow, dreamy motions, I was caught there in my black underwear and bustier when Malin emerged from the bathroom with the strop of his straight razor hanging from his hand.

I flinched back from the bedside upon which he tossed the heavy looking leather strap. My blood raced with delight even as I protested, "That looks so painful!"

"You know what to say if you don't really want it… Thecla…come here."

At the snap of his fingers, my stomach twisted. What would have been an insult any other time relegated to another sweet aphrodisiac, I hurried to stand before him and gasped as he caught me by the arms to roughly kiss me. Again, I crumpled beneath the plunging desperation of his tongue, the hungry theft of my breath: then he tore back from me, sat upon the edge of the bed, and patted his knee.

The sudden numbness in my lips matched what had already overtaken my fingers. Heart pounding in its cage, I slid over Malin's lap. My rear was pushed into the air by his knee beneath my pelvis, as well as by the height of the bed, which kept my legs stretched to the floor at a rough forty-five degree angle.

"I just want to be clear," he told me, sliding his hand over my rump through a veil of lace that hid practically nothing, "I am jealous, and angry, and hurt, Thecla…but not as much as I am desperate to no longer be jealous or angry or hurt and instead be *happy* together with you."

"That's exactly how I feel," I whispered, the words easier to say when I couldn't face him.

"Then let's accept each other's flaws. Leave the past behind us." His hand slid into the dark fronds of my hair, fingers curling against my scalp as he said, "Start fresh."

The words had an unusually plaintive note given our respective positions; a yielding quality that indicated not a demand, but a request. I inhaled, at once aware of how desperately I, also, wanted to start fresh. Even more than I had been by our marriage, I had been changed by the truth: by Malin's mistakes, and Eleison's, and Glenn's, and most of all by my own. I had already noted the great change within me since waking from the animal. Now, at last connected to Malin in as truthful a way as I could ever hope to be until the time was right, I wanted to throw everything away and begin again to celebrate that change.

"Yes, please, sir," I whispered as he stroked my hair. "I love you, Malin."

"Thecla—Thecla. I love you, too."

The heavy leather of the strap cracked down upon my rear.

I cried out, my entire body twitching across his lap.

"I can't tell you how happy I am that you're yourself again," he went on, his hand tightening to a fist in my hair. The second strike came, equal in measure yet somehow more intense than the first. While he let the heavy strop do the work against my twisting upper thighs and flinching backside, the thumb of that possessive fist ran along the skin behind my ear.

"I thought about you every day, darling, all day, all the time…it's a miracle Gudrune hasn't fallen to pieces, I've been so preoccupied. You selfish little animal! While you enjoyed the idyllic wanderings of an innocent doe, I was sick with worry."

Gasping at the fire of each strike, I clutched the quilted bedspread and protested, "I hardly knew—I wasn't myself, oh! Sir—"

"You can make any excuse you want. That doesn't change how I've pined for you, Thecla, every day, every night…especially at night. This empty bed; an empty hand. I was very grateful for the reprieve afforded me by Eleison."

The next snap had an extra sting, as the strop wrapped just slightly around the edge of my cheek and left a welt along the back of my thigh. While I hissed in pain, Malin responded by sliding down my underwear to expose my rear.

He dropped the implement at once, his teeth audibly gritting as he groaned, "Oh, Thecla, darling, you hot little bitch…I think I'll use my hand."

With an economy of movement that indicated his expertise, Malin folded his left arm around my waist and raised the right to snap his hard hand quickly down again. I cried out, kicking, looking back to watch him spank me with a joy I couldn't hide.

"Oh, Malin! Oh—Master, yes, I missed you, yes, oh, please, I've been so wicked—"

Each spank landed harder than the last, the resulting bonfire developed overtop my existing welts surely a sight to behold. At the very least, Malin was riveted to the sight. He sucked in a breath while he paused to slide a finger down between my thighs.

"*Malin,*" I moaned as he brushed the dampening signs of my excitement, "my husband, my good, devoted husband—"

And my stepfather, said a little voice in the back of my head.

Yet—at the whisper, a kind of perverse shudder rattled out through me. The absolute decadence of it, I would have then been ashamed to admit, provoked a devious thrill. Just as the grotesque nature of any pleasure achieved with the dharmine sweetened that pleasure threefold, so did I suddenly understand the taboo shadow Malin had wished to avoid.

I was not so sure I wanted to avoid it.

The next wave of strikes began again, sharper, more frequent. Gradually, they adjusted down, and the pressure of his rapid blows against my upper thighs had a way of quivering all through me.

"Malin," I gasped, "your hand is so heavy—worse than a paddle, oh, darling—"

"You say that as though you don't like it…I can tell you do, though…it's got you dying for a good, hard fucking. That's what you want, isn't it?"

As he stopped spanking me for the moment, his middle finger instead eased slowly, steadily into me. We gasped together at the digit's delving into the slick channel. I ground my forehead down against the bedspread, begging, "Please, yes! Yes—Malin! Make love to me—fuck me! Take what's yours as my husband—oh—yes—"

His breathing ragged with lust, Malin raised his hands to unfasten the hooks of my bustier. We let it fall to the floor. Then, pushing my underwear all the way down my legs and off my feet, he slid me from his lap and rolled me upon my back on his bed.

"Ah"—the pain in his cry was profound, and true—"ah, Thecla! Oh—"

His hand pressed to his scar, then slid up into his hair while he said in a tone of lamentation, "You're even more beautiful than my mind made you out to be in your absence. Oh...gorgeous, Thecla..."

His expression wild, Malin bent over me and was no longer focused on undressing himself. Instead, his mouth clamped over mine. His hands ran over my stomach, down my hip, then slipped between my thighs. Groaning, I spread my knees and marveled at the frictionless glide of his big fingers south and north again, never penetrating but always teasing that they might before they slid back up to my clitoris. As pleasure wept from me, I arched my hips against his petting and moaned into his mouth.

"Oh"—he pulled his mouth away with a gasp, his hand still working—"that's it, my good little strumpet...Master loves it when you're dripping wet and desperate for a cock, Thecla..."

"Yes! I am, oh, sir, please—Master, oh my husband, I missed you, oh, yes!"

He watched my face, entranced, his fingers stroking me to an ever more intense state of erotic bliss. Each time they slid down, his fingertips nudged farther into me; a bit deeper into the confines they barely dared to breach.

"You really are just like before, aren't you...oh, my jewel..." While his fingers curled into the slick center of my body, I gasped and clutched at the fabric of his shirt. His thumb contorted to find my clitoral nerve, and as his fingers coaxed within me, savoring their opportunity to reexplore the secret chambers of my body, the pleasure that built left me lewdly splayed in encouragement of his caress.

"Even for you," he remarked wryly, breathless as my fingers trembled down the buttons of his shirt, "you're awfully wet...oh, Thecla...just soaked, aren't you..."

"I need you so badly, Malin. I've missed you—I want you…"

"And I want you…darling! I want you more than anything. When Eleison was fucking me, all either one of us could talk about was you…you're my every fantasy, the star of every dream and nightmare. Thecla…ah, Thecla, my hot little wife, that's right, that's it, let me feel it—"

"Oh! Malin, oh, sweet hell—oh, yes, yes, yes—I'm sorry, I'm so sorry, I love you—!"

His mouth fell upon mine while the orgasm claimed me, contorting my limbs and annihilating my sense of space and self. I felt it in my frontal lobe, my fingers and toes. A terrible veil was torn from my eyes, which saw clearly for the first time in months. When I came to, the tidal wave ebbing away from the ruins of my being, my hands were upon Malin's face. He had freed his fingers to finish stripping off his clothes. There it was—there *he* was. I gasped and reached for him as soon as I recognized the golden instrument bobbing free of his trousers; and, as I slid my hand around it, he shuddered to bend his head over mine.

"That sordid undercurrent is there now." His nose brushed mine while he slid between my welcoming legs, his hand running along my open thigh. "I could ignore it before, angel, but now that we both know—I feel closer to you, yet more like a cad than ever…"

"You are," I whispered, raising my head to kiss him. The heavy weight of his cock made me gasp as it probed, then nestled against the swollen cleft open between my thighs. "Yes! Oh, yes, you're a cad, Malin—a conniving, evil, cruel old rogue—my stepfather, oh—oh *yes*—!"

That conniving, evil, cruel old rogue's cock pushed slowly, torturously, into me. The pace of his impalement felt so good all I could do was rock my head back and scream in pleasure. Inspired, he plunged deeper, and faster, and a shuddering moan wracked him along with me. Soon, his hand sliding beneath my rear, his cock plowing down into me, Malin found a natural, nearly barbarous pace that was so perfect it only served to reinforce my dysphoric sense of having lost no time at all. By the stroke, he grew more brutal, his breath panting from between his bared teeth while he pounded me full with his wonderful prick.

"I'm sorry I hurt you," he whispered between his bruising kisses, one hand fit just below my jaw while the other anchored my hips to leave me accessible to his strokes. "I'm sorry I had to keep anything from you—but, Thecla! I would do it again, a million times over again, to have you! Thecla—"

"Malin, oh! Darling, harder, please, yes, just that way—I know, I know I should care, I know that I should! But oh, darling, I can't...I can't, I can't. I don't care. As long as—as long as you love me for me—"

"I do! Of course I do, oh, angel—my dearest partner of greatness, my only peer—"

"Then it doesn't matter." Whispering hotly, I caught Malin's face and stared deeply into the devouring voids of those somehow alien eyes. "Nothing matters, Malin. Nothing, nothing. I want your child now more than ever."

"Thecla!"

"I forgive you." I stroked the scar along his brow while his eyes misted over. "After all you've done for me, before and after I found out—the truth doesn't matter. I love you, Malin...my husband."

"Oh—sweet Madame Farrow—Thecla—"

He groaned, bowing his head over mine for another kiss. The static of our contact was sharpened by the hammer of his pelvis into mine, each push down into and against me another slap of pressure against the enflamed nerve at the crown of my sex. I cried out, open to him, limp in his grip to allow him complete access to my body, my mind, my soul. My breath slipped into his lungs, and his into mine; his tongue penetrated to my very throat, working in time with the thick, throbbing cock that avidly reclaimed its territory; our hearts hammered together, the sweat of his chest hot against mine and leaving me to feel as though I were about to combust.

Above me, his body tensing, Malin seemed poised to do the same.

"When you cum," he commanded me, "I want you to call out to the dharmine."

"Oh, but darling—"

"Do as I say. Summon your pet closer at the peak of your pleasure. Invite it to the feast. One of these times, it won't be able to resist appearing before even me, the reward exceeding the risk. Thecla, sweet girl, oh, my radiant wife. Home!" Laughing, catching my chin, he admired me with the kind of joy he showed on our wedding day. "My wife is finally home."

"Never let me leave again," I begged, inspiring a dark laugh from him as we reached our crescendos.

"I won't, Thecla…rest assured—ah, hell—"

"Oh!" The sudden degree of additional stiffness within me made it impossible to resist the edge where Malin had me suspended. I slipped down the cliff face, paralyzed by my beloved's appreciative stare into my eyes until at last I remembered to cry, "Oh—! Dinon—Dinon, my servant, oh, come to me, come to me! Dinon—sweet dharmine, oh, sweet fuck, come feast on your mistress's love for her husband. Oh, joy—"

Watching my face, riveted as always to hear me calling for another man, Malin hammered home a few more overwhelming times. As my orgasm reached its height and I felt, in the base of the pleasure, the dark throbbing backbeat of Dinon's eager response, my husband's pace reached its peak and crashed back down in the form of a few steadier, deeper, slower strokes that brought the climax bursting from him. As he gasped my name, Malin descended upon me to kiss me with one hand stroking blindly into my hair.

In the aftermath, as both our eyes boiled with tears, he pressed my head to his warm chest as though to pull me into his heart.

"Your next child will be mine by blood," he announced, tipping my head back to look into my face with absolute confidence. "But, without having yet had that privilege, Thecla…I am so happy to have you home. So happy to have a proper family with you. Thank you for letting me be with you. Thank you for opening your heart to me."

38

To SAY WE were altogether healed would be wrong. In those first days of our recovery, Malin and I tiptoed overcautiously around one another's lingering bad feelings. I felt somehow afraid to even acknowledge the passage of time by asking about what had happened in Gudrune during my leave, or by inquiring whether Malin had seen fit to write to my stepmother and sister on my behalf. He had, I found—and had announced to the people of Gudrune that, discovering myself to be pregnant, I had fled home to our territory from my Valquist tour and was shying from the public eye until such time as the baby and I were ready to debut.

When we had been fully reunited for three days which he took off work, he reluctantly asked if I would be willing to subject Rosina to a few press photos of the three of us together. I think, when each of us realized how happy the other was to think of such a thing, it suddenly dawned on us that we didn't *have* to hold on to any kind of bad feelings for one another. That we could choose to move on, and to forgive, and to do it completely.

So, without discussing it at any further length, we did. The cover of a certain bi-monthly magazine published out of Saalast was, that same week, devoted entirely to a picture I still treasure: of me, smiling at Rosina's gentle fussing in my arms while Malin, out of frame, rested his ring-ornamented hand upon my shoulder.

Oh, we were both smitten with the girl, as was Eleison… and all of us were very grateful for Nellie, who dealt with those things that would, in other books by other storytellers, make for relatable and perhaps heartwarming tales of childrearing. The truth, however, is that I have not in either instance of parenting had the typical experience of motherhood, or even for that matter of birth. I was less responsible for the intricacies of caring for my own child than I had been for my sister when I was barely out of the nursery. When the baby was not hungry or in need of changing, I took great pleasure in holding her or singing to her. A few times in those early weeks of her life I bathed her, though I confess that novelty soon wore off and became just another of Nellie's tasks.

I must sound so very cold to you! It is true that I never had the opportunity or desire to develop a knack for the custodial aspects of raising a child; but I adore my children, and would do just anything for them, and in those early days most especially, I was so heart-full of love for Rosina that I must have spent eight hours a day doing nothing but holding and singing and reading to her.

But she had to sleep sometime, no matter how sporadic or combative. And when she did, the loom was always ready for me.

I seemed to work best on my tapestries when they had a definite purpose aside from their contribution to the developing series. For instance, the first had been meant as Malin's wedding present; the second, the small one in our villa, came as an inspiration during our honeymoon, and had been meant to communicate my patience with those very secrets that went on to cause us such problems. That was not to say that the next tapestry, completed in the months after our return to Saalast, had been sub-par—but it had not flowed as well as had the first in the series.

Now, with the child sleeping in the other wing and Malin joining us to complete our happy family when his work was finished in late afternoon, my time was bounded into a more regimented schedule than ever. This restraint somehow had the effect of instantly throwing me into the flow, I suppose because now I had a clock to beat. I would simply sit and marvel at the grace of the threads weaving in fulfillment of the template I designed in Valquist.

And, as I worked on it, I oftentimes pondered the dharmine.

There was no doubt about it. As, night on night, Malin coached me to call up the creature while stoking my pleasure to ever-higher peaks, the presence of the dharmine grew in me until it was clearly on the property with us—albeit, always at a distance just slightly too far to be detected by ordinary senses. Knowing Malin was on the lookout for him, Dinon hid himself from me. He shunned the building altogether and neglected even my dreams. Malin was right…it was a poor servant that served me only at its own leisure.

I did not dream of the black loom during this time; but more than once, in the dark of my bedroom—while Malin slept and I, glad to listen to his breathing, watched some distant wildlife prowling across the park I admired with soothing half-memory—I caught hints of what I thought might be the dark shape of a man watching our private fortress from the trees beneath us, or from a hill in the distance.

Even when I called to him in such moments, however, Dinon refused to come to me. I confess to feeling put out, much as one does when the housecat abruptly takes to favoring some other member of the family without any just cause. But Malin took the defiance lightly.

"I'm sure it will give in and appear before us," he consoled me, kissing my neck while I pouted in half-jest. "Any night, my angel, any night, you'll have your pet...must keep *my* pet happy, mustn't I..."

He certainly did his best to. Throughout the first weeks of my reunion with Malin, I did find myself increasingly happy. Though at first I had been eager to return to Saalast, I was growing content to remain where we were until Malin tamed the dharmine in what was a relatively isolated and hassle-free location to do so. We wanted for nothing, anyway. Eleison was there with us, and Rosina, of course, and everything was well taken care of.

Taken care of thanks in no small part to Charlotte.

If there was one thing I *was* unhappy about in those peaceful weeks, it was her. Oh, how embarrassed and heartbroken I was to reflect on the things I had said of her, *to* her. To remember all that while knowing she saved my life was an unbearable punishment. My gut twisted in horror every time I saw Charlotte and, ashamed but hardly knowing where to begin, I avoided her for something like six days whenever I heard her on my floor.

Then, one afternoon, my weaving was interrupted by an unusual knock, and I looked back, expecting Nellie with the baby in her arms. "Come in—oh—"

Her expression neutral but braced for difficulty, Charlotte stepped into the room and folded her hands over the manila folder she carried. "Madame," she said with a little curtsy.

"Oh, Charlotte—" My shoulders slumped. "You know— you really *can* call me Thecla. I would prefer it, even."

"If that is what you prefer," she said placidly, stepping forward with the folder extended. "I asked Master Farrow when you awoke if I might have this brought to us for your perusal…it just arrived today."

Even as I asked, "What is it," my eye fell upon the faded label that told me all I needed to know. *Terranova, Giselle*

"I was dishonest with you when we arrived in Saalast. I'm sorry." As, amazed, I flipped through the scant collection of documents and photographs pertaining to my mother's alteration, Charlotte said, "I went up to Sigma Labs on Master's request and pulled every string I still had to squirrel this file out before that godawful doctor got his hands on it."

"Then your mother…?"

Despite herself, Charlotte managed a paper-thin smile. "She's in a Karris rest home. My cousin looks after her."

With a little scoff—not offended by the deception so much as amused —I shut the folder. Charlotte had already turned to the door, intent on escaping, but I cleared my throat.

"You know," I said delicately, "Malin told me what you did for me."

It was not often Charlotte hesitated before speaking. "It's not what I did do, Thecla, but what I couldn't do."

"And I'm so grateful, Charlotte. Oh—Charlotte—I'm sorry, too sorry for words—"

"It's not necessary for you to apologize."

"Yes, it is. Of course it is. You saved my life!"

"And I lied to you, too. Just like Malin and Eleison…and just like them, I'm sorry. You deserve better than fabrications. Because I was too selfish to risk my comfort, all I could do was warn you that the more you loved Master Farrow, the more you would be hurt by him… And wasn't I right?"

Those first country house days seemed so long ago, yet not so long ago at all; a lifetime ago, and yesterday. Only just over a year— and a year already, somehow already a year of this strange dream that each day became more anticipated, normal. More my life.

"Yes," I confessed to her, worrying my hands before me. "Yes, Charlotte, you were right…but his love, that same love—it's healing, too. It can be. I think it's healthy to forgive, you know, when it's within reason, and I just—oh, Charlotte—"

A certain liquid shimmer brightening her eye, Charlotte looked up at the corner of the ceiling while I hurried to embrace her. "I hope you'll forgive *me*—"

"I keep telling you, Thecla, it's all right." One hand raising to pat me upon the back of the shoulder, Charlotte gradually gave up trying to encourage me to let her go early and instead returned my embrace. "We're all just relieved that you're back…and I'm relieved the air's been let out." Sighing, shaking her head as I unwound my arms from her, (and stepped away at last convinced she hadn't come to hate me in the past five months!), Charlotte looked at me in deep scrutiny. Beholding me in some way she hadn't before. "I'm a little surprised you're still here…but, maybe I shouldn't be."

"He hasn't exactly encouraged me to leave."

"His encouragement shouldn't be a problem for you. Weaving ropes and climbing out of windows?" The crisp white edges of her teeth flashed with her soft laugh. "You're resourceful. And, well—"

"What is it?"

My heart swelled as, with a glance toward the door she quietly shut all the way, Charlotte was at once herself with me. In a second, it was like nothing had ever happened between us and we were still in Saalast, our friendship—her mentorship—uninterrupted.

"Perhaps I shouldn't disrupt your image of Master Farrow, but he came to me in terrible condition about two weeks before the child's birth. It had occurred to him that he really *might* need to let you go; that he was willing to keep you here a long time, but it had suddenly dawned on him your heart might not be moved, and he needed to prepare for the possibility. I confess I was not particularly charitable in what I said to him on the subject, as I had been interrupted from my sleep and had spent the previous five months nursing my own irritations over the consequences of his poor decision."

"What did you tell him?"

She shrugged. "That he'd be lucky if you ever saw your way to bedding him again…and he is lucky, very lucky."

"More persuasive than lucky," I argued, cut off with a yelp when Charlotte slapped the back of my hand.

"He *is* lucky, Thecla. When you're dealing with these men of yours, never forget—no matter how powerful and seductive they are, *you* are the one privileging *them* with your presence. It's not the other way around. He can be persuasive *and* lucky you would deign to forgive him."

Inhaling a little, I admitted with a guilty laugh, "I still can't help feeling I've done plenty myself that requires forgiveness."

Charlotte shrugged. "Not against Malin. He made the decision to obsess his way across the continent to ensure you were safe. Why did he *have* to be there? He could have been in Saalast, running the territory in person rather than remotely, and left the logistics of your care to someone else. I have no doubt his support inspires love in you, and makes you feel very special...but it is both his duty to see that you're cared for and his personal choice to do it himself. It is his choice to *actually* love you, instead of to perceive you as some whimsical accoutrement of his bed and ballrooms. Malin is an adult; near infinitely more an adult than you, I should remind you, at least insofar as the time he's spent at it. While I know he was stung and frightened by your flight, I also know he had and has something that you don't, Thecla: the power to *do* something about it when the person he loves defies him. Frankly, the way I see it—"

Charlotte opened the door of my workroom with an aggressive wrench of the knob.

"You punished him for deceiving you, and he did his best to accept that punishment with dignity...and the fact that he *has* accepted that punishment, when coupled with your decision to forgive his errors, makes me suspect you two will be together for a long time."

I hoped forever.

At the very least, Malin's audacious claim rang through my ears as Charlotte left me to my work.

What had he meant by that? He told me not to be afraid—afraid of what? I turned that intimate moment over and over in my mind, but I dared not speak on it again. That was part of the trust, that silence. But I could not help speculating. Did he mean he would pursue alteration? I was not sure first-generation altered individuals lived forever, per se, but they did live a long time. Or—perhaps he referred to some phenomenon of his riftborn nature?

The silver eyes of a bad dream flashed into and through me and then disappeared. I shivered as I left my loom to dress for dinner.

Due to some call-in conference of Malin's, Eleison and I had the chance to eat together at a dinner table for the first time in what seemed like ages. How his demeanor had changed with his liberation! I'd hardly had a chance to enjoy it, as he had given Malin ample space and time with me to allow us to reconnect. But oh, having him there at dinner, I found him different at once. His collar was loose and his manner, posture, smile—all were at such ease that it felt like I saw him *truly* for the first time. Best of all, Eleison was different in the way he interacted with me. He coached me to change chairs at the table so I sat beside him, then pulled my seat close enough to slide his arm around me while we unwound with a digestif. It struck me while he laughed at my reaction to some bad joke of his that this was what had truly been missing in our relationship. At last, we were permitted to be friends.

And when, as Eleison teased that he had expected me to convert to a vegetarian diet after our time as animals, Malin stepped into the room, that must have been the first time my mate didn't release his embrace as some automatic response to my husband's presence. He showed no sign of shifting at all, in fact, and smiled. "Hey, Malin."

"There you are," I said, plucking up a grape left upon my plate. "We missed you at dinner."

"So sorry, dear, had to eat early…just thought I'd drop in when I heard from Charlotte that you two still at the table." One big hand fit to the back of my chair while Malin bent to receive the grape. With it tucked into his cheek, he kissed me, his tongue sliding coaxingly beyond my lips until he pulled away. Then he straightened, his eyes glittering as he rapidly chewed the grape, and Eleison's contemplative face was revealed. I smiled at my mate shyly, not wanting to incite his jealousy; when he smiled back, there was something about it that was new to me. The smile of one relenting to some indulgence, as when the waiter presents the dessert menu after a luxuriant meal.

Malin swallowed to speak. "I'm glad to find you here. I was hoping to catch you two before you grew occupied…would you consider joining me upstairs for a few drinks?"

"That sounds fun," agreed Eleison, delighting my heart… and my body. "I don't know, though. It's Thecla's call. You feel up to tolerating both of us, baby?"

That grand old fire licked out from my chest and across all my limbs more fiercely than it ever had in my life. Stomach tightening, I said in a tone of playful reluctance, "So long as you both promise to be interesting, and to avoid discussing politics or gun engineering."

"Ouch," said Eleison, slapping a hand over his heart while I accepted chuckling Malin's help out of my seat.

"No one can be fascinating all the time," I told my mate. "I know when I talk about weaving you start entertaining yourself by undressing me with your eyes."

Poorly combating his smile, Eleison opened his mouth to respond, but Malin jerked me around to look into those glinting jet irises of his.

"I assure you, Thecla, neither of us needs you to talk about anything for us to spend our time doing that."

Eleison rose from his seat with a meek shrug and a spread

of his hands that only deepened the scarlet of my face. "That is true…very true. Shall we?"

"You're trembling," Malin observed of me, causing Eleison to pause before he could fully step in the direction of the elevator. "What's the matter, angel?"

"I'm—oh, nothing, nothing at all. I'm just cold, of course."

"Mm." His arm tightening me against his body while, with a handsome smirk, Eleison called the elevator, Malin studied my face. "Could it be you're frightened of something?"

"Oh, no, Master, please. Nothing like that at all."

"Then it must be that you're excited about something." Sliding his palm beneath mine and regarding my twitching, adrenaline consumed hand upon his, Malin wove our fingers to lead me hand in hand to the elevator. "I wonder what it is you could be so excited about…should I try to guess?"

"You're a very cruel man to tease me this way."

"I'm genuinely curious…what do you think is going to happen, darling?"

"We're going to write poetry," said Eleison wryly, holding the elevator doors open for us as the car arrived, "and weave flower crowns, and play hopscotch."

Chuckling, Malin agreed, "That's certainly one way to put it," while the doors slid shut before us.

The car lurched up. Eleison slid his arm around my waist and said to his former employer, "Before I forget: You're going to keep the master apartment in the country house, right?"

"Oh, no, I've already had them move me out of it—the master suite, anyway." With a wry smile, Malin nudged me with the same hand that still held mine. "Seems I'll be staying in your old quarters when you're sick of hosting me in your boudoir."

"My room is your room, Malin, just like it is Eleison's…I never tire of you, neither one of you."

"Then you see, Eleison?" As the elevator doors opened once again, Malin said, "No need for me to worry about a bedroom when we visit your estate. I'll always have somewhere to sleep. Just take what's yours, and enjoy it."

"I will." Eleison spoke with a glad light in his eye, a certain edge of happy disbelief to his smile. "You know, I think I'm still in shock."

"Please, this was inevitable." While Eleison led me toward the bedroom, Malin released my hand to collect a bottle of wine and a tray of three glasses arranged upon the bar. "As soon as I realized you were Thecla's mate, I knew your days as my footman were numbered."

Looking at Eleison, I clarified, "But you are still employed with us?"

"That's right…cavalier servente of Gudrune."

What a career title! Not only for the traditional connotations of the cicisbeo, but for the ambiguity of the formal phraseology. "So does that make him your cavalier," I asked my husband while Eleison settled into the sofa, situated in the small sitting area across the room from the bed, "or mine?"

"It makes him ours in equal measure." A sly smile flitting across my husband's face as I lowered into Eleison's lap, Malin set down the tray and opened the bottle while speaking. "I am Gudrune, and therefore so are you. When Master Farrow dies, his appointed heir will take control; and, as it is possible Master Farrow's children will not be fully grown when he dies, he has appointed his consort the next Matrix of Gudrune. What's mine is yours, angel…the Overseer will probably contest it, but let's not worry about that today."

My mouth opened and shut a little, the gravity of the sentiment rendering me mute. Me, Matrix of Gudrune? Permanently, not as steward between heirs? Would I be able to cope with that, especially given what would be required for me to take the position?

If he was sure he was going to live forever, why was he always so preoccupied by plans for his death?

Now, of course, I feel silly not to have understood it. At the time, I could only protest, "I realized I would have to maintain your affairs for some time, at least until your heir could take over. But—*me*—"

The cork popped. "You told me you were interested in learning the duties of the position, didn't you? You'll learn more and more as we spend more time together…particularly once we return to Saalast. No need to worry…you will have a bevy of advisors, and Eleison, of course."

"What a light-hearted turn our conversation has taken," my mate rebuffed while Malin chuckled over the sound of pouring wine.

"I only mean to say…*you* are Gudrune, my pretty little rib. Just as much as I am." Upon setting the bottle down, he plucked up the first glass and handed it to me. "Who is to say where you end and I begin, at least so far as authority over our employee is concerned? Let's not worry over the details. He's your mate before he's anything else to either one of us, anyway."

After handing Eleison his glass, Malin settled next to us and draped a hand over the legs I slid over his lap. He, meanwhile, fit an arm along the back of the sofa, behind Eleison's shoulders.

A circuit completed, electrons rushing eagerly between our bodies.

"I just can't seem to believe how happy I am," Malin

murmured, raising his arm from my lap to bring the wine to his lips. "After these long months, to have everything at peace—I feel like I'm dreaming. I would be so grateful if this would continue."

"It will." Smiling, I leaned toward my husband and brushed my lips across his for a kiss that paused his respiration. Malin shut his eyes, absorbing every second, responding with the same steady sensualism I delivered, until at last I leaned back into Eleison's arms. My head poised against his shoulder, I gazed expectantly into my mate's fiery eyes. He didn't hesitate. One hand, warm and wide, cradled my cheek; but as his mouth found mine, that vast palm slid down my throat and over my heart, where it rested just above the shelf of my breasts. Feeling my pulse, Eleison murmured something into my mouth and bore down against me, his tongue more demanding of mine by the second.

When he raised his head enough to look me in the face, his stare ferocious with desire, Eleison's pupils had grown, and his breath had deliciously quickened.

"You haven't had a chance to make love to her yet,"— Malin reached past Eleison to take the glass from my quivering hand and set it aside for later, along with his own—"I've only just realized. Or am I wrong?"

"No." Tearing his gaze from mine, Eleison leaned forward to likewise retire his glass for the moment. "You're not wrong, Malin…I've wanted to give you two plenty of time to be together. But you seem like you're doing just fine right now, at least…"

His eyes crinkling with his slight but pleased smile, Malin slid his hand over my calf and up beneath the hem of my frock. Casually, almost innocently, as though he only meant to massage my limb. For a moment, he did, stroking the muscle and studying my face as he said, "Yes, yes indeed. I think we seem to be getting on excellently…don't you, darling?"

"Yes, oh—" The words caught in my throat as Eleison's hand slid down over my bodice, that powerful hand cupping my breast through layers of stiff fabric and forbidding wire. I arched back against my mate, then stretched my head toward my husband. Malin got the message and bent for a tender kiss, his caress making its natural progression up my thigh while I fit my hands to his face. How solemn those august features could appear—yet how alive they were in that moment, sharp from one angle, dreamy from another, the metamorphic qualities of his lust lending a kind of occult increase to his beauty.

"Yes, Malin, darling—I'm so grateful, so glad for your love. Ah—hm—"

His hand's exploration pausing at my lingerie, Malin slid his thumb and forefinger beneath the edge of the lace and teased his way along the inner crease of my thigh. The trembling of anticipation rolled into the quivering of bliss as every inch of my flesh grew sensitized. I sank my teeth into Malin's lip gently but firmly, then released him and turned to partake of Eleison's mouth.

It was so natural, yet almost practiced; as though choreographed by the god of love. I was afraid at first of Eleison's possessive nature, for as Malin's fingers slid over the mound of curled hair and down to the abyss of my supreme ecstasy, the gasp this first contact induced made me separate from Eleison's plunging tongue with glance of bright shock. When my gaze struck Malin's, his fingertips circled the bead of my passion far more deliberately than before. I looked back at Eleison, the receipt of such pleasure before him only provoking a greater, more obscene urge of ecstasy to rush through me.

And, oh, the jealousy was there, all right. The slight

hardness of my mate's features; the heavy hoods of the conflicted garnet eyes, through which he regarded my growing pleasure at my husband's experienced hand.

But rather than withdrawing, or perhaps trying to gain some upper hand over Malin, Eleison caught my jaw in one hand while the other plucked open the back of my gown.

"Does it feel good, baby?"

"Yes, yes, oh, Eleison—I love the way Malin touches me—"

"And I love to touch you..." Malin leaned in to kiss me again, our lips heavily fused as his teasing trailed down, down, to discover the river raging from me. Groaning, he leaned back to hear me scream with bliss at the slow penetration of two fingers.

"What a hot little tart you are! She's so wet, feel her with me, Eleison—pull up your skirt for us, darling, you're not doing anything else right now..."

Groaning at his command as much as at Eleison's low chuckle, I did as I was bidden and drew my gown and the layers beneath high up my legs. While I did, Malin slid his fingers from me only long enough to pull my underthings down; by the time I had the dress up high, he was back at the apex of my thighs, his middle and ring finger slipping easily into me on the lubrication of my lust.

Inhaling sharply to see me penetrated by another man, Eleison slid his hand from my bosom, down my stomach, and along the track of my thighs. While his mouth met mine, the taste of him rich and dense with wine and flavored tobacco, that hand wandered smoothly back up toward the center of my body. His caress trailed against my husband's hand so tenderly I swore I felt it myself.

I certainly felt it as, cautiously at first but with increasing confidence upon seeing my face, Eleison slid two of his own fingers along the track provided by Malin's.

"Oh yeah"—my mate gasped as, in shock to have somehow never considered this form of collaboration before, I crushed the fabric of my frock in my tightening fists and wantonly splayed my legs to encourage them—"oh, Thecla, baby, you're soaked…ah, honey…"

Though Malin preferred the gentle, deliberate coax, Eleison could not help but slowly pump his fingers in and out of me against my husband's. "I don't know why I resisted this for so long." Though his tone was still a bit gruff, my mate exchanged with Malin the arrogant, conspiratorial look of men who knew their inarguable prowess. "Thecla's always so hot for it when it's just the two of us, after all…I should have considered how excited she would get with both of us here to fuck her."

As I groaned, Malin's teeth flashed in a wicked grin I swore I felt in the pit of my stomach. Those wolflike eyes swiveled upon the unnatural ones of my truly animalistic lover while their fingers worked within me, and the air thickened with expectation as Malin agreed. "She's such a fun, sexy woman, gorgeous and free…I'm glad you're truly sharing her with me."

Nostrils flaring, Eleison regarded Malin's slight smile for a few long heartbeats.

This time, it was Eleison who initiated the kiss between the two men. His head ducked against Malin's and their mouths enfolded in a sudden eruption of long-building attraction. With a staggered sort of gasp, Malin pushed back against Eleison's kiss and at the same time stroked his fingers knowingly within my sensitive core.

I nearly screamed in rapture to glimpse their exchange of lip and tongue and occasional teeth, instead gasping sadly as Eleison slid his fingers from me—but I found myself crying his name as he took to working that irresistibly powerful nerve hidden within the crests of my sex. While my husband's digits worked within me, my mate's worked without, and their kiss ended only so each man could turn and feast next upon me. Eleison's free hand once more caught my jaw so his tongue could plunge to the depths of my mouth; whereas Malin, reaching behind me to finish what Eleison had started, tore open the loosened bodice and wrenched it down my body along with my bustier. While I cried out, my husband's kisses at once covered my breasts. His fingers found a steadier rhythm as his licking and nibbling crept lower; lower.

"I can never resist kissing this gorgeous pussy." Murmuring, he slid his fingers from me to tear my remaining clothes away and leave me naked, shaking with a torturously near orgasm, in Eleison's lap. Groaning to see me so, Malin slid down to his knees and buried his face between my thighs. Though I let my left leg fall widely from the other, Eleison kept his hand there to part my labia with his fingers. After pressing a few lingering kisses to that sensitive jewel that made me scream, Malin's tongue teased against my sex, and Eleison's slithered into my mouth along with his breath on our next kiss. Every time our master's tongue lashed the edge of Eleison's fingers in the pursuit of my pleasure, my mate would respond by exhaling the promise of more bliss and twitching a finger or thumb along my clitoris as though to pass along the ecstasy due to me.

Eventually, as Eleison's hand slid up from my thighs to instead cup a breast his head bowed to kiss, I clutched at his head with one hand and Malin's with the other. "I can't take it," I begged, "please, one of you, both of you, fuck me! I need it, I—oh! Oh!"

"You know she's getting close when she starts talking like

that," observed Eleison, lifting his head with a wry chuckle.

"Oh, I know…now is always when I'm tempted to stop and tease her." I groaned in misery—Malin *had* stopped, of course, to say such a thing—and pushed on my husband's head while he laughed. "But…she's been such a good girl since she got home…I think good girls deserve rewards. Don't they, Thecla?"

"Yes, Master, please, oh—Malin! Aha, ah—"

More relentless than ever, my husband's tongue whipped to work—now against my overstimulated clitoris, which was not left unattended for an instant, and which with each strike delivered a surge of pleasure that swept as far as my toes and fingertips. The resulting swell that careened upon me was so sharp and so fast that I jolted, my legs twitching around Malin's head as my hand tangled in the short locks of his silvered hair.

"Malin—darling, oh, sweet fuck—"

His crimson eyes drinking in my face with hedonistic appreciation and only the slightest traces of his usual possessive streak, Eleison observed, "Malin sure is good at eating you out, angel…you can barely even think when he licks your pussy, huh?"

"Yes! Yes! Eleison, oh, he's so good, Malin is so talented, he makes me—he—he—ah! Malin!"

Like an archer's bow, my taut stomach tightened to a point of maximum tension, then released into the vibration that propelled from my center and into my skull. I screamed, panting, the animal sounds of my ecstasy rising through the bedroom and across the otherwise empty floor. The only witnesses to my abandon were those men that caused it, my loves, my darlings, Eleison and Malin, who both lifted their heads to enjoy the sight of me as my mind dissolved and my body seized before its collapse into limp fluidity. I sagged back in Eleison's arms, and Malin, letting out a breath, stroked his hand along my stomach. Brow slightly furrowed by his admiration, Malin lowered his head to plant a final chaste kiss upon the apex of my thighs.

"I think we can take turns, can't we?"

His question to Eleison was as heavy with desire as it was with playful irony. My mate chuckled while my husband helped me up in the direction of the bed.

"Yeah…I think I'm learning more about fairness all the time, Malin. Would you like to go first?"

While I reclined upon the bed, gasping as I took the meaning, Malin smiled at me slightly and told Eleison, "If you really don't mind."

"Not at all…it's your bedroom, your property…your wife."

"Your mate," Malin said. His smile turned upon me; I took advantage of him shrugging off his waistcoat to unbutton his shirt. "What a girl you are, Thecla…delicious, fuckable, devious Thecla. Ah…"

Having run out of buttons, I bent my head to kiss him through his trousers, and Malin sighed to stroke my hair. "You can feel how hard you've made me, can't you…here, angel, lie back, take this."

While Malin slid a pillow under my rear, the bed beside me depressed. I smiled to find Eleison, his shirt already open while he loosened his trousers, his eyes on mine in silent declaration of his intention to kiss me.

Breathless, I turned my mouth toward him. He devoured me while Malin finished undressing, those black eyes never far from the scene.

"Do you ever notice how she displays herself when she's ready for a nice hard cock, Eleison? Ah, I love it…you couldn't close your legs right now if I paid you, could you, Thecla, darling…"

I moaned. It was really true. Once either one of these wonderful men worked me into such a state of unyielding fire, my legs fell apart and stayed apart. With a glance down and a grunt of agreement, Eleison reached between my thighs to slide his fingers along my clitoris a few more gasping seconds.

"I can see that…you're waiting for Malin's cock, aren't you, baby…"

While Eleison's thick fingers teased slowly into me, I arched against him in throbbing desperation. "Yes"—I gasped, sliding my hand into Eleison's opened trousers to draw his twitching cock into the open—"and yours—oh—oh! Malin—"

Eleison's fingers had slid from me, but as he absented himself, the unmistakable pressure of Malin's turgid anatomy fit heavily against my sex. While Eleison's hand remained on my open thigh, Malin stared into my face and gradually worked himself toward the mouth of my aching cunt.

"You're such an obliging little harlot…oh…my gorgeous slut of a bride—"

At last, at long last, Malin pushed inside me, and I moaned in desperation from the first inch. While stroking Eleison's cock and watching Malin's plunge into me, I whimpered, "Yes, yes sir, Master Farrow—I'm your dirty slut, oh—my husband, my good husband, oh, your cock feels so good—"

"Oh, Thecla! Eleison's presence really has done something wonderful to you…ah…Eleison…" Filling me to the hilt, Malin stroked his hand along my abdomen, then drew back to find the perfect pace with which to fuck me. "Now that you're here with us once," he went on to my mate, "it's going to happen again…and again…"

Eleison groaned, his wonderful prick pulsing in my hand

as he rocked against my touch. "I know it is," he said, pushing away his trousers and sliding his shirt from his shoulders. "I want to give you plenty of alone time…and I want us to have time alone together, too, Thecla, but…I kind of like the idea of this becoming a regular thing, too."

"That's good…because it will be. I can tell how much Thecla wants it to be. Don't you, darling…"

"Yes! Yes, please, oh, Eleison—oh, I want it to be like this all the time, this is so wonderful, this is—ah—Malin—"

"Getting close again, aren't you…I bet if I give you a nice"— he took hold of my hips to keep me still as he abruptly hammered into me, the sudden speed and heavy pressure producing a blinding increase in my pleasure—"rough fucking…if I pound you until you scream…"

"Malin! Malin, oh, yes, please, yes—"

"I'll bet you'll cum in an instant—aha—"

"Oh! Malin! Yes, yes, just like that, don't stop!"

"That's right…ah, Thecla, that's right…" Bending to kiss the corner of my mouth, my cheek, my ear, my throat, my mouth again, Malin caught my face to watch the orgasm that burst through me and tightened me around him. Almost pained by the sight, he exhaled raggedly and grit his teeth.

As my muscles' contractions reached their end, my husband slid his cock from me and took a step back.

"Your turn, Eleison," Malin coached, his glistening anatomy straining up with angry lust. "She's sensitive tonight… you really *do* need a good fucking from both of us, don't you, angel…"

"Yes! Yes, please, I'm desperate—"

With a chuckle low in his throat, Eleison bent to kiss me,

then stood from the bed to take his place between my thighs. My husband extended himself along my other side, taking up the job of kissing me, and raised his head only to watch Eleison make himself at home against my body.

"Here," said Malin, reaching out to slide a ringed hand around Eleison's prick. I gasped in astonishment at what a pulse of pleasure the sight could bring me while Malin went on, "Allow me to help you, Eleison, darling…"

"Ah, Malin—fuck—Thecla—"

I could not even manage a name, as incoherent with pleasure as I was to watch Malin's expert hand slowly, steadily stroke, then carefully guide Eleison's cock along the valley of my sex and into the tight, wet heart of me. While Malin fed him into this heat, Eleison groaned for me, his eyes flicking quickly away from my husband and down into me without hesitation.

The deeper Eleison plunged, the fuller I was, and the more ecstatically I screamed with relief to have my emptiness abated. Griping first the sheets, then Malin's free hand, I basked in the sight of my mate's thick prick marking the territory my husband had just taken as his.

Of course, Malin did not think like that. My pleasure was his pleasure; Eleison's pleasure, his pleasure. While Malin's hand slid over my abdomen to feel Eleison work within me, each thundering strike of his cock reverberating through my entire body, my husband watched my face with his own arranged in absolute sublimity.

"Oh, darling…I'll never get tired of seeing Eleison fuck you. Promise you'll always let me watch…"

"I promise!" I cried out, my body fluttering around my mate's as I glanced down to find Malin's hand had left us. Instead he worked his own cock with a slow, deliberate stroke that was, I suspected, intended to prolong and agonize rather than satisfy. The sight excited me as I cried, "Please, yes, oh, Malin, what a good husband you are to me!"

"Anything for my wife. Ah...my sexy, sweet, willing bride..."

"Baby"—Eleison's words were laced with a growl as he shifted my hips up and back, plunging deeper into me while his mouth covered mine—"I've never felt you like this..."

"Because I've never had you both! Oh! God! Please, I need this as often as possible. I love you both, oh, Eleison, Malin—I love you, I love you so much, oh, never let me leave again—fuck, oh! Oh!"

Another storm of pleasure overtook me, the resulting destruction rattling through my body to leave me panting for air while Eleison slowly worked his cock through my orgasm.

"That's nice," he said, the words another set of low rumbles in his chest. "That's nice, baby...you sure do love it when we share you..."

"Yes, oh, please...my body belongs to both of you in equal measure...I want you both to use me, to take me, to give me to each other...oh—"

Baring his teeth at the height of pleasure my words caused him, Eleison pulled free of me and nodded at Malin. With one last kiss of my mouth, Malin rose and took the offered place.

Now things occurred more quickly. The heat of the room intensified by the second and both men were gradually worked to a new crest of erotic need. Eleison stood by my knee, watching with that blazing gaze as Malin slid into my vacated body and animated me with euphoria. While my mate stroked my thigh and bent to kiss my bosom, my husband urged my hips higher by putting pressure on the underside of my thigh. With me so displayed, my legs wide and high in the air, he pounded so deeply and intensely into me that I lost all sense of place and time, and somehow briefly felt we were back in Saalast.

Then, as my pleasure neared its crescendo, he pulled himself from me and reached for Eleison's arm.

Now Eleison took his turn—and a kiss from Malin, who caught him by the back of the neck. With this grip, Malin held him still for the hungry stab of a brutal tongue that took its pleasure as Eleison pushed deeply into me. Holding my legs up as Malin just had, Eleison worked himself in and out of me, and the vigor of his fucking rushed me back to the climax cruelly denied by Malin's exit.

Yet, just as I began to approach it, Eleison reenacted that cruelty with the removal of his prick.

The pattern repeated. Against the pressures of instinct, delaying their own pleasure in the process, each man would penetrate me, work his cock deliciously within me, then slip away before either one of us could approach orgasm. While I cried and whined, his counterpart would take me, and tease me, and leave me for the first's pleasure, again without relief. On and on it went, until I was nearly delirious.

Gradually, as their turns became quicker, the men stood closer, and their kisses grew more frequent. It was during Malin's turn that at last, incensed by the sight of me sliding my hand down to toy with my own tender nerve, my husband grasped my mate's cock in another set of long, luxurious strokes that guided Eleison's throbbing tip against us. While I moaned, quaking at the sight and sensation, Malin drew our cavalier's cockhead back and forth along my clitoris. He tugged Eleison's prick to sweeten the moment, and Malin sometimes worked that sacred scepter along the shaft of his own while he drew back from me to give a particularly deep, almost vicious thrust.

This time, when Malin seceded his territory to permit Eleison his turn, as his twitching prick slid free of me, it throbbed against the length of Eleison's. Their cockheads ground together against me, and all three of us seemed to moan in unison as, with another kiss shared between them, Eleison pushed his prick against Malin's before sliding past and plunging into me.

By three strokes, I was a gibbering fool; I had lost track of my orgasms and collapsed into this latest one, clenching with desperation at my mate's thick shaft as he gave me everything I so desperately needed. While I cried out, Malin groaned; overwhelmed, he bent his head between us. I was astonished into an immediate second climax to feel my husband's tongue lash along my clitoris and down the cock of the man who savagely fucked me.

"Oh, Malin"—Eleison's growl was purely animal as he lowered a hand to stroke my husband's hair—"careful, you'll make me cum…"

"I want you to, Eleison…I love fucking Thecla when she's still dripping with your load. You love it, too, don't you, darling… love feeling Husband's cock getting nice and slick from your mate's cum…"

"Yes! Yes, oh, please, oh, Eleison—just promise you'll play with us again and there's no trouble at all with you giving in now, oh—Eleison! Oh, Malin, your tongue, oh—"

"Fuck—" Eleison gasped with sudden sharpness. Malin had slid a hand under my mate's testicles to coax him to the finish line with a gentle, almost tickling caress. His head tipped back, Eleison groaned from his diaphragm as he pounded heavily into me.

"Fuck it, ah, baby…I'll give you what you want, Thecla. I'll give you every drop you and your husband could ask for, right in this thirsty cunt—"

"Eleison! Oh, Eleison, darling, yes, please—please—yes!"

At last, he cried out. Malin groaned, smiling in epicurean pleasure while my mate pounded me as deeply as he could: until I screamed with the overwhelming sensation of being so stretched, so filled. While I twitched with my own nearing climax, Eleison throbbed within me, each distinct pulse of his prick marking another urgent jet of cum deep inside.

"That's right, Eleison," encouraged Malin, watching my mate's face just as I did, "give my wife everything you have, oh, yes, she needs this big cock to blow in her as often as possible, doesn't she…ah…beautiful…"

While, groaning, Eleison bent over me to swallow my mouth in a kiss, Malin watched us with a look of profound appreciation. When at last he finished, my mate growled in affection and drew back from my mouth, then from my body.

Then, reaching down to catch Malin by the cock, Eleison looked him in the eyes and stroked the territory master with such a steady, eager hand that I nearly screamed again to see it.

"Go on," said Eleison, drawing surprised but lewdly pleased Malin to his marked territory, "something tells me she's not done yet."

"Can she ever be…I love you, Eleison." With an intense, famished look, the men exchanged a consuming kiss. Then, turning to me, his look of sharp male affection softening, melting, gliding away, Malin took my face in his hands and bent over me to slide into my center one last time that evening. Gasping, I clung to him, lost in his beauty while he shuddered to feel within me.

"Isn't that a well-fucked girl...oh, flooded. That's nice. That's very nice. You had fun playing with your mate, didn't you, Thecla..."

"Yes, sir, oh, Malin—Husband, please, promise me we can have Eleison up all the time..."

"Of course...as much as he wants...I love to see you enjoying yourself, darling. Oh—" Malin's eyes fluttered shut as he buried himself to the hilt in me, rocking back again to repeat the pleasure. "And, of course...I enjoy it, too...it's so nice to feel Eleison's cock working inside of you..."

"Yes, oh, and to see you two kissing, touching each other— oh, Malin, oh—you're so hard—"

"I'm nearly on the verge myself, angel..."

"Oh, Malin! Please, darling, yes, I want you to cum in me, I want it so badly—nice and deep, please—ah!"

Malin went at it harder, and as he did, Eleison lay beside me with a low chuckle.

"You always look like you're being hurt when you're just about to cum, Thecla..."

"No," I answered my mate hoarsely, staring into my husband's face as though in breathless shock, "no, no! It feels good, it feels so good—Malin, Malin—deeper, oh—"

"Here's what you want," my husband said, plunging into me mercilessly, his thumb pressing discreetly along my windpipe while his hand rested against the side of my neck and jaw. "You want to be fucked nice and deeply, darling—oh, yes, that's it, isn't it—"

"Malin! Malin! Yes, yes, it is—"

That thumb compressed my words, my air, sweetening the pleasure with the denial as he murmured to me. "Just like this—just like this—well, angel, we'll be sure to give it to you whenever you want…beg me to cum in you, my hot little pet—"

When his thumb raised and I gasped for air, that air came with rapid words. "Oh, Malin! Please, yes, please! Cum in me, Husband, oh—mark your wife, fill me up—Malin, oh darling, oh darling, fuck me while my mate watches, I love you, I love you both so much—"

His body tightening above me at the ripple of the night's final climax, Malin swept over me for a kiss. I cried out, trembling, my pleasure increased and extended to feel it echoed in what he expressed within me. Moaning with ecstasy into my mouth, Malin hammered up inside me, spending himself while staring into my eyes.

Everything was peaceful.

Beside us, Eleison looked away to light a cigarette.

While my generous mate got up to fetch the wine, my husband emerged from his suspension in spacetime to press kisses along the fluttering lid of my left eye.

"I love you," Malin murmured, drawing carefully out of me while I returned his oath with my whole heart. "I missed you, Thecla. Oh, angel…if I was ever tempted to take you for granted before I had you home, I never will again. Never. I'm so glad to have you back. Come—ah—"

While I melted into his arms before he could even finish the request, Malin kissed my mouth again and said with a tired sort of chuckle, "You know, I thought for sure this would be the time the dharmine wouldn't be able to resist…oh, but I forgot to tell you to call to him, didn't I. Just as well…Eleison would have pitched a fit, I'm sure."

"What would Eleison have pitched a fit about," asked Eleison merrily, returning with the tray and its glasses balanced upon his right hand. As I giggled in a guilty way, he perched upon the edge of the bed and lowered the tray so the wine was in grabbing distance.

"How would you feel about getting Thecla a pet?" Malin's innocuous question came as he sat up. After taking his wine, he slid back against the pillows and extended his right arm to summon me back into his embrace. I settled in, and Eleison sipped his own wine with a scoff before putting the tray aside to stretch out along the foot of the bed.

"Why would that bother me?"

"Oh, well, who knows...after you spent the past five months or so as a semi-conscious borro, I would have expected you to grow more sensitive to animal welfare."

"Now that you mention it, I probably am." Chuckling, Eleison ran his free hand over his forehead while looking at me for a few thoughtful seconds. Then, lowering that hand upon my foot to massage me while I sighed, he said, "Anyway, no, it wouldn't bother me. You think, like, maybe a dog?"

"That's exactly what I'm thinking," said Malin from behind his glass while I smiled on between them. "Something protective...obedient—it must be obedient—but cunning in its own right. Properly suited for Thecla's disposition."

"I'd probably feel better about her being out in public in Saalast if she had a dog with her...a big dog."

"Yes, that was my thought."

It *had* been so freeing to walk through the gate at Valquist with Dinon wearing Eleison's form. And although the dharmine still partly revolted me due to its parasitic, predatory nature, I could not help but remain intrigued by it...nor could I help the crackle of attraction, the pull I felt toward it. Toward him.

And Malin, surely knowing what I felt, was eager to deliver Dinon to me all the same. More eager, perhaps.

How I loved him! How I loved both my husband and my mate, each love a flame that combined with the other into a greater light whenever I tried to compare them. Each man was too sublime, and each man's love, too individual and intense, for either to truly be in competition. And to have them both? To find all three of us falling asleep together in the same bed, spent, Eleison showing no sign of getting up to retire to his own quarters?

I had never felt so happy. So safe. Like a child, I clung to consciousness as long as I could, basking in the richness of the night while I still had it fixed in the present.

Eleison slept heavily on one side of me; Malin, with great soundness on the other. The sleep problems that had plagued me in Valquist disappeared on my waking from my strange sabbatical, but there was absolutely no sleep as wonderful as the sleep to which I gradually succumbed when still vibrating with the warmth of our ménage.

And in the depths of that sleep, the black loom stood in the center of its formless home.

Compelled as ever, I wandered up to it in the belly of my dream and studied its dark weaving. Such a small part had been completed before I disappeared from myself. The phantom weaving was slow-going.

In the dark, I slid into the little bench and resumed the work. While the pedals cranked beneath my feet and my fingers flew at a speed unhampered by time or matter or even by thought, footsteps approached me. They echoed from behind; yet, in that strange space, the figure that emerged from the dark was before me. Gradually, I perceived that the space ahead of me was a vast mirror in which the loom and I were not reflected, but the figure approaching was.

My work slowed. I straightened up, expecting Ba'al-Dinon with a chastisement already on my tongue.

Then the man stepped near enough that even through the dark he was visible to me, his blue eyes pained, the dark curls of his hair unkempt with time in the wilderness.

While my mouth opened in shock, Dinon's voice awoke me in a shout that seemed directly in my ear—in dream or waking, I am still not sure, just as I was not sure about the other times the dharmine's voice called me from slumber.

"Madame!"

That single urgent word, that sharp title, had an essence of desperate command. I snapped awake in the dark bedroom, eyes fixing on the ceiling.

To my left, Malin had rolled in his sleep and faced the edge of the bed. Likewise, at my right, Eleison was now upon his stomach, his arm having slipped off me.

And in the darkness at the foot of the bed, Glenn considered me for the time it took the surreality of dream to transform into limb-numbing panic of reality.

With a look that demanded I follow, he exited the room in perfect silence.

I DON'T KNOW how I managed to leave the bed without disturbing the men. In retrospect, I didn't, though at the time it seemed their patterns of respective breathing continued unabated while I slithered out from between the sheets. My body contorting in a series of automated, seemingly impossible angles by which I slid my legs up to my chest and hooked them over the edge of the sheet, I pushed myself down the length of the bed and rose from the foot.

All this happened in approximately six seconds, or seven, or eight. I tried not to make it more than that because I was already on the verge of trembling beneath the weight of the knowledge settling upon me: the absolute certainty of why Glenn had come.

My palms slickened with sweat. I caught my frock from the couch and yanked it on while I padded to the door.

He stood just to my left as I stepped from the room, the dress undone in the back and my hair streaming wildly around and across my face. Though I was frightened to see him so close as I stepped out, I endured the immediate evolution of my fear into fury: absolute and raging.

Before Glenn could raise a hand to ask my silence, I ignored his gesture—and the lowered gun, too. As though he had not broken into my house with the intention of murdering my husband, I grabbed him by the front of his shirt and shoved him away, far away, from the open bedroom door, then pushed him down the short corridor to the open sitting area. The hunter consented, if only owing to his surprise. He even stopped when I stopped and made no move to rejoin me for the rough treatment. Instead he regarded me through the sorrowful blue orbs that revealed his lonely vision of the world.

"What the *blazes* are you doing here?" I glanced quickly over my shoulder and pushing him on just a little farther.

Now, at the sound of my voice, or perhaps the true answer to the question, Glenn snapped from his stupor: enough, at least, to slide his arms around me and draw me to his heart. His empty hand fit to the back of my head while the cold metal of the gun's hard edge dug into my spine, the muzzle pointed at the floor.

"I wasn't expecting you to have forgiven him," Glenn remarked softly, bending to kiss the top of my head, then tipping me back to look into my eyes. "Have you?"

"Of *course* I have." The words hissed from me, scalding as a brand as I gestured back to the door. I was eager to get Glenn as far away as possible before he ended up shot—or before somebody else did, as he'd obviously intended until realizing I was also in that bed. My heart hammered as, by the second, I realized more clearly what had been avoided. Teeth clenched, I squirmed in his grip and pushed back against his chest. "Malin took *care* of me, damn you, the whole time I was trapped in that ventil—and what did you do? Where have *you* been all this time?"

Stung, he begged, "Don't talk to me so cruelly. Where do you *think* I've been?"

My eyes filled with angry tears to think of Rosina downstairs. Did he even realize she existed? "Stalking my husband, apparently, waiting for your chance."

"No! Thecla—I was following *you*."

A constellation of emotions—everything from shame to love to fear—swept through me. After a delay of a few shocked seconds, my open mouth stuttered automatic words. "Why? Why would you *do* that? We hardly know each other—"

"But I know enough to know you're not here by choice."

It was so much more complicated at that. No, I wasn't here by choice, not really. But I chose to stay, and was glad to stay now that things were mended. That did not morally justify my husband's actions, but it also didn't mean that I, an adult, required rescuing from the relationship I not only consented to, but craved. My mouth opening and closing in mute protest, I told my would-be hero, "Glenn, please, listen to me: I care about you more than you could know—"

"And I care about you, Thecla." His sad eyes regarded my face, then grew much too firm of purpose when they flickered down the hall behind me. "I knew from the moment I met you that you needed help; and I knew, on the night you ran away, that you would never be able to ask me for the help you really needed."

"My *husband* helps me," I insisted, earning a bleak look from the hunter.

"Your husband is the one you need help escaping from. That's why I came here. It's why I've *been* here. Why I followed you out of Valquist and let that borro chase me off without a fight."

Eyes widening, I asked, "Eleison saw you?"

"I was hoping he'd turn back to a man and let me talk to him...that maybe I could get him to see reason. But that didn't happen."

And it was less likely to happen than ever before, with Eleison's debt discharged and his obligation to Malin now a spiritual one far more than a financial one. Eyes blazing with frustration, especially as I was still in Glenn's clutches, I told him, "I'm glad you didn't press your luck—he would have torn your throat out if you tried getting close to me. Glenn, darling, I don't *need* your help. I need you to go back to your poor neglected house in Valquist and—"

"Who do you think got the blame for all the death that night?" With a sardonic, soft half-laugh, Glenn assured my falling features, "I'm a wanted man, Thecla. Valquist, it's not safe for me. The Hunter's Guild put a price on my head themselves, offering a reward for my arrest...or my body."

"But they can't *do* that! They have no proof—you didn't *do* anything—"

Pained by my indignation on his behalf, Glenn said, "I know."

More guilt flooded me, even as I stayed tense in his grip. How had I managed to hurt every man I loved with one single gesture? "Why not let us petition Valquist and the Hunter's Guild on your behalf? We all know you didn't do anything that night. The dharmine killed all those men."

"Almost all of them," he reminded me, contemplating my face until his hand slid from the back of my head to instead envelop my ear and cheek. "That dharmine, Thecla—why did it leave me alive?"

"Because I commanded it to," I whispered, paralyzed by the intensity of his stare and all the insanity in it.

His features tensed as if in response to a sharp, sudden pain. "I have to get you away from here," he said simply, releasing my face to grab my arm and haul me along to the elevator. While I dug in my heels and whispered urgent protests, Glenn ignored me, muttering on, "A dharmine—maybe I should go back and—"

Panic flooded me as he glanced toward the bedroom. Desperate to keep his thoughts well away from their present trajectory, I stopped resisting at once and caressed his face with my free hand. A scar from Eleison now trailed along his cheek above his beard; my finger fit to it as naturally as it fit to Malin's scar while I begged, "No, Glenn—don't do anything rash, please!"

"This is all rash, isn't it? But I have to. I have to do this, Thecla. I can't let you stay a prisoner to this life. Either you come with me, or I'll find some other way to free you."

Yes, he was insane. In that moment, there was no way for reason to reach him. After losing his own freedom for a crime he did not commit, Glenn had become obsessed with liberating me from a life that was not the burden he imagined it to be. It was my fault, I thought at the time—if only I had remained at the palace and grit my teeth around the Overseer for the length of a Rift Event, Malin would have arrived to meet me. Everything would have worked out. Instead, I had gone crying to Glenn, and in so doing I had given him the impression that I was more unhappy than happy.

And then, he had given me a child.

The inspiration struck me with a bolt of extreme urgency. Looking down at myself, then at Glenn and his gun, I adopted a displeased tone of imperious assent.

"Very well. I'll come with you if you swear not to hurt my husband or my mate. But we can't leave without some clothes."

Scoffing, Glenn protested, "Thecla—"

"You're a wanted man and I'm *naked* under here." I tore the shoulder of my bodice down from my arm and bared a breast for Glenn's shocked, then achingly moved eye. "Not to mention the size of this park, *shoes*—I'm going to need something to wear for the immediate future, unless you want me to leave as a ventil. And if I become a ventil, I cannot guarantee I will know you, or myself, or anything else without Eleison around."

Of course—I realized with a sudden start of some embarrassment that Glenn was also my mate now, in the technical sense that the Overseer had explained to me. The mated, the fated, and the bonded. Glenn and I were bonded, whether he knew it or not; and I ventured a guess that, since not even Eleison had seemed aware of developing research on altered mating, an unaltered human like Glenn, who did not even seem to know he had sired a child, had no prayer.

Therefore, he didn't question me when I told him I might not know him in my other form. To my undying gratitude, he relented.

"I'll give you five minutes to pack," he told me, using his gun to hit the button of the elevator and gritting his teeth at the immediate and very audible opening of the doors. "Which floor?"

I answered, my throat miserably dry, and stepped into the elevator with him while praying that one or both my lovers had been awoken by the sound. Glenn hit the button and turned to face me as the doors slid shut again. Seeing my features, the tension in his own relaxed once more into that perpetual sorrow.

"I know you can't see that I'm trying to help you," he said. "Not yet. But when we're away from here and living differently, you'll *feel* different. You'll be relieved. You don't want to get tangled up in his world, Thecla."

"You realize"—I was unable to help the cold edge to my tone, no matter how it hurt us both—"you are kidnapping the next Matrix of Gudrune."

His chest swelling in a deep inhalation, he shook his head and turned away while saying, "I have to get you out of here," again. A mantra. His only point and priority for half a year.

On the fourth floor, the elevator spat us into my sitting room. Its white carpeting and cream furniture, augmented with splashes of color here and there by way of a pillow or a painting, was normally far brighter than Malin's, and the room raised its very modern lights automatically when we stepped past the RMS panel. Given the late hour, it kept them to a low setting. Unfortunately I was not sure it would be enough to disturb Rosina or even Nellie's baby, assuming the nursery door had been left ajar. Holding my breath, I took a step in the direction of my bedroom. How could I make as much noise as possible without Glenn becoming alarmed?

Innocently smiling, still up from feeding her child or mine, Nellie appeared around the corner from her room while tightening her robe.

Glenn's gun whipped toward her in time with my scream; in time with Nellie's hands, which flew from her waist and into the air with an immediate cry of sharp fright. For the flutter of a second, I vividly imagined the worst—but Glenn was too well-trained and lowered the weapon from my petrified nurse even before, one at a time, the startled infants took to crying.

All three adults looked in the direction of the nursery while, pierced by my daughter's alarmed wailing, I told Nellie, "Take your son and stay in my bedroom. I have to say good-bye to Rosina."

As, with a few wild looks at the gun, Nellie hurried to obey, Glenn's brow furrowed. "You have a child?"

"Yes," I told him tersely, putting myself half-consciously between him and the corridor to the nursery. One door burst open, then another quickly slammed. "Yes, Glenn, I have a child."

"You didn't tell me you were a mother."

"Because I didn't have her at the time. She's not Malin's, you see."

Somewhat understandably taken aback to hear all this, no doubt as befuddled by the math as anyone not privy to certain details, Glenn asked, "Then whose could she be? You—"

The answer to his own question came into his eyes. While his mouth closed into a paralyzed part of shock, I stared him down unflinchingly.

"I was a blasted ventil for five and a half months, Glenn. Do you understand?" My eyes misted over and my throat tightened, but I kept staring, my own mad smile tweaking up the edges of my lips. "I'll tell you whose child she is. She's the child of—of a *good* man. Of a kind man. One too gentle for the world he lives in. Rosina—"

"Rosina." He repeated the name, fully hearing it now, the word soft with awe as I went on above his wonder.

"—is the daughter of a *hero*. You understand? She's the daughter of someone very different from me."

684

"That's not true." Glenn spoke quickly, at last looking away from the sound of the infant whose wails grew more ghastly by the second. "You're the same as me, Thecla. There are things, people in this world that want to corrupt us—you're right. But we don't have to let them."

"Then you'd let them corrupt our daughter on my behalf," I said with an agitated wave. "You'd have me leave her here, this child with a hero's blood in her veins, to be raised by the very men her father would regard as villains!"

"We'll take her with us."

My mouth open, I insisted, "Do you have the least idea what's required to care for a child? You want me to, what—bear this infant in my arms across the park? And then? Into the wilds, I suppose, to your dream log cabin."

"She'll be fine as long as she has you," he said with a reflexive glance to my bosom, which had been barely covered by my sloppily replaced sleeve. "Look, I was thinking we would take one of the safari autos and—"

"My *breasts* have no *milk*, you ignorant man!" My head jutted toward him while my arm flailed in an aggravated gesture that made him flinch as though he had been slapped. "Can't you tell to look at me? *I* wasn't pregnant with our child—the ventil was. My body is not *equipped* to feed Rosina. I can keep her warm and change her and bathe her"—my tears spilled over in real frustration I hadn't let myself fully feel until that second, and I wiped them quickly away—"but I can't provide for her most basic and important need. So, unless you also want to kidnap the blasted wetnurse and *her* baby, we are *not* taking Rosina. And if *Rosina* is not leaving, then I am not leaving, damn you, Glenn Stone, damn you."

Half a year of obsessive planning, completely annihilated with the addition of this one factor he had failed to note while keeping tabs from a distance that would alert neither Eleison nor Malin's staff. Visibly shaken, Glenn looked between my raging features and the door from which emanated sobs that had me more in knots than finding the hunter in our room.

Just so, the square of his shoulders softened.

"Can I see her?"

Regarding the weapon in his hand, then his haunted face, I took a breath to regain some control of my temper. "Holster your weapon," I told him. "Guns don't belong in a nursery."

His nostrils flared with a slow exhalation. Nodding, Glenn looked sheepishly down at my feet and, to my great astonishment, reached back to slide the gun into the holster at his hip.

My poor fool!

My poor Glenn.

That was the moment he sealed his fate: I see it now so clearly. Before then, before that fatal moment in which he followed me down the hall to the nursery, he had every ability to flee from me. To flee into the night forever, and forget me as much as any man ever could.

But the second he set eyes upon our child, he was mine forever.

The doom showed in his face as it had in the blackly shadowed mirror of my so-called dream.

"There, darling." I swept Rosina from her crib and drew her against my heart while she sobbed. "Oh, dear, Mama's here, Mommy's right here...yes"—I smiled at the ever so slight abatement of her weeping, and took her little hand to wave it while joggling her against me—"we're all right, we're all right, oh, we're better, aren't we..."

I sank into the rocking chair to sing her back to sleep, offering her my milkless breast in lieu of a soother—in large part, because I knew the effect it would have in further disarming Glenn. I am not proud to say I was right, and that, devastated, he stood in the nursery's door as though afraid to approach; but neither would he be proud, if penning this chronicle, to recount this particular episode of our then fraught relationship. In these pages, I am honest as I can stand to be: even as concerns my shames.

The baby's alarm ceased to ring, though still she sniffled, her little cheeks quivering as they puffed fruitlessly for milk. I inhaled into the uncomfortable sensation, my back straight and stomach tight, and mourned that I had nothing to give her—but quickly decided that was not true at all. It was by my lovers that she had all this.

The men who truly loved me already loved this child like their own, even though she was not their own. Now, here was the man who *was* the actual father of this child, maddened—and standing at a crossroads with us both.

"I must do what is best for Rosina," I told him firmly, my tone low with respect to the easily disturbed child and my expression clear of anything but the expectant neutrality of formal negotiation. "Aside from my own feelings for him—which are, I must tell you, deep and intense—Malin has promised Rosina the kind of life that most of the world can only dream about. She will never have to worry for anything. I *know* you understand what that means. We're both normal people, Glenn. That's the sameness you sense in us: it's our backgrounds, our craving for simplicity. Our introversion, as my dear friend Charlotte calls it, God bless her forgiving soul, her compassionate soul.

"But—you know, Glenn, the truth about me? I crave more than simplicity. I crave a simplicity of living, yes, of course. Who doesn't want living to be easy? But what I want is—oh, *luxury*. I *deserve* luxury! Don't we all? You know—Malin gave me my first-ever taste of chocolate, when he brought me to his property. It wasn't long after I arrived, anyway." I pondered the memory, the flavor flooding in my mouth at the behest of my mind. "And I realized—my goodness, how easily I might have gone my whole life *never* tasting it, ever! How easily I could have lived and died, in fact, never even having *heard* of it if I had been someone else's daughter. Or if I had been blind and deaf, some poor, deformed orphan, no tongue or nose to experience the world by any means but fearful grasping!

"But I am not those things, Glenn. I am me. I, Thecla of Lescaut, may be unknowingly distinguished by some heritage about which I know next to nothing; but I have chosen to take advantage of the opportunities extended to me. I put myself where I am—have decided to submit to the feelings at which others might dismay—through my *will*. I have chosen this, Glenn, this life. I have made it for myself with Malin's help, and Eleison's. And if you do not love the life I have made, am making, for myself, then I suppose I can accept we have a difference of opinion. But I will not be forced to change my life in a way I don't prefer for you or any other man's benefit, and I certainly will not respect any man who forces me to part with the child he made—or who abandons the both of us outright."

"That's not—"

"Softly," I urged him, causing him to clench his teeth with a look at the baby.

"That's not what I want," he said.

"Then what do you want, Glenn?"

His chest swelled, then receded with the final, defeated sagging of his shoulders.

An unformed word on his lips, he stepped toward us.

The elevator's chime caused us both to bolt in surprise. While he jerked the gun in the direction of the corridor and called, "Who is it," my heart sank. I launched up from the chair, already shouting, "He has a gun, stay back!"

The tap of Malin's house shoes paused for less than half a second before hurrying on to the corridor's end.

With a breathless sort of scoff, Glenn raised his head as though to convince himself he really had Malin Farrow in his sights; then, he leveled his aim.

"Glenn"—the vermillion outrage swirling in me had reached its peak, and I no longer cared that my shout disturbed the girl out of her doze and into a new batch of tears—"if you don't put that gun down, I will kill you *myself*, now stop this at once—"

"Mr. Stone," said Malin, stately in the red quilting of the robe that fell to his worn-in house shoes. His hands open and empty, my husband stood without the least trepidation across from a man who had the power to kill him in an instant.

"I'm glad you came here," my husband went on, his cautious tone yet somehow warm. A forced affect, given the circumstances, but drawn from a real place. "I've wanted to talk to you about your role in Rosina's life—I imagine you already explained about her, darling?"

"Yes." The word was hoarse. I was sure Eleison waited around the corner, within touching distance of Malin, and would be able to yank him away in an instant…before springing out with his own shocking quickdraw. Glenn's life was more at risk than ever, and I allowed all involved to hear the pleading note in my voice as I said to Glenn, "Please, think of the good of the child. Think of *yourself*. How little will be left for you if you prove the killer of Malin Farrow!"

"I'm already a fugitive," Glenn said, his gaze never straying from his target.

"But an innocent fugitive," I reminded him. "A wrongful one. I tell you, we can help you."

"We can more than help you, Glenn," my husband assured him with half a step forward. He halted mid-stride and returned to his original place at some twitch in Glenn's facial features. "There's no need for us to be rivals. Just as with Eleison and myself...he and I love the same woman, the same woman loves both of us. Isn't that a reason to be friends, instead of enemies? Isn't it a boon to have three watchful and well-rounded chaps assisting Thecla in young Rosina's upbringing?"

"That would be true, maybe, in another world, where you're not a war criminal...where you have lower odds of being responsible for exposing mankind to the Rift."

"No one can know that," I snapped, aggrieved. "My husband is a scapegoat, abused so the Overseer can maintain her status quo."

Without looking over, Glenn said, "I know you want to believe that."

"Only time will tell how right I am. In the meantime, you'll have made yourself as much a murderer as I am. As Malin is."

The hunter scoffed in disgust, his head jerking down for a few seconds of thought.

With this potential inroad, Malin pressed on. "We all know

my reputation precedes me, my friend, but rest assured…when you get to know me, you might change your mind about what you've heard."

Glenn's jaw tightened beneath his beard; his hand clenched around the gun.

He raised his eyes.

"That's what I'm afraid of."

The twitch of Glenn's forearm telegraphed a terrible decision that inspired from me another, now more articulate scream.

"Eleison!"

The events of the next seconds—beginning with the implosion of the nursery's glass wall and the blowing inward of the curtains on the cold winter air—occurred in such an overlapping tumult of confusion and terror that it would be impossible to truly express the scene as I experienced it: lost, unknowing, trapped in the eye of a cyclone while its sinistrorsal winds raged wildly around me.

As I screamed and the glass behind me shattered, Malin lurched beneath the body of Eleison, who, clad in only boxers, sprang out from exactly the place I'd expected him to be. He shoved Malin down while raising a pistol to return fire. Ba'al-Dinon, meanwhile, rocketed into the room through the free-flying curtains. I didn't even see him until, on the hellish shriek the dharmine unleashed while exercising my order to intervene on a threat to Malin's life, Glenn wrenched his gun toward Dinon with a shocked jerk of his head. More smoke and shadow than man at that instant, Dinon tore the gun from Glenn, then raised a suddenly clawed white hand that ripped across his chest and shoved him back in a crack of violet Rift radiation.

At the other end of the hall, Eleison's target changed.

I cried again, shielding the baby's head against my bosom, while the dharmine endured a hail of bullet fire across his chest and shoulder. Amid a splash of unnaturally purplish blood, Dinon lunged toward the hunter he had flung into the devastated changing table. The flash of Dinon's exposed fangs made me scream again. Knowing the hopelessness, I choked out a desperate command that he release Glenn unharmed—

But Malin, at last recovering since hitting the floor, pushed himself up amid a bellow that echoed down the corridor and brought the chaos to a complete halt.

"Dharmine! Ba'al-Dinon, you speaking animal: you are *but* a speaking animal, and like all animals, subject my will—and I will that you leave him unharmed."

The howl erupting from the beast at the very first word was unearthly, to say the least. As Malin spoke on, Ba'al-Dinon flung himself back from Glenn in such a sharp recoil it seemed some effect of magnetism. Gnashing his fangs, the demon lurched back toward me, one hand pressing over the shoulder that oozed unearthly blood from beneath his dark cloak.

"But"—Dinon gasped in a tone that, discordantly, implied a kind of breathless pleasure at the gunshot wounds, or perhaps at Malin's complete dominion over his will—"Master, please! I am already Madame's slave—"

"Because I eternally bind you in service to her this very instant. Eleison—put down the gun."

Eleison growled. Malin looked at him sharply and rose fully to his feet. Before me, Dinon panted, then flinched as Malin told him, "For all time, Dinon, for so long as you walk this entropic land, you will be the devoted slave to Thecla and myself. You will obey our orders without question; and if ever you disobey them, you pitiful dog, you will retreat to the Rift and never return, never experience the sweetness of existence, never again darken our consciousness with your parasitic subservience. You are Gudrune's, mine and hers. Now that our human wills have involved themselves in this contract in time, and now that my will has been concretely spoken as words you have no choice but understand, there will be no more wiggling out of it for you. You are nothing but an animal, Dinon, a speaking animal; and the Rift animals, every one I care to control, yield to me."

Crying out, having sunk to his knees with one hand upon the floor and the other upon his slowly healing chest, Dinon enthused, "Yes, Master! Yes, sir, I am so sorry—you are right, so right! I've taken advantage of Madame."

"Because you forget she and I are one flesh. You have obeyed her word as her word, and not as my word. Do you now understand the mistake you were making?"

While I marveled, excited and a little frightened to see my husband openly exhibit his power, (and over what a choice of animal!), Dinon scraped to press his head to the floor. "Please, Master, forgive me, forgive me. This world, the static direction in which time runs—I can only abide by events of the future so well before they happen."

"I know," agreed Malin in the patronizing sympathy with which one greets a dog's whines for table scraps it will never receive, "chronology must be confusing for you, Dinon…but now, it's all very simple."

"Yes!"

"What's past is past."

"Yes, yes!"

"I'm not through speaking. You will work among my properties, loyal to my servants as well as to myself; and, so long as you are in service to us, never shall you harm any servant, friend, guest, or relative of our household. Not unless Thecla or I should clearly tell you otherwise. You will eat what you are given without thieving more. And you will work in your heart for the sincere wellbeing of my wife—not for your own ends, or even, slave, or mine."

"Malin," I whispered gently, folding my arms tighter around the infant at a sudden shudder of cold, or excitement.

For just a second, my husband's dark eyes slid to me; then, they returned to the dharmine.

"I reserve the right to add or omit from this verbal contract with you, speaking animal that is bound by your knowledge of the words you now hear, at any point in the future of this world which operates under the constraints of linear time. Is that clear? You may speak when addressed."

"Yes, sir, thank you, it is clear."

"Good. Then I forgive you for taking advantage of my wife. I can only imagine the desperation one of your kind must feel to be perceived."

"Thank you, yes, sir. Thank you for your forgiveness."

"You are welcome." After regarding the dharmine for a few long seconds, Malin extended the toe of his house shoe beyond the hem of his robe. "Come greet your master properly, then, dog. We can start off as friends."

With a ghastly sort of moan that was half of pleasure and half of pain for his many injuries, the dharmine struggled to drag itself down the corridor's length. Lip curled, Eleison glanced at Malin.

"You must be crazy."

"I told you, I've been thinking about getting Thecla a

dog…and you'll be a loyal dog now that I've caught you, won't you, Dinon."

While Malin's eyes lowered to follow the crawling demon, Dinon collapsed at my husband's feet. "Yes, sir," gasped the dharmine while Eleison watched in disgust, "yes, Master Farrow! Thecla already knows how helpful I can be…"

"But now you'll *always* be that way…and not disingenuously, either. That's a good boy." As the dharmine pressed kisses upon Malin's house shoe—and even extended its tongue to lick—my dutiful husband raised a crinkling eye toward me.

"You know, I think if we can stop Eleison from killing him, this dharmine of yours will be a very useful member of our household."

With a sneer of revulsion I caught while rushing down to check on Glenn, Eleison stepped past the dharmine and said, "That's a big "if.""

I had no attention with which to remonstrate Eleison for his needless dislike of the dharmine. We had both witnessed multiple times Malin's control of Rift beasts. I had no doubt that Dinon was ours forever, and that, trapped by his knowledge of speech, he would have little choice but fulfill the verbal contract into which he had been forced. Accordingly, I was not worried about Dinon, or Eleison, or Malin.

Only about Glenn, who looked even worse than he had after Eleison had finished with him. In point of fact, he was unconscious. I cried out just as Eleison hurried around the corner and crouched at my side to listen for Glenn's breathing.

"He's alive," Eleison said while I inhaled in sharp relief. "I don't like the way his breathing sounds, though."

"He may have broken a rib, or worse." Having kicked Dinon away to stride in after Eleison and regard the damage with bleak displeasure, Malin turned to me. "If we are going to save him, we need to move quickly; and I do not know that feats of healing are within your new pet's purview, Thecla."

"What can we do? Oh, darling, can we get him to a hospital?"

"The nearest is some ways, but..." My husband glanced over at Eleison, who rose to call for help via the RMS panel in the hall. "If we have him airlifted and, crass as it is, send one of the veterinarians from the park along with him—"

"Please," I begged, "anything. Oh, Malin, I..."

Tears surged down my cheeks. My lips trembled in panic. Terrible possibilities played out in my mind. I dared not speak: luckily, I didn't need to.

"Sh, darling."

Far away, Eleison barked orders into the RMS panel. Malin knelt beside me to take me, along with weeping Rosina, into his arms.

"Just let me take care of this. Let your husband take care of everything, Thecla. I promise...I know just what to do."

# EPILOGUE

I T MUST HAVE been almost six months later that Malin, Eleison and I next saw Aleister.

Exhausted from the night prior, my husband, my mate and I lay sprawled in bed in the dim hours of early morning. I am not sure what called me back to consciousness a little early. A premonition, perhaps; although, in truth, I almost always find myself stirring early when sharing a bed with both Malin and Eleison. This is probably due to having one more person in bed, and therefore enduring an increased likelihood that one or all of us will disturb the others, but I have never minded. Early awakenings, especially in those days, were but extra time to bask in the sensual heat of last night's memories, and to fully, conscientiously feel the love with which these two fine men blessed me.

And, anyway…eventually, one man or the other would stir, and sleep would quickly be revealed as a mere pause to seeming endless proceedings of love.

That morning, it was Malin who rolled against me as, hand resting lightly upon my stomach, I contemplated Eleison's extraordinary form. My mate's body represented a pinnacle of physical achievement few had the discipline to earn, let alone maintain, and there were days I felt I could look at him for hours.

Weight, movement, flesh interrupted my rumination. As Malin's lips brushed the ridge of my ear, the heat of his body always extreme when first he awoke from deep slumber, I couldn't help but think the way I felt toward Eleison, the thoughts I had, often echoed the thoughts my husband expressed about me…and the mere possibility that Malin should hold me in such high regard practically made me purr as I tilted my head back against his kiss.

"Isn't he stunning," Malin asked softly, his hand sliding down along my stomach and then, without straying too far, up again to cup a breast.

"I just wish he slept on his back more often."

My murmur earned a chuckle and a smiling flash of Malin's hard teeth against my ear.

"Then we'd never leave him alone…this is the only way he can sleep at all, I'm sure…"

The lingering kisses Malin pressed along the curve of my neck sent sparks of pleasure rocketing to my thighs. I turned to accuse him with an arch look. "I think you mean *you'd* never leave him alone…goodness knows, it's a miracle *I'm* ever able to get any sleep at all."

"It is, isn't it." Chuckling against me, the distinct prod of his cock urging me to shift apart the thighs, Malin slid his hand back down the length of my body and this time didn't keep his fingers from wandering into the dark shadows of the woods. While I gasped, he sighed; and, as my thigh draped up and over his to permit his explorations, Malin's appreciative exhalation rolled into a low groan against the curve of my jaw.

"Especially when you're so wet and inviting all the time… Thecla…what a good wife you are. Always eager to satisfy your husband's needs."

The weight of that wonderful instrument fit perfectly against me, our bodies more familiar with one another each time we made love. While his hand slid away from me to caress my inner thigh and fold my leg against my stomach, my hand stretched between my legs to stroke his stony length.

"How would you feel about having dinner tonight? Just the two of us." He murmured the question in my ear, his breath barely hitching as I coaxed him into me inch by agonizing inch.

"Oh," I whimpered, flush and trembling to twist my head and meet that empty, agonized look of Satanic hunger that gripped his expression from the second of penetration, "oh, no—"

The corner of his mouth drew back in a sly half-smile. "No? Whyever not…"

"Because I know what that means."

Still reaching down between my legs as I was, I let my fingertips trail along his scrotum. The caress produced a grunt of pleasure from the base of his throat as he softly demanded, "What does it mean, Thecla?"

"It means," I continued on in a hot whisper while his nose brushed mine, "that you're in the mood to whip me."

"So you're on to me already, are you… I'd better teach Eleison to enjoy watching you take the cane if I'm ever going to surprise you again. Allow me to rephrase."

Malin's hand clamped down upon my mouth to mute my shocked moan when his slow draw back out of me turned into a violent stab of his prick up against that internal hot button of intensity. All at once he fucked me fast and hard, and I was thrust into a dimension of pleasure so intense I was grateful he'd covered my mouth.

"You'll be dining privately with me tonight," my husband informed me, each commandment a strained murmur into my ear, "and entertaining me before, during, and after, you little strumpet."

I could do nothing but helplessly choke back more keens of pleasure as his pace increased. That hand tightened against my mouth, perhaps anticipating my difficulty with staying silent as he went hotly on.

"After dinner, you're going to follow me to my suite, and you're going to get down on your knees and beg me to cane you… and you're going to love it. Is that clear?"

Moaning softly against Malin's hand, then remembering to choke back my exaltations as his other slid down to the apex of my thighs, I nodded.

"That's my good girl." Malin slowed as, at last unable to enjoy (or feign) sleep any longer, Eleison craned his neck to assess the scene through eyes all the redder for their exhaustion.

"You two," he observed, shutting his eyes and pressing his face to the pillow with a laugh, "never, ever stop."

"Isn't it what you love about us," my husband asked with a low chuckle, then a hum of appreciation when my mate raised his head again and this time leaned in to kiss me. I groaned at the sleepy tempo with which his tongue mined the depths of my mouth, my hand sliding down his chest and beneath the sheet across his hips.

"Oh," I moaned, "Eleison!" He strained so hot and hard with the night's sleep and the stimulus of the morning that simply brushing my knuckles against him gave me a pulse of pleasure. Intrigued, Malin slid his hand beneath the sheet along with me. Though Eleison's breath hitched into our kiss, he certainly didn't stop what he was doing any more than Malin did.

"You are *very* ready to fuck her this morning, aren't you, Eleison…" While my mate groaned to be fondled and petted by both Malin's hand and mine, my husband sank his teeth into the lobe of my ear and slid free of me. He released Eleison only to tug the sheet away, urging, "Come here, Eleison, darling. Come fuck your mate. I don't mind. I know she wants it…don't you, Thecla…"

"Yes! Oh, yes, please—both of you, oh, I want both of you so badly—"

Eleison's hard body pressed against mine, and I cried out in frenzied pleasure as the tip of his cock nestled against my drenched center.

"Wow, baby…you're not kidding."

"That's just what I said." While Malin's hand enveloped my breast, he arched against us both. I happened to glance down as my husband's prick slid slickly along my mate's, both men visibly twitching; moaning, I slipped my hand down between myself and Eleison to hold both cocks still so I might grind against them, stroke them, tease them at the same time. While Eleison groaned, Malin gnashed his teeth with a whispered curse, then resumed his grip of my thigh against my body to regain his control of the situation.

"Now she's trying to tease us, Eleison. Go on, fuck her senseless for it. I'll hold her still for you…"

Baring his teeth in a wicked grin that seemed more energetic by the second, Eleison swallowed up my mouth while driving home in one smooth motion: no hands required, for as well as he was acquainted with my anatomy. Somehow withholding a scream, I instead managed to pant out my mate's musical name while he laid claim to my body with my husband's assistance. As my hands flew to Eleison's face to hold him for a perpetually deeper kiss, Malin nipped and kissed my throat and ear, where he murmured with great appreciation.

"Isn't he a stud…oh, yes, I love to watch your mate fuck you. Darling, you take that big prick of his so well. Oh, don't you love it…oh, hell! Aren't you a slut for him, Thecla…"

"Yes! Yes! Oh, Eleison—*Eleison*—"

Malin's hand was there again, sliding past dewy curls and to the lips splayed apart by the thick shaft that worked between them. While his fingers teased along my clitoris, occasionally brushing against the cock that fucked me, my husband murmured on to me, "I love hearing you moan his name…say it again."

"Eleison! Oh—Eleison, yes, please, harder—fuck me harder, fuck me in front of my husband—oh! Oh—!"

With a growl, Eleison pushed me back against Malin, and my husband gasped with pleasure to relent. Malin folded his golden arms around my body, his mouth pressing against my ear, my hair, my neck, while Eleison spread my legs and plunged back in. I choked on bliss, my tongue swollen in my mouth by the pleasure of my sweet mate fucking me so deeply as I lay upon

Malin's chest. Already splayed as I was by the angle, the men's hands caught my thighs and arms to hold me all the wider. I lost all sense of sanity, humanity, tangibility as Eleison, maddeningly hard as he always was in the morning, pounded us both to an early morning finish line.

"Beg him for his cum, darling," Malin murmured in my ear. "Go on…ask him, you trollop. I want to hear it…"

"Oh, but—ah, hm—you know what I really want this morning, Master…oh, Eleison—"

My teeth sinking into my lower lip, a sudden shyness coming over me even in those circumstances, I murmured to Eleison, "Would you let me take it in the mouth?"

Both men groaned a little, their appreciation a bolt of pleasure that streaked right through me.

"I'll never turn you down, baby. Not for that, not for anything…" Bending down, his next kiss a vacuum for all its pressure against and within me, Eleison extricated himself sharply from my body and left me quivering while he suggested, "Go ahead, Malin…she's all yours."

"Such a gentleman…" While the men swapped places, I rolled upon my stomach and glanced back over my shoulder to see Malin kneeling comfortably between my legs. That gorgeous cock of his looked full and ready to burst, and it certainly felt that way as, meeting my eye, he caught my hip and eased back into me with an expression that telegraphed every thought he had about what he was going to do to me that night. I whimpered with pleasure, then glanced back as Eleison settled against the headboard to allow me to slide my upper half into his lap.

What a sight he always was! I marveled at the instrument which had provided so me much practice in the art of satisfying a man—"practice," if only because taking him deeply into my throat proved something of a challenge. It was the girth that was the difficulty; but I was always keen to push myself, and I had learned there was plenty else I could do. For instance, what my mouth could not contain, my hand worked adamantly, with one sliding along the shaft and the other fitting beneath his sensitive scrotum in a manner gentle but supportive. As my head bobbed and my tongue lashed against the firm, tense heat of my mate, Malin reached forward and drew my hair back from my face. Seeing me, he emitted a sigh of pure pleasure.

"Doesn't she look hot with a cock in her mouth, Eleison... ah, fuck, and it makes her so wet. You love sucking cock, don't you, beautiful..."

Moaning, I raised my head and nuzzled my lips against the reddened helmet of Eleison's prick. "It's much more fun than I would have expected it. The sight and the taste, oh, it all excites me— I want yours more often, Malin..."

"Hm, I know. Well, don't worry." The hand that gripped my hair pushed my head back down over Eleison's cock. I accepted a few inches with a full-mouthed moan, then gasped with pleasure as Malin pounded me in a new, more relentless dedication to my orgasm. "When I've gotten you pregnant again, you can suck my cock however much and however long you want...I'll even give it to you up the ass like you've been begging me for, you dirty slut. Ah, darling, wherever do you learn such naughty things..."

Groaning through a mouth too occupied to tell him it was all ultimately his fault, and Eleison's presence precluding the proper spanking my response would surely otherwise merit, I redoubled my efforts to savor my mate's pleasure. Oh, how Eleison tensed in my mouth while Malin worked within me! The tip of my mate's spear prodded hard against the back of my throat, often causing my uvula to strain and tickle; but I soldiered on, my head's every bob avid and my legs spreading wider to encourage Malin.

"That's right, darling," Malin coached, watching me all the while, his eyes coals of burning lust. "Suck your mate's cock, precious, make sure you've earned his cum…and mine, of course… only very good girls get their husband's load…"

"Malin, ah…" Eleison laughed, his tone bleary with pleasure and tight with his impending orgasm. "Some of the shit you say is just…out there…"

"Oh, if you like that, just wait until Thecla realizes what it will do to her to call me "Daddy" from time to time—ah, aha— oh, yes…"

Shocked, mortified—and inexplicably aroused—I found myself tipped into a climax without intending to be and cried out in pleasure against Eleison's prick. Hammering into me all the faster, Malin watched with appreciation while my hurried, strangled motions catalyzed Eleison's orgasm before mine was finished.

"Hm," my husband murmured, "you do like it, don't you… you dirty girl…I love how naughty you are. You let yourself have fun, ah, it's sexy, so sexy to me. We'll talk about it more later. Go on, that's right, make him cum, ah, Thecla—suck your mate, go on—yes, oh, fuck, yes, don't swallow it yet, darling, just let me see—"

Eleison's body stiffened and his hand enveloped Malin's against the back of my head. On the contact, my husband's thrusts increased in their intensity for about five seconds before, enamored by the white ropes of Eleison's semen jetting out against my lips and tongue, Malin succumbed to an explosion of his own, and cried out. All three of our bodies stiffened with the intensity of pleasure that worked us in waves, vibrating, dissolving, until the boundaries between us were so negligible they may as well have been dreams.

All that lay between us was love. The same love that had made us now inhabited us, fusing our souls while our bodies vanished into nothing.

We dozed together an hour, both men holding me closely, each kissing me repeatedly and occasionally tilting his head to kiss the other. Soon, the time closed in on six, and Malin looked at the clock with a resentful grumble before he peeled himself away and slunk off to shower in what once was my suite there in the country house. Eleison and I remained intertwined a little, chatting softly and making plans for the day—horseback riding with Kyrie, ping-pong to compensate for the day off from physical training, a walk around the gardens with Rosina—until a knock at the door interrupted our conversation.

"Come in," I called, neglecting the sheet as I sat up and provoking from Eleison an intolerant grumble for my indecency.

I hated to be the one to tell him it didn't matter how Dinon saw me…the dog had already seen plenty enough already.

A very fine-looking dog, though. Since joining the staff as Malin's new footman, the dharmine had adopted the uniform of a far more traditional one than Eleison had ever been. Consequently, his tailed suit and gray waistcoat only increased the offputtingly alien air of his unreachable personality. Dinon was far too pretty for the male staff to befriend, and far too distant for the female staff to find any opening. Very quickly, all had given up, and it came to be understood that my personal servant dwelled in a sphere of his own, maintaining my needs and occasionally Malin's without participating in life at the manor.

I was Dinon's life in the manor—in the world—and he smiled in feline pleasure to see me. He bowed, the neatly plaited braid of his white hair hanging, then falling back against his chest as he straightened.

"Good morning, Madame; Lord Eleison. Breakfast will arrive in an hour. Would Madame care to attend her toilette now, to make the morning stroll after the meal?"

I confess there are times even now that such address gives me a flush of pleasure; an artifact of the girl I was, occasionally still awakening in the woman I am like a sleeper snapping lucid in the middle of an endless dream.

"Yes, Dinon, very good. I'll have my bath now…Eleison—"

At my stretched arm, he leaned in to kiss me one final, lingering time, then released me with his eye on me as I slid my robe around my shoulders and walked through the door Dinon held. "See you later, baby," Eleison called before it shut. "Enjoy your bath."

Given my late spring wedding and the events of the subsequent autumn and winter, I had not enjoyed the country house as its peer in ownership. Now, of course, I would not have that chance, as Eleison's tie to me was not legal in the same way as Malin's; yet all the same, Eleison had naturally kept me in the position of lady of the house, and had worked with Malin to ensure I had ample space in which to exist independent of them both. The master apartment of the west wing, therefore, had a lovely set of rooms that were all mine, consisting of a boudoir with a dressing room, a washroom, a small study, and, of course, a space for a loom. With my needs seen to for the morning, Dinon dressed me with greater professionalism and precision that Brea had ever showed; that finished, he sat me at the vanity and just as excellently arranged my hair into an array of fabulously ornamented coils and vines. While his deft fingers worked, I watched him in the mirror...and, I confess, myself.

"Do you find me fair, Dinon? I feel so assured in my beauty these days...it's all the attention the men pay me that makes me feel that way, but one occasionally worries it's all in one's head, or theirs."

"You are exceptionally fair, Madame..." His reflection smiling at me, he drew one last stray lock back into the chignon of his scrupulous arrangement. "The fairest of them all."

Smiling wryly at the thick praise, I took his offered hand from the vanity and advised him while he turned to get the door, "Such hyperbole! That's how I know you're still disingenuous, Ba'al-Dinon."

But his hand, which had not released mine, dared to tighten, and remained there unflinchingly as I shot him a shocked look.

"I meant it, Madame. None on this Earth are fair to me as you. None, not one."

Blushing, I glanced down at my hand in his again, then jerked it quickly from his touch and stepped through the door.

"Try not to be so informal," I told him curtly, sure I heard the intake of a pleasurable breath as I strode on to breakfast.

By then, both Malin and Eleison were dressed and waiting, Malin with his paper, Eleison with his cigarette. It was a pleasant day—we ate on the terrace, the morning wind sweet and cool— and all concerned were in fine moods.

Then, with a brisk but polite knock, Charlotte stepped into the apartment and came out to us with her placid face prepared for bad reactions. Recognizing her look, Malin sighed and folded up his paper, slapped it down beside his empty plate, then hooked his thumb in the pocket of his waistcoat.

"Tell me it's good news."

"That all depends…will you be glad to hear Duke Montagne has arrived for an unannounced visit?"

While the men groaned, I perked—though not without trepidation Malin reflected while raising his head from where it had dropped to his chest. "I hope you warned him that if he intends to take my bride away again, he's looking at a public horsewhipping, at best."

"I did advise him of something to that effect. He assured me he and his sister are simply here to visit."

"*And* his sister," Malin said dryly. "Oh, goodie… if I so much as say "Hello," that's a three-hour, high-intensity conversation right in the middle of my eight-thirty. I'm so sorry, darling, but—"

"I'd be happy to entertain them," I said, adding, "I owe Aleister an apology, anyway…the last time we spoke, I was cross."

"Weren't we all…frankly, I'm surprised he had the chutzpah to visit at all. Almost wonder if he's on the run from the law."

Half an hour later, while accompanying me on my morning walk through the gardens, Aleister affected a laugh that had the good sense to be more breezy than annoyed. "Did Malin say that? Goodness, *he'd* ought to know I haven't been up to anything too terribly illegal since I stopped breeding designer ertiz. No, erm—"

Pausing beside a row of neatly manicured roses, Aleister drummed his fingers along the handle of his walking stick and, much to my surprise, actually managed to look embarrassed.

"I have to say, Thecla—I've had a good bit of time to think about what you said to me at Stone's house there in Valquist…and it occurred to me you do have a point."

My eyebrows raised in surprise that must have seemed too eager, for he added tersely, "Don't get *excited* about it, for Heaven's sake. Even I can admit I'm wrong. But—" Lips pursing, he looked back at the manor and shook his head.

"I owe Malin too much to place any value on the people who despise him, no matter what they can do for me socially, or politically, or even financially. I've been so preoccupied with elevating my status that I just—well—I was willing to tell myself that it didn't matter what those people thought of my *actual* friend. That I could be friends with Malin *and* the Valquist politicians who most despise him. But...having heard some downright harrowing rumors of your loyalty to Malin, I admit...I admire you. Rather makes one want to do better. So..."

As though not knowing what else to do, he chucked me lightly in the shoulder like I was a lad. "Good show, Thecla."

Laughing, I assured him, "Well, whatever it took, I'm happy you understood where I was coming from... Ah! There she *is*—good morning!"

All conversation was gone and forgotten as soon as Rosina and I set eyes upon one another. While my happy baby squealed in her nurse's arms, I cried in delight and hurried to meet them halfway.

His smile the mildly horrified sort worn by people for whom child-rearing is a baffling and frankly somewhat upsetting idea, Aleister attempted a pleasant noise. "Oh, and *there* she is, the young lady herself. My!"

While I turned back to him with softly babbling Rosina nestled cozily in my arms, Aleister's strained smile forced itself into better shape. His uninspired words, however...

"She certainly is...a *baby*, isn't she?"

"I can't wait to hear what kind of uncle you'll make to your sister's children."

"God willing, the distant kind! Now, if you'll excuse me, Madame, I appreciate the greeting, but my word, I am famished. Is that maid of yours still here? Brea? No? Pity! You're like my sister, she's always going through help."

Following me to the back door as he was, Aleister only now looked up and caught a glance of Dinon. The dharmine waited with a patient, pleasant smile for me to return to the house, obviously prepared to deliver some bit of news or other.

"Who's *that*," whispered Aleister, his eyes bulging and his voice hoarse with terror.

Recalling his nearly fatal dream, I responded rather coyly, "My lady's maid," and smiled down at happy Rosina while Dinon held the door for us. "Enjoy breakfast, Aleister. Let's all plan to have dinner together tomorrow to celebrate your visit!"

When my baby, my shadow and I reached the busy foyer of the house, Dinon bent to murmur into my ear from just behind my right shoulder.

"I believe his mood is such that he will consent to see you today, Madame."

Joy bolted through me at the news. "Oh! Will he, really?"

"I expect so. He has eaten, seems to have slept, and his beard is looking well-trimmed. It would appear his humor is better than usual."

My heart pulsed with hope. "Will you help me with the door?"

"It would be my pleasure."

Upstairs, in the north corridor, the door to what was once Eleison's suite was now almost permanently shut. Two people in the house had a key: Dinon and myself. Neither Eleison, who now owned the property, nor Malin, who controlled the territory, had means of entry—in part, to decrease the chances of escape.

Largely, so Glenn would never forget what his confinement was about.

At the sound of the door, he was already emerging from the bedroom and into the living area. His entire countenance brightening to see Rosina, Glenn hurried across the room to say, "Good morning—hi, Rosina, hi, sweetie, good morning! Can I—"

Smiling with pleasure to find Dinon had been right, I carefully passed the baby into her father's arms and enjoyed their identical grins. "I like her little flower," he said of the rose on her headband, turning to look me in the face as one does when in conversation.

Suddenly he saw me more clearly, and sobered: but not in a manner unpleasant.

"You look beautiful, Thecla."

"And so do you, Glenn, darling..." I leaned toward him, and he tensed. Sighing, I leaned back.

No matter. Eventually, he would capitulate. The unreasonability of his position would be made apparent. He would understand I was only giving him what he wanted.

I could wait.

"The Duke Montagne arrived today. If you promised to behave yourself"—that was, to make no effort to escape—"I'm sure I could see to it that you came out to dinner."

Laughing dryly, Glenn said, "That's not the most tantalizing incentive I've ever heard."

"Well you *must* start behaving yourself sometime, Glenn. You can't spend eternity in this apartment, can you?"

"That seems to be your plan for me."

"Only until you've seen *sense*," I reminded him, "and you're no longer so dead-set on leaving."

"Holding me captive isn't going to persuade me that fleeing is the wrong course of action."

Mouth tight, I stared Glenn in the purple sparks that now inhabited his once purely blue eyes.

"No…but holding you captive is what you want, in and of itself. Don't pretend you want anything resembling a choice, Glenn, darling. I'll just work all the harder to disabuse you of the notion."

Exhaling, Glenn looked away but still studied me from the corners of his wary eyes. He then nodded toward the sitting area that, at my command, had been decorated with full bookshelves: one for Glenn, and one for our baby.

"You want to read to her together for a while?"

Coolly, so as not to be disappointed, I considered the books and walked over to pick one at random. "Very well…if it won't bother you to have me here, at any rate."

"You know that's not the problem. Thecla…"

"Come along." I settled in and patted the cushion beside me, all the while smiling at the oblivious baby who was too happy to sense the distorted atmosphere in her father's rooms. "Let's just have a nice time with Rosina, shall we?"

While tiny baby hands flailed against the pages and happy babbling emanated from her damply working mouth, I smiled at the fun it was to read to Rosina. Soon enough, she would understand more; but, even as little as she comprehended, her enthusiasm for this strange new reality of hers compensated every gap. Happily snuggled against her mother while in the crook of her father's arm, Rosina watched the pages leaf by, and squeaked and thrashed, and sometimes almost seemed to listen. Her eyes, whipping from page to page, already looked eager for the next word.

And her softening effect on Glenn's guarded heart grew more powerful with each successful visit.

After an hour and a half, the child had grown tired, bored, and fussy. "I think she'd better eat and have a rest," I announced after the latest repetition of the third book, which I shut and set aside before taking the baby from Glenn's reluctant arms. "And it must be a bath day for her, too…say good-bye to Daddy, angel…"

While I waved her pudgy hand for her, Glenn rose. "Wait," he said, "please—"

At the unusual request, I paused, then tried not to enjoy too much the feeling of his broad hand resting gently upon my arm. The gesture was only to allow him to brace himself on me as he bent to kiss the baby, who squealed at his beard and patted him in approval.

Then, smiling, he raised his head. That happy expression lingered as his eyes questioned mine.

He leaned down. Shock rippled through me.

For the first time in months, for reasons I dared not speculate, Glenn pressed his lips to the corner of my mouth; then, with only a second's hesitation, to the temple of my forehead. While my breathing quickened, he leaned back and surveyed me.

"Maybe you could bring her by for another hour after lunch?"

Let Eleison play table tennis with Aleister that afternoon: poor Glenn was all alone. I adjusted Rosina from arm to arm and told my captive lover, "It sounds like a date."

Glenn said nothing as, from the center of his living room, he watched us go.

With a respectful half-bow, Dinon locked the door behind us.

DON'T MISS THE BONUS CONTENT!

Want more of Thecla's tale between now and Book III? Sign up for Ada's mailing list! As a thank-you, you'll receive the **ultra-steamy novella-length bridge story between RIFTBORN and WIDOW, only available for subscribers. Sure, you can enjoy the rest of the series without it, but do you want to? Not if you're into dark romance…**

INTRIGUED? VISIT ADA'S SITE TO SUBSCRIBE!

http://www.adadartromance.com

OTHER WORKS
FROM PAINTED BLIND PUBLISHING

REGINA WATTS

INDUSTRIAL DIVINITY (2020)
WILD GIRL RUNNING (2020)
DOTTIE FOR YOU SEASON 1 (2021)
THE BURNINGSOUL SAGA (2021-)
I WAS AN OP DEMON LORD (2021-)
BE MY BULLY (2021)
SEDUCED BY SABINE (2021)
MAYHEM AT THE MUSEUM (2021)
IDOL (2022)

M. F. SULLIVAN

DELILAH, MY WOMAN (2015)
THE LIGHTNING STENOGRAPHY DEVICE (2017)
THE DISGRACED MARTYR TRILOGY (2019-2020)

ABOUT THE AUTHOR

Ada Dart is an author of reverse harems and romances with undercurrents so dark you'll only want to read them at night. Her brooding, intellectual heroes defy boundaries and straddle conventions: whether older or younger, commanding or sensual, the men Dart writes are sure to keep readers' imaginations going long after the final page. In addition to writing other pulp genres under the pen name Regina Watts, Dart enjoys spending time watching opera with her cat and her real life age-gap partner of over half a decade.

ABOUT THE PUBLISHER

Painted Blind Publishing and its erotic imprint, Painted Blue Publishing, are the brainchild of M. F. Sullivan. Founded in 2015 while Sullivan resided in Tucson, PBP is a house dedicated to bringing readers the finest in consciousness-expanding fiction. Be sure to check out the wide variety of essays available for free at paintedblindpublishing.com to learn more about the company, Dart, and Sullivan.